D1389939

Silver Fountains

ALSO BY THIS AUTHOR FROM CENTURY

Mayfair Rebel
Song of Songs
Roses Have Thorns

SILVER FOUNTAINS

Beverley Hughesdon

Century · London

First published 1994

1 3 5 7 9 10 8 6 4 2

Copyright © Beverley Hughesdon 1994

The right of Beverley Hughesdon to be identified
as the author of this work has been asserted
by her in accordance with the
Copyright, Designs and Patents Act, 1988

First published in the United Kingdom in 1994 by
Century Limited
Random House, 20 Vauxhall Bridge Road,
London SW1V 2SA

Random House Australia (Pty) Limited
20 Alfred Street, Milsons Point, Sydney,
New South Wales 2061, Australia

Random House New Zealand Limited
18 Poland Road, Glenfield
Auckland 10, New Zealand

Random House South Africa (Pty) Limited
PO Box 337, Bergvlei, South Africa

Random House UK Limited Reg. No. 954009

A CIP catalogue record for this book is
available from the British Library

ISBN 0 7126 5490 9
Typeset in Pegasus by
SX Composing Ltd, Rayleigh, Essex
Printed in Great Britain by
Clays Ltd, St Ives plc

Chapter One
Belgrave Square, London – April 1916

It was the night he gave me the rose.

I'd been waiting for him all evening, and he was late – but I didn't mind because I held my baby in my arms. She was called Rose, too – the most wonderful gift he'd ever given me. Just a week old that evening, she was growing more beautiful with every day that passed.

Bending my head I breathed in the sweet scent of her, and whispered, 'Oh my Rose, thee bist beautiful – the most beautifullest baby I ever did see.' Her bright eyes gazed up into mine as I murmured to her, telling her of my love. Then, nestling closer to my heart, she let the dark-fringed crescents of her eyelashes fall until they rested on the plump curve of her cheek – and slept. Oh, I loved her, how I loved her.

She didn't wake up when he came in. I smiled to him over her head and he came closer, and stood looking down at us both. Very gently I moved my arm so he could see her properly. 'There, baint she beautiful?'

'Yes, she is.' I heard the tenderness in his voice; he loved her, just as I did. Then he asked, 'How are you, Amy?'

'I'm brave and well, thank 'ee Leo. That doctor, he do fuss too much.'

I was going to ask him about his journey, but he spoke before me. 'I've brought back a present for you.' Going over to the parcel he'd left on the table he began to unwrap it. When he came to the wooden box inside he reached down into it, and lifted out the rose. I recognised it at once: it was the new golden rose that he'd bred himself.

I exclaimed, 'Tis so early for her – tis only April!'

'I had a bush brought into the glass-house last year. Hicks had instructions to telegraph to me as soon as she came into bloom.' He swung round with the rose in his hand, and held it out to me, 'This is for you, Amy.'

Settling my baby in the crook of one arm I reached out my hand and took the rose from him. 'Thank you, Leo – thank you.' Lifting the rose to my face I breathed in the delicate lemony scent, then lowered it a little so I could admire those silken frills of golden yellow petals. With a smile I raised my eyes to his face and told him, 'She's far too beautiful to have no name.'

His grey eyes looked steadily back into mine. 'Yes, she is – so I'm christening her this evening.'

'Then – what be her name?'

His slow smile curved his lips and transformed his face as he told me, 'I am giving this rose your name. It is to be called "Amy, Countess of Warminster."'

I was so excited. I'd always loved roses, ever since I was a little girl, dancing round my Granfer and demanding to know the name of every one he grew in our cottage garden. Now I had a rose named for me! I felt my face light up with joy as I looked at the man who'd given me this wonderful gift. And then I saw it – the blaze of love and longing in his eyes.

At once my pleasure turned to pain and guilt. For he'd given me this perfect gift, but all I could feel in return was – gratitude.

I saw the uncertainty dawn as the hope in his mismatched eyes began to falter and fade, and I couldn't bear to watch. Looking down at the rose, his beautiful rose, I whispered, 'She be beautiful, the most beautifullest rose I ever did see.'

He replied, his voice heavy and dull now, 'I am glad – that you like it.'

I repeated again, uselessly, 'Aye – aye, I do like her.' And heard in my voice the unspoken message: like, but not love. Not love.

My husband heard it too, and his hand moved in a small, hopeless gesture. Then he said, 'Take care Amy, she has sharp thorns.'

I looked up at him. 'I know. Granfer told me, when I were only a liddle maid. I remember him saying as roses, they were like life. Joy and sorrow, pleasure and pain, they be all twined together like brier roses in a blackthorn hedge.'

He spoke so quietly I could scarcely hear him say, 'And I – am the blackthorn hedge.'

'No – no, I – ' My voice faltered and stopped. What could I say? For I did not love him as a wife should love her husband, and he knew it.

Silence fell, a silence that seemed to stretch and stretch – until it was broken by a small snuffling sound: Rose was waking up. At once I put down the golden rose and lifted her up, close against my heart. She nuzzled my blouse and with quick fingers I undid my buttons and gave her my breast. He sat there opposite me, not speaking, but watching: watching me feed the child he'd tried to deny me. When after a little while her steady rhythm slowed I looked up and said, 'She baint really hungry. I fed her not long afore you came back – but she does like her milk, my Rose.'

At my words he forced a smile, and I smiled back. He spoke, slowly, 'She looks – blooming.'

At once I offered, 'She's finished now – would you like to hold her?' As I lifted her up I smiled into her bright eyes and told her, 'Now, my Rose, thy Dada do want to say "Good evening" to thee.'

He took her from me and went back to his chair, holding her to one side, so that he could look directly into her eyes. 'Good evening, Rose.'

She hiccoughed in reply, so I suggested, 'Mebbe if you lifted her up, to ease her wind.' Raising her up he placed her gently but firmly against his shoulder, then his large hand stroked her small straight back until she gave a small, satisfied burp. 'There – baint thy Dada a clever nursemaid, then?'

He spoke to her softly. 'Is that better, my Rose?' His finger touched the satin-smooth skin at the nape of her neck. 'You have a fine dark curl already, I think.'

There was pride in my voice as I told him, 'More'n one. You can take her bonnet off if you want – tis warm by the fire.' His broad fingers tugged at the ribbon, unfastening the bow before easing off her bonnet and dropping it into his lap. His dark-furred hands gently stroked the curling black down on her head, and her tiny hand came up in response; at once he raised her up higher, so that her head rested against the waving grey hair on his temples. With her small fingers she reached out to pat his face, and catch hold of the curve of his nostril; and I watched them together – my beautiful, perfect baby, and the twisted, humped-back man who was her father.

He looked over at me, his eyes in shadow now. 'You're tired, Amy. I've kept you up too late.' Standing up he came across to give me back my precious baby daughter. He waited until she was safely settled in my arms before leaving go of her, but as he withdrew his right hand it brushed mine – and his fingers jerked away as if they'd been burnt. He backed away repeating, 'You're tired, Amy – you should be in bed.'

Quickly I replied, 'Tis no matter, I've been in bed most o' the day.'

'That is only right and proper, over the period of your confinement.'

That reminded me of what the doctor had said earlier. I'd been disappointed then, but now I was almost glad as I asked, 'Did he tell you – the doctor?'

The old hesitation in his speech was very noticeable as he replied, 'Yes. I was rather – concerned – '

'Oh, my temperature'll soon be down again, only he did say – '

'Of course, he's quite right. Even without that rise it would be unwise for me to enter your room once I am back assisting in the wards.' He sighed, 'So many of the patients' wounds have become infected in France.'

France, where men were even now fighting and dying. The tears welled up and I could not prevent my shiver of fear, for he was there, too – the man I loved.

My husband began to move awkwardly towards the fireplace. 'You are cold, Amy, you must go back to bed. I'll ring for Mrs Chandler.' His finger was poised over the bell push but he didn't press it. Instead he asked, 'You are – pleased with your rose?'

I said quickly, 'Aye, she's beautiful.'

In a low voice he replied, 'As – are – you.'

At once I exclaimed, 'She's the most beautiful rose I've ever seen.' And in that moment before his hand pressed the bell I saw the last flame of hope flicker and die. As he moved towards the door I seized the rose with my free hand and held it up, calling after him, 'Thank you, Leo – thank you.' But he didn't look back.

Tears threatened, but I heard Mrs Chandler's footsteps outside and her soft tap on the door, so I blinked them away. Mrs Chandler, who'd once been nursery maid to Leo's own Nanny, had come up from Eston to be my monthly nurse when Rose was born. Now she was full of admiration for the golden rose.

'Fancy that, a rose in April! But then, he's always been main clever at bringing 'em on in thic glass-house, his lordship has.'

I told her he'd named it for me, and she exclaimed, 'Baint that a treat for 'ee, my lady! You must be main pleased.'

I said quietly, 'Aye, twas very kind of him.'

Her smile broadened. 'Tis more'n kindness, I 'low, my lady.' She didn't see my guilty flush because she'd already gone to the basket to fetch a clean nappy. She returned to fetch Rose, 'Do 'ee come to I, my pretty maid.' Her hands moved briskly. 'And who's Dada's little pet, then?' She spoke over her shoulder to me, 'It's been such a pleasure to see his lordship this past week. He's been like a dog wi' two tails – and both on 'em wagging at once.'

She handed my daughter back to me, then I felt the warm pressure of her hand on my shoulder. 'My lady, I don't want to presume, but seeing the two of you together while thic liddle maid were agetting herself born I couldn't help noticing – I said to myself then, they've learnt to care for each other at last.' My head turned towards the rose, and following my gaze she said, 'I'll just go an put thic blooms in water, then I'll bring 'em straight back to 'ee. I know folks say as tisn't healthy to have flowers in a sickroom overnight, but I 'low those roses'll perk you up better'n a tonic, any time.'

She was soon back, carrying the vase full of his perfect golden roses. 'I'll set them down here, where you can see 'em, then I'll say goodnight, my lady. But don't you forget to ring if the liddle maid needs changing.' I smiled, and thanked her, but we both knew I wouldn't. I liked to care for my baby myself. Besides, it didn't come naturally to me to ring for servants – not when I'd been a servant myself.

The door closed with a soft click, and I was alone with my sleeping baby. But she wouldn't see the tears on my cheeks, so I let them slide down unchecked. All my calm confidence of the last few days had gone now, taken away by the rose – his gift. Just recently I'd been so comfortable with him, enjoying his company, learning to call him Leo, instead of 'my lord'. And I had learnt to care for him, too – Mrs Chandler was right – but caring wasn't love. I knew the difference. And tonight, watching my face, waiting for my reply, he'd known the difference, too.

Those hot tears of shame and guilt burnt my cheeks. I owed him so much, yet I could not give him the love he longed for – because it was given to another. The scent of his roses had brought summer into the room, and with summer came the memories: memories of that golden time before the war – memories of Frank.

I couldn't help it. Suddenly it was as if I were back there in that time, in the Park, with Frank. I saw his boyish smile, heard his teasing laugh – and then, all at once, he was running ahead of me, tall and slim and young. I ran panting after him until I saw his glossy top hat tilt and fall from his sleek blond head. I stopped to pick it up – and in that moment I'd known that I loved him, and always would.

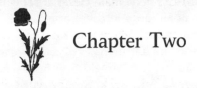

Chapter Two

But in the morning I woke to the joy of Rose – and of Flora. Ellen, the nursemaid, brought my elder daughter down to say good morning, and as soon as the door opened Flora was running across the carpet to the steps beside the bed. Scrambling up them she threw herself straight into my arms. I hugged her close. She seemed so big and sturdy compared with new-born Rose; but then Flora would be three next month and she looked every inch a little girl, from the pink satin bow in her hair to the white kid shoes on her feet. With a sudden backward leap she threw herself out of my arms and began to bounce up and down on the bed, eyes sparkling, curls dancing.

Ellen reached out a restraining hand. 'Careful now, Lady Flora.'

I said quickly, 'Look, Flora, see thic roses – and tis only spring.' She turned to look at them. 'Papa brought them last night, all the way from Eston.'

Her bright blue eyes swung back to my face as she told me importantly, 'Papa came to see me – *before breakfast.*'

Ellen smiled, 'Yes – you were still in your nightdress, weren't you, Lady Flora?'

Flora nodded her head vigorously so that her curls shone pale gold in the April sun; she was so beautiful. Smiling with love and pride I reached out a coaxing hand, 'Thee hasn't said "good morning" to thy new liddle sister.'

'Shan't.' Flora's lower lip jutted and one hand reached out towards Rose, stubby fingers ready to poke; quickly I eased her back. 'She's feeling sleepy, we'd best not disturb her. Would you like Mama to read you a story, Flora?'

Her mouth pursed, considering, then her head nodded firmly. 'Cind'rella.' I opened my mouth but before I had time to get out the automatic reminder she'd added, 'Please.'

Ellen's smile met mine as she handed me the story book. 'Thank you, Ellen. You can go now.'

'You'd best ring for me as soon as she starts getting boisterous, my lady.'

I smiled my thanks, then began to leaf through the pages to find today's favoured tale. As Flora settled herself heavily against my side I started to read: 'There was once upon a time, a gentleman who married for his second wife – ' faltering a moment, I remembered that I too was a second wife – then Flora's impatient wriggle recalled me to my duties and I read on: 'The proudest and most haughty woman that ever was known . . .'

The elder stepsister was determinedly trying to force the glass slipper on to her too large foot when there was a tap at my bedroom door. Flora's head jerked up and as soon as the door flew open she was slithering off the bed crying, 'Aunt N'bel, Aunt N'bel.'

Tall, slim, dark – and so very beautiful, even in her ugly VAD uniform, Miss Annabel swooped down to swing a shrieking Flora up into her arms.

'Good morning, Flora – how are you, Amy?' She didn't wait for a reply. 'I can't stop, I'm due at the depot – I was in so late last night I fell asleep again this morning after I'd drunk my tea and that wretched maid of mine let me sleep on. She doesn't seem to realize I've got a job to do.' She detached my daughter's clinging hand, 'No, Flora – I only looked in to say good morning to you because I promised I would, but I really must go.'

'Aunt N'bel – ' Flora's voice rose in a wail of protest, but Miss Annabel was firm. 'You must be a good girl and remember the poor soldiers who aren't at all well. They need your Aunt Annabel to drive them to hospital, so they can all be tucked up cosily in bed – and then your Papa can nurse them better again. I must go.'

Flora ran after her pleading, 'Flora wave goodbye – '

At the door Miss Annabel swung round again, 'Oh, all right, you can come downstairs with me. Amy, I'll tell Tims to send her back up with the housemaid after she's seen me off.' My daughter seized the slim hand with a crow of triumph. 'Quickly, I'm in a hurry.' She was always in a hurry, Miss Annabel.

Lady Quinham she was now, but I still thought of her as Miss Annabel because that's how I'd known her when I'd first gone to Nether Court to be her lady's maid.

Flora was sobbing when Bertha brought her back and at first she thrust my outstretched arms away. 'Aunt N'bel gone, Aunt N'bel *gone*.'

'She'll be back later, then she'll come and see you up in the nursery. You know she will, she always does.' Grudgingly she allowed herself to be comforted, then I reached for the book of fairy tales and held it out to her invitingly.

At once she exclaimed, ''Nother story, Mama.' There was a thoughtful pause, then she added, 'Please.'

I hugged her before asking, 'Which one would you like, Flora?'

'The Beast.'

So I began to read: 'There was once a very rich merchant, who had six children, three sons and three daughters . . .' I scarcely needed the words, I knew the tale so well: Beauty and the Beast had been my favourite story ever since I was a child in Borrell, and now I told it to my own daughter.

Flora listened intently, but I had to gabble the ending because I could hear Rose waking up. '"And so they lived happily ever after", and here's Ellen, come to take thee for thy walk.'

Flora's face became stubborn, 'Don't want to go – '

Glancing at Ellen I gestured towards the cradle; Ellen's voice was firm, 'Now, Lady Flora, if we don't go directly we'll miss seeing those big boys in the park.' Flora scowled; then, ignoring Ellen's outstretched hand, she rolled over on the bed and slithered off the other side with a bump before heading for the door.

Mrs Chandler closed it behind them with a smile. 'They're a handful at that age – take all a body's energy. That's why tis a good thing to have 'em while you're only young yourself – eh, my lady?' Suddenly her smile changed to a flush of embarrassment, which she quickly masked by turning her attention to the vase of roses. 'I'd best freshen this up, roses are thirsty creatures.'

I'd only been eighteen when Flora was born; young, but old enough to know better. With a sigh I reached down for Rose and gently eased back the frill of her bonnet, so that I could stroke the soft silken down on her head – as silken soft as the fine black hair that covered her father's body. Fur, I'd called it once, but it wasn't fur like a dog's fur, it was far softer than that . . .

Mrs Chandler interrupted my thoughts by setting the vase down beside me again. My eyes flew to the yellow rose: Beauty's rose, that bound her to the Beast. Mrs Chandler sighed, 'Tis a shame for his lordship, not being able to come and see you and the liddle maid just now – and tis a shame for you, too.'

Guilt returned, because I was relieved. I didn't want to see him, I didn't want to see that look of hopeless longing on his face as he came into the room. I couldn't bear it.

But it was my fault. I'd been so frightened while Rose was being born, and he'd been so good to me, helping me, holding me – that ever since, I'd tried too hard to please him. I'd chosen a special name to call him by, talked to him in a special voice, all low and soft – and so I'd led him on, to hope.

If only I'd remembered the fairy tale – remembered that what the Beast had really wanted from Beauty, was love. But it had never even crossed my mind that Leo would want the same: he never had before. Over these last years I'd learnt to care for him, respect him and trust him; and we'd been content together. Oh, why couldn't he be satisfied with that?

I got up and dressed for tea, and after Rose had had hers she dropped off to sleep, so I rang for Ellen to bring Flora down again and we played with her Noah's Ark on the bedroom floor. I pretended to be an extra elephant who wouldn't go up the gang plank so Flora caught hold of my hair to haul me up – and managed to pull most of it down. Of course then she tugged even harder until we both tumbled into a laughing heap on the floor. But when Mrs Chandler came back with the clean linen I realized how untidy I must look so I got up very quickly, brushed myself down and told Flora, 'I'll have to put my hair up again – do 'ee come and help me.'

She rushed over to the dressing table and clambered up on to a chair beside mine to help me untangle my remaining hairpins. Then as I picked up my hairbrush she began her favourite game, 'See Flora build castle, Mama.' My hand mirror took up its accustomed place in the centre with comb to one side and hat whisk on the other. Drawing the brush through my hair in long sweeping strokes I watched her chubby fingers busy with glove stretchers and shoe horn, boot button hook and blue velvet pincushion. When they'd all been precariously propped up I admired my daughter's handiwork before reminding, 'Tis nearly time for thy bath, Flora. Ellen'll be down presently.' Ignoring my warning she seized the second hairbrush and reached out for my carved horn dress combs. Then her head jerked up, she'd heard Ellen's footsteps outside. As the tap came at the door Flora dropped her trophies and dived to hide herself under the sheltering curtain of my hair; I felt the tickle of her breath on my neck as she buried her head in my shoulder.

In the mirror I could see Ellen's smile as she asked Mrs Chandler, 'Is there a little girl in here, Aunt Grace?'

Mrs Chandler's reflection pursed its lips, considering, 'Well now, Ellen, I thought as there were – but she maun up an' gone now, I cassent see her anywhere.'

'Bo!' All of a sudden Flora's beaming face burst through my hair.

'Well I never!'

'Fancy that – Lady Flora were here all the time, an' I didn't realize!'

With a crow of delight Flora tumbled heavily down into my lap to hug me before wriggling round to stand up on my knees and demand, 'Brush Mama's hair.' I gave her the brush and she dabbed at my head; Ellen came forward to guide her hand.

'Nice long strokes now, tis the brushing as makes thy Mama's hair shine – there.' She sighed, 'I wish mine did have a curl in it.'

Flora exclaimed, '*My* hair got curls like Mama.' She seized one of her own blonde curls and held it against mine: pale yellow, daffodil pale, against my deeper golden brown. In the mirror I saw the two women exchange knowing glances, then Mrs Chandler spoke, too quickly: 'I had a letter from our Clara this morning, Ellen. She's had another postcard from young Jim Arnold, o' one of thic towns they been marching through, in France.'

'She'll be pleased wi' that. Clara did allus have a soft spot for Jim.' She came closer, to look down into the cradle, 'And how's liddle Lady Rose today, Aunt Grace?'

'Glad as a bird – she's a good-tempered maid. Though she be a mite fussy about her bath, she likes to have a nice kick afore she'll settle. You'll have to remember that, Ellen, when I hand her over to you at the end of the month.'

'Aye, I will.' My heart sank. She was *my* baby; but not for much longer. All too soon she'd be banished to the nursery, and for a moment I almost hated Ellen; but it wasn't her fault that I'd have to stay down in the big, empty drawing room, it wasn't her fault that I was Lady Warminster.

I heard Rose's wakening murmur and turned towards her. Mrs Chandler glanced warningly at Ellen who immediately spoke briskly to my elder daughter, 'Come along, Lady Flora, tis bath time. Say goodnight to thy Mama.'

'But – '

'Lady Quinham did say as she might come up and read you a story *after* you've had your bath.'

Flora's protests stopped abruptly as she considered this, then she flung her arms around my neck. 'Nightie night, Mama.'

I kissed her soft cheek and stroked her hair, 'Good night, my Flora.' As soon as the door closed behind them I reached down for my younger daughter.

I'd just put Rose back in her cradle and picked up my brush again when I heard rapid footsteps on the landing followed by Miss Annabel's brisk rat-tat.

'How are you, Amy?'

At her quick nod of dismissal Mrs Chandler began to move towards the door; I called after her, 'Mebbe you'd like to go down for a cup o' tea?'

Miss Annabel shook her head at me as the door closed. 'There was absolutely no need to say that, Amy. Servants *always* go down for a cup of tea, *you* should know that.' She came and stood behind me, her eyes looking directly into mine in the mirror. 'It used to be the other way round, didn't it? My sitting at the dressing table and you standing submissively behind – do you remember, Amy?' All at once she seized the brush from my hand. 'Shall I brush *your* hair, my lady?' Raising the brush in a shining silver arc she brought it swiftly down in a single sweeping stroke – then suddenly she threw it on to the dressing table and sent my hairpins skittering across the polished surface.

Her voice was shaking as she asked, 'Do you remember, Amy, do you remember that summer? The summer I came out? I'd dance all night and when I came home you'd be here waiting up for me, and your quick clever fingers would be unhooking my dresses, unpinning my hair, combing it, brushing it – while I kept jumping up and rushing around, telling you about all the exciting young men I'd danced with. And when at last you'd got me to bed I'd lie there and dream about them.'

She paused for a moment, before asking, 'Did you dream as well, Amy? Did you dream of love and moonlight and roses?' Her reflected eyes held mine in the mirror. 'You did, didn't you? But it never crossed my mind that you dreamt too. I should have realized. After all, Great Uncle Thomas noticed, you know; he warned me. "That maid of yours, she'll cause trouble, just you wait and see – she's far too good-looking." But I wasn't bothered, I was so confident every time I looked in the mirror,' she bent to look at both our faces reflected there, 'I only saw my own face. You were always there in the shadows, behind me – but I didn't look at you. It's only now I can see you: see the perfect crescents of your eyelashes; see your soft, golden-flecked eyes; see your shining hair. I couldn't see you then – yet you were there all the time, glowing behind me like a summer peach on the wall, all golden ripe and ready to fall.' I covered my face with my hands but still I could hear her pain and regret as she whispered, 'Oh Amy, if only you'd stayed there, stayed in the shadows! Then you could have kept your dreams – and I could have kept mine.'

I heard the tears in her voice and I wanted to reach out to her – but I couldn't. And then it was too late: there was only the sound of the door closing behind her.

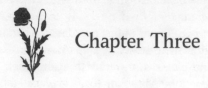

Chapter Three

I didn't see Miss Annabel again until the next evening. As she came through the door my eyes went to her face, but I couldn't read her expression. She stood before me, straight and slender in deep blue satin with her beautiful head held high and diamond combs sparkling in the glossy wings of her upswept hair. 'How are you to-day, Amy?' She raced on, 'I'm dining with Leonidas before I go out – since he's banned from your room I might as well keep him company. You don't mind my borrowing your husband, do you Amy? And after all, he is my father-in-law.'

'No, o' course I dussent mind. He do enjoy talking to you.'

'Yes, I think he does, doesn't he? Look, I really must go now – I promised Flora I'd run upstairs to show her when I was dressed. Good night, Amy.'

In a moment she was gone; she was always so quick and confident and sure. And she was right: Leo did enjoy talking to her. It was different when he dined with me: then he'd just sit there listening, while I chattered on about Flora or the roses. He'd make the odd brief comment in reply – but he didn't really talk to me, like the way he did with Miss Annabel.

All of a sudden I snatched at that thought and gripped it, like a twig to save me from drowning: he *didn't* talk to me – yet surely if he'd really fallen in love with me he would? When you truly loved someone you wanted to talk to them, tell them things as I had with – quickly I thrust the thought away. I mustn't think of him, I mustn't. But that first thought stayed with me. Perhaps I'd misunderstood Leo's expression, and that special look he'd given me had only been a trick of the light. How silly I'd been to read so much into it: yes, he had given me the rose – but only because he knew how much I loved roses.

And this rose meant so much to him. After all, he'd taken years to breed it, and it was very beautiful. No wonder he'd given it my name – because calling the rose after his wife was as near as he could get to calling it after himself.

It was all very simple now; he hadn't fallen in love with me at all – it had just been my imagination. I'd always been one for making up dreams, right from when I was a little girl. And I'd been daft enough to believe them, too. But now I was older I knew better – except the other night, when I'd been silly again, and I'd got myself in such a caddle – all over nothing!

I felt as if a great weight had rolled off my shoulders – and only just in time, too, because when the doctor called the next day he said that my temperature was well down now, so Leo could visit me again of an evening. Then he added with a shake of his head, 'But I must insist that until your confinement is over there is no physical contact at all. Not even a kiss, I'm afraid.'

Not even a kiss. But Leo never had kissed me. I'd borne his child, but he'd never kissed me, never. And I remembered, too, what he'd said to me after Rose's birth: 'You must make the most of her. There will be no others.' He had made it quite clear that we were not to live as man and wife again – so now I had the final proof. How stupid of me ever to have thought anything else.

Even so, the minute he came in next day my eyes flew to his face – but I saw that he wasn't even looking at me. Why ever should he, when he had his new-born daughter to love and admire instead? Smiling, I held her up, so he could see her properly.

'How are you, Amy?'

'I'm very well, thank you,' I added firmly, 'Leo.'

I began to relax; he was just the same as always, and as always he waited for me to talk. So I did, telling him of how wonderfully good Rose had been since I'd last seen him. 'She never do cry.'

He half smiled. 'She scarcely has the need to do that, since all her wants are instantly attended to.'

I looked down at my perfect Rose with a smile, 'Tis my pleasure.'

I waited to see if he wanted to say anything himself, but of course he didn't. Reassured, I began to tell him how Flora had brought her least-favourite doll down for her sister – and then had snatched it back the minute Rose had reached out her hand towards it! He smiled, so then I asked him 'And what have you been doing these last few days, Leo?'

'I've been quite busy, at the hospital.' And that was all he said. So obviously he didn't want to talk to me, and I'd been right yesterday. It was such a relief. And I wouldn't have liked to hear about the hospital anyway: I knew he was working as a Red Cross orderly, but I didn't want to know any more than that. I was such a coward, and I'd always been terrified of blood. Leo knew that.

Mrs Chandler arrived with the tray and the coffeepot: but as soon as she'd put it down she slipped discreetly away, so reluctantly I had to surrender Rose to her cradle, and pour out our coffee. He drank his two cups without speaking, but now that I was at ease with him again I was quite happy to do the talking for both of us, and he seemed equally content to sit there listening. Then of course Rose wanted to join in, so I put my cup down, and lifted her up into my arms.

He came again the next evening, and every evening after that he visited us, sitting quietly sipping his coffee while listening to my news of Flora and Rose. When Rose woke I'd put her to my breast, and he'd sit silently watching as she suckled. Sometimes I'd glance up to catch the tender expression on his face; he loved her so much, just as I did. And then I'd tell myself again how silly I'd been that evening when he'd given me the rose.

So I retreated into my little cocoon, wrapping myself snugly in my love for my daughters, and it kept me safe from the cold world outside.

But every day at tea-time Miss Annabel opened my bedroom door and let the chill air come surging in with her talk of ambulances and stretchers, hospitals and wounded soldiers. Then one day she ripped my cocoon apart. It was only a little tear at first.

'I *am* glad to be doing something useful at last – and I'm not the only one to feel like that. Amy, do you remember Lucas Venn?'

Yes, I remembered him. He was the artist who had painted Miss Annabel's portrait the year she came out. I'd had to go with her to his studio for sittings because in those days before the war a young lady must never go out unaccompanied, not even to visit Mr Venn who was fifty that summer and looked even older, having lost most of his hair, as well as being pigeon-chested. But Miss Annabel was in full flow: 'Well, I met him today, and you'll *never* guess what he was wearing!'

She paused expectantly, so I hazarded, 'A velvet smoking jacket?'

Miss Annabel burst out laughing. 'No, quite the reverse. A tunic of coarsely woven wool – khaki wool! He's enlisted in the RAMC. Lucas Venn, a soldier, can you imagine it?'

I couldn't. 'No, he must have been wearing something like it.'

'Don't be silly, Amy, there isn't anything like it. He was wearing puttees, huge boots – the lot. He's even got a stripe – I couldn't believe it. When he took his cap off I could scarcely keep my face straight: just a few wisps of grey hair straggling over that shining bald pate. I know lots of older men are joining up, but not men like Lucas, and not in the ranks.'

'But he was always so poorly, and then he had that trouble with his arm.'

'Oh, he hasn't changed a bit, Amy, except that his neuritis has cleared up, at least. Just as well, since he spends hours carrying stretchers now. He's an orderly at the Third London General, down at Wandsworth. That's how I met him. I had to drive some men down there and Lucas, of all people, came out to carry them in. I couldn't imagine how he'd managed to persuade the army to take him, so just before I left I asked him how he'd done it, and he said that when he'd got more time he'd tell me the whole story. I simply can't wait to hear it.'

Then her face changed, and became still. She moved across to the window and stood staring out for a moment before continuing. 'One of his friends is down there, too, that sculptor, Derwent Wood. I don't suppose you ever saw any of his work, but he had a real knack for catching a likeness.' She turned to look at me directly. 'Do you know what he does now, Amy, with those clever fingers of his?' I shook my head. 'He still makes likenesses, but of faces that don't exist any more.'

I whispered, 'Portraits – for grave stones?'

'Oh no, Amy. The men who owned these faces aren't dead – but their faces have been blown away by the big guns in France. So Derwent Wood makes masks for them – masks for handsome young men whose features have been destroyed – yet they're still alive.' I was shaking by now, and she saw it. 'Amy, you've no idea what modern weapons can do to a man. Those poor fellows have been so hideously disfigured that they daren't go out in the daytime. Even their own families can't bear to look at them. So Mr Wood – Sergeant Wood as he is now – makes masks of very thin metal and paints them: eyes, noses, mouths – all painted. Lucas took me into the studio, and there were "before" and "after" photographs on the walls. The "befores" were just too unbelievably awful.' She shuddered. 'To think that men can be damaged like that and survive.'

'Tis terrible, terrible!'

She glanced down at her watch. 'Good heavens, is that the time? I must fly, Amy – I've promised to read Flora a story before I leave.' But before reaching the door she turned round again and said, 'Amy, after seeing those photographs I thought of Leonidas. If only he could go down and see those pictures it might just jolt him out of his self-consciousness. He's so obsessed with his own deformities, yet they're nothing, absolutely nothing, compared with what those poor souls are having to live with. After all, you can't wear a mask all the time, can you?'

After she'd gone I lay shivering with cold. Those poor young men!

The doctor told me I could get up straight after breakfast in future: I'd made an excellent recovery from the birth, he said, and before long I would be able to go down and sit in the drawing room again. But I didn't want to do that, because of Rose. The end of my confinement would come all too soon and then I'd have to surrender her to the nursery and pretend to be Lady Warminster again. I knew I had no choice – I *was* Lady Warminster after all – but at least we'd have spent her first precious days together, so I was determined not to waste a single minute of them.

After breakfast next morning I put Rose to doze in her cradle while I got myself up. I'd just finished putting up my hair when Bertha, the housemaid, came in. 'My lady, Mr Tims says as could he have a word wi' you.'

When I went to the door I saw that the butler's face was creased with worry. 'My lady, Lord Quinham's downstairs.'

I stared at Mr Tims in disbelief. 'But – he can't be – he's in France!'

'No, my lady, he's downstairs now, and he's asking for her ladyship. She went out half an hour ago. I told him she wasn't at home, but he said he *must* see her.' His old knuckles cracked as he clenched them anxiously. 'I really don't know what to do; his lordship left for the hospital first thing – not that his young lordship asked for him – it was just Lady Quinham, and he wouldn't believe me when I told him she wasn't at home.'

I said, 'I'm up and dressed, I'll go down.'

Mrs Chandler's voice broke in from behind me. 'But, my lady, tis only just over a fortnight since the liddle maid were born. You've not even been downstairs yet.'

'I'm quite well, I'd best go.'

There was silence. Mr Tims' red-veined eyes peered, full of concern, into mine. 'My lady, if you would – '

Mrs Chandler said reluctantly, 'Mebbe if you were to lean on Bertha's arm – '

I shook my head. 'There's no need. After all, I been going along to the bathroom for more'n a week now.'

But as I started to go down the stairs my legs were trembling. I gripped the bannister firmly, and forced myself to go faster, ahead of the butler and housemaid. Reaching the drawing room landing before tackling the last flight, I still couldn't believe it. I knew his next leave wasn't due for months. But as my slippered feet padded noiselessly down the last few steps I could see through the open library door to where a khaki-clad figure stood, facing the empty hearth. The morning sunlight shone on the sleek fair head and straight slim back of the man who was Miss Annabel's husband, Lord Warminster's son – and the father of my daughter Flora.

I couldn't tear my eyes away from him; my heart was racing and my legs trembling so much I could scarcely make them carry me down that last step into the hall. At the bottom I stumbled, and hearing me, he swung quickly round, his face alight with pleasure. Then he saw who it was and disappointment darkened his eyes. 'Oh, it's you, Amy. I thought – ' He shrugged and gave a little half-smile as I came into the room. 'I didn't expect you to be in Town. Is Flora with you?'

'Aye, she's upstairs in the nursery.'

'Then at least I'll manage a glimpse of *her*. But, Amy,' he came closer, and now I could see the dark shadows under his eyes and the lines of exhaustion etched on his face, 'I must see Annabel – I simply must. Where is she?'

I said, 'She's driving ambulances now, so she went out, more'n half an hour ago.'

'Damn! I knew she was in Town, and I thought at this time of the morning I'd be sure to catch her.'

I whispered, 'I thought you were in France.'

'I was, last night. But I've been on temporary liaison duty with the French, so the powers that be suddenly decided I'd got to come in person to deliver a report on what's been going on recently.' He closed his eyes for a moment. 'God – Verdun! I've never seen anything like it. Those bloody Boches are tearing the heart out of my beautiful France. If Maman were alive to see it today! Anyway, I wangled myself on to an earlier boat so the brass hats at this end aren't expecting me for a couple of hours yet, and I thought if I came here first I'd catch her.'

He sounded so unhappy, I said quickly, 'She do go to lunch round one o'clock at her club, always.'

His face lightened. 'Thanks Amy, you're a sport. Right, I'll run up see Flora for a few minutes, then I'll go straight round to the War Office and insist on their seeing me early – I'll think of something – then I can join her for lunch.'

He smiled at me, and for a moment my heart stopped. 'And at least in the meantime I've had the unexpected pleasure of seeing *you*.'

He came closer. 'To think that only yesterday I was over there! It's like falling asleep in hell and waking up to find a particularly luscious angel hovering over you, except that you're not an angel, are you, Amy? You're a real flesh and blood woman, *I* know that, don't I?' He laughed, and I felt my face growing hotter and hotter. 'Even your forehead's blushing now!' Then his voice lost its teasing note. 'But Amy, what are you doing in Town?'

I took a deep breath before telling him, 'I came up here because of the baby – my baby were born the first day o' this month.'

He stared at me in disbelief. 'Your baby? *His* child?'

I said quickly, 'Tis all right – she's perfect, she baint twisted at all.'

For a moment he was totally silent, then he exclaimed, '*She* – so his child's a girl?'

'Aye – a lovely liddle maid.'

He let out his breath very slowly. 'So he didn't give you a son?'

'Leo, he's main pleased to have another little girl.'

His only reply was to move towards the door. With his hand on the doorknob he announced, 'I'm going upstairs to see *my* daughter, now.' He glanced back to tell me, 'Oh, and Amy, if Annabel should come back for any reason, don't tell her I'm over here, will you? I want to give her a surprise.'

The door closed firmly behind him, and I heard the thud of his boots running up the stairs.

Chapter Four

I could hardly drag myself up the stairs again; by the time I reached the top I was shaking as though I'd run a measured mile. Mrs Chandler came fussing out of my bedroom. 'There, I *knew* you shouldn't 'a gone downstairs – tis too soon, you're the colour of skim milk. Come in and rest on the sofa.'

I was glad to lie down and close my eyes; I couldn't bear to look at her. Behind her concern I sensed the disapproval. I said, 'He did only want to find Miss Annabel – Lady Quinham. I had to go and tell him where she was.'

Mrs Chandler's voice was polite but firm. 'My lady, *I* could have given a message from you.' And, of course, she could. There was no need for me to have gone down. But how could I not have done so, when he'd just come back from France, and only for a few short hours?

In desperation I told Mrs Chandler, 'I think I'll have a little nap. Mebbe you'd like to go downstairs – I'll ring if I need you.' She left.

As soon as the door closed behind her I reached down into the cradle and lifted out my sleepy Rose, seeking comfort in her warm young body. I was so shaken by the strength of my feelings that I almost wished I hadn't gone downstairs. I'd known I still loved him but I'd been trying so hard not to think of him too much. I'd made such an effort to shut him away in the little house in my head, keeping the memories behind that small front door; but now, seeing him had let them out again and I was too weak to control them. As I lay on the sofa, they came rushing back, golden as sunlight: golden as the summer had been, that summer of joy and hope. I could see Frank now, that day in Hyde Park, twirling the carved ivory handle of the dainty parasol on his forefinger, looking at me with the flashing smile of his blue eyes. I could hear the gaiety of his laughter, and feel the warm strength of his hand holding mine as he spoke those magical words: 'When can I see you again, Amy?'

And so it had begun. I should have known better: Grammer had brought me up to know right from wrong. But I'd thought he loved me, needed me, so I'd given him all I had – and sinned. Just as my own mother had sinned. For a moment I was a child again, hearing Grammer's harsh voice croak its judgement, 'You be conceived in sin and born in sin. You be a sinner.' I turned my face to the pillow and wept.

Miss Annabel came back at tea-time. As soon as she walked through the door, I saw the two red spots of anger burning on her cheeks. She said sharply, 'You may go, Mrs Chandler,' and the door was barely closed behind Clara's mother before she rounded on me in a blaze of fury.

'How could you, Amy, how could you? You knew I never wanted to see him again – and then you told him where to find me! He walked into the club, into the dining room, and informed them he was joining me for lunch – so, of course, they let him in – my *husband* back from the Front. I had to sit and eat with him in public – and pretend nothing had happened!' She came closer, and I cringed away from her anger. 'Do you know what he dared to suggest? That we both forgive and forget. Francis has decided to forgive *me*! He gives me a dose of the clap on my wedding night which damages my womb beyond repair, and then he deigns to forgive *me* for having it removed without his permission – the cheek of it!'

'I be sure as he didn't never mean to hurt you – '

Her furious voice broke across my words. 'How can you *dare* to defend him?' She was silent for a moment, before continuing, her voice low and bitter now. 'Still, I suppose it's easier for *you* to forgive him; he may have treated you in his typically irresponsible way but at least your baby lived – you were left with a child at the end of it all. Anyway, you knew what you were doing, didn't you, Amy? It wasn't *your* wedding night – you went to him with your eyes open.' She paused to draw an angry breath before accusing me again, 'But what about the child you so thoughtlessly conceived? Didn't you even *think* of that possibility? What would have happened to Flora if Leonidas hadn't been a man of honour?' Her eyes never left mine as she told me, 'We know the answer, don't we – because it happens all the time. She'd have been dumped in the workhouse – or worse still, brought up by a mother who was on the streets!' There was no reply I could make. Every word she'd said was true. With one last look of contempt she abruptly turned away and left me.

I huddled in my chair, the tears coursing down my cheeks. He hadn't meant to hurt her, but he had. He'd been careless, he hadn't thought. But I knew he'd never have deliberately hurt her because he loved her, he always had.

When Bertha brought my tray up later I forced myself to eat and drink for Rose's sake, but all the time I was worrying: however would I tell Leo? But as soon as he walked into the room I knew there was no need – Miss Annabel already had. His face was dark as a thunder cloud and he didn't sit down; he just stood lowering over me.

'Did the doctor give you permission to go downstairs?' He knew the answer, but he waited, forcing me to give it.

'No. I – '

'So why did you go?' He was simmering with rage.

'He – Lord Quinham – he wanted to know where Miss Annabel was.'

'You had no *right* to tell him of her movements if she had not chosen to inform him herself.'

In my panic I heard myself lapsing even further into dialect. 'But she do be his wife.'

He stiffened, forcing his twisted shoulder and humped back up to his full great height, and each word was a lash of anger as he replied, 'As you – are – mine.' Then he added bitterly, 'Whatever the circumstances of our marriage.' There was silence, but only for a moment, before his next accusation. 'You allowed him to see Flora.'

'He – he be her . . . ' I couldn't complete the sentence, but the unvoiced word hung heavy in the air between us.

He shouted, 'She is *my* child! In law she is *mine*! *I* acknowledged her. He has no rights over her whatsoever. There is no legal relationship – ' He broke off, his face suffused with blood, because, of course, we both knew that wasn't true. In law, my daughter was Frank's sister. Leo suddenly swung round and lurched out, slamming the door shut behind him. He'd not even looked at Rose.

I was shaking, not just from his words but from the intensity of his anger. I heard again the fury in his voice as he'd shouted, 'She is *my* child! In law she is *mine*!' And she was, she was – because he was my husband. But I couldn't stop loving Frank, however wrong it was. Guilt weighed me down, crushing me. Because what I had done had been wrong, very wrong – a sin. And when the price of that sin had had to be paid only one man had held out his hand to save me – this man who was my husband.

Leo didn't come back that evening, but Miss Annabel did. She moved restlessly round the room, first twitching the curtains straight, and then fidgeting with the vase of wooden spills on the mantelpiece.

Eventually I broke the silence. 'I'm sorry, terribly sorry I told him, if you didn't want him to know – '

She turned to face me. 'Oh, I suppose you couldn't help it, you're so totally infatuated by him. You always have been. Otherwise I doubt if you'd have behaved as you did. After all, you were never flighty, were you, Amy? I can remember Mama commenting approvingly on that, before – ' Her face tightened.

Quietly I admitted, 'I know I did wrong – but Miss Annabel, at least I didn't break one of the Commandments. What I did, 'twere fornication, not adultery.'

Her voice was sharp with mockery as she retorted, 'You betray your humble origins there, Amy. Society is far more tolerant of the latter sin.'

I flinched, but kept on trying to defend myself. 'But it were only the one night. And if you hadn't quarrelled with him, and sent his betrothal ring back, I wouldn't *never* have let him do what he did then.'

Her expression eased a little, then she said more quietly, 'No. I don't think you would.'

I pressed on, 'And afore that in London, I thought he was courting me. I never knew he were your Lord Quinham – not wi' him teasing me the way he did by calling himself "Mr Dunn". I was too slow, I should have realized – he told me afterwards he thought as I'd guessed the truth.'

'Did he? Really?' She sounded disbelieving. 'As I said, you're more forgiving than I am, Amy. If you ask me, I think he enjoyed every minute of that deception. In fact when you told me about it I rather assumed he'd spent the entire summer laughing up his sleeve at the pair of us.'

She came closer. 'Oh, don't let you and I quarrel over him, Amy – after all, we've both had to pay the price of loving him. Now the only sensible thing is to make sure we don't go on paying it. I'm certainly not going to – I've learnt my lesson. Loving Francis hurts – it hurt more than I could ever have believed possible. So I'll never, ever make that mistake again.' I could hardly bear to look at her face as she exclaimed, 'Yes, I loved him once – but now I hate him!' Then her voice steadied as she added, 'And if you've got any sense, Amy, you'll do the same.'

'No! I cassent – '

'After the way he left you in the lurch – '

Desperately I shook my head, 'No, he never meant to do that – because he knew I were betrothed to Joe, Joe Dempster. He didn't know as I'd tell Joe the truth. He thought I could just marry Joe, quick as quick – then Joe wouldn't 'a found out till Flora were born.'

'And what sort of future would that have been for poor little Flora! So he was willing to let his own daughter down, too.' Then the anger died from her voice and she said softly, 'Life is very odd sometimes, isn't it? I thought I'd hate Flora – but I don't. I suppose it's because she looks so like Francis must have done when he was young and innocent.' She smiled, and for a moment it was the young Miss Annabel I saw in front of me again. 'I'm glad Leonidas married you, for her sake.'

Then her eyes held mine as she told me firmly, 'Leonidas is a good man, Amy. He deserves more than mere loyalty from his wife. I hope you realize that.'

After she'd gone I wept over Rose's sleeping head.

Leo came in briefly after dinner. He was still brooding and angry and refused my timid offer of coffee. So I offered him Rose instead, and he held her, talking softly to her for a while; then as he handed her back to me, he told me that I was to go back to Eston with the children as soon as my month of confinement was over. I didn't argue, for in London now I feared for my daughters.

It was Mrs Johnstone who'd told me, just that morning – Mrs Johnstone the housekeeper, who'd disliked me ever since I had first gone to Eston as the new Lady Quinham's maid. She'd had her own way in that house for so long – lazy, slovenly, and overfond of the bottle as she was – so she'd not been best pleased when Miss Annabel arrived on the scene. And when I'd come back as Lady Warminster she'd resented me ever since – her and her crony Mrs Procter, who could cook well when she wanted to, but generally didn't bother.

This morning Mrs Johnstone had insisted on coming to my room on some pretence of consulting me – although she *never* consulted me: she despised me too much. More than once, knowing that I was nearby, I'd heard her say to Mrs Procter: 'Now in the time of the *first* Lady Warminster, of sainted memory – she

23

was a true lady, she was – ' then she would turn towards me with a feigned start of surprise, 'Oh, I didn't hear *you* coming. Did *you* want to speak to me?' Followed by a long deliberate pause before the exaggerated, 'My lady?' So now I wondered why she'd come; I wasn't long finding out.

'Them Zeppelins've been over again – there was people killed the very night his lordship's daughter was being born.'

I exclaimed, 'In London?'

Reluctantly she shook her head. 'They was *aiming* for London – but one on 'em was shot at on the way, by our guns, and it fell in the sea, all on fire. But it'll be only a matter of time afore they have another go, stands to reason.' She watched me, gloating; she knew I was a coward.

I asked Miss Annabel later if it were true. 'Certainly, and there've been other raids since, all over the place. Scotland, Norfolk – East Anglia's been hit more than once – obviously Eastern England's bound to be vulnerable. But Leonidas swore me to secrecy, and ordered Mrs Chandler and the nursemaids not to say a word of it to you. He thought you might be frightened.'

I shivered. 'I *am* frightened.'

She laughed. 'Goodness, Amy, there are four million people in London. What makes you imagine the Germans are aiming at you?' Then her smile faded. 'Just remember how much worse it is for my poor wounded soldiers, not even safe in their own capital. But you needn't worry; as soon as your confinement period has ended, you're to go back to Eston. Leonidas is concerned about the children, and he's quite right to be: they shouldn't be exposed to danger unnecessarily.'

'Is he coming back to Eston as well?'

'I shouldn't think so. He volunteered for Red Cross work, just as I did – he won't simply chuck it in.'

'But the roses, his roses, they'll be coming out soon – '

Annabel interrupted curtly. 'Amy, don't you *dare* suggest that Leonidas gives up what he's doing to spend the summer simply pottering about in his rose garden! Don't you understand him at *all*? With his family tradition he'd have been in the army as soon as he grew up if he'd been normal and even if he'd left by now, he would have been back again the minute this war broke out – he's still on the right side of fifty. Why, only last night, when talking to me over dinner, he gave me a long list of names of just about everyone who was a contemporary of his at Eton. They're all in uniform now. Even some men ten years or more older than him – they may be only in charge of remounts, that kind of thing, but they're all serving their King and country. All except poor Leonidas! I feel so sorry for him. It's such a dreadful humiliation for a man with his background, not to be holding the King's commission at a time like this.'

I dared to say, 'Lord Quinham – he's in the army.'

'Of course. I wouldn't still use his name if he wasn't.' Her face stiffened, and I heard the pride in her voice as she said, 'Francis will do his duty and fight bravely. I have no doubts on that score.' Then her voice hardened. 'There's nothing wrong with his patriotism – only his morals.'

I said, 'But he do love thee.'

There was both anger and regret in her voice as she replied, 'Amy, you may still believe in fairy-tale happy endings – but I don't.'

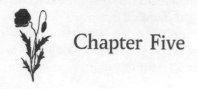

Chapter Five

The four weeks of my confinement would end on the Saturday; on the Sunday we were to return to Wiltshire. Leo had decided and the doctor had agreed. I wanted to take my daughters back to the safety of the countryside – but I didn't want to lose Rose. For a few last precious days I would have her to myself; after that, the nursery would claim her.

I dreaded the thought of it: how could I bear to be separated from her? Already Ellen had mentioned casually, 'Aunt Grace says Lady Rose is settling into a nice routine now, taking a proper long feed every three hours – so you'll soon be able to get back to normal, my lady.'

I said quickly, 'She do like a suck more often than that.'

Ellen laughed. 'I 'low she does. We'd all like a cup of tea every ten minutes if we had the chance, wouldn't we? But we don't need it.' I gazed down at my beautiful Rose; it was true, she didn't need it. Ellen was brisk. 'You mustn't spoil her, my lady.'

'No, but . . . ' I sighed.

After Ellen had taken Flora away, I lifted Rose up, caressing her cheek with mine, whispering to her, telling her of my love. Her small hands reached out in response and I hugged her close, settling her down in my arms again. It was I who was getting spoilt, having her with me all the time. After all, if I'd married Joe Dempster and lived in a cottage, I wouldn't have been able to nurse her all the time: there would be meals to cook and the house to clean. And although I'd liked and respected Joe, I hadn't loved him, either – at once my thoughts winged to the man I love. But I would still have had to give my baby up to the nursery, even if he'd been my husband – Suddenly, I realized where my thoughts were leading, and seizing hold of the door of the little house in my head I slammed it tight – shutting away my memories, battening them down, just as I had done ever since I was a child. But they wouldn't always stay shut away. Sometimes the door was prised open, and they'd come bursting out – to leave me weak and shaken until I could force them back inside again.

It was Mrs Chandler who let the memories out this time: she didn't intend to do it, she meant to be helpful. I told her that I wanted to choose the material for Rose's christening gown while we were still in London: 'I'll just slip out to the shops on Saturday.'

She looked quite shocked, 'My lady, 'tisn't fitting for you to go outside o' thic house afore you've been churched!'

'But I'm chapel, Mrs Chandler.'

She looked even more shocked at that. Then she shook her head firmly. 'No, my lady, not now. His lordship be church, so you maun be too.'

So after lunch on Friday I had to leave Rose behind, put on my hat and coat and go downstairs with Bertha. Outside the front door I stopped to lift my face to the spring sunshine; Bertha's grip on my arm tightened. 'You maunt dawdle, my lady, you maunt go straight to the church – otherwise tis bad luck.' Her voice dropped to a whisper. 'A woman just risen from childbed, her's unclean till she's abeen properly churched.'

But I didn't speed up. I was rather enjoying my outing. It wasn't far to the church on Eaton Square and I'd left Rose fast asleep; I was sure she wouldn't wake up before I got back.

The verger was waiting in the porch with a square veil of white linen. I put it over my hat and followed him into the quiet gloom of the church, and down to the front pew. The Rector stepped forward and began to address me: 'Forasmuch as it hath pleased Almighty God of his goodness to give you safe deliverance, and hath preserved you in the great danger of childbirth . . .'

I shivered at the memory of my fear and pain – then forced myself to concentrate as he began to read the Psalm on my behalf: 'The snares of death compassed me round about: and the pains of hell gat hold upon me . . .'

The pains of hell.

Those words burst open the door of my memory. In a moment I was back in the chapel at Borrell, the preacher's harsh voice loud in my ear. 'Ye will all burn in the fires of hell!' The leaping flames, the devils dancing old and evil – but the flames were leaping up between the apple trees behind the cottage as I watched them burn my Dimpsey, watched devils with pitchforks tossing burning straw on to her beautiful golden hair. And I was a child again – hearing the frantic scrabbling of her little bound trotters – seeing the pigsticker's knife slicing down – watching her lifeblood drain away –

'Lady Warminster, are you feeling faint?'

Somehow I dragged myself back from the past, and managed to control the shudders that racked my body. I drank the water they brought me, dousing the flames of my memory with its flat coolness. 'Do you feel well enough to continue with the service of thanksgiving now, Lady Warminster?' Thanksgiving. Giving thanks for Rose: I nodded. 'Gracious is the Lord . . .'

Bertha took me home in a cab, and she had to help me up the stairs. But the minute I was through the bedroom door I was almost running to the cradle to pick up Rose. Mrs Chandler didn't want to send up for Flora: she said I looked pale and should lie down, but I insisted. I wanted both my daughters with me. I must love them, care for them, protect them – never let them see what I had seen, or feel what I had felt under the apple trees that evening when Grammer made me stand and watch my Dimpsey die.

Leo came back early, just after tea. 'You shouldn't have gone out this afternoon.' His voice was accusing. 'Tims tells me you were scarcely able to walk up the stairs on your return.' He came a step closer, 'And you don't look much better now.' Accusation turned to concern, 'What's the matter, Amy? What's upset you? Tell me, tell me what it is.'

Before I could stop myself I'd blurted out like a frightened child, 'I were thinking o' Dimpsey.'

His eyebrows came together in a questioning frown, 'Dimpsey?'

The name was a question, but now I remembered that I wasn't a child any longer. Quickly I said, 'Flora'll be expecting you, you'd best go straight up to her – she'll have heard you come in.'

He hesitated. 'But Amy, you look so pale – are you sure I can't – '

I didn't let him finish. ''Tis nothing. You go on up to Flora.' He turned and left me at once.

By the time he came up after dinner the door of the little house in my head was bolted and barred once more.

As he sat down his eyes searched my face, 'How are you, Amy?'

'I'm fine now, Leo – 'twas just the shock of going out for the first time.'

'Grace Chandler should never have allowed it.'

'I had to be churched, else I couldn't go outside.'

'Superstitious twaddle! In any case,' his bushy eyebrows came together in a frown, '*you're* not a member of the established church – you couldn't even find your way round the Book of Common Prayer on Christmas Day.'

''Tis true as I were chapel, only Mrs Chandler said as I be – am, church now, because you are.'

'I don't consider myself anything.'

'You do go to church at Eston, sometimes.'

He snapped, 'Custom.'

It wasn't a very promising opening, but I knew I had to ask for my daughter's sake. 'When were you thinking of having Rose christened?'

'I was not thinking of having my daughter baptized.'

'But she must be christened. Flora was.'

'The sister at the hospital was insistent. I – On that occasion, I did not choose to dispute the matter. There were – other things on my mind.'

I said, 'I think Rose should be christened.' He didn't answer. But I had to say it, and I managed to keep my voice level as I did. 'If she isn't christened then she'll go to – hell.'

His grey eyes looked straight into mine. 'There is no hell – except that which we make for ourselves on earth.' His voice was bitter as he added, 'And in my experience baptism has provided no defence against *that*.' He glanced towards the coffeepot before saying in a tone that brooked no argument, 'It is a meaningless ritual, so I see no necessity whatsoever in having *my* daughter christened.'

I said swiftly, 'She be half mine.'

He blinked, then replied smoothly, 'Have *your* half christened, then.' With that, he settled himself back in his chair, looking rather smug, his eye on the coffeepot again.

I chose my words carefully. 'If you think it don't mean anything, then it

28

doesn't matter to you whether she's christened or not, does it?' His smug expression slipped slightly; I pressed on. 'But seeing as it does mean something to me, then it might as well be done as not. Bain't that sensible?'

Suddenly he gave a sound that was part grunt and part laugh. 'Yes, I suppose it does. Who taught you to argue logically, Amy?'

'I'm not *arguing*, I'm simply pointing it out.'

'You *are* arguing – in the true sense of the word – and I accept your arguments. Very well, then, have my daughter christened, if you must.' He reached out for the coffeepot and began to pour.

Getting up to leave later he said, 'If you insist on going through with this christening performance, you might ask Annabel if she would care to be a godmother.'

I asked her next morning. She said no.

'But – '

'I said no and I mean no. Since I can't ever be a mother to my own child, I won't be a godmother to anyone else's.' She walked out.

She came back again later, before she left to drive her ambulance, and I saw her eyes were red and swollen. I started to say, 'If only I'd – '

She shook her head. 'If onlies are useless, Amy. In any case, you weren't to blame on that occasion – we both knew whose fault it was. Tell Leonidas I won't be able to get away from Town. He'll probably guess the truth – he's no fool – but I don't want to talk about it.'

When I told Mrs Chandler I'd be going out to buy the materials for Rose's christening gown, she looked rather flustered, then said, 'His lordship, he says as you've not to go out again, not afore tomorrow, when we go back to Eston. He said as I shouldn't 'a let you go out yesterday, you weren't fit for it.'

'I know he were a mite put out.'

She just looked at me. 'Aye, you could put it that way.'

'He weren't best pleased wi' me, either.'

'Men,' she sighed. 'They don't understand what matters to a woman.' Then she brightened. 'Still, tis only 'cause he wants to take care of you.'

'And Rose,' I added quickly. 'He be powerful fond o' Rose.'

She smiled. 'Aye, that's true. Some men, they'd want a son; but his lordship, he were just as pleased with a little maid.' Her smile broadened. 'And you're young, my lady, you got plenty of time for boys yet. Now, Bertha can go and fetch what you wants from the shops – or I'll go, if you can spare me.'

'You go, Mrs Chandler. I dare say you'd enjoy a little outing. His lordship has an account at Harrods, and they've got everything I need there.'

She came back full of excitement. 'I've never seen the like of it afore. That baint a shop – tis a fairy palace. Now, I brought thic parcel with me. I know as you'd be wanting to make a start.'

Eagerly I opened it: finest white silk, Valenciennes lace, yards of satin ribbon

– my fingers itched to pick up the needle. I'd drafted the pattern while Mrs Chandler was out shopping, so I cut out and tacked the pieces at once. One seam was almost complete when there was a tap at the door. Bertha put her head round. 'You got a visitor, my lady – Mrs Thomson.'

It was Beat. Beat Harris she'd been when I first knew her, my Aunt Agnes' closest friend. When Aunt Agnes had been dying, Beat had promised her she'd look after the boys – and she had, by marrying Uncle Alf. Now she'd come all the way up from Lambeth to see me.

She bustled in, gave me a smacking kiss and tickled Rose under the chin. 'My, just you look how she's grown – and what a little beauty she is n'all.'

'Aye, she be as good as gold. Do 'ee sit down, Beat. Mrs Chandler – ' She was already discreetly heading for the door. 'Mebbe you could ask Bertha to bring up a cup o' tea for Mrs Thomson.'

'I wouldn't say no, ducks, ta.' Beat dropped heavily into a chair and it creaked protestingly – as did her corsets. 'It ain't arf warm in here, Amy. I'll take me titfer off.' It was her best hat, with the bobbing red cherries. She carefully skewered her hairpins through the crown, then put it on her lap. 'Nah then, Amy, howy're keeping? I thought as how I'd just pop in before your month was up, and you started gadding about again – dances, theatres, and what not, like what you ladies do.'

I'd never been to a dance in my life, and only ever been inside a theatre once, and that hadn't been a proper theatre, just a music hall, with Frank – but I mustn't remember that. ''Tis good of you to call, Beat. How are the boys?'

As Beat settled herself more comfortably, her corsets creaked again before admitting defeat. 'Ned's got his second stripe up already, and he's not nineteen till the summer. What with Albie already made up to sergeant, Alf's right proud of the pair of 'em. Aggie would've been, too.' She sighed. 'Poor Aggie – I still misses her, even arter all this time, but at least she was spared the worry of her two eldest boys going for soldiers – and the way it's dragging on, George and Jim'll be off n'all. Though they 'ave been saying down at the Rose and Crown as there's going to be a big battle in the summer and then we'll send them Jerries packing.'

There was a tap on the door; Bertha had arrived with the tea-tray. When Beat was settled with her cup she said, 'You knows, Amy, when Alf comes home again, I reckon as 'ow I'll 'ave to make a proper fuss of him, after what he's had to put up with in France. After all, he didn't have to go, at his age. You got to admire Alf for that, ain'tcha?'

Uncle Alf had been my stepfather, but I hadn't known that when Aunt Agnes was still alive; she'd never told me she was really my mother – and then it had been too late. I looked down at Rose, and felt the tears threatening as I listened to the latest news of the boys.

Then Beat asked me, 'And 'ow's young Flora – had her nose put out of joint, 'as she?'

'She be a mite jealous – but Leo, he do make a fuss of her.'

Beat smiled. 'Well, she is his granddaughter, when all's said and done. He won't go off of her just 'cause he's got one of his own, will he?'

I couldn't help it, I blurted out, '*He* came the other day – Flora's father. They sent him over from France with a message for the War Office, and he came here first.'

Beat was watching my face. When she spoke, her voice was kind but firm. 'Look 'ere, Amy, it ain't no use. You're somebody else's wife now, and he's somebody else's husband.'

'Miss Annabel didn't want to see him. She says she hates him.'

Beat shook her head. 'That's her business. Couples is always falling out and then making it up later. But anyways, you got your own 'ome and family to think about now. And his lordship's been a good husband to you, you can't deny that. I know it weren't easy, marrying him the way you did, but you made your bed, and now you got to lie in it.' She winked. 'Besides, when it comes down to it, all tomcats is grey in the dark – you should know that by now, Amy.' She hauled herself up out of the chair. 'Must go, duck. Ta-ta for now – and ta-ta to you, little Rose. Ain't she a little love, eh?'

After she'd gone, her words stayed with me: 'You made your bed.' But I hadn't. I hadn't knowingly made that decision. I'd never told Beat the truth, nor Miss Annabel, but Frank knew – and so did my husband.

Pushing that memory aside, I thought instead of Beat's news of Albie and Ned; they were my brothers, but they didn't know that, and I would never tell them. With a sigh I picked up my sewing and began to set the tiny, regular stitches. Rose's christening gown must be perfect.

I was sewing again when Leo came up for his coffee; putting my work safely aside I reached for the pot. As I poured, I saw him go to my sewing and pick it up; it looked very white and delicate in his huge black-furred hand. He carried it back to his chair, took out his spectacles and put them on to inspect the seams. I smiled to myself, confident of my stitches: even Grammer wouldn't have ripped *them* out. Leo looked up. 'Surely these stitches don't need to be so small? You'll strain your eyes.'

I almost snatched it off him. ''Tis Rose's christening gown.'

'I am aware of that, but I really don't see the necessity for – '

'You don't sew lace and silk with a *darning* needle.'

'Oh.' He fell silent. We were both halfway through our first cup before he spoke again. 'Did you ask Annabel if she would agree to be godmother?'

I replied without looking at him, 'Yes, but she said she didn't, couldn't – ' I stumbled to a halt. I heard his soft exclamation: 'That damned young fool!' Then his voice rose again. 'Tell her I quite understand. So whom have you decided on instead?'

I was silent. I couldn't think of anyone else. I should have liked to have asked for Mrs Chandler's daughter, Clara, but I knew you couldn't have housemaids for godmothers. So I just sat there. He was watching my face intently and I thought, he's won. He didn't want Rose christened and now – Suddenly I said, 'Would you mind if – could I ask Beat?'

'Mrs Harris?' He sounded surprised, then he shrugged. 'Why not? I hardly suppose she's a communicant Anglican, but I am in no position to quibble at that! Once the date is fixed, write and invite her down to Eston for the weekend. You will no doubt be pleased to have her company. Ask Selby for a postal order to cover her fare and incidental expenses.'

I heaved a sigh of relief. 'Thank 'ee – though she's Mrs Thomson now – Uncle Alf said as they'd best get wed afore he went to be a soldier 'cause of the allotment.'

Leo frowned. 'He enlisted, your stepfather enlisted?'

'Aye, he said if his boys were going, then so was he. He's a sergeant now.'

I knew what the next question was going to be before it came, but I had to answer it: 'How – old is he?'

I looked down at my lap. 'He were just turned fifty, last spring. Only he were a sailor when he were younger, so naturally –'

'Naturally.' When I sneaked a look I saw his lips were set in a tight line – a lopsided line. He was as he was; there was nothing he could do about that.

When he spoke again he sounded almost angry. 'You will still need a godfather, if you insist on going ahead with this performance, and a second godmother.'

At last I said, 'I don't know anybody else to ask.' I reached out a hand to the christening gown, then drew it back again. I was near to tears.

Leo looked away, then in a voice that was deliberately casual, he suggested, 'I could ask George Burton. I've known him all my life and he's still in England.'

'Would you?'

Still not looking at me, he added, 'And there is his mother. I don't suppose Ettie Burton would mind. Do you wish me to write to her?'

'Oh, please, Leo. Thank you – thank you so much. You been very thoughtful.'

He flushed brick red. 'Not – always. Indeed, I have frequently been extremely remiss. I do, however, intend to remedy one of my omissions.' He reached into his pocket and drew out a small box. Leaning across, he placed it on the tray beside me. 'That's for you.'

'For me?' Eagerly I opened it; inside was a ring. It was beautiful. When I'd been Miss Annabel's maid I'd looked after her jewellery, and seen her mother's jewels, too, putting them away of an evening when it had been my turn to wait up. They'd had lovely jewels, but I'd never seen a ring like this before. It was a half-hoop of five matching diamonds, the largest stone set in the centre and the others slightly smaller. They were fine lustrous white diamonds – nothing cold about these stones – and as I moved them they shimmered with light. The gold setting was lovely too: intricately carved with a flowing pattern of leaves and tiny roses, each one perfect. I exclaimed, 'Tis beautiful. I bain't never seen the like afore!' I looked up at him. 'Thank you, Leo, thank 'ee so much.'

His face was still flushed. 'Aren't you going to – to put it on?'

'Aye.' I spread out my right hand and began to slip the ring over the knuckle – then something in his stillness alerted me. 'Be it, is it – an engagement ring?' He shifted his head slightly in assent and at once I pulled the ring off, and slid it instead onto the third finger of my left hand, pushing it down to rest in its proper place above my wedding ring. I held it up so that he could see it. 'Thank you, Leo.'

His voice was low and halting as he said, 'I have – been – negligent. I should have given you such a ring before.'

I tried to lighten the atmosphere. 'Well, you didn't have much of a chance, did you? After all, we weren't betrothed for very long, were we?'

His face stiffened and his cup and saucer came down heavily on the tray. 'We were never betrothed at all – not as far as *you* were aware.' Suddenly he jerked himself upright. 'I will see you – in the morning.' The door almost slammed shut behind him.

There had been such anger in his voice, yet I knew that this time the anger was not directed at me – but at himself. Only it hadn't been his fault, it had been mine. Mine at the first sinful step, and mine at the last unwitting stumble into the trap of marriage. Yes, he had set that trap, but he had never intended it as a trap; simply a refuge.

I had been desperate, and he had helped me. To him I was merely a servant, dismissed in disgrace by his daughter-in-law, but because he was a responsible employer, and I was carrying the child of his son, he helped me. He'd given me money, and told me, 'Take this, and secure respectable lodgings until the birth. Tell the landlady that you will be receiving a weekly allowance.' 'Until the birth': those words had tormented me, because what would happen after that? But I'd known the answer already: the workhouse or the streets.

So I'd been desperate. In my despair I'd thought of my own mother, who'd been in the same plight – but at least she'd been able to send me back to Granfer, where I was safe. And that had given me the idea: for the child I was carrying had a granfer too – Lord Warminster. So I'd offered my baby to him, before she was even born. And he'd accepted.

I could still remember the pain of knowing that I must lose her – but there was worse even than that. Because although I was handing her over to a man who could give her everything, there was one thing even he could not give her. Like me, she would be a nameless, a bastard – and so she would have to pay the price that I had always had to pay.

Then when the time of her birth drew near I'd become very ill, and Beat had had to take me to the hospital. I'd been terrified, and kept calling like a child for the man I loved, crying for 'my lord' to come and comfort me. Yet even in the midst of my pain and confusion that one awful thought had haunted me still:

my baby would be born without a name. So when Beat had brought Lord Warminster to the hospital I'd cried out to him in my despair, 'My lord, canst thee not give her a name?'

My cry had sprung the trap. Because the doctor, hearing me, believing that Leo was the 'my lord' I'd cried for and that he was the father of the child I was about to bear, had replied, 'Only marriage can legitimize a child.'

Even then, the jaws wouldn't have snapped shut on me if it hadn't been for Beat. She'd meant to help, to save me from having to lose my child, so she'd suggested to Lord Warminster that he should marry me to claim his grandchild – for hadn't the doctor told them I was dying? I knew he'd had no time to think – the birth was due – so he'd gone for the marriage licence at once.

But he'd told the doctor that in the meantime, he *must* ask me if I were willing to make such a marriage. Only what the doctor had said when he came to me, was: 'Your precious "my lord" had agreed to marry you.' I was a servant: to me even the man I loved was 'my lord' – so I'd thought he meant Frank.

Despite the state I was in I'd known Frank wasn't free to marry me, but to my muttered protests the doctor replied, 'He informed me that his wife is dead.' And I'd believed him, because I knew Miss Annabel had been very ill, expecting their first child.

So it wasn't until I was huddled in my wheelchair in front of the chaplain and heard Frank's father's halting voice behind me say, 'I – will,' that I'd realized my mistake. At once I'd cried out, 'No! No!' But my labour pains had started, the doctor misunderstood my cry – everyone misunderstood. And so they'd coaxed me to reply, to put my hand on Leo's, to stammer my vows – just as he'd stammered his. All I could do then was to cling to his black furry hand as the pains gripped me – until the first convulsion racked my body, and there was nothing left but fear and darkness. By then it was too late: Leonidas Arthur Hector Fitzwarren-Donne, Seventh Earl of Warminster, and Amy Roberts, bastard grand-daughter of a country labourer, had become man and wife.

I didn't tell Lord Warminster that I'd only agreed to the wedding because of a mistake, I didn't tell anyone – until months later when I told Frank. I wished, how I wished, that I'd held my foolish tongue, because at once Frank had thrown the truth in Leo's face. Ever since, my husband had been tormented by guilt. His guilt and my guilt: because I did not love him, could not love him.

I looked across at the golden rose, and saw that its last petals had fallen now. Tomorrow we would go back to Eston.

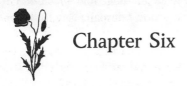

Chapter Six

We were to leave after lunch. Mrs Johnstone, Mr Tims, and Mrs Procter were to go down in the morning, to be ready to meet us there. Leo had gone to the hospital at the usual time, as he was coming back to fetch us later. Meanwhile, Ellen and Dora, the young nursemaid, would be busy packing up the nursery equipment, so I was able to have both my daughters with me for one last morning. I took them out into the gardens in the square; it was the last day of April and the sun was shining, but as I cuddled Rose and kept a watchful eye on Flora's blonde head I couldn't help a feeling of sadness. I did want to leave London – but I didn't want to go back to Eston.

Mrs Chandler had said only that morning, 'You'll be glad to be getting home, my lady,' but I wasn't. I did not belong at Eston: it was his home, not mine. It was a house for a lady, and I wasn't a lady and never would be. I was a servant; worse than that, I was a servant who'd gone astray.

Worse still was the thought of losing Rose. I didn't want her banished to the nursery. I wanted her beside me, where she belonged, and where I could hear at once her first questioning call. Why should she wait if she needed me? And why should I deny myself the pleasure of giving her what she needed, the minute she needed it?

But I knew it was no use asking those questions; I was a countess now, a lady, and ladies did not sit in the nursery all day waiting to suckle their babies. Ladies didn't cook or bake or clean either, or do any of the things I enjoyed doing. I told myself I could read, but I didn't want to read in the morning; reading was a treat, to be saved for the evenings, after a hard day's work – only I hadn't any work to do. I would simply sit in the huge gloomy drawing room waiting until my baby was brought to me. I sighed. Then Flora came running to show me a smooth round pebble, and as I admired it I remembered that I would be able to take her for walks at Eston, and I could sew; that at least was allowed.

Mrs Chandler, Ellen, Dora and I travelled with the children in a 'Ladies Only' compartment, so I could feed Rose without any embarrassment. At Salisbury, Leo escorted us to the ladies' waiting room until the Yeovil train was due. For the last part of the journey he joined us; Flora ran to scramble up on his knee, and she perched there stabbing her finger at the window, asking endless questions all the way to Eston.

The carriage was waiting outside the station, old Mr Tyson up on the box, the boy standing proudly on the steps. There were no young men in the stables now; they'd all gone to the war.

With a clip-clop of hooves, we set off out of the station forecourt and down the slope to the village. Leo leant forward, keen to look out; Eston was his village. Every house and garden, every stick and stone, belonged to him. He was a good landlord: each pointed window frame, each neat porch, each lacey patterned bargeboard was shining white on those brick-built cottages. And there wouldn't be a tile out of place on the steep-pitched roofs, either; I knew that. But I couldn't see them, because I was crouching back in my seat trying to hide. Although it was a Sunday afternoon there were a lot of people out in the main street. They'd known which train we were arriving by, his lordship coming home with his new daughter – obviously they were curious. As soon as caps had been lifted and bobs politely dropped, faces craned up, trying to peer in. I shrank even further back into my corner; I couldn't hear what they were saying, but I could easily imagine it: 'Tis her, as were Lady Quinham's maid.' 'No maid, her!' 'Twasn't Lady Quinham as she served – twas his young lordship.' 'He served her, more like!' I could imagine the nudges, the knowing winks, the sniggers among the men, and the shocked looks of the women, despising me for what I'd done. I drew Rose closer to me, gazing down into her face until I felt the carriage slow, and turn through the gates. As the gate creaked shut behind us, Leo muttered, 'Those hinges need oiling.' Then his voice rose: 'Yes, Flora, sheep – they always come into the park in spring, to graze.'

We rounded the final curve and the house came into sight. The first time I'd seen it, I hadn't been at all impressed; fresh from the glories of Nether Court, and all the big houses I'd visited that summer with Miss Annabel. I'd thought Eston rather dull, built of plain brick, with its long rows of matching windows. Now I was glad it wasn't as grand-looking as those others – but it was still so very big: looking at it, my spirits sank even lower. I didn't belong here.

We finally drew up at a flight of stone steps. The huge front door opened, and Mr Tims stepped out. The boy came running round and pulled out the steps, Leo jumped down, turned to lift Flora out – and a yellow streak flew down the front steps like an arrow from a bow. It was Nella. She danced around Leo, golden tail wagging furiously. He bent down to pat her, and she gave a deep woof of welcome. Mrs Chandler was out of the carriage next; she lifted her arms up and took Rose from me, and then I followed. I bent to pat Nella, but she hardly acknowledged my caress; her brown eyes were fixed on Leo. She was his dog, not mine.

I stood there, blinking in the sunlight, then he turned to me. 'Can you manage, Amy?'

He half held his arm out to me, but I knew he didn't want me to take it. So I replied, 'Tis all right, I can manage.' I crossed the gravel and began to climb the stone steps.

Mr Selby, Leo's agent, came out of the door as I reached the top. He greeted me politely: 'Good afternoon, Lady Warminster,' then he turned to Leo and drew him to one side, and at once they were involved in a deep discussion.

Clara, the head housemaid, had come out on the front step too, to greet her mother. Now she was admiring Rose in Mrs Chandler's arms. I began to move towards them, but Ellen was there first, with Flora. Ellen ordered the nursemaid, 'Dora, you take Lady Flora's hand now.' Then she glanced at Mrs Chandler. ''Tis the end o' the month, Aunt Grace.'

The two women smiled at each other. 'Here she is then, Ellen.' I watched as my baby was handed over. Straight-backed Ellen bore her off. Flora looked round to find me, but Dora spoke briskly, 'Now, Lady Flora, Dobbin'll be waiting for you in the nursery.' Flora scampered ahead, tugging the nursemaid after her. Both my children had gone, and I was bereft. Leo had his humpback to me as he listened intently to his agent's report; Clara and her mother stood talking together, heads close; I stood on my own. I didn't belong here.

Then Mrs Chandler broke away. 'I'll say goodbye now, my lady.'

Leo heard her and bent round. 'Thank you for all you help, Mrs Chandler; her ladyship and I are most grateful. Selby here will arrange your remuneration.'

'Thank 'ee, my lord.' She bobbed a curtsey.

I said quietly, 'Thank you, Mrs Chandler. I be main grateful for all you've done.'

I overheard Clara's quick whisper, 'I'll see thee later, Mam – mebbe run down after supper, if Mrs Johnstone don't object.' They hugged each other.

I walked into the hall, dark after the sunlight outside. Mr Tims hovered politely, but I had nowhere to go, I didn't belong here. Then Clara came to my rescue. 'We lit the fire in your bedroom, my lady, I dare say as you feel like washing some o' thic London soot off afore tea.' I followed her obediently through the hall to the wide staircase – the *front* stairs. But as I climbed up them, the portraits of the red-coated generals seemed to glare at me scornfully.

The bannister was cleaner than I'd ever known it; so as I reached the top I said, 'You been busy, Clara. This wood do have a lovely shine.'

She flushed with pleasure. 'While Mrs J was away, I took Sal Arnott out of the scullery and between us we gave everything a good clean. She's a steady little worker, is Sal, for all she's not turned fourteen yet.'

There was a jug of hot water on the washstand in my room. 'I thought as you might rather freshen up in here, near the fire, 'stead of in thic draughty bathroom.' Clara was right. I knew Leo had had the adjoining bathroom fitted up for his first wife, the French Countess, but she'd been born a lady. I didn't like the cold bathroom, empty except for its iron bath and china washbasin. I preferred to wash decently, behind the screen.

Once I'd washed and changed, there was nothing for me to do except sit down on the sofa and miss Rose: my arms were aching for her already.

It was even worse down in the big drawing room. I'd never liked that room: it was so enormous, it made me feel like a pigmy. The mottled marble mantelpiece was so high up, I had to stand on tiptoe to look at the picture hung

37

above it; and then the picture was only of a ruined building and a steep cliff, all under a dark thundery sky. There were several other pictures, but they were all the same, showing dark gloomy places where no one would ever want to go – not a bit like those bright, sunny paintings of women and girls and babies that Leo had had in his flat at Kew. These pictures seemed to be sinking back into the heavy red walls, as if defeated by them; the windows were defeated too. There were four of them, great tall windows – but the thick maroon velvet drapes all around them seemed to smother all the sunlight before it could reach the room. The upholstery on the chairs and sofas was the same dark red, so that you could hardly see the pattern on the brocade. And what wasn't red was dull gold in the most elaborate, involved patterns. Every chair leg and arm, every window surround, every picture frame was the same – and when you craned your neck up to the ceiling, even *that* was covered by oblongs and circles and patterns of dull gold and dirty white. There was nowhere in the whole room where you could rest your eyes.

Mr Tims came in and set the tray down on one of the huge oval tables. 'I've brought two cups, my lady. I don't know if his lordship will be . . . ' His voice trailed off anxiously.

'You'd best leave them, Mr Tims, just in case.' I wasn't expecting the other cup to be used, and it wasn't. But just as I was finishing, Leo came in. He stood awkwardly by the door. I asked, 'Did you want – I could ring for a fresh pot – '

'No, thank you. I must get back to Selby. I just wondered how you – ' He took a step forward and asked, 'You look very tired, Amy. Perhaps you would rather not dine downstairs tonight?'

I suddenly realized that if I went to bed early I could take Rose with me, so I said quickly, 'Aye, I would rather go to bed now,' and I rang the bell for Mr Tims to clear. In a moment I was on my feet, ready to leave.

He stood to one side, saying, 'I shall be returning to Town first thing on Tuesday morning.' But I hardly heard: I was thinking about claiming my Rose.

Ellen didn't give her up without a struggle. When I told her, 'I'm going to bed now, so I've come for Rose,' she offered to bring her down later. I shook my head. 'No, I might be asleep then. His lordship says as I must go to bed and rest now.' Reluctantly, Ellen handed Rose over, and I almost ran downstairs with my prize. That big bedroom became almost cosy now that I held Rose in my arms. I wasn't so tired, though I did go to bed because I'd said I would, but once there I simply sat up holding Rose, talking to her, playing with her. I sent Clara up for some spare nappies and a pail when she came up with the supper tray. I could hear Leo in his dressing room, but I knew he wouldn't come in through the connecting door to say goodnight. He never did.

Next morning, I asked for breakfast in bed; I wanted to delay the parting from Rose for as long as possible. But when Clara came to fetch my tray she had a message from Ellen. 'Ellen says as could you give Lady Rose a good long feed at nine o'clock, then she can go upstairs till midday.' At half-past nine

Ellen came herself, and bore Rose away. But she did offer to send Flora down at ten, if I wished. *If I wished!*

Flora and I went for a little walk round to the stables, and met Tabby Cat again; but after half an hour Leo appeared and said he was going up to the Home Farm, would Flora like to come too? So of course I lost my elder daughter as well. I went back to the drawing room and picked up my sewing.

But I couldn't seem to concentrate. I kept looking at the clock. It was a very irritating clock, the one in the drawing room. It was made of brass and wood, all swirls and patterns that didn't seem to go anywhere or mean anything. Even the clock face was like that, so it was quite difficult to pick out the hands. And the hands moved so slowly, I kept getting up to peer at them, not believing they'd only moved on five minutes since the last time I'd looked. Yet I knew it was keeping good time, because I could hear the stable clock striking.

At eleven o'clock I simply couldn't bear it any longer. I almost ran up the three flights of stairs to the nursery. As I opened the door, Ellen looked up – and Rose called. I got to the cradle before Ellen, lifted my baby out and put her to my breast. Ellen looked at me reproachfully. 'My lady, she's not due for a feed until midday. Every three hours the lady at my last place used to nurse, and every four after three months.'

I said, 'But, she needed me, she were calling.'

'Not until *you* came into the room.' Ellen was tight-lipped.

Rose wasn't really hungry, so after ten minutes I had to go downstairs and sit watching that clock again. It was like when I'd first come back to Eston with Flora, and the hospital-trained nurse Leo had engaged had rationed me to one precious hour a day with her. But I knew that comparison was unfair to Ellen, who never usually stopped me going up to the nursery; it was just that she wanted to get Rose into a routine. And naturally, she saw the children as *her* job, whereas I was Lady Warminster, who should sit in the drawing room. I sighed, and tried to force myself to get on with my sewing.

At twelve o'clock, Ellen brought her down at last. 'I'll be back for Lady Rose in half an hour, my lady,' and she was. Rose wasn't too pleased at being taken away, but Ellen was firm with both of us.

At one o'clock, Mr Tims announced lunch. The table in the morning room was only set with one place; Leo didn't eat lunch. Knowing this, Mrs Procter had only sent up cold mutton and left-over potatoes, but I didn't care. I wasn't interested in food: I only wanted Rose.

At two o'clock I couldn't stand it any longer, but Ellen politely yet firmly barred my way to the cradle. 'She's asleep.'

Half an hour later I was up at the nursery door again. 'I thought I heard her crying – '

Ellen looked at me in disbelief. The drawing room was two floors below the nursery. I slunk downstairs again. At a quarter to three I decided to go up to my bedroom to fetch another spool of silk thread, so I crept up the next flight of stairs and went to listen at the nursery door keyhole – and she *was* crying. I burst in and snatched her up. We had half an hour together on the window seat, while Ellen sat in a disapproving silence by the fire. At least I would be allowed to have Flora downstairs for tea, but as I left Ellen said, 'Lady Rose's next feed will be at *six*, my lady.'

Then Flora, clever Flora, told me, 'I saw the lambs with Papa.' Papa! I seized on the idea eagerly. 'Ellen, his lordship'll likely be in for tea at half-past four, and if he is he's sure to want to see Lady Rose, with him going back first thing tomorrow morning. So mebbe you could bring her down to tea?'

Reluctantly, Ellen agreed. His word was law. I knew that he almost certainly wouldn't come in, but I'd only said 'likely'. Anyway, if he did, he'd scold me for having my baby downstairs, but I was so desperate that I was prepared to risk that. I sat downstairs watching the clock again. The hands crawled so slowly, they looked as though they'd *never* get to four o'clock, and when they did I still had another half an hour to wait. I felt so exhausted I could scarcely bring myself to sew.

Then the door opened: it was Leo. He came halfway in and asked, 'How are you, Amy?' Coming a bare step closer he said, 'You – look – tired.'

I just couldn't stop myself. ''Tis wi' running up and down thic stairs to see Rose.' Once I'd started, the words came pouring out. 'I know she maun get into her routine, and Ellen, she be annoyed wi' I – she do say as I be waking her up – only Rose, she were wanting me that time, needing me – I know she was. And once, I were listening outside the door and I did hear her crying. I dare say Ellen's right an' she would be settling if *I* weren't disturbing her, and I dare say she *bain't* missing I – only I, I be missing her so much, my arms they be aching wi' not holding her in 'em . . . ' I held out my arms to him, but he only stood unmoving and my voice trailed away. 'So I been running up and down they stairs all day.'

He spoke harshly, decisively. 'That must stop – at once.' He turned and walked out. I collapsed back on the hard red sofa, crying tears of despair.

Several minutes later, the door opened again. It was Leo, and he was carrying the cradle. I gazed at him, scarcely daring to hope, but Ellen was behind him – with Rose. He set the cradle down beside the sofa. 'Put the child in there, Ellen.' Ellen bent over in a huffy crackle of starch, but I didn't care; my eyes were fixed on Rose.

'My Rose, my Rose,' I called to her and she called back. Before Ellen had even left the room, I had Rose in my arms, at my breast, and I couldn't stop the tears of relief from running down my face as I murmured, 'Oh Rose, my Rose, I did miss 'ee so much.'

After that first intense joy of reunion was over, I remembered who'd brought her, and looked up at the man standing in front of me. 'Thank 'ee, oh thank 'ee for bringing her down. Can I keep her until tea-time now?'

'You may keep her here as long as you like.'

I couldn't believe it. 'All day?'

'All day, and every day.'

'But Ellen said her routine – '

'*You* are her mother, *you* decide on the routine appropriate to your daughters.'

I whispered, 'But proper ladies, they do have nurseries, and nurses for their children – and I be Lady Warminster now.'

'Yes, you are Lady Warminster now.' He paused before adding more strongly, 'Therefore the house must be run as *you* wish, not for the convenience of the servants.'

I just sat there, looking at him: I still could not believe he meant what he said. But he went on, 'There are times when you will have to make use of the nursery: you can scarcely bring an infant into the dining room during dinner, for example; but on other occasions, you may decide.'

'But, with Flora, you said then, I had to – '

His face changed; he began to back away. 'I – ' he was stammering badly, 'I – one's – experience – changes one's views. I hope, I will try to understand – a little more – now.' By the time he'd finished he was out through the door.

I was so full of relief and gratitude that when Flora arrived I dared to send Mr Tims to ask if his lordship would come to the drawing room to take a cup of tea. He came. As soon as he appeared at the door Flora ran to greet him; she squealed with delight as he swung her up in his arms. After he'd set her down again, he perched his huge body awkwardly on the red gilt sofa on the other side of the mottled marble fireplace. At once, Flora clambered up on to his knee to tell him her news of the day. He listened to her seriously, exclaiming and questioning in all the right places, just as Granfer had done with me. I offered to refill his cup, and when he brought it over to me he glanced down at Rose. 'The child – has settled?'

'Aye, I put her cradle near the fire. Tis a mite chilly in this room, even in May. It never do seem to get properly warm.' I sighed. 'Tis so big.'

He gazed round, as if looking at it for the first time. 'Yes, I suppose so. And you are not – very big, are you?'

I said quickly, 'I'm five foot three.'

He half smiled. 'Then you will never be tall enough to wear tails at Eton. For that, one must have reached five foot four.'

'I 'low you didn't have no trouble then.'

'No, I fulfilled that particular requirement – despite my sideways inclination.'

I was so surprised at his referring openly to his being twisted that I stared at him – and saw that he looked as if he wished he hadn't mentioned it, so I said swiftly, 'Well, in this room I feel like one o' them liddle pygmies we read about in the Standard Four schoolbook, 'cept tis all dark red in here, instead of a nice bright green, like in a jungle.'

He looked round again. 'Yes, I suppose it is rather – overwhelming. I so rarely come in here I just hadn't realized.' He put his cup down. 'Why don't you consider moving upstairs?'

'Upstairs?'

'Yes, to the end room on the south front. I believe that that is where my mother – ' His voice dragged; he *never* mentioned her. Then he went on more firmly, 'My mother had her boudoir. It is customary for a lady to have a personal sitting room of her own; after all, I have the library for myself. If you sit upstairs in the morning, you will be nearer the nursery – and if visitors should choose to call in the afternoons, you could still receive them in here.'

I didn't expect any visitors, so that wouldn't be a problem. 'Mebbe we could go up and look at it when you've finished your tea?' He gulped it down.

It was a nice square room, and being on the corner, it had windows on two sides, so it would catch the afternoon sun. Even though it looked neglected and bare now, with all the furniture under dustsheets, I liked it at once. Flora burrowed under one of the sheets, and when I lifted it up she was hiding on a sofa seat that was covered in a nice blue brocade. The legs were of plain polished wood, with just a gentle curve to them. I said, 'Tis a mite old-fashioned, but none the worse for that.'

'Order new furniture,' he exclaimed. 'Carpets, curtains – Maud Winterslow will make those up for you, she attends to all the household sewing when required. The Harrods catalogue is in the library, on the fourth shelf up to the left of the fireplace. Fetch it whenever you need it for making your choices.' He glanced down at Rose in my arms. 'And obtain a new hat for yourself, for the christening; and a complete new outfit, several new outfits.'

'That'd be a mite extravagant.'

'Amy, *be* extravagant. I order it.' He half smiled.

'But I could get my machine out, and do my own sewing.'

'You can hardly use a sewing machine when you're suckling that child every fifteen minutes.' Now he was smiling fully.

'Tisn't every fifteen minutes.' Just at that moment Rose started tugging at my blouse and of course I was unbuttoning without even thinking: he watched me, laughing, and I had to laugh too. I settled her at my breast, then walked over to the window. 'Tis a lovely view, right across the autumn rose garden.' He came to stand behind me, and I pointed. 'Look, I can just see Aimée Vibert's corner.'

Then Flora came running back from her explorations to seize his hand. 'Lady, lady in picture.' She dragged him across the floor and I followed, more slowly. There was a picture propped against the wall in the alcove. Flora lifted the dustcover triumphantly. 'Lady!' Beside me he went very still.

She had a pleasant face, not pretty, and not young; but she looked very happy. I crouched down a little to read the title at the bottom: 'Elizabeth, Countess of Warminster,' and the date, '1868'. Leo's mother.

He didn't speak, so after a moment I said briskly, 'She must've got lonely, under that sheet. I dare say she'll be glad to be hanging on thic wall again.'

I could barely hear his reply: 'Thank you, Amy.' Then he crouched awkwardly down to speak to my daughter. 'Flora, Papa must leave you now, he will see you again later.' Her lower lip jutted ominously as she watched him leave the room, and I tried to distract her; but she'd obviously made up her mind to throw a tantrum, so throw it she did.

By the time I'd soothed her, seen her bathed, read her goodnight story and heard her say her prayers, he'd arrived. He always came to say goodnight to Flora if he were in the house. He stroked her hair and patted her cheek – he never kissed her – and then we walked downstairs together. In the hall I asked, 'Would you like me to dine with you tonight?'

He swung round so suddenly, he almost hit his shoulder against the newel post. 'Yes, please, Amy.'

I felt a sudden tinge of uneasiness, but I said briskly, 'I'll go up and get changed then.'

I had to wear my old dress blouse, because of going up to feed Rose straight after; and then there was the milk: I couldn't let it stain one of my best evening dresses. I'd hoped he might simply wear a dinner jacket, but instead he was in full evening dress: white tie, white waistcoat, and tails. He came to meet me. 'Shall we go in?' He didn't offer me his arm; he never did.

We sat at the long table in the gloomy dining room – the walls were a dark green, and the huge mottled marble pillars at either end were all of different shades of mustard – I didn't think they went together at all.

As fried whiting succeeded mulligatawny soup and was followed by chicken cutlets, we managed a halting conversation about the weather. Then he asked, 'Did you keep Rose with you until dinner?'

'Aye, we did have a little cuddle, afore I came down, I thought if I – ' I broke off; it didn't seem right to talk about suckling in that gloomy dining room, to a man in full evening dress. But just thinking about it had done the damage. I felt my milk coming. I squinted surreptitiously down: my muslin pads had soaked through, and two damp patches were appearing on the faded blue satin of my blouse. I looked up and saw he'd noticed too. Both our faces were aflame with embarrassment, and he spent the rest of the meal staring at the wall above my head.

As soon as Mr Tims had cleared away the remains of the savoury patties I said, 'I don't think – mebbe I'd better – ' I half rose. At once he stood up and went to open the door for me. I left him to his oranges and nuts and went directly to Rose.

By the time she was fed and settled in my bedroom, I knew he'd have finished his coffee and been halfway round the rose garden with Nella, so I might as well go straight to bed. But then I realized I'd left my sewing downstairs, so I ran quickly to the drawing room. He was sitting hunched over the dying fire, the untouched coffee tray beside him. I went right in, saying, 'Oh, I'm sorry, you shouldn't 'a waited.'

43

'I expected you to bring Rose down here.' He sounded grumpy.

'I couldn't feed her in the drawing room.'

'Why not? You did earlier.' His voice was aggrieved now.

'That were *afore* dinner.' I offered hastily, 'Shall I ring for fresh coffee?'

'No, you needn't bother. I don't feel like it anyway, now. I'll go and fetch Nella. Goodnight.' He stamped off. I sighed; he was a very difficult man to live with sometimes.

Next day, he'd already breakfasted when I came down. I'd told Mr Tims to fetch me from the drawing room when Leo was ready to leave, but instead Leo himself came, with Mr Selby.

'Selby here will be writing to me regularly; apply to him if you have any problems. And let him know once you've decided on a colour scheme for your sitting room.' He turned to Mr Selby. 'You'll arrange for the painters to come up from the workshop then?'

'Certainly, Lord Warminster.' Mr Selby smiled politely at me.

I looked at Leo in excitement. '*I* can choose?'

'Of course you may. I'll be going now. I've said goodbye to Flora.' As he turned to leave, I scooped up Rose and followed him out on to the front step to wave him off. He looked back in surprise. 'Don't get cold.'

I shook my head. 'Not now – twas the first of May, yesterday.' And then I suddenly realized. I went down the two steps to him. 'Leo – '

All at once I was shy as I said, 'I do wish thee a happy birthday.'

He replied, 'Thank you, Amy,' and smiled fully, properly.

I said, 'Goodbye, then.'

He repeated, 'Thank you, Amy – and goodbye.' He almost ran down the steps to the dog cart, moving very lightly for a man of his age. He sat down on the opposite side, facing me and Rose, and waved. I waved back, then stood watching as he was driven away – and I saw that all the time he was looking back at me – and Rose. And at Rose: I told myself firmly that it was Rose he was determined to catch that last glimpse of, not me. Then I went back inside.

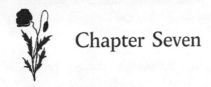

Chapter Seven

I played with the children all day. I didn't sew a stitch of Rose's christening gown – I knew I'd have to get on with that tomorrow, but today was like a little holiday. It was lovely having them always with me, and being able to romp on the floor with Flora while Rose was having her nap, then nursing Rose with Flora pressed close to my side, demanding a story. So yet again I began to read: 'There was once a very rich merchant . . .'

As the story unfolded I became as absorbed in it as Flora. It was Beauty's father who sprang the trap, when he stole a rose to take home to her. At once the terrible Beast appeared and demanded a payment for that rose: the merchant's death – or his daughter's life. And so Beauty, for love of her father, became the prisoner of the Beast.

She came to the enchanted castle in fear and trembling – but the Beast never harmed her, and soon her fear turned to compassion. Flora repeated after me, 'Com – pass – ion.' She liked long words, did my Flora.

'It means she felt sorry for him, because he was so ugly and so lonely.'

So lonely that Beauty was happy to talk to him kindly as she dined with him of an evening. Only there was a problem – the Beast had fallen in love with Beauty, and wanted to marry her. But Beauty always said no, because she didn't love the Beast.

'Why not, Mama?'

'She just didn't, Flora.'

'But he was a *nice* Beast, wasn't he?' Yes, he was. And so generous to Beauty that he surrounded her with every luxury in his enchanted castle, while each afternoon she could walk in his rose garden and admire the beauty of his roses. So she lived contentedly enough with the Beast – until one day she looked into the Beast's magic mirror and saw that her father had fallen ill, through pining for her.

Beauty longed to go to him, and the Beast, ever generous, set her free. But he warned her that if she did not return to him within seven days then he would die of grief, because he loved her so much. And he gave her a ring, a magic ring, that would bring her back to him.

Flora caught at the band of gold on my finger, 'Like *your* ring, Mama.'

'No, Flora – mine is a wedding ring.' But then, was it so very different?

Beauty was so pleased to be home again she forgot all about the Beast. Ten whole days had passed before she remembered and used her ring to return to him. But when she got back to his castle she couldn't find him anywhere. Poor Beauty became quite frantic with worry, and by evening she was out in the garden running up and down the grassy paths between the roses searching for him – until at last she found him, lying senseless on the ground. And in that moment, her pity turned to love. Kneeling down beside the dying Beast she told him that she loved him, and so brought him back to life.

Flora gave a great sigh of satisfaction. 'And she said she'd marry him, didn't she?'

'Yes, she did, Flora.' In a specially loud voice I read of the clap of thunder and the magic fireworks exploding across the sky, then dropped it again to tell of the handsome young prince who now stood in front of Beauty. The miracle had happened: Beauty's love had lifted the spell put upon him so many years ago.

Flora triumphantly finished: 'And so they got married, and lived happily ever after. Did they have a little girl?' I nodded. 'And did they call her Flora?'

'I daresay they did.' But even as I spoke I was remembering the rose that Leo had given me. Then I looked down at Rose in my arms and told myself firmly that I'd been silly that evening – I'd read too many tales. The golden rose had been merely a gift to the mother of his new-born daughter. Gratitude had prompted that gift – nothing else. I turned back to my elder daughter. 'Which story would you like me to read next, Flora?'

I could hardly bear to tear myself away from the children to go down to dinner. I left it to the last minute before I dressed: it didn't matter, since I was dining on my own. Mrs Procter obviously had the same attitude, since she'd sent up only three courses, and the vegetables for the turnip soup hadn't been properly sieved, while the rice pudding had been left in the oven a shade too long. I wasn't going to spoil my lovely day by complaining to Mrs Johnstone now – especially not in the evening when she was generally tipsy – but I decided I really would speak to her, sometime. My thoughts returned to Rose, and the minute I'd swallowed the last mouthful I was on my way to fetch her.

But even with Rose in my arms the drawing room seemed especially big and empty as I drank my coffee. Still, soon I'd be able to go and sit in my room upstairs. I could even start choosing the decorations now, since Leo had told me to use the Harrods catalogue. I put my cup down. 'Come along, my Rose, we'll go and find thic catalogue.'

I'm not sure I'd have had the courage to go into the library if I hadn't had Rose with me: it was so very much *Leo*'s room. It wasn't at all like the drawing room: there were no fussy ornaments and everything was very plain. The carpet was patterned with flowers, but they'd faded over the years. Bending down for a closer look I smiled, because the flowers were roses. I wondered if the Beast had had a rose-patterned carpet in his library at the enchanted castle – I was sure he had. I straightened up and looked around me – I'd so rarely been in here before, and never on my own. Although it was always called the library, and every wall was lined with books from floor to ceiling, it actually looked more like a study; I suppose because Leo spent so much time in here. I noticed now that the pattern on the heavy silk brocade curtains was of roses, too; and the cluster of pictures on the wall above the chimney breast were all delicate water-colours of his roses. There was his favourite pink Blairii rose, tiny Persephone he'd bred himself – and down in the corner my special white rose, Aimé Vibert. 'See thy Dada's roses, my Rose?' But she wasn't interested, she only yawned.

I looked round at his books; at the big comfortable armchair by the fire, with its cushion hollowed in the middle where he'd sat so many evenings; at the massive wooden desk, leather topped, with blotter lying in front of the pair of inkwells, and pen waiting for him to pick up. It was as if he'd just slipped out for a minute to give Nella her run. I almost expected his footstep in the hall, his hand on the door knob, so strong was the sense of his personality in that room.

And I remembered the first time I'd come into this room, as a disgraced, penniless servant. Clara had told him of my plight, and so he'd sent for me to give me help. I owed him so much: not just the food that I ate, the clothes that I wore, these walls that sheltered me. No, those were generous gifts – but I owed him much more than that, much much more.

Now it was another night I remembered – that night when he'd made himself drunk, just so he could talk to me. I'd cried out, 'I did sin!' But he had questioned my cry. 'Did you sin? Or did you simply love too well? If loving too well be a sin, then let sin prevail – so that those of us who are not loved at all may hold out our hands to the reflected warmth.' And then had come that simple, decided command: 'You need feel no guilt.'

Those words of his had shaken the foundations of all that Grammer had taught me, and that night the claws of my guilt had begun to loosen their grip. By saying what he had, he had given me the beginnings of absolution. Yes, I owed him so much, more than I could ever repay.

I left without the Harrods catalogue: I'd go and fetch it later. I couldn't carry it anyhow, not with Rose in my arms. Besides, she was damp, so I had to go and change her now.

I took her all the way up to the nursery to do it, so that I could have one final peep at Flora. Ellen was there on her own, and she started to get up when I came in.

I said, 'Don't disturb yourself, Ellen – Rose only needs changing. I'll see to it,' and I saw her face drop: she looked so upset. Because of course, it was her job. She'd become a nurse because she wanted to look after children, and she could look after them, very well: she was kind but firm, patient, gentle – yet full of ideas for keeping Flora amused. But I wouldn't even let her change Rose's nappy. I said, 'Ellen, I be terrible sorry, only . . . ' I didn't know how to go on.

Ellen looked me straight in the eye. 'Don't you trust me with your baby?'

I exclaimed, 'O' course I do, Ellen, you know I do. But,' I looked down at

Rose, 'tis only a little more'n a month since I were carrying her all the time, carrying her under my heart and – ' I looked up at Ellen, trying to explain. 'The doctor, he did cut the cord, but while I be nursing her, she's still a part o' me. Do 'ee understand?'

She looked at me for a long time, then at last she managed to smile. 'Aye, I 'low I do.' My legs were shaking with relief. Ellen's smile reached her eyes. 'I remember my first place. The lady went out for the evening, soon as her month was up, to the theatre; she come back later than she said, all laughing and gay she was, and that poor liddle boy – he'd been bawling fit to bust for nigh on four hour, wi' needing her. I thought it were dreadful. I said to Nanny Fowkes, "How could she *do* it?" And Nanny Fowkes says, "Ellen, ladies are different from you and me; the sooner you gets used to that, the better."'

I said, 'But I baint a proper lady. You knows that.'

We looked at each other for a moment without speaking. Then Ellen drew herself up. 'Well, I'll just have to get used to another way o' doing things now.' She gave a wry smile. 'Aunt Grace did warn me as you'd be forever running up and down them stairs – only she said as you'd have to leave her in the nursery most of the day, because of him, his lordship. She said, Aunt Grace said, as he'd be wanting you to himself.' I felt my face flushing hot, but then Ellen didn't seem to notice as she went on, 'But o' course, what with him having to go back to London – and you'll be missing him, too, so tis only natural – '

I interrupted quickly, 'Ellen, his lordship told me to fetch a book from his library, and tis so big as I couldn't take it off the shelf, or even sit with it on my lap, when I got Rose there. So if you'd see to her for a liddle while – '

Ellen held out her arms. 'It'll be a pleasure.' She took Rose, cuddling her, '*Who's* a pretty liddle maid, then?' I left them admiring each other.

I found the catalogue straightaway, exactly where he'd said it was. Sitting down with it in the chair opposite his, I began to turn the pages. But I wasn't really concentrating; instead, I was thinking of what Ellen had said. 'He'll be wanting you to himself' – but surely, Mrs Chandler was wrong. We'd never spent any time together during the day; he was only interested in the children, not me. 'You'll be missing him.' I felt guilty because I wasn't – or only a little, in the evening, over dinner. I looked up at that big armchair: it seemed to be accusing me. I said aloud, 'You shouldn't have married me,' then I felt so ashamed of myself, because he hadn't meant to marry me against my will, poor Leo; he'd felt guilty ever since; yet in truth, it was *I* who was responsible for our marriage, it was my fault.

He'd told me that night in here, when he was drunk, and I'd dared to ask him, 'Why did you marry me?' I recalled the way he'd drained his glass in one gulp to nerve himself up to tell me. 'Why did I marry you? Because you asked me to.'

I hadn't *meant* to ask him, only I'd been so confused, so desperate that my baby should not be branded in the way that I had been, that I'd asked her grandfather, 'Canst thee not give her a name?' And he had. I remembered him telling me that night: 'I thought, why not? My name is of no value to me – but if it matters so much to her, then she can have it.' It had been an act of casual kindness, that was all. And when he'd understood, later, he'd offered to set me free by means of an annulment, because it had been no marriage then.

But now another memory came from that night, forcing its way in: 'Don't leave me, Amy, please don't leave me.' But he'd been drunk, very drunk, when he said that; he'd warned me himself he would feel differently when he was sober, and he had. He'd wanted me to leave then, but I still hadn't gone. I wasn't Beauty, with a family of her own – I had nowhere else to go. Besides there was Flora. I couldn't take her away from him, because he loved her, and he'd always wanted a daughter of his own. And suddenly I realised: *that* was why he'd wanted me to stay – to be a daughter to him. He'd told me so himself, earlier that night, when I'd asked him why he'd married me. He'd said then: '*You were only a child yourself.*' To him I was just a child, because he was so much older than I was.

A warm tide of relief washed over me – I understood it all now. He'd invited Miss Annabel, his daughter-in-law, to live at Eston first – but then he'd quarrelled with Frank and lost her, so he'd had to make do with me instead. I wasn't his first choice – how could I be? I wasn't educated or able to converse about plays or literature, but over the past year or so he'd grown used to me. It was my fault that I'd turned him into a husband for a little while – desperation for another baby had made me selfish – but we were back to normal now, he'd made that quite clear. He'd had one wife when he was a young man, and he didn't want another. Only sometimes he liked to listen to my chatter, just for company – that was all.

I picked up the Harrods catalogue and took it upstairs to look at in bed, with Rose nestled cosily beside me.

By next morning, I'd decided on the colours I wanted for my sitting room and sent off for wallpaper pattern books, and curtain and carpet samples. I'd also chosen two new hats, a pair of shoes and the material for the dress I would wear at Rose's christening. Then I began to worry: how would I arrange the christening? Leo only went to church at Christmas and Easter, and I'd never even spoken to the Rector of Eston.

It happened like an answer to my prayers. Ellen had just taken Flora up for her nap when Mr Tims opened the drawing room door. 'Mr Beeston has called, my lady. Are you at home?'

I stammered an assent, and plump Mr Beeston came trotting in. There were beads of sweat on his forehead and his hand was quite damp as it shook mine: I realized he was as nervous as I was. Apparently Leo had written to him, telling him when the christening was to be.

'Is that convenient for you, Mr Beeston?' I asked.

He looked rather surprised before answering, 'If *Lord Warminster* wishes that date . . . ' then his voice trailed off nervously.

I said hastily, 'Of course, if his *lordship* did say – ' We exchanged timid glances; it was obvious that neither of us would dare to gainsay Leo, so the date was fixed.

'And how is she, the little one?' I turned to look down into the cradle and he exclaimed, 'Ah, she's here with you! *May* I peep?' He seemed really pleased to see Rose. 'What a *beautiful* baby – and *so* plump and healthy-looking. Ah, these innocent babes bring such joy to a home.'

'Oh, she does, Mr Beeston, she does.' We beamed at each other. I asked, 'Do you have any children?'

He said regretfully, 'I'm afraid no young lady saw fit to grace my hearth, Lady Warminster. My sister shares my humble abode.' Then his face changed to a mixture of pride and anxiety. 'But our nephew Cyril makes his home with us; though with this dreadful war – he's in France.' His face puckered.

'Oh, Mr Beeston, what a terrible worry for you.'

'It is, Lady Warminster, it is. Cyril has always been as dear to us as a son; but naturally, he went to do his duty at once – only,' he leant closer, 'he does have a weakness of the kidneys. He had scarlet fever as a child.' He shook his head. 'A terrible disease, Lady Warminster, terrible, and it's left him so prone to nephritis.' He sighed. 'This last winter, Lucinda and I were quite unable to enjoy the warmth of our domestic hearth for thinking of our dear Cyril in those damp trenches.'

I put my hand on his arm in sympathy, and he patted it gratefully. 'Dear Lady Warminster, so kind.' Then he straightened his short back. 'But we are proud, very proud.' Rose murmured in sympathy and at once he smiled down at her. 'Ah, your little one is awakening. I shall tell Lucinda that I have seen her. And if you are ever in the village, *do* call. We don't stand on ceremony, you know.'

Mr Beeston had gone, and I had my thimble on again when Mr Tims came to the door a second time. 'Lady Burton, my lady.'

She swept in, surrounded with her usual cloud of violet scent. 'Do sit down, dear. *So* lovely to see you.' She sank onto the sofa. 'And how *are* you? Quite recovered from your ordeal? You look blooming, quite blooming – such a shame the little one was a girl. Still, *next* time – ' She smiled. 'And how *is* baby?' She jumped up and came to look into the cradle. 'Rose is a *most* appropriate name for this little one. They always look their best when they're asleep, don't they? And so much less trouble. Of course, she isn't walking yet, *so* exhausting when they are – into everything!' She smiled. 'Much as I adored having darling George downstairs at tea-time – and dear Joan and Helen and Cynthia, of course. Females are just a twitch more civilized – ' She broke off to ask, 'Where was I, dear?'

'Sir George, he were coming down at tea-time.'

'Ah, yes, how clever of you to remember – and you weren't even born then – yes it *was* such a relief when Nanny whisked him back upstairs again.' She settled back on the sofa. 'Now, what did I come for? Ah yes, I remember – to say that of course we'll both be here on the twenty-first. Leonidas saw George in town and asked him what was most convenient for him. George said to let him know when he'd consulted with the Rector, but Leonidas didn't appear to see the necessity for that.'

'Leo did send him a letter.'

'Leo? Is that what you call him? It sounds almost jolly – how misleading names can be. Now, poor little Beeston – so *unbeastlike*, especially when it comes to standing up to Leonidas – but then, Leonidas can be a frightful bully sometimes,' she gave me a sharp look, 'as I'm sure *you* know, dear.'

I shook my head. 'Leo, he don't bully me.'

'How wise you are to stand up to him!' She didn't give me time to protest. 'That was poor dear Jeanette's mistake.' Her voice dropped. 'His first wife, you know. Such a sweet girl, but she never learnt to stand up to him, and he led her such a dance – not that he could, with his short leg – dance, I mean.' She nodded her head. 'Such a blessing, that accident, he barely even limps now – so nice for him after wearing a built-up boot from the day he was born. Now, where was I? Ah, Jeanette. Mm, but perhaps the mistake was his – perhaps *that* was the trouble; he cared for her too much.' She paused, and I sat waiting, my ears pricked. 'Yes,' Lady Burton's voice was reminiscent, 'he couldn't bear to let her out of his sight – he *hovered*, you know. A wife does want some time to herself; being doted on is all very well during the engagement period, but after marriage a degree of restrained affection is *quite* sufficient. But then, Leonidas has never known the meaning of restraint – and he can do such *extraordinary* things – ' She came to an abrupt halt. 'Well, *you* know that, dear. How is little Flora? She was growing to be the image of her grandmother last time I saw her – no wonder Leonidas thinks the world of her, such a pretty child. But then, so is your little Rose; quite amazing when one considers – ' She smiled brightly. 'Still, you've got looks good enough for two.'

I said firmly, 'Leo would be a handsome man if he weren't twisted.'

'But he is, dear, isn't he? Twisted, I mean.'

I took a deep breath. 'Lady Quinham – ' I got it out almost without a tremor – 'she said once that if he weren't lopsided Leo'd look like an actor – Mr Forbes Robertson, she said.'

Lady Burton held up her plump gloved hands in disbelief. 'But Mr Forbes Robertson is such a *handsome* man; I recall when I saw him as Julius Caesar, his profile – ' She broke off, her voice becoming excited, 'D'you know, she could be right. That noble furrowed brown and strong jaw. Leonidas' nose is rather more – er, *forceful*, but those piercing grey eyes . . . Yes, imagine him in a toga and a laurel wreath – I simply *must* tell George, next time I see him!

How *clever* of Annabel to spot the resemblance. George tells me she's driving ambulances; how *brave* young women are today, not just sitting at home. Still, it's different for you, dear. Is that the time? I simply must fly!' Rose and I were enveloped in violet scent once more. 'Such a delightful child – and don't worry, I'm sure it will be a boy next time, you're obviously so much more sensible than poor dear Jeanette; but men don't look for sense when they're young, do they? They simply fall in love! Goodbye, dear, we'll see you on the twenty-first.'

Flora came down soon after. As I looked at her blue eyes and blonde curls, I remembered the French Countess, Leo's first wife. I'd only seen her once, but I'd never forgotten her. He hadn't either, I knew that: because he'd loved her.

Chapter Eight

My order from Harrods had arrived by the time I'd finished Rose's christening dress, so I drafted the pattern for the outfit I was going to wear. I'd decided on a costume frock in deep rose-pink serge: the top was shaped into a neat little low-cut jacket with a high turned-over collar and deep cuffs, all faced with paler pink satin to match the inset blouse front. I'd chosen a satin with a narrow woven stripe, so that I could cut the blouse bodice into a vee with ten little rose-pink buttons down the centre where each pair of stripes met. The skirt was fitted at the waist and over my hips, where it fell into a slight flare – but only midway down my calf, since hemlines had lifted so much with the war. I decided that if my ankles were to be on show, they would be clad in pure silk, so I'd bought two pairs of silk stockings, just in case I laddered one. And seeing that Leo had ordered me to be extravagant, I sent for a pair of glacé kid shoes as well, with the highest Louis heels I'd ever worn, and kid gloves to match. I couldn't make my mind up about a hat at first – most of them seemed far too decorated to me – but in the end I settled for a plain cream straw with a wide curving brim, and sent for a ribbon and two satin roses in the same shade as my costume frock. I would trim my hat myself.

I was in the middle of tacking the skirt panels when Mr Tims came in to say that Mr Selby had a message for me. As he came through the door, Mr Selby looked rather surprised to see the blanket spread over one of the huge drawing room tables, and pieces of rose pink serge cut out on top of it, but he was too polite to comment. He simply told me the decorators were coming tomorrow, so would I ask Mrs Johnstone to prepare the sitting room for them.

My spirits sank at once, but it had to be done so I sent Mr Tims to ask the housekeeper to come and see me. She came in with her lips shut tightly together, and when she saw what I was doing she tightened them still further. I made my request, and at first she didn't reply; then she said, 'The *first* Lady Warminster always used this drawing room.' She looked at me, meaningfully.

I told her, 'His lordship said as I could use the sitting room.'

She knew she was beaten, but she wasn't one for retiring gracefully. She looked at my dressmaking and her nostrils flared as if she'd caught a bad smell. 'She'd sit in here, embroidering like a lady, with her dainty needle flashing in and out.' She pointed to a chair. 'While his lordship'd be sitting there, just watching of her.' Mrs Johnstone came closer, and almost hissed in my ear, 'She was the great love of his life, you know. Why, I remember the day she died – '

I dared to interrupt. 'But Mrs Johnstone, she didn't die *here* – she were in France. She'd left Eston years before.'

She gave me a look of pure venom. 'I remember the day the telegram came to say as that beautiful lady had passed on to the heaven she surely deserved. That evening, his lordship were in her bedroom, the countess's bedroom – the room as *you* sleep in now – well, Mr Wallis went up to valet him as usual and found him in there, just standing, looking as though he'd been struck dumb with a thunderbolt.'

I tried again. 'But they'd parted; she went back to France, Clara told me – '

'It didn't make no difference to him, he never changed.' Her hand took hold of my arm, gripping it like a claw. 'He loved her, he did, and he always will. You best believe that.' I did believe it. Her voice rose, crowing, 'When she went back to France, everything had to be left, just as it was, nothing touched – his lordship's orders. Her clothes in the wardrobe, her books on the shelf, her jewel case on the dressing table. She left in such a hurry, she only took her brushes with her. The jewellery that *he'd* given her – lavished jewels on her, he did – it was all left, just as though she were still living here. And the night she died, he was in there, with the wardrobe door open, stroking her dresses, as though she were still wearing them. Eerie it was, Mr Wallis said, like as if he were looking at her ghost.'

I stood drinking in every word, until she must have realized that it was the despised second wife she was talking to, and drawing herself up she said, 'If you're *certain* his lordship wants you to sit upstairs – '

I couldn't help it, I had to know. 'What did he do about 'em, her clothes and things?'

She hesitated, but couldn't resist finishing the tale. 'He gave orders, that very night, as they was all to be packed up and put away in a boxroom. Said it had to be done at once, straightaway – even though it was suppertime in the Room by then.' She sounded aggrieved. 'I wasn't going to miss my supper, so I sent Clara, she saw to it.' Her eyes dared me to protest, I didn't, and she left triumphant.

I couldn't get her story out of my mind, and when Clara came to say she and Bertha would be clearing out the sitting room for the decorators after lunch, I began, 'Mrs Johnstone says as her ladyship – her *first* ladyship – never had her own sitting room.'

'No, that's right: she used to sit down here, so I've heard.'

I went on, 'Mrs Johnstone, she said as how *you* put her things away, after she died.'

'Aye. It should've been Mrs J, but you knows what state she's in by the evening.' We grinned at each other. I didn't need to prompt Clara any more: she was obviously ready for a chat. 'She wouldn't have dared to send me to do it, 'cept that his lordship had gone out. Never came back all night. His boots were all caked in mud the next morning – terrible job for Mr Wallis to clean – chalky mud it was, he must have been up on the Down, just walking. Still, as Mr Wallis said, you don't lose your wife every day.'

'So Mrs J sent you up to her bedroom . . .'

'Yes. Course, I was only second housemaid then, but I 'low she thought if he did find out he'd be less angry if it were me,' her left hand went up without thinking, to touch the large port-wine birthmark which stained her cheek, 'with Mam having been his nursemaid once. He do shout, even at me, but I knows he don't really mean it – tis just his way. So Mrs J sent me. I wished she hadn't. Proper spooky it was, all her ladyship's things just as she'd left them. We'd always cleaned the room, o'course, put camphor bags in the wardrobe and suchlike, but knowing she was dead, and him out there mourning her . . . he'd 'a been mourning all them wasted years, too, as Mam said. So I packed 'em all away as quick as I could.' She leant towards me. 'They was all there, must have been her trousseau, lovely fine stitching it was – beautiful her nightdresses were.' Then Clara shook her head, puzzled. 'Strange for a woman to go without her nighties. Her maid, she'd took all her things, and young Lord Quinham's nurse had packed for the nursery, so there must've been time – but she just left the lot. Only her brushes had gone. Lovely hair she had, my Mam told me – silver-gilt. Mam said she'd never seen the like of it afore, not on a grown woman. Even Lady Flora's is darker, like her – ' Clara broke off, flushing.

I managed to keep my voice level as I said, 'Granny Withers told me as Flora do take after her grandmother.'

'Yes, she do – my Mam says the same.' She went on quickly, 'She'd left her books behind, too. A dozen or more there was, as he'd given her. Some of 'em English and some of 'em foreign – French, I suppose. I told Mrs J and she asked him next day did he want them put in the library – lovely leather bindings there were, with gold lettering. Anyway he shouted at Mrs J, lost his temper good and proper, even worse'n usual. Quite upset her, it did, took more'n a couple o' glasses of his lordship's brandy to bring her round that time! But the gist of it was as he didn't want 'em. They was all to be packed away with her other things and put in the furthest boxroom – that's what he said, "the furthest boxroom". So that's what we done wi' 'em – and there they've stayed, till this very day.'

'And there they've stayed till this very day.' Clara's words kept running round and round in my head; and eventually I went to find them – of course I did. I crept up like a thief, after dinner, and went to the furthest boxroom. Clara had put the things in old trunks; but she must have packed in a hurry, because the clothes were all tumbled about. I put my hand amongst them. Silks and satins, lawn and cashmere – one of her nightdresses was thrust down the side: it was of the finest white lawn, trimmed with yard upon yard of delicate lace, sewn on with the most exquisitely tiny stitches, just as Clara had described. But she'd still left it behind, that French Countess.

Guiltily I folded it properly, and slipped it back down the side of the trunk – and as I did so, my hand touched a book. I pulled it out and opened it; someone had written several lines on the flyleaf. 'My chère Jeanette,' I glanced down, 'Je t'adore . . . ' I knew I shouldn't read it, and I didn't, but I could see what it was: a tiny love letter, to her. And beneath it was the signature, 'Léonide.'

The other books were in the next trunk, with her furs and winter coats and jackets. I only looked quickly, because I knew I had no right to look at all, but the books were all dedicated in the same way. In the French books he'd written to her in French, in the English books, in English; each one held its message of love. They were all love letters, love letters from my husband.

Next day, I took Rose for a walk. It was fine and sunny, and I tied her round me in her shawl, carrying her close to my heart. I crossed the park to the wood and took the path between two big old oak trees, the path that wound its way right into the heart of the woods. Turning aside on to a still narrower trail, I came to the hedge. The dog roses weren't flowering yet, but they would be soon. Shielding Rose with my body, I slipped through the gap into the sunlit clearing and walked on over the rough turf to the ruined house. The rose stems here were sturdier and thicker, because they'd been planted deliberately, many years ago. But I didn't stay to look for early buds. Instead, I went on, through the roofless hall, and into the courtyard, where she stood: the French Countess, my husband's first wife.

The sun on the marble seemed to give her statue the pink flush of life. I looked at her lovely face, at her hair sweeping up from her smooth forehead in a flowing wave – so finely carved that you could see the single curling tendril which had escaped and twined itself around the delicate curve of her ear. You could see every feature of that finely chiselled face – except for her eyes, for they were lowered to gaze at the sleeping child she held cradled in her arms.

I stood there, looking up at her, at Jeanette Joséphine Marie-Louise, only daughter of the late Marquis de Montjean, who had married Leonidas Arthur Hector Fitzwarren-Donne, Seventh Earl of Warminster. I'd found her statue here that first summer after I'd come back to Eston as his wife. I'd known who she was. I'd recognized her, because once, as a living woman, she'd visited our school at Borrell. We had known nothing then of Lord Warminster. Her husband, he was just a name to us at Borrell: a great landowner with estates at Pennings, a few miles from our village. But he never came to his estates there, so no one I knew had ever seen him. That year I was eight, though, his wife had come to stay at Pennings and visited Lady Blanche, who'd brought her along on one of her regular inspections of our needlework.

When it had been my turn to take my sewing out to the front of the class, I'd gazed up into that lovely face, into those eyes, blue as forget-me-nots – and worshipped her. She had looked own at my tiny, even, stitches and praised them. Then she'd told me, 'You must be a lady's maid when you grow up, *ma petite.*' And so my young dreams had begun.

I had dreamt that I would be *her* lady's maid, and meet Lord Warminster, who in my dreams was tall and distinguished, with silver-grey hair. My dream Lord Warminster would find my father for me, the father I'd never met; and my father would be a lord, too, and take me back into his own home. But one day I would leave it again, to marry Lord Warminster's son and be welcomed back by his mother – my beautiful Lady Warminster.

So beautiful, and so full of deceit.

For my dreams had been wrong, all wrong. I'd dreamt that her son loved me – and he didn't. I'd dreamt that she'd loved Lord Warminster – and she hadn't. I'd hung on to that dream much longer; much longer than all the others. I'd been told soon after I'd come to Eston that they'd lived apart from the time her son was very young, but I'd assumed that Lord Warminster had treated her badly, as men do – taking mistresses, being neglectful – but still I'd been sure that despite his faults, she'd loved him. But now I knew the truth. Not only had she not loved him, never loved him; she had deceived him. She had married him with another man's child already in her womb.

Yet he'd still loved her, loved her so much that when her son was born too early and he'd realized the depth of her deceit, he still forgave her, and promised to acknowledge her son as his heir. So Frank had become Lord Quinham, and one day would be Earl of Warminster in his turn.

Her husband had never backed down on his promise, but she had not kept hers: she had promised him a child of his own, but instead she'd left him, and gone back to her lover in France. Leo had never betrayed her secret. Instead, he had set up this statue of her, here in the depths of the wood, and he'd planted roses, his favourite roses, all around, because he'd loved her. And he loved her still, even though she was dead.

I wandered back through the woods, talking to Rose. I showed her the dancing butterflies, with their wings of yellow, of blue, and tipped with orange. I showed her the jackdaw with his sleek black head cocked to one side as he watched us, I showed her the bright pink campion and the delicate mauve-veined leaves of the wood sorrel; I showed her the starry-petalled stitchwort, and the hidden blossom of the holly tree. It was May, and every leaf in the wood was green and alive with promise.

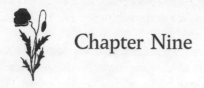# Chapter Nine

That evening I went up to the corner sitting room before dinner: the faded paper had been stripped from the walls and the old paint burnt off. It was all ready for a new beginning and I felt a ripple of excitement at that thought. Going over to one of the long windows I lifted Rose up against my shoulder. 'Do 'ee see the roses? They'll be in bloom afore long – soon as thee've been christened, most like. And one day thy Dada'll name a rose for thee, just as he did for thy Mama.' She crowed with pleasure, and I kissed her rose petal cheek and nuzzled the perfect shell of her tiny ear.

As soon as I'd left her safe in the nursery I went down to find Clara, and asked would she send down to Miss Winterslow about coming to sew the curtains, 'When tis convenient for her, o' course.'

Clara grinned. 'I 'low it'll be convenient tomorrow morning. There's nothing Maud Winterslow likes better than to come up here and poke her nose into his lordship's affairs!'

Next morning Clara came down to fetch me. 'Miss Winterslow says as she'd best see you, my lady – to be certain sure she's making 'em the way you wants. She's in the sewing room. I told her you'd step up – she'd 'a been down here, running her eye over everything if I'd given her half a chance, which I didn't. I've brought Dora down to keep an eye on Lady Rose while you're upstairs.'

Maud Winterslow looked very trim in a close-fitting black dress; I could see from her face that she was getting on, but she held her back straight as a young girl's as she looked at me from bright, unblinking eyes. I said politely, 'Good morning, Miss Winterslow.'

'Morning, me lady.' Her eyes flicked over me as alert as a lizard's. 'So *you're* her ladyship. Martha told me all about you.'

'Martha?' I was bewildered.

'My sister, Martha Withers.'

'Oh, *Granny* Withers.'

She snorted. '*Granny* Withers! Trust Martha to give herself a highfalutin name like that just on account of having spent a year or two in Lunnon. *Grammer*, that's the proper Wiltshire name. "Your *Grammer*", that's how I talk of her to her young 'uns.' She smirked. 'Martha don't like it at all, but I don't take no notice of her, for all she's a year older'n I am.' She suddenly rapped out, '*You* been to Lunnon?'

'Aye, I used to live there.'

She smiled approvingly. 'So did I – lived there for years, a sight longer'n Martha ever did – but you don't catch *me* boasting of it, like her. I keeps myself to myself. I was never a flighty young piece, not like Martha.'

I just couldn't believe it. I remembered Granny Withers from when she'd come to help out in the nursery with Flora: wearing her heavy big boots and puffing her clay pipe between her remaining two stumps of teeth!

Maud Winterslow's smart button boots creaked as she stepped forward. 'Now, let's have a good look at you.' I began to back nervously away but a hand darted out and caught me, pinioning my arm. 'No, stay where you are, I'm inclined to be near-sighted these days. And that day, the *only* day, as you ever got yourself to church I couldn't see more'n the crown o' your hat. You'd upped and left by the time I'd got meself to the front o' that crowd o' gawpers as had collected outside. I can't abide nosy folk, no manners, any of 'em. Now, what have we got here?'

I felt the blood rising to my face as those shrewd dark eyes raked me from head to foot. When she was satisfied she released my arm and stepped back again. 'Well, well, just for once Martha weren't gilding the lily. First I heard, I didn't believe it – catching both on 'em, father and son, but I can see how you did it, now. You're a looker, you are, and no mistake.' As I blushed she turned and headed for the sewing machine. 'Now, me lady, you tell me exactly what you wants done and I'll be getting on with it. As folks'll tell you, Maud Winterslow's never been one to waste her time gossiping.'

I showed her the curtain material and told her the measurements. She nodded. 'Got the lining?'

'Aye – tis here.'

'Right. I'll soon have these done for you.'

'If you're busy – '

'Don't you worry bout that. If I tells my customers they've got to wait they'll wait. I'm the best dressmaker for miles around, and I charge a fair price, too.' Her eyes flicked over me again. 'Who made that skirt you're wearing?'

'I did.'

'Mm – you've got a good fit there. Let's see the back.' I turned around.

'Yes, I likes a gored skirt myself, you don't see 'em so often with six panels these day. Where'd you get the pattern from?'

'I drafted it myself.'

Maud Winterslow's sallow face creased into a smile. 'I could hardly've done better meself. Where did you learn your trade?'

I told her and she nodded approvingly. 'A proper apprenticeship, that's the way to do it. O' course there weren't no money for a premium for me at first, so I started out as a sewing maid.'

I asked, 'Did you never think of being a lady's maid?'

Her chest swelled. 'Me? At the beck and call of some female as thinks she's my better just because of the cradle she happened to be born into? Near as bad as being married, that.' She snorted. 'You look around at women as've married, and see the damage it's done to 'em! Spent their lives wi' one in the belly or one at the breast – both, if they're not careful. Childbearing wrecks a woman and ruins her figure.' Her eyes sharpened as she studied mine. 'You've kept your trim little waist, but you wait: once this one's weaned you'll find those bosoms of yours have dropped.' She leant forward. 'But don't you worry, my lady – you come and have a word with me and I'll show you how to put 'em back to how they was before the pair of 'em got to you. A strong piece of fabric, cut on the bias, nicely shaped according to how you was before, rather than how you is now. But you'll have to be firm with his lordship, no point bothering if he's just going to start you off again, is there?'

I was blushing again as Clara came in with a tea-tray. Maud Winterslow gestured to the big table. 'Just put it down there, Clara, thank 'ee. I see you've not forgot my fruit.'

''Tis only apples and oranges today, Miss Winterslow.'

The dressmaker explained to me, 'I like a bowl of fruit when I'm up at the house. I allus comes to check the linen when the peaches are nicely ripe.'

I picked up the teapot. 'How do you like it, Miss Winterslow – mebbe a mite stronger yet?'

'That'll do nicely, my lady, with a couple of sugar lumps, well stirred in.' I fetched an upright chair and set the tray with the filled cup down on the seat beside the machine. 'I can see *you've* been brought up proper, with respect for your elders. Now, mebbe you could give me the benefit of your thoughts. A lady's bought me a nice length of midnight-blue velvet for an evening gown, and she's a bit scraggy round the shoulders so I'm wondering what's best for softening the neckline . . .'

We were deep in discussion when the door opened and Mrs Johnstone came in with a face like vinegar; when she saw me the vinegar curdled. 'I wasn't aware as you'd been sent for, Mrs Winterslow.'

Maud Winterslow's eyes narrowed. '*Miss* Winterslow, if you please. I've never been married and I'm proud of it – unlike some as try to pretend, calling themselves *Mrs* when they've no more right to the title than my little tabby cat.'

The red veins on Mrs Johnstone's face deepened in colour. 'There was nothing wrong with the old curtains.'

'Her ladyship here has chosen new fabric.'

Mrs Johnstone ostentatiously turned her back on me. 'Hardly necessary, so wasteful – especially in time of war when our gallant soldiers are in need – '

Miss Winterslow cut in sharply: 'I haven't heard as them young men are in need of *curtains* in thic there trenches.' Before Mrs Johnstone could reply she leant over and tapped the teapot. 'I'd offer you a cup, Mrs Johnstone, only I knows it's not *tea* as you're so fond of.'

Mrs Johnstone turned purple and the next minute she'd flounced out, slamming the door behind her.

Miss Winterslow said sternly, 'If there's one thing I can't abide, tis to see a woman taking strong drink. I never touches a drop meself, 'cept for medicinal purposes. Can't abide a woman smoking either – Martha everlasting puffing at her pipe! 'Baccy allowance, a 'baccy allowance for women! Tis different for men, they don't know no better.' She leaned forward. 'Do you know what Martha did? Dan Withers wasn't cold in his grave and she stops his lordship in the street and says can she have his 'baccy ration now, seeing as twas her that'd allus smoked it not him! An' his lordship, he's so daft he gives it to her.' She paused, then nodded to the door, her eyes on my face. 'He's daft wi' her as has just gone out, too. Tis time *you* started checking her books.'

However did she know I didn't? But of course, Clara – Mrs Chandler – Granny Withers – no doubt the whole village knew.

I said defensively, 'His lordship do check.'

'Do 'ee?' Her lizard eyes watched me, then her head cocked to one side. 'That's your liddle one crying for her feed – nothing wrong wi' *my* hearing. Off you go then, and tend to her.'

I went back later to see how Maud Winterslow was getting on, and to show her Rose.

She admired her, then said, 'For all she's a pretty maid she's the very daps of her Pa. Now, you can both of you sit down here and keep me company. Curtains are boring to make I allus think.'

Above the whirr and clack of the treadle she told me about Mary Dawson who'd been second housemaid at Eston when I'd first arrived, and married Mr Tyson the coachman's grandson last time he'd come home on leave. 'Due in July, she is – Grace Chandler won't get her month's work there seeing as Mary's living wi' her mother. Widder she is, Mrs Dawson, lost her man through the pneumonia, that bad winter two, three years back.'

I learnt the names of the other women who were expecting later in the summer; Mary's sister was one of them.

'I don't know what thic government were thinking of, sending the men home on leave like that one after the other! Ten days and they were off back again – but they mostly left something behind 'em, they did. Poor Mary Ellis, she's a grandmother.' She shook her head disapprovingly. 'Looking for a rest, she were, and who's to blame her after seven reared and two in the churchyard? Now she's got it all to go through again. I told her, I told her when she comes to me for a new blouse, all excited because her Jim's coming due for his leave, I said, "Mary, you'll regret dressing yourself up," I said. "A nice shapeless potato sack, that's what you should be wearing when he walks through the door." Still, nothing stops 'em, do it? When they puts a ring on a woman's finger they thinks they own her – well, in law they do. That's why I kept myself single!' She glanced over to the door. 'Clara now, she's got a soft spot for Jim Arnold.'

'Baint he younger'n her?'

'He is, me dear, but the Watson women, they allus go for men younger'n them – same with Grace when she took Bert Chandler. Ellen Watson now, she won't be in a hurry, you'll see. Mind, she's a choosy girl, Ellen is. Just as well, it baint so easy for girls as is nursemaids to meet young men, not down here. Tis different in London when you sees 'em walking their prams wi' a pair o' strapping young guardsmen either side of 'em.'

By the time Maud Winterslow packed up and left at the end of the afternoon, I knew more about Eston than I'd learnt in the whole two years since I'd come back with Flora. I was quite sorry when she said she'd only be coming for another morning to finish the cushion covers for the window seats.

But at the end of the week I had another visitor. Mr Tims came up with a smile on his face. 'Mr Wallis is downstairs, my lady – he's back on leave and he's run down from Town for the day. He wondered if he might come up and have a word with you?'

I was so pleased. Mr Wallis had been Leo's valet, and not that much younger than him, but when his brother's ship had gone down last spring, he'd decided to enlist. I'd always liked Mr Wallis, and he'd been so kind to me, especially in those dreadful months before Flora was born.

He looked his usual trim self in his uniform, and I saw he'd already got two stripes on his sleeve. 'How are you, Mr Wallis?' I ran to him and took his hand in both of mine. 'I'm so pleased to see you!'

He shook my hand vigorously. 'How are you, my lady?' He looked across at the cradle. 'And what have you got there then?' I rushed across and scooped out Rose to show him. He tickled her under the chin and she gurgled to him. 'My, *aren't* you a little beauty – just like your Ma, eh?'

I glowed. 'And she's such a good baby, she never do cry.'

'I bet his lordship is as pleased as punch with her.'

'He is, Mr Wallis, he is.'

He glanced up at me. 'And you look well, you've grown up this past year, too; I can see it in your face.' He smiled. 'I was so pleased when Eustace wrote to tell me the little 'un had arrived safely.'

Eustace? Then I realized who he meant. 'I didn't know as Mr Tims wrote to you.'

'Oh yes – he keeps me in touch with what's going on. And Clara drops me a line from time to time. She's a good girl, is Clara. So young Mary got herself married, did she?'

Thanks to Maud I was able to tell him some gossip. Then I asked how he was getting on now. He gave a wry smile. 'I'd got meself into a nice comfortable rut here at Eston, and after that, soldiering took a bit o' getting used to, I can tell you. Still, I reckon if I hadn't gone, I'd never have forgiven meself later. You got to do what's right, when all's said and done. Anyway, I'll enjoy the fleshpots of Town all the more for having been away from 'em for so long.'

As he stood up to go I said, 'Come and see us next time you're on leave, Mr Wallis, do.'

'I will, my lady, I will. Though that won't be all that soon. Leave's only coming round once in a twelvemonth for us in the ranks, for all the promises they've been making in the papers. Officers do better, of course. Still, I don't begrudge them, poor devils. When the whistle blows they're the first to go over the top.' He bent to say goodbye to Rose, so he didn't see my shiver.

Straightening up again he said, 'All the best, my lady – and I hope to see you this time next year.' We shook hands and then he went back downstairs.

I felt rather bereft after he'd gone; I knew they'd be having a lively tea-time in the servants' hall, with Mr Wallis there; but it was no use, I was Lady Warminster now. Then I thought that at least Lady Warminster would be able to sit in her own sitting room soon. It was almost ready, so I took Rose up to look at it.

The marble fireplace had a delicate tracery of pink veins in it, so I'd chosen wallpaper of the same shade, plain, but with a glossy stripe to it that was ever so slightly darker. The ceiling was pale pink, too; and I'd had all the woodwork painted white. I knew it wasn't usual, because of showing the dirt, but it had made the room look so light and airy. I'd chosen a carpet that had a pattern of ivy leaves entwined on it, all in shades of dark green, so it wouldn't show the dirt too much when the children came running in, and the new sofa and chairs were upholstered in a good strong fabric for the same reason. The background was buff with a pattern of darker pink roses. I was especially pleased with the curtains: I'd managed to find a rose-patterned chintz for them, which picked up the green from the carpet in the foliage and the pink from the walls in the blooms.

The rest of the furniture was what had been in the room already: when the dustsheets came off I'd thought how elegant it was, made of polished wood in simple curving lines. I particularly liked the small desk, and someone had worked all the chair seats to match – I guessed it had been Leo's mother, so I kept them. I'd hung her picture, too, in the right-hand alcove; she looked so serene and happy. I took Rose over. 'See, tis thy grandmother.' She put out one tiny starfish hand and the woman in the picture looked just as if she'd like to reach out and take it in hers. My eyes filled with tears.

When I stood back that one picture did look rather lonely; but most of the others at Eston were of scenes, rather dark, with hardly ever any people in them. There were the portraits of the generals on the stairs but I didn't think they'd approve of my sitting room at all. Besides, they really belonged at Pennings; Clara's mother had told me that. Old Lord Warminster had sent them over when he realized that his newborn son was twisted, and so couldn't ever be a red-coated general himself. Poor Leo.

But I did need at least one other picture in the left-hand alcove to match – perhaps one of the ones in the drawing room. No, there wasn't one nice enough to be worth the trouble of fighting Mrs Johnstone over moving it.

Thinking of that made me remember what Maud Winterslow had said about the household books. It wouldn't surprise me at all if she were overdoing the perks – but surely Leo would have noticed when he checked her accounts? After all, he'd been to Eton and Cambridge; and he was so clever he could read Greek as easily as he could English.

Rose patted me; she was getting bored and Flora would be coming back from her walk in five minutes. 'We've just got time to go and look at your christening gown, Rosy-Posy.'

I took one last look round my new sitting room; it was still being aired, to get rid of the last lingering smell of paint, but by the time Beat arrived for the christening we'd be able to use it. The christening! I was so looking forward to it.

Chapter Ten

The twenty-first was a Sunday, so Beat was to come down on Saturday morning and stay the night. On Friday, Clara and I rearranged the furniture in my new sitting room yet again, until we'd got it just so. I hadn't sat up there yet; Beat and I would christen it the next day. I was telling Clara how the sitting room would be cosier for Beat, so she suggested that we had dinner in the morning room on Saturday evening. 'Thic dining room, tis main big and gloomy, and Mr Tims, I've heard him say as he'd rather serve in the morning room, with it being smaller.'

I liked eating in the morning room better too, so I suggested, 'If tis all the same to him, mebbe we could shut up the dining room when his lordship's not here – be less trouble for cleaning, too.'

Clara nodded. 'Aye, even Mrs J should see the sense in that. Now, me and Bertha'll just give the drawing room an extra turn out, first thing tomorrow, ready for the party on Sunday.'

'Party! Tisn't a party, Clara.'

She grinned. ''Tis the nearest we've had to one for years! Even Mrs Procter's bestirred herself to make a nice job o' that cake. And Mam says Maud Winterslow's told the whole village about your fine stitching in Lady Rose's christening gown.' I blushed with pleasure, as Clara bent over Rose, cooing, 'She heard me. Look at that smile! And hasn't she grown?' She tickled Rose. ''Tis just as well tis thy christening this weekend – else thee'd a bin too big for thy dress!'

Clara was right: Rose was growing fast. And she had such a beautiful smile, now – I did wish her father could have seen her, but Mr Selby had told me Leo had written to say he was very busy. Besides, he wouldn't be coming to the christening because he disapproved. But Lady Burton had sent me a violet-scented note that morning to say that Sir George would definitely be able to come with her, since he'd not been posted back to France yet. I was glad for her sake: I knew how she worried at the thought of her precious son going back to the war. I tried not to think of Frank; at least it was nearly summer now, and surely it must be easier to jump out of the way of the bullets on the lighter evenings? Mr Tims had told me the government had passed a Summer Time Act, to start on Sunday. 'The clocks are to be advanced an hour, my lady, so when should I serve breakfast?' His forehead wrinkled into a worried frown.

Mr Beeston arrived soon after, looking even more worried: when should he change the church clock? And did we want Rose's christening to stay at the real time or the government's time? I told him firmly that we'd obey the government, and sent a note to Belling to tell Lady Burton.

Clara said Mrs Johnstone was in a terrible state about the clocks changing, and down in the village the women were complaining they'd never get the children in from play to go to bed of an evening now. But I must admit I rather liked the idea: I could go for a walk in the rose garden in the evening sun.

On Saturday morning I asked Mr Tims to order the governess cart to meet Beat's train, and as soon as I heard the wheels on the gravel I rushed out into the hall. Mr Tims swung the door open and I went out on to the step, blinking in the bright sunlight. Beat waved, then a slim figure in khaki jumped down to help her out. For a moment my heart stopped – I thought, no, it can't be – and of course it wasn't. It was a man in an ordinary soldier's uniform, with three stripes on his sleeve – Albie.

Beat came puffing up the steps. 'Ow are yer, Amy, duck? And 'ow's the little 'un? I brought Albie,' she looked at me meaningfully, 'your *cousin* Albie. He got home on leave Thursday and I thought a couple o' days in the country'd be a nice break for 'im. He can find a room in the village if it ain't convenient.'

'Of course it's convenient!' I exclaimed. 'We got *lots* o' room here.' I ran down the steps to where my brother stood waiting. 'Hello, Albie. I be main glad to see thee. Do 'ee come in now, for a cup o' tea. Rose, she's in the drawing room.'

Beat chattered away about the boys and the letter she'd just had from Uncle Alf. Then Ellen arrived with Flora, who ran straight to Albie and began to drag him and Ellen round the room, showing them her treasures. Beat bent closer. 'Poor Albie were a bit low, having to leave Ned out there. Why they can't send brothers home on leave together I don't know, but they never do. That's why I brought him, really. Now you'd best have a quick word with his lordship, and tell him not to call me your stepmother – explain as Albie don't know, see. 'E can always say as I was a friend o' your auntie's – and never a truer word was spoken than that.' She sighed.

I told her, 'Leo won't be here, he's busy in London. And he don't approve of christenings.'

Beat looked surprised, then Flora ran up and tugged at her hand. 'Come and see my ark, Auntie Beat.' Ellen began to move towards the door, and at once Albie sprang forward and flung it open for her; I thought how good-looking he was now, and what nice manners he had. I wished I could have told him I was his sister, but it was no use; he'd worshipped Aunt Agnes, and he'd have been terribly upset if he'd known the truth.

I slipped out to have a quick word with Clara but she'd already put bottles in to air a bed for Albie, and Mr Tims had laid an extra place. We had lunch in the morning room, then we all went out for a walk in the rose garden. Ellen brought Flora, too, and Albie gave my daughter piggyback rides.

We had tea up in my sitting-room. Beat was full of admiration for it, 'But them walls looks a bit bare, Amy. What you needs is some nice pictures; something a bit more lively than that muddy lane you got in the alcove downstairs. A bit o' sun and blue sky, now, that'd be the ticket. It'd cheer you up no end when it's blowing a gale outside.' And I suddenly thought of the answer: Leo's pictures from Kew; but I didn't know whether I dared ask him if I could borrow them – and come to that, they weren't all quite suitable for a lady's sitting room!

Albie and Beat came up to the nursery with me to see Rose and Flora bathed, and Albie read Flora her bedtime story; she'd really taken to him, and Ellen had to be quite firm when bedtime came.

It was lovely having company all evening; I couldn't remember when I'd enjoyed myself at Eston so much. But after we'd gone to bed I began to get nervous. Beat had said to me before I'd wished her goodnight, 'You'll have to tell me the drill for tomorrow, Amy. I ain't never been to a christening in a proper church afore. I was chapel as a girl.'

But so had I been; I realized with a jolt that I didn't 'know the drill' either. I'd thought Mr Beeston would tell me, but he'd been in too much of a state over the church clock. I became more and more worried: suppose I ruined Rose's special day? And there was the tea party afterwards: how would Beat get on with Lady Burton? They were very different. And I'd only met Sir George once before and he was so distinguished – whatever could I say to him? I was so worried by now that I had to wake Rose up to give me a cuddle before I could get to sleep.

I'd said breakfast would be at nine the next morning, and I thought Albie would appreciate the lie-in, but when I went up to the nursery to see Flora he was already up there, having breakfast with her and Ellen and Dora. Ellen explained, 'Clara, she said it were no trouble to bring up another tray.'

Albie added quickly, 'I've got so used to turning out first thing, Amy. I just couldn't stay in bed.'

I smiled. 'I dare say you could manage some more breakfast, wi' me and Beat later.'

Ellen chipped in, 'I dare say he could. A boiled egg's not much for a grown man.'

Mrs Procter sent up devilled kidneys and kedgeree as well as the usual bacon and eggs; she seemed to be making an effort this weekend. Clara said it was because she didn't want to be shown up in front of guests. Then Clara asked if I'd mind if her mother came to the church for the christening.

'I'd be main pleased,' I said, 'to see anyone as cared to come, Clara.' But of course I began to worry still more. Suppose I did something stupid in front of everyone? I should have asked Clara if she knew what to do, but it was too late by then, she was so busy getting everything ready: Bertha wasn't much help and Mrs Johnstone was worse than useless.

We were in the drawing room before lunch when Mr Tims opened the door and announced, 'His lordship.'

I jumped up and Leo came straight towards me. 'Good morning, Amy.' Then he saw Albie standing to attention behind me and looked very surprised. I collected my wits together and explained, 'This is my *cousin*, Albert Thomson,' adding, just to make quite clear to him, 'Beat, she's *Albie's* stepmother.' As I watched his face I saw he understood. Then, with the briefest flicker of reassurance to me, he turned to greet Albie, 'How do you do, Thomson?'

Albie looked flustered. 'Very well, thank you – my lord.'

Beat came surging forward to the rescue. 'Good afternoon, me lord. I 'opes you don't mind me bringing young Amy's cousin down with me, but Albie here come home on leave a coulpa days ago, and I didn't want 'im 'aving to stay at home fending for hisself.'

'I'm delighted to entertain any of my wife's relations, especially on such an occasion as this. And thank you, Mrs Thomson, for agreeing to stand sponsor for our daughter.'

Beat beamed. 'The pleasure's mine, me lord.'

Leo glanced down at his tweed suit. 'You must excuse me now, I have to get changed. I presume Flora is upstairs, Amy?' When I nodded he said, 'Then I'll just run up and see her for a few minutes.'

As the door closed behind him Beat said, 'I thought he'd turn up, Amy, never mind how busy he was.' She turned to my brother, 'Real gent, ain't he, Albie? Young Amy's done well for herself, an' no mistake. Your Ma'd be that pleased if she could see her now.'

'He's not as old as I thought,' Albie said. 'The way you talked about him, Amy, you made him sound as if he were over the hill.'

'He's getting on for fifty.'

Beat spoke firmly. 'Getting on isn't there, and besides, his lordship's wearing well. Now then, Amy, don't mind us; you just run along and say hello to him proper, and I'll keep an eye on Rosy-Posy here.'

I didn't really know what more I could say than 'Good morning', but Beat seemed to expect me to go, so I followed Leo up the stairs. Hearing me, he turned to wait on the top landing. As I came up the last steps he smiled, so I smiled back before saying, 'I weren't expecting you to come.'

He looked surprised. 'Obviously, I always intended to be here. I assumed that *you* would wish it.'

The way he said '*you*' made me feel a mite uneasy, so I told him briskly, 'Of course you wouldn't want to miss Rose's christening, seeing as you're her father.'

There was a little silence, then he said, 'I *wasn't* expecting you.'

I was puzzled. 'But you knew I'd be here.'

He moved his head slightly. 'I was correcting your English grammar. "Wasn't" is the first person singular of the past tense of the verb "to be". "Weren't" is the plural form. "Weren't" would only be correct if we were together, but we aren't, are we?' He looked at me with a strange expression on his face as if he was really trying to say something else.

I stood hesitating, not knowing what to reply, but then he asked, 'Is there anything I can do to assist with the arrangements?'

I blurted out, 'I don't know what the arrangements are. I've never been to a christening afore. I don't even know when to give Rose to the Rector.'

'You don't. Ellen does.'

'Ellen? But I'm her mother – '

'It is the nurse's role. If you intervened it would be a blow to Ellen's professional pride – not to speak of depriving her of the traditional nurse's gratuities.'

'Oh. I didn't know. Beat doesn't know, either.'

'Then I'll have a word with her beforehand.'

'Thank you. What do I – '

His voice was reassuring now. 'Don't worry, Amy, the child's parents are onlookers on these occasions. You may relax and enjoy the spectacle, and my responsibilities are confined to dispensing the usual monies, and the traditional bottle of wine to the servants, so they can drink the health of the child downstairs while the guests are doing the same in the drawing room.'

In a small voice I told him, 'I've only ordered tea.'

His lips curved upwards. 'It's all under control. I've told Tims to bring up the champagne.'

I said fervently, 'I'm main glad you did come down.'

He was smiling fully now. 'Are you?' He sounded pleased.

'Yes, I'd have been in a terrible muddle else.'

He stopped smiling and said politely, 'I think I should go along to see Flora now, or I won't have time to get changed before lunch.'

We were waiting in the hall when Leo came down the stairs, almost running. I thought how distinguished he looked, and yet younger than usual, because he was wearing a morning coat instead of the old-fashioned frock coat he'd always worn in the past in Town or on formal occasions. And he moved much more quickly now; I suppose it was with working at the hospital when they were busy.

Beat chatted away over lunch, but she took the trouble to draw Albie into the conversation; he was very shy with Leo at first, but when Leo asked him about the war, Albie responded. As they talked, it struck me how much less noticeable the hesitation in Leo's speech was nowadays, even when he was talking to a stranger.

After lunch I changed quickly into my new outfit. I was getting nervous again, and it was a relief to see the reassuring bulk of Leo waiting at the bottom of the stairs. He turned, and standing very still, watched me coming down. Perhaps my skirt was too short?

Then as I reached the hall he said, 'You look most elegant, Amy.'

I smiled with relief. ''Tis my new heels, they make me look taller. With them on I'll be able to wear tails at Eton after all.'

Throwing his head to one side, he burst out laughing, before commanding, 'Come along, Amy, it's time for us to leave. We're going down in the motor, so that Ellen and Rose will have more room for their finery in the carriage.'

'But – '

He was already out on the steps. 'No harm will come to your precious daughter between now and three o'clock.'

I'd never been in the motor before. It was strange, the two of us sitting so close to one another in that cramped space. I watched his hands reach confidently for the levers; although the hair on his head was going grey, that on his hands was as black as ever, and still reminded me of fur.

As we swung round the curve of the carriage sweep he enquired, 'Have you asked Beeston back to the house afterwards? It is customary to invite the officiating clergyman.'

'Oh, I didn't know – '

His lips curved. 'No cause for alarm, Amy. A word after the ceremony will be quite sufficient.' He steered smoothly down the drive. 'The Burtons should be arriving any minute. Ettie is notoriously unpunctual, but George always tells her maid to put the clocks forward half an hour on occasions like this; though even that doesn't always work. I recall she was very nearly late for the christening of George's own boy.'

I stared at him in surprise. 'I didn't know Sir George had a son – I didn't even know he was married.'

'Young Geoffrey is at Eton now; George is a widower. His wife died a year or so after their son was born.'

'Did he never marry again?'

'No.' He hesitated before adding, 'George was devoted to Betty.' His voice was a little strained.

'How sad.' Leo did not reply, and I thought, he must be remembering her, the French Countess.

Another car had arrived outside the church just before us, and as we got out the chauffeur went round to open its rear door. Lady Burton swept out and I was engulfed in a violet-scented embrace. 'My dear – what a beautiful day! I'm afraid that wretched government has made us late, but fortunately your church clock is behind, so it really doesn't matter at all!'

I saw Sir George wink at Leo, then he held his hand out to me. 'Good afternoon, Lady Warminster, and my heartiest congratulations. I know your new daughter is a paragon of all the virtues' – as I blushed with pride he glanced at Leo, laughing – 'because her father assures me of this every time I meet him!' I looked up at Leo, with a smile, then there was the sound of hooves behind us. As I spun round, I heard the amusement in Leo's voice: 'There now, Amy, you see they haven't run off with her!'

Albie sprang out first, and helped Ellen down the steps with her precious burden. I went forward to greet Rose, who gave me her wide toothless smile of welcome; she did look beautiful in all her finery. As I was murmuring to her I heard Albie exclaim in a whisper, 'Amy, that chap's a general!'

'Tis only Sir George,' but Albie, looking quite pale, had already retreated behind Ellen's starched skirts.

Leo performed the introductions, making me thankful all over again that he was there with me. Then I saw Mr Beeston hovering by the church door in his smart white surplice; there was a small plump woman with him, bobbing up and down like an anxious thrush. I began to move towards him, and at once he darted forward. 'Lady Warminster, I do *hope* you don't mind, but Lucinda is so longing to see your little one baptized – '

'She's very welcome, Mr Beeston, and mebbe she'd like to come with you up to the house for a slice of christening cake?'

'So kind, Lady Warminster, so kind. Ah, my lord – '

'Good afternoon, Beeston. Are you ready to start then?'

'Certainly, certainly.' Mr Beeston fluttered off.

As my eyes adjusted to the twilight gloom inside the church, I saw a whole row of women's faces beyond the font: Clara, her mother, Maud Winterslow, Granny Withers, Mary Tyson with old Mrs Tyson – then I heard Rose whimper and quickly turned round. Leo said firmly, 'She's fine, Amy,' and ushered me to where two kneelers were set ready for us. The three godparents took up their position close to the font, with Ellen holding Rose a little behind them. The Rector turned to the godparents and I heard his low voice asking, 'Hath this child been already baptized, or no?'

At Sir George's confident 'No', the service began: 'Dearly beloved, for as much as all men are conceived in sin and born in sin . . .'

The words hit me with the force of a blow, then I thought, no, she *wasn't* conceived in sin, she's my husband's child; and in that moment, the bulk of him standing beside me was infinitely reassuring.

I tried to listen carefully to every word, though I couldn't help taking peeks through my fingers at Rose while I was kneeling; and when we were standing up my eyes never left her: my baby, my beautiful baby. I watched Ellen discreetly slipping off her frilled cap before handing her to Lady Burton, who then handed her on, like a gorgeously wrapped parcel, to Mr Beeston. I craned my neck; Rose was looking distinctly suspicious by now. As the water flowed down over her head to the words, 'Rose Agnes, I baptize thee in the Name of the Father . . . ' she looked even more suspicious. By the second wetting suspicion had changed to indignation, and at the third shower she let out a loud yell of protest. I strained forward, but Leo's hand barred my way; then I realized he was shaking with suppressed laughter.

I'd enjoyed the service, but in the motor on the way back, I began to panic. 'Suppose nobody speaks, suppose they just sit – '

'Amy, I am quite sure that no social gathering which contains Ettie Burton will *ever* fall silent.'

He was right. Even Beat could hardly get a word in edgeways; Lady Burton spoke enough for everyone. When she began to talk about the war my ears pricked up. She insisted it would be over by next Christmas because we were going to rout the enemy in a big battle at midsummer. Sir George interrupted, 'Shush, Mama, you mustn't spread rumours. The Germans might get to hear.'

'Don't be silly, dear, I'm sure they know already. It's all round Salisbury.'

The three men gradually formed a group to one side, but I could see that Albie was still rather nervous of Sir George; then the next time I looked, he'd disappeared altogether. I went to pour more tea, and Leo came to help me hand the cups round. I whispered, 'Albie – he's gone.'

'I gather his presence was required in the servants' hall, to open more bottles of champagne.'

'*More* bottles?'

'Apparently the party assembled there has been considerably augmented by the arrival of such luminaries of Eston village as Martha Withers and Maud Winterslow – and the presence of those two ladies has considerably increased the demand for alcoholic beverages.'

I shook my head. 'Miss Winterslow, she doesn't drink – she told me herself she never touched a drop, 'cepting for medicinal purposes.'

Leo raised his busy eyebrows. 'Doubtless she omitted to inform you of the distressing frequency with which her bouts of ill-health occur.'

I stared up at him. 'Well, I never! And after the way she spoke to Mrs Johnstone, too!'

'The world is indeed a wicked place, Amy.'

I realized he was laughing at me; he must have had quite a lot of champagne too for him to be so cheerful.

There was a loud yell from the cradle; I'd insisted on Rose being present at her own christening tea, and now she'd decided she wanted a drink as well. Leo smiled, 'You'd better take her upstairs, Amy, she obviously won't take "no" for an answer.'

I didn't want to risk her making my new dress damp, so I slipped it off, before removing Rose's christening gown and lying down with her on the bed. We curled up together, both of us in our lace-trimmed silk petticoats.

It was so cosy there, just the two of us, that I almost fell asleep; then there was a tap at the door. I called, 'Come in,' thinking it was Clara, but it wasn't – it was Leo.

He closed the door and came over to the bed. 'I had to come up myself – all the servants are – downstairs.' The old hesitation was back in his voice, and very noticeable now. 'The Burtons will have to leave soon. George must return to Town tonight.'

He stopped and simply stood there, looking down at me; suddenly I felt very self-conscious. He came even closer, and held his arms out. 'Shall I – hold her for you – while you get dressed?'

I'd suckled Rose in front of him dozens of times, but somehow, lying on my bed in my petticoats seemed different. Very quickly I buttoned up my chemise, and the minute I'd handed her over I slid down the bed and off it. Luckily my dress was hanging ready nearby, so I slipped it over my head with my back to him. Only when I'd tidied my hair did I turn round to say, 'I'll put Rose's dress back on. She did look beautiful, didn't she?'

'Yes.' Then as he reached the door he said something so softly that for a moment it sounded like, 'And so did you'. I told myself I must have misheard – yet after he'd gone my fingers were shaking so much I could scarcely fasten the small pearl buttons.

Once the guests had left it was a little flat in the drawing room. Beat sighed, 'Rose Agnes – that brings back memories, that does; it was a lovely thought, Amy. Aggie would have been that proud.'

Leo stood up. 'If you'll both excuse me, Selby said he'd run up for a word whilst I was here – one or two matters are rather pressing.'

Beat and I sat quietly talking of Aunt Agnes and the boys, then Clara came in to see if we wanted a fresh pot of tea. Her cap was crooked and her face flushed. 'That cousin of yours is a real card, my lady. Had us all in stitches, he did. Made a real hit with Maud Winterslow and Granny Withers – but they aren't the only ones.' She leant closer. 'I've never seen our Ellen so taken with a fellow afore. Allus been choosy, Ellen has.' Clara was humming a catchy little tune as she went to the door and I wished I could have joined in the fun downstairs.

Beat and Albie were leaving on the six o'clock train. Leo told Beat, 'You must visit us again – and you too, Thomson, if you should fancy a spell in the country next time you're on leave.'

Albie brightened noticeably at the invitation, so I added, 'Albie, I dare say Flora'd like to say goodbye to you. You've just got time to run up to the nursery.'

There was a streak of khaki as Albie took the stairs two at a time. Beat gazed after him. 'My, he ain't half took a shine to that Ellen. Still, she could do worse – always been a steady one, has Albie.'

The governess cart was waiting by the time Albie came down again, looking rather flushed. So we all said our goodbyes; and very soon only Leo and I were left standing in the evening sun.

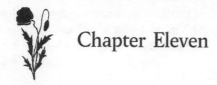

Chapter Eleven

I didn't know how to behave with Leo. I'd convinced myself that he still loved the French Countess, so there was no need for me to feel shy when I was alone with him – yet I did feel shy, shy and uncomfortable. He moved a little closer – not very close, he never stood close to anyone – but closer. And then he tilted his big body to one side so that he could look me fully in the face as he asked, 'Did you – enjoy – your daughter's christening?'

In a polite, formal voice I replied, 'Yes, thank you,' but when I saw the pleasure in his face begin to drain away, I quickly added, 'I did, Leo, I did – thank 'ee. And thank you for taking the trouble to come.' And at once the pleasure returned, to blossom into a smile.

I said firmly, 'I must go up to the nursery now. Tis time for Rose's bath.'

Turning away, I headed for the stairs – but he followed me, saying, 'I seem hardly to have seen Flora today.' I felt such relief – So *that* was why he was staying a little longer, just to spend time with Flora – and of course, she was the grand-daughter of the French countess. The minute the door opened, Flora ran straight to him, and he swung her up into his arms; there was no mistaking the joy in his face as he greeted the grandchild of the woman he loved. I could relax again.

We stayed in the nursery for more than an hour. Flora was still full of excitement after her party in the servants' hall; she told us she'd had a drink of champagne. Ellen broke in hastily, 'Just a sip, my lady – only a sniff at the bubbles, really. They made you sneeze, didn't they, Lady Flora?' She shook her head so vigorously her blonde curls bounced, and pierced my memory with love. Oh Frank – please stay safe. A big battle, Lady Burton had said – but once it was over, the war would be won, and then he would come home.

When Leo moved towards the door saying, 'I will see you at dinner, Amy,' I looked at him in surprise: he'd told Flora he was going back to London, and wouldn't be seeing her tomorrow.

'I thought you'd be getting the seven fifteen.'

'No, I've decided to catch the milk train.'

''Tis main early.'

He gave a small grimace. 'I know, but a couple more of our patients have developed this wretched fever, so I'll be needed.'

Mr Tims had laid the table in the morning room, but when I apologized Leo said, 'I'm quite happy to dine in here, Amy; by all means make the change permanent if you wish.' He smiled. 'I think I might even indulge myself in a dinner jacket for the duration of hostilities.'

I blurted out, 'Do you think it will be over by Christmas?'

He hesitated before saying, 'History tells us that when foes are evenly matched the outcome tends to be delayed. Consider the Napoleonic conflict, Amy.'

'How long did that last, then?'

'With the exception of one brief intermission, the wars between Britain and France continued for twenty-two years.'

'Twenty-two years!'

'The circumstances were rather different: modern weaponry will no doubt force an earlier resolution.' I shivered. 'Come, Amy, let's forget the war for this evening – I'm no Tiresias, I cannot see into the future. Ettie Burton may well be right. I know George is optimistic.'

I let my breath out in relief. 'And he's a general.'

'Quite. Emptying bedpans scarcely qualifies me to make pronouncements.'

The way he said that, I could tell he'd be in one of his black moods if I didn't act quickly. So at once I began to tell him about the children: all the clever things Flora had said and done, and how Rose was already holding her head up nice and strong. 'She likes to look around, does Rose – and she do smile so lovely now.'

He listened, and every so often smiled one of his slow smiles. But he never said much himself, he never did, to me. I imagined him sitting having breakfast with the French Countess in this same room every morning; he'd have talked to her, I knew that – even just giving her a book, he'd written a love letter in it. My heart was pierced with pity for him, thinking of what must have been. And knowing what I knew now I felt closer to him than ever before, because we had something in common: both of us loving hopelessly where love could never be returned.

After dessert I asked, 'Would you like to drink your coffee in the drawing room, Leo?'

'Thank you, Amy, that would give me great pleasure.'

As we stood up he said, 'Selby tells me your new sitting room has been decorated.'

'Aye, tis all ready now. I've hung the curtains. Would you like to come and see it?'

'I would be – interested.'

Upstairs, he stood looking round, then said, 'I expected you to prefer more – elaboration, a more ornate style.'

'Oh, don't you like it?'

'I do like it, very much. But it's not what I expected you to choose.'

I said doubtfully, 'Beat did say as the walls looked a bit plain, with only the one picture.'

'Then choose some more. Come up to London one day if there are none at Eston to your taste.'

I took my courage in both hands. 'There *are* some here I'd like – only they're yourn.'

His bushy eyebrows came together in a question. 'Mine?'

'Those picture you had in Kew.' I added hastily, 'Mebbe not *all* on 'em.'

He glanced at me, sideways. 'No, one or two are hardly – suitable – for a lady's sitting room.'

'But the one o' the girls with the baby, Flora'd like that one.'

He was watching me. 'But maybe not Aphrodite.'

'I did like her.'

'So – do I.'

I looked up at him from under my lashes. 'Mebbe you could send her back to the artist, ask him to paint some clothes on her – a nice high-necked blouse and a navy serge skirt, the same as schoolteachers wear.'

'What?' He sounded horrified. 'You can't be serious.'

I started giggling, 'No, o' course I weren't – she looks just right as she is.' For a moment I wondered if he was annoyed with me for daring to tease him, then he started to laugh too. It must have been the wine we'd had at dinner on top of all the champagne; it had made me feel a bit light-headed as well.

Downstairs in the drawing room I played with Rose in between drinking my two cups of coffee, while he just sat silently watching. I realized he'd let his own coffee go quite cold in the meantime, so I asked, 'Would you like a fresh cup afore you take Nella for her walk?'

He seemed to shake himself, like a great bear just waking up from its winter sleep, and it was a moment before he replied, 'No, thank you. I was wondering if I might take Rose with me for a walk round the garden.'

'Rose? But – '

'Naturally, she would be happier if you came too.'

'Well, I don't know – tis late.'

'But the government have decreed this is the first day of summer, and have kindly moved the clocks forward to give us more sunlight. Besides, I think Rose should celebrate her christening.'

Why not? The sun *was* still shining. 'I'll wrap her up warm, then.'

We went through the white gate in the high brick wall, down between the tall hedges and under the leafy green arches. At the clearing he led us to the left, along beside the ramblers. There he stopped. 'Do you remember, Amy, that afternoon when you spoke to me for the very first time? I was pruning these Dorothy Perkins and you thought it was the wrong season to be doing it – that I was making a mistake. So you spoke to me, to put me right. Do you remember?'

At once I became very brisk. 'Aye, o' course I do. Now, you come along here – I want to show you General Jack. He's looking very lively this year.' Resolutely I led the way ahead. Silently he followed me.

We toured the entire garden. I told him how each of his roses had been getting on, and he listened, asking the odd question. Rose dropped off in his arms, she'd seen it all before.

Then we came back to the top of the steps, looking down at the bronze boy proudly holding his dolphin aloft – and at the Garland Rose, twining her new green leaves around the boughs of the old apple tree. Leo began to walk down the steps. Slowly I followed him. He halted at the seat midway. 'Shall we sit down for a little while?'

In truth I didn't want to, but I supposed Rose was getting a bit heavy, since he wasn't used to carrying a baby about with him all day like I was, so I sat down. Nella flopped on her belly at my feet, as he lowered his bulk down beside me. He had seated himself sideways, so he could look directly down at the Garland, but he didn't speak, and all of a sudden I couldn't think of anything to say. We sat in silence, until at last he shifted round so that he was facing me and said, 'It seems unbelievable, doesn't it? Here I am, holding Rose in my arms – yet a year ago she didn't exist, she wasn't even thought of – '

I thought to myself, *you* might not have been thinking of a baby – but I was. I couldn't think of anything else last spring. I reached out and stroked the face of my sleeping daughter. 'Mebbe I was selfish wanting another baby – but I can't regret it.'

His voice was low but quite distinct as he replied, 'No, nor can I.'

I felt uneasy; I fixed my mind on the French Countess. He must have brought *her* here – but she was dead now. Only her son, he was still alive. I couldn't help it, I couldn't help loving him; though I wanted to cry with the pity of it, I still couldn't help myself.

It was no use staying here in the evening sun, sitting next to the man who was my husband, so I stood up. ''Tis chilly, we maun take Rose in.'

He replied quietly, 'Yes, it is. We'll go in now, Amy, if that would make you feel happier.'

On the way back, my flow of chatter seemed to have dried up completely. He didn't speak either, except to say as we came into the hall, 'I'm not sure if I'll be able to get down next Saturday for Flora's birthday. I'll send her presents in advance, then perhaps you would give them to her if I can't make it. Here she is, your precious baby.'

I took Rose from him. 'Thank you, and thank you for letting me keep her downstairs with me all day.'

His voice was formal now. 'I am pleased that you find so much joy in her. Good night. I will not, of course, be seeing you in the morning.'

I'd been wondering whether to get up, but clearly he didn't want me to see him off; I was relieved. 'Good night, Leo. Do 'ee have a safe journey.'

'Thank you.' He turned and went into his library without a backward glance; Nella followed, a faithful golden shadow at his heels.

Next day I asked Clara to tell Mrs Johnstone that his lordship had said I could unpack his paintings and hang any I wanted. Jesse, the oddman, came in, and young Ben from the stables, and I chose where each painting should go. After the men had left I walked round with Rose, showing them to her. It was like meeting old friends again, only better, because now I knew the stories of several of those who had names in the title; I'd read about them in a book of Greek myths and legends that Leo had given me. My favourites were still those three paintings that showed mothers with their children. They were so bright and happy, those pictures, you seemed to feel the warmth of the sun just looking at them.

I moved on to the painting of Nausicaä, leaning against a pillar with her chin on her hand: likely she was wondering what to give Odysseus for his dinner, seeing as he'd dropped in unexpectedly. I knew all about her now; but Balneatrix wasn't in the book he'd given me, nor was Clytie. I liked Balneatrix, who was holding a tray with linen towels on it, giving a little smile as she offered them; but I couldn't work out what Clytie was doing at all. She was kneeling down full in the sun, with her arms stretched out and her head tipped right back so that her long hair fell rippling down behind her; it was a golden colour like my hair, and was waved just the same, but I thought mine was longer: I could sit on mine, but I didn't reckon she could sit on hers.

Last of all I came to Psyche. I liked the picture, but there was something disturbing about it. I knew who Psyche was now: the beautiful princess whom Eros fell in love with. But although he was God of Love, he feared that his jealous mother, Aphrodite, might harm his bride, so he took her to his enchanted palace. Each night in the darkness, he came and loved her, but she never saw his face, so in time Psyche came to believe that maybe she was married to a loathsome monster. She found out the truth in the end, but only after terrible trials. Poor Psyche!

Flora's parcels arrived, and I put them away with my present. I'd been dressing a new doll for her every evening this week; now it had a complete set of new clothes, right down to a miniature pair of corsets. Then first thing Saturday morning, I went up to the nursery to help my daughter unpack her presents. We undressed her doll together, then she picked up the kaleidoscope Leo had sent. I showed her how to look down the peephole, and then give it a quick twist so that the shining coloured glass fell into a new pattern. She watched it change intently, then dived into the gaily coloured alphabet bricks he had sent. With a frown of concentration she squatted on the floor and began to position one above the other, pushing my hand away. 'No, Flora do it.'

I picked up the discarded kaleidoscope, and put it to my own eye. I'd only ever seen one once before. Now I turned and turned, slowly, quickly, slowly again – fascinated by the way the same chips of coloured glass could make so many different patterns. Suddenly, Flora swiped at her tower of bricks. They all tumbled to the floor and she shrieked with excitement. Then she stopped in mid-shriek and turned towards the door; her whole face lit up and within seconds she was on her feet and running across the room.

'Papa! Papa!'

He swung her up in his arms. 'Good morning, my Flora – many happy returns of the day!' But beneath his smile his eyes were pouched with fatigue, and I could smell the scent of carbolic where he'd scrubbed himself clean after leaving the hospital; obviously there were still problems with that fever. He turned a moment to smile at me: 'Good morning, Amy,' then Flora was tugging him down beside her, so that he could help her build another wobbly tower of wooden bricks.

Mr Tims arrived, 'My lord, breakfast will be served in five minutes.'

Hearing him, Flora grabbed hold of Leo's hand. 'Papa not go.'

He looked up, his eyes dark with tiredness. 'Perhaps I might eat up here, I don't have very long.'

Ellen nodded. 'Dora, lay the table – and a place for her ladyship, too.'

So we ate in the nursery. He told me he'd been awake for the past twenty-four hours; and he was due back this afternoon. Two of the VADs had gone down with this mysterious fever, so he'd been doing double duty. He would be returning on the eleven o'clock train.

'But Leo, surely you can stay and rest.'

'I promised.' He shrugged. 'I can always sleep on the train.'

He looked better once he'd had breakfast, but soon it was time for him to go. I left Ellen consoling Flora and carried Rose down with him to say goodbye.

A couple of days later another parcel arrived with Flora's name on it. It contained a beautiful doll with a delicate wax face and flowing golden hair, all dressed in silk and satin and lace. It had been sent from Gamages, but there was no clue as to who had ordered it. I wondered if it were an extra present from Leo – or Lady Burton perhaps, in case Flora had felt left out when they sent Rose her christening presents. But the second post solved the puzzle. Mr Tims brought in a letter. I stared down at the envelope, my heart in my mouth. He said anxiously, 'I know it's to Lady Flora, but I thought, seeing as she can't read yet . . .'

'Thank you.' As I took it off the silver tray I could hardly keep my hands from shaking. I waited until the door had closed behind Mr Tims before I began to lift the flap. Even though I'd only seen it once before, I'd recognized the sprawling handwriting in an instant.

My darling Flora,

I've ordered a present for you so I hope it won't arrive too late for your birthday. In the meantime, your Uncle Frank wishes you many happy returns. Have you got lots of presents? I dare say you'll enjoy playing with them. Did your pretty Mama give you a birthday kiss? I'm sure she did. Perhaps you could ask her to give you another one from me. Now, Flora, once in the past your Uncle Frank behaved very thoughtlessly to your Mama, and this caused her some distress. He's sorry now that she was

79

upset by what he did (though he isn't sorry he did it!) and he'd like you to ask her to forgive him. If she is prepared to forgive him, perhaps you could write a little letter and tell me so, Flora my pet; and even if she isn't, perhaps you could still write – we poor soldiers get very cold and lonely in these nasty draughty trenches, so a letter is always most welcome.

Underneath was the bold, scrawling, signature: 'From Uncle Frank, with love.'

I read it over and over again; my hands were trembling and my breathing uneven. 'If she is prepared to forgive him.' Of course I was, how could I not help forgiving him? Then I tried to force it out of my mind; after all, it was *Flora* he'd written too. But he knew she couldn't read. The doll was for Flora, the letter was for me.

I carried it around in my pocket all day, sneaking it out whenever I was alone with Rose. Soon I knew it by heart, but I still kept on taking it out, just for the sake of holding the paper he'd held, and reading the words he'd written.

But every time I read those words I saw the other words, too, those printed starkly at the head of the page:

On Active Service
WITH THE BRITISH EXPEDITIONARY FORCE

I'd known, of course, where he was, and the dangers he'd faced, but that letter with its uncompromising heading brought the situation home to me like the crack of a shotgun.

He'd asked me to write back – but I knew I shouldn't: it was wrong, he was not my husband. But he was Flora's father, and it was Flora he'd written to; I would write back on her behalf, and tell him how pleased she was with her doll, and how she'd put the kaleidoscope to the doll's glass eye and turned the tube, knowing the patterns were changing despite not seeing them – my clever Flora.

I went to my desk, and taking up one of those sheets of paper headed 'Eston, Wiltshire', began to write:

Dear Uncle Frank,
My Mama is writing to you because I'm not old enough to write yet. Thank you very much for the beautiful doll. She has golden hair and blue eyes. I have been playing with her, and I showed her my kaleidoscope.
Mama wants to tell you that of course she forgives you.

I paused, then underlined 'of course'. I wanted to write more, but I knew I mustn't. Only I couldn't help adding: 'Mama hopes that the trenches are not too draughty for you, and that you are able to light a nice warm fire of an evening.'

I didn't know how to end it, since it was supposed to be from Flora. In the end I wrote simply, 'Mama and I send our best wishes. From Flora.'

I sealed it quickly and took it down to the post box in the hall. I could have walked across the park with it tomorrow, since there was a post box in the lane that led up from the church, but I didn't want to be deceitful. Besides, when Mr Tims handled it he would know it was only a short letter.

All evening I tried not to think of him, but that night I had a dream. Just a simple dream: I was walking through the woods with Flora, and he was beside me.

I woke up weeping: tears of loss, and guilt; because I held my husband's child in my arms. I mustn't think of Frank, I mustn't. But it was so difficult not to.

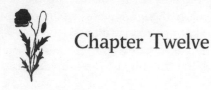

Chapter Twelve

On the last day of May the first buds of the golden rose opened, in all its perfect beauty. I showed it to Flora, 'See, tis Papa's new rose.'

By early June more of his roses were in flower. I went to see his favourite Blairii roses; they would be blooming around the statue in the woods now. Here in his garden they greeted me, laughing with delight as they climbed up their pillars and nodded their fragrant heads in triumph at the top. Gently I drew one of those perfect blooms closer to me so I could breathe in the delicious sweetness of her scent. Poor Leo, trapped in dusty, dirty London; he would be missing his roses, knowing that the first buds were opening.

I walked on with my own sleeping Rose in my arms, noticing how the roses were a little unkempt this year: a briar straggling here, a thinning of foliage there. It couldn't be helped; the younger gardeners had all left and gone to the war. My heart jumped. But I must not think of him.

Instead I thought of Mary, who wasn't due for another month; but her pains had begun this morning, Mrs Tyson had told me as I'd passed her cottage on the way out of the stableyard. So Mary was in labour even now; I would go in and ask Clara if she had any news.

She hadn't. 'Mam's with her. Tis a worry, her having started early. Looks as if it'll be a long time, too. Tis her first, and she was allus thin as a lath, Mary – and then she's been pining for Tom. I told her as tis no use doing that, but she can't help it.' Clara sighed.

By next morning no message had come up to the house. Clara said old Mrs Tyson was fretting for news. 'So I'm going to run down during dinner, if we've heard nothing by then.' It was an hour or more before Clara came back. I was up in the nursery, with Ellen, both of us worrying, when Clara rushed in. 'Tis a boy! Only a tiddler, wi' coming early, but Mam's got him well wrapped up.'

'And Mary?'

'She's all right now, but she had a bad time: terrible slow at first, Mam said. With him coming early the liddl'un weren't lying right, so the doctor had to be sent for, to use his instruments.' I shuddered. Clara glanced at Flora, playing out of earshot by the window, then whispered, 'Mary, she were torn – Doctor had to stitch her. But Mam says as she were brave, all the way through. She told Mam after, she couldn't have stood it, but for thinking o' Tom's face, when he walked through the door and saw her holding his son in her arms.' Clara dabbed at her eyes with the corner of her apron, before adding, 'Be a few months afore that happens, though.'

Ellen was practical. 'Still, she's got the longest part of the waiting over. Has she picked a name yet, Clara?'

Clara smiled. 'Tis to be Tommy, o' course.'

Later, Clara said to me, 'Be a busy old time for Mam, in a coupla months. Another three due afore the autumn, and then our Emmy. Never mind, at least they sent the men home one after the other when they'd got back from Egypt; if they'd all come on leave at once poor Mam wouldn't have known which way to turn.'

I thought of the women all carrying their babies together, and wished I was living down there in the village, too. As it was I likely wouldn't even see Mary's little boy, unless I happened to pass her in the stableyard when she brought little Tommy up to see his great-grandparents.

That afternoon Mr Tims came to say Mr Selby, Leo's agent, would like a word with me. I went down to the hall and he was waiting with a letter in his hand. 'Lord Warminster wished me to inform you that the hospital in London is to close down – a problem with the drains, apparently – so he will shortly be returning to Eston.' He stood politely waiting but he was obviously wanting to go, so I didn't ask any questions.

I thanked him, and then went straight upstairs to tell the children. 'Flora, thy Papa's coming home, to stay!'

She shrieked and went rushing round and round the nursery in a whirl of starched petticoats. Then, skidding to a halt beside her bricks she exclaimed, 'Papa build Flora a house – big house!'

I smiled. 'Soon, Flora, soon.' Rose gurgled up at me – I could see she was pleased, too.

It was late the following evening when he arrived; I was already up in my bedroom, but Clara ran up to tell me.

I bent over the bed. 'Thy Dada's come back, Rose.' She reached out to me and I knew he'd want to see her, so as soon as I'd pulled on my blouse and skirt I scooped her up and hurried out to the door.

Mr Tims was still in the hall, and as he saw me coming down the stairs he opened the library door to announce: 'Her ladyship's come down, my lord.' By the time I reached the bottom of the stairs, Leo was already there waiting for us.

I held his daughter out to him. 'There, baint she grown?' He admired Rose, then I told him how she'd learnt to roll over just this last couple of days, and how she liked to listen to her rattle. 'Tis lucky about those drains – you'll be able to see more of her now.'

'It was most unfortunate for the patients who were affected, but I must confess, I am not sorry to be home.'

'And the roses are all coming out, too.'

He smiled. 'Yes, I'm looking forward to my customary evening stroll. Now you must go upstairs again, Amy – I can see that you were preparing for bed.' At once I put my hand to my blouse to check that the buttons were all done up. His smile broadened. 'No, I deduced it from your plaits!'

I'd clean forgotten about them, hanging down my back. He laughed at my confusion. 'Run along now, I will see you tomorrow.'

He'd already been up to visit Flora first thing, but by the time I went down to breakfast only a few stray crumbs on the table showed he was back. Mr Tims told me that Mr Selby had arrived early, 'Very anxious to see his lordship about the County War Committee, he said.'

'War? But his lordship's not a soldier.'

'He's a landowner, my lady. The government's naturally very concerned that adequate food supplies are maintained. Then there's the timber, terrible to see so much of it being cut down, Mr Selby says. Still,' he brightened, 'they say this big battle that's coming will send those Germans packing.'

Clara came in, pretending to check the hot water, but really to tell me the latest news of her youngest brother. 'He wrote to say as he's staying in a nice village, so he's well away from all that nasty fighting. I *am* doing well for letters, wi' Mr Wallis writing only last week.' She bent over the table to rearrange the marmalade spoon, 'And yesterday, I had a letter from Jim, too – came by the late post. Nice of him to take the trouble to write.' Even the back of her neck was blushing. I knew Clara had missed Jim Arnold, ever since he'd left the stables to go to war.

I said, 'You'll have to be sure and write back quickly, Clara. Soldiers, they realy do appreciate letters from home.'

She didn't look at me as she muttered, 'Well, mebbe I can spare a minute this afternoon, then.'

I went to fetch Rose, and then took her into my sitting room. It was so much cosier than the drawing room and I was grateful to Leo for letting me have it – that gave me the idea. 'Rose, thee and me are going on a treasure hunt.' I found what I wanted in the billiard room, and Jesse and young Ben brought it upstairs; it looked a bit odd at first, but I'd soon get used to that.

I ate lunch alone; Leo never had taken lunch. Flora told me on our walk that he'd been up to see her. 'But Papa busy, very very busy.'

'That's right, Flora, because of the war.' It was strange not to have Nella padding along with us, but I knew that now Leo was back she wouldn't leave his side unless he ordered her to. Later, Mr Tims brought a message that Leo would be joining me for dinner at the usual time. I said, 'I'll lay his clothes out, then.'

'But, my lady – '

'You've got quite enough to do. And 'sides, he won't know as long you're up there running his bath at the usual time.'

I settled Rose down on the armchair in his dressing room, wedging her in with a pillow. Her bright eyes watched me as I laid out clean vest, underpants, shirt, cufflinks, collar stud – just as Mr Wallis had taught me before he left last year. But recalling what Leo had said, I put out a dinner jacket, and so I had to find a black tie to go with the stiff white collar.

Leo and I dined together as usual. I chattered, and he listened, but after I'd told him about the children and the roses I asked what the County War Committee did.

He corrected, 'The County War Agricultural Committee,' before saying dismissively, 'But you needn't bother your head about things like that, Amy.' I didn't ask again.

As he held the door open for me to precede him, he asked, 'Are you taking – coffee – in the drawing room?'

I shook my head. 'No.' Without a word he began to close the door behind me. I turned back to prevent him shutting me out, and repeated, 'No, 'cos I do take my coffee in my new sitting room now. Mebbe you'd care to drink yours up there, too?'

'Thank you, Amy. I would be honoured.' He suddenly looked cheerful; he was a terribly changeable man.

I told him, 'I'll just go up and fetch Rose then, I won't be a minute.'

When I came back down from the nursery he was standing outside the sitting room door like a great uncertain bear. 'You should have gone in, Leo.'

'I – that is – it is *your* sitting room.' He was still hesitating on the threshold, then he noticed. 'You've brought up one of the billiard room armchairs.'

'Aye, I reckoned the others were a mite on the small side for you.'

'For *me*? You brought up that chair for *me*?'

He sounded very surprised, yet pleased, too, so I replied briskly, 'I know you like to see Rose of an evening, and seeing as she's generally in here with me, I reckoned it made sense. Now sit down, do.'

He sat there drinking his coffee while I nursed Rose, and seemed in no hurry to leave for his walk. Nella had settled down comfortably, too; I was sure she'd never really liked the drawing room, either.

I said, 'The pictures, they do brighten up the room, don't they?'

'Yes, I'm pleased to see them on show again. They were like old friends to me.'

He was in such a good mood I said, 'I know some of their stories from that book you gave me, mebbe you could tell me about the others, now?'

'Certainly.' He jumped up so quickly he almost upset his empty cup and saucer.

Rose was dozing, so I settled her in her cradle and stood up, too.

He went straight to Psyche. 'Do you know the story of Psyche?' He pronounced her name as though it began with an S. I was glad I hadn't said it first, and made a fool of myself.

'Aye, I do, she were in the book, so I read all about her.'

He still stood in front of the picture, gazing at Psyche as she timidly pushed open the door of Eros' rose garden. Then he asked, without looking up at me, 'Do – you still – read the story of Beauty and the Beast?'

I smiled. He knew I'd thought of him as the kindly Beast, sometimes.

'Aye, I read it to Flora only yesterday.'

'Some – have suggested that – the myth of Psyche and Eros was the original of the tale of Beauty and the Beast.'

I thought that one over, then said, 'I suppose, with Beauty being alone all day in the castle, this picture could be of her.'

'Yes.'

Then I changed my mind. 'No, tisn't the same. I know Psyche did think mebbe her husband was a loathsome monster, like the Beast – but he wasn't, was he? He was the handsome God of Love.'

Speaking very slowly now, he said, 'Perhaps – in his heart – the Beast too felt as though he were the God of Love.'

'But he weren't, were he?'

'No.' There was a long pause before he asked, 'So there is no hope for the Beast, then?'

I was puzzled. 'Yes, there was, because he turned into a handsome prince when the spell was lifted by the magic fireworks – and then he and Beauty got married, and lived happily ever after.'

Abruptly Leo moved on to the next picture. 'Nausicaä – you know *her* story, I presume?'

'Aye.' I told him how I imagined her standing there, wondering what to give Odysseus for his dinner, with him having dropped in so unexpectedly, and he gave a short bark of laughter.

Next came Balneatrix. 'I looked her up in the book, but I couldn't find her name anywhere.'

He began to laugh, proper laughter this time. 'It's not a girl's name, it's a Latin word for a bath attendant.'

'So *that's* why she's offering towels – she's a servant.' I felt so stupid, then I began to laugh, too. 'An' I thought it were such a pretty name. Now I don't know what she's called.'

'Why not call her Flavia?'

I nodded approvingly. 'That's pretty too. Is it Latin? I don't know any Latin names.'

'Yes you do, you use one every day.'

'But yours is Greek.'

'And you don't use it every day. Flora is the name of the Goddess of Flowers.'

'Of Flowers! So now I've got *two* flowers for daughters – well I never!'

He smiled: he was back in his good mood again, thank goodness. I led him on to Clytie, kneeling in her green dress with her arms stretched out to the sun. 'I couldn't find her story, either.'

'Poor Clytie. She fell hopelessly in love with the sun god, golden-haired Apollo himself. But she never found favour in his eyes, and was simply languishing from unrequited love, until the gods took pity on her and turned her into a sunflower.'

And though it was a warm evening, I felt my body go cold. Clytie, who loved golden-haired Apollo hopelessly, uselessly . . .

But Leo hadn't finished. 'To this day, sunflowers turn their faces to follow the sun as it crosses the sky in memory of Clytie's constancy. Moore wrote a poem about her; let me see if I can remember it:

> *No, the heart that has truly loved never forgets,*
> *But as truly loves on to the close . . . '*

He paused, repeating the lines softly to himself before continuing:

> *'As the sunflower turns on her God when he sets,*
> *The same look which she turned when he rose.'*

The heart that has truly loved never forgets – and I couldn't forget, I couldn't. I didn't want to forget . . .

I realized that my husband was still speaking to me. 'Don't you think so, Amy?'

'What? Do I think what?'

'That her hair is so very like yours. A slightly darker gold, perhaps, but the wave in it resembles how I've always imagined yours would look when it's let down.' He stopped a moment, then his voice continued lower, yet stronger. 'Amy, I've never seen you with your hair flowing loose – would you unpin it for me, now?'

I faltered, '*Now?* But – '

He was insistent. 'You'll be going to bed soon, so you'll have to take it down then to plait it. I would be grateful if you would do so now.'

Grateful – I was grateful to him, so what could I say? But I felt very embarrassed as I removed all my hairpins. When my hair had all fallen down, I shook it out, and it fell around me like a curtain. I turned my back on him, hiding beneath it.

I seemed to stand there for ever; there was silence behind me. Then he spoke again.

'May I – touch it?'

'Yes, o' course.'

'Thank you.' His touch was so light, I could barely feel his fingers as he stroked my hair.

At last I whispered, 'Can I – can I put it up again now?'

'Yes, yes – '

The door had closed behind me before I could turn round.

Chapter Thirteen

Now Leo was home again, he'd spend the first part of the morning with Mr Selby, then he'd take Flora out for a walk. Once he took her over to the Home Farm with him in his motor, and when she came back she was full of the excitements of the morning: the chicks, the hens, the geese. So next day, when he came to fetch her, it was, 'Farm, Papa – Papa go to farm.'

He smiled, 'If there is time, my Flora.'

Of course he made time, so she came running in later with mud on her socks and straw clinging to her pinafore.

I hugged her close. 'And what did you see today, my flower?'

'Pigs – baby pigs.' She beamed with delight. 'I scratched their ears, they made noises.' She drew a deep breath and gave a high-pitched squeal in imitation. Looking at her young face, I could not control my shiver.

As Leo came back from the nursery, I barred his way. 'In future, when you take Flora to the Home Farm, don't take her to see the pigs.'

He gave a half-smile. 'I can assure you, Amy, that I only held her on the field gate. The scratching was performed by means of a stick. In any case, pigs are clean animals when kept in the proper conditions; indeed, they are generally the most amiable of creatures, I find.'

I remembered Dimpsey in her sty coming running to be petted, her little eyes so full of love. I could hardly keep the tears out of my voice as I exclaimed, 'Pigs, they be lovely animals, but – ' I couldn't bear to go on. Instead, I finished flatly, 'There's Nella. Flora's main fond o' Nella, and o' Tabby Cat in the stables; she can stroke them. I just don't want her making a pet of a pig, and getting fond of it.'

There was silence, then he said, 'Flora only looked at the pigs once. She did not make a pet of one, and will not be allowed to do so.' He paused, then added, 'I'm going into the garden for a few minutes – perhaps you and Rose would like to accompany me?'

But I was still fighting my tears. I shook my head. 'No – thank 'ee.' He turned and went on down the corridor without another word. I couldn't get Dimpsey out of my mind all afternoon, and that night I had a nightmare. The pig-sticker's knife flashed, Dimpsey's red blood spurted out. I awoke shivering and cold; as cold as if I were back in the cottage at Borrell, kneeling on the stone flags to mop up the brine that oozed from her body. But I hadn't eaten her, I hadn't. I clung desperately to that thought; to have eaten her would have been the final betrayal.

Next day when Leo came to fetch Flora, he turned down her request. 'Papa is not visiting the farm this morning, Flora.'

'Pigs, Flora see pigs.'

He ignored her wail of disappointment. 'We will go to the stables to see the horses, and Tabby Cat.' He glanced across at me. 'Perhaps your Mama would like to come too? I think the fresh air might do her good.'

I shook my head. 'Rose'll be waking up soon.' As he began to turn away, I called to his humped back, 'Mebbe this evening we could have a walk in the rose garden?'

Immediately he swung back to face me. 'It would be – my pleasure. Your favourite cabbage rose is particularly fine at the moment.'

Most evenings after that, we walked in the rose garden together; as he rarely saw Rose except after dinner, he'd ask to take her with him for his evening stroll, so naturally I went too. He told me that once the outstanding business of the estate was sorted out, he'd offer his services as a Red Cross orderly to the military hospitals over at Sutton Veny. But at present the hospitals were only half full: they were waiting for the great battle to start. We were all waiting; every time I looked at the picture of Clytie worshipping her golden-haired sun god I remembered – and prayed for his safety.

Maud Winterslow came up to do some household mending; I went along to see her and she talked of the men of Eston who'd gone away to the war. 'Clara there, she's fretting after her brothers – and for young Jim Arnold, too, although she won't thank you for mentioning it.'

I told her, 'Ellen had a letter from her brother this morning.'

'That'll be Ben. He's one as is next in age to her, always close they were, Ellen and Ben. Now Mary Tyson – Dawson as was – she's only got the one brother. They runs to females in thic family, they do – though she's got a son of her own now.'

I asked, 'How's she getting along, Miss Winterslow?'

She pursed her mouth. ''Tis lucky she's with her mother. That baby takes so long over his feeds he's started the next one afore he's finished the first. Awkward he is, like all male creatures!' As she finished her seam she leant towards me. 'Look at thic there Kaiser now, he's just the same: typical man, allus wants to be upsetting folks. They should 'a put a woman in charge, we got more sense – most of us, that is.' She darted a sharp glance at me from under her lizard lids. 'You checking them books o' Mrs Johnstone's yet?'

'No, his lordship do do that.'

She snorted. ''Tis no use relying on him, he's a man.' She cocked her head. 'And here he is, coming this way. That's his footsteps – nothing wrong with *my* hearing.'

'He'll be going to the nursery, to see Flora – tis just along the corridor.'

But she smirked knowingly as the footsteps slowed before the sewing room door. 'No, tis you as he's after.'

Leo came in. 'Good morning, Amy.' He looked across at my companion. 'And good morning to you, Miss Winterslow. Don't trouble yourself getting up.'

'I weren't intending to, as you very well know. I'm not one o' them lackeys, always dipping and swaying whenever they sees you a-coming. I've never bent my knee before any man, and I never will.'

In horror I turned to look at Leo's face; he didn't seem at all put out – quite the reverse. 'Nor sat on any man's knee, eh, Miss Winterslow?'

Now it was Maud Winterslow's turn to receive my horrified glance – but to my amazement she burst into a cracked peal of laughter. 'You don't know what I got up to in my salad days, young man.'

I couldn't believe my ears; she'd called him 'young man' – and not a mention of 'my lord'! And Leo was laughing, actually laughing. 'Miss Winterslow, I can believe anything of you.'

She sniffed. 'You can keep your beliefs to yourself. I don't agree with gossip, as you well know.'

'Indeed.'

She continued, 'I suppose as you've come for your lady here. Well, you can take her away now, we've had our little discussion.'

'Discussion? Or was it a goss-'

She was too quick for him. 'A *business* discussion – about seams and plackets and facings and suchlike important things as you men knows nothing about.' She turned her approving nod on me. 'She can handle a needle, I can't say higher than that. You run along with him now, my lady – afore he starts getting fidgety.'

I stood up, looking uncertainly at Leo; I was sure he didn't want me at all. He continued light-heartedly, 'It would appear that we are dismissed, Amy.'

'By the way,' Maud Winterslow detained us at the door, ' I been telling your lady tis time you let her check the housekeeping books – she's the mistress here.' Her eyes caught mine, in a look full of meaning, then the treadle began to whirr.

Outside the door Leo asked, 'Do you really want to check the books? There is surely no necessity for you to take the trouble – '

But now she'd brought up the subject I was decided. 'Miss Winterslow's right: it *is* my job.'

'Very well, they're due tomorrow – I'll send Mrs Johnstone on to you.'

I wondered if Maud Winterslow had known they were due tomorrow; then I thought, of course she did, nothing got past her sharp ears.

When Mrs Johnstone appeared at my sitting room door the next morning, it was obvious she wasn't at all pleased. 'His *lordship* said,' from the tone of her voice it was clear she thought he was suffering from a temporary mental derangement, 'He said as he wanted *you* to sign the books.'

'Yes, Mrs Johnstone.'

I went over to my desk. She dropped them down on the top. 'Sign there.' Her broad finger with its none-too-clean nail jabbed at the bottom of the page.

'I never signs accounts I haven't read, Mrs Johnstone.'

There was a momentary flash of fear, then her usual confidence returned with a smirk. 'Is that so? Then I'll leave them to your expert eye, my lady.' She flounced out.

I opened the first of the books; it began more than two years ago. Mrs Johnstone had obviously meant to be sarcastic, but in fact I did know a thing or two about book-keeping. While I was an apprentice dressmaker I'd regularly checked the business books, and finished up doing the housekeeping ones as well, because everyone knew I was handy with figures. Naturally, the Eston books were more complicated than the household ones I'd seen before, Eston being so big, but I soon saw they'd been made more complicated than they needed to be. Maud Winterslow had been right; not that I'd seriously believed she wasn't.

Only I'd thought it would be a matter of a few pennies dropped off a total here and there; but it was much cleverer than that. As I compared one set of figures with the other and spotted the discrepancies, I was quite surprised; I wouldn't have expected Mrs Johnstone to be so clever; she must have worked the system out before she got fond of the bottle. I soon discovered that Mrs Procter had been cooking her books better than her food. The pair of them had to have been in it together, or it wouldn't have worked.

The housekeeper came back in half an hour, demanding her books. I replied, 'No, Mrs Johnstone, and I want all the earlier ones, too – ever since you came to Eston.' And this time there was more than a flash of fear in her eyes.

Clara brought up the older books. 'Whatever have you been saying to Mrs Johnstone? She's as fidgety as a flittermouse. I never seen the like afore.'

'I been checking her books.'

Clara looked interested. 'Ah, well, I have wondered. I said to my Mam more'n once, I wouldn't share a farthing with that one.' So that was why Maud Winterslow had been suspicious.

In the earliest book I got a shock: the signature wasn't Leo's. Instead, in a round hand, was the name 'Jeanette Warminster.' The French Countess. But she'd signed those books too. She might have been a lady and been taught by nuns, but the village school at Borrell had taught me more about arithmetic.

I left a message with Mr Tims, to ask his lordship to kindly step upstairs when he came in. As he came through the door, Leo looked anxious. 'Is anything the matter, Amy? Are you ill? Or one of the children – '

'No, tis these books.'

'I'll sign them if you'd rather.'

Looking him straight in the eye, I said, 'Nobody's signing these. And I reckon as you shouldn't have been signing the others, either – not without looking 'em over first.' He looked quite deflated as I asked, '*Did* you check?'

'Well, I, er – I usually cast an eye over them.'

I said firmly, 'Draw up a chair, and we'll look at them together. Then you can check as it baint me as is wrong.'

Obediently he fetched a chair and I began to explain. 'Now, I'll just open it at any page. Right, look here,' I pointed. 'Seven at 4s 11¾d, let me see, that's £1 14s 10¼d.' I turned over the page and ran my finger down the column. 'Well, she's got that right. Let's check this one: ten at 5s 8½d.' After a moment's thinking, I said, 'That should be £2 17s 1d, shouldn't it?'

'Well I – '

'Course it should.' I flicked through the pages. 'Now, here it is again, correct, but,' turning to the grocery supplies book, 'see the date, see the money, it's come through right, but she's entered 'em together here, instead of separately. Now add them together.' I waited a moment before stabbing a triumphant finger down at the entry, '£4 10s 4¾d – that do really stand out, don't it? – is 6½d short! Only she's done it so it *could* 'a been a mistake, but when you look here – now, you add up that column – '

He pleaded, 'Amy, I can't add up that quickly, not in my head.'

I turned and stared at him. 'Didn't you do mental at Eton?'

He looked abashed. 'Clearly not frequently enough; I will need a piece of paper and a pencil.' He had to write each sum out and add it up with a 'carry one', just as though he were still in Standard II; I could hardly believe it. And him being able to read Greek as though it were English!

He was so slow to see how she'd played her tricks that eventually I decided to pretend he *was* in Standard II and explain accordingly. I finished, 'So that's whats he's been up to. It's obvious. Soon as you start looking a bit careful, like.'

'Not to me, it wasn't obvious to me.'

He did look rather embarrassed, so I said, 'Never mind, you do know Greek instead.'

'I'm beginning to think book-keeping might have been more useful; but wherever did you learn how to deal with figures so rapidly?'

'You don't *learn* figures, not after Standard I: they just, well, you see 'em in your head like little soldiers, marching to their places, don't you?'

'No, *I* don't. Nor I think do many others. Selby's a good man with accounts, but he is certainly not as quick as you.'

I glowed with pride, then I remembered the whole point of it. I tapped the housekeeping books. 'There's money been going astray for years. Mrs Johnstone and Mrs Procter, they've been cheating you almost since they first came.'

'Yes, you're right.' There was a pause before he asked, 'What are we going to do about it?'

He sounded as if he really didn't know, as if he wanted my opinion, so I said firmly, 'What they've been doing, tis thieving – they got to be turned off.'

He sighed, 'Yes, I'm afraid you're right. But it may be difficult to replace both a cook and a housekeeper at short notice, especially in wartime.'

I wasn't having any shillyshallying. 'They're both of 'em lazy as cuckoos, so I don't reckon as we'll notice any difference.'

'I think I might rather notice the absence of dinner.'

I reassured him, ' You'll not go without your vittals – I can cook your dinner for you, if need be.'

He looked quite startled at this prospect, then he smiled. 'That is kind of you, Amy, but I hope it won't be necessary. Besides, you can scarcely take Rose into the kitchen, can you? It wouldn't be a healthy atmosphere.'

'Then I dare say the kitchenmaid could manage for a while.'

'You favour instant dismissal?'

'At the very least. I know cooks are entitled to their perks, but that baint what we're talking about here. And it's been going on so long, too.'

He reddened. 'As to that, I confess that I have been culpable in failing to scrutinize the figures.'

'But even if you had looked, she were main cunning – '

He raised his bushy eyebrows. 'Are you implying that I lack the necessary skills to detect such a fraud?' I didn't know quite how to answer that one, but he saved me the trouble. 'No doubt you are right, but I could have asked Selby to run an eye over them. As it was I simply didn't bother, so I feel I must bear some of the responsibility. Since I signed those accounts, I will not take legal action.' He turned so that he could look at me directly. 'But you are right: they must be dismissed at once.'

He rang for Mr Tims. 'Send Mrs Johnstone and Mrs Procter up here. Her ladyship wishes to speak to them.'

While we were waiting my confidence began to ooze away. 'Mebbe if *you* could tell 'em?'

He didn't reply, but I thought by his expression that he'd do it, and he did. 'Mrs Johnstone, Mrs Procter, her ladyship has discovered certain persistent irregularities in your household accounts. Under those circumstances I have no option but to dismiss you both, at once.'

Mrs Procter blenched, but Mrs Jonstone turned red as a rooster's wattles. 'Her *ladyship*?' She almost spat the words. 'She's no more a ladyship than I am – and when it comes to her morals – '

Mrs Procter caught at Mrs Johnstone's sleeve. 'Ethel, be quiet. His lordship'll have the law on us.'

Leo was on his feet, his voice very loud. 'I had not intended to prosecute, but now you have dared insult my wife I will invoke the full force of the law.' I saw the panic in Mrs Johnstone's eyes and then Leo was shouting, 'Get out! Get out, the pair of you!' They jostled each other trying to get through the door as it closed. I flinched from the fury in his face as he said, 'How *dare* she! Don't worry, Amy, I will write to my solicitors at once.'

Recalling Mrs Procter's agonized expression, I said, 'Leo, Mrs Johnstone were drunk. She's always like that when she's had a drop too much – '

He didn't wait for me to finish. '*Always?* Do you mean she's spoken to you like that before?' He read the answer in my face. 'Why didn't you *tell* me? Why

93

didn't you *tell* me?' His anger was turned on me now; then suddenly he almost threw himself across the room and out of the door.

I was upset all morning, until Clara told me Leo had simply sent them packing. 'Mr Tims reckons Mr Selby talked him out of it; said it wasn't worth the trouble, not a court case an' all.' I gave a great sigh of relief. I didn't want to think of either of them behind bars; besides, Leo had spoken true: he should have checked, and so should I, much sooner.

He was in a terrible mood at dinner, just sitting brooding over lumpy soup and under-done mutton served with cabbage that had been boiled to a slime. He'd got a black dog on both his shoulders tonight. When the rice pudding came in, all dried up round the edges, I asked, 'Do you want me to – should I advertise for a cook?'

'*You* are Lady Warminster. You decide.' He refused the offer of coffee in my sitting room, muttering that he was taking Nella for a long walk.

Mr Tims seemed even more anxious than usual when he brought the tray upstairs. He went to fidget with the curtains, then came back and stood in front of me, shuffling from one foot to the other. I asked him, 'Is anything the matter, Mr Tims?'

His words came in a rush. 'My lady, I was wondering if I might speak on behalf of my cousin. She had a place as a cook, only she fell ill, and when she had to go to the hospital the lady turned her off.' He looked at me, his forehead wrinkling as he explained further, 'There'd been problems: Emily, she'd got very hard of hearing, and it used to irritate the lady, so when she fell ill the lady wouldn't wait. Emily's recovered her health, but now she can't hear at all: she's stone deaf. She's written for posts, the lady gave her a good character, but as soon as she goes to be interviewed,' he sighed, 'she can't hear the questions.'

I made up my mind at once. Going to my desk I took out some pound notes. 'Mr Tims, send her a postal order for her fare and tell her I'll write the questions down.'

He must have sent down for the postal order first thing, because just before lunch on Thursday he shepherded her in. 'Emily Carter, my lady.'

She was younger than Mr Tims but with the same anxious expression. As she came closer I saw that her clothes were clean but very shabby; and the way they hung on her gaunt frame, they were obviously from before her illness. She reached into her pocket and held out a cheap pad and pencil; her hand was trembling. 'Good morning, my lady.' Her voice was flat; she'd been hard of hearing for a long time, I reckoned.

I took the pad and pencil with a 'Thank 'ee, Mrs Carter,' but as I knew she couldn't hear it I gave her a big smile, and her lips twitched nervously in response. 'Mebbe you could fetch Mrs Carter a chair, Mr Tims?'

He brought it forward and gestured to her to sit down; she did so, looking very surprised.

I raised the pencil she'd given me – and then couldn't think of a question; I'd never interviewed a servant before. I thought of asking Leo to come, but the mood he was in, the poor lady would probably have fallen off her chair in a dead faint. She was watching me, her face getting more and more worried; if she'd been a sewing maid I could have judged by looking at her work. That gave me the idea. I wrote, 'Would you like to cook his lordship's dinner tonight?'

I held it out to her and she nodded vigorously. 'Yes, yes. How many courses?'

I wrote, 'Just soup, fish, roast, and pudding. Send the orders down for anything you want. And you must stay the night afterwards, of course.'

She jumped up. 'I'll be starting now.' Ten minutes later Mr Tims arrived with a menu for me to approve. I put a tick by each dish. As I handed it back, Mr Tims said, 'Emily's very grateful to you for giving her a chance, my lady. I'm sure his lordship will be pleased.'

But that evening as I came downstairs, my heart sank at the sight of Leo's expression. He didn't look as if anything would please him tonight. I glanced at Mr Tims; he looked as nervous as I felt.

Mrs Carter had suggested a clear soup with chicken quenelles. I began to relax at the first mouthful: that soup had been so well sieved it was like drinking liquid silk and the marble-sized bites of minced chicken made you want more. Leo looked round for a second helping, and Mr Tims fairly leapt towards the tureen. The fried sole was a beautiful golden brown and Mr Tims must have told her how fond Leo was of anchovies, since she'd made a sauce of them. I was sure he was enjoying it, but he was so determined to sulk he wouldn't admit it.

The joint of beef arrived looking very tempting, decorated with its sauce and little clumps of onions and carrots. The potatoes had been cooked with onions and parsley – lyonnaise she'd written on the menu – I'd never had them before but they smelled delicious. Then I saw Mr Tims' agonized expression as he lifted the lid of the first vegetable dish. The cabbage wasn't green slime this evening, but it was definitely overcooked. He mouthed, 'The kitchenmaid.' I nodded and said loudly, 'There's your favourite creamed parsnips, Leo.' He grunted, but I could see that the scent of the beef had set his nostrils quivering, so I just hoped he'd be too busy enjoying that to notice the cabbage. Mr Tims' eyes went straight to Leo's plate when he came in to clear; he almost sagged with relief when he saw it was completely empty.

The first mouthful of the caramel pudding told me I could relax now; Leo always liked a good egg custard, and this was a good one.

After he'd finished his dessert, I asked him, 'Did you enjoy your dinner?'

'Did *you* cook it?'

'No, I couldn't cook anything fancy like that. Twas Mr Tims' cousin as sent these dishes up. She's applied to be the cook. May I engage her to replace Mrs Procter?'

He almost snapped, 'It is your decision, as I told you.'

'Then I will.'

He stood up, went to open the door and waited for me to go past. I stopped. 'Leo, she's deaf, and having problems getting a place because of it, so tonight she did try awful hard to please you. Mebbe I could tell her you did enjoy your dinner?'

He replied curtly, 'Tell her that, then.'

I went straight down to the kitchen. Everything was neatly tidied away and Mrs Carter was sitting bolt upright near the range. As soon as she saw me she jumped up, holding out her pad. I wrote on it, 'His lordship enjoyed his dinner, so if you'd like to stay – ' I stopped writing because she'd burst into tears, great racking sobs. I put my hand on her arm. 'Is there anything the matter?'

'My lady, thank you, thank you! I've been so worried. I thought, I thought – ' she could hardly get the words out – 'I thought it'd be the House.'

The workhouse: I felt so sorry for her. I squeezed her hand. 'You needn't worry, Mrs Carter, nobody do go to the workhouse from Eston. His lordship don't allow it.' Then I realized she couldn't hear me, so I wrote it all down and she cried even harder. I remembered how desperate I'd been when Miss Annabel had turned me off, but that had been my own fault; poor Mrs Carter hadn't been to blame for her trouble.

I left her sitting with Mr Tims in his pantry, drinking a nice cup of tea that Clara had made. I thought as I came away how uncomfortable the chairs looked in there; as soon as we got a new housekeeper I'd tell her to order some better ones.

But where was I to get a new housekeeper from? It wasn't likely Mr Tims would have another cousin free. Meanwhile I went up to the nursery to find Clara – she always had her evening cup of cocoa up there – and ask her, 'Mebbe you could keep an eye on the kitchenmaid, and Sal in the scullery, to see as they don't take advantage of Mrs Carter, with her being deaf.'

Clara agreed. 'Aye, I will. I'd thought o' that myself.' That was typical of Clara: you could always rely on her. And I saw the answer, just like that. 'Clara, why shouldn't you be housekeeper now?'

Clara gasped, open-mouthed. It took me a while to persuade her, and I might not have succeeded if Ellen hadn't joined in. Clara kept saying she was too young to be a housekeeper, and because she'd never been housemaid anywhere apart from Eston she'd never had any training in the right way of doing things – Mrs Johnstone having been the way she was.

I joked, ''Tis easy, you just think what she did, and then do the opposite!' We all giggled, then I added, 'Clara, I knows his lordship'd rather have you. He don't like new faces. Mebbe you could ask your Mam how to housekeep?'

She shook her head. 'No, Mam was always in the nursery, afore she married – ' Then her face brightened, 'There's Mrs Whittle, Jim's Aunt Mags, down at the East Lodge. She were head housemaid over at Belling for years. And Lady Burton's housekeeper then were Mrs Rogers, a real tartar – everything had to be just so.'

I could tell Clara was getting tempted, and so could Ellen. We looked at each other, and then Ellen said firmly, 'You go down first thing tomorrow, Clara, and ask Mrs Whittle if she'll kindly step up and give us some advice.' She grinned at me. 'What she's said in the past about Mrs J's slammocky ways don't bear repeating, my lady – so now's her chance to tell us how to put the place to rights.'

The first thing Mrs Whittle said was that Clara must ask me to look at the state of the still room and linen cupboard and suchlike, so I'd know just how bad things were, and wouldn't blame Clara for not being able to put them to rights overnight. As soon as Clara gave me that message, I ran up to the nursery to leave Rose there, and went straight down to the Room. Mrs Whittle stood up and gave me a bob when I came in, but from then on it was clear who was in charge – although she was very polite about it. I was only too happy to let her explain how things should be done, though I did put my penn'orth in about Mrs Harper at Nether Court. 'Now Mrs Harper, she told me she allus dried rose leaves and mixed 'em with clover and mace, in little bags to put in the linen cupboard.'

Mrs Whittle nodded approvingly. 'Nothing better for keeping the linen sweet. Now, you take a smell o' this pillowcase. Tis sour as curdled milk!' If Mrs Johnstone could have heard us, her ears wouldn't just have been burning – they'd have gone up in flames. 'Look at this soap, tis all cracked.' 'Been dried too quickly, that has.' 'And this is sugar in thic packet right next to it – she's stored soap next to sugar!' 'You cassent believe it!' 'I'd believe anything of that woman, my lady, after seeing the state o' this store room. Now what've we got in this cupboard? Well, I knew she was a lazy slammock, but there's *mould* in them preserves!' We tut-tutted and shook our heads before moving on to discover the shocking state of the peppermint cordial. 'Now Mrs Harper, she *could* make a peppermint cordial, she could. By the time you'd just taken a sniff o' that your indigestion had gone.' 'I reckon it'd only take a sniff o' *this* to put you in bed for the week – under the doctor. Tis a wonder his lordship hasn't been poisoned years ago, wi' the state o' these cupboards.'

I did enjoy that morning. When we'd ended our tour in the housekeeper's sitting room Clara said, 'Mrs Whittle were wondering if she could have a liddle peep at Lady Rose afore she goes.' I ran up and fetched her at once, and by the time Mrs Whittle had finished admiring her even I was satisfied with the praise.

When Clara had made us a cup of tea and we were all sitting down drinking it together, I asked, 'Have you any family, Mrs Whittle?'

'Only the two boys – I married late, my lady – but I couldn't ask for better sons than my Bert and Joe.' She sighed. 'Both of 'em are away now, o' course. Tis a terrible worry, thic war.'

'Aye, it maun be that. Still, they say as thic big battle'll settle them Germans for good an' all. Come the midsummer the church bells'll be ringing for victory, you see.'

'I do hope so, my lady. But a mother, she just waits from one post to the next. They're both such good boys, too.'

I was watching Leo warily as I came down the stairs that evening; he'd sulked all through dinner for two days now. But when he stepped forward he said, 'It's all right, Amy, I won't bite – not tonight, anyway.'

I smiled up at him. 'You don't bite – only bark a bit, sometimes.'

He didn't smile back and his voice was formal now. 'I have been blaming you for my own deficiencies: a reprehensible fault. I must shoulder my own guilt.' He gave a rueful almost-smile. 'Goodness knows I've had enough practice at doing that.'

I said briskly, ''Tis time you let that fox escape from under your cloak. Thic Spartan boy, he were a gurt fool – foxes, I doubt they taste nice, not considering the smell on 'em.' At last he was smiling properly.

Over soup I told him that Clara was going to be our new housekeeper; he looked relieved, then said he'd raise her wages from what Mrs Johnstone had got, since prices had gone up with the war and he was sure that Clara was going to work twice as hard.

'A lot more n' twice, I'm sure o' that.' I leant forward. 'May I give Mrs Carter part of her wages early? I doubt if the poor woman's got a shilling left, after all her troubles.'

'Of course you may, Amy. Remember, you are Lady Warminster.'

When I saw the relief on Mrs Carter's face after she'd read my message, for the first time I was glad I *was* Lady Warminster.

I fetched Rose and went along to the sitting room; Leo was already waiting. As soon as I'd poured our coffee I began to tell him about my day. ' . . . And you never seen anything like the state o' that store cupboard! But I weren't surprised, 'cos the very first afternoon I came to Eston, I had a peep behind those carved leaves on the mantlepiece in the hall, and do you know', I steadied Rose so that I could lean forward, 'The dust on the back on 'em were thick as a rabbit's fur!'

He threw back his head and started laughing. I said, 'Tweren't funny, that.'

He was still smiling as he retorted, 'No, but the horrified expression on your face as you told me certainly was.'

I sniffed. 'Well, we're not having that in future. Clara's new black dresses have been ordered this very day. And we're looking for Sal Arnott's sister Lily to be the new housemaid – she's ready for a change and she's a good worker, Clara says. We'll get this house running properly, you just wait and see.' I sat back in my chair. 'Now, anything you wants sorted out, you've only to say.'

He reached for his cup. 'There is one point: about my valeting.'

'Oh yes?' I was alert. 'Baint Mr Tims doing it the way you wants?'

He swallowed a mouthful of coffee before replying, 'He is most efficient.' I relaxed. 'Everything is to hand when I come up to dress, and my suits are brushed to a very high standard: quite as good as Wallis ever attained.' I felt so pleased, it was hard not to smile. Then he added, 'It's just that after he'd laid out my evening clothes last night, I noticed a damp patch on the armchair; so perhaps you could mention to Tims that if he wishes to have Rose there with him he might just change her first.' My mouth dropped open in dismay – then I saw that he was laughing at me.

I tickled Rose under her chin. 'You naughty girl, Rose. You did give me away!'

He shook his head. 'I would have known in any case, your method of laying out my clothes is slightly different from that of Tims – your style is more after the school of Wallis. Presumably he trained you before he left.' His voice altered, becoming more serious. 'Amy, I'm not sure you should be – '

I broke in swiftly, ''Tis my war work. 'Twill be different once the war's over. Likely Mr Wallis'll come back then.'

'I did tell him his post would still be open to him should he wish to return to it, and he indicated that that would be his preference. He said he'd been happy at Eston. In fact I gather he still corresponds with Tims.'

'And Clara.'

Leo's bushy eyebrows lifted. 'Indeed? Well, she could do worse, Wallis is a steady fellow.'

'Clara, she do like Jim Arnold.'

'Hmm, but in the vulgar terminology Wallis is the better catch – looking at it from the worldly point of view.'

I shook my head. 'Women, they don't think like that.'

His face went still. 'Many women do. But obviously you and Clara are not amongst them.'

Abruptly he stood up. 'I'll take Nella out now.'

'I'll just run up and change Rose – '

'No, it's too cold for her. Good night.' It wasn't really cold at all, it was just that his bad mood had come back all of a sudden; I'd seen it in his face.

Next day he told me he'd been over to Sutton Veny and arranged to begin work as an orderly. But as yet there was only routine work to do, so he'd be home by tea-time most days, in time to see Flora.

Each evening we dined together, and then we walked in the rose garden with our Rose. He said little, and I rarely broke the silence. Yet even as the roses bloomed, so too did the rumours of battle. In the morning Flora would run across the grass so that her fair hair shone in the sun – just as her father's did. *Please, don't let him be killed in the hour of victory, please let him come home.*

Mr Beeston called with his sister: they sat in the drawing room telling me of their fears for Cyril – and my thoughts winged again to Frank. In the nursery Clara and Ellen talked of their brothers, and when Miss Winterslow came up with Clara's new dresses and stayed to mend the linen she told me of family after family, all waiting for news of their sons. One evening I went up to fetch Rose, and Ellen was reading a letter. 'Be that news of thy brother Ben?'

'No.' She blushed a fiery red, so I guessed that the letter was not from her brother, but mine. Albie, Ned, Uncle Alf – so many men were in France now – and Frank was there too, waiting for the battle to begin.

On the first day of July Mr Tims lingered after he'd brought in the tea-tray. 'They say it's started, my lady. In Kent they've been hearing the guns for more than a week now – pray God give us a success.'

When Leo came home at tea-time he told me not to wait dinner for him. 'I'll be eating at the hospital in future, so as to be ready for the arrival of convoys.'

'But they say as we're going to win a great victory.'

'Even in victory,' he replied quietly, 'there are casualties; we must be prepared.'

But on Sunday morning Clara came almost running into the nursery, her face flushed. 'We're winning! Mam read the bulletin at the post office. It says as an attack was launched north of the Somme – tis a big river in France, Dr Matthews knows – and our troops've broken forward on a sixteen-mile front! Sixteen miles, baint that good? Oh, and the French, they be doing well an' all, so we'll soon have 'em beat, and our men back home again.'

We were so excited, we kept making her repeat her news over and over again. Our men were winning, the war would be over soon. All we had to do was wait.

We waited that evening, and the days that followed. We knew the church bells would ring when we'd won our great victory, and I strained my ears to hear them. But they didn't ring. Instead, the telegrams began to arrive.

Clara's white face came to the drawing room. 'Aunt Emma says, can Ellen come – tis our Ben.' She was crying.

I spent all day up in the nursery until Ellen came back, red-eyed and grieving for her brother. I spoke halting words of sympathy. She whispered, 'Joe Sykes and Herbie Dawson – Mary's brother – they be gone too.'

'They did die bravely, winning the war. We'll hear the church bells soon.'

But we didn't. Leo began to leave earlier and earlier in the morning, and return later and later. He barely answered when I spoke to him. 'Go to bed, Amy, I'll take Nella for her walk.' With a shocked face Clara told me of two more telegrams, bearing news of Eston men who'd been wounded. The next day another buff envelope came, this time for Mrs Whittle at the Lodge; her Bert was dead.

I picked up Rose and went straight down to the Lodge to see her. She wept in her bright clean little kitchen. 'He was such a good boy – they both were such good boys.' She raised her face, her plump red cheeks sunken now and scoured with tears. 'My lady, I remember the day my Bert was born, and I remember when he was no older than thy liddle one, lying in his cradle there by the range, smiling up at me.' Her voice broke. At once I went to her, and put Rose in her arms; she cuddled my daughter closer, seeking comfort from her warm young body.

I waited up to tell Leo; his face was gaunt and grey. 'So many of our young men joined up together, joined the same regiment, some even the same battalion – how many more will there be?' He spoke like a man who'd looked into a nightmare and seen that it was true. 'Ensure that Selby knows of the bereavements. He will make any financial arrangements which may be necessary.' He stood up. 'I'll go into the garden for a while, then I shall be returning to Sutton Veny tonight. I have taken a room at the inn near the hospital. Perhaps you would be so good as to pack several changes of undergarments and nightwear, I don't know when I shall be home again.'

'Be you – be you *very* busy?'

His reply was the one bleak word, 'Yes.'

He didn't come home the next day, or the one after. I walked in the rose garden with my daughters, Flora running excitedly from bush to bush exclaiming and calling to me to see her new-found treasures. The roses were so beautiful, but all I could think of were those telegrams. The same regiment, the same battalion – how many more would there be? Yes, the roses were beautiful, but how could I dare to enjoy their beauty while down in the village women mourned their dead and waited for that next telegram?

But when it came, it came for me.

Chapter Fourteen

I looked down at that small buff envelope lying on the silver tray. It was addressed simply to 'Warminster, Eston.' Mr Tims' voice seemed thin and far away as he said, 'We don't know when his lordship will be back. You must open it, my lady.' So with shaking hands, I did.

'Will telephone after ten tonight. Annabel Quinham.'

I was trembling with apprehension all evening, and by 9.30 I was sitting in the telephone cubby hole with Rose bound close to me in my shawl; but it was nearly half-past ten before the bells on the top of the wooden box began their shrill ringing. Rose jumped and I snatched the receiver from the hook, pressing my ear into it. A tinny voice asked, 'Is that Eston 12?' Somehow I managed a squeak of assent. The voice continued, 'Hold the line please. I have a trunk call for you, from London.'

I heard a series of whirrs and clicks and then, at last, sounding faint and far away, Miss Annabel spoke. 'Hello?' I tried to call back, but I was too far below the mouthpiece. Clutching Rose I managed to unlock my cramped knees to half stand up as she asked again, 'Hello? Is that you, Leonidas?'

Jamming the receiver still harder against my ear I shouted back, 'No – tis I, Amy.'

'Tell Leonidas that Francis has been wounded.'

My whole body seemed to feel his pain. 'Be it bad? Be he very poorly?'

'I don't know. That's why I'm telephoning. I want Leonidas to go and find out. Ask him to come up tomorrow – '

I broke in, 'He baint here. He be gone to Sutton Veny, to the hospital there, and he be staying over. We dussent know when he be coming back.'

I strained my ears, but I could hear only the whirrs and clicks. Then at last she spoke again. 'In that case *you'll* have to come up instead. He's at Lady Upton's hospital, 24 Arlington Street.'

I was bewildered. 'But – baint *you* going to visit him?'

Her voice came very clear and sharp. 'Only if he's dying, and I doubt that. But things are so confused up here at present – messages do go astray – so just in case,' her voice faltered a moment, then gained strength again. 'If he *is*, then I will go and see him. But not otherwise. Only I think someone should go. If Leonidas can't, you'll have to. But Amy – *don't* tell him I sent you, you must promise me that.'

I whispered, 'Aye.'

'When you've seen him, come to my club. I'll tell them to expect you; wait for me there. I'm sorry to telephone so late, but I had to wait for a line – and I've not been in long. It's hell in town at the moment, the wounded are pouring in. I'll see you tomorrow, Amy. Good night.' There was a click and she'd gone.

Mr Tims was hovering anxiously outside in the passage. I told him what had happened and his face creased, 'Oh dear, oh dear! I'll go and order the governess cart now, my lady.'

'For the early train, Mr Tims – thank 'ee.'

I went to bed but I couldn't sleep. Frank, Frank – but surely if he'd been very bad someone would have told Miss Annabel, and she'd have gone to him? But with so many men wounded, maybe a message had gone astray.

All the way to London the next morning I held Rose close for comfort; and when I got out of the cab at Arlington Stret I could hardly walk for the trembling of my legs. A butler opened the big door and for a moment I was reassured – then the starched white cap of a nurse appeared behind him. I stammered out my request to her and she frowned. 'It's rather early to visit a patient. What name shall I give Lord Quinham?'

'Amy.'

When she came back she was smiling and at once I stepped forward in relief, then glancing down at Rose she said, 'You must leave the baby with her nursemaid, we don't allow children in the wards.'

'But I didn't bring her nursemaid with me.'

She pursed her lips, then looking down at Rose again said, 'Has Lord Quinham seen the little one yet?'

'No.'

Her smile returned. 'Then in that case we'll bend the rules. Come along.'

I followed her up a fine staircase, but the smell of disinfectant permeated the air and I shivered with fear and apprehension. We climbed up still more flights of stairs until we were on the top floor. 'We're so busy at present we're having to use some of the servants' rooms as two-bed wards. Here he is.'

She opened the door and at once I saw that Frank was sitting up in a chair. My legs nearly gave way with relief. His blue eyes flashed in their familiar smile. 'Hello, Amy.' My lips were so stiff I could barely smile back. He turned to the nurse, 'Would you ask Matheson to stay next door for a while, so I can be alone with my wife?'

'Certainly, Lord Quinham.' As she rustled out I just stood there gaping at him.

'Do close your mouth, Amy, you look like a goldfish – though an extraordinarily pretty goldfish, I must admit. I'm afraid you'll have to find yourself a seat, I can't move without help.' He gestured to his leg; it was wrapped in white bandages and propped up on a footstool. A pair of crutches rested against the arm of his chair.

As I sat down I exclaimed, 'But I *baint* thy wife!'

He shrugged. '*We* know that – but they don't. It was the easiest way to persuade them to let you in. I gather visitors aren't encouraged before lunch.'

'But suppose Miss Annabel did come . . .'

His face hardened. 'But she isn't going to, is she? I worked that out as soon as they said it was you downstairs. Typical of her sense of humour, to send you as a substitute.'

Flushing scarlet I broke my promise. 'She did say she'd come if you were dying.'

'Well, tell her I'm not – and I don't intend to die just to oblige *her*.' He leant forward, 'I suppose I'd better have a look at this baby, since I've laid claim to it.' I pulled back the shawl so he could see Rose's face. 'Good God – it's got black hair! A most unlikely infant for the pair of us to produce. You really should have been more careful, Amy. They'll all be laughing at me for a cuckold in the nurses' sitting room. Couldn't you have borrowed a blond one for the day?' He was laughing, but as he sat back in the chair his leg jerked up and he gave a gasp of pain. Seeing the sweat break out on his forehead I asked, 'Do it hurt?'

He grimaced, 'Yes, you could say that. Still, it might've been worse – much worse. Like it was for the poor devils either side of me.' His voice was bleak.

'Were it bad – the battle?'

'Yes, pretty bad.' Then he gave a shrug. 'Oh, forget the stiff upper lip. Actually, Amy, it was bloody awful. I've never been so terrified in my entire life.' His blue eyes held mine. 'And do you know, before it started we were looking forward to it! Said we were fed up with skulking in those damned trenches like rats in a sewer. "Let's get out in the open and have a crack at them. It'll be good sport," Linley said. Like fools we all agreed – except for Rimmer, he'd been some sort of engineer before the war and he had the temerity to question whether high explosive really did cut through barbed wire; we all laughed at him for a Doubting Thomas. Still, he got the last laugh – he was probably saying "I told you so" as he keeled over in front of me. Not for long, though, the bullet had sliced through an artery.' I couldn't take my eyes off his face as he added, 'Anyway, by then we knew it wasn't sport – any more than it's sport for those rabbits who're stupid enough to get caught in the standing corn at harvest time. I used to wait there with my shotgun cocked all ready to bag the little blighters as the reaper drove them out of their last shrinking patch of safety. God, Amy, now I know exactly how those poor bloody bunnies felt and it's not pleasant, I can tell you. Better to be a sewer rat any day. Still, I was lucky, at least they potted me before I'd gone too far. Lucky twice over: I went down near some kind of drainage ditch, so I managed to drag myself into a bit of cover. It still felt pretty exposed though, lying there gazing up at the sky waiting for the next one to get me and feeling as if I'd been kicked by half a dozen particularly evil-tempered mules.' He glanced up at me under his lashes. 'I suppose I should have lain there contemplating my past misdeeds and generally repenting my sins, but to be honest, Amy, all I could think of was whether I still had a cock and balls left! Fortunately that little anxiety proved to be unfounded, but it was damned unpleasant while it lasted, I can tell you.'

Then his voice softened. 'Stop shivering, my pet, you'll wake your baby up. Let's talk about something else. Tell me about Flora. Did she like her doll?'

So I talked of Flora and her doll, and of all the clever things she said and did. And as he listened the tightness went from his face and the colour came back into his cheeks.

He said softly, 'I like to think of her, so young and happy in her nursery – just as I was. I remember Marie, my foster mother – she called me her little prince. I suppose you could say she spoilt me,' he laughed. 'Yes she did – and I loved every minute of it!' His voice became teasing, but his smile was gentle as he told me, 'I like to be spoilt, Amy – and you're so good at it. You sit there listening to me with your eyes never leaving my face. Looking at me as if I were some sort of wounded hero – instead of a chap who got knocked into a ditch the minute the battle started! Thank God.' I shuddered. 'Oh Amy, I am so glad you took the trouble to come and visit me.' His smile faded, 'Unlike my dear wife, who neither forgives nor forgets.' He sounded so hurt.

I said quickly, 'She did ask me to go and tell her how you were, after I'd seen you.'

'Did she?' His voice had become very casual.

'If I told her what you said, about being frightened – '

He broke in sharply, 'No, Amy – don't you dare! I've still got some pride left. I'd never tell her that, never.'

'But you told me.'

'Telling you is different. *You* don't have any pride yourself. You wouldn't be here if you had.' He smiled. 'That's what I like about you, Amy, a few little faults in a man doesn't put you off him – not even quite a lot of rather large faults!'

Outside there was the sound of footsteps and the rattle of cutlery; I began to lift Rose up to my shoulder.

'Thank you for coming, my pet. It's nice to know someone cares.' The footsteps came nearer. 'I think that's lunch arriving, some top medico's coming this afternoon to give us all a going-over.' He grimaced. 'I'm not looking forward to *that* much. Those fellows do nothing but poke and prod. Time to go now, Amy. Give me your hand.' I held it out, but instead of shaking it he lifted it to his lips, then laughed at my flustered expression. 'Don't forget, I am a Frenchman – through and through.' His face hardened. 'I don't forget, either. It's *my* country that's been invaded, *my* soil I'm fighting for. We'll send those bloody Boches packing, just you wait and see.'

The door opened; he turned his head towards it. 'Perhaps you'd show my wife out? Bye, Amy, look after yourself.'

I ate a poached egg on toast in a tea shop, then I went round to Miss Annabel's club. She'd left a message that I could wait in her bedroom until she came back. I changed Rose on her washstand and packed away the wet nappy in my basket. I couldn't stop thinking of him, wounded and frightened; I began to shudder and Rose, sensing my distress, became fretful and started to cry. I carried her over to the bed and lay down on it, rocking and cuddling her until eventually we both fell into an exhausted sleep.

'Have you seen him, Amy?' Miss Annabel was standing at the foot of the bed looking tall and strong in her blue uniform. I nodded. 'Well, is he dying?'

'No, but – '

'So he isn't. I knew he was all right the minute I walked through the door and saw you lying there so peacefully.'

'His leg, tis paining him – I'm sure he'd like it if you went to see him.'

She replied with a decisive shake of her head. 'No. I've got more pride than that.'

'But you sent me – '

'I hope you didn't *tell* him that, Amy.' Luckily she'd turned away to take her tunic off, and couldn't see my guilty expression. She shrugged. 'Well, I had to send someone, didn't I? When he'd been wounded in the service of his country. And since Leonidas couldn't go – ' She sat down at the dressing table. 'After all, you *are* his step-mother.' She began to unpin her hair. 'Besides, I knew I could rely on getting the truth from you, Amy. He isn't that badly wounded, is he, after all?' Her hand trembled, and the hairpin she was taking out slipped and jabbed into her scalp. Jumping up I went to help her, but as I unfastened the last heavy coil her face in the mirror stiffened and she thrust my hands away. 'Stop it Amy – you're not my maid now!' And I realized she'd seen Rose, in the mirror, as she lay kicking her small feet on the bed.

Quietly I turned away and went to pack my basket. Miss Annabel said behind me, 'Amy, I'm sorry I snapped at you – it's just that I'm rather wrought up. A man had a haemorrhage in the ambulance today. Dorothy managed to stop it at last but by then the floor was swimming in blood, so I had to borrow a mop at the hospital to swab it out.' The bile rose in my throat and I had to fight not to retch. Moving forward she caught sight of my face, 'Poor Amy, you've gone quite green.'

'I be frightened o' blood.'

'Then it's just as well it's Leonidas who's doing the nursing, not you. Give him my best regards, Amy. Oh, and tell him it was me who asked you to come up and visit Francis.'

I had to try again. 'Mebbe you could go and see him, too – just for a few minutes?'

She shook her head. 'It's too late, Amy. I know that, even if he doesn't.' She added quietly, 'I loved him once – and he hurt me so much. So now I won't let him hurt me ever again.' Then her voice lost its certainty. 'But – I hope your visit cheered him up. He must be feeling a bit low at the moment – '

'No!' She was strong again now. 'No – I'm not going to be a sentimental fool just because he's been wounded. God knows, he's not the only one, and he's obviously got off lightly.' There was no softening in her voice as she went on,

'He would – the Devil looks after his own! No doubt he'll soon be back to normal, the old selfish Francis.' Her face tightened. 'Leopards don't change their spots, Amy – they can't. Goodbye.'

Abruptly she turned and opened the wardrobe. 'Now, what shall I wear to-night? I think I'll go dancing, Jack Osborne's on leave. Goodbye, Amy.'

All the way back on the train I kept thinking of him: wounded, in pain and longing for her to go to him. She would go, she must go.

But as the train drew into Eston I began to worry for myself. What would Leo say when he found out where I'd been? Perhaps he wouldn't come home tonight, then I wouldn't have to tell him yet.

Clutching Rose and my basket I scuttled through the ticket barrier, head down. It was a cool evening and with luck most people would be indoors. Although I was tired and footsore I walked as quickly as I could up the main street and turned towards the drive – and as I did so I heard the splutter of the motor behind me.

It drew up beside me. The door opened and Leo clambered out. 'Wherever have *you* been?'

'To London.'

His eyebrows drew together in a frown. 'To Town?'

'Lord Quinham, he's been wounded.'

'What!'

''Tis his leg – but he baint too poorly. I've been to see him.' His face changed, hardening, so I raced on, 'Miss Annabel telephoned to tell you, to ask you to go, but you weren't here.'

'So *you* went in my stead?'

'She asked me to – '

He shouted, 'She had no *right* to ask you, and you – you had no right to go!' At the sound of his voice Rose began to wail. 'And what of her, your child – how could you be so foolish as to take a baby into a hospital, exposing her to infection?'

'I – I didn't think – '

'Get in!'

He drove me through the gate and up the drive without speaking. The motor shuddered to a halt outside the front door: Mr Tims was lurking there already. 'Go in. I'll see you at dinner.'

He didn't say a word all through dinner, but I could feel the heat of his anger. As he stood by the door at the end of the meal he spoke for the first time: 'I *offered* you your freedom. It was *you* who chose to stay, you chose it.'

I was so tired and choked with tears I couldn't answer. As soon as I was outside he slammed the door behind me. By the time I got up the next morning he'd gone back to Sutton Veny.

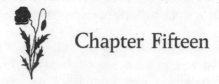

Chapter Fifteen

Leo came home twice over the next four days, but he didn't speak to me; instead he asked the wall above my head if Rose was well, and then went up to see Flora. I could have followed him up to the nursery, but I didn't. He'd been unfair: Miss Annabel had asked me to go. Besides, Frank was legally his son; Leo had promised after his birth that he'd treat him as his son – yet now, when Frank had been wounded, he hadn't even gone to see him – and nor had Miss Annabel. Then I chided myself; surely she wouldn't stay in London, while he lay wounded nearby, and not go and and see him? She *must* have gone.

But she hadn't. Mr Tims brought the letter up to my sitting room at tea-time. My heart jumped when I saw the writing on the envelope and I could hardly control the trembling of my hands as I unsealed the flap.

Dear Amy,
   I'm still stuck in this place, tethered by this wretched leg of mine. Now I know how a horse feels when it's been hobbled and all the particularly desirable grass is over the hedge. I'm completely browned off – I could kick the bucket tomorrow for all anybody cares. When are *you* coming to see me again? After all, you are my stepmother!
Yours in anticipation,
Frank.

I read his words over and over again; my chest thumped like an anvil under the blows of a blacksmith's hammer. Whatever was I to do? I couldn't not go and see him, but if I went, Leo would be so angry. 'For all anybody cares.' She hadn't gone, Leo hadn't gone, and Frank was lying there, lonely and in pain; I seemed to feel that pain in my own leg.

Then there was Rose – even if I defied Leo and went myself, I couldn't take Rose, I couldn't put her at risk – and even if I went straight to London and came straight back, it was too long for her to wait. Then I thought, but I can take her to London, I just can't take her into the hospital – and I remembered Beat. I would take Rose to Lambeth. Ellen would be pleased to come too, to talk about Albie; and while she and Beat were doing that I could leave Rose with them and take a cab to Arlington Street. If I wrote a letter to Beat now it would go off by the first post tomorrow, she would get it by the following morning, and I would go up the day after. If I were lucky, Leo wouldn't come home in between; I knew he'd be very angry afterwards, but by then I'd have seen Frank and it would be too late for him to stop me.

Only, of course, I wasn't so lucky. Leo came home the following evening.

Clara came up with a message. 'His lordship's here. He said to tell you he'll be staying for dinner.' She glanced at me before adding, 'I know Ellen's none too pleased about tomorrow, but she won't give you away, not Ellen. She won't tell him.' Maybe not; but it wouldn't make any difference, because I'd have to; obviously I couldn't sit all through dinner with him and not tell him what I planned to do. But suppose he forbade me to go? What would I do then?

There was no point putting it off. I went straight downstairs and tapped on the library door before going in. He was at his desk; he stood up at once when he saw me, and his face was a little less remote. He almost looked at me as he asked, 'How is – Rose?'

'She's quite well, thank you, Leo.' Then, drawing the biggest breath I could to give me courage, I went on, 'But Lord Quinham, he's feeling lonely. I had a letter from him, and he asked me to go and visit him, so I'm going tomorrow.' I hadn't dared to look at his face while I was speaking; now I did, I wished I hadn't. Before he could say anything I rushed on, 'But I won't take Rose into the hospital. I'm taking her to Beat, and Ellen'll look after her there.' My words speeded up until I was gabbling, 'And Dora, she'll see to Flora while Ellen's away – and Clara'll pop in every half hour or so to keep an eye on her.'

There was silence, a very long charged silence. Then he shouted, 'I forbid you to go! I forbid you!'

Only the thought of Frank's letter gave me courage, and even then my voice quavered as I said, 'I be sorry, terrible sorry – but tis no use you forbidding me, I be going. 'Cos there baint no one else as is willing to go.' Then I turned round and quickly left the room.

He went straight back to the hospital. Mr Tims told me later, without ever looking me in the eye. I said, 'Then I'll dine alone, in the morning room.' If it hadn't been for the thought of my needing to feed Rose I wouldn't have been able to swallow a single morsel. But how could I not go and see Frank when he was so lonely?

Having made my mind up I was determined to take no notice of Ellen's obvious disapproval as we sat on the train the next day. As we came closer to London I looked eagerly out of the window: each rushing street we passed was bringing me nearer and nearer to him. I imagined his face, and how it would light up as I came into the room; how pleased he would be to see me. Then for a moment, I remembered Leo's face and the fury in it – but I thrust the memory away. I would endure the full onslaught of his anger later; for today I would think only of Frank.

I was still thinking of him when we reached Waterloo. Ahead of us at the ticket barrier stood a tall young soldier gazing down at the woman in front of him. His whole body spoke of his love and concern. She reached out her bare hand to him, and I saw the flash of new gold on her wedding finger. Then all at once he dropped his pack and flung his arms around her small body, kissing her as if he'd never let go. Turning my face away from their private farewell I hurried on to the cab rank.

Beat opened the door in Lambeth. 'Hello, Amy.' But it wasn't her usual broad welcoming beam. Bending over Rose she tickled her chin, 'My, haven't you grown!' She glanced up again. 'Ellen, duck, I've just had a letter from Albie, I'll show you in a sec – but p'rhaps you could just step into the scullery and light the gas under the kettle, while I has a word with Amy here?'

I caught the meaningful expression in Beat's eyes, and so did Ellen; her, 'I'll be glad to, Mrs Thomson,' came just a little too quickly.

I said, 'Rose, she's smiling at you. She do know her godmother.'

But Beat wouldn't be diverted. 'Now then, Amy, what are you up to?'

'Lord Quinham, Frank – ' She frowned. I began again. 'Miss Annabel, she hasn't been near him, not once since he been hurt, so he wrote to me saying as he's lonely – so I'm going to visit him.' I added firmly, 'After all, I am his stepmother.'

Beat's snort was so loud it made Rose jump. My face flushed as she exclaimed, 'Stepmother! That's not the way *I* sees it, and it's not the way his lordship sees it either, I'll be bound. Does he know you've come up here?'

'Yes, I told him.'

'Oh did you now? Then I don't reckon he was very happy about it, to judge by the guilty look on your face!'

I didn't reply. I just stared down hard at Rose's face until the pink curve of her mouth seemed to blur into her plump cheeks.

Beat continued heavily, 'I can't stop you, Amy, but I reckons as you should have thought more careful like about how your husband'd feel about this little outing o' yours. You just think about it now, while I goes and gives Ellen an hand.'

I gulped down my cup of tea very quickly, and as soon as Rose had drunk her fill I got up to leave. But once I was in the cab I couldn't control the surge of excitement. In a few minutes I'd be seeing him!

As the door opened at Arlington Street I smelt the terrifying hospital smell, and fear caught at my throat; but by the time the nurse came – a different nurse – the anticipation was back and I asked confidently if I could see Lord Quinham.

She hesitated. 'His temperature was a little raised this morning, though that's hardly surprising with so many visitors. Are you a relative?'

'I didn't realize – ' Then I pulled myself together and told her firmly, 'I'm his stepmother.'

'Oh.' She looked very surprised. 'Oh well, in that case I suppose . . . Come along then.'

I followed her up the stairs. So many visitors: she must have been thinking of the other officer, who shared his room. But when she pushed open the door Frank was the only man inside – and the two ladies sitting either side of him were quite obviously *his* visitors. The nurse announced loudly, 'This lady says she is your stepmother, Lord Quinham.'

Glancing up, he waved his cigarette in greeting. 'Yes, that's right. Hello, Amy, find a pew if you can.' He looked casually round; the two ladies settled themselves even more firmly in their chairs. So he patted the bed, 'Come and perch here. Now have you all met before?'

The lady on his left shook her head very decisively, but the one on his right smiled slyly. 'I do believe I have met your – ' she paused deliberately 'er, *stepmother* at the Belgrave Square house.' Her lips curved in an oversweet smile. 'As I recall, Lady Warminster, your accent was so delightfully countrified. Do say something now. I know Moira would be *fascinated* to hear it.'

Frank smiled, but shook his head at her, 'Don't tease poor little Amy, Muriel – she isn't used to it. By the way, Sylvia Mayhew dropped in to see me yesterday. How is she getting on with that new beau of hers?'

I stayed silent while the three of them chattered together. If they wouldn't speak to me, then I wouldn't speak to them. But I did feel dowdy. Those two ladies were so smart in their close-fitting hats and slim skirts; hemlines were obviously higher than ever this season and although it was only the afternoon both pairs of long shapely legs were clad in sheer silk hose. Then I thought, but it takes more than fine feathers to make fine birds – tis time they learnt some manners.

At last the pair of them stood up. 'We simply must go now, Francis – we promised to look in on Rory James. He's a guest of Sister Agnes, you know, in Grosvenor Gardens. *So* typical of him, wheedling his way into the most exclusive hospital in Town!'

'Now be fair, Muriel, he does need all the help he can get. He is going just a teensy-weensy bit bald.'

She reached out and ruffled Frank's blond hair. 'Not like *you*, darling.'

Muriel chimed in, 'He hasn't got bonny blue eyes either, Francis my sweet.'

'In fact, all in all, it's not surprising that we always put you at the top of our list! Goodbye for now, darling, and do *try* to be good.' I heard her whisper as she kissed him, 'But not *too* hard!'

She was still holding his hand as Moira intruded, 'You've left rouge on his cheek, Muriel. Here, let me, Francis.' She took out the tiniest of lace-trimmed handkerchiefs and dabbed at his cheek. He sat patiently while she attended to him; then she bent closer. 'I'll be terribly careful myself, darling – just a butterfly.' But all of a sudden, Frank slipped his arm round her neck and pulled her mouth right down on his. When she finally drew back she was laughing. '*Naughty* Francis – whatever would Edward say?'

Frank grinned. 'He'd say I was a lucky so-and-so!'

Both ladies were laughing now, a delighted rippling laughter. 'It's the French blood, Moira. It makes him so terribly, terribiy wicked!'

'And terribly, terribly charming. Rory will be so dull after visiting you,

Francis. The poor fellow wouldn't know a compliment if he tripped over one in the street, let alone how to pay one. But duty calls. Bye-bye for now, darling.' Two gloved hands were raised, two kisses blown. 'Oh, and Lena said she'd pop in later. Byee . . .'

Frank stretched and sat back in his chair. 'They always keep a fellow entertained, those two. And now *you've* come to cheer up poor old Frank, Amy, my sweet.' He patted the seat of the chair on his right. 'Come and make yourself comfortable. You'll fall off that bed if you sit right on the edge like that.' Slowly I went over and sat down beside him. 'And are you pleased to see me, my pet?' He grinned. 'I don't need to ask that, I can see the answer in those soft golden eyes of yours. Pity those two were here when you came. You should have slipped along earlier – this seems to be the favoured time for visits *à deux*. Those females who hunt in pairs always arrive late. They get distracted by the shops when there's two of them.' He smiled indulgently. 'Still, I'm not complaining, there's nothing like a bit of female company to cheer a fellow up – and I find that a lot of female company cheers a fellow up even more!'

'I thought – I thought as you didn't have any visitors.'

He looked very surprised. 'Whatever gave you that idea? Obviously most of the chaps are overseas, but the girls left behind seem to view hospital visiting as their war work, I'm glad to say. And even one or two of the fellows have dropped in. There's always someone on sick leave, or with a temporary posting in Town.' His face clouded. 'And George Burton's looked in a couple of times. Not that I've anything against George, but it was only too obvious why *he* turned up.' He snorted. 'My wife sent a substitute and so did my so-called father.'

I said quickly, 'Leo, he be terrible busy. He's gone over to Sutton Veny to look after the wounded soldiers there. Often he doesn't even get home of a night.'

He shrugged. 'Oh, you don't have to make excusese for the old man, I wasn't expecting a visit, not after what I said to him the last time we met. Anyway, if our positions were reversed I wouldn't visit him, either, so I can hardly blame him for staying away. Now forget the old man, Amy. *You're* the one who's visiting me. And do you know, you haven't even said how do you do to me properly yet!' He held out his strong slim hand. 'How *do* you do, Amy?' I put my hand in his and he shook it vigorously; but he didn't let go. Instead his warm fingers gently fondled mine as he told me, 'You look more desirable than ever, today.' He grinned. 'The Muriels and Moiras of this world are as smart as paint, and they certainly know how to stir a man's senses – but there's something extra about you, Amy.' I couldn't tear my eyes away from his as his voice became low and caressing. 'Something so quintessentially feminine. I always think you're the sort of woman who'll conceive the moment a man so much as takes hold of her hand.'

I snatched my fingers away and he burst out laughing. 'Too late, Amy, too late! And where is Flora – where's our daughter?'

'She's at home, at Eston.' I could hardly find my voice.

He grinned again. 'And what about that black-haired baby?'

'She's at Beat's, with Ellen. I had to leave her there because Leo said I shouldn't have brought her into a hospital for fear of infection.'

I flushed guiltily and his eyes narrowed; I couldn't meet them. 'I'm surprised he allowed *you* to come and see me, then.' His voice was probing. '*Did* he give you permission, Amy?' I shook my head. He laughed. 'So you've slipped out behind his back?'

'No, I told him, I told him I were going to come and visit you.'

'And no doubt received a tirade of stammered abuse for your pains. But you still came to visit your wounded warrior, didn't you? Loyal little Amy.'

All at once I knew I should go. I began to stand up.

'Oh, you can't go yet – you've only just arrived. You still haven't told me about Flora. And while you're doing that I'll have one or two of those grapes the two Ms brought – no pips and no skin, thank you, my pet.'

Subsiding into my chair again, I reached for the fruit bowl. As I carefully peeled each grape before squeezing the pips out of its juicy heart I talked of Flora, while he lay back with his eyes closed and his mouth open, like a fledgling waiting to be fed. As I gently slipped the first grape between his lips I noticed how his face had grown thinner; there were hollows under his cheekbones, and the dark shadows beneath his eyes told their own story of pain and suffering. I felt as though I were being torn in two.

He didn't move as I fed him grape after grape, then, without opening his eyes he commanded, 'One more, Amy.' But this time, as I inserted the peeled grape, his hand came up and caught my wrist, holding it in place while his lips closed over my fingers. I felt his warm tongue licking their tips, caressing, stroking. Slowly he released my hand, to let me draw back. Then he smiled, his familiar lazy smile. 'That was delicious, Amy – and the grapes tasted quite good too!' He laughed at my confusion, then he said, his voice soft and coaxing, 'But do you know what I'd like even more than that, Amy? I'd like a kiss.'

'No!'

'Come on, Amy, just one.'

'No, tis wrong.'

'Don't be prissy, Amy. How could one little kiss possibly be wrong? All the others girls do it, and besides, you're here as my substitute wife.'

I drew a deep breath and shook my head. 'No, I be Leo's wife, not yourn. Miss Annabel, she be your true wife.'

At once his face darkened, and his voice came sharp and bitter. 'Not so's you'd notice. One measly postcard! She'd have sent as much to her blasted dog if he'd lied about his age and enlisted! Love, honour, and obey – I remember her making those vows even if she doesn't.'

I said, very quietly, 'And I did make the same vows – to him.'

Frank's reply was quick. 'But you never intended to make them. You know that: I know that. And *he* knows that, too. So you can't be bound by them.'

But I was, I was. My breasts were heavy with milk, for my child, his child. 'Tis I who made him be a proper husband to me.'

There was silence. We both sat looking at each other, then there was the tip-tap of high heels in the corridor outside. He said, 'That'll be Lena. You'd better go now, Amy. Thanks for calling.'

The door opened. 'Francis, *darling* – how are you, my sweet? I've brought you some grapes, and a whole box of those special ciggies you like so much – '

I slipped out as she came in, and almost ran down the stairs. Beat was right: I shouldn't have come . . .

I was fortunate, I found a cab very quickly. All the way back to Lambeth the tears ran down my cheeks while the milk soaked my blouse. As soon as the cab slowed I could hear Rose's hungry wails, and the moment I got through the door Beat thrust her into my arms. There was too much milk and her face became red with fury as she coughed and spluttered. 'Rose, Rose! I be sorry, I be so sorry!'

'You shouldn't have left her so long,' said a stony-faced Beat. 'She's been crying her little heart out for you this past half-hour or more.'

'Leo said I couldn't take her to the hospital.'

'Then you shouldn't 'a gone yourself.'

'I won't go again – not never.'

Beat heaved her great sigh. 'Well, I'm glad to hear *that*. Ellen, turn the gas up under the kettle, there's a duck. Amy here'll need a few good cups of tea, by the looks of her.'

Beat gave me the news of Albie and Ned and Uncle Alf and the other boys while I nursed my hungry daughter and drank cup after cup of tea. Then it was time to go and catch the train.

Chapter Sixteen

All the way back on the train I kept thinking of what I'd done: I was so ashamed. 'Loyal little Amy,' Frank had called me; but it wasn't to him I owed my loyalty, it was to my husband – yet I'd been so determined to see Frank I'd defied Leo to do it. I'd made excuses for that defiance, telling myelf that I had to go because Frank was lonely – but I should have known better, and I certainly knew better now.

Obviously he had lots of friends and plenty of women to flirt with; he'd only wanted me to play his substitute wife because his true wife had neglected him. It was Miss Annabel he loved, it always had been. I was just Clytie, hopelessly loving my sun god for ever.

But I must not visit him again, because unlike Clytie I had a husband to consider. Leo didn't know I still loved another man and he never would know, because I'd never tell him. But he'd know I'd defied him, and he would be so angry. And as the train carried us closer and closer to Eston, my fear of his anger increased.

It was after eight when we drew into the station. Ellen spoke for the first time. 'Did you telegraph for the carriage, my lady?'

'No, I – ' I faltered to a stop.

Ellen's face became even stonier. 'I naturally supposed you'd wired from London before you got back to Mrs Thomson's. After all, my lady, you had plenty of time.' She hadn't supposed anything of the sort; she was punishing me for having gone to London in the first place. All I wanted to do was get home as quickly as possible. I'd gladly have walked, tired though I was, but Ellen had no intention of allowing that. 'I'll ask Mr Soutar to send a boy up, my lady.' She spoke quickly to the stationmaster, then swept ahead of me up the platform, back erect.

Shoulders drooping, I followed her. In the waiting room Ellen waited until I was seated, then sat down opposite me. I couldn't look her in the face; instead I gazed down at my sleeping daughter. But even that pleasure was tainted with guilt.

The door was pushed open and I jumped up – but it was only the stationmaster's wife. 'I thought you might like a cup o' tea, my lady, while you was waiting.'

I subsided back on to the seat. 'Thank you kindly, Mrs Soutar.'

She set the tray down, but didn't seem to want to leave; glancing at Ellen she asked, 'Have you heard?'

'We've been in London all day.' Then Ellen's face changed. 'No – not another telegram?'

'Aye, this morning.' For a moment all three of us were still, then Mrs Soutar's hands crumpled her apron as she told us, 'Tom Tyson, he's been killed.'

'Tom – Mary's husband?' Ellen's face was white.

Mrs Soutar lifted one corner of her apron to dab at her eyes. 'Aye. First her brother, now her husband – and young Tom, he never even saw his son. And Mary, with the shock she's lost her milk – gone, just like that. And the baby, he won't take it from a rag. Doctor fetched a bottle but he won't have that, neither. He's been screaming all day and Mary, she's sobbing her heart out. They sent for Granny Withers, but even she can't get that baby to take a drop.' She sighed. 'Maggie Arnold weaned her liddle maid more'n six weeks ago, and Mary's own sister's not due till next month, so there's nobody as can help.'

Before she'd finished speaking I'd put my cup and saucer down and was on my feet. Although I'd only fed Rose a short time ago the milk was already coming tingling into my breasts. 'We'll be on our way now, Mrs Soutar, and thank you kindly for the tea.'

Looking puzzled Ellen followed me out. As we turned into the station road, I asked her, 'Which is Mrs Dawson's cottage?'

'The second one after the post office.' Then I saw her face change in understanding. 'But, my lady, *you* can't. His lordship, he'd never – '

I interrupted her. 'Mebbe you could take Rose now.'

'But – ' Then her protests died; we could both hear the screaming, the high-pitched, desperate screaming of a very young baby.

I was almost running by the time I reached the cottage, and my blouse was already damp with milk as I began to unbutton it. Lifting the latch I went straight in. There must have been half a dozen women crowded into the small front room, but all I saw was that frantic baby in Mrs Chandler's arms.

'Gi' him to I.' He was in such a state that for a moment or two he thrashed around in my arms screaming; then his cheek touched my bare breast, he smelt the milk, tasted it – and opened his mouth for more. Suddenly there was silence in the small room save only for the sound of a woman sobbing upstairs.

A chair was pushed behind me and as I sank down on to it I saw Mary's mother go creeping quietly up to her daughter. The baby was hungry, so I gave him both breasts. When he'd finished Mrs Chandler took him from me. 'I'll take him up to his Mam, now.'

Ellen gave Rose back to me; she nuzzled my breast but she wasn't really hungry; when she was, there'd be milk enough for her, too. Mrs Dawson came back down the narrow stairs. 'My Mary says thank 'ee, my lady – thank 'ee.'

It was Granny Withers who broke the silence. 'Whatever will his lordship say when he hears what you done?'

I looked up into her veined old eyes. 'I be the only woman in Eston as is in milk.'

She shook her head. 'But you bain't a woman in Eston, you be her ladyship – and the carriage is waiting outside to prove it.'

There was a circle of anxious faces around me; I knew I had to decide, nobody else could. But there was only one choice I could make, however much it angered Leo. 'I'll have to take Tommy back wi' me. He'll need feeding again tonight, more'n once it's likely, wi' him being so young.' And now the anxiety was mingled with relief. I stood up. 'It'd be best if Mary could come up to the Hall as well, she'll not want to be parted from him.' I looked over at Mary's mother. 'Mebbe you could come too, Mrs Dawson, to keep her company?'

Mrs Dawson bobbed, 'Thank 'ee, my lady. I'll just put our things together. It won't take long.'

All the way back in the carriage Mary kept repeating, 'Both on 'em gone, I cassent believe it.' She looked down at her son, dozing in her arms, 'He do be the daps o' Tom, baint he, Mam? And he's got a look of our Herbie, too.' She rocked him, the tears trickling down her cheeks all the while; but it was only a trickle. These past weeks she'd cried herself dry.

As soon as we got home I sent for Clara and asked her to make up the big bed in the room on the other side of mine. 'That way, Mrs Dawson can bring him to me as soon as he starts crying.'

Clara's face was anxious. 'But his lordship – '

'Clara,' I said, 'there weren't nothing else I could do.'

She sighed, 'Well, mebbe he won't be home for a day or two yet.'

I ate my supper quickly, then began to feed Rose. Before she'd finished I could hear Tommy screaming for me. Rose was very good, though. She looked a bit surprised to be put back in the cradle so soon, but once there she lay murmuring contentedly to herself while I attended to little Tommy. He wasn't an easy baby: Mrs Dawson told me he never had been. 'Crying and fretful from the day he were born, poor little mite.'

'Tis only natural, with him coming early the way he did.' I bent over him, coaxing, petting, 'Choo, choo, my Tommy – now doan that taste nice? No, no little puss – thee maunt nibble – now open thy mouth wide like a good boy there.' At last I had him suckling properly.

As I nursed him my thoughts went to his mother. Poor Mary: first her brother, now her husband. My heart wept for her. But after a while my mind returned to its own worries: Leo was already so angry with me for disobeying him by going to see Frank and now . . . I quailed just at the thought of his fury. Then Tommy relaxed his hold, and turned his head a little to gaze up at me from his round blue eyes. Gently I stroked his soft cheek. 'Doan 'ee fret, my bird, however much he do shout I'll still nurse 'ee.' Reassured, his mouth found my breast again and resumed its steady sucking.

I seemed to be feeding babies all night. Tommy didn't seem to know what he wanted sometimes, but I was learning his little ways and how to coax him. Mrs Dawson said anxiously, 'He be a lot o' trouble to 'ee, my lady, he's taking all o' thy time.'

I looked at her over Tommy's bald head. 'My Rose has always been so easy to manage, I reckon as I got time to spare. He's getting used to me now, baint thee, my Tommy?' I smiled down at him, and he smiled back.

When he'd finished I cuddled him for a while, talking to him, kissing his damp forehead, nuzzling his soft cheek, telling him what a good boy he was, stroking him, soothing him until he was sleepy and relaxed in my arms. I smiled up at his grandmother. 'He's nicely settled now. I'll just bring him along and slip him in next to Mary. He'll likely sleep for an hour or two now, and twill give her comfort.'

Mrs Dawson looked down at her drowsy grandson in my arms, then her eyes lifted to mine. 'My lady, there's folk in Eston as say you're not a proper lady – but I says as no proper lady would've done what you done, not in a thousand years. I thank you, my lady, I thank you from the bottom of my heart.'

Chapter Seventeen

The next couple of days, it was as though we were all treading on eggshells. The following evening I asked Mr Tims, 'Has his lordship come home?'

'No, not yet, my lady.' His expression was even more anxious than usual.

I took a deep breath. 'Mr Tims, tell everyone – all the staff – not to say a word. I'll tell him myself, as soon as he gets in.' I saw the relief on his face. I just hoped that Leo wouldn't arrive while I was feeding Tommy. Not that he'd come in unexpectedly, there was no fear of that; he never came up to my sitting room uninvited. Besides, when he did come home he'd be keeping out of my way, he was already so angry with me. But I'd have to tell him eventually; I shuddered at the thought. Suppose he tried to make me send little Tommy away? What then? But I knew the answer already: I'd have to refuse, however angry it made him.

He arrived back after tea on the third day. The babies were between feeds when Clara came up to tell me, so there was no putting it off. I said, 'Would you tell Mr Tims to say as her ladyship would take it kindly if his lordship would step upstairs to see her, when he's got a free minute?'

She came back to say he'd come as soon as he'd had his bath and changed, so I just sat praying Tommy wouldn't start crying before Leo got to me. Then I heard his heavy tread.

He came in but didn't walk across the room to me. He just stood there, in front of the door, his face unmoving. 'Well?'

I got up and went to stand in front of him; he towered over me as I said, 'There's something I got to tell you.' I licked my dry lips before making my first confession. 'I did go to London to see Lord Quinham, like I said I would.' His lips tightened and I added quickly, 'But I shouldn't 'a gone, and I won't be going again.'

There was a long silence. I dropped my eyes to the toes of his huge boots; they were dull, Jesse must have cleaned them and not made a good job of them.

Then his voice above my head asked, 'Is that – all – you wish to inform me of?'

I dragged my eyes away from those toecaps and lifted them up to his waistcoat buttons. 'No – I done something else – ' I corrected, 'I be doing something else. And you'll be angry about it, very angry – only I baint a-going to stop doing it, whatever you say. I can't stop, because he do need me.'

His whole body went rigid. 'Well?' In that one word I could hear all the intensity of his anger.

I tried to marshal the words, to explain, excuse: 'The telegram came three days ago. It were Tom Tyson, Mary's husband – he's been killed. And Mary, with the shock of it coming on top of her brother's death, she's lost her milk.'

I didn't dare to raise my eyes to his face, but I heard the frown in his voice as he queried, 'Her *milk?*'

'For the baby, for liddle Tommy.' My words came faster now in my anxiety to get them in before he exploded. 'Tommy, he were born early and he's less'n two months now and small for his age. Mary, she's allus had problems wi' the feeding of him and now she's lost her milk – but he wouldn't take no food by hand. Everyone tried, Dr Matthews brought a bottle but even Granny Withers couldn't get him to take it.' I took a quick breath, 'And you see, nobody else in Eston was nursing, 'cept for me.' Gathering all my courage, I added, 'So I been feeding him.' And now my hands began to tumble over one another in my anxiety to reassure him. 'Rose, she baint going short, not at all. I got plenty o' milk, enough for two – it do come, when tis needed, and little Tommy, he do need it, so I baint a-going to stop.' I still didn't dare to look at his face; I just stood there with my eyes fixed on that waistcoat button, waiting.

I seemed to have waited a long time before he asked, 'You – are feeding – another woman's child?'

'Aye.'

He repeated again, as if he couldn't believe what he'd heard. 'You – my wife – are feeding the child of one of my former servants?'

I said quietly, 'I'm sorry, but I got to do it.'

He just turned on his heel and walked out.

As soon as the door closed I began to cry. I'd rather he'd shouted at me, I could have stood that; but just to walk out like that, without a word – suppose he never came back again?

Rose was still asleep but I went to the cradle and lifted her out, cuddling her close for comfort. 'Oh Rose, thy Dada be so angry with me.'

Clara told me later that he'd gone straight out again. 'Mr Tims asked him about dinner, but he didn't even answer.'

'Mebbe he's gone back to Sutton Veny.'

She shook her head. 'Not in the motor, he hasn't. 'Sides, Mr Tims reckons as he saw the dog slip after him, so he'd have to bring her back.' We looked at each other, then Clara said, 'I suppose he'll calm down eventually.' She didn't sound too sure.

I pleaded, 'But I couldn't have done anything else, could I, Clara?'

'No, I reckon as *you* couldn't have,' she admitted. I noticed that slight emphasis on the 'you'. My eyes stung.

'Should I bring your dinner up on a tray?'

'I don't think I want any dinner.'

Clara was firm. 'My lady, you've two young 'uns depending on you, you maun eat.'

I'd just finished feeding Tommy at half-past nine when Mr Tims appeared, looking flustered. 'My lady, his lordship has returned. He asked, would you be prepared to see him in half an hour or so, as he wishes to have a few words with you? If you haven't gone to bed, that is.'

I was tempted to say I *was* going to bed, but it was no use, I'd have to face him sooner or later; only I did so wish he'd just come in and shout at me then and there: the waiting made it so much worse.

The minute hand on the clock moved as slowly as a slug until the last five minutes – then it raced like a hare to the hour. Perhaps he'd changed his mind? But then I heard his footsteps outside, and the rap of his knuckles on the door panel. My 'come in' quavered.

He closed the door very carefully behind him before saying, 'I must apologize for my intrusion on your privacy at such an unconscionably late hour.' And as soon as he spoke I knew why I'd had to wait: he was drunk. 'May I turn the light out?' His hand flicked down the switch without waiting for my reply. There was a moment of darkness, then I could see his ungainly shape once more in the fading evening light. 'Summer Time is a presumptuous conception, is it not? Man has defeated the passing hour, but his conquest is a mere illusion – ' He stopped himself. 'I must not let myself be diverted. I did not come to expound on chronometry, I came to talk to you – to my wife.'

I tried to keep my voice steady as I said, 'I be terrible sorry I made you angry, only I – '

He interrupted, sounding surprised. 'Angry with you? I'm not angry. I am a prey to many emotions this evening, but anger is not one of them.' I stared at him in disbelief and he came closer and snapped on the lamp beside my chair. He tipped up the shade, so that the light fell full on my face while his own remained hidden in the shadows. 'You are frightened? Frightened of me?' His eyes dropped. 'Of course you are frightened of me. When Beauty heard the roar of the Beast how could she help but be frightened? Only I thought – I thought that if I were drunk you might be a little less frightened.' His voice was heavy with sadness as he asked, 'Shall I go away again?'

At last I found my own voice. 'No, no, o' course not. Mr Tims said as there were something you wanted to say to me.'

'Yes, that's why I got drunk – but naturally you realize that. May I sit down?'

'Of course.'

He dropped heavily down into his chair. 'Where is he, the child you are feeding?'

'With Mary. He'll sleep now for a couple of hours, so Mrs Dawson won't be coming back.'

'So I have a precious two hours alone with my wife.'

I said quickly, 'Except for Rose, o' course.'

At once he sprang up and came to look in the cradle, 'Rose, such a beautiful Rose. How fortunate that she took after her mother.' I shivered. 'Are you cold, Amy?'

I shook my head. 'No.'

'Just frightened. I'm sorry, Amy, I'm sorry for everything – but that's not what I came to say to you tonight. I came to tell you something, but I don't know how to begin.' Restlessly he moved away and began to prowl around the room until he came to an abrupt halt in front of the portrait.

'Elizabeth, Countess of Warminster. That's the place to start – with my mother.' He swung round to face me but in the dim light I couldn't see his expression. 'She was many years younger than my father, though not as many as the difference between us. The army was his first love, and so he elected to wait before choosing his bride; Ettie Burton told me that. My father was a handsome man, a man of stature and proven courage, so he gained the young wife he wanted. But more than a wife, he wanted a son, and that did not prove so easy an accomplishment. My mother, too, wanted a son, for his sake, and for her own; but for nearly twenty-seven years she was barren. Then one day, when she'd given up hope – hope came. She found she was with child.' His voice dropped. 'She never knew, she never realized, what it was she carried in her womb. Instead she dreamt over her sewing as women do, sewing perfect garments for a perfect son. And while she sewed she chose the names her soldier son would bear: Leonidas, Arthur, Hector; the names of her three favourite heroes. Then I was born.' His voice was suddenly loud in the quiet room as he exclaimed, 'And I killed her.'

I started to say, 'That weren't *your* fault – ' but he wouldn't listen.

'I didn't know until I saw you labouring with my child, I didn't know how women have to suffer to bring forth their young. I'd seen puppies born, foals, calves: a little straining, a little effort, and the young ones are there, at their feet. But women are different, aren't they? God ordained it in his wisdom: "In sorrow shalt thou bring forth thy children." And so in sorrow and pain and fear you delivered Rose. I would have endured it for you if I could – but I couldn't. But then you took her in your arms, and in that moment I understood. The rose and the thorn; the thorn and the rose. For my mother there were only the thorns, and if she'd lived on, still sharper thorns. So maybe at the end her death was a mercy, because she died without seeing me.'

I tried to speak but I didn't know what words to use. Instead his anguished voice continued, 'But *he* saw me, and seeing, banished me from his presence. So I came here, to Eston, to my mother's girlhood home. He hated me for what I was, but I was his only son, his heir; he could not let me die. So he was forced to procure a wet nurse to share my exile. I don't remember her; I only remember Nanny Fenton, who was everything to me. She'd been my mother's own nurse, so naturally she was an old woman, but I didn't realize that. All I knew was that she loved me, and loving me, would never leave me.

'My eighth birthday came and I was sent away to school. It is – the custom. Children can be cruel, very cruel – you know that. They single out those who are – different. Later I understood, but then – ' His shoulders moved in one of his awkward, sideways shrugs. 'But I knew that when I came home again Nanny Fenton would be waiting for me, and that knowledge enabled me to survive. Only when I did come back, she wasn't waiting, she was dead.'

He paused. He closed his eyes for a moment, remembering, then he continued. 'But there was still Helmsley, the incumbent before Beeston. I'd learnt my first lessons from him, and he helped me, he helped me so much. He taught me to enjoy Latin, to love Greek – and to worship roses.' His voice became lighter now. 'He even taught me to box. What an odd pair we must have looked: an old man in a clerical collar and vest and a hump-backed boy, sparring. So I was able to defend myself from the bullies until I grew larger, and they left me alone. I owed him so much – but he died, too: the summer after I was seventeen. His roses were in bloom and I gathered his favourites together and strewed them on his grave.

'The following year my father died. It was quite sudden; although he was a very old man he had remained active until the day of his death. So I chose to believe that if it had not been so sudden, then he would have sent for me. We all believe what we want to believe; unfounded optimism is in the nature of man, else how would he survive at all? But I was young and confident and determined to do my duty by my inheritance. So I began my study of the estate records; and it was only then that I discovered I'd had a wet nurse, a young married woman from the Pennings estate. I can still remember the excitement I felt as I made that discovery; somebody was left from my childhood after all. And I reasoned that if she'd been a wet nurse then there must have been a child: I had a foster brother or sister, too. Of course I decided to go in search of them.

'Apart from Helmsley all the kindness I'd ever known in my life had come from servants. I imagined her pleasure at meeting me again, and I had dreams of bringing her over here, to Eston: offering her a better cottage, a better job for her husband, for the child – my foster brother or sister. My father had paid her well, but so precious was the gift she'd given me, I told myself I owed her more.' He paused before admitting quietly, 'But in truth my dreams were selfish, I wanted somebody of my own. And as always, selfishness was punished.

'I discovered the full story from her sister. There was no foster brother because my father had made her leave her own child behind. Apparently it is the custom with wet nurses – I hadn't realized. In order that the interloper be nourished, the natural child must be deprived of its birthright just when it needs it most.' He was watching me, but I didn't move. 'You've guessed what I'm going to tell you, haven't you, Amy? You who are always so quick. I was born in May, at the start of the summer, when hand-reared children are at especial risk. The woman's sister, the one I spoke with, had been left to care for the child. She told me, "Come midsummer, he took sick of a fever, and died in my arms. Such a fine boy he would have been." That was all she said, but as she said it she looked at me standing there in front of her, twisted and misshapen as I am.'

I exclaimed, 'Tweren't *your* fault, that wet nurse, she could 'a said no.'

He shook his head. 'Don't be foolish, Amy. As I told you, she was a young woman from the Pennings estate. She and her husband had no choice. Their livelihood, their very home depended on her acquiescence, and so she lost her first-born son. But she didn't forget. With the blood money my father paid her they bought a passage to Canada. She told her sister she was going "to a land where there were no lords nor ladies". When the sister told me that I simply turned and walked out. But I have never forgotten that I was responsible for that child's death. I have carried the burden of guilt ever since.'

He got to his feet, and came over to stand in front of my chair. 'I had gone to Pennings intending to pay a debt, but I found that the debt was a greater one than I could ever repay. Yet this very day, my wife tell me that she is repaying it. I thank you, Amy. I thank you.'

I said softly, 'An' I thought you would be angry.'

'Not anger, never anger – but so many other emotions,' and I heard the intensity in his voice. As he came closer, leaning over me, it was all I could do not to shrink away from him.

Suddenly he exclaimed, 'Amy, they are all yours, all those emotions. I lay them at your feet. Which of them do you want? Choose, Amy, choose. Whichever you want I will give you.'

'I cassent – '

He drew back a little, his voice uncertain now as he said, 'But you must want something from me. I must be able to give you *something*.' Then it became stronger again. 'Tell me, what can I give you? What do you want?'

'Nothing. I don't want nothing!'

He flinched back, then turning his twisted shoulder away from me he began to blunder towards the door, like a great defeated animal.

I cried out after him, 'Just a rose! Gi' I a bunch o' thy roses, tis all I do want.' He paused a moment, so I knew he'd heard, then with a final awkward lurch he thrust open the door and left.

In bed that night I cried and cried. I cried so much I became frightened I'd lose my milk. But the strong mouths of the babies drew it from me, as I held their warm young bodies close, cradling them to me.

He must have gone to bed very late because I didn't hear him passing my door, and Clara told me next morning that he'd left very early to go back to Sutton Veny. She glanced at me uncertainly as she spoke, as if expecting me to be upset by the news; but all I could feel was relief.

After breakfast I went along to my sitting room as usual – and as I opened the door I was overwhelmed by the scent of roses. The whole floor was covered with them. They lay just where they'd been tossed, bloom after bloom: tea roses, moss roses, Bourbons, Noisettes; sweet briars and Albas, Rugosas and Damasks. He must have cut every rose in his garden, and carried it inside. I couldn't move without treading on their fragile petals, because he had heaped all of his scented blooms at my feet.

Clara brought every vase in the house, but it wasn't enough. I sent for the pails from the stables, but even they weren't enough. When they were all filled, more roses still lay wilting on the floor. Flora came in, and ran shrieking amidst the fallen petals, scooping them up, tossing them into the air and then running to the cradle to scatter handfuls of bruised petals over her sister. 'For Rose, roses for Rose!'

Clara came back with another stone jar she'd found in the stillroom. 'There, this'll hold a few more.' She turned and saw my face, 'My lady, they're only flowers. You maunt upset thyself. See how beautiful they bist for their liddle hour.'

They were beautiful, beautiful and brave; but I wasn't weeping for them, but for him, for the man who had laid them at my feet.

Chapter Eighteen

Clara came back again, followed by Jesse, the oddman, carrying a long metal trough; she must have got it from the garden. 'I thought as we could put this down on a piece of sacking. Mr Hicks says as he's sure there's a couple more like it if he can find 'em. We can get the rest o' the roses crammed into these. A drop of water'll soon perk 'em up. Mr Hicks weren't best pleased bout his lordship picking 'em all like this, but I explained as tis your birthday next week, and likely his lordship's afraid he won't be home then. He left your other present wi' me, I told Mr Hicks, but likely he wanted to give you something hisself.

Tis raining now, so you wouldn't have been able to walk out today – tis just as well you've got a rose garden indoors instead. There's a wind coming up, too – all the petals would've been blown off outside, so they're best off here, really.'

She spoke in a firm, reassuring tone and Jesse agreed, 'Aye, you'm right, Clara.' He grinned his cheerful, vacant grin. 'Do look proper purty, don't they? I'll go and see if Mr Hicks has laid his hand on t'other troughs.'

We got them all into water somehow, except for those that had been trodden on. We couldn't help doing that, there were just so many of them. Then we swept up the drifts of pink and white and red petals and Bertha and Lily Arnott carried them away.

Clara wiped her hands on her apron. 'There, don't they look pretty? I allus used to say to my Mam as twas a shame his lordship wouldn't ever cut his roses and bring 'em indoors. Last night he must 'a thought the same hisself.' I opened my mouth to speak, then I closed it. Clara was right; it was better to pretend.

Only, as I stood there, surrounded by the scent and the colour and the beauty of his roses, I knew I couldn't go on pretending any longer. I'd pretended too much in the past; now it was time for the truth. But I didn't know how I was going to tell him.

It was Flora who gave me the clue. That evening after I'd towelled her dry from her bath and sat her on my lap she asked for a story, as she always did. 'The Beast, Mama, "Beauty and her Beast".' And as I read that well-loved tale, it told me what to do.

It was long after dinner when he arrived. He didn't tap at the door; if I hadn't been straining my ears listening for his footsteps I wouldn't have known he was there. I called, 'Come in,' and the door opened very slowly. He sidled inside like a great clumsy bear, and sat down in his armchair without looking at me. I said briskly, 'I'll ring for some coffee,' but he still didn't speak, and we sat in silence until Mr Tims had put the tray on the low table beside me, and left us. Then Leo looked up, at his roses: vase after vase, pail after pail, and the three long troughs all crammed full of them.

His face went crimson as he stammered, 'I'm so sorry, Amy. I won't get drunk again, I promise.' I didn't reply, but when I poured the coffee and took his cup to him he flinched away as if I'd struck him.

As soon as I was sitting down again I began to speak. 'The other day I were reading a fairy tale to Flora, the tale of Beauty and the Beast – she does like that one.' He didn't look at me, but I could sense his wariness. I went on, 'I like that tale, too – truly, tis my favourite. I allus did feel sorry for the Beast, him getting fond of Beauty, but her saying no to him each evening when he asked her to marry him.' His huge body had gone very still now. I continued quietly, 'But Beauty, it weren't easy for her, either. You see, she did *like* the Beast, she looked forward to dining with him of an evening, and he'd always been kind to her; kind and generous. He'd given her so much, that naturally she was grateful.' I repeated, 'Very grateful. So when he did ask her to marry him every night she were upset at having to say no, because it made him unhappy, but you see, she couldn't say yes.' I faltered, glancing across to where he sat. He still held the cup and saucer in his hand, untouched; he hadn't moved the whole time I'd been speaking. I found my voice again: 'She couldn't say yes because she didn't love him.'

There was silence as I watched the knuckles of his hands whiten under their dark covering of hair. I added, speaking faster now, 'Only it must have been difficult for Beauty, because there'd have been times when the Beast looked tired and out of sorts, and likely she'd have wanted to fuss over him, only she didn't feel as she could – because it would've given him false hopes.'

I stopped; I couldn't go on. At last he raised his huge head; I couldn't see his face clearly, but I knew he was looking at me as he asked, 'So there – is not – even hope?'

I couldn't answer; I just shook my head. He turned his whole body away and stared at the trough full of roses, his roses. Then he put down his untouched cup and began to stand up. Quickly I said, 'But if she thought he understood, then it would've been easier for her, because she could've fussed over him without the risk of him thinking it meant more than it did. And she would've felt free to give him a cuddle or suchlike, if he wanted it, so long as he knew it were just in friendship – as long as she were sure he understood.'

When I'd finished he didn't reply at first; then he said in a low voice, 'But – even if – he understood – ' He broke off, before resuming more loudly, 'Beasts are hasty, ill-disciplined creatures, it is in their nature. They might not intend to behave badly, but they do.'

I whispered, 'I dare say Beauty wouldn't mind that too much, not so long as she knew he understood.'

'Oh yes, he understands.' He spoke very quietly. Then, reaching down he picked up his untouched cup of coffee and carried it over to the tray beside me. 'It is late. I will leave you now.' He left so rapidly there wasn't even time to say good night.

I went straight to bed with Rose. I felt wretched and unhappy; but what else could I have done? I had to tell him the truth.

He didn't come back again until the day after my birthday. We spoke to each other formally, politely, almost as though we were strangers who just happened to be living in the same house. Clara had given me his present the previous day: it was a painting of a little girl in a sun bonnet, feeding the hens on a patch of grass outside her cottage. There were flowers in bloom in the garden: moon daisies, poppies, tall purple lupins – and roses. Pink roses were climbing so high up the old brick wall that they could peep into the window under the thatched eaves. I did like that picture, and I'd already hung it over my desk; but when I came to thank him for it I couldn't think of anything to say, beyond, 'Thank 'ee, thank 'ee very much. Tis beautiful.'

'I'm glad you like it,' he said, and I repeated, 'Aye, tis beautiful,' and then we both fell silent until, ducking his head and shoulders in an awkward sideways movement, he asked, 'Perhaps I might take Flora for a walk now?'

'O' course, she'd like that.'

When he brought Flora back to the nursery I told him about the letter Mary had had from an officer in France, telling as how her Tom had died bravely. He ducked his head again; then, bending over Rose, held his hand out to her. She seized his finger, laughing, and he almost smiled back. 'Mebbe you'd like to hold her?'

He lifted her carefully out and held her close against his shoulder. Then Mrs Dawson came for me; Tommy was crying for his feed. By the time I came back up again Leo had already left for Sutton Veny.

Chapter Nineteen

On the last day of July, three more telegrams came to Eston village. Two men had been killed and a third wounded. We were all very quiet in the nursery that day. Then Clara came up in the evening to say that Mr Tims had told her we were still winning. We'd captured a wood called Delville – 'The Devil's Wood' they were calling it in the papers.

I said, 'That is good news, Clara,' but underneath I couldn't help wondering how one wood could ever be worth the lives of two young men.

Three days later, Clara met me in the hall as I came in from the garden. Her face was completely white, except for that dark birthmark stain on her cheek. She said simply, 'Tis Jim.'

'Clara, no – '

'Wounded, the telegram said. Not dead, wounded.'

I put my hand on her arm. 'You run down and see his Mam, Clara. She might know more.'

But she didn't. I tried to reassure Clara. 'Jim'll be safe in hospital by now. Thic doctors, they'll be taking good care on him.'

Clara's hands were still trembling. 'A man from Tilton – the son o' Greens, the drapers in the High Street – were wounded a couple o' weeks back, and they sent for his mother and she went all the way to France, but when she got there he were already dead. He'd died the night afore she got there. Lots on 'em do die, even in hospital. My cousin Jane lives over by Sutton Veny, and she do say as they be burying 'em all the time. Tis the bugle, they blow the bugle at the burying, and she can hear it, up on the hillside.'

I said quietly, 'Lord Quinham, he were wounded, but twas only his leg. He were sitting up in a chair by the time I went. You mustn't be afeared, Clara. Gunshot, tis only liddle pellets, when all's said and done. Tis different when a rabbit or a hare be shot, but a man, he's bigger.'

But of course I couldn't stop thinking about Jim. The other men had just been names; I'd felt for their families, but I hadn't known them. Jim was different and I kept remembering his sunburnt laughing face as he'd met me at the station the first time I'd come to Eston.

After lunch the next day I'd just got little Tommy settled when Clara came in; she didn't even tap. 'Jim's sister come up. She says they've sent for his Mam.'

'Oh, Clara! To France?'

'No, he's in Lunnon, Bet says.'

'That's got to be better than France, Clara. He must've been well enough to be moved.'

'Bet said, would it be all right if I went wi' Jim's Mam? She's never been further'n Tilton afore. Just for a day, my lady.'

'O' course.' Still holding Tommy I ran awkwardly to the desk. 'Clara, you maun take some money, in case the pair of you have to stay.'

'But – '

'His lordship'd say you maun take it. You go now – and stay as long as you're needed.'

After tea, when Leo arrived, his back was even more hunched than usual, and he looked very tired, but I had to tell him about Jim and the other telegrams.

He closed his eyes for a moment then said, 'All the young men of Eston. They went to do their duty: to serve their King and country, and now – ' He broke off, before saying abruptly, 'Helmsley told me once that there were men from Eston at Agincourt.' Then his voice became angry and bitter. 'My mother's family lived here even then – they were lords of Eston. And a lord of Eston was at Agincourt, too, and led his men into battle – *led* them. But I, what do I do? I skulk at home while the young men die! Day after day they die, and all *I* can do is carry out their bodies for burial.'

I didn't know what to say. I whispered, 'But Jim, he baint dead yet.'

He looked at me as if he'd forgotten I was there. Then he swung round and started to walk back down the stairs. I began to run after him, but halfway down I heard Tommy wailing, so at the second of the red-coated generals I stopped. Leo left the house with Nella at his heels.

He didn't come back until long after dinner. Standing in the doorway of my sitting room he said, 'I'm sorry, Amy, so very sorry. I had no right to upset you.'

Before I could reply Mr Tims had appeared behind him. 'My lord, Mrs Carter has kept dinner for you, if you come down now.'

Leo gestured to his tweed suit. 'But I'm not dressed.'

I told him, 'You don't need to dress for the morning room, and you can drink your coffee up here afterwards.' He still hesitated, so I said firmly, 'You maun eat, Leo. You go downstairs now.' Slowly he went.

As I waited, I worried: he still looked so strained. My eye caught the picture he'd given me and I sighed. If only we'd lived a normal life in a cottage he could have sat in the kitchen while I cooked him something myself – not that Mrs Carter didn't cook tasty meals, she did – but it was a wife's job. Besides, it would have been better for him to eat in the kitchen with the children round his feet. Then I thought, Flora may be upstairs in the nursery but I've still got Rose with me, alive and young and full of hope.

She was asleep when he came back, but I bent down and lifted her out of the cradle. 'Wake up now, my Rose. Thy Dada, he do need thee.' I carried her over and set her down on his lap. 'There, baint she beautiful?' I tickled her cheek, 'Gi' thy Dada a smile, Rose.' And bless her, she did. Then she raised her perfect starfish hands to his face, trying to catch hold of his mouth. I told him, 'You nurse her for a while, she'll like that.'

He held her for a long time, until at last she fell asleep in his arms. Then he fell asleep, too. He must have been exhausted because he didn't waken, not even when Mary brought Tommy in for his feed, and he was still fast asleep when I tiptoed out with Tommy again. But I had to wake him in the end. 'You'd best go to bed now, Leo.'

His eyes opened, and he looked up at me as if he were still dreaming – then he flushed. 'I mut apologize for my appalling manners –' Then Rose woke up and interrupted him.

She needed changing – I saw the damp patch on his waistcoat as I took her from him. 'You'd best take that waistcoat off, Leo. I'll sponge it down for you.'

He carefully turned his back before removing his jacket, and the nape of his neck was bright red by the time he was down to his braces. He very quickly shrugged his jacket back on and left without looking at me.

Clara came back two days later. I was up in the nursery and she came straight upstairs, still in her hat. 'Jim's holding his own, but his Mam's staying for a while yet.'

'Oh Clara, that is good news!'

She just stood looking at me. 'They've taken his leg off. Jim, he's lost his leg, an' he were such a good cricketer. Now he'll never run between the wickets again.' She collapsed sobbing into a chair.

Ellen sent Dora to take Flora out for her walk, while we sat with Clara in the nursery. She was shaking. 'It were terrible, terrible. The state some o' them poor fellows were in. I'd never've believed it. The one next to Jim, his whole head were just a big bundle o' bandages, wi' a pair of eyes peering through. And all the time he'd lie there trying to catch your eye, as if he were desperate to say something, but he couldn't.' She shuddered. 'And then the one on the other side never stopped talking – but none of it made sense, just groaning and muttering he were and throwing hisself about. Tis the poison in their blood as does it they say. And the smell! The whole place were stinking like meat as has gone off in the warm weather. Terrible it was.' She tried to drink her tea, but her hand was shaking so much she could hardly get the cup to her lips.

'Jim's mother, she were so brave. I couldn't have stayed if it hadn't been for her. Jim, he were coming round from the operation, looking so ill I couldn't bear to look at his face, but when I looked down at the rest of him all I could see were – were – nothing, just this sort o' lump of bandages where his leg should 'a been. There weren't even a blanket over it in case it started to bleed – they got to be able to get at it quick, so I kept looking at it, in case. I don't know how the nurses stand it. Jim's mother said, "We got to be brave for Jim's sake, Clara," and she were, she were. Then after a coupla days they said as how Jim had turned the corner, so Mrs Arnold told me I'd best come back, seeing as I'd got work to do.'

I said, 'Clara, you could 'a stayed.'

She shook her head. 'No, I couldn't. I couldn't have stood another day of it. I wasn't brave enough. So I came away. I let Jim down. My Mam allus did tell me as I were too squeamish – and now I've let Jim down.'

Ellen went over and put her arm round her cousin's shoulders. 'No, you haven't, Clara. You told us yourself you waited until he'd turned the corner. You wouldn't have left otherwise, I know you better'n that.'

Clara spent most of the day in the nursery. I kept Flora downstairs with Rose, and Mary and Mrs Dawson watched them for me whenever I popped upstairs to see how Clara was.

She'd calmed down by the evening, but she still sounded so helpless. 'Jim, he'll never be able to work again.'

Ellen shook her head. 'Look, Clara, you know as his lordship said at the start, anybody who went, their job'd be there waiting for them when they came back.'

'But Jim were a *groom*.'

'Then he'll have to turn his hand to something else.'

'But – '

Ellen looked her straight in the eye. 'Clara, don't 'ee think as I'd give my right hand to have our Ben back, leg or no leg?'

Clara's face changed. I put my arm round her shoulders, shocked at Ellen's blunt words. But when Clara replied the tears had gone from her voice. 'Aye, Ellen, thee bist in the right of it.' She turned to look at me. 'My lady, if I could have a free day next Saturday I'll go up to see how Jim's getting on. I'll make the time up later, o' course.'

'You go, whenever you want to.'

I knew Ellen was right, but I knew just how Clara felt, too. I was squeamish as well, and I'd have been exactly the same in her place. However did those nurses stand it? Then I thought, but it's not just the nurses that have to stand it, it's the orderlies as well. Leo must be seeing the same sights, hearing the same screams, smelling the same smells – no wonder he'd been upset the other day. If only there was something I could do for him. Then I realized there was: I'd start cleaning his boots; Jesse simply hadn't got the knack of making a proper job of them.

But next morning I didn't want to take Rose into the boot hole – it was far too dirty and damp – so I fetched his boots into the brushing room. I kept a laundry basket there for Rose, on the counter top. I asked Mr Tims for some old newspapers and he spread them out to protect the table. Then I rolled up my sleeves and got to work. Rose slept as good as gold so I cleaned all his footwear, finishing off with his patent leather evening shoes. Then I stood back to admire my handiwork. I was glad Leo had such big feet; you felt you'd really done a good morning's work when you'd got his shoes all cleaned and polished.

I began to fold up the newspapers – and then I saw the lists. I didn't realize what they were at first, those lists of names: I thought they were just the names of those men who'd joined the army this month. I was thinking what a lot there were, and how we'd soon be beating the Germans at this rate. Then suddenly I understood. They weren't lists of recruits, but of casualties – and not lists for a month, but for a single day. The fifth of August 1916: 5,472 men killed or wounded. There was a whole page of tiny printed names, men in the ranks, name after name. With the officers they told you how many were dead: 41 out of 292 – and another 49 'missing', whatever that meant.

Quickly I scrabbled for the other paper, the one for the day before – maybe the fifth was a special day, a battle – but the day before there were 114 officers dead – though only 2,610 other ranks as casualties. Then I realized what I was thinking: *only*. Only! And for that we'd won a wood. I'd thought a wood wasn't worth two lives – but standing looking at those lists I finally understood. Not just Eston; every village, every town, every city, telegram after telegram, street after street: tiny cottages, huge mansions like Eston – and inside each one of them women weeping, women mourning for their men. It was too much to hold in my head for more than a moment – but even that moment was almost more than I could bear. My hands were all grubby with newsprint but I went straight to the basket and lifted out Rose, cuddling her desperately to me while I wept.

I didn't say anything to Clara; she'd got enough to worry about, what with Jim, and her two brothers out there as well. But even as I walked in the rose garden that afternoon I seemed to see those names, and for every one of them, somewhere a woman was weeping.

Leo came back the following afternoon. I'd left Rose with Ellen so I could take Flora for a walk. We went round by the stables on our way back, and found Tabby Cat stretched out in the sun, her full belly swollen with promise. Flora crouched down to stroke her soft fur until she began to purr lazily. Mr Tyson came out of the harness room; bending over my daughter, he said, 'There'll be kittens for thee to play with soon, Lady Flora. That cat, she drops 'em regular as clockwork.' He creaked slowly upright, as if his joints were paining him. 'Mary brought young Tommy in to see me and the missus this morning.' He shook his head. 'Poor bird, pale as a shadder she is. She baint never got over it.'

'Tisn't likely yet, is it, Mr Tyson.'

'No. A body don't get over something like that. Tom, he were such a lissom lad – never still for a moment – I still can't believe he's gone. Still, at least Mary's got the little 'un for comfort, and he's growing, too, thanks to you, my lady.' He raised his cap before shuffling back inside. He'd looked his age, these past few months. Then Nella, who'd been sitting patiently by while Flora petted the cat, pricked up her ears and gave a short woof.

I couldn't hear the motor yet myself, but Nella was never wrong. Flora jumped up. 'Papa?'

I took firm hold of her hand. 'Now, doan 'ee run in front of the motor.' We could both hear it now.

It drew up with a spluttering jerk. Leo got tiredly out, but his face lit up when he saw Flora standing there with me. I released my squirming daughter and she ran full tilt across the cobbles behind Nella. After he'd greeted them both he walked slowly over to me. 'Good afternoon, Amy. Is there any more news of young Arnold?'

'He's holding his own, but – ' I glanced down at Flora, hanging on his hand.

Hastily Leo said, 'Flora, I've lost my hat. Please would you go and look to see if it's in the motor?'

As soon as she'd sped off he repeated, 'But?'

'They've had to take his leg off.'

His eyes closed for a moment, then Flora, jumping down from the running board, came rushing back. 'I seed it, I seed it!'

'I *saw* it, my Flora. Right, we'll go and fetch it, shall we?'

'Are you staying for dinner?'

'If I may. We're between convoys at the moment. I must see Selby now, though.'

After dinner I invited Leo up for coffee. When we were sitting down he said, 'Clara tells me Mrs Arnold is still up in town.'

'Aye. Clara, she's going back at the end of the week.' I sighed. 'She's main upset about his leg.'

'It is – a high amputation: the most mutilating.' He stared down into his coffee cup.

'She said as he wouldn't be able to be a groom, not any more.'

'No. But he's a quick-witted young fellow. There'll be something he can do.'

'Ellen said as you'd promised anyone who went that they could have a job when they got back.'

He looked up at me, his eyes dark, 'The way things are going at the moment I will not have to keep many of those promises.'

He sounded so bitter; and remembering that single wood and all those names I couldn't help asking, 'But we are going to win, aren't we?'

He straightened up – as much as he ever could – before replying, 'We have to, Amy, we have to.' Then he repeated, 'Yes, there'll be something for Arnold – in the estate office, perhaps. But he won't like it. That boy loved to be outside. He used to swing on gates you know, young Jim. I was always shouting at him for it when he was at school; he'd jump off and run away with that deer-like leaping run you only see in boys and young men – and now – '

I thought he wasn't going to continue, but then he said, 'Do you know, in the ward to which I am attached at present there are five young men who've lost a leg, and one who's lost both. And that's not the worst of the mutilations – ' He broke off again, then went on quietly, 'I seem to see nothing all day but young men who have been maimed or crippled.'

Lifting up Rose, I untied her bootee and slipped it off. She kicked up, pleased at the new game, and I kissed her pink toes. Then I carried her over to Leo and plumped her down on his lap. Bending over them both I said to him, 'Today I were looking at Rose's foot, now you look at it, too. Tis beautiful. See her liddle toenails, like pearls they be. And her foot, tis so plump and smooth. Do 'ee tickle it.' Taking hold of his hand I guided the tip of one finger to stroke the sole of her foot until her toes crinkled with pleasure. Then placing her foot in his huge palm I told him, 'There, tis the most beautiful thing I ever did see.' He looked down at it, so soft and pink against the calloused skin of his hand. Then his strong fingers gently closed round his daughter's small foot in the briefest of caresses before setting her free.

Slowly he turned his twisted shoulder round so that he could look into my face. 'Yes, it is beautiful, Amy. Thank you.'

I said a word or two to him while he was drinking his coffee, but I kept my voice very low because I could see he was tired, and sure enough he soon nodded off. I sat there with Rose on my lap watching him. At first he slept heavily, but after half an hour or so he began to get restless; it was awkward for him, sleeping in an armchair, because of his hump. So putting Rose back in her cradle, I picked up one of my own cushions and tiptoed over to him. He didn't move, so gently I slipped the pillow in behind his shoulder, to give him more support. He shifted a moment, then settled back, but he still wasn't quite right, so very carefully I sat down behind him, to ease the pillow further down – and as I did so I knew he was awake. His eyes didn't open, he hadn't moved, but I could tell it from his breathing.

Bending forward I slipped my other arm round his neck and gently drew his head towards me, until it came to rest on my breast. I held it there, with my chin touching the hair of his head. Soft it was, softer than any woman's hair, soft as his daughter's dark curls – and turning my head a little, I pressed my cheek close against it.

He didn't move, and nor did I. He was pretending to be asleep, and I was pretending that I didn't know he was awake. We'd have stayed like that for a long time – only Rose began to call. The man in my arms stiffened for a moment and I gave him a quick, close hug before letting go of him and tiptoeing back to Rose.

As he yawned and stretched and made a show of waking up I said, 'Naughty Rose, thee's woken thy Dada up – and he was so tired.'

He asked, 'How long have I been asleep, Amy?'

'Getting on for an hour, I 'low.'

'I really must apologize, it's abominably bad manners to fall asleep in a lady's sitting room.'

'But I baint no lady,' I told him, 'I'm your wife.'

He blinked, then started laughing. I didn't know what the joke was, but I was so pleased to see him more cheerful I laughed, too, and Rose joined in as well; she didn't like to miss anything, Rose didn't.

135

Chapter Twenty

It was more than a fortnight before I saw Leo again. He sent a message to Mr Selby to say he wouldn't be having any free time for a while. 'There are increased casualties as a result of the renewed offensive, Lady Warminster, and several VADs are on sick leave, so the remainder are having to undertake extended responsibilities.'

'But Leo will be falling sick himself. Tis tiring work, carrying stretchers, and he isn't a young man.'

Mr Selby spoke kindly. 'Don't worry, Lady Warminster, your husband is strong – and I've rarely known him fall a prey to illness.'

After Mr Selby had gone I thought of what he'd said. 'Increased casualties'; but there'd been so many already. I sighed and went upstairs to feed little Tommy.

But not for much longer; Mary's sister's baby was born at the end of the week. She was a bit early but Poll had no problems; and the baby was a fine little maid, Mrs Dawson told me when she came back from the village. I was pleased, but when I fed Tommy that evening I felt a pang; I'd grown so fond of him these past weeks; he was such a loving baby once he got used to you.

When Poll's milk had come in I handed him over to Mary after giving him his last feed and told her how much I'd miss him.

'My lady,' she said, 'Mam and me were wondering if mebbe you'd care to come down and drink a cup o' tea with us one afternoon – ' she flushed – 'if we're not presuming, that is.'

'Oh Mary, I'd like that fine.'

Mrs Dawson said, 'The door'll always be open to you, my lady, always. We can't ever thank you enough for what you done.' There were tears in my eyes as I waved them goodbye; I would hardly know what to do with myself with only one baby to feed.

I said to Clara next morning, 'It does seem strange without Tommy.'

She replied, 'You maun go down and see him this afternoon.'

'But, Clara – ' My face crimsoned.

Her voice was firm. 'My lady, tis a long time ago now, and folk have likely forgotten. Anyway, you got to, else Mary'll be main upset.'

So I went. I took Rose with me like a shield, but I was still nervous, feeling as though everyone was peering at me through their curtains. I was scurrying down the High Street with my head down, counting the cottages, when Mrs Dawson appeared, almost running down her garden path. 'Come you in, my lady. The kettle's on the hob.' She looked so pleased to see me that all at once I was glad I'd come.

After I'd had my cup of tea I went next door to admire Poll's new baby. 'My, baint she a pretty one! And look at her, eyes on everything already – she'll be a quick liddle maid when she do grow up.'

I sat nursing Rose while Poll nursed her little Marjorie and Mary cuddled Tommy – and we talked about babies. It was a wrench to tear myself away, but Flora would be expecting me and Poll's three elder ones had come in wanting their tea and their Mam.

As I came out of the door blinking in the bright sunlight, a dark figure came hobbling towards me: Granny Withers. 'Next time, thee maun drink thy tea along wi' me.'

'Why, thank you, Mrs Withers – I'd like that.'

'Maud were going to ask you, but I were set on getting to 'ee first. Now doan 'ee be forgetting.'

I drank tea all week: Granny Withers, Maud Winterslow, Clara's mother, Ellen's mother. Other women spoke to me in the street: 'Be that Lady Rose you got there? My, baint she the daps of his lordship? I were wondering, you maun be tired carrying her all the way down from the house. Mebbe you'd like to rest your legs for a little while?'

So I'd find myself ushered into another trim kitchen and offered the best seat by yet another shining black range. All different, and yet all the same: babies, children, the smell of baking – and the photographs. 'My Jim', 'My Tom and Dickie', 'George – he allus did want to see the world, our George.' The voice dropped, and the corner of the apron was lifted to wipe away a tear.

'I be terrible sorry, tis such a loss for you and his father, but you maun both be main proud of him.' Then the letters: 'Lovely letter thic officer wrote. Would you like to read it, my lady?'

'I'd be honoured to, Mrs Hale.'

Dear Mr and Mrs Hale,
    I know that by now you will have received the usual notification from the War Office . . . be relieved to hear that death was instantaneous . . . a brave comrade . . . a great loss to us all . . .
Yours sincerely,
Edward Bradbury, Commanding Officer 'B' Company.

'I'd be pleased to see it, Mrs Sykes.'

My hand would be shaking as I gave back each letter. 'He died for his country, Mrs Sykes.'

'Aye, that's what Rector said: "He gave all he had for the sake of others." Only, my lady, Feyther and I – we keep thinking as how we'll never hear the ring of his boot on the step ever again.'

I'd be weeping with her, then she'd say, 'I'll fill your cup up again, tis thirsty work, nursing. I remember when I was trying to wean my Joe – I tried everything, but thic boy, he just didn't want to stop. His Da used to say, "Leave him to cry, he'll soon learn then," but I couldn't 'a done that; I allus picked him up and gave him a cuddle.'

'You maun be glad o' that now, Mrs Sykes.'

'Aye, that I am.' I'd feel the grip of her hand on my shoulder and we'd talk of babies and children – and what a good boy Joe had been.

Next day, another cottage, another photograph, another letter . . . I'd come home, my eyes red with weeping. That Sunday morning, I left the children with Ellen and went to church to pray for all the men in the army; it was the least I could do. Later, as I looked after my children while Ellen and Dora went to evening service as usual, I decided I would go every week in future. It was only right. I did hope Leo wouldn't mind; but he was never home of a Sunday now, anyway.

But the following Thursday Mr Selby told me that Leo had written to say the situation at Sutton Veny was improving, so he'd be coming over on both Saturday and Sunday evening. I found out the reason why, when the afternoon post brought a letter from Miss Annabel to say she'd written to Leo inviting herself down to Eston this weekend because she wanted to 'lay old ghosts' – and to see Flora.

I went to see Clara at once and we decided to give the drawing room a really good spring clean, even though it was summer. Clara was nearly as nervous as I was, so she didn't stop at the drawing room, and we were still putting the finishing touches to the hall when Leo arrived home on Saturday afternoon. I was relieved he'd come back early. I'd never entertained a guest before, and besides, I couldn't forget that the last time Miss Annabel had been at Eston she'd been the mistress and I'd been the maid.

She arrived looking as poised and confident as ever. 'Good afternoon, Amy, how lovely to see you. Goodness, Leo, the country does smell so fresh after the frowst of Town. As soon as Amy's given me a cup of tea you must take me to see your roses.'

I watched her as she sat chatting to Leo. From the crown of her glossy dark hair to the arch of her elegant slim foot she was beautiful. More beautiful, even, than when she'd first come to Eston as a bride. Only the faint purple shadows under her dark eyes betrayed what she had endured these past years.

Uncrossing her slender silk-clad ankles, she rose to her feet in one graceful movement. Leo's misshapen body followed in a clumsy parody. 'Are you coming with us, Amy?'

I shook my head. 'No, thank 'ee, I was out in the garden with Flora this morning.'

Miss Annabel turned to Leo with a smile. 'Shall we go then, Leonidas?'

When they came back she said, 'Now, I must see darling Flora. Would you send for her, Amy?' So the time until the dressing bell passed easily as she and Leo allowed Flora to bully them into play.

I dressed carefully, but I suspected that my evening frock would seem out of date now; and as soon as I saw Miss Annabel I knew that it was. Over soup she told me about the latest fashions, while Leo looked on indulgently, then as the fish was served she turned her attention to him. They talked of plays and paintings, of people I didn't know, and then, inevitably, of the war. He never talked to me like that, and soon I couldn't even follow easily as they used initials: MO, CCS, ADMS; it was clearly all to do with doctors and hospitals, so I closed my ears. I didn't want to hear about them.

'Shall we leave Leonidas to his port now, Amy?'

'Oh, I be sorry – ' I stammered in confusion. Miss Annabel was waiting for me to rise; after all, I was supposed to be the hostess. But when I led the way into the drawing room Leo followed us at once.

As soon as I'd poured the coffee I excused myself so I could go up to check on Rose, and when I came back they were deep in conversation again. Leo was so obviously enjoying her company that I was glad she'd come. When he stood up to take Nella for her final walk she rose to her feet too: 'I'll join you if I may, Leonidas. The scents will be delicious this evening.'

He looked over at me. 'Are you coming too, Amy?'

I shook my head. 'I'm a little tired, thank you.'

Turning to her with a smile he said, 'Amy has been officiating over some kind of out-of-season spring clean, Annabel, in preparation for your arrival.'

'Goodness, I am honoured.' Her silvery laugh rang out. 'But, Amy, I really must congratulate you on your new cook – a great improvement.' Flashing her brilliant smile, she asked, 'Shall we go, Leonidas? Nella is getting impatient.'

I had been worried about how to entertain her the next day, but there was no need, she didn't get up until it was almost time for lunch.

'Sorry to be so slack, Amy, but I couldn't resist the chance of a long lie-in. We've been so infernally busy recently, and then every spare moment seems to be taken up. When chaps are on leave you feel you can't refuse them your company. And so many of the men one knows have been wounded in this show, I feel the least I can do is visit them.'

I took a deep breath before daring to ask, 'Did you visit him?'

Her voice hardened. 'If by "him" you mean my husband – no, I didn't. In any case, he's been out of hospital for ages.'

My head jerked up. 'He's gone back to France?'

'Do you mind if I smoke?' She lit a cigarette without waiting for a reply, then she answered my question. 'No. His leg hasn't fully healed yet – but they're so short of beds because of this Somme affair that anyone who can possibly be turfed out of hospital has been, so he's on extended sick leave.'

I knew I had no right to keep asking but I couldn't help myself. 'Have you seen him?'

She inhaled deeply, and I thought she wasn't going to reply until she said, 'Unfortunately – yes. There are so many busybodies in this world who feel it's their duty to try and effect reconciliations between happily estranged couples, that on two occasions I was tricked into spending an entire evening in his company – in a party, naturally. If you wish to know, Amy, and obviously you do, apart from a fashionable sympathy-inducing limp he appears to be quite his old self, and as arrogant and selfish as ever. I think we'd better change the subject now.'

She began to talk instead of her fellow ambulance drivers who'd been suffragettes before the war. 'I do so admire them. Milly was arrested twice and then went on hunger strike. *They're* not content to lurk in the shadow of a man, to be mere ciphers.' She leant forward, her cigarette forgotten in its holder. 'Once this war is over they'll have to give us more than just the right to vote. We'll *demand* equality. After all, women can do anything men can do.'

'But tis men as are over in France, doing the fighting.'

'So they should be. They started it, didn't they? But even there, women are needed to help them out.' Her face was flushed, her voice excited, as she exclaimed, '*I'm* going to France, Amy. I'm going to drive an ambulance there, instead of in boring old London.'

I just sat staring at her. France, where men were fighting and dying. Miss Annabel was so brave.

After lunch she said, 'Would you mind if I went out for a ride? I haven't been on a horse for ages. I suppose despite the War Office, Leonidas has still got one or two riding hacks in his stables?'

'Aye, o' course.' As soon as she'd gone out I went up to the nursery to fetch Rose; but all the time I was nursing her I kept thinking of what Miss Annabel had told me – and wondering when *he'd* be going back to France, too.

She returned just as Mr Tims brought in the tea-tray. Flora was with me and she ran to her at once, 'Aunt N'bel, Aunt N'bel – play games.'

'Of course I will, my pet.'

They began a counting game on Flora's fingers and I heard my daughter squeal in delight as Miss Annabel's clear voice exclaimed 'And this little piggy went wee wee wee wee – all the way home!'

Then the door opened and Mr Tims' cracked voice announced, 'Lord Quinham, my lady.'

He stood there in the doorway, tall and slim in his uniform, his sleek blond hair shining in the sun. He looked around: at Annabel with an open-mouthed Flora on her lap, and at me with Rose wide-eyed at my side. Then he said lightly, 'Well, it's no mean achievement to reduce an entire roomful of females to silence.'

Miss Annabel's voice rang out high and clear, 'Dear me, Flora – it would appear that the little piggy-wiggy has arrived. What shall we play next?' But Flora didn't respond; her blue eyes were fixed on the tall figure of her father.

He limped across to a chair and threw himself down in it. 'Pour me a cup of tea, Amy, there's a good girl.' My hands were shaking so much as I handed it to him that the cup jumped in the saucer. He thanked me with a smiling flash of his blue eyes before turning to ask, 'Hasn't my ever-loving wife a word of welcome for her wounded soldier?'

Annabel looked straight back at him. 'Who told you? Who told you I was down here?'

He shrugged. 'Does it matter? Besides, why assume that I came to see *you*? After all, Eston is supposed to be my home, and it's not without its attractions. There's Flora, for one.'

At the sound of her name Flora slid off Miss Annabel's lap and made a tentative move towards him – but Annabel put her hand on her arm to restrain her. 'No, Flora, you don't want to get your hands dirty.'

His mouth tightened for a moment, then, looking directly at her he said, 'What's this nonsense I hear about your going to France?'

'It isn't nonsense. I'm leaving next week.'

'France is no place for a woman. I won't allow it.'

'You can't stop me.'

His chin came up. 'I most certainly can. The Red Cross won't allow *any* VAD whose husband is on active service in France to go there herself, and I'll be returning shortly.'

Her beautiful mouth curved in a smile of triumph. 'But I'm not going as a VAD, Francis. I've joined the FANYS, and they couldn't care less about outmoded conventions like that.'

He looked baffled for a moment, then said firmly, 'I absolutely forbid it. I have the right to do so – you are still my wife.'

Still smiling, she said, '*That's* easily settled.' Raising her left hand, she began to tug at her finger; I saw what she was doing but at the expression on her face my 'no' died in my throat. Once the circlet of gold was freed, she casually tossed it over her shoulder. The shining golden hoop rolled along the carpet and came to rest beneath the window. 'There, that solves the problem, doesn't it?'

I turned my eyes away from the stricken look on his face. Then suddenly Flora began to run straight to that golden circle. She picked it up, her face one smile of delight, then she bore it in triumph to me. 'Mama, look – ring.' She dropped it into my lap.

I heard the silvery peal of Miss Annabel's laughter: 'Oh, how deliciously symbolic.'

The gold burnt my fingertips as I pushed it back into Flora's hand. 'Flora, take it to Uncle Frank. It do belong to him.'

She looked surprised, then obediently trotted off with it. 'Thank you, Flora my pet.' Carefully he put the ring in the breast pocket of his tunic, and buttoned down the flap again, before asking, 'More tea, perhaps, Amy? It is a warm day.'

There was silence as I fetched his cup and topped it up with fresh tea. He took several mouthfuls then said, with a glance at Miss Annabel and me, 'Please, *don't* let me interrupt your girlish gossip.'

Our silence continued for a moment longer before being broken by Miss Annabel's voice, high and conversational: 'By the way, Amy, I saw George Burton in Town. He asked after you specially. Apparently his wretched arm still isn't right from when he was wounded, but he's hoping to get back to France before too long – so brave, at his age.' Her smiling glance in Frank's direction was a deliberate challenge as she added, 'Of course, it's different for *young* men, they enjoy shooting people and all that sort of silliness. It's a game for them, just a great game.'

Frank sprang to his feet, tall and angry. 'Everything's a game for you, isn't it, Annabel? Even marriage.' He marched to the door, and slammed it shut behind him.

I exclaimed, 'Miss Annabel, you shouldn't 'a done that. You shouldn't have taken his ring off.'

She turned on me angrily. 'You fool, Amy. How can you, of all people, plead for him?'

'He didn't mean – it were *my* fault – '

'Don't flatter yourself, Amy. You just happened to be available. If it hadn't been you it would have been some other woman – it *was* some other woman. There always are other women, where Francis is concerned!' She stalked out.

Flora gazed at the door, her lower lip trembling, then she burst into noisy sobs.

'Oh Flora, Flora.' I hugged her close and we wept together.

When Mr Tims came for the tray he said, 'Lord Quinham has sent his bag upstairs, my lady, to his old room.'

I tried to be calm. 'Perhaps you'd ask Clara to check as the bed's aired?'

'Yes, my lady. And, my lady, will you be using the dining room tonight?'

'Aye. I suppose so.'

Leo came back while we were up in the nursery. Miss Annabel looked up at him over Flora's blonde head. 'Good evening, Leonidas. Has Amy told you? Your *son* is joining us for dinner.'

His face darkened; deliberately he turned his back on me as he bent down to greet Flora.

I came downstairs early; I was the hostess. Leo came out of the library in full evening dress. I told him, 'I didn't invite him. He must've heard Miss Annabel were here, and followed her down.' I stopped abruptly as I heard her step on the stair.

We talked – they talked – of the weather and the harvest. Then the front door opened, and Frank came in, still in khaki. He gave the briefest of nods to Leo before saying, 'Sorry to keep you waiting, Amy, but it's such a lovely evening I walked further than I intended. I trust I may dine in my uniform – the King's uniform.' His gaze lingered on Leo's spotless evening dress.

Then Mr Tims announced, 'Dinner is served, my lord.'

Annabel stepped forward. 'Shall we go in, Leonidas?' They walked away without a backward glance.

As Frank turned to me, I caught the smell of whisky on his breath. 'Then that leaves us, Amy, doesn't it?' He held out his khaki-clad arm. Resting my fingertips on the woollen cloth, I walked beside him into dinner. My heart was thudding like a drum.

Chapter Twenty-One

We began with royal soup, clear as a summer stream. Mrs Carter had been so anxious that everything should be 'just right for your guest, my lady', she'd brought me several menus and we'd studied them anxiously together before making our choice – but her satin-smooth consommé might as well have been Mrs Procter's lumpy turnip for all the notice any of us were taking of it.

It was Miss Annabel who broke the silence. 'I think it was very sensible of you to move into the morning room for family meals, Amy. Oval tables are quite the thing now. These endless expanses of white linen have altogether gone out of fashion except for the most formal of meals.'

Frank looked up. 'How right you are, Annabel my pet. I remember Mama telling me how much she used to hate dinners at Eston – "those interminable evenings" was how she described it.' My eyes flew to Leo; his face had stiffened. Frank continued, 'Poor Maman, she was always so sensitive to her – er – surroundings.'

Miss Annabel spoke very quickly. 'I must admit, Leonidas, this dining room is not the jolliest of rooms. It tends to be gloomy of an evening.' She glanced around her. 'I think perhaps these paintings are too dark for the wallpaper.' Frank tried to interrupt but her voice continued sharp and bright as an icicle, 'Perhaps you might consider replacing one or two of them with the work of some more modern artists.' Frank opened his mouth again but she was too quick for him. 'And talking of modern artists that reminds me, Amy, I quite forgot to tell you earlier – I saw Lucas Venn in Town.' She turned to Leo with only the lightest of pauses. 'You'll be familiar with his work of course, Leonidas. His portrait of Lady Londonderry was much admired.'

Frank's voice was harsh. 'So was his portrait of you – especially by your husband.'

Miss Annabel faltered; suddenly she was on the verge of collapse. Desperately I seized on the name, 'Mr Venn – did he tell you? He said as how he were going to tell you how he did come to join the army.'

Miss Annabel caught my ineptly thrown line and held it tight. Then she began to reel it in, her voice controlled and confident once more. 'Yes, he did tell me – an extraordinary tale, so typical of these impulsive artists. You'll all be fascinated to hear it'. She looked directly at Frank, daring him to disagree. With a shrug of surrender he reached for his glass, leaving Miss Annabel to tell her tale.

'I was down at the Third London again, and Lucas had a half-day pass, so I offered him a lift up to Town, and all the way back he was talking about his bad chest and weak heart.' Her voice was light and conversational; she was in control again. 'I'd suggested he drop into the club later for tea, so when he did I asked him how on earth he'd managed to get through an army medical – and he told me the whole incredible story. Apparently Colonel Porter – he's the CO of the Third London General Hospital – was desperately short of orderlies, since they'd sent all the halfway reasonable ones to France, and it was before the army agreed to use female VADs. So he, Colonel Porter that is, went along to dinner at the Chelsea Arts Club, and asked if any of the members would be prepared to enlist in the ranks, and the very next day all these middle-aged artists and sculptors and writers joined the army as private soldiers. Some of them had tried to join up before, but been turned down for medical reasons. Poor old Lucas is C3 you know – you can't get any lower than that without actually being wounded – but the army took them all the same, they were so desperately needed. They'll never be sent to the Front, of course, or even to a base hospital in France. Lucas actually sounded rather regretful about that, but they're doing a vital job over here, and above all, they're really in the army! Lucas told me confidentially that he's ready to burst with pride every time he goes on a bus and the conductor shouts: "Move along there, Tommy." Just fancy, a famous Royal Academician and he's far more proud of being Lance Corporal Venn.' She laughed. 'Fascinating, isn't it, how people's values have changed since the war began.' She smiled at Frank, a hard brilliant smile, then lifted her spoon. 'This soup is quite delicious, Amy.'

Frank looked up from his glass; his face was unreadable, but when he spoke his voice was normal, even pleasant. 'Your story reminds me of a rather similar one, Annabel, that old Geoff Carey told me. You'll remember him, I expect – he joined the Engineers. Anyway, he copped rather a nasty packet this summer, so he's on sick leave too. We did a show together last week, and in the interval he told me of a close shave he'd had when he was up in front of Ypres back in the winter. There'd been a bit of shelling but nothing to get upset about on his particular patch, so old Geoff was snatching a few hours' sleep in his dugout when the major turned up from Vlamertinghe.' He gave a short laugh. 'They always seem to do that when a chap's having a bit of shuteye. So poor old Geoff had to haul himself out of his bunk and trek up to the front line with him – and no sooner had they arrived there than a damn whizz-bang burst slap bang in the middle of them.'

Annabel's eyes never left his face as he went on, 'Three men killed outright and the major sprawled on the ground bleeding like a stuck pig.' I gasped, but he took no notice. 'Geoff said he was a great tall fellow, so it was probably him they'd spotted. He ran back for the stretcher bearers, and they got the survivors to the dressing station, but it was a bit of a shambles down there, apparently – the Boches had been whizz-banging nearby for a couple of days – so what with that and the state of the major Geoff didn't have time to notice that his own gumboot had a nasty gash in it. Anyway, he reckoned it was only a couple of crushed toes so he had his antitetanus jab and hobbled off back to his dugout. Obviously he didn't want to leave his men, so he kept hopping about for a few days while the regimental MO dressed his toes. Then the medico chappie put his foot down – not literally, fortunately.' Frank laughed, and even Miss Annabel smiled. 'So Geoff was packed off to the nearest Casualty Clearing Station at Hazebrouk. Spent three weeks there having bits of dead bone picked out of his foot and listening to sentimental love songs on this gramophone they'd got there. Made a nice little Christmas break he said.'

The fish had arrived while he was speaking. He looked down at his plate and prodded the baked sole with his fork before reaching for his glass again and drinking deeply. Then his head snapped back and he looked straight at Leo. 'But I've forgotten to tell you the end of the story. Quite amusing, it was. When Geoff arrived at the CCS an RAMC corporal met the ambulance and carried his bag inside for him. Geoff gave the fellow threepence for his pains – never has much spare cash, Geoff! But he said the corporal seemed quite satisfied. It was only later that Geoff discovered he'd tipped Scotland's premier earl!' Frank burst out laughing, but his eyes never left Leo's face. 'You probably know Crawford, don't you, sir? Must have been a contemporary of yours at Eton. Evidently he had some perfectly good job in government but he felt he wasn't doing enough, so he chucked it in and enlisted in the ranks. Damn plucky thing to do at his age – don't you think so, sir?' Leo's eyes dropped to his plate. Frank's voice rose, as Mr Tims left the room. 'Don't you think so, sir?'

Leo muttered, 'Yes, yes.'

Frank smiled. 'I was sure you'd agree.'

Two red spots appeared in the centre of Miss Annabel's cheeks. She spoke quickly. 'Mama had a letter from her cousin in America last week; I gather attitudes have considerably changed over there with regard to Germany. Of course, the *Lusitania* made such a difference . . . ' She moved on to rumours of more cuts in the railway services, and Frank drank steadily as she talked.

Then, as she spoke of labour shortages he broke in: 'It can only get worse, with the move towards conscription. Good news for females, though. Apparently a lot more men have been doing the decent thing and marrying their girls since conscription came in for bachelors,' he paused before adding, 'and widowers.' He looked directly at Leo.

Annabel spoke sharply. 'You're out of date, Frank. Since March there's been no distinction between married men and bachelors. And only those of military age are affected – men under forty-one.'

Frank raised his glass, his voice studiedly casual. 'So far, but rumour has it now that the army'll be needing the men up to fifty next, for home defence.' He turned to address Leo. 'Still, I don't think *you've* anything to worry about, have you, sir?'

Leo just sat there, hump-backed, twisted-shouldered; he was like a huge stricken bear. Without stopping to think I cried out, 'Leo, he be working hard, carrying stretchers – just like thic artist fellows!'

Leo's voice was harsh. 'Be quiet Amy!'

Frank's eyes held mine for a moment. 'What a loyal little wife you are, Amy my pet.' Then he swung right round until he faced Miss Annabel. 'It makes a change from the attitude of my own dear helpmate.' He reached up to pat the pocket of his tunic, his eyes glittering recklessly. 'But still, there are plenty more fish in the sea. In fact, I landed one only last night – and she was more than happy to be hooked.'

Miss Annabel's face flamed as she cried, 'I hate you! I hate you!'

'Never mind, as long as somebody still loves me.' Turning to face me now, he said, 'And someone does, don't they, Amy?'

'Francis – ' Miss Annabel's voice died away.

Frank's eyes were holding mine. 'You still love me, don't you, Amy? After all, you never meant to marry him, did you? He forced you into marriage, so there's no need to be ashamed of admitting the truth.' I was drowning in his blue eyes, I couldn't look away. 'Go on, Amy, tell me who you really love.' I didn't answer but all at once he seized my hand, holding it in a grip so tight it crushed my fingers. 'If you don't love me, say "no".'

I gasped for breath, I tried to move my lips – but I couldn't say that one word. It was Frank who broke the silence. 'He may be your husband, but *I'm* the man you love.' As he slowly released my hand, I looked up – and saw Leo's face.

Stumbling to my feet, I blundered towards the door. Behind me I heard Miss Annabel's furious cry, 'Francis, that was unforgivable!' Running out into the hall, I heard someone following me, so desperately I sought for shelter – rushing straight across into the library, to collapse sobbing in the big armchair.

I heard the door opening, and hid my face. The door closed again and footsteps came towards me. 'Amy?'

I couldn't look at him, I could only whisper again and again, 'I be sorry, I be terrible sorry.' A hand rested for a moment on my hair; it was the lightest of caresses but I felt it and turned towards him. He was kneeling on the carpet in front of me and as I looked at his awkward twisted shape I repeated again, 'I be sorry. I know he don't care for me, but I cassent help it.'

When at last he spoke his voice was very gentle, 'None of us can help where we love, Amy.'

I raised my head fully so that I could see the expression in his mismatched grey eyes and whispered in disbelief, 'Thee baint angry wi' I?'

'How can I be angry with you, when I've committed the same folly myself? For I too am guilty of loving where there is no hope of return.'

And now there was no more pretence, I could only whisper, 'I be sorry, I be terrible sorry – but I cassent.'

His voice was so gentle as he replied, 'I know, Amy, I know. It's all right, the Beast does understand.' He smiled and I began to shake with relief.

Awkwardly he pulled his cumbersome body upright and went to the cupboard in the corner. There was the chink of glass and then he stood in front of me again. 'Drink a little, Amy. It'll make you feel better.'

The brandy made me cough and splutter. Carefully I put down the glass before repeating again, 'I am sorry.'

'It's not your fault, Amy. He's right, I forced you into marriage.'

'But nobody realized when I cried out "no". Twere a natural mistake, the way things were.'

'Amy, you should never have been in front of that altar at all. I should never have offered to marry you in the first place: I was quite wrong to make that decision.'

'But that were my fault – you told me it were. That evening in here, you told me you only offered to marry me because I asked you to give my baby a name!'

He shook his head. 'No, those words of yours were merely the trigger.'

I stared at him in astonishment as he continued, 'I only told you part of the truth that night. You were so unhappy, so distraught. How could I have told you the whole truth, and so burdened you still further?' He turned his head and shoulders a little sideways so that he could look me straight in the eye. 'But it's time for the truth now. Besides, why should you carry the responsibility for my folly? No, Amy, I married you because I wanted to.'

'But – why ever did you want to marry me?' I was completely bewildered.

'Because you spoke to me in the garden. May I have a little of your brandy?' Dumbly I handed it to him. 'Thank you.' He took a sip before beginning to explain. 'That first time, when I was pruning my roses, you spoke to me – with all the confident certainty of youth, yet with kindness, too. And then, when I turned round, I saw the face of Aphrodite.' His voice was very quiet, but I could hear every word. 'A very young and innocent Aphrodite. But it wasn't your face I was looking at, it was your eyes: I always look at the eyes of strangers when they catch sight of me for the first time. I could see that my appearance took you by surprise – you hadn't been warned – and you looked startled, yet still you smiled: fully, openly, smiling at me as if I were no different from other men. You're so transparent, Amy, you can hide nothing. You hid nothing then; yet as you looked at me from your beautiful golden eyes it was as if, despite your awareness of how ugly I was, you were not one jot disturbed by it.' He stared down into his glass, then raised his eyes to mine. 'And that was how it began.'

I looked at him, startled, but he shook his head. 'No, I'm not talking about love. Not then, not later. I did not intend to love; not ever again. Besides, you were simply Annabel's maid. If it hadn't been for your – seduction, you would have remained nothing more. But then, here in this room, I learnt that you had no home, that you were as alone as I was – but so much younger and more vulnerable. You were so unhappy, so desperate – I couldn't just cast you adrift. So I sent you to Kew.'

His voice was gentle. 'But then I began to worry about you. You can't imagine what a luxury that was, to have someone to worry about! No one else seemed to care about you – and you'd offered me the child you were carrying, so I felt I had the right to be concerned about you, the right to look after you, just a little. Only then I became greedy and wanted more. So that in the hospital, after you called out, the temptation became too much for me. You wanted a name for your baby, you were desperate for one, and I had a name going begging that no one else would ever want, so why shouldn't I offer it to you?'

His voice dropped lower. 'And I was lonely, Amy – so terribly lonely. You'd offered me your child, and I wanted her, but I'd have to wait until she was grown up before she'd be a companion – while you, you were almost grown up already. I know it was the crassest of follies to even think of such a thing, but there was so little time, and the dream was so seductive that I succumbed. You see, I thought that if I offered you my name, my title, my status, my wealth, then you might be willing to live in this house with me – and all I would ask of you in return was that you would talk to me each evening without flinching.' Then he added softly, 'And you have done that, over and over again.'

He raised the glass and his voice became firmer and stronger as he told me, 'But now I promise that I will expect nothing from you, not even that. I ask *nothing* of you, nothing.'

Looking up into his face I said quietly, 'I do like to talk to thee of an evening.'

For a fraction of a second his eyes closed then he replied, 'Thank you, Amy, thank you.'

Silence fell. He turned and went to the window. When he spoke again it was with his humpback still towards me. 'Once I was a young man, walking in the park. It was summer and the whole world was warm with promise – but I was alone. And then I saw her; I saw Jeanette. A bumble bee had become entangled in the gauze trimming of her hat so she'd taken it off; she stood there, with the silver-gilt of her hair shining against the green of the leaves, watching her maid trying to shake that bee out of her hat – and she was laughing. In that moment I fell hopelessly, irretrievably in love. I couldn't help it, any more than you can help loving her son. She didn't know me, she didn't want to know me, but I was determined to have her. So I pursued her, I married her – and I never heard her laughter again.'

He turned and I saw the desolation in his face as he said, 'I swore I would never do that to another woman, never again burden a woman with the weight of my unwanted affection. And when I broke that vow I made another, that at least I wouldn't burden her with the knowledge of that affection. But I broke my second vow, too. I'm sorry, Amy. I'm sorry.' He asked quietly, 'It was the rose, wasn't it?' I couldn't trust myself to speak; I simply nodded. 'Yes, I saw it in your face that evening: the flash of awareness that turned to fear. Fear of me. But you weren't always afraid, and so I began to hope. I pretended, deceiving myself, telling myself there *was* hope – and so I would frighten you again. But you needn't be frightened any more, Amy, the Beast accepts that there *is* no hope for him.' His lopsided mouth curved into a sad smile. 'After all, this is real life, not a fairy tale.' He moved over to the door. 'Stay here, Amy, I won't be a moment.'

When he came back he was carrying Rose. He held her out to me, 'Here's your daughter.'

Taking her into my arms I hugged her close, burying my face in her sweet-smelling neck, kissing her cheek, nuzzling her hair. She blinked at me with sleepy dark eyes, and I asked, 'Were you asleep, my Rose? Did thy Dada wake thee up? Oh dear!'

He said, 'She doesn't mind being woken up – she loves you.'

Her small hand reached for my dress and at once I unfastened it, and put her to my breast. Leo sat in silence, watching me suckle his daughter, until she fell asleep again. Then he said gently, 'It's time you were in bed, Amy.'

'Where's Miss Annabel?'

'She went straight up to her room.' Then he answered my unspoken question. 'And he's gone. He told Tims he was catching the evening train.'

I felt the emptiness and began to shiver. Rose's eyes opened, startled, so I forced myself to be calm. 'Tis time I took thee to bed, my flower.'

He waited at the foot of the stairs until I was safely at the top, then he turned away, and I heard the library door close behind him.

Chapter Twenty-Two

I lay cuddling Rose's warm young body all night. My thoughts kept going back to Frank. I couldn't help it. I remembered his face as he first looked at Miss Annabel; and his face as she'd thrown his wedding ring over her shoulder. Because he loved her. It had always been her he loved, never me; I'd simply been a toy, a plaything to be made use of and then tossed aside. He hadn't meant to make me love him: it wasn't his fault. And I had no right to love him, especially not now, when I had a husband. But my husband understood; I clung to that thought like an anchor. Leo understood; and he expected nothing of me, wanted nothing from me – only that I should talk to him of an evening, without flinching. I wept with relief and gratitude.

I could hardly bear to look at Miss Annabel as she came into breakfast next morning. I told her, 'I'm sorry. Last night – '

She shrugged. 'You can scarcely be held responsible for the appalling manners of the man I was fool enough to marry.'

In a voice barely louder than a whisper I said, 'He do love thee.'

She was furious at my presumption. 'Don't be stupid, Amy, he's incapable of love. All he cares about is his own self-gratification.' She leant forward, her dark eyes hard. 'Forget him, Amy, he's worthless – absolutely worthless.' Then, reaching for a slice of toast, her voice became bright and social. 'Isn't it a lovely day? I think I might go for a really long walk before plunging back into the heat and dust of London – if you've no other plans for me, that is?'

'No, no – if you do want to go out – '

'Then I will. Perhaps you'd ask your cook to put me up some sandwiches – nothing elaborate, bread and cheese will do. Oh, and a bottle of lemonade. I won't be back much before tea-time.'

I took Flora out into the garden before lunch. Papa hadn't come to say good morning, she told me; he must have left very early. Then as we were coming back up out of the garden we heard the motor and Flora dragged me up to the drive to meet him. He swung her up into his arms while she squealed with delight. Then, setting her down, he bent to pat Nella. As he straightened up he looked directly at me; I couldn't read the expression on his face – I'd never seen him look like that before. His hand still rested on Flora's golden head but it was to me he spoke: 'I've seen the CO at Sutton Veny; he gave me a thorough going-over and it appears that there's absolutely no reason why I shouldn't pass my medical, so I'm going to enlist. I'm joining the RAMC – in the ranks, naturally, just like Crawford.'

I was stunned.

He gave me a lop-sided half-smile. 'So you see, I will be able to keep my promise.' He bent down to Flora again. 'I'll come up and see you, my flower, but not before tea-time. Papa has to go and find Mr Selby now. You must go in with your Mama.' Turning back to the motor he called for Nella, and in a surge of golden fur she leapt into the passenger seat; then the car headed off down the drive again. My mind was in turmoil: I could hardly believe I'd heard aright.

Miss Annabel came back first, her cheeks glowing with exercise and the sun. 'Ring for tea early, Amy – there's a good girl.'

I said, 'Leo, he came back afore lunch and he said he's going to join the army.'

'What?'

She made me tell her word for word what he'd said, then she closed her eyes a moment before exclaiming, 'Why ever was I so stupid as to tell that story?' Then her voice hardened. 'But it's Francis who's to blame for taunting and belittling him. He provoked Leonidas into doing this. Damn him, damn him! Look, Amy, you must talk Leonidas out of this madness.'

'But you said as all the men he were at school with, they'd joined the army.'

'It's not the same. They're officers, with men of their own sort – gentlemen. But Leonidas can't be an officer. You've just told me, he's going in the ranks.'

'So did that Earl o' Crawford. He were carrying *bags*.'

'Amy, there's always been the odd gentleman ranker – but they've not been men like Leonidas, who's led the life of a recluse. And besides, there's his appearance. Men of that class will make fun of his – his physical peculiarities. You *must* stop him.'

He came in when we were halfway through tea, but he didn't say anything to Miss Annabel about enlisting, and she didn't broach the subject either.

He took Flora with him when he drove Annabel down to the station to catch her train. When he came up to the nursery after getting back, he was smiling.

'Can you spare me a few minutes, Amy? It seems ages since I've seen my roses in the afternoon.'

I kept stealing glances at him as we walked down through the rose garden. When we came to his favourite Blairii rose her full summer flowering was over, but a few of her buds had opened later, as they always did. Pausing beside her, he gently drew one fragrant bloom towards him, and breathed in its sweet scent. 'I shall miss my roses, and my daughters.' Slowly he straightened up again. 'And I shall miss your talking to me of an evening, Amy.'

I blurted out, 'Please don't go because o' me.'

'Because of you?' He sounded puzzled, then said, 'Oh, because of what I said about keeping my promise. It's all right, Amy, you needn't worry. I've come to my senses now – though I admit it will be easier to keep to my senses if I'm away from you. But that's not why I'm going.' He swung round to face me, and I saw that he was smiling fully. 'I'm going because I want to go. No doubt there'll be times when I'll call myself all sorts of a fool, times when I'll hate it, hate being always cheek by jowl with other men – strangers. I've got no illusions on that score: I won't take kindly to losing my privacy. Nor will I suffer gladly the loss of my independence: I will not like having to do what I'm told, I've had my own way too long now to want to be at the beck and call of others. But none of that matters one iota – as long as I'm wearing the King's uniform.'

I changed tack. 'But, if tis only to do what you're doing now – '

'You don't understand, Amy.' He smiled again. 'How could you? You're a woman. You can't understand the shame of it, of seeing other men, ordinary men – labourers, shepherds, carters – all of them going to be soldiers, to fight for their country while I stay skulking at home. I've been so ashamed, so bitterly ashamed.' He turned a little to look at his roses, and in profile I saw it: the hawk nose and high forehead of his father: 'Arthur, Sixth Earl of Warminster, Afghanistan and the Crimea'.

I exclaimed, 'Tis because of the portraits – because of the pictures of the generals.'

His eyes came back to me, his face surprised. 'So you do understand. I didn't think you would.' There was a long pause before he spoke again, and when he did, the old hesitation was back. 'When – I was a child, my nurse used to tell me – stories of my father, and of his father and grandfather before him. She'd been my mother's nurse before she'd become her maid, so they were very close. My mother had told her tales of all the Earls of Warminster. She was so proud to have married into the family, since her own father had served, too. Both of my grandfathers had fought at Waterloo, you know. I knew that from infancy, and so I used to dream of how one day I would fight, too, and win battles and defeat evil men. The Napoleons, the Tsars: in the nursery I fought them all with my toy soldiers.

'I was fighting one of those battles when my father came. Once a year he came to see me: an old, fierce man with a stick. I was so engrossed in my game I didn't realize he was there. When I turned and saw him I had a French soldier in my hand – a galloping dragoon, brandishing his sword. I'd just captured him, so I went to my father and held it out to him, saying, "*I* will be a soldier when I grow up."

'And he just looked down at me with utter contempt on his face; then he said, "You, you'll never be a soldier – you're a cripple," and he turned and stumped out. I can still feel the point of that tiny sword biting into my hand.'

He took a deep breath; he was fighting for words. 'I knew – I knew I was twisted, but I thought – I didn't see many other children – I suppose I thought I'd grow out of it, grow straight. Nanny Fenton had never said that I was – damaged. I ran to her, shouting, "I *will* be a soldier! I *will*! It's not true!" and then I saw her face: she was crying. Helmsley came later. She must have sent for him specially; he never normally came after bedtime. He sat beside me, holding my hand, and explained that I could become a scholar, a great landowner – but never, never a soldier. So then I knew it was true. I've carried

153

that shame with me all my life; but now, now I will be a soldier!' And for a moment he was transformed: he looked like a young boy. I could hardly believe it was the same man.

He smiled at me, almost gaily. 'And it's you I have to thank, Amy. I've been so slow to realize. Even when Annabel spoke of those artists I didn't think; Crawford's almost my age, but then, he's not a cripple. All I could hear were Francis' jibes – and then *you* said: "He's carrying stretchers, too, just like thic artist fellows!" I didn't see the significance, I shouted at you; and then afterwards, when he – said what he said – you were so distressed, I couldn't think of anything else – I – '

He looked away for a moment, and his face wasn't young any more, but then his voice rose again, 'But that night, it came back to me: "He's carrying stretchers" – just like those artists, and all at once it made sense. Sutton Veny's a military hospital, there are RAMC orderlies there – only those not fit to serve abroad, of course – but I *am* doing the same as they are, just the same. So I went to see the Commanding Officer this morning. My heart was beating like a drum when I went into his office. It seemed too much to ask; I could barely get the words out. Until I saw his face: he didn't even look surprised, he just reached for his stethoscope. It didn't take long. Then he told me I would be quite acceptable to the Medical Board. He offered to give me a note, but then he said, "You won't need it if you tell the usual lie about your age – and even that's scarcely necessary as you're on the right side of fifty." And I realized that was all he was thinking of – my age.' He laughed, 'I can still hardly believe it. I wish I could enlist tomorrow, before I get cold feet, but I owe it to Selby to spend a week sorting things out before I go.'

He sounded so sure, only I couldn't help thinking of Uncle Alf – he was in France, in danger. I exclaimed, 'But thee might get shot at!'

Leo shook his head. 'There's no prospect of that, Amy; I'll never get past the base hospitals; not even out of Britain, I don't suppose, any more than those artists have done. But once I've taken the King's shilling I'll have to go where I'm told, there'll be no more slipping home for an hour or two at the end of the day; I'll miss you and the children and my roses – ' he bent down for a quick pat – 'and my faithful Nella, eh, girl? But,' he stood up, 'despite all that, I can't wait to go because then, at last, I will be able to look the world in the face.' He smiled at me, a very gentle smile.

Oh yes, I understood; I understood better than he realized. Because I would have done anything to take the shame of my birth from my shoulders. There was no restitution for me, but for him, at last, it had come, and I understood. I looked up at him and smiled, because he in his turn understood that I loved Frank, and always would. And as we stood there, in the garden, it was as if a great wall between us came tumbling down. I bent my head, and buried it in the Blairii roses.

Above me I heard the sound of his voice, calm now, asking 'Shall we go in? I expect Rose will be wanting you, and Selby will be waiting in the office.'

Back indoors I fed Rose and bathed Flora and tucked her up in bed. Just as I finished reading to her, Leo came up to say goodnight. As he bent over her bed and put his hand to her cheek as he always did I saw the difference: he was looking at her like a man seeking to remember, like a man going away.

Then he stood up and came out into the day nursery with me – and even the way he walked was different. His back was still humped, his neck twisted, and yet he seemed to hold himself straighter. He carried himself with a confidence I'd never seen in him before.

It was still there as he walked across the hall towards me before dinner; almost a jauntiness. He watched me as I came down the last steps, and again there was the look of a man storing memories. When he spoke his voice was light, 'Is Beauty ready for her dinner? Then let us go in.'

As we spread our table napkins I asked, 'Has Mr Selby gone home now?'

'Yes, looking even more careworn than usual. I'm afraid I'm leaving him in the lurch. And today was not a good day to tell him, since he'd already arranged to go over to Pennings tomorrow.'

'I didn't know he were agent at Pennings as well,' I said while the soup was being served.

'He was only nominally in charge until war broke out. Young Parry is a very able youngster, and he was running the Pennings estate practically single-handed – but he was one of the first to volunteer, so Selby had to take over again once Parry went. Now that I'm leaving at this end, he'll have to carry the entire burden of Eston as well. Arnott at the Home Farm is a capable fellow, but he's under a lot of pressure, too, with so many men having enlisted. Besides, Arnott's gifts are very much in the practical field, so Selby's always done the Home Farm accounts on top of everything else.' He picked up his spoon and dipped it into Mrs Carter's fragrant game soup.

Recalling that the Home Farm at Borrell simply supplied the Hall, I suggested tentatively, 'Mebbe I could help Mr Selby with them?'

Leo's spoon halted just before his lips. 'With the Home Farm accounts?' He sounded surprised.

'Well, Home Farms, they aren't so big.'

He swallowed his mouthful of soup before saying, 'The Home Farm at Eston is more than twenty-one thousand acres.'

I stared at him, while mentally multiplying the Ten Acre Field at Borrell two thousand one hundred times – I couldn't believe it.

Smiling, he asked, 'Didn't you realize that I had most of the Eston estate in hand?'

Puzzled, I repeated, 'In *hand*?'

'The farms at Pennings are let, but not here at Eston. I only have eight tennants; I farm the rest myself.'

'But, I thought the gentry always had tenants.'

'Drink your soup, Amy – it'll get cold. Yes, it is the normal practice and it was at Eston until the 'eighties, when the depression began to bite.'

I was lost. 'The depression?'

'Surely you've heard of – ' He broke off. 'Of course you haven't: you're far too young.' He was closing up again.

I said loudly, 'I'd have heard of it if you told me.'

'What?'

'You're saying I haven't heard of it, but how can I hear of it, if you don't tell me?'

He said slowly, 'Do you *want* me to tell you?'

'Yes.'

'I don't quite know where to start.'

'Mebbe if you had a drink of brandy – '

He gave a small shake of his head. 'I don't need the effect of alcohol to enable me to expound on the state of British agriculture.' But he still didn't start.

I prompted, 'Sir Harry, at Borrell – *he* had tenants.'

'As I have at Pennings because the western half of the county weathered the depression rather better; rents stayed relatively stable.'

'Rents – you mean the rents the farmers do pay them as owns the land?' Sudden light dawned. 'Like the wages of the gentry.'

'Yes, that's right.'

I was getting so interested I'd hardly noticed that the soup plates had gone and been replaced by boiled turbot. 'But the rents went down at Eston?'

'All over southern and eastern England: the arable areas, the wheat-growing areas; but at Eston my father was still alive, and he refused to reduce the rents.'

I grappled with this idea along with the turbot, and concluded, 'So he couldn't get anyone to look after his farms, because there were others as were cheaper.' He nodded. 'But *why* did the rents go down everywhere else? Did they go on strike and refuse to pay?'

'Not exactly; they couldn't afford to pay.'

'But why not?' My mind jumped, struggling for an answer. 'They must have been able to sell their wheat. After all, everyone do eat bread, every day.'

'True.' He was watching me intently.

'But not for so much?' He nodded. I thought of fruit stalls in a market – a glut – and wondered, 'Then where did the extra come from?'

He half smiled. 'That was very quick of you, Amy. Now tell me where you think it was coming from.'

I recollected the map of the world on the wall of the school. 'Canada? Tis a new country.'

He was pleased with my progress. 'Yes – and America, and Russia.'

'But Russia's an old country. It could've come from there afore.'

'Heavy stuff, grain.'

'Did they build railways later in Russia, then?'

He laughed. 'Much later. In fact, they were still building them when this damned war broke out.'

'But Germany's in the way now, so they can't send their wheat by train. So has the price gone up again? It has, hasn't it – what with the ships from America being sunk as well? So more fields have to be ploughed, only all the men have gone to be soldiers, and ploughing, tis skilled work.' I shook my head. 'No wonder Mr Selby's in a caddle.' I looked down at my plate: I'd hardly started my fish, and he'd almost finished his. I seized my fork.

As I tried to eat my turbot and hollandaise sauce as quickly as I could without gobbling, Leo said quietly, 'You know, Amy, there are times when I can scarcely credit that you left school before your twelfth birthday.' I glowed with pleasure at the approval in his voice.

As soon as we were sitting in front of our chicken cutlets I asked, 'But why didn't you just put the rents down when you,' I remembered the word from Debrett, 'succeeded?'

'Because I was young and foolish. In any case, even with lowered rents it simply wasn't possible to find enough efficient farmers to take leases over that period – especially not for the larger farms. So I decided to farm them myself. Although I wasn't of age, George Burton's father was one of my trustees and he persuaded the other trustee to let me have my head.'

'But,' I hesitated, until his smile encouraged me to continue, 'but if the farmers couldn't sell the grain to make a profit, how could you?' Then my mind went racing on. 'Unless you knew some way of growing it cheaper?'

'That was the original idea; I decided that if I had a large enough farm, then I could practise economies of scale – invest in better machinery, for example. So I bought a steam ploughing set, and portable engines to do the threshing.'

'So it was like using a sewing machine instead of setting every stitch by hand? You don't need so many hands, so you save on wages.'

'Exactly – and that's where I ran into trouble, because one of the reasons why I'd chosen to farm myself was that if I didn't nobody would, and then there'd be no work for the men on the estate.' He put down his knife and fork. 'As a landowner, it is my duty to provide work, so I finished up in the ludicrous situation of using machinery which saved labour, but still employing the workers who would otherwise have been dispensed with.'

He rang the bell and Mr Tims came in to serve the beef. 'As a result of my reforms, the Home Farm was as spick and span as my rose garden. Every ditch cleaned before it became clogged, every hedge laid, every weed removed when it would have died of frost in any case. In addition, my wilder and more foolish schemes provided yet more employment. Irrigating part of the Down, for instance, kept a number of men busy digging the channels – and then provided work for others when the whole scheme had to be dismantled. Then there was the Eston stud: a short-lived folly! I'd heard that Lord Wantage had done something similar over on his estate in Berkshire, but the truth is, a man shouldn't dabble in horse-breeding unless he's seriously interested in horses, and I'm not. Those buildings must be the most expensive sheepfold in the

157

country now!' He laughed, and I thought what a shame it was that he was going away – just when he'd started talking to me properly.

When he'd finished his beef I said, 'I think you were right, though – folk do need work.'

He shrugged. 'It was no virtue on my part. I was fortunate in that I inherited no mortgages – and I've got the London property, which has greatly increased in value over recent years. I could afford to do what I did. Moreover, as I told you, with the Pennings estate being in the west of the county, rents there held up.'

As we began our trifle I asked, 'Why was it different over there?'

'Because – ' Then he broke off with a smile. 'No, Amy, use those quick wits of yours and work it out. I'll give you a clue if necessary.'

It was like a problem in arithmetic: at once I began to puzzle it out. 'They must grow something different from wheat. And it must be something that they *can't* grow in Canada.' I watched a tiny frown begin to form on his face and amended hastily, 'Or that doesn't travel well.' The frown vanished. 'And folk must eat a lot of it, regular,' I thought back to shopping in Lambeth, 'Vegetables?'

'Not at Pennings.'

I ticked off a list in my mind. 'Not meat, that comes frozen from New Zealand, and frozen meat, tis cheaper; cheese, butter – ' and suddenly I knew: 'Tis milk! All of London drinks milk, every day, it has to go up on the milk train. But there's a station at Eston, and trains to London. So why didn't you do the same here?'

'I have done, but we're on the edge of downland, so not all the fields are suitable. I couldn't make a complete transfer – and there's the employment question again: arable mops up the labour of more men. Besides,' he smiled, 'I had to make use of my precious steam ploughing set, having once invested in it.'

I finished my last spoonful of trifle before saying, 'I don't reckon as I've ever seen a steam ploughing set.'

'There are catalogues in the estate office. Perhaps you'd care to look at them sometime?'

'Aye, I would.' I smiled at him, as Mr Tims came in with the anchovy toasts.

When he'd finished his usual orange Leo said, 'I'll fetch a catalogue and bring it upstairs to show you over coffee.' As I went up to the nursery for Rose it struck me that that was the first time he'd ever suggested coming up to my sitting room for coffee; before, he'd always waited for my invitation.

My coffee grew cold while I pored over the illustrations and did sums in my head comparing the price of coal with the cost of a horse and its fodder – bearing in mind that the steam plough had six plough shares instead of one. But then there was the high first cost of the steam ploughing set; and if that money had been invested instead of spent on the plough it would have earned interest. Altogether I thoroughly enjoyed myself, and Leo was so patient, answering all my questions. I was sorry when the time came for Nella's run, and as I reluctantly closed the book I said, 'I'd like to see one o' those.'

'You shall. I'll take you up to the Home Farm with me after lunch tomorrow. I need to have a word with Arnott.' As he stood up he added, 'Do you think Rose would care for a stroll in the rose garden tonight?'

It had been raining earlier, and the scents hung heavy on the still air as we came into the autumn rose garden. I went first to greet Aimée Vibert, then we strolled from bush to bush, each enjoying our special favourites.

We were on our way back to the house when he said abruptly, 'I'm glad that you have some interest in farming, because the Eston estate will be yours one day.'

I turned to him in surprise, but I couldn't see his face in the twilight shadows as he explained, 'Because of the wide discrepancy in our ages, it is in the nature of things that you will outlive me.'

I still didn't understand. 'But – surely tis *his*.'

'Pennings is the Warminster estate, together with the property in London: Eston came from my mother and I am free to dispose of it howsoever I wish. Therefore I have left it to you, with the reversion to the children.'

'You're shivering, we'd better go in now.'

Chapter Twenty-Three

We went up to the Home Farm in the motor. It was further by road but we took the children; I had to take Rose, of course, and Flora begged to come too. On the way Leo told me about Mr Arnott.

'He's the son of one of George's most conservative tenants and he was always at loggerheads with his father, wanting to try out new ideas, so he said he'd had enough of the old country and emigrated to Canada. He'd been out there half a dozen years or so – managing to lose an eye in a saloon bar brawl in the meantime – when he heard that the girl he'd wanted to marry had been widowed, and he caught the next boat back. Arnott tried to persuade her to marry him and return to Canada – he'd established his own claim out there – but she refused, so he looked for work in England. George knew my head bailiff was ready to retire so he suggested I give young Arnott a trial. He's not the easiest of characters to deal with, but he's a very hard worker, and since the start of the war his colonial experience has been invaluable. Before that he was always telling me I wasted labour.' Leo pulled up at a gate, and got out to open it.

As he slid back in I asked, 'Did she marry him, then?' He looked puzzled so I added, 'The widow?'

'Yes, eventually. She couldn't have had an easy time, on her own with three youngsters.' He got out to refasten the gate and didn't speak again until the motor drew into the farmyard, scattering a group of flustered hens and two indignant geese. 'No doubt Arnott will be out in the fields. His wife should tell us where.'

I gazed at Mrs Arnott with interest as she appeared at the door of the trim-looking farmhouse. She was tall, with jet-black hair swept back from a pale oval face and she carried herself like a queen.

'Good afternoon, my lord, my lady. James is up in High Hams.'

'Thank you, Mrs Arnott. I'll just show Lady Warminster round the buildings. She hasn't visited the Home Farm before.'

A miniature version of Mrs Arnott suddenly came rushing through the doorway to seize Flora's hand; they scampered off across the yard and Leo and I followed them. The hens were back again, scratching in the straw, picking up insects with quick darting movements of their beaks. A watching cockerel ruffled his shining feathers in the sun before strutting over to select some particularly choice morsel.

Behind the cartsheds was a barn. Leo opened the small door set into the larger one and I stepped inside. I blinked in the dimness after the sun outside –

and gasped in astonishment: the steam plough was enormous, its great back wheel higher than my head. Leo chuckled at my surprise, and then began to explain what was what. Flora and her companion soon retreated to the superior delights of the chickens outside but I was fascinated. Walking all round the nearest of the two monsters I tried to match the small flat picture in the book with this looming reality.

As we came out again into the bright sunlight Leo said, 'It's even more impressive when it's in steam. You'll have to get the finer points demonstrated then – by Mrs Hawkins.' He glanced at me slyly.

'*Mrs* Hawkins?'

'Her father, Butty Williams, was in charge with Jem Hawkins as his mate; when he enlisted Judith Hawkins insisted on taking her husband's place.' He added, 'There is no end to the talents of the Williams family, her sister Jael took the place of the other son-in-law in the workshop.'

'I don't believe it, you're teasing me – especially not *Jael*!'

He was laughing outright now. 'I assure you, Amy, that that is her name. Williams gave his daughters names of power and they've certainly lived up to them. They're both big strong women, naturally – or they wouldn't have been able to take on those jobs.'

I glanced up at him under my eyelashes. 'You'll be telling me next as Jael's husband be called Sisera.'

He grinned. 'No, merely Bob. Just as well, as his wife is quite capable of hammering a tent peg through a man's temple. Though she is much the better-looking of the pair – quite Junoesque, in fact.'

'Fancy you noticing that!'

'Oh, I notice, Amy, I do notice.' I felt my cheeks go warm. He added briskly, 'However, I am truly grateful to those two Amazons for stepping so ably into the breach.' He cocked his head. 'I can hear voices, the men must be bringing a waggon in.'

I followed him round the barn to the stackyard. Several straw ricks had already been completed, and another one was in progress. As I stood looking at the horses pulling that waggon piled high with golden sheaves, the man leading the horses saw us, and lifted his cap. 'Arternoon, me lord.' I could hear the surprise in his voice as he added, 'Me lady.'

They began to unload, their strong brown arms moving in a steady rhythm as they worked. Leo said, 'It looks easy, but it's skilled labour to stack a waggon so it can be unloaded without mishap.'

'Aye, thic sheaves at bottom maun always be lengthways, wi' their heads to the middle – else load'll slip.'

He raised his bushy eyebrows. 'How do you know that, Amy?'

'Granfer told I, an' I used to watch him doing it when I took his nammet out to the field of a harvest time. He told me lots o' things about farming, did my Granfer.'

'Good. That'll be useful to you now, Amy. Come, we'll have a stroll up to High Hams and see Arnott.'

Flora didn't want to come with us. She was nicely settled in with her friend, and Mrs Arnott said she'd keep an eye on the pair of them, so Leo lifted Rose from my arms and we set off up the winding track. I'd never been this way before so my eyes were everywhere; Leo kept my curiosity satisfied. 'That shed below the water tower is where we kept the traction engine. Unfortunately it was requisitioned by the ASC – the Army Supply Corps – for baling forage; luckily all our other engines were only portables. The buildings beyond are the estate workshops. Jael Drewett will be busy there now.'

'Whenever does she find the time to do her housework?'

He smiled. 'The Williams sisters have many skills, but I gather the domestic arts are not numbered among them: they have always been much happier outdoors. But their children seem healthy enough, even if the sheets they sleep between are less than pristine white. Ah, here are the Jerseys.' He stopped at a field gate. The dainty fawn-coloured cows inside lifted their pretty heads to gaze at us. 'It's their milk we drink in the house; I bought them when Flora's arrival was – ah – imminent. I get Hill over to test them regularly with tuberculin – against the possibility of tuberculosis – though I'm glad to say that this disease hasn't reared its ugly head in any Eston herd as yet. Open air is the best preventative, and we keep our cattle outside as long as possible; though Arnott accuses me of pampering these creatures.'

I said to Rose, 'We seen them down in the park, baint we, Rose? Flora do like to pat 'em.'

'Yes, they're docile little beasts, but when the bull's running with them we have to keep them up in the field: Jersey bulls are notorious for their aggression. Regrettably, extreme docility in the female seems to encourage a correspondingly bad temper on the part of the male,' he glanced down at me, 'A character trait not confined to Jersey cattle, I'm afraid.'

I looked up at him, 'You baint *that* bad-tempered – not these days.'

'Perhaps because you aren't so docile – these days.'

I didn't quite know what to say to that; I was relieved when he went on, 'George Burton keeps a couple of Jerseys for the house, so he borrows the bull from time to time; that's where he's gone this week.'

'What's his name?'

'Antinous.' Antinous, the most handsome and yet the most treacherous of the suitors of Penelope. Leo added, unnecessarily, 'I name all the stud animals myself.'

I said briskly, 'Then I hope as you haven't called one o' the other bulls Odysseus – or there will be trouble.' He threw back his head and shoulders and laughed. Rose looked a bit put out at the disturbance so I took her back into my own arms. Besides, we could already hear the shouts of the harvesters, and it would be embarrassing for Leo to be seen carrying a baby.

As we came closer, I saw that a lot of the workers in the field were wearing khaki. Leo explained, 'Many of those soldiers still in England have been detailed to assist with the harvest, thank goodness: we'd be in serious trouble without them.'

I heard a man bawl out at the top of his voice, 'What's up wi' you – squint-eyed or summat? Get thic stook straight!'

'That's Arnott!'

'Well,' I said, 'Mrs Arnott, she did look main docile.'

Leo laughed. 'He's not always as short-tempered as that, but harvest is an anxious time.'

The machine at the end of the field turned and began to head towards us. I exclaimed, 'Why, tis a binder! I heard tell of 'em, but I never seen one afore – in Borrell the farmers only had reapers. Well, I never, baint it clever!' Instead of great wide sails, the binder had shorter, spindly ones, and they whirled round, nipping the stalks off and then tossing the corn into a canvas sheet before throwing it out again, all bound into sheaves. 'My, that *do* save some work, that do!' I couldn't take my eyes off it, until Mr Arnott came striding over the stubble to see us. He was a short, stocky man with a black patch over one eye, like a pirate. He raised his bowler hat. 'Arternoon, me lord, me lady.'

'Lady Warminster is admiring our self-binder, Arnott.'

He grunted. 'Does its job, when it's not broke down – tis main hard on the horses, though.'

Leo explained, 'The mechanism is driven by chains from the ground wheel, so the horses have to provide the power, as well as pull it.'

There were four horses, in pairs, and a man was riding on one of the back ones to drive them. Those horses did look as if they were working hard, even harder than the team of soldiers and boys picking up the sheaves and propping them into stooks. Hiles we called them in Borrell – and now half the field looked as if it were lined with miniature golden tents. Leo pointed to them. 'The corn has to dry, Amy, before it can be carted.'

I retorted, 'Well, o' course it do. Stack 'em now and the rick'll be on fire afore you knows it – wi' the heat on 'em. Three Sundays for oats to dry and wheat must stand for a fortnight in their hiles – depending on how much rubbish there is in it – weeds and suchlike.'

Leo looked surprised and I was feeling rather pleased with myself until he turned to Mr Arnott and said, 'By the way, Lady Warminster will be taking over the Home Farm accounts.'

I stared at Leo, but Mr Arnott only shrugged, 'So long as you don't expect *me* to do 'em, me lord.' His body stiffened. 'Look at that! Thic soldiers think as they're here on holiday. Hey you – ' He was back over the stubble again.

I turned to Leo. 'The Home Farm, tis too big for me to do the accounts.'

'You'll manage, Amy, you'll manage. Selby will give you any help you need.'

'But – ' Then Rose started tugging at my blouse.

Noticing, Leo said, 'We'd better find you somewhere to sit down.' He led the way over into the shade of a large elm, and spread his jacket for me to sit on. Leaning on its trunk I suckled Rose, while Leo lay stretched out in his shirt sleeves beside me, gazing up into the branches with a straw in his mouth. He'd been so at ease today; it had made such a difference to him, knowing he could join the army.

Out on the field two of the horses were changed over, and a man led the sweating pair into the shade of the next elm to rest. They stood there, heads hanging down. The man plodded over to us and took his cap off his glistening bald head. 'Arternoon, me lord, me lady.'

Leo pulled himself up. 'How are you, Jenkins? And how are your sons?'

'Had a letter from our Toby only yesterday – mebbe you'd care to read it?' He drew the doubled sheet out of his waistcoat pocket, and carefully smoothing it out, handed it to Leo. As Leo was scanning it he looked down at me and Rose. 'The missus was pleased to see you and the liddle maid t'other day, me lady. You maun call again afore too long.'

'Why, thank 'ee, Mr Jenkins.'

'My sister, Missus Hale that be, she says it were a real comfort talking to you about her George – and you shedding tears wi' her in her loss – so thank 'ee again.'

Leo looked at me sharply before handing the letter back. 'Your son appears to be finding things to amuse him, Jenkins.'

'Oh – ah – they do, don't they, the youngsters.' He hesitated a moment before enquiring, 'Be it true as *you* be a-going to join the army?'

Leo flushed. 'I hope to do so.'

Mr Jenkins wiped his sweaty hand on his trousers and then held it out, 'Good luck to 'ee, me lord.' Leo stood up and they shook hands. 'I'd best get thic 'osses watered, then.' He trudged off.

Leo said quietly, 'So you've been visiting the bereaved?'

''Tis all I could do.'

'And you weep with them for their children.'

'I cassent help it.'

'No, of course you can't.' He turned and said, 'I love you, Amy.'

'I – I – '

Very quickly he added, 'Don't be afraid. I won't say it again. I just couldn't help saying it once – but I won't say it again, I won't, I promise – because I do understand. Let's go back and collect Flora now, shall we?'

He started talking about cattle as we walked back and I relaxed again; he did understand. He told me he preferred Shorthorns for milking and Herefords for meat. 'If we take a slight detour, by this track, you can have a look at some of my Shorthorns.' He patted his jacket pocket. 'Luckily I remembered my crusts today.'

We came to a gate. 'There they are – fine-looking beasts, aren't they?'

They were fine animals, and the bull was the finest of them all. There was nothing graceful about him, with his massive red-brown shoulders and heavy haunches; yet he had his own dignity as he plodded forward a few paces to position himself in front of his cows, almost as if to guard them.

I said, 'My, baint he a handsome fellow, what be – '

'Percy.'

'Percy!' I was suspicious. '*You* never named him Percy.'

'That's what Arnott calls him.'

I thought for a moment before exclaiming, 'But you named him for Perseus, who did rescue the maid Andromeda from the dragon.'

Leo smiled. 'And he's defending his heifers now from the dragon of Nella. He doesn't like dogs, in case they snap at the heels of a cow in calf.'

'Nella wouldn't do that.'

'No, and he knows that really, but he won't allow even her near them. Back, Nella.' She retreated obediently down the track and sat down. The bull gave a little nod, as if satisfied, and came lumbering a few paces towards us. Leo began to climb the gate. In alarm I put out my hand to stop him but he smiled. 'There's no cause for anxiety, Amy. Percy and I are old friends. Besides, under that ton of bone and muscle lies a very sweet nature.' He sat poised on the gate, waiting for me to remove my hand. As soon as I did so he dropped off on the other side and began to walk forward. Percy started to move. Bull and man walked towards each other, with the same heavy yet firm gait. As they met, Leo reached into his pocket and the broad nose of the bull came down, snuffling. Watching Perseus eat a crust from Leo's big hand, I realized why I'd so often had to shake crumbs out of Leo's jacket pocket – but I'd always thought it was the horses he'd been feeding!

Seeing the two of them together like that, I suddenly thought how alike they were, bull and man, both with heavy shoulders and strong flanks. Leo gave a final pat to the massive roan neck. The bull waited a moment, then backed away with a slight toss of his head, as if to say, 'Thank you', before turning and walking back to his heifers. I let out my breath.

Leo turned, too, and walked back to me. As he put his hand on the gate and began to climb over he said, 'Some bulls are born short-tempered, but most of them get like that from being cooped up in a pen. I won't permit that, it's cruel and unnecessary. Here, I'll carry Rose the rest of the way.'

When we'd arrived home I said, 'Thank 'ee, Leo, I enjoyed my afternoon so much.'

He flushed with pleasure. 'Good. I want to spend this week having a last look round the estate, so I'll take you and the children with me sometimes.'

So that became the pattern: we visited a different part of the estate each afternoon, and in the evening after dinner we looked at the maps in the estate office. The office was in the corner of the service courtyard, overlooking the back drive leading to the stables. It smelt of Mr Selby's pipe and it was quiet and private, with ivy hanging down over the two windows. The estate records were shelved on one wall, with the maps stored in a cupboard underneath. Leo would put his spectacles on, then spread the maps out on the huge leather-topped desk, but they were so large I had to kneel on the seat of the chair to see the upper corners. I was fascinated; I'd never seen maps on that scale before. Leo taught me to read them the first night. 'See, here's the farmhouse at the Home Farm, the barn behind, the track leading up to High Hams.' We traced our route of that day. Then we came back to Eston, and he began to take me through the woods. 'There's the field boundary, the path curves here, round, up past that cottage . . .'

As he explained, the map made a picture in my head, and fitted the world I'd seen.

I said, 'Show me the footpath that winds round to the lane behind the church.'

'Here.' His black-furred finger stabbed the map. I craned to look, and in doing so I touched his shoulder – and felt it go rigid under my arm.

At that moment I knew I had a choice. I could move away easily, casually, to look at some other part of the map; and if I did so I knew he would never let himself come so close again. His face was turned a little, so I couldn't see the expression in his eyes, but he was so close that I could see the dark pits where the black stubble was already seeking to grow again after his evening shave. I could see, too, the curve of his ear and the way the hair above it was trying to curl, just like Rose's; because he was Rose's father, and my husband. Gently I shifted a little, until the full weight of my body rested against his shoulder; then he began to speak again. 'The path dips here, through this coppice, then comes out into the open . . .'

Each evening after that we went to the estate office and I traced the route we'd followed that day. Then he would show me where we were to go the following afternoon, and each evening he would arrange the map so that I had to crane a little and lean against his shoulder should I choose to study the far corner. And each evening I did choose to study that far corner; because he understood now. So we sat close together, looking at the maps. But otherwise we never touched.

One day when the weather was set fine he brought round the governess cart with Bessie between the shafts. I'd never seen him driving a horse before. He jumped down and gave the reins to the stable boy while he lifted in Flora, the rug, and Rose's basket. 'Can you manage, Amy?'

'Aye.' When I was settled with Nella at my feet he sprang up and took the seat opposite me. 'Giddup,' he called, and we rolled smoothly off. 'Thank goodness Bessie is too old to be requisitioned. Now, we'll go down to Harbin's Bottom first. I took it back from the plough in '93 . . .'

We talked about farming, always about farming. Every field, every hedge, almost every ditch had its own story. He talked of the fertility of the land, he talked of the damage done by the war: 'We've had to take too much from it too quickly. You must give to the land, as well as take from it.' He sighed, before continuing, 'But our country needs bread today, so the grain must be grown.'

We drove down the winding lane to the small cluster of cottages in the bottom of the river valley. We left Bessie in the mill-yard, where the white-dusted miller wiped his floury hand before offering it to Leo. 'I hears as you're off to be a soldier, me lord – so I wishes you all the best, then.' We walked up the narrow path beside the great splashing wheel, Flora firmly clasped to Leo's chest, Rose to mine. Then on beside the swiftly flowing millrace to the deep water behind the dam. I stared down into its dark and secret depths, then hastily stepped back, frightened of its power.

Leo led the way on to where the river flowed between its lush green banks, under the damp shade of the willows and out into the sunlit edge of the field where half a dozen of his red and white Herefords stood knee-deep in the cool water. We stopped to look at them. 'They're hardy animals, but not in the first rank as milkers – though Herefords are remarkably free from tuberculosis . . .'

As we came back to fetch Bessie, Leo said, 'Just one more visit this afternoon. There's something you and Flora will enjoy seeing.' He smiled. 'And so will I.'

He drove us into a trim farmyard, 'Jackson is one of my tenants; you'll recall that we looked at his land on the map last night.'

A golden dog came running to meet us. 'Why, tis Nella's twin!'

Leo laughed. 'No, her son. I bred her – let me think – it would be the year before you first came to Eston; Jackson took one of her pups.'

Watching the two dogs greet each other I asked, 'Is he what you wanted to show us, then?'

'No, that's something more unusual. Jackson's eldest boy has reared an otter cub by hand.' When I heard that I was even more excited than Flora. I'd never seen an otter before, because normally they only came out at night – except when they were being hunted.

The otter was beautiful, with her soft brown fur and quick, lithe body; she frisked and played around Bob Jackson's legs and the boy told us proudly, 'She don't miss a trick, she don't – she can smell the fish in thic pail.' He grinned down at the otter. 'You got to work for these, my girl, and show her ladyship what a good liddle swimmer thee bist.'

As soon as we reached the river bank the boy threw in the first of the silver trout, and in one smooth movement, the otter was in the water, chasing after it. A quick dive and then in a moment her sleek dark head triumphantly broke the surface, her catch in her mouth. 'Ah, baint she beautiful – the most beatifullest creature I ever did see!'

I watched entranced. She was so swift and sure in her movements: one moment she would be a slim dark shape gliding silently under the surface, with only a chain of bubbles marking her passing, then the next she'd be rearing up to look us straight in the eye, demanding another trout. When all the fish were finished, Bob nodded to his dog, 'Your turn now, Tom.' With a streak of golden fur he was in the water, too, and the pair of them, otter and dog, were romping together: playing, teasing, frolicking – so light-hearted and happy. The boy turned to me. 'She were only a liddle mite when I found her, so twere Tom as taught her to swim.'

I asked, 'And what be her name?'

He grinned. 'I calls her Tinker cos she's allus on the move.'

Back in the trap on my way home I thanked Leo; he'd had the fish sent down specially for Tinker. She normally ate rabbit, Bob Jackson told me.

Leo became reminiscent. 'The first otters I ever saw were a whole family, fishing by moonlight. George's father took the pair of us boys down the Wylie to look for them. I'm afraid that later he regretted his kindness, since I was so charmed by what I saw that I've never allowed the otter hounds to hunt my rivers.'

I said fervently, 'I'm main glad o' that.'

'It's been an extremely unpopular stance, Amy. However, I justify it on the grounds that otters breed all the year round, so there can be no open season. But the truth is much simpler – I fell in love with the creatures that night. Amy, look over there,' he raised his whip to point, 'All that ground was pasture before the war . . .'

The next day he took me to see his sheep. On the open Down we left the motor and walked across the springy turf to where the sheep grazed, and for the first time I saw Dorset Horn ewes with their curving horns like the brims of elegant hats, and the ram with his great swirling loop of horn either side of his lively white face. 'He's in fine fleece today, Amy, almost golden in the sun. Aren't you going to ask me his name?'

I glanced up into Leo's teasing eyes before turning to say, 'Thee bist a fine ram, Jason,' and Leo's laughter told me I'd guessed aright. 'They lamb a couple of months earlier than the other flocks . . .'

We met their shepherd, an old man with pure white side whiskers and pale, far-sighted eyes. He raised his hat.

'Arternoon, me lord, me lady.' His blue eyes went up to where Flora rode high on Leo's shoulder. 'Arternoon, young 'un – have 'ee come to see my dawg, then?' Flora's blonde curls bounced as she nodded her head. The shepherd gave a high piercing whistle, and an arrow of black and white came streaking towards him, long and low. As Leo lowered my daughter to the ground the sheepdog eyed Nella warily; but both were too well-trained even to sniff at each other.

'Best of my Dainty's pups. You remember my Dainty?'

'Yes, Caleb, I do – a fine bitch.'

'Aye, she were.'

'And how is Mrs Brewer?'

'A touch of the rheumatics, we'm neither of on us getting any younger.'

'And your grandson?'

'At a place called Ypers – been crossed through with a red pencil, only our Mary, she puzzled it out, the way a mother does.' His old eyes creased with worry. 'I remembers how he came up on the Down wi' I when he were no bigger'n' your liddle maid.' He sighed. 'The missus, she prays fer our Davy every night. I dunno. Seems to me as if there were a God he maun 'a gone back home now, wi' what's going on in thic old world. How be your son getting on, me lord?'

'He's still on sick leave.'

'Aar. I 'ears as *you'm* thinking about going yourself?' Leo gave a small nod of assent. 'Then good luck to 'ee, me lord.' He held out his hand.

I saw Leo differently, that last week. Now I saw him as a man who cared for his land, and the people on it; who looked after his estate and saw it as held in trust from the past – and for the future.

Once I said, 'You never talked to me about farming afore.'

'I didn't know you were interested. I assumed you only wished to speak of the children and the roses.' And when he said that I realized he was seeing me differently, too.

I looked forward to each afternoon, not just because I wanted to learn more about the estate but also because for the first time it was as though we were a real family, Leo, the children and I. But always when he spoke to the men in the fields would come those final words: 'I hears as you be going to join up, me lord,' followed by the out-thrust hand: 'Good luck to 'ee, then.'

And all too soon the last day came.

Chapter Twenty-Four

'Where are we going today, Leo?'

'I'd like to go up on the Down again.' We drove part of the way, then he stopped the motor on the edge of the wood. 'This is a favourite walk of mine; I'll carry Rose until Flora becomes tired.'

Flora ran from flower to flower, asking names. Then she'd suddenly stop to crane upwards, her eyes following the red flash of a squirrel's tail. Leo scarcely spoke today; he'd say a word or two about the timber, or about coppicing, and then he'd fall silent again.

The trees were beeches, standing tall and straight either side of the grassy lane, their upper branches meeting over our heads to form a dappled canopy of green and blue. Already we could see the open air in front of us, and soon we came to the sweep of the open Down. Flora ran on ahead, circling round and round like a puppy, then back to Leo, arms upheld, 'Ride, Papa, wanna ride!' I took Rose from him, and bound her safely round me in a shawl as he swung a squealing Flora high into the air and set her on his shoulder. Firmly anchoring her legs with his arms, he strode on, her little hands gripping his neck while she rested her chin on the crown of his panama. The ribbons of her sunbonnet flapped in the breeze; the air was never still up here on the Down.

When we reached the top of the ridge she clamoured to be set down, and she and Nella went running across the springy turf. Taking his jacket off, Leo spread it on the ground. 'Rest a while, Amy. Rose is getting heavy these days.'

'Aye, thee bist a fine big girl, baint thee, my Rose?' I lowered myself to the ground and he sat beside me, but a little way off on the grass, his eyes on Nella and Flora. With the scent of thyme warm in the air I watched the restless blue butterflies flit from one purple thistle to another. Larks were singing overhead, and as I gazed up, one dropped like a stone from the sky – so swiftly it looked as if it would be dashed to pieces on the ground – then its wings spread out and it glided those last few yards safely to earth.

Beside me Leo said, 'I've always found comfort on these downs. They are so open, so empty, as if mankind had never existed. The world is left below, up here there is only the sky and the birds and the forgiving turf under one's feet.' He fell silent again as abruptly as he'd spoken.

Flora came running back to drag us to our feet and we walked on, with the shadows of clouds chasing each other across the grass in front of us. Leo kept by my side, curbing his long strides to suit my shorter paces. There was no sense of hurry, yet I knew he wasn't roaming aimlessly, and his steps quickened as we rounded the shoulder of the Down and saw the valley below.

The whole of Eston lay there beneath us: fields, woods, village and church. And there, a little apart but still close, as if guarding them, stood the house: his home.

For a long time he stood gazing down, as if trying to fix that picture in his mind for ever. Then he said, 'Look after it for me while I'm away, Amy.'

'Aye, I will.'

We came down by another path, clinging steeply to the edge of the slope; then we walked back through a small farm where one of Leo's foremen came out of the shippon to wish him godspeed, while his wife gave us cups of water to drink, cold from the well.

As he opened the door of the motor for me outside the house, Leo said, 'I promised Selby I'd have a final word with him – I'll see you at dinner, Amy.'

He was very quiet over dinner. As soon as we'd finished he followed me up to my sitting room for coffee. 'I'll hold Rose while you pour.' She babbled to him cheerfully as she played with her feet, so I left them together and sat down opposite with my own cup.

Leo looked up from his daughter's face. 'Obviously Selby will get in touch with me in the event of a major problem, but I've told him to consult you about day-to-day matters.'

My cup went down with a bump. 'But Leo, I don't think I – '

He ignored my interruption. 'He's an able man but he fusses, and finds it difficult to reach a final decision, so you will have to do that for him. Especially as he and Arnott don't always see eye to eye. You'll have to act as umpire if the need arises.'

'But I can't – '

'Yes you can; I have every confidence in you, Amy. By the way, it will be easier for you to get round the estate if you use the motor. The garage in Tilton will send a man over to teach you to drive.'

'But – '

'I've often noticed how dextrous you are, so it won't take long to pick it up. But don't take the children out with you until you're quite confident. Your Mama,' he told Rose, 'is an extremely able young woman, and your Papa is not going to listen to any of her protestations of weakness.' So I was silenced.

Then he suggested, without looking at me, 'Perhaps you'd care for a final look at the maps – just to get everything clear in your head.'

'Aye, we'll do that.'

Down in the tobacco-smelling estate office I climbed up to kneel on the chair; he drew his up beside me and put his spectacles on. As we studied the maps I glanced at his face: it was tense and unhappy. Deliberately I moved over to lean against his shoulder before asking, 'What train will you be catching tomorrow?'

'The nine o' clock.' He paused before adding, 'I shall lose my nerve if I leave it any later.' Then his broad finger pointed. 'Here's the beech wood we walked through today . . .'

At last he began to roll up the map. 'Nella is waiting for her walk.'

'I'll fetch Rose.'

He said quickly, 'She'll be asleep – don't disturb her.' So we went out in to the rose garden for the last time, just the two of us.

Inside the autumn rose garden we made our way from one favourite bloom to another, not talking, just looking, touching, breathing in the scent of each rose in turn. Coming to the corner, Nella slipped into the little round room set in the wall there. Following her, we sat side by side, looking out into the darkening garden through a veil of roses.

It was he who broke the silence. 'I'm a coward, Amy – I don't want to go.'

There was no reply I could make, because I knew he had to go; he would never be able to live with himself if he didn't. So instead I moved very gently along the seat, until my shoulder rested against his arm. He stayed quite still, not even turning his head. I looked up at his profile: strong like a hawk, like the generals; but they were portraits of heroes, while he was a living, breathing man – and frightened. I reached out to where his hand lay on his knee, and as my fingers touched it, his answered, twining themselves around mine. So we sat, holding hands in the scented darkness.

It grew chill and I shivered. His hand tightened a moment round mine before slowly releasing my fingers. 'You're getting cold, Amy. It's time I took you in.'

At the foot of the stairs he wished me good night, and I replied before beginning to mount them. But halfway up I knew I couldn't go on. I paused for a moment, thinking – and the answer came at once. Turning I saw he still stood in the hall, watching me. Quickly I went back to him.

'Leo, tonight I'll bide with thee.' His whole face changed; I couldn't bear to look at him, but I'd made up my mind. 'Rose and I will keep thee company.' He was struggling to speak, but before he could get the words out I added, 'Only I'll leave her in the cradle at first, and come by myself, so you can act as husband to me.'

'But I – I – must – not – '

I said quietly, 'There won't be no harm taken, just this once, because o' Rose. Being as I'm still nursing her my monthlies haven't come back. They didn't afore, until after Flora were weaned.'

I saw that moment of hope before he shook his head. 'No, there may still be a risk – '

'Then you can use one o' they little gloves, to be on the safe side.'

He went very still before admitting slowly, 'Yes – I – suppose – I could. But, Amy, are you willing?'

'I just said I was. Tis why I offered. After all tis only natural for a man to want to – '

He broke across my words. 'No, Amy, please listen.' He spoke very clearly, 'Are you willing to allow me to make love to you? Because that is what it will be.' The tread of the stair seemed to shift under my feet. He was watching me intently. 'If it is merely wifely duty, I would rather – not.'

'But,' I whispered, 'you did say you understood.'

He closed his eyes for a moment. When he opened them again his voice was firm. 'Yes, I do understand. But – I love you, I can't help it – so it will be – love.'

I felt as though I were teetering on the brink of the deep mill pond, terrified of falling in. I wanted to step back, but he was going away tomorrow, he was my husband, so what else could I do? I said quietly, 'I'll come to your room, soon as I've fed Rose and settled her.' I almost ran up the stairs.

I was very nervous; it seemed a long time since he'd used to come to my room. When I'd settled Rose in her cradle I walked across to the dressing room door. Then I realized my hair was still in plaits. Hastily I ran to the mirror, undid the tape bows, shook out my hair and swiftly brushed it out. Returning to his dressing room door, I opened it and walked through, into my husband's bedroom.

He was sitting up in bed, waiting, his head turned towards the door. I saw the blaze of excitement light up his face as I came into the room and it frightened me, so I made myself brisk. 'Rose's asleep, I'll get in wi' you now.' Lifting the bedclothes, I clambered in; we sat side by side, not touching.

He didn't move towards me, but instead he said, 'I'm not sure I know – how to – make love to a woman.' He sounded almost despairing.

Quickly I suggested, 'Mebbe if we had a little cuddle, to start with . . . ' I put my arms around his neck and at once he caught hold of me, clutching me so tightly I could scarcely breathe. Then he realized and loosened his grip. 'Amy, I'm not sure if I can – ' He was as uncertain as a young boy.

Still brisk, I told him, 'You did it afore.'

'But – ' He was getting himself into a real old state. It was obvious one of us had to take charge – and just as obvious that it wasn't going to be him. I instructed, 'You take your pyjama bottoms off and I'll pull my nightie up, and we'll lie nice and close – then I dare say your rod'll remember how to do it.' He struggled with his pyjamas under the bedclothes and then we were lying close. I put my arms around his behind, and feeling the silkiness of his hair, it was only natural to stroke it. Meanwhile his rod obviously was remembering, and quickly, too. I whispered, 'There, what did I tell you? All you got to do now is slip him inside, I 'low he'll know what to do after that.'

'Yes, Amy,' and to my relief, I realized he was almost laughing. 'But I must put on – ' He turned over, and fumbled in the chest of drawers beside his bed. When he turned back again and put his arms around me his rod felt different – cold; but if it made him happier . . . I turned on my back and felt his fingers gently easing open my cunny, and then he was inside. It was a bit of a shock that first time, as it always was. He asked me anxiously, 'Am I hurting you?'

'No, no, tis fine. Tis quite comfortable now.' And oddly enough, it was. I'd never liked having It done to me, but it didn't seem to be bothering me tonight. I told him, 'You get on and enjoy yourself.'

I thought he muttered, 'Thank you,' but his voice was all muffled in my hair. I didn't think about my sewing, as I'd always done before: it didn't seem polite. So instead I just concentrated on stroking his behind, which he seemed to like; in fact he seemed to be enjoying it altogether now he'd got properly started. He kept giving little gasps of delight, and I was pleased. It was such a simple thing to do really, to give him so much pleasure, that I wished I'd thought of it sooner.

I held him extra close as he began spending himself, and gave him a little hug when he'd finished, just to let him know he was welcome to stay as long as he wanted – but, of course, he had to pull away quite soon to get the little glove off. When he'd seen to that he lay back against the pillow as if he were exhausted. Then he murmured, 'Thank you, Amy, thank you.'

I whispered back, 'Let's have a cuddle now, shall we?'

'Please.' We put our arms around each other for a proper cuddle – and Rose woke up.

It was only a little cry at first, a questioning, 'Where are you?' but then the 'Where are you?' got more puzzled, became surprised, and Leo knew that I never left her calling, so his arms had already loosened. 'She wants a cuddle, too. I'll go and fetch her.' I came back with Rose and put her between us. It was strange lying like this, and knowing it was he who had begotten her.

After a little while he said, 'I am so heavy, and I'm not used to a child in the bed, suppose I fell asleep and crushed her – '

'Then I'll turn over with my back to you, and cuddle her the way I usually do, and then you can cuddle the pair of us.' So that's what we did.

I woke in the night and couldn't lift my head; he must have been sleeping with his cheek in my hair – then he realized and released me. 'Go back to sleep, Amy.' But before I dozed off I felt it: the flutter of butterfly wings on my cheek as he kissed me. But I knew that if I moved, and he guessed I was still awake, he would stop at once. I lay quite still, sensing the gentle touch of his secret kisses.

I woke at dawn. Leo was awake, too. 'I'd best go, now, Leo.' As I pulled my hair free and sat up I saw his eyes were dark with anxiety, with fear of the unknown. Reaching out, I gently stroked his cheek, all bristly now with his overnight growth of stubble. 'You must have a good breakfast afore you go. I'll bring Flora down and we'll all eat together.' Then I left him.

We all sat round the table in the morning room; it was the first time he and I had ever broken our fast together. I kept Rose on my lap, she enjoyed a spoonful of egg in the mornings now. But her father didn't have much more than that himself; despite my urging he only drank cup after cup of coffee. His face was haggard: he looked every year of his age this morning.

He gave his crooked, almost-smile. 'I keep telling myself that even

174

Aldershot can't be worse than my first term at school,' though that thought didn't seem to be giving him much comfort; I was grateful for the distraction of Flora's excitement at eating downstairs.

But in the hall later, her lower lip trembled and the big tears came squeezing out of her eyes as he said, 'Goodbye, Flora.'

Ellen took her hand, soothing her, as Mr Tims announced, 'The dog cart is at the door, my lord.'

We went out on the step. Leo put his hand down to rest for a moment on Flora's blonde curls, then turned to bend over Rose, touching her cheek. He looked up from his daughter at me. 'Goodbye, Amy.' And I knew I couldn't just let him go like that.

I swung round to Ellen. 'Do 'ee take Rose, I'm going down to the station. Flora, Mama won't be long.' He held out his hand and I climbed up into the dog cart; he followed me up, and Nella leapt in behind us. Leo sat with his hand on her head as we bowled along the drive. Mrs Whittle was standing by the open gate. 'Goodbye, my lord – good luck.'

As we drove down the village street hands were raised to lift caps and knees were bent in bobs. 'All the best, me lord', 'Good luck', 'Godspeed'. Children running to school skidded to a halt as the trap passed them; pinafore skirts dipped in bobs, and caps tugged off tousled hair.

We turned into the station. Mr Soutar came forward, hand outstretched. 'Goodbye, my lord. I wish you the best of luck.' He escorted us on to the platform, and then withdrew a discreet distance, leaving Leo and me alone together.

Leo turned towards to me. 'Thank you for coming down with me, Amy. And thank you, too, for last night.' I felt my cheeks grow warm as he continued, 'I would be grateful if you could spare the time to send me reports on the children, and the estate.' He added quickly, 'If that's not too much trouble for you.'

'O' course it's not, only I don't know where to write to.'

'I'll send my direction to Selby, he will inform you.'

After that we just stood there, neither of us knowing what to say; then I saw the plume of grey smoke.

When the train was in, the porter picked up Leo's bag and put it in the rack of a first-class compartment, then stood to one side, holding the door open for him.

'Goodbye, Amy.'

'Goodbye, Leo.' He turned and walked towards the train; his humpback and twisted shoulder seemed very noticeable today, and he looked so lonely.

Suddenly I ran after him. 'Leo!' The guard was waiting, with his green flag in one hand and whistle in the other, but I didn't care. I remembered Waterloo – the soldier – the butterfly wings. Reaching my arms up to him I said, 'Leo, thee hasn't kissed I goodbye.'

175

His face was stunned. 'You want *me* to kiss you?'

'Aye.' Raising myself on tiptoe I put my hands to pull his head down. His face came closer and closer until I felt the butterfly wings brush my cheek. Then all at once he pulled away and almost threw himself up into the waiting train. The porter slammed the door and there was the shrill sound of the whistle, then slowly the train drew away. Leo's huge lopsided figure filled the window, his hand raised.

I lifted mine in reply, and kept on waving until the back of the last carriage dwindled into the distance.

Chapter Twenty-Five

I felt so guilty as I comforted Flora. Young as she was she knew about soldiers, she knew they went away for a long time, and now her Papa had gone for a soldier, too. So she sobbed at her loss, because she did love him so much. But as I cuddled her and kissed the tears from her soft cheeks, I felt more and more guilty – because I knew I didn't love him. Respect, trust, affection: all these I could give him – but not love. And I knew I held the reason in my arms. Even now, just after my husband had kissed me goodbye, my treacherous thoughts kept returning to Frank.

I told myself that since Leo would soon be in the army, too – both of them serving their country – that I had no right to think of Frank. But there was a difference. Frank was a young man, tall and straight, so he would go back to France, into danger, whereas Leo would only ever serve at a base hospital. So I still couldn't stop thinking of Frank – however guilty I felt.

That guilt drove me down to the estate office in the afternoon. I knew Mr Selby wouldn't want me to do the Home Farm accounts, I'd only be a nuisance to him. I didn't think I could cope with them myself, but Leo had wanted me to do it, so I went.

Mr Selby stood up politely as I entered, but it was obvious that he disapproved of my interfering. I could see it in his face, even though he masked it with a formal smile. I'd decided to ask if I could simply take away the account books to look at, which would be less of a nuisance to him than my staying and pestering him with questions. Politely he handed them over, and I carried them apprehensively away.

I didn't get a chance to look at them until the children were in bed, then I carried them over to my desk. There wasn't even room there to lay them all out because there were six of them: Day Book, Cash Book, Ledger, Corn Account, Stock Account, Charge and Discharge. I quailed before their leather-bound haughtiness, and although when I opened them I could understand some of the words and terms used, there were many more I couldn't. I'd thought I'd known about farming from listening to Granfer, and then I'd listened so hard to Leo – but I'd never heard of guano; and I only knew of washing soda – whatever was nitrate of soda? I began to panic: I'd let Leo down, I couldn't do what he wanted. Words that I thought I understood like valuation and inventory I began to lose confidence over; I knew what a creditor was, but were 'sundry creditors' what I thought they were? I hardly dared even look at the figures, my nerve had gone completely – and when I did and saw how high the sums were I just closed the books, and went over to Rose and took her off to bed.

Next morning I went down to Mr Selby to confess. 'I did want to help you, because Leo asked me to – he *wanted* me to – only I baint never even *heard* o' guano, or nitrate o' soda.'

'My dear Lady Warminster, it's hardly likely that you would have done.' I was crushed. Then he added, 'I hadn't heard of them myself when I first went to assist my uncle in his office. But Lord Warminster wanted you to help because you have a natural talent for figures – those were his very words. And he said you'd had prior experience of book-keeping.'

'Those were *dressmaking* books, so I knew what voile or galatea or twill were.' I admitted miserably, 'These books, I never even looked at the figures, because I didn't know what they stood for.'

He took out his watch, then said, 'I've half an hour to spare, perhaps if I looked at them with you now ... Guano, by the way, is simply a type of imported manure.'

Surprise at that diverted me. 'But don't we have enough o' that already? And with the war on surely it must be main dear to import?'

He actually smiled properly. 'Yes, you're quite right, we do need to consider other options. Now, if you'd care to take a seat –'

He was really very kind. And the odd thing was, as soon as I had Mr Selby to explain to me, I didn't seem to need as much explanation. In fact he was pleased that I already knew the difference between a chilver and a gimmer, and a wether and a tup.

After that the figures began to march like soldiers again, all back into their lines. It was just that they were very big soldiers, that was all: once I'd got used to seeing £376 at the end of a line instead of £3 7s 6d, it wasn't really all that different. There was a ready reckoner in the drawer I could use, but I'd only ever referred to them for checking, because the teacher at Borrell had said they made your brain lazy – and Mr Selby laughed, and told me his uncle had always said the same.

After half an hour he left me alone with the books. By the time he came back they were still a foreign language, but one I thought I could learn, given a bit of time.

I spent another hour with Mr Selby in the estate office that afternoon, and he seemed pleased with my progress. 'Rome wasn't built in a day, Lady Warminster, but you've laid the foundations. Lord Warminster was quite right, you are a nimble-witted young lady.' I glowed with pride.

We arranged that I would sit with Mr Selby while he did this month's accounts, and that in the meantime I should read an article on the keeping of Home Farm Accounts in the 1910 issue of *The Country Gentleman's Estate Book*. 'It does, of course, refer to the more usual Home Farm of two to three hundred acres, but I'm sure you'll find it helpful.'

'I'll read it tonight, Mr Selby, thank 'ee, thank 'ee so much.'

Just as I was leaving, the postman arrived, and Mr Selby called me back.

'Lady Warminster, here is a letter from your husband, who will have enclosed his address for you.' He had, and now I had something else to worry about: I'd never written a letter to Leo before, and I had no idea how to start.

I got as far as 'Dear Leo', then I stopped. 'What shall I say to thy Dada, Rose?' She beamed up at me from her cradle; she didn't really care now she'd been fed. Sighing, I picked up my pen and dipped it in the inkwell. I managed half a sheet, but it seemed a very dull letter, saying only that the children were well, and so was Nella; I was well, and Mr Selby had been showing me how to help him with the accounts. Then I added that I hoped he was well, and signed off, 'Your obedient wife, Amy.' It did seem a rather short letter, but at least I'd got it finished in time for the next post, so it would get to him quickly. I took it down to Mr Tims myself.

Leo's reply arrived a couple of days later: it was even shorter. He was glad the children and I were in good health and that I was learning to do the accounts.

I hadn't said I was learning to *do* them; I wasn't at all sure about that, with so much money involved. But Mr Selby had said it would be helpful to him to have someone to check with a head for figures. We both knew Leo didn't have much of a head where figures were concerned. Only as I'd said, 'He's main clever at reading Greek.' Mr Selby had agreed. 'He's a considerable classical scholar.'

'And he do know so much about roses.'

'Yes, he does indeed. Lord Warminster is a man of wide interests and talents.'

We both nodded our heads together. I couldn't think why I'd been so nervous of Mr Selby before; he was a very kind person when you got to know him – just rather shy.

Clara had told me his wife had died some years ago, and they'd never had any children, so she thought he must be lonely of an evening. 'Though he's very friendly with Dr Matthews, the doctor being a widower, too.' She sighed. ''Tis hard for a man when he loses his wife, especially when he's not as young as he was.' I thought of Leo. The French Countess had only died six years ago but he'd lost her long before that. Poor Leo.

I told Mr Selby I'd better run up and see how Rose was, and he replied that although he knew Lady Flora, he'd hardly ever seen Lady Rose. I didn't need the hint twice. 'I'll run and fetch her down now.'

After admiring her he said, 'She's very like her proud Papa.'

'She is, isn't she? For all she's so pretty.' Then I added hastily, 'But Leo, he'd be a fine handsome man if he hadn't been born twisted.'

Mr Selby gave a little cough before saying, 'Lady Warminster, I don't wish to presume, but I would like to say how pleased I am that you have been such a helpmate to Lord Warminster. I know your being at Eston has transformed his life.' I stood there holding Rose, fighting back the tears; because I knew that however much I helped Leo, I couldn't give him what he really wanted.

I went upstairs to write another letter to him. I'd decided to write faithfully every week with news of the children, as he'd asked, and he'd obviously decided on the same interval. I'd had three letters from him by now, and I kept them carefully in my desk – but they didn't really say anything. He just commented on what I'd already told him about the children. Before he'd gone he'd arranged for the delivery of a little Shetland pony for Flora, and I'd written to tell him how fond she was of her pony, and how she'd called it Porridge, because of his colour. I'd said she was having a little ride every day in the basket seat Mr Tyson had found for her in the harness room. He wrote back to say he was pleased, and we'd have to decide whether to put her into a side saddle or a cross saddle when she outgrew the basket; more women were riding astride these days, and he thought that might be safer. Then he wrote that he'd consult Annabel on the matter, so he was clearly writing to her. He always had done, but he didn't seem to be able to think of anything much to write to me, any more than I could to him.

I did try to ask him how he was finding it in the army, and he wrote back the next time that it was 'Very different from my old life, as I'd expected; however, it is also at variance from previous expectations.' But I still didn't know whether he'd settled down or not, although I spent ages trying to puzzle it out from his stilted phrases. I sighed. I knew he'd wanted to enlist, but it was a shame he'd done it just when we'd been getting to know each other better; now he'd gone away I could feel the barrier rising up between us again with every brief, formal letter.

I stood up to go and look out of the window at his rose garden – and saw the picture of Clytie. I just stood there, thinking of Frank, remembering the first time I'd seen him, remembering the last time – I knew he didn't love me, I knew it – but I couldn't help loving him. Then I remembered Leo's voice: 'I do – understand', and felt again the relief of that moment.

After reading the article about Home Farm accounts, I started reading the others, too. I became quite engrossed in 'Estate Law 1909', and I was so fascinated by 'The Equipment of the Estate Office' that I asked Mr Selby if I might have a look at the other ledgers, for the corn mill and the brickyard and suchlike. He said certainly, I could borrow any of them I wanted.

I learnt so much from those ledgers. Not just about the estate, but about Leo, too. I knew he was a good landlord, but I hadn't realized just *how* good. It wasn't simply a case of seeing that cottage roofs were mended and so on; it was much more thorough. Take butchers' meat for example; in Borrell, labourers' families never shopped at the butcher, except for a joint of pork on a Sunday, and big families not even that. It was just too dear; a man might spend a lifetime looking after the farmer's sheep, yet couldn't afford to eat mutton. But Eston was different because all meat from the estate was sold at cost. The Home Farm had taken over the butcher's shop years ago, Mr Selby said, so anyone from the estate could buy their meat cheaply. It was the same with flour for making bread, and butter and cheese, and milk for the children – which was cheaper than cost. Allotments at Eston were big, too, and everybody who wanted one could have one. A piglet came free every year, and rents were lower than they'd been at Borrell, despite higher wages as a result of the war.

All Dr Matthews' bills were paid by the estate, too, and there'd been a system of sick pay and old age pensions at Eston long before Mr Lloyd George had given them to the whole country. When I talked about it to Mr Selby he said that there were other landowners doing the same things: 'Lord Wantage, for example, set up a profit-sharing scheme on the Lockinge estate, and established local co-operative stores. But Lord Warminster has never followed this route,' Mr Selby smiled, 'He favours benevolent, rather than enlightened, despotism.' He laughed at his little joke.

Up in my sitting room later I thought of Leo. I'd married a good man, a caring man, a man who deserved to be respected by everyone – and loved by his wife. But I was no better than Clytie, gazing hopelessly at Apollo, her sun god. And a fool, too, because my sun god didn't care for me any more than Clytie's did for her. Likely he'd go back to France without even bothering to come and see me.

But a couple of days later, the postcard arrived. 'I'll be down for lunch on Thursday. Send the trap to meet the 1.10. F.'

There was no address so I couldn't have put him off even if I'd wanted to. I knew I should have more pride, I knew he'd behaved badly to me at that awful dinner; but, after all, he'd only forced me to admit the truth – that I loved him.

On Thursday morning I did my hair very carefully and put on a new blouse, then I sat down to wait. No sooner did I hear the clip-clop of hooves than I was in the hall. Mr Tims had already opened the door so I went out on to the steps – and there was Frank. He wasn't in uniform and he was driving himself; when he saw me he tossed the reins across to Mr Tyson and raised his hat. Wearing a light suit and with a creamy straw boater on his head, he looked so young and dashing. My legs were trembling so much I could hardly stand upright.

He sprang down from the driving seat and came running up the steps; his limp had altogether gone. My racing heart slowed to become a lump of lead in my chest.

'Your leg – tis better.'

'Yes, 'fraid so. The holiday's over.' He lobbed his hat to Mr Tims – who only just caught it – and turned to me. 'Good afternoon, Amy. Beautiful as ever, I see.' And at his dazzling smile my heart began to race again until I thought it would never slow down. 'Aren't we going in to lunch? I'm starving.'

Over lunch he talked about the holiday he'd just had in Scotland: the fish he'd caught, the grouse he'd shot and the stags he'd stalked. Then, when Mr Tims had served the coffee and left us, he lit up a cigarette. Squinting at me through the smoke he said, 'Well, it's apologies again, eh, Amy? I behaved abominably that evening – any other hostess would have forbidden me the house for ever after that performance.'

I looked down at my hands. 'Eston, tis thy home.'

'It was never that!' he exclaimed. Then all at once his face changed, and he continued, 'Yet it seems now that it's the only home I've got left.' I couldn't answer and he fell silent for a little while before saying, 'I am sorry, Amy. I did behave extremely badly, but you know why, don't you?'

Remembering the gold circle spinning through the air to drop discarded to the floor, I whispered, 'Yes.'

'Do you remember that summer before the war, Amy?' I nodded, I couldn't bring myself to speak. 'I thought then that I was fooling you. Now I wonder who really was the fool.' Abruptly he stabbed out his cigarette and jumped up. 'Come along, Amy, we'll go for a walk.'

'No – I mustn't.'

He grinned. 'I was going to suggest that Flora accompanies us – as a chaperone.'

'Mebbe, if Ellen came too, with Rose.'

He shrugged. 'Oh very well, if you insist.'

Ellen's face was prim, but when he smiled at her she softened and went for her hat. We all set out in a little procession: Flora tugging him along in front, me following, and Ellen bringing up the rear with Rose and Nella. We went through the park and into the oak wood, where he was content to let Flora drag him from tree to tree, showing him her treasures. We came to the most exciting of all – we'd only found it yesterday – a dormouse asleep in its nest. We'd gazed in awe at the round golden ball of fur, but when Flora had reached out to it I'd drawn her hand gently back, 'No, sweetheart, don't touch. He's very tired, you must let him sleep.'

Now the two blond heads bent over the nest. 'Dormouse – asleep.' Flora's voice was breathy with excitement.

'Let's wake him up, shall we?' A long brown finger shot out and poked the golden fur. There was a flash of terrified eyes, a frantic scrabbling of small pink paws, then in a streak of gold the tiny creature vanished. Flora's shrieks of glee were echoed by his deep male laughter.

I said reproachfully, 'You shouldn't have done that, not while he were sleeping.'

Frank lifted one lazy eyebrow. 'Why not? The Boches are always doing it to me, while *I'm* asleep. Come along, Flora, let's see how much noise we can make!' Catching hold of her hands he began to run, lifting her up, whirling her round high above his head while she screamed in an ecstasy of fear and delight. Two golden heads, two pairs of sparkling blue eyes. Then, slowing, he kissed her first on one cheek then the other before setting her gently down with a final kiss on her rosebud mouth. They walked on, hand in hand, and my whole body seemed to melt as I watched them together.

We came back for tea in my sitting room. Flinging himself down in a chair he looked around him. 'You've made this into quite a bright little room, Amy. I like your pictures, they're rather jolly.' Then he frowned slightly, 'But I'm sure I've seen some of them before.'

'They're Leo's, from his flat in Kew.'

'So they are. I only went there once or twice, when I'd run through my allowance and the old man happened to be up in Town.' He sprang to his feet and began to walk round. 'How curious, not a man to be seen, they're all of women and children.' He paused. 'Bizarre, isn't it? He couldn't keep a wife or beget his own children, so he made do with paintings instead.' His tone was mocking.

I said defensively, 'He's main fond o' children.'

Turning, Frank faced me directly. 'Flora is *mine*, Amy.'

'Not in law.'

'No. But in everything else that matters. He stole her from me.' His eyes were hard. 'Where is he, by the way – over at Sutton Veny?'

I stared at him. 'Didn't you know? He's in the army now.'

'What?' He looked astounded.

'I thought Miss Ann- , somebody would've told you.'

'*She* wouldn't tell me anything. If she knew the end of the world was coming she'd leave me to face the Last Judgment with my defence unprepared. But, Amy, he must just be in a military hospital, he *can't* have – '

'The day after you were here he went to the doctor in charge at Sutton Veny to see if he could enlist, and the doctor said yes. So he joined the RAMC. He's Private Warminster now.'

'In the ranks! But he's a peer.'

'So was that earl you told us about.'

'Crawford's back in the Lords now – he's got some job in government. In any case, he'd had some sort of connection with the territorials before the war. His was a different kettle of fish altogether.' He shook his head. 'I just can't believe it. I never thought he had it in him. God, I must have really flicked him on the raw with my jibes! But he's a bloody fool. If he was so desperate to get into uniform he could have pulled a few strings and got himself a cushy little number as an officer in charge of remounts or something. God knows there's enough of them hanging around London, and younger than him, too.'

'Sir George, he's the same age as Leo, and he's been in France, fighting.'

'But George Burton's a regular! For goodness' sake, Amy, the old man's only going to spend his time humping bodies and bedpans at a base hospital. He might as well have carried on doing that as a volunteer at Sutton Veny – there was no need for such an absurd and quixotic gesture!' Then he glanced at me, 'Still, I suppose it's not the first absurd and quixotic gesture he's ever made, is it?' Then he asked abruptly, 'did you tell him I was coming down to see you?'

'Not yet. I'll tell him when I write next, o' course.'

He laughed. '*Of course*. Prissy, prim, little five foot three Amy! Well, I wish you joy of his reply. Good lord, is that the time?'

I stood at the door and watched his slim back go down the drive until at last there was only the clip-clop of hooves fading into the distance. My eyes were so blurred I could hardly see my way upstairs. In my sitting room there was only the faint lingering scent of his cigarette.

After dinner I sat down to write my weekly letter to Leo. Following the usual news, I told him about Frank's visit: I wrote that he'd sent the postcard and come to lunch, and we'd all gone for a walk in the woods. 'Ellen, she came too, all the time.' That looked so obvious I added, 'Flora showed him the doormouse we found on Wednesday. Lord Quinham did leave as soon as he'd had his tea.' Then I sent the letter off and waited apprehensively for his reply.

It came at the usual time.

Dear Amy,

Thank you for your letter and all your news. I trust that you and the children remain well and that the dormouse continues to thrive. (Spelt with one O, incidentally, Amy, as in *dormire* the Latin for 'to sleep', not as in the opening kind.) Tell Flora not to disturb their nests: they are pretty, harmless creatures who, if awakened from hibernation, may not survive the winter.'

He then went on to make some comments about the estate. But his last sentence read: 'As to the question you did not write, but merely implied, the answer is that I trust you, as my wife, to do whatever is right.' He'd signed himself off in the way he always did, 'Your affectionate husband, Leo Warminster.'

I let out my breath in a great sigh of relief.

But as soon as I'd folded up his letter and put it away I began to worry again – about Frank. Had he reached France yet?

I picked up the newspaper that Mr Tims always left beside my plate at breakfast now; the British were attacking again. I couldn't help it, my fingers turned to that long list of names, the casualty list. Oh please, please don't let him be hurt.

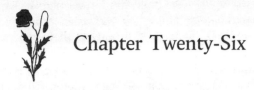

Chapter Twenty-Six

I made myself concentrate on learning to do the accounts. I was glad I'd got something like that to do: the busier I was, the less time I had to worry. In fact when Mr Selby suggested I might find it helpful to look at the Estate record books, I went back down to the office after dinner the same day. Mr Selby had said he was running down to see Dr Matthews, but he'd probably be in himself later, if I had any questions. I'd asked him one straightaway: could I take Rose with me in her laundry basket? He smiled and said of course I could.

I couldn't resist playing with her for a little while first, she was such a lovely baby; she liked to pull herself up on my lap and bounce up and down there, bending her knees and then straightening them again, all the time looking *so* pleased with herself as she did it. And the way she babbled now was almost talking. She was such good company. I wished Leo could have seen her. She'd got a tooth now, and she'd cut it with hardly any grizzling. She was growing up; soon she'd be running about like Flora, and there wouldn't be another baby. I sighed, before opening the first of the huge green leather-bound books.

Each one covered five full years, their dates stamped in gold on the spine, and I'd decided to start with 1881-1886, because that covered the time when Leo had taken charge himself. I leafed through to September 1884, when Leo would have been sixteen and his father still alive, and read a bleak account of rent cuts refused, farms unlet, others losing their tenants that year. The Home Farm was making a loss. There were accounts of damage reported, repairs not even started – or left incomplete. Eston was sliding further and further into decay.

I imagined the estate as it must have looked then: buildings dilapidated, fields untended; and the people – what was happening to them, with jobs disappearing? There must have been despair in those pretty houses.

Then Leo's father's death was noted and almost at once the record changed. Orders for repairs and rebuilding were given, while the recorder's writing became less even, as if his hand were becoming shaky under pressure of work. Soon the entries were in Mr Selby's familiar sloping hand.

Between them, Leo and Mr Selby must have surveyed the entire estate before Leo went up to Cambridge in the autumn, and he'd obviously left the agent with a long list of instructions, since over the next few months cottages and farm buildings were repaired, hedges laid, ditches cleared, fences rebuilt, roads improved. It must have been like a glorious spring-clean – only better, because he was building, too. Tenants were found for the outlying farms at lower rents, but it was the change in the Home Farm which was most noticeable: it expanded under my very eyes. The estate workshops were enlarged, new roads were constructed, barns and a water tower were built, timber was planted, and land put down to pasture. The steam ploughing set had been purchased, together with a traction engine, while in the woods beyond the park a stream had been dammed and a deep pool turned into a lake, with rocks piled high up at one end. I'd seen it often because Nella preferred to take her swim in there rather than in the pond, but I'd never realized the lake had been made deliberately, and now I wondered why. By the time the wash houses were built, each with its own copper and coal store at the back, Eston must have looked a very different place from three years earlier. And all this was achieved before Mr Selby recorded the coming of age of Lord Warminster in May 1889, followed shortly by the award of his first-class degree from Cambridge. I read on.

June 25th. Lord Warminster was married today, in France. I wish them both long life and happiness.

September 27th. Lord Warminster and his bride returned from their honeymoon tour. They were welcomed to Eston with the appropriate celebrations.

October 28th. Lord Warminster left today to escort his wife to France, to visit her relations there.

Leo came back, she didn't. So he travelled to France to visit her early in November, and then again later in the month. And all at once I began to add up. I knew the date of Frank's birth: February 2nd 1890. Except he couldn't have been born then, because he'd told me himself that his mother was over four months gone at the time of her marriage. Quickly I turned the pages to 1890.

February 2nd. Today Lord Warminster informed me by telegram of the birth of his heir, Lord Quinham.

And as I read these words I knew that Mr Selby knew the truth. He had been 'informed' of the birth, not that Frank had been born that day, and not a 'son and heir', but merely the legally correct term, 'heir'.

It was clear that apart from that one brief visit to France to register the birth at the official time Leo had stayed at Eston, nursing his hurt and betrayal here, alone and in silence. It was May before he brought the French countess and Frank back home.

The estate business continued: improvements were still being made, but not so rapidly – and then I realized they'd stopped. After November of that year nothing was being recorded except essential repairs, and routine maintenance; and these were all arranged by Mr Selby. It was as if Leo had ceased to exist.

I went to fetch the next volume. It wasn't until October 1892 that the improvements began again, and then came a whole range of new dairy buildings at three of the Home Farm farmhouses. After that abrupt beginning other improvements slowly accumulated once more.

I was so involved in the past it took me a moment to realize Mr Selby had come in – but Rose was crowing and cooing to him already. His face softened. 'How delightful to see Lady Rose down here!'

'Aye, she's such good company. Show Mr Selby your rattle, Rose.' I put it in her hand and at once she shook it for him.

The dark curl on her forehead bounced up and down and Mr Selby laughed. 'Her hair is such a deep true black, just like her father's when he was younger.' And the minute he'd said it, without thinking I looked down at that first record book. Mr Selby's eyes followed mine, saw the dates – and his face crimsoned. 'Oh, I thought you'd to be looking at the more recent volumes, dear me.' Then catching hold of himself, he said, 'I hardly expected you to be bothered about delving into such ancient history. Let me put it back.'

'I've already read it,' I said. 'Besides, I did know.'

He said 'Oh,' again, and reached into his pocket for his pipe. Then with a glance at Rose he pushed it back again. 'I suppose, if his lordship told you – '

'Aye, he did.' I didn't say which lordship.

But Mr Selby still looked bothered. 'I thought I'd – obscured the situation.'

'You would 'a done, for anybody as didn't know already.' He still looked rather bothered so I asked, 'Mr Selby, what I don't understand,' I gestured down at the records, 'is why did the improvements stop like that, all of a sudden? Did Leo fall ill?'

'No, not exactly.' Mr Selby moved over to the window, before turning round to face me. 'The first Lady Warminster left Eston at the end of 1890, and although she made periodic visits after that date she did not live here again.'

He paused a moment before continuing, 'Lady Warminster, I'm not the right person to talk about your – predecessor. I scarcely knew her – I only knew of the harm she did to Lord Warminster. I told you that your husband did not fall ill after she left, and that is true in that he was not ill in body, but he became prey to an extreme melancholia, so much so that I became most concerned about the balance of his mind. My dear Laura was still alive then, and she would often invite him over for dinner, but only very occasionally would he agree to come. His spirits would appear to lift a little with the spring. Then in the summer *she* would come back.' Mr Selby shook his head. 'Lord Warminster has always been a man of strong feelings, with few close friends. Sir George came down from Town whenever he could, and his mother and sisters visited – people did try, but it is difficult when a man is totally unresponsive. I spoke to Beeston, but unfortunately relations were never good between those two: Lord Warminster resented Beeston for taking the place of the previous incumbent, Beeston being his father's choice. In any case the Rector is too timid a man to – I'm afraid that Lord Warminster does not react well to timidity.'

I prompted, 'But then Leo started making improvements again, so did he get better?'

'He was shocked out of his own personal misfortune by that of others, Lady Warminster. There was an epidemic of scarlet fever in Eston.' Scarlet fever – I went cold, remembering how mothers in Lambeth had dreaded it. Mr Selby continued, 'Two children died in the village, and then Cyril Beeston went down with it. He pulled through, but his younger brother and sister did not. Their mother had recently been widowed in India, so she'd brought her children back to make their home with their aunt and uncle.'

There were tears in my eyes. 'Their poor mother – how could she have stood it, losing both of them, after her husband?'

'I'm afraid she did not stand it, Lady Warminster. Worn out with grief, and the exertions of nursing her children, she took the fever herself, and succumbed. Even Cyril did not recover unscathed, his kidneys were weakened as a result. He really should not have been accepted by the army, but he persuaded a friend to pull strings to enable him to pass his medical.'

'Like Leo did.'

Mr Selby looked surprised. 'Lord Warminster had no problems at all – indeed the Medical Officer at Sutton Veny apparently told him he had the heart and lungs of a man half his age. His physical health has always been excellent. But I digress. With scarlet fever there is always the possibility of infection having originated in the milk supply, and although stringent tests proved this could not have been the case at Eston, Lord Warminster decided to take all possible precautions against another outbreak.

'Having planned a thorough overhaul of our milk production, he was then prevented from lapsing back into his previous melancholia by the appointment of Robson as schoolmaster. He insisted on the man being given the post because he was far and away the best qualified of the candidates, but Robson's also an out-and-out radical. He began an immediate campaign on the state of the school buildings. Having obtained new earth closets, Robson moved on to the question of piped water – and after that Lord Warminster seemed to turn a corner. Though it was a long time before he was back to – er – normal.' His voice softened. 'Indeed, I would venture to say that only in the past few years has his recovery been completed. Domestic affection is a great blessing to a man, especially a lonely man, as he has been.'

I didn't know how to reply; I knew I didn't deserve Mr Selby's smiling approval. Hastily I asked, 'Why did he dam the stream, and make that lake? Tis a bit big just for Nella to swim in.'

'It was *his* bathing pool – he used to be a very regular swimmer at one time. Has he not told you?'

I shook my head, and was going to ask more but Rose had got bored. It was time I took her back upstairs.

But later, in bed, my thoughts went back to Mr Selby's story. I felt so angry with the French Countess, who shouldn't have left him. He loved her, he'd forgiven her; she should have stayed.

Next day it was time to write my weekly letter. Deciding I simply *must* make it a bit longer, I wrote about the roses. Only when I read it through it mostly seemed to be questions, so I scribbled underneath, 'I dare say you haven't time to answer all these questions, especially if you are very busy, so don't fret about them.' Then I said I hoped he was remembering to change his socks if they got damp, and signed off as usual. It was longer than normal, at any rate.

When his reply came that was longer too. Following the regular comments about the children and the estate he'd written: 'As to your questions about my roses, do ask any you wish; I have the instincts of a paedagogue, so your assumption of my omniscience is deeply flattering.' I reached for my dictionary. 'However, I am not, in truth, omniscient so I may on occasion have to refer you to various titles in my library, for your further elucidation.' The dictionary was opened again; I wondered if he was doing it deliberately, since he'd given me the dictionary in the first place. 'But obviously, I can explain my system of encouraging roses to bloom in winter. Hicks and I use an American method: we take cuttings from shoots which have flowered in February and strike them in a hot bed . . .'

The letter went on in great detail, but when I read it through again, I realized that he hadn't explained how you got the first roses to bloom in February in order to make a start. I was glad of that, since it gave me something to ask him next week. After that he'd written: 'We are fairly busy at present. Thank you for your concern for my health; fortunately dry socks are readily procurable here. Your affectionate husband, Leo Warminster.'

I'd just picked up my sewing again when Mr Tims came to the door. 'Lady Burton has called, my lady, and Mrs Tomlinson.' I jumped up in a panic. Lady Burton often called now, but I'd never heard of this Mrs Tomlinson.

'Show them into the drawing room, please, I'll be down directly.' I rushed Rose up to the nursery, and went running downstairs, patting my hair into place.

But even before Lady Burton had introduced her as her youngest daughter, I knew who Mrs Tomlinson was: they were so alike, even to the flowery scent they wore.

Lady Burton enveloped me. '*So* long since I've seen you, dear. I said to Cynthia here we simply *must* go and visit little Amy, now Leonidas has gone away and left her. How is he, dear? Quite *heroic* of him! As I said to George, I do admire what he's done, but such a rash step to take – so typical of Leonidas. How is dear Flora? And how *is* dear little Rose?' She murmured aside, 'My goddaughter, Cynthia – such a sweet infant.'

I pressed the bell. 'I'll send for her.'

'Do, my dear – Cynthia's youngest is a litle older than your Flora, you know.

189

I am quite blessed with grandchildren: George's boy, Joan's pigeon pair, Helen's four – but they're in Canada at the moment, so they don't count – and then Cynthia's three girls.' She leant forward confidentially, 'Cynthia was my little surprise. I quite thought at my age – still, you never can tell, can you, like Leonidas' poor mother? So her three are younger than the others – '

'Mama, *do* let Lady Warminster get a word in edgeways.' Mrs Tomlinson smiled encouragingly at me.

But at first I couldn't think of anything to say; then I took the plunge. 'Three girls, that must be nice.'

Mrs Tomlinson sighed, 'They do look so sweet – all matching like that – but obviously John wants a boy.' She brightened, 'Still, as he's in France at the moment, I don't have to worry about that just now, so I've come to stay with Mama.'

I smiled at Lady Burton. 'That must be nice for you, to have your grandchildren to stay.'

Mrs Tomlinson looked surprised. 'Oh I haven't brought the children. They're at the seaside with Nanny. Rather late in the year, but the poor little things have all been down with the measles. Darling Pamela was quite poorly, so Dr Gardiner *insisted* they must have a month of sea air – a little place in Wales, I never can pronounce it, but Nanny assures me it's *quite* satisfactory.'

'So darling Cynthia came to me for a rest.'

Both paused at once for a second so I ventured, 'You must be fair worn out with it, the measles can be nasty.'

Mrs Tomlinson leant forward, 'Yes, my dear, such a worry. Nanny was wonderful, of course, but we did have to obtain a hospital nurse for poor little Pamela since Nanny was quite worn out by then, and the doctor was afraid of complications.'

'It must've been an anxious time for you. Tis terrible to see a little 'un ill.'

'Oh my dear, you can't imagine! My heart was in my mouth every morning while I waited for my maid to bring the latest report from Nanny. Then, after breakfast each day, I would walk in the garden in front of the nursery window and wave. I could just see their little white faces pressing against the panes as they looked out for me. Once I'd done that I would feel a little happier – but I never left the house for more than a few hours the whole time they were ill.'

Lady Burton patted her daughter's hand. 'Cynthia is a devoted mother – just like you are, dear.'

I couldn't think of a reply to that so it was fortunate Ellen arrived at that moment with Rose – who looked beautiful. Ellen had dressed her in her best frock. I offered her to Lady Burton, who made a fuss of her, and then Mrs Tomlinson held her. 'What an engaging infant! And so cheerful – my youngest always started squawking the minute she came down to the drawing room – but then,' beckoning to Ellen she handed Rose back to her, 'children are only really happy up in the nursery, aren't they? I was so relieved when dear little Isabel was weaned, and I could get back to normal. Are you still feeding your little one, dear?'

'Oh yes, she likes her milk, does Rose.'

'Try bitter aloes, my dear, applied to the breast before a feed's due. They soon learn to do without then.'

Bitter aloes! On my breast, for Rose! I could hardly keep from saying something, but luckily Ellen distracted me. 'Shall I take Lady Rose back upstairs now, my lady?'

'Aye – yes, thank you.' Ellen winked at me before disappearing through the door in a rustle of starch.

After my visitors had gone I couldn't stop thinking about what Mrs Tomlinson had said. I knew real ladies did things differently, though at least she'd fed her babies herself – but bitter aloes! And however could she have borne it, her children ill and her just looking at them through the window?

Next time I took Flora out for her walk, we took the footpath that came out beside the church, and we went through the lychgate into the churchyard. I soon found the gravestone I was seeking: of white marble, in the form of an angel with folded wings perched on top. The first names on it were Alice Mary Beeston, aged five years two months, and James Alfred Beeston, aged three years five months. They had both died within a week of each other. And then below, 'Also, their grieving mother, Mary Jane Beeston, aged 26 years.' She'd died less than a month after her two children. The tears filled my eyes and flowed down my cheeks. Then Flora tugged hard at my hand, wanting to be on her way.

We took the winding lane that led back to the East Lodge. Although we were well into autumn now, it was a fine day. The bryony trailed in looping curves along the hedgerow, its red berries glossy in the sun, while the purple dogwood nestled below in the white whiskers of old man's beard. A may tree flaunted its scarlet haws, and beyond it a single maple stood straight and true, its golden leaves fluttering gently in the breeze. Flora pulled forward; I steadied her as she clambered across the ditch to touch the flower-like berries of the skewer tree. She tipped one up, and cried out in triumph to see the pink skin already splitting open to reveal the orange seeds within.

'Careful, my Flora. They be poison.' She quickly drew back her searching finger, her round blue eyes anxious as they turned to look into mine. I lifted her back across the ditch and held her close, kissing her soft cheek as I told her, 'Doan 'ee fret, Flora my maid, thy Mama will keep thee safe.'

As soon as I'd taken Flora home and fed Rose I went down the estate office. I seemed to be on the go all the time these days, and I preferred it that way, since I'd always liked to be busy. I enjoyed seeing more people, too. I'd met the Williams sisters: big rawboned Judith wearing her husband's boots and flat cap as she tended her hissing monsters, and Jael in the workshop, greasing the self-binder before putting it away for the winter. They were so obviously sisters, and yet they looked so different. Jael wore her husband's boots, too, but on her they might almost have had dainty Louis heels, and she perched his old peaked cap at a jaunty angle above her sparkling brown eyes.

'How's his lordship getting on, me lady? I do miss him popping his head round the door of the workshop – always got a cheery wave and a civil word for a body, has his lordship.'

I stared at her in surprise; then looking again at the full, ripe curves of her body I decided that perhaps they explained Leo's good humour.

It certainly wasn't the case with everyone. Mr Arnott said to me one day, 'His lordship is a fair man, but he doesn't know how to keep a rein on that temper of his.' Then he shrugged. 'But I suppose he doesn't have to, seeing as he's the great Pooh Bah around these parts. I still can't get over the difference from Canada. Out there all men are equal.'

'Mr Robson says they are here, too.'

'Oh, Robson!' Mr Arnott laughed, looking more like a pirate than ever. 'He's an idealist. The rest of us live in the real world, and if an earl says jump, we jump.'

I glanced at him sideways. 'I don't reckon as you always jump, Mr Arnott – not from what Mr Selby's said to me.'

He threw back his head and guffawed. 'Me and his lordship has had our ups and downs, but he knows what I'm worth – and even the longest sulk comes to an end sometime. Now, I suppose I'd better find those receipts for you, or I'll have old Selby breathing down my ear.' He grinned, 'I must say, I much prefer it when he sends *you* to pester me.' His single eye flashed. He was a bit of a flirt, was Mr Arnott, but I didn't mind: it was just his way. And when I saw him looking at Mrs Arnott I knew why he'd come back from Canada.

People talked about Leo down the village, too. 'Aar, his lordship'll be finding it strange, with him being so pertic'lar about his clothes.' 'Miss his roses he will. Used to prune my liddle bush fer me, 'e did. Got out his knife and did it hisself, every spring. He knows I can't see so well these days.' 'I misses seeing him going past. I hopes as he's not finding soldiering too much of a trial.'

Granny Withers was more robust. 'When's he going to shoot all thic there Germans, then?'

'No, Mrs Withers, he won't never go to France, not being the way he is. 'Sides, RAMC, they don't carry guns, tisn't allowed.'

She snorted. 'Spoil 'is fun, that will. Writing to you reg'lar, is he?'

'Every week, without fail.'

'Then I hopes as you keeps him waiting for 'is reply, you dussent want to spoil thic there men. Keep 'em on their toes, that's what I says.'

Mr Robson was leaning over the schoolyard wall, the children racing around behind him. 'How's Lord Warminster, Lady Warminster?'

'Getting along pretty well, Mr Robson.'

He grinned. 'You wait and see – a few months in the ranks will make a good socialist of him yet!'

Then it would be Dr Matthews on his way out of a cottage. When we'd had a word about whoever was ill, he'd ask, 'Warminster getting along all right, is he?'

'I think so, doctor, but he don't say a lot about what he's doing.'

'I dare say he doesn't want to bore you.'

But I reckoned it more likely that it was because Leo knew how squeamish I was: even the thought of a hospital frightened me. I stopped at Mary's gate. I'd just got time to say hello to little Tommy before going in to see Mrs Chandler. 'See, Rose, tis Tommy – do 'ee give him a wave.'

I knew Mrs Chandler was quite worried about how Leo was coping, like I was. 'I know he's with grown men now – but they can act like children sometimes. And tis a shame he's had to go away just now, but I'm main glad he's got you to come back to, my lady.'

Walking back that afternoon, Rose weighed heavy in my arms; but the weight of guilt was heavier still on my shoulders. If only I could give him the love he needed – but I couldn't.

His weekly letter was waiting when I got back home; it had arrived by the afternoon post. I took it up to the nursery with me. 'Look, Flora, tis a letter from Papa. Would you like to help me open it?' Together we pulled up the flap and tugged out the sheet of paper inside – then I stood there, dumbfounded.

Ellen asked anxiously, 'Is anything the matter, my lady?'

I held it out to her without speaking. In each top corner of the sheet was an upside-down triangle, with YMCA written across it – but it was the words printed in between I pointed to: 'On Active Service with the British Expeditionary Force.' On the right-hand side he'd written as usual his number and the initials RAMC – but beneath he'd added the one word 'FRANCE'.

Chapter Twenty-Seven

Ellen looked as surprised as I felt. 'You'd best read it, my lady.'

Dear Amy,

Please forgive the somewhat ostentatious notepaper, but our unit embarked in rather a hurry, and I find I have left my usual stationery behind. However, I am not ungrateful to the YMCA, as their hut provides some kind of haven in this extremely crowded camp. I am now stationed at one of the larger base hospitals in France; I must not divulge its name for fear of the censor's pencil. The realization that from now on every word I write will be read by a third unintended pair of eyes is a most distasteful one; however, the officers have to do their duty.

Then it just continued as usual; nothing about the journey or why he'd gone, simply replies to my queries and comments on my news, until the final: 'Your affectionate husband, Leo Warminster.'

I turned to Flora. 'Papa's gone to France!'

She wrinkled her nose, and said, 'Uncle Albie's in France.'

I looked at Ellen in alarm, but she shook her head. 'The base hospitals are right back on the coast, my lady. Stands to reason as they wouldn't put the wounded anywhere they were in danger.' The rapid pace of my heart slowed as she continued, 'Albie did tell me a month or two back that they weren't sending men back to England so quick now; if they've not been hurt too bad they keep 'em in France, ready to go and fight again. But in the meantime someone's got to look after them, and that's what his lordship'll be doing.'

I knew Ellen was right, and yet: 'On Active Service'! For all Leo's talk about ostentatious notepaper I was sure he'd be pleased he was in France – even if his activity was only carrying stretchers and emptying bedpans.

Everybody else was impressed as well. I saw Mr Tims in the hall and told him, and after his: 'Well, I never!' he shuffled off backstairs much faster than usual; he wanted to be first to tell the other servants. I went along to the estate office to see if I could catch Mr Selby, and then out to tell Mr Hicks in the garden; I was still a little in awe of the head gardener even after all this time, but I knew he'd want to know. By the next day it was all round the village: 'Just fancy, at his lordship's age!' 'And him being the way he is!' 'There's not many in his position as'd do what he's done.'

Mr Beeston came up specially that evening to say he and Lucinda would be remembering Leo in their prayers. I thanked him, though I wasn't sure Leo would be very pleased about that, but as soon as I asked about Cyril Leo was forgotten – and that was only natural since poor Cyril was in the front line, and him with his weak kidneys, too. Mr Beeston talking about Cyril reminded me of Frank – not that I ever forgot – and after he'd gone I went upstairs to the night nursery where Flora lay asleep. Bending down I kissed her tumbled curls. *Please, pleaase, keep him safe.*

It was as if my plea had been heard, because a couple of days later another letter arrived from France. My hands trembled as I took out the single sheet with its brief scrawl.

Dear Amy,

As my real wife won't speak to me I'm writing instead to my substitute one. Life is a little less bloody at present as I've been seconded for liaison duties with the French army. I feel very much at home with them, as indeed I should, and the food's certainly better. It's also a great deal more comfortable back at HQ – those damned guns were giving me a headache!
Yours, in whatever way you wish to take me,
Frank.

I stood there, shaking with relief. It was a minute or two before I deciphered the PS: 'It's all right, I'm not expecting a reply – I've no doubt your conscience forbids it.' I was tempted, but I knew I shouldn't. In the end I went down and asked Mrs Carter to make one of her special fruit cakes; I put it in a tin, bought some cigarettes and made up a parcel. With a lot of help from me, Flora managed to write a wobbly: 'To Uncle Frank, with best wishes from Flora.'

I'd got it all ready to post and then I suddenly realized what I'd done, so I asked Mrs Carter for another cake – she always made them in batches – packed that up, too, and wrote: 'To Leo, with best wishes from Amy.' Flora traced her name again and then I dabbled a little ink on Rose's thumb and pressed it down with a note of explanation at the side. As soon as I'd sent it off I remembered the cigarettes, but I'd never seen Leo smoke anything other than a cigar of an evening, so I ordered a box of his usual brand from Harrods and asked for them to be sent directly to France. When that was done I sat down to write my weekly letter.

November arrived. I'd learnt to drive the motor by now and Mr Selby told me that this month I could do the Home Farm accounts myself; proudly I wrote of it in my weekly letter to Leo. In his reply he said he was sure I would do them well, but otherwise his letter was even briefer than usual. It was written in indelible pencil, so obviously he'd run out of ink and didn't want to be bothered writing more.

Soon after, papers arrived from the military authorities: we had to fill in the particulars of all the young men who worked on the Home Farm. Mr Selby sighed as he showed them to me.

'All the men under thirty will be called up now, unless we can give a good reason for retaining them. I don't know what Arnott will say to this. We can ill afford to lose more men.' But as I pointed out to him, it wouldn't be all that many; most Eston men that age had gone already, even those who'd been married. And my thoughts went to Clara's sister, Emmie. Her time was very close now, and she'd not seen her Bill for the whole nine months; men in the ranks were still having to wait a year or more for leave – but Frank, he was an officer; he'd gone back in September, so come the end of February . . . I caught at my thoughts and held them fast.

There'd been a scrawled note from him for Flora, thanking her for the parcel, and as I'd decided to send one every month to Leo now he was in France, surely he'd understand if I sometimes sent a parcel to Frank as well? I must be content with that; and it would be from Flora, of course. So when I wasn't reading books on farming I'd pick up the Harrods catalogue and search for delicacies while my hands were busy knitting Leo a nice warm muffler. I'd have liked to knit one for Frank, too, but Flora couldn't knit.

I had to learn as much about farming as I could because Mr Selby was having to spend more and more time on government business. As well as the main County War Agricultural Committee there was a smaller executive committee now, set up to decide how land should be used and what crops should be grown; Mr Selby was a member of that, too. With ships being sunk all the time Britain needed more wheat to be produced at home. Leo had put more pasture land under the plough last year, but there'd been no guaranteed price so other farmers hadn't. In practice, by the autumn shortages had pushed the price up, so the Home Farm had made a good profit. But of course now the government was beginning to impose price controls – milk was controlled already – so obviously it wouldn't be worth the trouble for farmers to put more land under the plough, especially not with labour so short. Now Mr Selby told me that the County Committees were going to have to force farmers to plough up more land. 'It's unheard of, Lady Warminster, unheard of. So very much against our British traditions. There's bound to be hostility – but what else can we do? The people must be fed.'

Poor Mr Selby was looking very drawn these days, and then his cook went down with a chill. I was sure he wasn't eating properly so I invited him to have all his meals with me at Eston while his cook was out of action. We sat every evening talking about the war and the changes it was bringing to farming and how we might best cope with them. I learnt a lot during those meals, and I was especially pleased when Leo wrote, 'I've just received a letter from Selby; he states that you are being of considerable assistance to him.' I suggested to Mr Selby that he came for Sunday lunch every week, even after his cook was better, and he said that would be most useful, as we could work out together what needed to be done over the next seven days.

By the middle of November Clara was all on tenterhooks waiting for news of their Emmie, then one day she came rushing up to the nursery, 'Mam's sent up to say as our Emmie's started!'

'You best go down now, Clara, and lend a hand.' She was off in a flash.

Ellen and Dora and I sat wondering how long Emmie would take and whether it'd be a boy or a girl: Granny Withers had said she was carrying so high it must be a boy. Clara sent her niece up after tea while I was feeding Rose: 'Aunt Emmie's got a fine liddle boy – and she's doing well, Grammer says.'

We all laughed and cried with excitement and relief and Ellen said, 'Bill'll be so pleased!' I went down to tell Mr Tims, and then along to Mr Selby; it seemed to make the war go away a little, a baby being born.

I took the sovereign from the estate down next day. Mrs Chandler invited me up to see Emmie, who looked tired but so happy and proud. I rocked and cuddled her little son, and told Emmie I could hardly bear to give him back. I didn't want another baby yet – but the thought of *never* having another one . . .

Then a couple of days later Lady Burton arrived. When she was settled with her cup of tea and slice of bread and butter she looked round at my sitting room. 'I *am* glad you use this room so much. It brings back memories of Elizabeth. How well I remember visiting her here! She and my mother were *such* good friends – they'd been girls together. Eston was Elizabeth's home, of course – the Warminster seat was at Pennings, but she always made a point of visiting Eston several times a year after she was married.' She sighed, 'Poor dear Elizabeth, so many years longing for a child. And then one day, when she'd quite given up hope, it happened. Elizabeth was so happy those last months, radiant. I can remember her sitting by that window, sewing – she wasn't a beautiful woman, Elizabeth, but she looked beautiful that day. She was never in any doubt that it was a boy she was carrying. "He's to be called after my three favourite heroes," she said. "I asked Arthur and he's agreed. Our son – at last!" She couldn't stop talking about the child. "He's going to be as tall and handsome as his father, and become a dashing young officer. I can see him in his red tunic already."' Lady Burton sighed. 'That was the last time I saw her. Within a month she was dead and the son she'd had such high hopes for was born so crooked his own father couldn't bear the sight of him. Poor little Leonidas was banished to Eston along with the family portraits, and Arthur became a total recluse. It just shows: you should never count your chickens – all poor Elizabeth's dreams came to nothing.'

I said firmly, 'Leo *has* joined the army.'

'I know dear, but it's not quite the same, is it? The Fitzwarren-Donnes were always generals, and they led from the front, not emptying bedpans in the rear. Still, dear Francis is carrying on the family tradition.' She glanced at me shrewdly before adding, 'Such a shame about him and dear Annabel.'

I said quietly, 'Aye, it is.' Then luckily Rose woke up, so I had to attend to her. 'Still feeding her, dear? I suppose that means you're not expecting again. Such a shame Leonidas has gone away – but never mind, even private soldiers get leave occasionally.' Lady Burton smiled. 'A boy would be nice next time, don't you think?'

I shook my head. 'No – there won't be any next time.' It was such a relief to tell someone the truth that I blurted out, 'Leo says there mustn't be any more babies because they'll be born twisted, like him.'

And for a moment she was silenced. Then she asked, 'But why ever does he think that?'

So I had to explain properly. 'When he was married to the French countess – the doctors in London told him then.'

Lady Burton blinked in surprise. Then she leant forward and said earnestly, 'But my dear, I *never* believe doctors as a matter of principle. When George was a little boy they told me he had consumption, you know. I was devastated. We took him straight to Switzerland and within a month he was running up and down those nice clean mountains like a young hare! It was just a childish cough. He's never had another day's illness in his life until that nasty Hun shot him in the arm. It's still not right, dear – he's had to go behind a desk at the War Office in London, which he doesn't like at all – but I must admit I'm relieved, any mother would be. But this question of Leonidas,' her forehead wrinkled, 'you know I *distinctly* remember when Mama and I came over to see Nanny Fenton, after she arrived with poor little Leonidas, and she gave us a blow-by-blow account of poor dear Elizabeth's terrible ordeal – the way women of that class do – she said that Leonidas was born how he was because Elizabeth had growths in her womb, had had them for years. The doctor told her it was a miracle she'd ever conceived at all. So poor little Leonidas, being such a big baby, had grown all twisted sideways. And then he was upside down as well and in the end they had to pull him out and so he was damaged even more. And, of course, Elizabeth was exhausted and they couldn't stop her bleeding. Mama and I were both in tears by the time Nanny Fenton had finished, such a tragedy – Arthur blamed the baby for her death, though logically he should have blamed himself. But then men never do, do they, dear? But I'm sure Nanny Fenton was right in saying that that was the cause of Leonidas' deformities – after all, the doctor told her, so it must be true.' She glanced down at Rose. 'And then there's this little one – she's perfect, isn't she?'

I sat staring at her, my head in a whirl as she added, 'So the minute he comes home on leave you go straight ahead and give him a son – or two, perhaps – that would be better.'

'He won't believe me.'

'Then I'll speak to him.'

'He won't believe you, either – he's so sure. He said we weren't ever to be man and wife again.'

Lady Burton put down her cup. 'What! My dear, this *is* serious. Now he's finally got himself another wife he can't possibly live like a monk again, especially not when you're such a pretty girl, but,' her eyes sharpened, 'if he's been convinced of this for so long,' she leant forward and prodded Rose, 'Where did *this* little one come from?'

'I did want a baby so much that I took him by surprise.'

She jumped up and I felt her violet-scented lips press my cheek. 'My dear, Elizabeth would have been *so* grateful to you! How right you were. Leonidas needs a firm hand, he's his own worst enemy sometimes.' She put her hand out and touched Rose's dark curls, 'But now you've done it once, dear – it's time he had a son.'

I shook my head. 'He'll never let me – '

She cut across my protests. 'Don't worry any more, Amy. I'm going up to town on Thursday and I'll speak to George about the whole affair. He'll know what to do, he always does.'

After she'd gone I cuddled Rose and thought of her at Flora's age. By then there might be another baby at my breast, perhaps a boy this time. Then I stopped myself firmly; I mustn't dream, I'd done it too often before. But I was on pins waiting for Lady Burton to come back.

She was smiling as she came in. 'All sorted, dear. George has had a chat with one of his medical officer friends and apparently ideas have changed. A specialist would have given that advice to Leonidas twenty years ago, but they know better now. And the story Nanny Fenton told me confirmed it.' Her voice dropped to a hissing whisper, 'And you'll never guess what *else* that doctor told George: apparently the Kaiser had a torticollis, just like Leonidas, only they managed to straighten him! And now he's got seven healthy children – all Huns, unfortunately – so that proves there's no problem about passing it on. Only don't tell anybody, my dear – we wouldn't want anyone to think Leonidas had a *German* condition, would we?' She sat back in her chair with a satisfied smile. 'So as soon as Leonidas comes home you can tell him the good news.'

I still couldn't believe it, it seemed too good to be true. Then when I was down the village I saw Dr Matthews coming along the street. I went straight up to him. 'Could I – could I mebbe have a word with you?'

'Certainly Lady Warminster – shall I come up to the house?' Then he must have seen the disappointment on my face because he added, 'Or would you like to come along to the surgery with me? I was just on my way back.'

As soon as I was sitting down he asked, 'Now, what can I do for you? Is it good news?'

'No – I – that is – ' I stopped, flushing. He just sat there, waiting, but looking so kind that eventually I managed to tell him what Lady Burton had told me. Finally I asked, 'So is he right, Sir George's friend?'

Dr Matthews smiled. 'Almost certainly, I should think.'

I just burst into tears. He went and fetched me a glass of brandy.

After I'd drunk it he said, 'Lady Warminster, I had no idea that that was what your husband believed. If only he'd confided in me.' He gave a wry smile. 'A stupid comment to make; he is not a man who confides in anyone – except you, obviously. But in all fairness, if he'd asked me twenty years ago I would have felt bound to give him the same advice; although even then, in view of the circumstances of his birth I would have been less than certain. But even if there were a remote possibility of his torticollis being transmitted it can be corrected now, as long as action is taken while the child is still young.' He leant forward and tickled Rose under the chin. 'But with this fine specimen in front of us I don't think we need worry about that. I'm sure she'll convince him that he's capable of begetting another healthy child.' He looked up – and saw the expression on my face. His voice was quiet as he added, 'I've been rather slow, haven't I? Obviously he would not have confided in me since it would have involved betraying another person.'

I couldn't answer; I felt so guilty. Dr Matthews spoke gently. 'Don't look so upset, Lady Warminster. I had already realized there was a possibility. I have some knowledge of Mendelism, which indicates that certain patterns of inheritance are – less likely than others. And in any case, the person concerned is dead.'

I whispered, 'But her son isn't.'

His voice became even more gentle. 'Doctors do not betray confidences.'

'But Lady Burton, Sir George – '

'I'm quite sure Sir George will have mentioned no names when he consulted his friend: the British upper classes know how to close ranks. Indeed, I suspect Lady Burton and her son have been doing just that for the past twenty years or more. After all, they've known your husband a long time.' I recalled Lady Burton's firm: 'It's time he had a son,' and realized that Dr Matthews was right. He was still speaking reassuringly, 'Besides, since your husband's condition is almost certainly not transmitted by inheritance it makes no difference whether we refer to one unaffected child or two. You can tell Warminster I made the latter assumption, if you wish. Now, would you like me to get a second opinion on the case?'

'Please – and thank you for being so kind.'

Dr Matthews told me the result of his enquiry a few days later; it was exactly as he'd predicted. 'So when you next write to your husband you may tell him that precautions against conception are no longer required.'

Of course I didn't write to Leo; it would be difficult enough explaining as it was. He'd be so angry if he thought I'd betrayed her. Yet I was sure Dr Matthews was right: Lady Burton *had* known, just as Mr Selby had – and I wondered how many others had suspected. How often had people in the village commented approvingly on the colour of Rose's hair: 'And a nice little curl in it – just like his lordship's.' I prayed that Frank would never realize. But, of course, it was Pennings he would inherit, and Leo hardly ever went there – so it would be all right. And in the meantime I would give Leo a son for Eston.

Chapter Twenty-Eight

Every day now I read *The Times* over breakfast, so as to learn the latest news of the war. Our troops had launched a new offensive and reached a river called the Ancre, but two hospital ships had been sunk by mines in the Aegean. One of these was the great liner the *Britannic*, which had gone down in an hour; luckily she had had no patients aboard, but a doctor was lost, and so were a number of RAMC orderlies. I shivered; thank goodness Leo was safe on land.

Jim Arnold was in a hospital near Salisbury now. The place where his leg had been cut off had become infected, and he'd got terribly thin but he was on the mend at last. Clara visited him every week, and on Sunday afternoons she went to tea with his mother. Mrs Chandler told me that Mrs Arnold thought a lot of Clara. 'She's a good girl, my Clara, tis a pity – ' She sighed. 'Men, they only notice the outside of a girl. Women are different, they don't worry if a man's odd in his looks. They see inside, to his heart.'

By the end of the month most of Leo's roses had shed their last petals. I said goodbye to Aimée Vibert for another year and wrote to Leo of how I would miss her red-tipped buds and glossy green leaves. 'I do like her so much, I wish she really did carry my name.' Then I asked him: 'I know she's a French rose, and I remember you telling me once she was a Noisette – but she doesn't look quite the same as the other Noisettes. Why is she different?'

His reply arrived while I was in the storeroom with Clara; there'd been a lot of talk about food being put on ration, so she'd asked me to look over our supplies with her. As Mr Tims gave me Leo's letter I exclaimed, 'How odd. Tis in a green-printed envelope!'

Clara smiled. 'Our George has used one o' those, when he could get hold of it. He don't like his letters being looked over by his officer, George don't. See,' she took it from me and pointed to the printed words: 'Correspondence in this envelope need not be censored regimentally.' 'You has to sign on 'em as there's nothing inside about the war, that you've only written about family matters and suchlike. Look, there's his lordship's signature.'

Once Clara had explained, I wasn't at all surprised Leo had used that envelope. I knew he didn't like his letters being read by someone else; they'd become even more businesslike and formal since he'd been in France. I hoped that in this one he'd tell me a bit about what he was doing; maybe what the food was like at the hospital. I'd never asked because I knew he wouldn't want to write anything that sounded like a complaint to be read by his officer, but I'd often wondered.

Only when I opened it upstairs in my sitting room it seemed just the same as usual; he'd started by answering a question about the rose:

Aimée Vibert is not quite a Noisette, as you surmised, though she certainly has one in her ancestry: Champney's Pink Cluster: I had a cutting of that once, but it did not thrive. She inherits her distinctive foliage from Rose Sempervirens (semper = always, virens = green), and her late flowering she owes to Rose Moschata, the Musk Rose (Keats' musk rose, 'full of dewy wine'). However, she did not inherit the full musk fragrance, and I have even heard men deny her her claim to scent, but I disagree. She does not thrust her scent forward, like her more confident sisters – it has to be sought for – but once found its delicacy is unrivalled. So you see your little Aimée Vibert is of mixed parentage, but none the worse for that. Indeed, I always feel that it is that flaw in her parentage which gives her her tenacity and her fidelity: she will always offer me her flowers if she is able. Yet being a rambler she needs support and will twine herself around the most unpromising of props, until her very dependence gives that prop the strength to succour her. She is a vulnerable rose, my Aimé Vibert, with few thorns; but she will use those thorns, if she sees the need; and so, for all her apparent weakness, she is very strong.

I went back to the beginning and read his words again. My hand was trembling a little. Perhaps I was being foolish – surely he was only writing about the rose? I read on:

I am relieved to hear that Flora is over her recent cold, you were quite right to call Matthews in; we cannot be too careful. I trust that Rose is less fretful now her next tooth has come through. Thank you for your regular news of our daughters. I do not regret my decision to enlist, but I miss seeing my children grow; I wish I could at least have the Beast's magic mirror, so that I might look into it every evening and watch the three of you sitting cosily by the nursery fire.

Why did you write so wistfully of Aimée Vibert: 'I wish she really did carry my name'? Surely you know that she does: Amy is the beloved one. Please excuse my ramblings today. We are having a quiet spell at present, and having been the recipient of two green envelopes I could not resist squandering one immediately: the gift of privacy is most precious in wartime. However, I know you have very little time for reading letters, so I do not expect you to reply to what I have written today. I do understand, Amy.

Your affectionate husband,
Leo Warminster

'Amy is the beloved one.' And as I read those words again I knew he had not been writing about his roses.

It was a love letter – but such a very gentle love letter. And one that I might accept or discard as I wished, because he understood.

In the morning I dressed the children in their best clothes and drove them into Tilton. In the photographer's studio I sat with Rose on my lap and Flora leaning heavily against my shoulder. At the word of command we all smiled at the flare of sizzling white light. I couldn't give him the love he wanted, but at least I could send him a substitute for the Beast's magic mirror.

When I got back, Mr Selby told me he'd heard a rumour that Mr Asquith was going to resign, and Mr Lloyd George would be our new prime minister. 'I don't suppose Crawford will stay at Agriculture if Asquith goes,' Mr Selby sighed. 'We can be sure of one thing, Lady Warminster: whoever takes over, it will mean more wretched forms for us to fill in.' I knew he was right; I spent more and more time in the estate office these days. It was lucky Rose was such a good-tempered baby; she was quite happy up in the nursery, as long as I ran up to see her every couple of hours. She'd learnt to pull herself up and stand now; if I sat on the floor she'd come crawling eagerly towards me and haul herself up by my clothes until she was upright – wobbly but triumphant. It was an effort to drag myself away from my daughters to go downstairs again; but it couldn't be helped. We had to win the war.

Sir George had gone back to his regiment in France, Lady Burton told me on her next visit. 'He wanted to go, he felt he ought to go, but – ' She sighed; her face was shadowed and drawn. Then her eyes brightened. 'Still, Cynthia's here, with the children. She's closed the house in Rutland, it seemed pointless to keep it open while John was away. She is *such* a help with the convalescents – her music, you know – and, of course, the men love to see the children running around. Now, dear, Cynthia has invited your little Flora over to nursery tea one day. When shall it be?'

I was pleased; it was time Flora mixed more with other children. Ellen was even more pleased; she said she hadn't spoken to another nanny since before Rose was born.

Flora came back full of her afternoon, and I suggested a return visit the following week. Ellen agreed, but there was something reserved about her voice. I asked, 'You wouldn't mind, would you, Ellen?'

'I'd like to return Nanny Tomlinson's hospitality in *my own* nursery.' And then I understood.

I said quickly, 'O' course, I'd be busy in the estate office, but I dare say as you'd prefer to see to it all yourself.'

'Yes, my lady, I would.' Her agreement was a little too firm for politeness, but I should have realized earlier. After all, I'd been a servant myself. It would have been very hurtful to Ellen's pride if I'd come into the nursery and played with the children while she was entertaining a colleague. Nanny Tomlinson would have thought it very odd indeed.

When the day of the tea party arrived Ellen suggested that I should just look in for five minutes. 'Nanny Tomlinson would see it as a nice gesture, my lady.' So that's what I did. But I was sorry I couldn't stay longer, the little girls were obviously enjoying themselves so much. As Clara said, 'Our Ellen's allus had lots of ideas for games; even when she was only a young maid herself she'd have the little 'uns running up to her, asking her to play with 'em. Mam always said as she'd be a main good mother when the time came, Ellen would.' Clara glanced at me, smiling. 'Your cousin, he likes writing, don't he? Ellen's never without a letter from him in her apron pocket.' She leant closer. 'And I 'low she's quite smitten wi' him, for all they've only seen each other that one time.'

I was sure Clara was right, because often of an evening when I'd said goodnight to Flora, Ellen would pass a remark about London, and then sit waiting, looking hopeful. Then I'd dredge through my memories of Lambeth and come up with a little tidbit of a story about Albie.

Beat wrote to say that George had enlisted; he was eighteen this month. Then Jim had gone too and lied about his age, but Beat had marched straight round to the sergeant with Jim's birth certificate and got him back. She said Jim was sulking now and wouldn't hardly speak to her, but Alf had written telling Beat she'd been quite right to do what she'd done – three sons in the army were enough for any man to worry about. 'He's a good father, Alf, always thinks of the boys first. He's a good man, for all he can be difficult sometimes.'

'A good man, for all he can be difficult.' My thoughts winged to Leo, and all the things he'd be having to put up with in the hospital: the moans of pain, the smells – and the blood. I couldn't have borne even to go into one of those places, let alone work there, as he was doing.

Forcing the fear away I concentrated instead on the contents of his Christmas parcel. I'd thought very carefully about his main present, how he'd be living in a wooden hut, and how cold it would be in winter – especially with him not being so young, and his uniform likely not fitting properly on account of his hump – so I'd decided to make an inner jacket to go under his tunic. It buttoned right up to his neck and was of a khaki colour, like his uniform; but unlike his uniform it would be a perfect fit, because I'd drafted a pattern using his morning coat as a model; and even more unlike his uniform it was made of the finest quality mohair alpaca. When it was finished I embroidered his name and number in bright red inside the neck, in nice large letters, so that nobody else could 'borrow' it – not that it would have fitted anyone else, with him being such a peculiar shape. After that was done I spent half an hour with the Harrods catalogue, choosing a selection of his favourite foods, starting with anchovy paste and finishing with truffles in a tin. Mrs Carter had made several Christmas cakes, so I sent him one of those, too, along with his regular box of cigars and a pair of gloves I'd knitted while I was reading the latest regulations from the Board of Agriculture.

I wasn't expecting a Christmas present from him, but it came, direct from Harrods: a package containing a sleek silver fountain pen and a gold watch bracelet. They'd both be so useful, because these days I always seemed to be at my desk in the estate office filling in forms with Mr Selby or hurrying up to the Home Farm to see Mr Arnott. But as I said to Leo in my thank you letter, they were beautiful, too.

He seemed very pleased with his presents; he wrote back to me at once. And so did Frank. Obviously I'd sent a parcel to him, in case no one else did; I'd sent it in Flora's name, but the letter in reply was addressed to me.

> Do thank Flora for the Christmas parcel; it was much appreciated. She has quite a sophisticated taste in cigarettes, considering her tender years! Still having a good time with the French. I'll be deuced sorry when it's over. When I get my next leave I'll run down to Wiltshire to see you – it looks as if I'll have to make do with my substitute wife for good now.
> Ever yours, Frank.

As I read his words I felt a rush of excitement – I just couldn't help it.

After Christmas the short days became bleak and bitter. Mr Tims said he'd never known such a cold winter; I ordered two long-sleeved vests of llama wool and told him he must wear them under his dress jacket. When they arrived the vests were so soft and thick that I immediately ordered two more, and sent them to Leo; it would be just as cold in France. Coal was in short supply and we were ordered by the government not to waste fuel, so Leo wrote to Mr Hicks saying the glasshouses would have to be left unheated. He sent pages of instructions on how he wanted this done, and as they were all written in indelible pencil his tongue must have been purple for weeks from having to lick the point. Clara and I helped Mr Hicks pack the pot roses in straw, then he and Jesse draped tarpaulins over the glass roofs and we left the roses in the dark.

Out in the garden the fronds of the Garland Rose were only twigs against the steel-grey sky; they looked as if they'd never come to life again. Two more telegrams came to the village; the young men of Eston were being cut down and scattered like the petals of a rose in winter. I went down and wept with their mothers as they showed me the photographs of their sons: 'He was such a good boy . . .' The next week they handed me the letters which had followed: 'Would you like to read what it says about our Ted, my lady?' 'Dear Mrs Davies, I know that by now you will have received the usual notification from the War Office . . . shot in the head . . . died at once . . . his gallant conduct . . . a sad loss to us all . . . Sincerely yours, Philip Branson, Officer Commanding C Company.' I shared their tears of pride.

Leo's letters got shorter and shorter; perhaps he didn't like the taste of indelible pencil, since when he did write the odd one in ink it was longer – and generally from the YMCA hut. I wondered why he didn't use their ink all the time. I still wrote my weekly letter to him on the same day, but his replies came all on different days now; he said it depended how busy he was. At the beginning of February he ended one by writing: 'Incidentally, I now wear two stripes on my sleeve, so technically your reply envelope should be addressed to: "Corporal Warminster".'

I told Lady Burton the next time she called and she smiled approvingly. 'So the Warminster blood is still running true to form – even in the ranks.' As she walked down the stairs on her way out she nodded to the portraits of the painted generals, reciting the battles they'd fought in: 'The Boyne, Blenheim, Quebec, Saratoga, Waterloo.' She moved on to the last fierce portrait: Arthur, Sixth Earl of Warminster. 'He was in Afghanistan, one of the few survivors. Then he went to the Crimea. He'd been laid up with typhoid, so he didn't get there until '55, but he landed determined to sort them out – the British High Command, not the Russians – and so he did by all accounts. Not an easy person: he barked at everyone, poor Elizabeth worst of all. Leonidas takes after him, I'm afraid.'

I said indignantly, 'Leo doesn't bark – except when he's angry!'

'What a loyal little thing you are, dear – just like Elizabeth.' As we reached the hall she said, 'What a terrible winter. Poor George, I do wish he hadn't gone back to the Front.' Her face was suddenly pinched and old.

I put my hand on her arm, 'I'm sure Sir George will be all right, Lady Burton. He's been a soldier for so long.' For a moment I was suffocated by the scent of violets, then we heard the clatter of the motor drawing up outside and Mr Tims shuffled over to the front door.

Lady Burton turned to face me directly. 'By the way, I had a telegram from Francis this morning. He's invited himself down for a few days while he's on leave. I expect he'll run over here. It's only natural he should wish to see the little girl.' Her eyes were shrewd as they watched my face, then she added, 'We can't always have what we want, dear – not in this world. You will remember that, won't you? Goodbye for now, regards to Leonidas when next you write.'

But even under the watchful gaze of the red-coated generals I could not conceal my excitement as I ran back upstairs. Just to see him, to know he was safe – that would be enough.

Chapter Twenty-Nine

He arrived just before tea. I was up in my sitting room with Rose when he came in, ruddy-cheeked from exercise and the cold. 'Thank God old George has still got one or two decent horses in his stable.' Flinging himself down into a chair he held his hands out to the warmth of the fire. 'I had a thoroughly good gallop on the way over here.'

I sat watching him as he stared into the leaping flames. His face was thinner and the slimness of youth had given way to the lean strength of manhood: gone forever was the laughing boy who'd run beside me in the park. I shivered, and it was some time before I ventured to ask, 'Are you still talking to the French?'

His head came up, and I saw the fine lines around his blue eyes. 'Not officially. I'm back in the line now, with the old battalion. Except it isn't the old battalion any longer, so many good fellows have bought it.' This time he saw my shiver. 'No good looking like that, Amy. If your number's up, it's up.' He sat back in his chair, stretching out his glossy leather boots so that the steel tips of his spurs glittered in the firelight. 'Where's Flora?'

'She'll be down in a minute for tea. Shall I send for her now?'

'Please, Amy.'

He charmed his daughter all through tea; she was utterly entranced by him. Rose fell asleep on the sofa beside me, as I sat quietly watching those two blond heads so close together. But once the tray had been removed he said firmly, 'It's time you were back in your nursery, young lady.' So I rang Ellen to take a protesting Flora away.

As soon as the door had closed behind them he said abruptly, 'I saw Annabel on my way back to England. She was wearing a shapeless blue uniform, her lovely hair was crammed under a turban and her beautiful hands were covered in filthy grease. She'd been investigating the innards of her ambulance. We stood there, having a civilized chat about flywheels and sparking plugs – not that any of it meant a thing to me, I'm no engineer. We even had a cup of coffee together in some god-awful café in Boulogne – once she'd divested herself of the grease. She's ruined her hands, simply ruined them!' His voice had risen in anger; now it became level once more. 'She told me being in France had made her see things differently. She'd realized life was too short to waste in useless regrets – so she said she'd forgiven me.'

I whispered, 'I'm glad – I'm so glad.'

'No, Amy, you don't understand. Her idea of forgiveness is that she's now willing to set me free. She's already consulted her lawyer about starting divorce proceedings. I can't deny adultery, of course, but since it's a wife petitioning she has to prove cruelty as well.'

I exclaimed, 'You were never cruel to her!'

'But I was, Amy, that's the final irony. One of the definitions of cruelty is the transmission by one spouse to another of a venereal disease. And the law is right: it was the cruellest thing I could have done to her. I shan't defend it – I can't defend it.' He was silent for a moment, before continuing, 'She's playing totally fair, she said if I hadn't turned up she would have written to me. She's thought it all out very carefully. She's even been to see the old man – God knows how she managed that, but it seems she can manage anything these days. She wanted his agreement because if she set me free and I then married again my son would eventually inherit the title and the Warminster estates. He told her he wasn't bothered: he'd promised Maman he would acknowledge me as his heir and he would never go back on that promise. And since the Eston property came from his mother it's his to leave outright, so you and the girls will be well provided for.'

He looked up at me, his blue eyes hurt and angry. 'How damned civilized everyone's become these days! They talk about estates and property, and "doing the decent thing". No one talks of love and hate, guilt and anger any more. The cold-blooded English – it made me realize how totally French I am. I wanted to seize hold of her overalled shoulders and shake her while I bellowed to the skies of love and passion! I wanted to tell the whole world of how I'd loved her the first moment I saw her!' Then his voice dropped. 'The world might have listened, but she wouldn't have done.' His face was twisted with pain and regret as his blue eyes sought mine, and held them. 'So I'll tell you instead, my faithful little Amy.' His eyes became shadowed as he retreated into his memories. 'That evening I first saw her – it was the Doncasters' ball. I looked at her glossy dark hair, at her sparkling brown eyes, at the flashing delight of her smile – and I fell in love with her, there and then, before I'd even spoken to her. I'd gone with Tom Verney and he'd got his eye on her too – he was very reluctant to perform the introductions! But the minute the music started again I asked her to dance, so for the first time I held her in my arms. I was delirious with excitement, and afterwards I couldn't get her out of my mind. I hadn't intended to marry, not till I was old and grey – I was enjoying myself too much – but now I knew I was going to have to take the plunge, because I simply couldn't bear the thought of losing her.

'That day I met her in the park I was on fire with love, so as soon as I realized she'd left her parasol behind I mounted guard over it, holding it hostage for another glimpse, another word – even just for the lightest touch of her gloved hand. So I stood there, in the sun, waiting for Annabel to come back. But instead, you came.' His eyes lifted to my face. 'You came running towards me, the golden tendrils of your hair blowing in the breeze and your pretty face so flustered and pink – and then my eyes fastened on your rounded little figure, all curved and ripe with promise.'

He paused for a moment, and his voice became very quiet as he told me,

'Amy, I was in love with the girl of my dreams – but I was a young man, and you know what young men are. Yes, the minute I'd seen Annabel I'd fallen in love with her – but the minute I saw you I wanted you, too.' My eyes never left his face as he continued, 'I didn't see it as impossible – I didn't even see it as wrong. You were two such different girls. Annabel was a girl of my own class, the woman I'd already chosen as my future wife – while you were just – Amy, her maid. When I flirted with you I assumed you knew the odds. It never even crossed my mind that you were expecting more of me than I intended to give.'

'But – '

'I know, Amy, I know – but young men are like that. They believe what they want to believe. And they believe that whatever they want, they should have. And bluntly, I wanted to marry Annabel, and I was prepared to be faithful to her as long as I could. But then, when the children began to come and she – wasn't always available – I wanted you, as well.'

'But that would've been adultery – and adultery, tis one o' the commandments!'

He smiled wryly. 'Well, yes – so I gather. But I can't say I was thinking much about the ten commandments, that day I first saw you in the Park.' He gave a small shrug. 'I suppose if anyone had drawn my attention to their existence I would have simply quoted biblical precedent. After all, Sarah offered Abraham the services of her handmaiden, didn't she?'

I exclaimed, 'That weren't the same at all! Everyone *knew* what were going on – Sarah *and* her maid. It were different with me and Miss Annabel. If I'd known who you really were that day in the Park I'd never ever have started making up dreams about you.'

His smile was tender now. 'My poor Amy, I'm afraid the sad truth is I wasn't worthy of your dreams. I was only interested in having fun, in the excitement of pursuing two girls who lived in the same house, who spent so much time together. How I enjoyed it all: the scent of intrigue, the spice of danger! It was a wonderful summer for me: courting Annabel under the approving eyes of half the matrons of London – and then, whenever I had a spare moment, wooing you, too.'

I couldn't speak. Watching my face he said gently, 'You see it was just a game for me, Amy – I never thought you'd be taking it seriously.' He paused a moment. 'No, let's be honest, I didn't think at all, not as long as I got my own way. But that time here at Eston, Annabel dared to challenge me, calling me selfish and over-bearing, and announcing that she wouldn't marry me if I were the last man left in the world. I was so angry – and hurt, too. But there you were, so totally different from her, hanging on my every word, gazing at me so adoringly from your pansy-soft eyes. You were balm to my wounded pride. *She* might have spurned me, but you were there instead, available – and offering yourself to me in every glance, every gesture.'

I was almost crying as I told him, 'I didn't mean – I weren't a light woman – I did love you! And you, I asked you if you did love me – and you said yes. You said yes.'

He looked at me with his eyes in shadow as he said, 'The oldest lie in the book.' Then he added, so softly I could hardly hear his words, 'But it isn't a lie any longer.' My heart thudded in my chest as I strained to hear his low voice. 'She's right, Annabel: the war makes you think differently, feel differently – you become a different person. What I'm trying to tell you, Amy, is that *I'm* different now. When I saw Annabel this time I respected her, admired her – but I didn't love her, not any more. Perhaps it was seeing her like that, wearing a man's uniform, doing a man's job; these last years, she's grown hard, unfeminine. It was partly my fault, I admit that now – perhaps I do feel guilt after all, and feeling guilty towards her has suffocated my love. I don't know. But I do know it's gone for good. So I decided to come here, not to see Flora, though I have, of course – but to see you. To see if I'd changed towards you, too.'

I couldn't help it; in a whisper I asked, 'And have you?'

'I don't know. Maybe I have, or maybe it was always there, underneath – and I simply didn't realize. But I'm sure now,' he paused, then raised his voice to say loudly and clearly, 'I love you Amy – and I always will.'

There was silence in that room, except for the crackling of the fire and the soft breathing of my husband's baby, asleep beside me.

When Frank finally spoke again his voice was very tired. 'It's all right, I won't try and persuade you to break any of your precious commandments now. I think, I hope, that I've become less selfish.' He laughed, gently, 'I'd like to say it was all in my soul now, and that I didn't want you physically – but it wouldn't be true. I do want you, very much. But I won't seduce you because I know that your conscience would destroy you afterwards. Only I wanted to tell you, Amy, that if we were both free again then I would go down on my bended knee and ask you to marry me.'

Abruptly he stood up. 'I'd better be going now. I don't want to damage your reputation. Besides, I'm looking forward to one of Ettie Burton's good dinners, and a full night's sleep in a decent bed.'

Gazing up at him I asked, 'Will you be coming tomorrow?'

'Yes. I don't know exactly when, but you'll wait for me, won't you?' I ducked my head in assent. 'Even if you have to wait for me all day?'

'Yes.'

'Amy, whose love is unconditional.' He came towards me, very tall and straight. 'Give me your hand – I'm a Frenchman, remember.' He bent over it, and his lips brushed the back. Then he turned it over and kissed my palm. 'Goodbye, sweet Amy.' The door closed quietly behind him.

After he'd gone I sat for a long time with my palm pressed against my cheek as his voice told me over and over again in my head, 'I love you, Amy – and I always will.' And at the memory of his words my heart sang with joy.

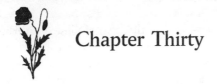

Chapter Thirty

At last I took my hand away from my cheek and kissed the palm, my lips touching where his had so briefly rested. 'If we were both free again . . .' Soon he would be free – but I would not. I would never be free. But even that knowledge could not dim the light of my joy tonight. I looked over to where Clytie knelt, in hopeless love; poor Clytie – but it was different for me, because my sun god loved me.

Beside me Rose snuffled and began to stir. I bent to kiss her awake then lifted her up close against my heart. For all the weight of her sturdy young body in my arms my step was quick and light as a young girl's as I ran up the stairs to the nursery.

Next morning I went along to the estate office as usual: Mr Selby was over at Pennings for the day and I had to do the corn accounts. But even as I entered the time and quantity of the wheat threshed last month, and amended the plan of the stackyard to suit, so my eyes kept veering up to the clock on the wall. All the time I was adding up quarters and bushels and calculating yield per acre, I was waiting for him. And when the last neat figure had been entered in its column I seized the blotting paper, slammed the book shut and almost ran out of the door like a child finally released from school.

I was only just in time. I'd hardly finished feeding Rose and picked up my sewing when Mr Tims announced: 'Lord Quinham, my lady.' Frank came striding into the room, so tall and lithe, 'Hello, Amy my pet. Are you going to give me lunch?' My heart leapt in my breast.

As we ate lunch together he talked of the shows he hoped to see in London before he went back, and of Paris in wartime: chatting to me lightly, casually – as if yesterday's conversation had never taken place. He smoked a cigarette with his coffee, after politely requesting my permission. Then as he stubbed it out he said, 'Let's take Flora for a walk, just the two of us.'

'Rose'll – '

He broke in, shaking his head, 'She'll be too heavy for you to carry.'

Rose complained a little when she realized I was leaving her, but Ellen distracted her. Then Flora, pleased and proud to be singled out, trotted downstairs by my side to where he waited in the hall. He held out his hand and she went to him at once. 'We're going for a walk in the woods, Flora.' Then he gave me a sidelong glance, his blue eyes teasing. 'But if we find a dormouse we mustn't wake him up or your Mama will be angry!'

Outside Flora chattered to him, pulling him along the path, demanding his attention; and he was content to let her have it. Then, as he held open the wicket gate that led into the wood he told her, 'We're neglecting your Mama, Flora – she'll be lonely.' He turned back to me, smiling, and although it was a cold February day I felt as though I were basking in the heat of a midsummer's sun.

As we walked on under the bare branches he said, 'Talk to me, Amy. I want to hear that soft, wood pigeon voice of yours.'

'What shall I talk about?'

'Oh, anything,' Then he checked himself. 'No, let's not talk about the past – or the future. Let's talk about the present. Tell me what you do all day: the little domestic tasks, the small trivial problems that vex the pretty heads of young women like you.'

I didn't think he really wanted to know about the problems of coping with all the orders being issued by the new food Production Department, so instead I told him of the frock I was sewing for Flora and the new bonnet I'd planned to make for Rose. He listened, smiling, and gradually the tired lines of his face relaxed and became smooth until he looked young again.

We came to the stile at the edge of the wood, and lifting Flora up into his arms he swung her in a great swooping arc over the wooden rail. She squealed with pleasure and excitement as she came to land in the lane beyond. He sprang over after her, then turned back to me, smiling. 'Give me your hand.' At the touch of his warm strong fingers my whole body seemed to come alive. He guided me up to the top step, but before I could climb over his hands were at my waist, holding me fast – and then, like Flora, I was swinging over, to land close beside him on the other side. His hands still held me; but his face was serious now as it bent over mine. 'Amy?' His voice was a whisper, and his mouth came nearer and nearer – then Flora tugged at my skirt. 'Mama, want to see ducks.' At once I pulled away from his restraining hands and he let me go. But as we walked on his breath came deep and fast, as though he'd been running; and my breathing echoed his. I bent and took Flora's hand in mine: Flora, my shield against him, and against myself.

As soon as we came to the pond Flora ran on, calling him, and he followed. I hung back in the shadow of the trees, listening to my daughter's excited voice as she clamoured for her father's attention. We let her do the talking as we returned by the lower path. It was getting colder now, and to speed us up he gave her a piggyback for the last stretch.

As soon as we got in, Frank carried her up to the nursery and handed her over to Ellen, ignoring her protests. Outside the door he grinned. 'Whatever would we do without nurseries! At that age a little of their company goes a long way; besides, I fancy a nice quiet cigarette in the peace of your sitting room. Coming, Amy?' He set off down the stairs, and I followed him.

As he smoked his cigarette I told him the story of Mary and the telegram and little Tommy. He exclaimed, 'You didn't actually *feed* it – a housemaid's child?'

'I couldn't let a baby starve.'

'Don't be silly, Amy, he wouldn't have done that. Obviously if he could get your breast he'd take it, but if you hadn't offered he'd have started guzzling from a bottle once he got really hungry. All healthy young male animals have a strong instinct for survival.' His face darkened. 'Even when the odds are all against them.' At the tone of his voice I shivered.

When he'd finished his cigarette I said, 'Rose'll have woken up by now, shall I fetch her down – '

'No, Amy – it's my turn today, I want you to myself.' I looked at him, startled. 'Oh, don't worry, I promise I won't lay a single wicked finger on you – I just want to talk to you.'

'What do you want to talk about?'

'Oh, this and that – anything will do.' His voice was rueful as he admitted, 'The truth is Amy, it's so long since I've had a woman hanging on my every word I want to make the most of the experience.' So he talked of France, and what a beautiful country she was; the sea, the mountains, the small villages. 'And now she's fighting for her life. Despite everything I'm glad I'm there, fighting with her.' He glanced at his watch. 'I'd better be off now, Ettie's invited some people round to dinner. I'll see you tomorrow, Amy, before I go back to Town. *Au revoir*.' Suddenly he was gone.

I loved him, oh, how I loved him. But it was too late. 'If we were both free again . . . ' But I would never be free, not now. If only, if only – I tried to rein in my thoughts but they careered on like a runaway horse, out of control. If only Leo hadn't married me, then when Miss Annabel divorced Frank – I caught at my thoughts again, trying to halt them, but they wouldn't be checked. If only Leo hadn't made me marry him, I'd have managed somehow, cared for Flora – and then taken her to Frank as a marriage gift.

And truth seized hold of those reins and pulled them tight. Because if Leo hadn't married me I would have lost Flora. I wouldn't have managed, not to keep her and myself. It would have been the workhouse, or the streets. By marrying me Leo had saved us both.

I stood up. I had to go down to the estate office; there was work to be done. But as I walked down the stairs my feet seemed to weigh like lead.

I spent most of the evening down in the office. I could control my thoughts better while I was busy; but I couldn't control my dreams that night. In them I saw Frank coming towards me like a knight of olden times, armour shining, spurs glinting. He held out his hands to me and I ran forward – only to wake weeping, because I had cut myself off for ever from the man I loved. It was a long time before I got back to sleep again.

Mr Selby arrived very early, his face creased with worry. He told me that the tenants over at Pennings were insisting that they couldn't possibly comply with the latest spate of ploughing orders. 'So many more men were called up in January, and the steam contractor that several of them customarily use has announced that he's given up his business. He's lost two of his ploughing team to the army and he's in poor health himself. He feels he simply can't cope any more. I gather he was keeping the business going for the sake of his son, so when he was killed just before Christmas ... I really don't know what we're going to do, Lady Warminster. Without that ploughing set even the normal work would have been delayed – and, of course, the weather's been so bad, too. But with the extra demands created by the ploughing orders the situation is impossible.' He sighed. 'And because I'm a member of the committee which signed those orders they all hold *me* responsible.'

I said automatically, 'Tisn't *your* fault, Mr Selby.' He looked at me hopefully, as if I was going to come up with an idea, but I couldn't seem to think clearly this morning. With another sigh he asked me if I'd finished the corn accounts.

Frank arrived in the middle of the afternoon. We walked in the garden and then we all had tea together. Afterwards he stretched out in his chair and watched as I played with the children on the floor, laughing as Rose tried to crawl over Nella's patient back, and allowing Flora to use his pockets as hiding places for the animals that escaped from the ark. But then he told them firmly, 'It's time you went upstairs now.' So I rang for Ellen.

As soon as she'd taken them away he sat back in his chair and stretched out his long legs. 'Nice little things, but they never give you a moment's peace, do they? And Flora's incessant questions soon pall. All those endless "whys". "Why does a duck swim, Uncle Frank?" she asked me yesterday. I told her, "Because they find drowning so inconvenient," and she gave me a very old-fashioned look. That's why women have that streak of childishness in their natures. They wouldn't be able to stand the company of young children, otherwise. They're like all young animals, basically boring.'

I leapt to the defence of my daughters. 'Leo says Flora's curiosity is a sign of how clever she is. He never minds answering her questions, however many she asks.' I took a deep breath and added, 'Rose coming, it could've made a difference to him, but it hasn't, he loves Flora just as much as her.'

Frank jumped up and walked over to the window. With his back to me he began to fiddle with the tassel on the end of the blind cord, before muttering, 'I know.' Then all of a sudden he spun round and said abruptly, 'I saw him over there – a month or so ago.'

'You didn't tell me.'

'No.' He dropped the tassel and came back, throwing himself down in the chair opposite me. 'The truth is, I've been wrestling with my conscience ever since I came down here, and conscience has finally won.' He gave a wry smile. 'It doesn't get many victories, so I'll concede this one, and tell you where I met him.'

But then he fell silent again, and it was left to me to prompt, 'Were you visiting someone, in the hospital?'

'He isn't in a hospital, hasn't been for months, virtually not since he arrived in France. He's with a field ambulance.'

Puzzled I asked, 'An ambulance – parked in a field?'

He looked up, half smiling. 'What an ignorant little pet you are, Amy. A field ambulance is a unit, a group of soldiers – it doesn't have anything to do with fields – not in the sense you think of them. Though I suppose there were nice, pretty green fields there once – before the Germans attacked and we dug our trenches and the Boches started firing their big guns, trying to destroy Ypres.'

'Ypres!' I heard the shock in my own voice, 'But they're fighting round Ypres!' Then I shook my head. 'Leo, he wouldn't be there. He isn't fighting, he's tending to soldiers as are wounded.'

'Exactly. And where do you think these soldiers are when they *get* their wounds?'

'But – ' I couldn't believe what he was implying.

'Oh, there are regimental stretcher bearers, but they only bring men in to the frontline trenches; after that it's up to the RAMC. And when there's a big show on there aren't enough regimentals – they need reinforcements, so we're back to the old man again. That's his job, lugging stretchers through that vile, unbelievable mud that tries to suck you under with every step, while the shells go screaming overhead. Rather him than me, I'll tell you. I like to get a move on in that kind of situation, but a loaded stretcher's damned heavy. It slows you down to a snail's pace, and at that speed you're a sitting duck for the Hun gunners.'

'But even the Germans wouldn't fire at men on stretchers!'

'You little goose, Amy – they simply fire. The big guns are way behind the line. They don't aim, they just try to blow up everything in front of them with their shells.' He grunted. 'Shells! What an innocuous word that is, redolent of sand castles on summer beaches. Typical of the English to give them a stupid name like that. I prefer the French *obu*, it's got the right note of menace.'

I hardly heard him, I was still grappling with the shock of what he'd told me. 'Leo's too old – and he's got a twisted neck!'

'He's certainly not the only volunteer on the wrong side of forty who's found himself in the thick of it, though I grant you the twisted neck's less common. But twisted neck or not, he's a big, strong man, and that's what they need up there. Actually, it was through that wry neck of his I found out where he was. I got a letter from Ted Gerard, who said after he bought his packet he was carried in by a man with a humped back, who held his head at a funny angle. He told me he was sure he'd seen this fellow before but he was so woozy he couldn't put a name to him until he reached the CCS. Then he became convinced it had been my father – so he said would I convey his heartfelt thanks. Apparently one of the other bearers was only a youngster and he began to break down – started shaking and saying he couldn't go on. Ted said he was sweating, thinking they'd have to leave him, but the old man kept this boy going somehow until they got to the ADS. Then the old man swapped the boy for some other poor so-and-so and went straight out again, lugging another empty stretcher ready for filling.'

Frank paused, gazing into the fire. I just sat staring at him, trying to take in what he'd been telling me. Leo, out there, plodding through dragging, sucking mud while the shells screamed overhead. I couldn't believe it – yet I knew it was true.

Frank turned his face from the fire and looked at me again. 'Not long after that I had to take a message back to divisional HQ, and as there was no rush I tracked down the dressing station Ted had told me about. It wasn't that far from where we were. Evil hole it was – been a farmhouse once but it was in ruins by now so they were using the cellar. The stench – I could hardly bear to go down the steps! And there at the bottom was the old man, feeding sips of tea to some poor sod who looked as if he were on the way out. I stood watching until the chap had finished his drink, and then the old man looked up and saw it was me. We just stared at each other for a few moments, then he said, "Good afternoon, Francis. Perhaps you would care for a cup of tea?"

'He made the tea and I offered him a fag, but he insisted I had one of his cigars instead. I'll say that for you, Amy, you've got the right idea there. He must be the only corporal on the Western Front whose wife's supplying him with Corona Imperials! You might send me a box as well, next time. Anyway, I gave him Ted's message, at which he looked distinctly embarrassed. Then I asked him how long he'd been with the field ambulance, and he told me; then he asked me where I was based, and I told him – and after that we didn't seem to have anything to say to each other.

'There was an MO there, a Scotsman – decent chap, though he looked absolutely exhausted – and I finished up chatting to him about the way things were going and suchlike. Really I wanted to talk to the old man, but I couldn't think of anything to say. Eventually I asked how the children were, and he said they were both in excellent health last time he'd heard. Then he added, "If you are in communication with my wife I would like you to give me your word that you won't mention this meeting. She is under the impression that I'm at a base hospital, and I would prefer that she retain that impression." He half turned his shoulder, as if he were embarrassed, before saying, "She is – soft-hearted – she might even – worry." So I gave him my word, and at the time I had every intention of keeping it. I think he sensed that, because he looked satisfied. Then he got up and said he had to call his section together, they were in some dugout at the back, and I still hadn't said anything – and the next minute he'd gone shambling up the steps and out.

'The doctor asked, "Do you know Corporal Warminster?" and I answered, "He's my father." It was the first time I'd ever called him that since Maman died, and even before, I'd always concealed the relationship if I could. When he'd got over his surprise the doctor started telling me what a stout fellow the old man was: apparently his sergeant had been killed a couple of weeks back, and he said he couldn't have kept the show on the road if it hadn't been for the old man. I stood there and listened, wishing I'd at least shaken hands with him before he'd gone, but the party of bearers had already left by then.'

216

He paused briefly before saying, 'You know, if he'd just wanted to get into uniform he could have wangled a desk job in London, he's got the right connections, but instead he chose to do it the hard way. And so there we were, the pair of us stuck in that god-awful sector, both of us up to our eyeballs in mud. And it was me that pushed him into it – though God knows, I didn't intend to push him all the way to the front line.' He broke off for a moment before adding quietly, 'I wasn't going to tell you, you know – not because he'd asked me to keep quiet about it but because I didn't want you to admire him. But then I thought, why shouldn't she admire him? I do.'

I didn't speak; I couldn't speak. For a moment he was silent, too. Then his eyes narrowed. 'Has the thought crossed your mind, Amy, that Annabel's going to set me free,' he paused before adding deliberately, 'and the old man could be blown to smithereens any minute?'

'No!'

'Oh come on, Amy, you're only human. The thought must have occurred to you.'

'No!' My voice was barely a whisper as I accused him, 'You said – you said you did admire him.'

'I do, but it doesn't stop me wishing he'd never married you.' He fell silent again, and when at last he spoke his voice was kind, 'Dry your eyes and we'll go and watch the babies being bathed. I feel like sitting in front of the fire in a warm nursery watching their strong, unmarked bodies splashing in the water. After all, that's what I'm fighting for – their future. Certainly not mine. Come along.'

Reaching out he took hold of my hands and pulled me upright. Then he squeezed my cold fingers with his warm, strong ones before letting them go. 'Can't have the servants talking, can we? Come on now.'

We sat in the warm nursery watching Rose splashing in her bath and listening to Flora's chatter. Then I took Rose next door while Ellen bathed Flora. As Rose fell asleep at my breast I heard his voice through the night nursery door – he was reading his daughter her bedtime story.

When Flora was tucked up in bed he kissed her goodnight, then outside in the corridor he told me, 'I'm off to Town first thing, and I'm hoping to get a few days' hunting in before I go back next week. Goodbye, Amy,' his voice softened, 'my golden girl, my might-have-been.'

We went downstairs to the hall, and waited in silence for his horse to be brought round. When we heard the clip-clop of its hooves he bent and kissed my hand in the French fashion. '*Au revoir*, my pet. Don't come out on the step, you'll get cold.' Mr Tims closed the door behind him and I went back up to my sitting room.

I went straight over to Clytie. Frank had gone. Next week he'd be back in France, again, in danger – yet still I seemed to hear his voice saying: 'I love you, Amy – and I always will.' But as I stood, facing that picture I heard another voice, halting, hesitant, as it asked: 'Would you unpin your hair for me now?' My hand still glowed from the warmth of Frank's kiss, but on my hair I seemed to feel that gentlest of touches, reminding me that another man loved me, too – and he, too, was in danger. My husband. And now I heard the other words Frank had spoken, those words I'd been fighting to forget: 'Has the thought crossed your mind, Amy . . . ' I cried again, 'No!' But he wouldn't be silenced. 'You're only human. The thought must have occurred to you.'

Had it? Had I thought that – even for one single moment? The ground beneath my feet was shaking, swaying. Had I? Had I? I gazed at Clytie – but she couldn't tell me the answer, she'd never been married. Turning away from her I ran out of the room and straight down the stairs to the hall. Seizing the handle of the door I almost threw myself into the library. For a moment it was as if I saw him there behind the desk – then I sank down into the armchair, my legs trembling. Because in that moment I'd known, known that if the price of a thousand lifetimes with the man I loved was the death of my husband, then that price was too high. I crouched in his chair sobbing with relief as Frank's words sank back into the mud and slime where they belonged.

Chapter Thirty-One

Drying my eyes I went out to the hall, to the portrait at the foot of the stairs: Arthur, Sixth Earl of Warminster. I gazed up at the high sweep of forehead, at the arrogant, jutting nose and stern unbending lips; then, looking him straight in the eye I told him, 'Your son, he's a brave man. You must be proud of him.'

As I went back up to my sitting room I knew that I was proud of him, too. He needn't have gone at all, and he certainly needn't ever have gone to the Front, into danger – yet he had. But for all my pride I couldn't stop worrying; and I was annoyed with myself, too. I should have realized. He wasn't a pigeon-chested artist, he was a strong, healthy man. Age was no bar to serving in France; Uncle Alf was there and he was older than Leo, and he wasn't the only one. I should have guessed when those letters came, written in pencil; a man as meticulous as Leo would never have written in pencil unless he had no choice. Then I became a little annoyed with him, too. Why hadn't he told me the truth, instead of trying to mislead me? 'I am now stationed at one of the larger base hospitals in France!' But perhaps he hadn't known then? No, I was sure he had; he'd simply chosen to write to me in that way over the brief time it was true, so as to mislead me.

As soon as Mr Selby stepped through the door of the estate office next day I demanded, 'Did *you* know that Leo was at the Front?'

Without looking me in the eye he said, 'I gather Lord Warminster is currently serving with a field ambulance.'

'Lord Quinham told me yesterday. He saw Leo out there, at *Ypres*.'

Mr Selby winced. 'I was not aware of the precise location of his posting.'

'Ypres, tis a main dangerous place.'

'Yes, I believe that is true. But I understand that RAMC personnel are not subject to quite the same degree of – risk as men in the infantry regiments.'

I just looked at him. 'Why didn't you tell me?'

'Lord Warminster expressly desired that I should not. He didn't wish to worry you.' Before I could say any more he continued hurriedly, 'Lady Warminster, I was going to consult you about a letter I've just received from Bedworth – he's one of the tenants at Pennings, I'm sure you remember. He's very anxious about the ploughing up orders. He says he's trying to obtain an exemption for his son on the grounds that he's needed on the farm as a ploughman, but he's short of horses and so behind because of the weather he's afraid he won't be able to comply with the orders and then his son will be conscripted, thus rendering the situation even more impossible.'

I said, 'Mr Selby, you write back to Mr Bedworth and tell him he'll be sure of an exemption for his son if he's working on a steam plough.'

Mr Selby looked surprised. 'But we don't need a steam ploughman at the Home Farm.'

'We will over at Pennings, though, for that pair o' ploughing engines we're going to buy from the contractor as is giving up his business.' Then I suddenly thought 'Tis a ploughman they're short of, isn't it? Foremen and drivers, they'd likely be older.'

'Yes, you're quite right. The foreman and driver are both above military age, but they've lost the spare driver, too – and the cook.'

'We'll have to ask the farmers' wives to let 'em have a bite to eat off their table, and they'll have to do without a spare driver; Butty Williams and Judith, they manage between 'em. They can have a boy to give a hand with the water and coal and suchlike, and we'll put up the wages all round, like you did at Eston, to compensate for the extra work.'

'But Lady Warminster, we haven't bought the steam plough yet – it would be a considerable capital outlay.'

'Mr Selby, we can afford it. And we got to win this war.'

He was still hesitant. 'Perhaps we should write to Lord Warminster first.'

I shook my head firmly. 'There baint time. 'Sides, he's got enough to worry about. You go over to Pennings this afternoon and make an offer, I'll take the responsibility for doing it.'

Mr Selby's face cleared. 'You're quite right, Lady Warminster, absolutely right. The tenants will have no excuse for evading ploughing orders then, and Bedworth will be so relieved. He lost his elder boy last year, on the Somme, and his wife, hasn't got over it.'

'You'll have to make it clear to him, though, as his boy'll have to stay with the ploughing engines. Once we've seen to our tenants we'll hire it out to recoup some of our outlay. Anyway, steam tackle's too precious to be lying idle these days.'

Mr Selby took out his watch. 'I'll just glance through the post with you, Lady Warminster, then I'll catch the ten forty.'

We finished the post with ten minutes to spare, just as the cups of cocoa arrived. Mr Selby was very partial to milky drinks and it would set him up before his journey.

As he put his cup down he said abruptly, 'Lady Warminster, I personally feel that Lord Warminster was mistaken in his decision not to apprise you of his current situation. You may be still a young woman, but calendar years are not the only guide to wisdom. It is right that you should know the true facts. However, if I may proffer some advice, I suggest that when you next write to your husband you do not refer to your recently acquired knowledge.'

'But – '

'If *he* feels happier protecting you from additional worry, wouldn't it be kinder to allow him to continue in that state?'

I rolled my pencil along the desk. 'But suppose, suppose – ' I looked up at Mr Selby and voiced my fears, 'Suppose a telegram comes?'

There was silence. Then Mr Selby said quietly, 'Lord Warminster has arranged that in such an eventuality the notification from the War Office will be addressed to me. I think that indicates the strength of his desire to protect you.' When I didn't reply he spoke more forcefully, 'Please, Lady Warminster, I have known your husband a long time, and over the years I have become aware that, because of his – physical and personal problems, he has a horror of arousing sympathy. I am quite sure that if he had wanted you to know his whereabouts he would have told you.'

In the end I agreed. But it was difficult composing my usual letter: it would have been difficult anyway, after Frank's visit, but it was even more so now. Eventually I began as I always did with news of the children, and a question about the roses. Then I wrote:

> Lord Quinham was on leave and he came to stay with Lady Burton for a couple of nights. He visited me and the children in the afternoons. He's gone back to London now, and then he was hoping to go hunting. The weather is still very cold here, it has been a bad winter. You must be sure and change your socks when they get damp, else you might catch a chill.

Then I went on to tell him about the steam ploughing set, making it quite clear that it had been my decision to buy it, in case he disapproved; but I didn't think he would. I was grateful to that steam plough, it helped me to fill two pages; I wouldn't have known what to write, otherwise. Then I signed myself, as always: 'Your obedient wife, Amy.' But as I wrote 'wife' I felt like Judas, because however hard I tried I couldn't get Frank's words out of my mind: 'I love you, Amy – and I always will.' Those words I'd longed for, hungered for – spoken too late.

The address on Leo's next letter was written in ink; I heaved a sigh of relief as I noticed. At least he was safe for a little while. Apprehensively I opened it, but I needn't have worried. After replying to my news of the children, and the query about his roses he'd written:

> You were quite right to instruct Selby to purchase the steam ploughing set; he informs me the transaction is proceeding satisfactorily. I trust Francis enjoyed the rest of his leave and was successful in his desire for a few days' hunting; however, I'm afraid he may have been disappointed, since there have been so many sharp frosts recently. I am concerned that my poor roses will suffer from the effects of this harsh winter, although Hicks is an able man and will, I know, do everything possible to obviate the most serious consequences. Do take care to wrap up warmly when you take Nella for her evening run.

Despite the cold I enjoyed those evening walks with Nella: it was pleasant to have a little time outside when I didn't have to worry about the estate. But as February gave way to March and the bitter weather of that spring which was no spring still held us in its icy grip, I had to spend even more time on estate business; and as a consequence I had to wean Rose. I didn't want to, but I had no choice. Mr Selby developed a bad chest, and although he insisted on coming over to the estate office each morning I couldn't let him go out on his usual round of visits, so I went in his place. Even if I'd been able to use the motor it would have been too cold for Rose, but petrol was in short supply and the motor was difficult to start in the very cold weather so I asked Mr Tyson to teach me to drive the governess cart. Bessy was so placid it didn't take long to get the hang of it, and then I'd set off each afternoon, leaving Rose upstairs in the warm nursery.

Then Mr Selby got worse, and Dr Matthews ordered him to bed. He was due over at Pennings, so I had to go instead. I didn't want to go and I was shivering with nerves on the train on the way, but as soon as Mr Bedworth met me at the station with his trap and his worries I realized that I wasn't little Amy Roberts any longer: I was Lady Warminster now, with a job to do and people depending on me.

I even had to take Mr Selby's place at a meeting of the County Agricultural Executive Committee. I felt extremely nervous at first sitting round a table with all those elderly, grave-faced men, but they were very polite and helpful, and obviously we all shared the same problems. Another thirty thousand men had been called up from the land in January, and although the War Office had promised us agricultural companies of soldiers to partially replace them they were to be made up of men who were unfit even for Home Defence, so, as Mr Arnott had said, they wouldn't be fit for much else, either. So we talked of how best to allocate the new tractors the government was lending us, and pinned our hopes on the promise that all skilled soldier ploughmen who were still based in Britain would be released on leave until the end of April. I was so glad we'd bought that second steam ploughing set, and so were the men on the committee.

Albie came home on leave. Beat wrote to invite Ellen to stay in London, because he only had five days. Albie brought her back the evening before he had to leave for France, and we all sat up in the nursery together, listening to Albie talk about the war.

Leo's next letter was in pencil, and I held it in my hand for a moment, almost frightened to open it. But after his usual replies to my news he simply wrote of the roses: how he missed walking in his garden of an evening because even in winter he liked to know how his rose bushes were getting on. So that evening I decided to take Nella a little further than usual, and make the walk for him; then next time I wrote I would describe everything I'd seen.

Although the moon was almost full the black clouds chasing across her silver face kept plunging us into darkness, and I was soon shivering because it was colder than I'd realized. But I didn't go back for an extra cardigan to wear under my coat because I knew that wherever Leo and Frank were, they were cold, too – so it was only right that I should suffer a little for their sakes. My feet soon took me to the autumn rose garden, to the place where Aimée Vibert's black branches clung to their supporting wall. Nella went to the corner of the walls, and into the little round room, sniffing for some lingering scent of him, and whined as she remembered.

And I remembered, too. Remembering how that first time I'd come into this garden I'd thought I'd stepped into a fairy story: the story of Beauty and the Beast. I'd woven a tale of how he'd grown this beautiful garden to please the French Countess, and to win her love. But I'd been wrong, quite wrong; he'd grown it as a refuge from the world in which she'd never loved him and never would. I couldn't bear to stay there any longer. With Nella close behind me I began to run across the frost-dried grass of winter, running away from his memories. I came to the gate in the wall and the minute Nella had whisked her feathery tail through I slammed it shut, closing the door on that garden Beauty had never wanted, grown by the Beast she had come to hate. I was sobbing as I walked back to the house, and up in my sitting room I threw myself down on the hearthrug in front of the fire and wrapped my arms around the golden-furred neck of Nella; Nella, who truly loved him.

All through March the papers had been full of news. There'd been a revolution in Russia and the Tsar had abdicated; the British had advanced on the Somme, the Germans were retreating – but by the end of the month the Germans were fighting back fiercely and the casualty lists lengthened. I read them each day with my heart pounding like a drum; please keep Frank safe. And Leo, where was he? If some men were wounded then other men had to carry them in from the battlefield.

When April arrived there were still very sharp frosts every night. Mr Selby said he'd never known a season when the crops had been so far behind. The winter seemed to be going on for ever – like the war. But on April 6th the Americans declared war on Germany, and the Stars and Stripes flew beside the Union Jack over the Houses of Parliament. When Lady Burton brought her grandchildren over to play with Flora she said it would be quite some time before their army would be ready to sail across the Atlantic, 'But as soon as they arrive we'll beat the Huns – there's no doubt about that.' But in the meantime our troops couldn't simply sit and wait – and the next week there were reports of a big battle near a town called Arras.

Leo's letters were in pencil again. I wrote back with news of the children: 'Rose do like to feed herself with her spoon, though she puts more on her face than she does in her mouth! She's learnt to drink nicely from a cup now, and what with her beginning to walk and starting to talk she's not really a baby any longer.' I thought of him out there in the mud missing all this and added:

I wish you did have the Beast's magic mirror, and could see her turning into a little girl. I dare say you still picture her as she was before you went away. Do you remember that last night before you left, how you held us both? She was such a good baby, wasn't she, settling down so cosily with us the way she did.

Mr Tims put his head round the door. 'Mr Selby's arrived, my lady.'

Hastily I scribbled: 'Now don't forget to change your socks when they get wet. Your obedient wife, Amy.'

When his reply came it was written with a pen; nowadays I was more aware of his writing implement than of the words he wrote. He told me Mr Selby had said he didn't know how he would have managed the estate without my help. I couldn't control my feeling of pride as I read those last words.

Leo's next two letters were in pencil, and I worried again; but the one after that was in ink, though I only had time to notice that from the envelope, another of those green-printed ones – because Mr Tims brought it up to the nursery, and the minute I'd pulled up the flap Flora snatched it out of my hand and the sheets inside dropped out on to the rug. Immediately Flora seized one and ran shrieking off with it; Rose tried to stagger after her, lost her grip on the chair and tumbled to the floor with a howl of protest. By the time I'd picked her up and kissed her better and Ellen had retrieved the scattered sheets of paper we were all flushed and panting. Ellen grinned, 'They've got the wind in their tails today, my lady – you'd best slip down to your sitting room and read his lordship's letter in peace.'

Downstairs I curled up on the window seat where there was plenty of light and smoothed out the crumpled pages; despite the way the letter had been tossed about the first page was still on top. The date was almost three weeks ago, so it must have been delayed in the post.

Dear Amy,

Thank you for your letter. Yes, I do remember the night before I left. I remember too, regretting the arrival of dawn that final morning, so delightful was the experience of holding you both in my arms. I have such happy memories of that night; even now I can see in my mind's eye the golden fringe of your lashes resting on the curve of your cheek as you slept. I didn't sleep, not for one single second: I didn't want to waste a moment of that precious time when I lay holding you. Holding your warm, scented body – milk-scented, flower-scented – the scent of a woman lovelier far than the most beautiful of my roses, and dearer, far dearer than any rose could be – because I love you, Amy, I love you.

But that last night when you nestled so trustingly against me, my heart was pierced with joy and sorrow mingled, for I knew you did not love me, would never love me. Duty, obedience, loyalty, compassion: all these you have given me, but love you cannot give, for your heart belongs to another, the son of him whom my first wife loved – and so the wheel has turned full circle.

My rose, my beloved one, my dearest, dearest wife – but therein lies the thorn. My wife, but not my wife from choice; for I seized you and made you captive as surely as the Beast trapped Beauty, holding her prisoner in his enchanted castle. You, like Beauty, talked kindly to the Beast each evening, and did not blame him for your captivity. But the Beast, how did he feel, wounded by the stabbing thorns of guilt, cursed by his hideous deformed body, and knowing the agony of loving where love could never be returned? Pity the Beast, Amy, pity the Beast.

But you are more generous than Beauty – for you give love even when you cannot feel it, and so you came to me that night and held me in your arms – and in so doing, broke my heart.

And next morning you broke my heart a second time, and now it will never be whole again. It was when you lifted your smooth young cheek to my lips – and commanded me to kiss you. To kiss! You do not understand, my Amy, what that gesture meant to me. You cannot know, and I shall never tell you, just as I will never tell you of my love. I should never have even let you glimpse it. There was no need. You believed my heart still lay with her, with Jeanette; and it would have been kinder to let you believe so still. After all, Amy, I did love her, my pale, silver-gilt Jeanette. I loved her with all the ferocious, selfish arrogance of youth, but it was love, nonetheless; and to love and be spurned is a terrible thing. You know that, my sweet Amy, you understand; and understanding, you have never spurned or rejected me.

How I love you, Amy, how I love you. Yes, I loved Jeanette, and when I understood that she could never return my love then such was my despair that I craved for death. I loved her; but my love for her was as the pale silver moon compared with the blazing golden sun of my love for Amy – for Amy who can never love me. Pity the Beast, Amy, pity the Beast – but pity me more, for he had hope and I have none.

I intended to write a moderate, considered reply to your letter; but I am not a moderate or considering man. Nevertheless I will have to pretend to be such, as I have done so often before. When I am rational again then I shall calmly burn these pages, and scatter their ashes in the mud where so many other dead bones lie buried. I was foolish to address this green envelope, it proved far too dangerous a temptation; my pen needs the curb of a censor's eye. So now I will proceed to write another missive, couched in the terms of restrained affection appropriate for a middle-aged husband writing to his young wife. But this letter I cannot send because I know you would not wish to receive it; it would distress you beyond measure. You do not want or need my love, so I will not inflict it upon you; yet while I am still in the grip of my folly I shall continue to write to you as I long to do, because I love you, Amy, I love you. I love you, I love you, I love you, I love you . . .

He had written it over and over again, filling the page. I turned over and still it was written, *I love you, I love you*. As he came nearer to the bottom of the paper his writing became smaller and smaller, so that he could fit it in more times.

One of my tears dropped on the page, blurring a tiny 'I love you,' and it was only then that I realized there was a fourth sheet – written in a different, unfamiliar hand.

> Dear Lady Warminster
> I know that by now you will have received the usual notification from the War Office . . .

My heart stood still.

The words blurred and jumped before my eyes and it was a long time before I could read on:

> However, I felt I should write and tell you that although Corporal Warminster's wounds were severe I have seen others recover from worse, and despite his age he is a strong and healthy man.
> He will be greatly missed by all of us in this unit, and especially by myself, for in these past difficult months he has been a tower of strength to me. I hope you will forgive my presumption in writing to you in this way, but I felt I wanted to express my sympathy with you in your anxiety. I have his small book and personal effects and will send them to the appropriate authorities, who will doubtless forward them on to you; however, since it was clear from the briefest of glimpses that the enclosed letter was of a personal nature I thought it best to post it to you directly, in the hope that it may be of comfort to you in this time of trial.
> Yours, very sincerely,
> David McIver (Captain, RAMC).

In a nightmare I looked at Leo's writing on the envelope – and saw the betraying rust-red smear. He was dying, Leo was dying!

Chapter Thirty-Two

He was dying, and I hadn't loved him. 'Pity the Beast – but pity me more, for he had hope and I have none.' No hope because I wouldn't give him hope, had not let him hope. And now he was lying wounded in France, and would die – unless I gave him the hope he needed. And so I knew what I had to do: I must go to France, and tell him I loved him. As I stood up my legs were shaking so much they would scarcely support me, but I had to go, because I was his wife. I looked down at the ring he had given me: my wedding ring. 'Love, honour and obey' – I had obeyed, I had honoured, now I must love.

By the time I got downstairs Mr Selby had arrived, with the telegram. I showed him the doctor's letter, then I told him, 'I'm going to France.'

'But, Lady Warminster, surely it would be better to wait until we receive further information?'

I shook my head. 'No, I've waited too long already.'

I went to Lady Burton, and asked her to help. When I showed her the letter – both letters – she understood. She took me to London to see a general with braid on his tunic and red tabs on his collar; he tried to reason with me, but I would have none of it, so he told us to wait. I waited, with Lady Burton's hand clasping mine, until at last he called us back into his office. 'Warminster has severe gunshot wounds of the left arm and leg; he's a patient in the Number 23 General Hospital at Etaples. Do you understand that, Lady Warminster? Etaples is in France, and France is a war zone. Are you quite sure you want to make this journey?'

My legs shook with fear but I had to go, I had to. 'Yes – yes, I'm sure.'

He pushed a piece of paper across the desk. 'Then you may leave tomorrow. Here's your Red Cross pass: it's made out in your name – yours alone. No one may accompany you, not even your maid. There's a travel warrant, too, and as Warminster enlisted in the ranks you will have to go third class.'

I shook my head. 'That dussent matter.'

His cheeks reddened as he said, 'Yes, of course – I'd forgotten – ' He rose to his feet and held out his hand, 'Good luck, Lady Warminster.'

I went back to Eston and packed my basket. That night as I lay in bed, cuddling Rose, I remembered those hours before she'd been born. I'd been so frightened. And then Leo had come to me, comforted me and given me strength. Now I must go to him and give him hope, the hope that only I could give.

Next morning I kissed Rose and Flora goodbye and then drove to the station in the chill dawn air, Clara by my side. On the platform she hugged me in farewell – and then I was on my own. As I sat on the train my thoughts darted hither and thither. Remembering my daughters' uncomprehending faces as I'd told them I must leave them for a while, my heart ached; but they were safe at Eston, while their father lay alone, wounded, dying. My hand tightened on his letter: 'Pity the Beast, Amy, pity the Beast – but pity me more.' Yes, I pitied him – but did I love him? At once I thrust the treacherous question from me; I would love him, I must love him.

Victoria was a huge mingled crowd of men in khaki uniforms and women with strained anxious eyes. Then the men began to separate, moving towards the barrier and through on to the platform where the train stood waiting. On legs that would not stop their shaking, I followed them.

At Folkestone I almost fled in panic from the signs of war: the long lines of soldiers filing down the path, the small group of serious-faced nurses following them, the drab ships in the harbour and the warships waiting further out to sea – all these struck terror in my heart. But I had to go, although my hands shook so much I could barely fasten the tapes of the bulky life jacket I was ordered to wear.

Slowly the ship left harbour, leaving England and safety behind. Already I could see the coast of France ahead. It was too late to turn back now, and with that realization came a measure of calm. Then I saw him. He stood tall and straight, his cap in his hand and his blond head bare as he gazed across the sea to France, his own country. It was Frank. Dropping my basket I began to run, twisting and turning between the groups of soldiers, my heart hammering in my ears, my breath catching in my throat, until at last I came to him and caught his arm crying, 'Frank – I be here!' And a stranger's face turned to mine.

He looked surprised before saying politely, 'I'm sorry, I don't think – '

I turned and dived back into the crowd, the tears of disappointment coursing my cheeks.

I found a hiding place in a dark corner behind the stairs and there I let myself cry: hopelessly, desperately, because it was no use. I should never have come – all I could offer him was a lie. It was Frank I loved, not Leo. If only I'd listened to Mr Selby, and waited for more news. But suppose, suppose I'd waited – and he'd died? He was wounded, badly wounded – and the letter . . . I'd read it so often I knew it by heart. 'I loved Jeanette, and when I understood she could never return my love then I craved for death . . . the Beast had hope, I have none.' I couldn't have waited, I couldn't wait now.

I would have to tell him a lie, tell him I loved him, even though I didn't. But after that first moment of joy he would know the truth, know that I was lying. I was certain of that, with a bleak, cold certainty. After all, why should I love him now, when I'd not loved him before he went? 'You have never spurned or rejected me.' But I had. All that summer I had rejected his love, choosing honesty instead – a pitiless, selfish honesty that had left him in no doubt about my feelings. And he had understood: he still understood, his letter proved that. It was too late for lies now: yet lies were all I had to offer him.

Hopelessly I dried my tears and went to retrieve my basket. I found a seat and sat staring out across the grey seas to France, trying not to think.

But as the coast came nearer and nearer those words of his came creeping back into my mind: 'Pity the Beast, pity the Beast . . . ' And I did, I did – but it was no use, because that was all I felt. Just like Beauty. Suddenly my head snapped up. No, I was wrong. Not like Beauty. Pity was all she felt *until she saw the Beast!* At that moment, pity turned to love – the miracle happened when Beauty saw him lying at her feet. And as it happened for her, so would it for me.

A strong tide of confidence surged through me – but even as it came flooding in I remembered that fair young officer, and felt its threatened ebb – *no!* I must not remember. Don't even think of fair young officers, don't think of – I knew I dare not even say his name. I stared at the coast ahead of me: no, think of Leo, lying in front of me, wounded and close to death. Leo, needing me, needing my love. Think of him now, and think of that moment when I'll see him and know that I love him – and loving him, will save his life.

At last the shuddering movements of the ship became calm as we began to move safely in between the sheltering arms of the harbour. And so I came to France – France where once Leo had taken me to safety.

But it was an alien France now, a khaki-clad France where bugles sounded and every man carried a rifle. As I came ashore a train with a red cross on its side drew up along the quay, and through its windows I saw the bandaged forms and pale faces of men who'd been wounded – wounded like him.

Then a woman in a grey uniform called out, 'Any more relatives? Relatives visiting wounded?' I stepped forward. She studied my pass carefully before saying, 'You must wait with the others. The train is delayed.' Like a sheepdog she swept me ahead of her into a small group of white-faced women, and one shaking old man.

We were herded into a hotel, still clutching our passes like talismans. A woman with a shawl over her grey hair turned to me, 'Are ye away to see yer man, lassie?'

'Yes – my husband.' Her thin hand reached out and patted mine, and I whispered, 'Is it your son?'

'Aye – my Jamie, and sich a guid laddie, too.' I saw the tears in her eyes as she said, 'But I've been two days on ma way already, and they dinna send fer kin unless – ' Then her shoulders squared under her shawl. 'But if only I can see my Jamie – I'll hearten him, I'm sure of it.'

In low-pitched voices women murmured of their hopes, because they dared not talk of their fears – and in the corner opposite the old man sat silent, his mottled veined hands clutching his stick and his chalky blue eyes blank with despair.

They brought us a meal, which I chewed and swallowed without tasting. Then at last the uniformed woman bundled us out, and into a compartment where two tired soldiers sat slumped in the far corner. We soon fell into silence, each of us weaving our own web of worries while the rhythmically turning wheels seemed to beat out their warning, 'The Beast is dying, the Beast is dying . . . ' I put my hands to my ears to muffle the sound – but I could still hear the insistent note: 'Dying – dying – dying – '

The wheels slowed, and stopped. Then the train began to clatter slowly backwards. I looked up in dismay and one of the soldiers spoke reassuringly. 'It's only a siding – to let another train through – an ambulance train, mebbe.'

But it wasn't an ambulance train that clanked slowly past: it was worse, much worse than that. Under their muffling tarpaulins the great guns poked their menacing barrels up into the sky; I'd seen pictures – we'd all seen pictures – but I'd never believed guns could be so huge, so enormous. 'Severe gunshot wounds of the left arm and leg,' the General had said. The soldier leant over and tried to talk to me, but I couldn't reply. All I could do was clutch at my wedding ring – Leo's ring – the magic ring that the Beast had given Beauty, to bring her back to him.

Stopping, starting, wearily the train crawled on. Every time it stopped I willed it to start again, every time it started again I willed it to go faster – but it never did, there was only the slow, clanking refrain: 'The Beast is dying, the Beast is dying . . . '

Finally, with a low expiring hiss of steam, it shuddered to a halt by the lamps of a station. I sprang up, then one of the soldiers said, 'This is Dannes-Camiers,' and I sank down on the hard seat again, watching the old man opposite pick up his hat with one shaking hand while the knuckles of the other whitened as he levered himself up with his stick. He climbed stiffly down the steps and stood still for a moment on the platform, then he began to shuffle away, out of sight. He'd never spoken a single word.

I turned to one of the soldiers, 'Etaples, when will we get to Etaples?'

His eyes were kind as he told me, 'It's the next stop. We'll soon be there.'

By the time we reached Etaples it had long been dark, and the dim light from the lamps was reflected on the shining wetness of the platform. My shaking legs took me down into the wind and rain – and people, and noise.

A grey-uniformed figure stepped forward: 'Relatives wait here.' A lady's voice, loud and authoritative. When we were all assembled she said briskly, 'I'll take you down to the hostel, you'll be in need of a good night's sleep.'

Before I could speak the Scotswoman asked, 'Jamie – my Jamie?'

'You can see him tomorrow. It's too late to go to the hospital tonight. Follow me, please.'

Too late, too late – the Beast was dying, I must find him now. Quite deliberately I slipped sideways, into the deeper shadows, and waited there until the sound of footsteps had receded. Then I went up to the soldier guarding the barrier. 'Please, which way is the hospital called Number 23?'

A thumb jerked. 'That way. Go straight through Eetaps village and out the other side. You'll see the signboard.'

Leaving the shelter of the station I stepped out on to the greasy cobbles and began to walk, my head down against the driving rain. I came to houses, then a dirty, rubbish-strewn square. Crossing it I walked along another filthy street until the houses ended and there was open space on either side. Slithering and slipping in the darkness, I was panting and frightened – but I must find him, I must. An engine whistled, and an ambulance rattled past, its red cross dark against a circle of white; I followed it, on and on. Then ahead of me I saw another pair of headlights, a second ambulance, turning off the road – and in the gleam of its lights I saw black letters on a white board: 'No. 23 General Hospital'.

Quickening my pace I hurried in pursuit of the ambulance, but by the time I reached the hospital entrance it was well ahead of me, and I slowed down, looking around. Lamps set high on posts cast a dim glow over the lines of huts that stretched into the distance. It was so big – I'd never thought it would be so big – but I made myself walk on, my eyes desperately searching for other painted signs. I found them, but their names meant nothing to me, and I began to panic. But I had to find him, I had to. I fixed my mind on Beauty, searching for her Beast: but her search had taken her running lightly over springy grass amid the scent of roses, while I slipped and slithered in the mud, and all around me was the stench of decay. A sob rose in my throat, but I fought it down – I must find him, I must. Doggedly I plodded on.

Then another ambulance rattled slowly past and ahead of me I saw lights, and heard the sound of voices. I speeded up until I came to an open space lit by roaring flares, where the ambulances were unloading. Men staggered along duckboards, stooping under the weight of loaded stretchers, while others followed, bowed and shuffling with bandaged legs and arms in slings. Three men came towards me, huddled close together, and I stepped forward – and then I saw it, the blood-stained bandaged stump of the man in the middle, swinging uselessly where his leg should have been. My 'Please' died on my lips unvoiced as I backed away in horror, eyes darting desperately around – and all at once it was a scene from hell itself, with the everlasting flames leaping and burning until they consumed utterly the staggering sinners who shuffled towards them.

The vision only lasted a moment – but it left me so shaken and trembling that I could not go forward into that scene and ask for help. Instead I turned, and stumbled back into the maze of huts. Vainly I searched, up one slippery path and down the next, up and down, up and down, until I came to a little hut. It was smaller than all the others, and it stood by itself in its own clearing; the size and simplicity of it reassured me. I would go up to its door and knock on it, asking for help. But even as I began to walk towards it the door opened and I saw inside: saw a man with a shining knife raised in one hand, saw the flash of steel as the knife sliced down into living flesh – and saw the blood spurt up in a plume of scarlet.

It was the pigsticker with his knife, and the blood was Dimpsey's blood – Dimpsey's lifeblood bubbling away into the can I held in front of her despairing eyes. Dimpsey, my Dimpsey – and the agony of betrayal overwhelmed me as I rushed headlong into the darkness.

I didn't stop until I fell over a rope to land sprawling against harsh wet canvas, with my knees sinking into the cold mud. While the wind wailed overhead I clutched at the rope that had tripped me up, and sobbed with fear and pain, because I was a child again, a child who'd betrayed her pet pig; and now the poison of that betrayal welled up to destroy me.

Blindly I reached out my other hand, and it caught on the tent peg, sharp and painful. I snatched my hand back – and gold gleamed through the rent in my torn glove. The ring. My wedding ring – Beauty's magic ring – because I was married to the Beast. Desperately I clung to that fairy tale, calling to it for help as I'd so often called before – and help came. Fighting down my panic I concentrated on the ring, Leo's ring. I must find him, find Leo. And when I found him I would love him, and so save his life. All I had to do was find him.

Gripping the rope I pulled myself up to stand swaying in the cold and the rain. Then I bent to lift my basket and began to pick my way over the slippery mud to the duckboard path. Once I reached it I set off back the way I'd come. I shuddered as I passed the small hut, but now the first panic had gone I knew what it was: a place where men used knives not to kill but to heal. And that knowledge kept my footsteps steady as I walked on past those flares – which were not the leaping flames of hell but a light to guide injured men to rest and shelter. My eyes searched for a sign – and saw it in a notice reading: 'Sisters' Quarters'. I walked up to the door of the nearest hut and knocked on it.

The two nurses inside helped me. One fetched hot water so I could wash the worst of the mud from my legs and hands and face, and while I was tidying my hair she sponged my coat for me. Meanwhile, the other nurse had gone to try and find out where Leo was. When she came back she told me she'd spoken to the sister who was in charge at night and she'd said I could go to the ward now. I set off beside her, her torch casting a bobbing circle of light in front of our feet.

We stopped outside one of the huge tents – as big as a marquee – and the sister came forward to meet me and take me into a small, canvas-walled room. 'So you're Corporal Warminster's wife.'

Her eyes were so kind that as I nodded I told her, 'I've come to tell him I love him.'

Her face creased in concern. 'My dear, I'm afraid you can't do that.'

Fear clutched at my throat and I could only gasp, 'He baint dead?'

'No, no,' she was patting my arm, reassuring me. 'His condition is quite stable. Captain Adams is pleased with his progress.' I was trembling with relief as she added, 'But I'm afraid you won't be able to speak to him because he's totally deaf: the force of the explosion has ruptured both his eardrums.

However, he should regain his hearing before too long, providing there's no serious infection. But come along now, and you can see him, at least.'

Picking up her torch she led me out into a long narrow ward of canvas. A row of beds was set either side of a central aisle, and in the dim glow from the red-shaded lights I could see the humped shapes of the occupants. A nurse was sitting at a screened table in the middle, her white cap tinged with pink as she bent over her sewing. I followed the sister up between the endless rows of beds until we came to the last one. She spoke softly, 'He's sleeping at present, but you may sit by his bed until he wakes. Here he is.'

She shaded her torch with her hand before switching it on. Then she raised it so that I could see him properly. He lay there before me, hump-backed, wry-necked, and with his lopsided face swollen by a great, livid bruise; and I saw that he was uglier and more grotesque than he had ever been. As I stood there looking down at him I was engulfed by a great surging flood of pity and compassion – but not love. Not love.

Chapter Thirty-Three

The sister murmured, 'See, he's only sleeping,' and I felt the pressure of her hand on my shoulder. Obediently I sat down on the chair beside the bed; there was nothing else to do. Switching off her torch she went away, and I sat on in the dark.

I could hear the gurgling, irregular snores of the other men, the sound of grinding teeth from the next bed – and all the time the steady, monotonous hiss-slap as the canvas sides of the ward bellied in and out in the wind. Gradually my eyes became accustomed to the dim glow from the red-shaded lights until the mound in the bed beside me became Leo's familiar hump-backed shape again. I shivered with the cold of despair. I had gambled everything on one last desperate throw – and I'd lost. I still loved Frank. I bent over the sleeping form of my husband and whispered, 'I be sorry, Leo – terrible sorry.' But he couldn't hear me, and he simply slumbered on.

All I could do was sit there, hopeless; then I felt a light touch on my shoulder. It was the sister again. Low-voiced she murmured, 'Nurse is making us all a cup of tea. Come down to the kitchen with me.'

I followed her back down between the beds and out into a canvas-walled kitchen where a kettle hissed on a Primus stove. As soon as the tea was brewed the nurse filled three cups and then carried her own back to her seat in the ward; the sister sat down opposite me. Her voice was kind as she said, 'Don't worry, my dear. When he wakes you'll find there are more ways than words of telling a man that you love him.'

Raising my eyes to hers I told her the bleak truth. 'But I don't.' And then it all came tumbling out: 'I do still love Frank – I cassent help it. Leo, he's been such a good husband to me. He did marry me to give my baby a name, and he does love her, my Flora – just as though she were his own. And now we've got Rose, and when she were being born I were so frightened – but Leo, he came to me and held me – he's been so good to me. And now he loves me – but I cassent love him back.'

I drew a long, quavering breath before going on to explain, 'I got the letter, the letter from the doctor saying as he'd been wounded, hurt bad – and I thought if I didn't come and tell him I loved him, then he'd die, like the Beast. In the fairy tale, the Beast was dying until Beauty came back. So I came, I left my babies and I came. Only on the boat there was an officer with fair hair, and he looked just like Frank. At first I thought he was Frank – but he wasn't. Only seeing him like that, it made me realize that it were no use. I still loved Frank, not Leo.' Her eyes were so kind that I confessed my last desperate folly. 'But I

234

thought mebbe I could *make* myself fall in love with him by pretending it were the same as the fairy tale; that when I saw him I'd love him – just like Beauty did. But I didn't. And now I dussent know what to do.'

There was silence, except for the hissing-slapping sound of the wind in the canvas walls. Then the sister began to speak. 'A long time ago, when I'd only just learnt to be a nurse, I went out on a private case to care for an old lady. She was very old, and she used to sleep a lot, so I'd sit by her bedside reading. One evening she picked up my book and looked at it; it was a tale of love and romance. After she'd glanced at it she put it down again, with a smile. Then she said, "You know, nurse, there are so many foolish ideas about love."'

The sister reached over and touched my hand. 'Drink your tea, Mrs Warminster, or it'll get cold.' Obediently I raised my cup to my lips, and the quiet voice continued, 'So I asked my patient why she'd said that. It was obvious she wanted to tell me, and I was curious. What she told me was her own story. When she was a girl she'd fallen in love with a young man – John, he was called – and he'd fallen in love with her. As she spoke of him her whole face lit up, and I could see that in her youth she'd been very beautiful. But they'd been headstrong, each wanting their own way, she said, and neither would give in to the other. So they quarrelled, and John went rushing off to India in a huff – and in a fit of pique she'd married his brother, Edwin. She hadn't loved him, but she wanted to show John she didn't care for him any more. But of course, she did. She told me: "As I walked out of the church on Edwin's arm I realized what I'd done – but it was too late. I was young and selfish, and I made Edwin very unhappy. He didn't deserve it, he was a good man and he loved me, but I didn't love him – and I let him know it; I punished him for my own folly. Then our first child was born, a boy, and I looked at Edwin's face as he held his son – our son – and thought, it's time I grew up. Edwin is such a good man: so kind, so patient, and now he is the father of my child – so I will make myself love him." Then her eyes closed in pain as she told me, "But I couldn't."'

My hands trembled so much on my teacup I had to put it down. The sister didn't look at me as she went on with her story. ' "I felt so guilty," the old lady told me, "because I knew it was all my fault, so I kept trying and trying. Then it got even worse, because John came back, and I knew I still loved him, and always would – and that he still loved me. So I realized it was no use trying to love Edwin any longer. I could only do my best to be a good wife to him."'

The tears began to trickle down my cheeks; the sister said gently, 'I haven't reached the end of my story yet. The old lady told me: "We had other children, two more sons – and then my precious daughter was born. Every summer their Uncle John used to come and stay with us, and every summer I used to hope that perhaps this year my heart would not leap in my breast as I saw him come striding through the door, but every year it did. And then one summer the two of them were standing by the window, talking, and I looked at John, so tall and strong and splendid – and knew that I still loved him, totally, utterly. And then

I looked at my husband: shorter, rather plump now, and going slightly bald – and I realized that I loved him, too. Not in the same way, but it was love, nonetheless." She smiled at me, such a beautiful smile, as she said, "People talk as if it's not possible to love two men at once, but it is. And they talk as if there can only be one kind of love between men and women – the love of passion, the love of romance – but that's not so, either. There is another kind of love, too: the calmer love that grows from trust and respect and affection." Then she said: "But that love cannot be forced, nurse: it will come when it's ready, and not before." Have you finished your tea, Mrs Warminster? Then why don't you go back and sit by your husband's bed for a little while? I'm sure your presence will be a comfort to him when he wakens.'

I dried my eyes before saying quietly, 'Aye, sister, I'll do that. And thank 'ee, thank 'ee for telling me that story.'

She went over to the cupboard and took out a small lantern. 'Here, take this with you. It's rather dark in that far corner. Put it on his locker, then he can see you clearly when he wakes up.' She smiled. 'We don't want him to think you're just a dream, do we?' She lit the lantern and I carried it up the ward to where Leo lay, and sat down by his bed.

He must have broken his left arm; it was in a splint, which was tied at one end to a wooden frame over the bed, to keep his arm stretched out. As I'd walked up the ward I'd noticed other men with their limbs tethered to the same contraptions, but it must have been worse for Leo, because his hump prevented him from lying flat on his back. He'd be so uncomfortable when he woke. And his face: I had time to look at it properly now, and by the light of the lantern I could see just how bad was the bruising from where the shell must have exploded, on his left side. I shuddered. If it had been just a little closer – then I thrust that thought away. It hadn't been, and he was here, alive, in front of me. And the sister had said Captain Adams was pleased with his progress, so he would get well again, and come back to his rose garden.

I felt a little warmer now, from drinking the tea – and besides, Leo could have been so much worse. But all the same, I was sure he was in pain: his uneven mouth was more lopsided than ever because of his lips being so puffed and swollen from the bruising, and there was a split in one corner that was encrusted with dried, blackened blood. Oh, my poor Leo, what have they done to you?

Then guilt came back: for what had I done to him, too? It was different for the old lady, she'd tried to love her husband – but I hadn't. No, all that summer before he'd gone away, I'd been trying *not* to love him; finally I admitted that to myself. I hadn't *wanted* to love him, because I'd thought that a woman could only love one man – and I hadn't wanted to stop loving Frank. Quickly I defended myself with the reminder that Leo had understood: yes, he'd understood, but understanding hadn't been enough, he needed love, too – my love. So now, at last I'd tried to love him – but it was too late. I couldn't.

The tears filled my eyes again. Whatever would I do when he woke up? For he was beginning to shift, uneasily. He must be so uncomfortable with his arm stuck out like that. With his eyes still closed he began to pull away from the frame and I murmured, 'No, Leo, thee maunt do that.' But, of course, he was deaf, so I reached out and touched his cheek to waken him fully and make him aware. His lids lifted, and his bloodshot grey eyes focused on my face; he stopped tugging at the frame and became absolutely still as he lay staring at me.

'Amy, Amy – '

His voice was no more than a hoarse croak, but it sounded loud in that sleeping ward, so bending over him I put my finger close to his swollen lips. 'Shush, my Leo.' He opened his mouth again but the dried blood at the corner cracked, making him wince with pain. 'Lie still a moment, Leo.' Taking out my handkerchief I licked it, and then carefully wiped the dried blood from the crack in his lips. 'My poor Leo, do it hurt?' Gently I stroked his cheek, rough with the stubble of his beard; he looked as though he hadn't shaved for a week, but with him it was probably only a couple of days. He tried to turn further towards me, and tugged at his splint again. 'No,' I pointed up at the frame, and he became still again. He was so patient – yet I could see how uncomfortable he was. Reaching for his pillow I gently began to shift it round. What with his hump and his wry neck he needed it placed just so, and I watched his face until I saw the discomfort had eased.

'Thank you, Amy.' Then in a hoarse whisper he asked, 'Amy, is it truly you – or just a dream?'

'No dream, my Leo.' Then I realized he couldn't hear, so I bent right down over the bed and placed my cheek against his, so that he could feel me there. I stayed like that for a moment, while the warmth of his breath tickled my ear, then I sat back in the chair again. With his eyes fixed on my face he began to pull his right arm out from under the bedclothes. Still watching me he very slowly lifted it – then let it fall back again on to the coarse woollen blanket. It lay there, waiting. I reached out both of my hands and took his uninjured one between them. At once his fingers closed round mine, like a child taking comfort from the clasp of his mother's hand. I tightened my grip – and saw the relief in his face.

Cautiously I hooked my foot round the leg of the chair and eased it gently forward, so that I could sit back in it without letting go of his hand. His eyes were still fixed on my face, so I smiled at him before whispering, 'Tis time thee went back to sleep.' I dropped my own eyelids for a moment to tell him what he should do, and obediently he closed his; but his grip on my hand didn't loosen. Easing my chair closer still, I settled down to wait for him to fall asleep.

His breathing slowed, and his clasp slackened, but still I held his hand in mine. It was warm and alive, and gently I stroked the soft black fur of his wrist. The Beast would live. Tears began to trickle down my cheek: tears of relief and of thankfulness – and of love. And of love. The old lady had been right: it wasn't the same love, but it was love. Bending over him I whispered, 'Leo, I do love thee,' but he was deaf and could not hear. He gave a small, grunting snort, and then began to snore.

As I sat there looking down at his poor battered face I realized that I must have loved him for a long time, but I hadn't known that I did, because it was a different kind of love from the love I felt for Frank, and so I hadn't recognized it. And besides, I'd never imagined, never believed, that a woman could love in such a very different way. So trust, respect, affection – all these had grown into love without my even realizing it.

His hold on my hand slackened further as he sank into a deeper, healing sleep, so gently I disengaged my fingers and shifted in the chair to ease my aching back. My thoughts made their way back to Eston, to the nursery where my daughters lay sleeping. They would miss me when they woke in the morning and I yearned for them now. If only I had the Beast's magic mirror and could catch just a glimpse of their sleeping faces. But tonight my place was with Leo, my husband.

My eyelids were drooping when I felt a hand on my shoulder; I jerked up in my chair to see the sister's smiling face. Putting a finger to her lips she beckoned to me, and when we'd left the ward she said, 'Nurse tells me your husband has woken and seen that you're here, so it's time you went to get some sleep. It's too late to knock them up at the relatives' hostel, so if I give you a blanket you can go and lie down on one of the night nurses' beds for now. You can come back to see your husband tomorrow afternoon.'

I stumbled after her bobbing lantern until we reached the main path where the tall lamps lit our way. Sister pointed. 'Those are the latrines, and that's the ablutions hut.'

'Be that where I maun sleep?'

She laughed. 'No, dear – but I dare say you'll want to pop in and use the facilities before you go to bed. Now, this way, the hut on the end – you'll find two beds inside. Will you be all right now?'

'Aye, sister, thank 'ee – thank 'ee so much, you been main kind.' She turned to go, but I ran after her. 'Sister, thank 'ee for telling me that story. The old lady, she were right – an' I be so thankful for it.'

'I am so glad, my dear. Good night, now.'

I put my basket down in the hut and then went to find the latrines, and to wash. Back in the little hut I barely managed to get my shoes and coat and skirt off before falling on to the bed; I was asleep before I was properly lying down.

'And who's been sleeping in *my* bed?'

A nurse stood looking down at me. I jumped up stammering, 'I be terrible sorry. I didn't realize – '

A second nurse spoke reassuringly, 'It's all right. Sister told us all about you, only Tilney will have her little joke.'

238

'You must admit, Mac, she does look awfully like Goldilocks, with those long plaits spread all over the pillow. Oh, Sister said to tell you: "Corporal Warminster has had a comfortable night." That means he's doing quite nicely. In fact your arrival is proving rather a mystery, since nobody remembers sending for you in the first place. Still, ours not to reason why – and it makes a nice change to have a relative arrive to good news.' She smiled, then bent to untie her shoelace. 'Oh no! Not *another* holey stocking! It must have been when I rammed that sterilizer. I do so hate darning – and I've completely run out of wool, too.' She looked up at me, 'I say, since they won't let you visit your better half until this afternoon, you couldn't possibly run out to the shop from the hostel, could you?'

The nurse called Mac interrupted, 'Don't be silly, Tilney. She won't be able to make herself understood.'

I finally gathered my scattered wits together. 'O' course I'll get you some wool, I can speak French – and I'll darn your stocking for you, if you want.'

They both stared at me; then the one called Tilney said, 'That Corporal Warminster's wife can darn stockings is not surprising, but to be able to speak French – ' Her eyes narrowed, 'Now, don't tell me, let me guess. You were in service before you were married?' I nodded. 'A lady's maid?'

I exclaimed in surprise, 'Aye, I were!'

Tilney burst out laughing, 'Elementary, my dear Watson! Well, if you don't mind going to the shop – here, I'll give you the money. Are you serious about mending them, too?'

'Aye, I'd be glad to. I do like to keep my fingers busy. Mebbe if you've any other mending wants doing . . .'

Mac's eyebrows shot up. 'Any *other* mending – oh, aren't you wonderful! She isn't Goldilocks, Tilney, she's an angel.'

'*Non Angli, sed angeli* – as the sainted Augustine so neatly punned it!' They both laughed.

'You've got the gender wrong, old girl. This angel's female.'

'Victory for the suffragettes at last. Now, where was that petticoat I tore? How *lucky* that it's our hut at the end of the row. Suppose Sister had sent you to rest on the bed of that lazy hound Hunter, and *she'd* nobbled you instead. A real live lady's maid offering to do all my mending – I haven't felt so cheerful since we started nights!'

As she said that I realized that I was feeling cheerful, too. I missed Rose and Flora, of course, but otherwise it was as though a great weight had rolled from my shoulders. It was all right, I did love Leo.

239

Chapter Thirty-Four

I loved Leo. It was such a relief I was almost skipping as I walked out through the hospital gates. I wondered how he was feeling this morning. He was bound to be uncomfortable tethered to that wooden frame, but I'd be able to go and cheer him up this afternoon. I decided that when I went shopping I'd see if I could find him some fruit; he'd be missing that, I knew.

The maid let me in at the relatives' hostel, and invited me into the kitchen to share an early morning bowl of coffee with herself and the cook. The French words and phrases came sliding easily from my tongue, just as I'd learnt that year I'd lived in France. Now with quick words and gestures the two Frenchwomen told me where I could change my English money into francs, and the whereabouts of the telegraph office. That was my first task, to send a message of reassurance to Eston.

I felt positively light-hearted as I set off to do my shopping. Obviously the nurses had been right: he hadn't been ill enough to have his wife sent for – but I was so glad I'd come. And I knew Leo was glad, too: he needed me to look after him when he was feeling poorly. I bought the darning wool and managed to find some quite good apples for Leo, then I went in search of a treat for him. I found just the thing at the *épicerie*: a row of bottles of preserved fruit in syrup. I bought one of apricots and one of figs. Then I couldn't resist adding some cherries, because they were in a curled bottle that was shaped exactly like a fat stick of barley sugar: it was so pretty I thought he'd enjoy looking at it on his locker. I finished up by buying an enamel bowl and a spoon, so I could feed him myself and not be a nuisance to the nurses.

At dinner I sat beside Jamie's mother. She'd been to see her son in the hospital that morning, and now her eyes glistened with the tears she would not allow herself to shed. Her Jamie was dying, but at least she would be with him at the end, and as she pretended to eat she told me again what a good boy he was.

As soon as we'd finished our meal we set off down the busy road to the hospital entrance, and passed through into that strange city of wood and canvas, where every citizen wore uniform. I followed in the steady wake of Jamie's mother. She reached her wooden ward and turned into it, while I walked on to the line of great marquees, to find the one I wanted.

Just for a second, as I went up the wooden steps to go in, my confidence slipped. Suppose that in the daytime I didn't love him after all? But as soon as I saw his humped shape with that poor arm of his tied to its frame I knew that I did. And had done for a long time. Nothing had changed; except that now I knew, and that knowledge filled me with relief and thankfulness. He was looking out for me, his head turned awkwardly so he could watch the entrance to the ward, and his eyes never left my face as I walked up the aisle to his bed. When I reached him he just lay staring up at me, as if he couldn't believe I was really there. I smiled down at him. 'Tis all right now, my Leo. I be come to look after thee.' Bending down I touched his bristly cheek in greeting, and watched his slow, awkward smile light up his swollen face.

I set down my basket and went to fetch a chair. A man in khaki came hurrying forward, ''Ere, let me carry that for you, me love. Come to see your old dad, have you?'

I shook my head, glad that Leo was deaf. 'No, I've come to see my *husband*.'

Bending down I took out the bottle of figs and mimed the question: now or later?

He understood, and in a voice that was still hoarse replied, 'In a little while, please, Amy.' He smiled again and I smiled back before reaching into my basket for the first of the nurse's holey stockings. Luckily they'd had a darning mushroom in the shop, so as soon as I'd set the first line of threads my needle was rapidly weaving in and out.

He lay there watching me, then he asked, slowly, as if talking was still painful for him, 'How are the children?' Setting down my stocking I took his hand in mine and began to trace letters on his palm: T-H-E-Y. Glancing at him I saw he understood and continued: ARE BOTH WELL.

'Good, good.' Then he spoke again, asking, 'How did you get here?' This time it was easier to explain: I simply took the Red Cross pass out of my pocket and showed it to him. He looked rather surprised, then said slowly, 'I would not have expected my condition to warrant your being sent for, but I am glad you came. Thank you, Amy, thank you.' The letter – his letter – seemed to give a betraying rustle in my pocket, so I sat very still – because I knew he'd never intended it to be sent, and this wasn't the time or the place to tell him. Besides, he was deaf.

When I'd finished darning the first pair of stockings I rolled them together, slid my needle safely into the lapel of my jacket and opened the first of my bottles. Choosing four fine figs I cut them up into small pieces with the edge of the spoon and then gently eased each tasty fragment into the uninjured side of his mouth. When they'd all gone I put the bowl and spoon down on his locker and picked up the second pair of stockings. Looking at the large hole I was stretching over the mushroom he asked, 'Did you bring the *entire* contents of your mending basket with you?'

I was a touch indignant. 'They aren't mine, I wouldn't never let *my* stockings get into such a state!' Then I remembered he couldn't hear me and wrote on his palm, THEY BELONG TO THE NURSES.

'I see.'

After that he didn't speak again, but just lay watching my needle. I fed him cherries between stockings until tea-time. Then when I saw the nurses busy with their trays I put away my darning and went to help. I sat down again with Leo while the cups of tea were being drunk, until it was time to collect the crockery and take it out to that curious kitchen of canvas. I washed up the tea things and then laid the cutlery out ready for supper before returning to the mending.

When it was time for me to go back to the hostel I took his hand and wrote: GOOD NIGHT LEO on the palm.

At once he croaked, 'Will you be here tomorrow?'

'Aye,' I nodded vigorously – and saw the relief in his eyes. He was so big, and yet so vulnerable. He lay there looking up at me like a child looking up at its mother. I felt a wave of tenderness flood through me. 'Doan 'ee worry, Leo – I'll look after thee.'

I stayed in France for four more days. Although I was never again overwhelmed with the panic of that first night I didn't feel at ease in the hospital, with its smell of disinfectant battling against the foul scent of decay; and every time I passed the shining instruments lying in wait beside those sinister white enamel bowls my legs seemed to turn to jelly. But it helped being so busy: I'd collected a lot more mending from the other nurses and sisters, and every afternoon I'd take my basket into the ward with me when I went to see Leo. Whether I was simply sitting sewing, or on my feet running errands for the nurses and the other patients, he'd be watching me. And as I came back towards his bed he'd smile. But he said little, and I spoke even less, knowing he couldn't hear me. I'd bought some notepaper in Etaples so that I could write a letter home to Eston, but although I took it with me to the hospital each day I didn't use it much, except for the briefest of messages. Leo seemed content just to lie watching me sewing, waiting patiently for me to finish each darn, then he'd open his mouth ready for a slice of apple or a fragment of fig. But those small pieces were growing bigger every day, because the cut at the corner of his lips was healing and his bruised mouth was gradually returning to its normal, lopsided shape.

His wounds were healing too, Sister said. She explained that they were being regularly washed out through little rubber tubes – irrigation, she called it; and that since this seemed to be successfully preventing infection the doctor would soon be able to sew the edges of Leo's wounds together. She smiled, 'Captain Adams is as skilful with his needle as you are, Mrs Warminster, and your husband will feel much more comfortable once the suturing's done – but it'll be a while before the bones in his arm knit together again, so I'm sure he'll be sent back to England soon. Won't that be nice for you both? Though we'll be sorry to lose you, Mrs Warminster. You've been such a help in the ward, and with our mending – your stitches are so beautifully neat and regular. Nurse tells me you were a lady's maid before you married?'

'Aye, I was.'

'And your husband? What was his occupation before he enlisted? Although he's a man of few words I couldn't help noticing that he has quite a superior way of speaking, so I wondered if he was in good service, too.'

I hesitated before replying; I knew how Leo would hate the surprise and the exclamations if I told her he was a lord. Then inspiration came, and I said firmly, 'He were a gardener.' And it was the truth.

She smiled. 'How lovely – I'm sure he'll be glad to get back to it when the war ends. So brave of him to volunteer at his age, and with his disability.' A man called her, and she rustled away; I returned to Leo.

By the end of the week he was obviously much better, and my bed in the relatives' hostel was needed for another wife, so I decided it was time I returned to England. We knew by then that Leo would be following me soon after, and Flora and Rose would be missing me. The nurses gave me a present for them, a book of children's stories written in French by a man called Aesop. It had lovely illustrations in it of all different animals. I decided to show them the pictures when I got back, and then put it safely away until they were old enough to learn French.

I left Jamie's mother to her soon-ending vigil. We were both weeping as we clung together and kissed each other goodbye. Then I made the slow journey to Boulogne and up the gangway on to the leave boat.

As I stood on the deck in my bulky life jacket looking across the grey sea to England I remembered my outward journey: the panic and the fears – and that dreadful moment of despair when I'd seen the fair-haired young officer and believed my journey had been useless. But it hadn't been. The clouds parted, and ahead of me I saw the cliffs of England – England, where my children were waiting. My heart gave a great leap of excitement and longing.

A few days later we heard that Leo had been sent to a military hospital in Bristol. I went there to visit him regularly. They'd put his arm in a new type of splint, so now instead of sticking out at an awkward angle it was neatly folded at the elbow, with his forearm held tidily against his chest. He was up and walking, though it was obvious his leg was still painful. His hearing was gradually coming back but we seemed to have got out of the habit of talking to each other – or perhaps it was the presence of the other patients making us both shy. I finished up sitting beside him doing my sewing, just as I had in France. I preferred it when Mr Selby came to Bristol with me. Apart from him being company on the train Leo could hear his voice better than mine, and it was the same with Mr Wallis, too.

Mr Wallis had arrived on leave the week after Leo came back to England. He said he felt like some country peace and quiet, so he was going to see about a room in the village; but I insisted he must have his old one at Eston. 'You stay as long as you like, Mr Wallis, you know you're always welcome here.'

After he'd thanked me he said, 'You could have knocked me down with a feather when I got Clara's letter saying his lordship'd enlisted! But then I thought, well, it's not so surprising – it's in his blood, when all's said and done. I'll run along and see him while I'm on leave.'

Mr Wallis came to Bristol with me the very next day. He and Leo actually seemed to have quite a lot to talk about; it was with them both being in the army, of course.

As we left, the two men shook hands, and then Leo gestured to the three stripes on Mr Wallis' sleeve: 'You outrank me these days, Wallis!' They both laughed.

On the train afterwards Mr Wallis said, 'It's done him good, you know, being in the ranks – rubbed a few of his prickly corners off, I reckon. He used to spend far too much of his time prowling round his garden brooding over his problems, but he's got something else to think about now.' Then he glanced at me, smiling. 'Mind, I don't think it's just being in the army that's cheered him up. When you walked into that ward, my lady, he looked like a man who'd dropped a ha'penny and found the Crown Jewels instead!' My cheeks flamed, but I'd seen that expression on Leo's face, too. I was so glad I loved him now, after all.

By the time Leo had been three weeks at Bristol his hearing was almost back again, and although he'd still got a limp he'd discarded his stick and was walking steadily. The sister told me he'd be transferred to a convalescent hospital shortly – but she'd reckoned without Leo. As soon as he heard that, he sent Mr Selby up to London with a letter to a general who'd been at Eton with him, and by the next day he'd received notice of his discharge. As long as Dr Matthews kept an eye on him he could convalesce at home, at Eston.

Chapter Thirty-Five

Mr Hicks went with Mr Selby to fetch Leo, in case he felt faint on the train. After the carriage had gone down to the station I waited in the drawing room with the children, and as soon as we heard the wheels on the gravel Flora and Nella rushed out into the hall. Mr Tims opened the door, and we saw Leo already climbing out of the carriage under Mr Selby's watchful eye. Flora squealed, 'Papa!' and went running down the steps – but Nella was ahead of her. Rose watched the scene from the safety of my arms, her mouth open in amazement; she didn't remember her father at all.

She was still wary of him in the drawing room as we all had tea together. But after she'd watched Flora sitting close beside him, chattering nineteen to the dozen, she finally decided to make a move. Clutching a piece of cake in one sticky hand she toddled over to the sofa and offered it to Leo. I smiled proudly 'She's a good little walker now.'

'Steadier than I am at present. Thank you, Rose, that's very kind.'

But by the time Mr Tims came to take the tray away Leo's face had lost all its colour; the journey had obviously been tiring for him, and when I told him that Dr Matthews had said he'd drop in after evening surgery and would expect to find him in bed, he only put up a token resistance. I was firm. 'You're still convalescent. Mr Tims'll bring your dinner up on a tray.'

Dr Matthews came to see me afterwards in my sitting room. 'Nothing to worry about, Lady Warminster. He's a bit done up with the travelling, though, so I've told him it's breakfast in bed for the time being and no getting up tomorrow until I've seen him to give the say-so. I'll be round after morning surgery.'

He was almost at the door before I called him back. 'Dr Matthews, tomorrow, would you tell him what the doctor in London said – about his neck not being passed on?' I was bright red with embarrassment by now.

Dr Matthews looked surprised. 'Didn't you write to him at the time?' I shook my head. 'Oh well, no matter. I'll have to have a word with him in the morning.'

I was glad Dr Matthews was going to explain about that, because I had something else to say to Leo: now he could hear properly again I wanted to tell him that I did love him, after all. But I didn't know how to begin.

It was clear when I knocked and went shyly into his bedroom after dinner that tonight wasn't the right time. He was already three-quarters asleep. I murmured 'Good night, Leo – sleep tight,' and gently cupped his warm cheek with my hand for a moment before tiptoeing out.

The day after wasn't the right time either: Dr Matthews had obviously given Leo his news. Every time I popped into the library with the children to see how he was, he went brick-red and wouldn't look me in the eye. We went for a walk in the rose garden with the children and he hardly addressed one word to me. I decided I'd have to raise the matter myself, or we might not be speaking for a week.

As soon as Ellen had taken the children back to the nursery after tea, I asked, 'Leo, did Dr Matthews tell you?'

His colour began to rise. 'Yes – yes he did.'

''Tis good news, isn't it?'

'I – er – I . . . ' He was stammering badly. Then he caught hold of himself and said, 'I can hardly – take it in. For so long – I have believed – the reverse.' His voice dropped as he added, 'For so long – I believed that I was doomed to a life of celibacy.'

I said firmly, 'Well, you needn't have done.' Then, realizing what I'd said, I became rather flustered. 'That is, even if you hadn't wanted to get married – I mean, men, they do have their needs – '

'No.' His voice was decisive. 'When I was – a young man, before I realized the full – implications – of my appearance, I was exposed to temptation. My position in society alone ensured that this would be so. But I decided then that the – act of love – should not take place except where there is affection and trust. And feeling thus, I resolved that – for me – such actions should only take place within – marriage. I have always remained faithful to that resolution – and I always will.' Then suddenly he thrust himself up from the armchair and headed for the door. 'I will – go along to the library now.' He'd gone before I could say anything, which was perhaps as well, as I couldn't think of a reply.

I was surprised at what he'd said; I'd thought it was only women who felt like that. Yet in another way I wasn't, because Leo had always been different than other men – and for that I was glad.

I went up to the nursery to bath the children and Leo arrived while I was reading them their bedtime stories. Flora jumped up and ran to tug him over to the sofa; as soon as he sat down she clambered on to his lap. By the end of the stories Rose's soft dark head rested trustingly against his arm. He looked so pleased to be back with his daughters again.

As I dressed for dinner I remembered how he'd looked forward to grandchildren when Miss Annabel had first got married. Now he had daughters of his own, and soon I would give him a son. My heart leapt with excitement at the thought. This time next year I might be holding a baby in my arms again.

We talked of the roses over dinner. They were racing into bud now because these past few weeks had been so warm and fine. Even the crops had almost caught up after the terrible winter, which was such a relief. But all the time we talked of the roses I was thinking of what I'd be saying to him later.

We had coffee in my sitting room, so that he could stay upstairs afterwards.

Clara had offered to let Nella out for her evening run for the time being, to save Leo on the stairs – they were still an effort for him with his injured leg. I'd suggested he use a stick, with Eston being so big, but of course he wouldn't. 'I'm not a cripple, Amy.' I couldn't even reach out to hand to help, without him almost snapping at me, 'I can manage, I can manage.'

Mr Selby said, 'He's always been the same, Lady Warminster. He never could stand the idea of people feeling sorry for him.' So I had to pretend not to notice when he finally reached the top of the stairs and stood swaying there, with the sweat standing out on his forehead in glistening beads.

Once he was settled in his armchair, with his coffee close at hand, I took a deep breath and said, 'Leo, I thought as 'twould be nice to have a little boy next, after Rose.' There was silence. I added, 'I dare say as you'd like a son, wouldn't you?'

He took a sip of coffee before replying, 'No, I don't think so.'

'You'd rather have another girl then? I know you like little girls.'

'Yes, I do, but I'm quite satisfied with the two I've already got. They are delightful children.'

I just sat there, as disappointment seeped through me. I realized that I'd been deceiving myself with all these thoughts of giving *him* a son. I was the one who wanted the baby.

I guessed from the way he was concentrating on his coffee cup that he wasn't going to help me out, so I took another deep breath and asked, 'Would you mind if *I* had another baby?'

His head came up. 'Do you wish me to co-operate in this – enterprise?'

I stared at him in surprise. 'Well, o' course. You're my husband.'

He spoke very quietly. 'I'm not sure that I can – beget a child on you.'

I shook my head. 'No, didn't Dr Matthews explain? He said as you could.'

'He indicated that there was no – inheritance bar. That does not mean that I *can*, that I am able.'

'But now the doctor's said – '

'I can't get used to the idea, after so long.'

I was crestfallen. 'I should've written to you in the autumn, then you'd have had time to get used to it.'

'The problem is not merely one of time. It is more – fundamental.' His face was crimson by now, but at least he was still trying to explain. 'I think that were the circumstances such that I knew conception was a possibility,' he looked at me directly and amended to 'was likely, then anxiety might preclude my – performing – as a husband – is required to do.' I could feel my face fall. He continued, 'You are obviously disappointed. I am sorry – ' He broke off and began again. 'No, that's not being honest. I'm not sorry, not at the moment. We are both aware of the dangers of childbirth. I don't want to go away again and leave you facing that danger. That would be – another inhibiting factor.'

So there wasn't really anything else to say. He started to talk of the roses again. But when he'd finished his coffee and began to pull himself awkwardly to his feet with his sound arm, I remembered that there was something else to be said. 'Leo – ' He paused. I began again, my face hot. 'Leo, would anxiety preclude – prevent you acting as husband if there *weren't* a possibility of a baby?'

I knew the answer before he spoke: it was written in his face. 'Are you saying that you would be willing to resume marital relations even though I wore a – preventative?'

'O' course.'

'Well, if you're sure, I – ' He tried to move his arm, then looked down at the splint with a disappointed expression. 'I'm afraid that at present this damned appliance will prevent – '

I interrupted firmly. 'Tis no problem, Leo. We'll manage. After all, we got three good arms between us.' He began to smile.

He'd lost his nerve again by the time he came to my bedroom in his pyjamas later; but oddly, the more nervous he became, the more confident I felt. He looked like a big clumsy bear, and I was determined to help him. 'Have you got your little glove with you? Then I'll just turn my back while you slip it on.'

It took him a while because of only using one hand, but at last he started to heave himself over. But then, 'Amy, I can't – this damned splint will crush you.'

'Then, you best lie on your back and I'll lie on top of you.'

'But will we be able to – '

I said briskly, 'Leo, tis only a case o' putting the one thing inside the other. It don't really matter which way up we are. There baint no law about always doing it the same way – leastways, not so as I've heard.'

I felt his body quiver, and then I realized it was with laughter. I didn't know quite what he was laughing about, but luckily it seemed to cheer up his rod, too. I wriggled myself round so that my cunny was nicely placed at its tip and instructed, 'You slip your hand down, and put it in now.' And he did.

I said, 'Right, now you won't be able to move your hips up and down so easily from there, so I'd best move mine instead. You just lie still.'

It was fairly hard work at first, and then I got into the rhythm of it, and it was just like dancing. He'd closed his eyes but he looked as if he were enjoying it. Just to be sure, I asked, 'Is that all right for you , Leo?' His eyes flickered open, and gazing up at me, he said, 'It – is – most exquisitely – pleasurable, Amy.' When I heard that, I seemed to feel his pleasure in my own body. Then all of a sudden his hips started jerking up, and almost before I realized it, he was spending himself. I stayed there, holding his rod safe in my cunny, watching his face and listening to the little grunts he was giving. My whole body was flushed with warmth – it must have been all the exercise.

It was a bit awkward disentangling ourselves, because of the little glove. I lay with my back to him while he tried to get it off and sort it out with only one hand. It really would have been much easier if only – I pushed the thought away, and lay waiting for him to turn back for his cuddle.

I was really looking forward to that cuddle, and I'd decided that that was when I'd tell him I did love him – but no sooner had we got ourselves arranged around his splint than he fell asleep. I was rather indignant as I felt the weight of his head on my arm and realized. After all, I was the one who'd used all the energy doing It – but then I remembered he was only just out of hospital, and besides, if I were honest with myself I had to admit I'd found it quite a nice change doing It to him instead of the other way round. I was still thinking that when I fell asleep myself.

He must have eased himself out of the bed later, very carefully, because he hadn't disturbed me at all. When I awoke in the morning there was only the dent in the pillow beside me to show he'd been there.

Downstairs, Clara told me he was sleeping late. 'Mr Tims put his head round the door but he never stirred, so I said we'd best leave him to his rest, with him being just out of hospital.'

I felt rather worried at that; perhaps last night had been too much for him and I should have waited before offering. But at midday, when he came into the estate office, he looked so cheerful I decided I'd been right after all. He only stopped for a brief word with Mr Selby before asking, 'Shall I be seeing you at luncheon, Amy?'

'Aye, o' course.' He disappeared with Nella while Mr Selby and I got back to our calculations on how many acres we'd have to plant with oats next year.

Over lunch, Leo told me he'd been to see the golden rose – my rose – and the first buds would be opening soon. I remembered that evening he'd given it to me – and the disappointment on his face because I couldn't love him. Then I imagined his pleasure when he learnt that now I did, and I hugged the anticipation to me. I would tell him tonight.

But Lady Burton forestalled me. She didn't tell him that, of course, but she did tell him about the letter. I hadn't been sure about mentioning that just yet, since after all, he hadn't meant it to be sent   but there was no stopping Lady Burton once she was in full flood.

She sailed into the drawing room in a swirl of violet-scented silk. 'Leonidas – you're back! No, *please* don't get up. We must *cosset* our wounded heroes. How *proud* your dear mother would have been!' Seizing his hand, she pressed it to her bosom with both of hers. Leo looked desperately round for deliverance.

I ventured, 'Won't you sit down, Lady Burton?' She cast Leo off, 'Thank you, dear – and how are *you*? *So* pleased to have him home, I know. But you mustn't spoil him, my dear.' She wagged a playful finger at me. 'These men *will* take advantage, and we can't let them get above themselves, can we?' She swung back to Leo, 'Your little wife has been coping splendidly with the estate while you've been away. Your man Selby is *constantly* singing her praises to George's Evans.' She made me blush, but fortunately she was soon off on another tack. 'How is my dear little goddaughter – and darling Flora? *That's* what I came about, not just to make a fuss of this dear man.' She reached out to take Leo's hand again, then, thinking better of it, contented herself with patting the arm of his chair instead. 'It's Laura's birthday next week and we're having a party. Cynthia says you simply *must* send Flora over. There's to be a conjuror with a white rabbit. Now I know Flora's rather younger than the others but she's so quick for her age, and Cynthia's girls have made quite a pet of her. That reminds me, Leonidas, I heard from George this morning . . .'

She rattled on, and I could hardly get a word in edgeways; Leo didn't even try. Then she lifted her jewelled watch and peered at it. 'Oh, my dear, is that the time? I *promised* Matron I'd be back for tea, though the poor dear soldiers scarcely need any attention these days – not at all like when you used to come over, Leonidas. We only take convalescents now, and all they need is a little spoiling. Just like you, Leonidas dear – but I know dear little Amy will see to that.' As I reached for the bell, she exclaimed, 'Ah, Leonidas, if only you'd been here when she discovered you were lying wounded over there. She was *so* determined. "I must go to him, Lady Burton," she said, "I must go to him." Selby tried to make her wait until we had more news but she simply wouldn't. So I took her straight up to Town to see Farquarson – you remember him, of course? When he gave her the Red Cross pass he warned her. "France is a war zone," he said, but she still insisted on going, although I could see she was frightened, naturally – but once she'd got your letter nothing could stop her.' Out of the corner of my eye I saw Leo's whole body go rigid, as she continued, smiling, 'Although the doctor's note was really quite encouraging, she kept repeating, "I must go to him, I must find him – or he'll die." *So* romantic!' Mr Tims swung open the door. 'Don't forget to send little Flora – three o' clock. But don't tell her about the white rabbit, will you? We don't want to let the cat out of the bag. Goodbye, dear.' She rustled out, and Mr Tims silently closed the door behind her.

Leo rounded on me at once. 'You told me the Red Cross sent for you!'

'No, I didn't. You asked me *how* I came, not why.'

'That letter – *that's* why you came. McIver posted that letter.'

'He didn't read it. He said he could see it were personal.'

'That damned letter! It was a morass of self-pity! I intended to destroy it, I should have destroyed it. I shouldn't have written it – and you shouldn't have read it!'

'But it were addressed to me – of course I read it.'

'And having read it, of course you came.' He quoted Lady Burton's words: '"I must find him, or he'll die."' His voice dragged like the links of a chain. 'What a fool I was to talk of the Beast. You were haunted by that damned fairy tale again.'

'But I did find you, and you didn't die.'

His voice was harsh and angry as he exclaimed, 'But I didn't turn into a handsome young prince, did I?'

'No, o' course not, I never thought you would. It weren't *that* I were expecting – ' I broke off, but he pounced at once.

'What *were* you expecting, Amy? What magic did you hope for?' I hesitated and his voice rose, 'Tell me, tell me.'

So I told him. 'I thought that when I saw you lying there, I thought – ' my voice dropped to a whisper – 'I thought as I'd fall in love with you.'

There was silence between us. Then he said flatly, 'But you didn't, did you? Because you still love Francis.'

I couldn't reply, and he knew it. His voice was quiet, almost conversational, as he asked, 'Tell me, Amy, what *did* you feel when you saw me lying there? Tell me the truth, Amy, tell me!'

So I told him the truth. 'I felt sorry for you.' His face went white and hastily I added, 'That were all I felt at first. But then the sister, she gave me a cup of tea, and told me about this lady who'd married the wrong man. Two brothers they were, and she fell out wi' the one she loved, and married the other, only she still loved the first one – John he were called – she couldn't help it. She did try to love her husband, but she couldn't, so she stopped trying. But one day when he were holding one of her babies she realized she did love him, too, but it were a different kind of love from the way she loved John.' Leo's eyes never left my face. 'And after the sister had finished telling me that story, I went back and sat by your bed, just looking at you, with your poor face all bruised, and your arm broken like that – and then I realized I did love you, too.' He didn't reply, so I added quietly, 'I told you then, but you were deaf, so you couldn't hear.'

His anger exploded. 'Would that I were still deaf! I asked for pity, and that's what I got!'

I shook my head. 'No, twas love, too – '

'The love of a woman for a sickly child!' His voice was bitter with contempt.

I cried, 'I do *love* thee.'

He moved suddenly, limping, lurching, towards the door. When he reached it he swung round to look at me one last time before shouting, 'I don't want your lukewarm love!' Then, flinging himself through the door, he slammed it shut behind him.

Chapter Thirty-Six

At first I just couldn't believe it. I stood there, staring at the door which was still vibrating from the force of his slam with his words hammering in my ears: 'I don't want your lukewarm love!' My eyes filled with tears at the pain of his rejection. I'd tried so hard, I'd even gone all the way to France – and now he didn't want me.

I was like a child again, facing the awful truth that Grammer didn't want me, didn't love me – then I pulled myself up. No, it wasn't the same, not the same at all. Because Leo *did* love me. That was the problem: he wanted more love than I could give him. I'd tried so hard, and made myself love him, but he *still* wasn't satisfied. Anger burnt away my tears. He had no right to shout at me the way he had: it was he who'd demanded that I told him the truth. Besides, he'd *asked* for pity; he'd written in his letter, 'Pity the Beast – but pity me more,' and I had done; and loved him, too – but that wasn't good enough for him, and because he couldn't have exactly what he wanted he'd thrown a tantrum like a spoilt child.

And I knew what he'd do next – still like a spoilt child he'd sulk: brooding over his imaginary wrongs until eventually, grudgingly, he would allow me to coax him out of his bad mood. I closed my mouth in a firm line, because this time he was going to be disappointed; I wouldn't pander to his childish behaviour. It was time he grew up.

I didn't see him again until dinner, when he stumped out of the hall ahead of me without even replying to my 'Good evening'. In the morning room he sat hunched at the table, scowling at his plate. Shaking out my napkin I said, 'There's quite a nip in the air tonight.' His scowl deepened, and he didn't even grunt in reply. I didn't try to converse with him again, and when he held the door open for me at the end of the meal I swept past him without a word.

The story was the same for the rest of the week. He stayed in bed until after I'd breakfasted and then sulked in his library when he wasn't out in the garden with Nella. He didn't come near the estate office; not that it mattered since Mr Selby and I could cope perfectly well on our own.

Once when Mr Selby and I were discussing the arrangements for haymaking he said, 'I wonder if Lord Warminster would prefer – ' Then he broke off, saying, 'No, there's no point troubling Lord Warminster with this while he's convalescing.'

I said briskly, 'No, no point at all.'

I was determined not to give in first. After all, he was the one in the wrong. Then, as I was leaving the morning room after dinner on Friday, Leo suddenly spoke.

'By the way – '

I swung round at once. 'Yes? Did you want to – '

He snapped, 'Annabel's on leave. She will be coming here tomorrow, and staying the night.' He started closing the door before I was properly through it.

Of course, he was completely different with Miss Annabel, talking all through dinner, but he never addressed one single word to me. We had coffee in the drawing room afterwards, and when Leo briefly left us to fetch a book he'd been telling Miss Annabel about she turned to me and asked, 'Have you done something to upset Leonidas, Amy?'

I said, 'No, he's done something to upset me.'

She raised her eyebrows in disapproval. 'I hardly think this is the time for you to behave so childishly to your husband – not when he's been wounded in the service of his country.'

I couldn't keep back my retort. 'He baint the only husband as has been wounded defending his country.'

Her eyes glittered, 'How *dare* you – ' At that moment Leo came back, so now there were two of them not speaking to me.

They scarcely even looked up when I muttered, 'I feel a mite tired. I'll go up to bed now, if you don't mind.'

I went straight up to the nursery. Ellen was sitting at the table in her dressing gown, writing a letter. 'Don't get up, Ellen.' She smiled, and went back to her pen.

I always came up to look at my babies last thing, but tonight I stayed longer than usual and Ellen came in.

'Is there anything wrong, my lady?'

'No, but they both be so beautiful I can't bear to tear myself away.' Bending down I tucked the blanket more securely round Flora's sleeping form, then with a last lingering glance I followed Ellen out into the day nursery.

Smiling she told me, 'Lady Flora's been that excited all day, couldn't stop chattering about the party tomorrow – and I'm looking forward to it myself. And Lady Rose is going to have a little treat, too. His lordship said as he'll take her and Dora up to the Home Farm for an hour after lunch.'

He'd not told me; I'd been looking forward to having Rose to myself for the whole afternoon. Ellen suggested, 'Why don't you go with him, instead of Dora, my lady?'

Quickly I shook my head. 'No, I'm too busy.' There was a slight frown on Ellen's face as she heard my reply, and as I went down to my bedroom I couldn't help wishing that I lived in a cottage with just Leo and the children. Then when we had a little disagreement the butler wouldn't be looking anxious and nor would the nursemaid be dropping hints. If we'd been under each other's feet all day and sharing a bed at night we'd likely have made it up by now; but I wasn't going to be the first to apologize, not when he was the one in the wrong.

Miss Annabel spent the morning in the garden with Leo and Flora. Then it was time for her train. I'd hardly spoken to her, but perhaps that was just as well: I'd have only finished up annoying her again. After lunch I waved Ellen and Flora off to their party and then went along to the estate office to work at the accounts until it was my turn to have Rose. Leo didn't even have the grace to bring her along himself, but sent her with Dora. And later it was obvious that he was waiting until I'd left the nursery before going up to hear about all the excitements of Flora's party. It was very easy to avoid each other in a house as large as Eston.

The day after, Flora was in a bad mood, too. The excitements of the party seemed to have gone to her head, and she was whining and grizzly. When Rose toddled up to play with her, Flora pushed her sister away. Rose's face crumpled and I picked her up and cuddled her. 'Never thee mind about Flora. She did get out o' bed the wrong side this morning, like her Papa.' Ellen glanced at me sharply and opened her mouth to speak – then thought better of it.

That evening Leo actually spoke. As he was slicing his apple he said, 'Flora is not her usual cheerful self today.'

'She wants another party, but she's got to learn as she can't have everything she wants. Life baint like that.'

'Life *isn't* like that.' He snapped the correction.

I retorted, 'As long as *you* realize.'

An angry flush crept up his neck. 'Don't try and treat *me* as though I were a naughty child!'

'Why not – if you behave like one?'

As soon as I'd said them I wished the words back again. The angry veins stood out on his forehead and he flung the half-eaten apple down on the table with such force it smashed in a splatter all over the cloth. With a lurch he threw himself to his feet, banging his splinted arm hard against the table. I jumped up and ran to him as his face contorted in pain. 'You've hurt yourself!'

He thrust my hand away. 'Leave me alone!'

'I were only trying to help.'

He cut furiously across my words, 'I don't want your pity! Get away from me – go!'

I just stood there looking up into his angry face; then I turned and left.

I went up to the nursery with tears smarting in my eyes. Flora was asleep. She'd be back to her normal cheerful self in the morning. If only I could say the same of her father. Then I recollected that of course he wasn't her father. Standing there looking down at her blonde hair and golden fringes of lashes I remembered her real father, laughing beside me in the park – and my whole body ached with the longing to see him once more, just to know that he was safe. I tried to force that longing out of my mind but I couldn't: Flora was a constant reminder. If only she were less like him – but I didn't *want* her to be less like him, she was his child.

I woke early and went straight up to the nursery. Flora was up, but she was sitting on the sofa, listlessly cuddling her doll. Ellen shook her head, 'She still seems out of sorts, my lady.'

But when I went to her she greeted me with her usual blue-eyed smile. Lifting her on to my lap I stroked her daffodil-pale hair, 'You'll feel better when you've had your porridge, my Flora.'

'Don't want no porridge.'

I glanced over her head at Ellen. 'I think she's a mite too young for parties.'

Ellen nodded in agreement. 'I dare say twas the jelly as upset her. She baint used to it, and she did have a second helping.'

I didn't stay long in the nursery; Flora seemed to be perking up, and besides, I didn't want to be still there when Leo came to pay his early morning visit to the children.

I was down in the estate office at eleven – the stable clock had just struck – when Mr Tims came to the door. 'My lady, Lady Burton is on the telephone, and she wishes to speak to you.'

I wondered why she hadn't just given the message to Mr Tims. It would have been much easier. I reached the telephone cubbyhole and picked up the earpiece.

'Good morning, Lady Burton, tis Amy speaking.'

'My dear, Isabel's just been on the line about her Jimmy. He was at the party and now he's quite feverish, and her doctor thinks it's probably scarlet fever. Apparently some child he visited last week has gone down with it and . . . ' Her voice went rattling on, but I didn't hear. Scarlet fever – scarlet fever! The Beeston children – Flora, my Flora – ' . . . and your little Flora was sitting next to him at the table, and although Jimmy's older he was so good with her, helping her in the games . . . ' Flora – scarlet fever – ' . . . are you still there, dear?' I managed to croak an assent, 'So do tell your nursemaid to keep an eye on her – and I think perhaps you should ask Matthews to have a look at her, too. It can be quite nasty, you know – especially in younger children. Good bye for now, dear.'

Somehow I managed to ask the operator to put me through to Dr Matthews' house and I left a message there – then I panicked. Scarlet fever: those graves in the churchyard. My Flora – and Rose! Suppose Rose caught it too? Both my babies! I stood frozen, with the earpiece still in my hand. Then all at once the ice encasing my limbs cracked and I began to run. Along the passage, up the step, into the hallway. I thrust the library door open. He was there.

'Amy?'

'Lady Burton – Flora – scarlet fever,' the words tumbled over each other. 'Flora, she said she didn't want her breakfast.'

I saw by his face he knew that already. He barked, 'Matthews?'

'I did telephone, but he were out.'

Leo was already heading for the stairs. He moved so quickly I could hardly keep up with him.

Flora was sitting listlessly on the nursery sofa. I went to her and lifted her on to my lap while Leo told Ellen, 'The child's been in contact with scarlet fever.' She paled as he turned to me, 'We must get Rose away. Ellen, carry her over to the door.' He jammed his hand hard down on the bell.

Clara came herself, and I heard his voice rapping out orders. Ellen and Rose were to have a bath of disinfectant, then put on a complete change of clothing fresh from the linen cupboard. He turned on Dora, 'How old are you?'

A frightened Dora squeaked, 'Sixteen, me lord.'

'Too young. You must do the same, and then go with Ellen and Lady Rose to the Tysons'. Ellen, tell them Rose is in quarantine. They must keep all other children away from her. She could be a risk to them. No, Amy, you must *not* touch her.'

'But suppose she's taken ill, too?'

'Then Ellen will bring her back – but only if Matthews is sure it's scarlet fever.' So all I could do was wave my daughter goodbye.

As soon as Clara had sent off Rose and Ellen she was to prepare two adjoining rooms in the bachelors' wing. 'Get the carpets out, take the curtains down, get rid of any unnecessary furniture – and if the bedsteads aren't metal replace them with ones that are. When you've done that mop the floor with disinfectant; wipe down her cot as well. We'll need a hip bath of carbolic solution for the soiled linen, too – and put a jug of boiled water ready on the table.'

Clara went off to fetch Bertha and Jesse, and we were alone. Flora's head lay heavy against my breast. 'But mebbe she hasn't caught it?'

'I hope to God she hasn't, but we must be prepared for the worst.' And at that moment Flora began to retch. Seizing the chamber pot Leo thrust it in front of her; her whole body shuddered as she vomited into it. Afterwards she collapsed limply back into my arms, and began to shiver. He fetched a blanket and tucked it round her with his free hand. 'This damned splint!'

Flora whimpered. I whispered, 'Doan 'ee fret, my Flora. Thy Mama and Papa will take care o' thee.' His black-furred hand gently cradled her cheek, and as she turned her hot face into his palm I saw my own fear reflected in his eyes.

Lowering himself on to the sofa beside me he took out his watch and balanced it on his knee. 'Let Papa hold your wrist for a little while, Flora.'

She lay unresisting, and I realized he was counting her pulse. I watched his face crease in concern and I whispered, 'Be it too fast?'

'I – I'm not sure, Amy. I believe it is normal for children to have a faster pulse.'

Flora turned her head restlessly. 'Neck hurts.' Gently I drew back the collar of her frock – and we saw the tiny red spots: it was the rash. I felt as though my heart had turned to ice.

Leo said quietly, 'Matthews will be here shortly, no doubt.'

'He were out on his rounds. He may not be back until lunchtime.'

'That's only an hour or two. We'll have her in bed by then.' I sat cuddling her, talking to her, and his low voice echoed mine until Clara came back to say that the rooms were ready.

Although I was as quick as possible Flora moaned as I undressed her – and then she was violently sick again. I'd never seen her like this before, her skin was so hot and dry. She asked for a drink, but when I gave her one she tried to push it away, 'Hurts, hurts.'

'She must drink, Amy. Fluid intake is vital with a fever.' Between us we managed to coax her to swallow a glass of water, and then she seemed to fall into a restless sleep. I sat back in my chair, easing my aching back.

Suddenly she cried out loud and I watched frozen with horror as her whole body went rigid: her back arched and her eyeballs shot up under her lids. 'Flora! Flora!' She'd stopped breathing. Then all at once her face was contorting, her eyes rolling, and her arms and legs thrashing against Leo as he crouched over her, preventing her flailing limbs from bruising themselves against the metal bars of the cot.

At last the fit was over, and she fell into a stupor, her whole body completely limp. Slowly her breathing returned to something like normal, but her eyes remained closed. As he straightened up I began to shake and shudder, 'Flora, Flora!'

I felt his arm come round my shoulder. 'Amy, calm yourself. You can't help her if you're hysterical.' His arm tightened, holding me close while I fought for self-control – dashing myself against the rock of his body until at last the battle was over and I was calm again.

I told him quietly, 'Tis all right, I won't be silly again.' Straightening my back I sat with my eyes on the cot: watching, waiting.

By the evening Flora's whole body was covered with red spots. Only her face was a pale white mask. Dr Matthews had been twice, his face grave. Leo had shown me how to take her temperature, and I managed to keep my hand steady as I read its unrelenting rise: 103°, 103.5°, 104° – . As the doctor peered down her throat I saw how my poor Flora's tongue was coated in a thick white fur now, stark against the vivid red behind it. Her neck was swollen and painful, and her stomach tender to the touch. It was obvious that she no longer knew where she was or who we were. Leo spoke gently, 'She's in a delirium now, Amy, but that isn't an uncommon occurrence with a severe infection. Keep talking to her – underneath she may well know it's you who are with her.'

Mrs Chandler arrived; Leo had sent for her. She'd been helping with a confinement, but a neighbour had stepped in to set her free. Leo told me I must go and lie down in the adjoining room. I didn't want to leave Flora, but he made me.

'You can't help her if you lose your own strength. Grace will call you if – ' He didn't complete the sentence.

There was food waiting on the small table next door. I shook my head, but

Leo's voice was firm. 'You must eat, Amy.' We sat down together to drink soup and swallow a chicken cream that slipped unnoticed down my throat. Leo had closed the connecting door, but all the time my ears were straining to hear every movement in the other room. I could feel the thread binding me to her. I mustn't let go of that thread or she would die.

'I maun have the door open.' He hesitated a moment, then went to do as I'd asked.

As soon as the table had been cleared Clara brought a can of hot water so I could wash. Leo stood up. 'I'll leave you now, Amy.' I scarcely heard him go; all my concentration was on her.

I slept, but even in my dreams Flora was with me. As soon as I woke in the night I slipped next door. Mrs Chandler was bending over my daughter, her hands moving gently and carefully as she made her more comfortable. In the dim light of the shaded lamp I gazed at my child's face. Was she better? No, she was worse. I knew she was.

Beside me Mrs Chandler murmured, 'She's holding on, my lady.' But that was all. As I straightened up I saw a dark shape huddled in a chair in the corner of the room, his splinted arm heavy against his chest. Mrs Chandler looked anxiously at me. 'He needs his sleep – but he won't go away.'

I went to him and spoke softly, 'You must go to bed, Leo.'

He mumbled, 'Too far away.'

'Come with me, then.' Reaching out my hand I took hold of his and led him next door. The springs of the other bed squealed in protest as they took his weight; I lay down on mine and fixed my thoughts on Flora so that even in sleep I would keep her there.

Morning came, and I sent Mrs Chandler away to her bedroom and resumed my vigil. Flora, my beautiful Flora – she tossed and turned as I sponged her burning skin and coaxed her to swallow more water. She didn't even know me.

Dr Matthews had shown me how to clean her mouth out for her with a glycerine mixture, but it was Leo who taught me to use the douche can on her throat. 'Flora, thee maun let I.' I turned to him. 'She doesn't like it.'

'Her throat must be kept clean, Amy. Come Flora, open your mouth, there's a good girl.'

When I'd finished he said, 'It's time we put her on the bedpan again.' She squirmed and panted and it was difficult to keep her there – but eventually we had what we needed. 'I'll test it myself.' I heard the hiss of the spirit lamp then Leo spoke again, 'No sign of albumen yet.' I didn't understand, but I knew from the tone of his voice that it was good news, and breathed a small prayer of thanks.

Dr Matthews came before morning surgery. I held her still while he peered down her throat, then it was her ears he studied. 'Any sign of a discharge?'

'No.'

'Tell me at once if there is – or if her joints start swelling. You must try and measure how much water she passes.' He turned away and spoke in a low voice to Leo. I couldn't hear what he said. I didn't want to hear. 'I'll be back at lunchtime, Lady Warminster.'

Leo came back to the bed. 'Amy, if she won't take nourishment by mouth Matthews will have to use a tube. Try to persuade her to drink a little milk. She'll do it for you.'

'She doesn't know me.'

'Yes she does.'

I held the feeding cup to her lips. 'Flora, do 'ee take a liddle drink. Now swallow, Flora – swallow.' Slowly, painfully, she did.

Taking her temperature: 104.5°. Cleaning her mouth, her throat. Coaxing, calming, loving. Taking her temperature: 105°.

Twice a day Ellen sent word of Rose: 'Quite well.' I breathed a prayer of thanks and then turned my attention back to her sister.

Leo tried to send me outside for a walk, but I wouldn't go. I didn't want to break the slender thread that bound her to me. It was thin as gossamer now, but still it held. He spoke to Dr Matthews. 'Tell her she must get some fresh air.'

Without even looking up I shook my head. 'I maunt leave her.'

Dr Matthews said quietly, 'Don't make her, Warminster. She'd never forgive you if – '

Another day, another night. Fight Flora, fight my pretty maid – fight. And she fought.

All my concentration was on Flora, but every so often I would ease my head back and look over at the still form of her father, hunched in his chair.

He and I ate in the bedroom next door. Then he would go downstairs to wave to Rose across the stable yard. 'Rose is fine, Amy.'

'Thank 'ee. You should 'a gone for a walk with Nella, to get a breath of air.' But I knew he wouldn't go that far, any more than I would.

At night he lay on the other bed while I dozed and woke and dozed again. Whenever I heard her hoarse, whimpering cry I would slip out of bed and go to sit beside Mrs Chandler, 'Flora, I be here. I be here wi' you.'

Silence was worse: if I woke to silence then fear clutched at my heart and I'd almost run to the door. Then Mrs Chandler would chide me gently, 'My lady, thee mustn't torment thyself. If anything were to happen I'd tell you.' And I would make myself go and lie down again.

A low voice would ask from the other bed, 'How is she?'

'No change.'

Fear closed its icy hand on my heart, but I thrust it away. Fear weakened the thread – and it was so finely spun already.

Chapter Thirty-Seven

On the afternoon of the fourth day I took her temperature – and it had dropped by half a degree. Disbelievingly, I showed it to Leo, and saw by his face that I had read it aright. Like two children we thrust the chart at Dr Matthews when he came for his evening visit, but his face remained grave. 'Perhaps, but we must wait and see.'

When Mrs Chandler arrived for her night vigil she said, 'She looks a mite easier to me, my lady.' But it was too soon to hope. Yet that night I slept more deeply, and when I awoke for the first time it was already well past midnight. I hurried into the other room – and knew by her breathing: it was steadier, calmer.

Mrs Chandler looked up with a smile. 'She be sleeping easier now, my lady.' I stood gazing down at Flora, and even by the dim light of the shaded lamp I was sure that the rash on her neck was less brilliantly red. Mrs Chandler murmured, 'She do look to be turning the corner.'

Raising my head I saw Leo standing on the other side of the cot; he'd followed me out. For a moment our eyes held – then we both looked down again, down at our daughter. Neither of us dared to hope yet.

Mrs Chandler was firm, 'You'd best get back to bed, my lord, my lady. You'll need to keep your strength up.' We crept back to the other room, and each lay down on our own bed.

At dawn I woke, and crept through again, and knew at once by the expression on Mrs Chandler's face. 'I've just taken her temperature, my lady. It's down two degrees from this time yesterday. And her rash, tis fading – she's over the worst.'

I stood looking at Flora, my whole body shaking with relief. Then I turned and almost ran back into the other room, crying, 'Leo, Leo – '

He was rearing up, awake at once, 'Is she – '

'She's getting better, she's getting better!' He began to shake, great racking shudders. I repeated, 'Leo, tis all right – she's getting better.' As I spoke my legs gave way and I collapsed on to the bed beside him. He reached out to me blindly, and we clung together, weeping in each other's arms.

At last we drew apart, and standing up I put my hand out to him. 'Do 'ee come and look at her now. Thic rash, tis already fading.'

We stood hand in hand beside the cot, looking down at our sleeping child. 'Her neck, tis a mite less swollen.'

'She's lost that febrile restlessness.'

'See, her breathing, tis more natural.'

'I'm sure her pulse has steadied.'

Eventually Mrs Chandler shooed us both away. 'There's no need for three nurses. Now, you both go back to bed till breakfast.'

But in the bedroom I turned to him. 'I don't think I can sleep any more.'

'Nor I.'

I glanced over at the window. ''Tis already light.'

'Then come, Amy, let us walk in the rose garden.'

He'd never properly undressed the last four days; now I held his jacket for him while he slid his good arm into the right sleeve, then I pulled it round his splint. He waited outside while I changed into a fresh dress. We walked down the back stairs together and out into the stable yard to where we could see the window of Mr Tyson's spare room. There was no light: Rose and Ellen and Dora must all be still asleep. Turning, we went round to the front of the house and on down into the rose garden.

We didn't speak, but just walked together in the quiet of the early morning, surrounded by the scent and colour of his roses. Today their petals were a deeper red, a rosier pink and a purer white; it was as though every rose in the garden was greeting us, and sharing our thankfulness.

When we came to the Crested Moss rose, I lingered before the full pink blooms. It was one of Flora's favourites; she would always insist on stopping here and searching for a bud at that intriguing stage when the mossy sepals arrayed to form a miniature cocked hat, with a sliver of pink petal peeping out from between them like a tiny face. Now I found one such bud, and stroked its mossy coat, before lifting my finger tips to breathe in the apple-like scent – just as she always did. Leo stood watching, as he must so often have watched her.

Abruptly he spoke. 'I was so sure we were going to lose her. These last years I've watched so many die. For a few weeks before I left England I was assisting on a fever ward, nursing Canadian soldiers who'd gone down with cerebral meningitis – spotted fever. They were big, strong men – yet they died. And she seemed so tiny, so frail. I thought . . . ' His huge free hand moved in a small, hopeless gesture. 'I didn't dare even to hope. All I could do was to try to make bargains with Fate: let me go back and die but let her live.' For a moment he closed his eyes and looked gaunt and grey as an old man.

Suddenly I was frightened. Looking at the splint I said, 'You've been doing too much, Leo – you're still poorly yourself. You must come back and have your breakfast, then you'd best get some sleep. Come along now.'

Obediently he followed me in. But he wouldn't go back to bed; he wanted to wait until Dr Matthews came. We were both anxious again now. Suppose Flora's improvement was only a temporary rally?

Dr Matthews examined her very carefully before pronouncing, 'I think she has turned the corner.' I was giddy with relief. 'But we aren't out of the wood yet. With scarlet fever there's always a risk of complications. Her throat has been badly affected, and there may be trouble with her ears. Keep a careful watch for any signs of a discharge. She must be kept lying down, too. Tell me if there's any puffiness of the joints, arthritis can follow. But above all, keep measuring her water and test it regularly.'

I told him, 'There isn't more than a trace of albumen. Leo checked again, this morning.'

'That is certainly encouraging, Lady Warminster, but kidney inflammation tends to strike later – generally not before the end of the first week. And it may develop as late as the third, so you must be very vigilant. Inspect her throat regularly, too. Scarlet fever is sometimes followed by diptheria, or there could even be a recurrence of the original infection.' I just stood there, looking at him. He continued, 'But it's generally the case that the more severe the first attack the less serious the relapse – so we won't worry too much about that one.'

By now all the euphoria of the early morning had vanished. I felt my shoulders slump. My eyes met Leo's. Then he said heavily, 'Thank you, Matthews. We will naturally heed your advice.'

As soon as the doctor had gone Mrs Chandler said briskly, 'Doan 'ee fret. She's a lot better today, we can all see that. An' doctor said hisself as she's turned the corner.' She sniffed, 'Thic doctors, they allus look on the gloomy side – then if things do go wrong, they dussent get the blame. But if they goes all right then everybody thinks what a clever fellow that doctor be, getting her cured like that!' She smiled reassuringly. 'Your Flora, she's a sturdy little maid, and she's a fighter. She's through the worst, I'm sure on it. I've nursed more sick children'n I can count, and I knows when they're on the mend.'

'Thank you, Mrs Chandler.'

'And you, my lord, tis time you got some sleep, what with your arm an' all. Off you goes to bed – you do as you're told, now.'

But of course he didn't, he never did. Once Mrs Chandler had gone off to sleep he came back and sat with Flora, reading her stories until he was quite hoarse. When she'd dozed off again he turned to me. 'That rash is fading.'

'Aye, it is. And look at her neck – you can hardly see the swelling now.'

'Her breathing is almost back to normal.'

'You can tell her temperature's gone down just from the feel of her skin.'

I did manage to persuade him to take Nella out for a walk in the afternoon, but he was soon back again. As he came through the door I exclaimed, 'Her temperature, tis down again!'

Hurrying to the cot he bent over it. 'Good girl, Flora. Papa is very proud of you.' She smiled up at him and his face lit up in reply. We stood together, gazing down at her, revelling in the miracle of that smile. Then he took his hand from behind his back and held out a spray of buds. 'See, Flora, I've brought you some little green cocked hats.' He laughed to see the pleasure in his daughter's face.

The next day he collapsed. Flora's temperature had gone down until it was almost normal. Her rash was only a pale pink, and the worst swelling in her throat had definitely subsided. She'd begun to talk again, and she'd drunk a full feeding cup of beef tea for lunch, and one of chicken for tea. I was feeling so much more cheerful – and then Leo collapsed.

He was sitting in the wooden armchair at the foot of her bed, just watching her, when he made an odd moaning noise. I looked up in time to see his face go ashen – and then he slumped forward. I just caught him before he toppled to the floor.

Mrs Chandler was already at my side. 'Tis only a faint, my lady. Let his head fall forwards. There, he's coming round already.'

He pulled himself back into the chair, his face the colour of chalk and the sweat standing out on his forehead as he muttered, 'It's nothing – too hot in here.'

But it wasn't; we'd kept the temperature just at sixty degrees for Flora, as Dr Matthews had told us. I glanced across at Mrs Chandler, whose voice was reassuring. 'Doctor'll be here shortly.'

Flora called, 'Papa!' She was sitting up.

Quickly I turned to her. 'Thee must lie down, my flower. Papa, he were only having a little nap.' We made Leo lie down, too, on the bed next door, and waited for the doctor.

After he'd examined Leo, Dr Matthews called me in and said, 'It's total exhaustion, Lady Warminster.' Leo tried to protest but the doctor was firm. 'You've not had a proper night's sleep for a week, Lord Warminster. You can't go on like this.'

'But Amy's not slept properly, either.'

'Your wife is nearly thirty years younger than you are,' Leo's face darkened, 'and more to the point, she has not recently suffered a couple of serious wounds. By rights, you shouldn't even be out of hospital yet – and you'll find yourself back there again if you aren't careful.'

Leo shook his head impatiently. 'Just give me a bottle of one of your vile potions – '

'The only medicine I'm prescribing is a fortnight's complete bed rest.'

'Rubbish! I'll turn in early tonight – that will put me to rights.' Leo began to get up, but his face was hollow-cheeked with fatigue.

I looked anxiously at Dr Matthews and his hand came firmly down on Leo's shoulder. 'Warminster, if you don't do as I say I won't be answerable for the consequences.'

'Then don't be. As you just pointed out, I'm old enough to make my own decisions.' He sounded angry.

I said, 'Leo, you're behaving like a gurt babby. You do as the doctor says.'

His scowl turned on me. 'No!' I could have hit him.

Dr Matthews intervened, 'Lady Warminster, I think we'd better engage a private nurse for him.'

263

Leo's head jerked up. 'No! Anyway, you won't find one now – they're all nursing in war hospitals.'

Dr Matthews ignored him. Looking straight at me he said, 'Both Mrs Withers and her sister, Miss Winterslow, have repeatedly offered their services to help care for your daughter. I really think we should call one of them in to nurse your husband instead.'

Leo erupted in a howl of rage. 'I'm not having either of those two harpies in *my* bedroom.'

I said, 'Leo, if you don't promise me to get to bed and stay there for two full weeks it won't be one of 'em as I'll ask to step up and help – it'll be *both* of 'em.'

Before Leo could reply Dr Matthews had added smoothly, 'They assure me they've each had scarlet fever so are not at risk.'

I suddenly thought. 'Leo, have *you* had scarlet fever?' Sullenly he shook his head. I turned back to Dr Matthews. 'Do you think – '

'Adults are generally less at risk, but Lord Warminster's constitution has been weakened by his recent injuries. There is some cause for concern – '

Bending over Leo I looked him straight in the eye. 'Leo, you be going to your bed now, and you be staying there for two full weeks by the calendar.'

He glared back at me – and then his eyes finally dropped. 'Tims will bring me my meals, but I don't need anyone nursing me. *You're* too busy.'

It was only the slightest of emphases, but I heard it and I told him, 'I'll come and sit with you for an hour of an evening, once Flora's asleep.'

With a gruff 'Thank you,' he stood up. He swayed slightly as he began to walk towards the door; and when Dr Matthews put his hand under Leo's arm, I noticed that he didn't shake it off.

After he'd gone and we'd settled Flora, Mrs Chandler said, 'He baint the easiest of men to handle, his lordship.' I agreed whole-heartedly. She smiled. 'He do need a lot o' loving – but he can be so stubborn at times that he needs a firm hand, too, just like now.' She glanced at me then looked away again before saying, 'The first Lady Warminster, she couldn't handle him, couldn't handle him at all. But then, as I says, he do need a lot o' loving.' Listening to her saying that I sighed inwardly, because I didn't love him enough either. 'I don't want your lukewarm love' – poor Leo. Mrs Chandler was right: he needed more than that; he deserved more than that.

Easing her chair round to get a better view of Flora's sleeping face, she said, 'Tis lovely to see her sleeping so peaceful – and Clara says Lady Rose is as hale and hearty as could be. You maun be missing her, my lady.'

I was. I was longing to hold her in my arms again. But when I spoke to Dr Matthews next morning he shook his head. 'She hasn't finished her quarantine yet. We can't be sure she's safe until the full eight days have passed. And then she must not return to the house until her sister is no longer infectious. This contagion possesses extraordinary tenacity, Lady Warminster: clothing, furniture, toys, letters – even Lord Warminster's Labrador bitch will have to be bathed in disinfectant before Rose is allowed to stroke her again. And since you are nursing your elder daughter, I'm afraid it will be several weeks before you can go near your younger one.'

'*Weeks*! But she's too young to be away from her mother so long!'

Dr Matthews' face was grave. 'It's *because* she's so young that you must keep away from her: the younger the child, the greater the risk of serious consequences.'

'But Dr Matthews – '

'Lady Warminster, for every five children of your daughter's age who catch scarlet fever, one will die.' I froze. 'That's why fever hospitals were built in our cities – isolation is our only defence. And while we're on the subject of contagion, before you visit your husband each day, you must put disinfectant in your bathwater, and then ensure that your hair is completely covered whilst you are with him. And there must be no physical contact whilst he's in this weakened state, not even a good-night kiss. Now, let me have a proper look at my younger patient.'

He was pleased with Flora's progress, but because of the risk of complications she had to stay in bed another two weeks, just like Leo. I don't know which of them was the more trouble. Flora was fractious and fidgety, wanting to be up and doing, so I'd have to play games and read stories to her every day. The only break I got was when she put her kaleidoscope to her eye and began to turn it, still fascinated by the ever-changing patterns. When I'd got her settled of an evening, Mrs Chandler would take over, so I could bath in carbolic and tie my hair up in a square of white cotton. Then I'd go along to Leo.

His first words were always, 'How is Flora?' But as soon as he was satisfied about Flora his lower lip would jut out and he would announce, 'I'm going to get up tomorrow.'

'No, you aren't.'

'Yes I am.'

'Dr Matthews said – '

'Old fool! why should I do what *he* tells me?'

'You're not getting up because *I* say so.' We went through the same little performance every single night.

The first evening he'd demanded, 'Why are you wearing that pudding bag over your head?'

'Dr Matthews told me I'd got to cover my hair.'

'But I want to look at it.'

'Well you can't, so there's an end to it. You'll have to look at Nella's fur instead.'

'Huh!' Then it was, 'I'm bored.'

I looked down at his bedside table. 'You got plenty of books to read. Clara says she's finding 'em for you all day, with Mr Tims not being able to see the titles so well.'

'My eyes are tired of reading.'

'I'll read to you, then. What do you want me to read?'

He muttered grumpily, 'Anything – I don't care.'

I thought, why not? Seeing as he's behaving like a child, I might as well treat him as one. So I went quickly over to the dressing room door.

His voice followed me, 'Where are you going, Amy? I've got another fifty minutes yet.'

'I'll be back in a second. I'm just going to fetch a book.'

I came back with it hidden behind my skirt. 'Now if your eyes are tired, you'd best close them while I read to you.' Obediently he did so.

'Once upon a time there were thic man, and he were so lucky, cos he had a goose as everytime it laid, it did drop an egg o' pure shining gold.'

Without opening his eyes he said, 'That's a children's story.'

'Aye. I thought it the right choice the way you been behaving tonight.' His mouth twitched with the beginnings of a smile as I read of how the man, who wasn't satisfied with a single golden egg a day, finished up killing his goose. 'So that were the end o' thic gold for him!'

Leo was smiling properly by now. 'Very well, Amy – I know what the moral of that story is. But how curious to be listening to an ancient Greek fable read in Wiltshire dialect.'

I shook my head triumphantly. 'No, tis a French story. Those first two nurses whose stockings I mended gave it to me for Flora – only I'm saving it for her till she learns to read French.'

'French?' Reaching out, he snatched it from me – then stared at the page in disbelief. 'It *is* in French. I knew you'd picked up the spoken language – but I didn't know you could read it, too!'

'Well, it baint so difficult once you get used to their odd way o' spelling things.'

That seemed to silence him for a moment, until he said, 'You asked me once if I would teach you Greek. Would you like me to do that?'

I hesitated, 'Well – '

'Of course, if you'd rather I didn't – '

He sounded hurt so I explained, 'It baint that, tis just as I don't have a lot o' spare time at present, what with doing the Home Farm accounts, and giving Mr Selby a hand in the estate office. Mebbe after the war, only – ' I paused, then said firmly, 'I dare say by then there'll be more babies – '

Abruptly he cut across my words. 'Read me another story.'

I started to read the story of the fox who took a fancy to some plump juicy grapes – but when he realized he couldn't reach then, he exclaimed, 'I dussent want thic grapes. I 'low they baint ripe, and bist as sour as sour can be.'

As I finished I saw Leo's face tighten, then he muttered, 'If only I could be as wise as that fox.' Hastily I moved on to the story of the race between the tortoise and the hare.

When the stable clock struck eight I closed the book. 'Tis time you went to sleep now. Dr Matthews said as I wasn't to tire you.'

'Damn Matthews!'

'You're as bad as Flora.' I stood up. 'Good night, Leo, sleep tight.'

Halfway across the room I heard him say, 'That's not the way you say goodnight to Flora.'

'Dr Matthews said as I wasn't to touch you, for fear of infection – not even a good-night kiss,' he said.'

His 'Damn Matthews' was louder this time. Then with his eyes closed, he muttered, 'I don't suppose you would have, anyway.'

'You don't deserve good-night kisses while you're in such an awkward mood.'

He opened one eye. 'But since I'm not going to get one anyway, I might as well enjoy the pleasure of being awkward, eh, Amy? An hour an evening isn't long, but I intend to make the most of it.'

And he did. So I had him and Flora both playing me up; but I didn't really mind because I was so glad to see them both getting better.

After a fortnight Dr Matthews said Flora could get up on the following day – though she'd have to stay in the bedroom, since she was still infectious. It took all my energy to keep her in that bed and I was quite worn out by the time I'd had my bath and gone up to Leo. Dr Matthews had already given him the good news about Flora. 'I can hardly believe she's fully recovered, Amy.'

'And Rose is as fit as a fiddle. I can see that across the stable yard. If you hadn't been so quick to get her out o' the nursery – ' I shuddered, then said briskly, 'We'll have to make certain sure we kill all those liddle germs.'

'You're doing your best, Amy. You've been smelling of carbolic for weeks!'

I retorted, 'Tis time you started playing up – or are you going to behave yourself tonight?'

'Certainly not.' He announced loudly, 'I'm getting up tomorrow.'

I smiled. 'Aye, Leo. Doctor told me to tell you you could.'

I saw I'd really taken the wind out of his sails, then he puffed himself up again. 'I'm getting up *now*.' He gripped the edge of the bedclothes.

'No, you baint.'

'Yes I am.'

'You're behaving like a gurt babby!'

'I've still got fifty minutes left and I intend to make the most of them.'

I exclaimed, 'I've had enough today with Flora. I were at my wits' end keeping her in bed. Truth is, these last few days she's been every bit as awkward and stubborn as you. Still, I suppose tis only natural, wi' you being her father.'

And all of a sudden there was silence. Then he said quietly, 'But I'm not, am I? Surely you hadn't forgotten that?' His eyes searched my face. 'Or had you, Amy?'

I was adrift, because sometimes these past weeks, I had. Guessing the truth, he pressed home his advantage. '*Have* you forgotten?'

I teetered on the brink of the cliff. She was *Frank's* child: I'd always thought of her as Frank's child and I still loved him. I didn't want to lose him as my child's father. Leo's grey eyes watched me intently. I tried to pull back from the brink, but it was already too late, I'd jumped over that cliff on that first night when Flora had been so ill and the great huddled form of her father had sat watching over her with me.

I looked down at my folded hands and told him the truth. 'Thee bist Flora's father, she knows that, and so do I.' As I lifted my eyes again I saw the blaze of triumph in his. Oh forgive me, Frank – but it's the truth.

He should have been content with that victory – but Leo always wanted more. And so he pressed me harder. 'I always felt she was mine, even before she was born. You were so sure she would be a girl. I'd wanted Jeanette to give me a daughter, and there you were carrying her granddaughter – and you'd given her to me before she was born.'

Bitterly I told him, 'Aye, I did. But then, I didn't have much choice, did I? You could give her everything, while all I could offer her was the workhouse – or a mother on the streets.'

He jerked his head up. 'But – '

I didn't let him interrupt. 'I couldn't earn the money to keep her! I could only have worked in the sweatshop – and what they pay wouldn't 'a kept me, let alone her. And even if I had managed, somehow, she'd 'a been cold, hungry – I couldn't let that happen to her.'

He exclaimed, 'But Amy, if the allowance I was making you was insufficient for you and your child to live on, you only had to tell me, or inform me through Wallis – '

Now it was my turn to be amazed. 'But that was only until she was born! You said, "Secure and respectable lodgings – *until the birth*".' And then I knew from the expression of horror on his face what I should have known before from the estate records, the accounts, the pensions. For he was a man who did not take his responsibilities lightly.

He was speaking, 'If Francis had failed to provide, then obviously I would have made the upkeep of you and your child a charge on the estate, just as I did with that girl at Pennings – ' He broke off, the sweat standing on his forehead. 'Are you telling me, Amy, that that was the only reason you offered me your child? Because you thought you couldn't afford to keep her?' His voice was very loud now.

'O' course I didn't want to lose her – she was all I'd got!'

His face was grey. 'Oh God – and all this time, I've been telling myself that you *wanted* to give me the child, you didn't want to keep it yourself. And that you made that choice long before I ever forced you into marriage.' He drew a deep, painful breath. 'But now I learn that you had no choice about that, either. I was simply the only alternative to the workhouse or the streets.'

'But if you hadn't helped me when Miss Annabel turned me off, it would've been the workhouse or the streets long before she was born. I didn't have nobody.'

Without looking at me he said, 'Perhaps Francis – '

'He'd already left.' Then, defending Frank I added; 'He thought I were going to marry Joe – Joe Dempster. He said I mustn't tell Joe I were already carrying.'

Leo continued, 'But you did.' Then he looked up into my face. 'I've always admired your honesty, Amy. But at the moment I wish – how I wish – that you'd lied to me.'

'I'm sorry.' The tears were stinging.

'That wasn't very fair, was it? No, Amy, you are right: tell the truth and shame the devil.' His voice dropped. 'Only it's hard on the devil, sometimes.'

'You baint the devil.'

'But having claimed your unborn child, I then forced you into marriage – and I can never put right *that* wrong. I'm sorry, Amy, so terribly, terribly sorry.' He lay back against the pillows. 'You'd better go now, you're tired.'

'But – '

'No, Amy, go – please go.' I hesitated a moment, but I had no more comfort to offer him, so I turned and left.

Chapter Thirty-Eight

Outside in the corridor I realized my legs were trembling so much I could hardly stand upright. His distress had forced me to face the truth. As I'd waited in such pain at the altar I'd believed it was Frank who was coming to my rescue – until the moment when I'd heard that deep voice behind me stammer: 'I will'. The wrong voice. The wrong man. And the end to all my dreams. Because I had dreamt, right up until then: foolish dreams, wrong dreams – but very precious ones. And Leo had destroyed them. My mind knew that I had no right to resent what he had done – but deep in my heart I resented it, and he knew it. But there was no point brooding over the past now; it was done, and we were man and wife.

I tried to control my thoughts; but they would not be controlled, because I knew that however often I'd spoken to him in the garden the idea of marrying me would never have crossed his mind – if I hadn't already offered him Flora. And now I'd discovered that I need never have done that; he would have supported us both anyway. And I would have been free. Free to live in a little cottage with my darling daughter. Free to entertain her own father for tea when he came to visit her – and free now, when his wife was divorcing him. 'If we were both free again . . . ' As I stood there in the corridor a whole different life unrolled before me, sweet and seductive, and I longed to move towards it.

With a geat effort I thrust it away, deep down, out of sight. Because it was too late now: the past could not be changed, only the future.

I went along to see Flora: she was fast asleep, a healthy, healing, sleep. Mrs Chandler was sitting beside her bed, so there was no need for me to stay. 'How is his lordship, my lady?'

'Quite well, Mrs Chandler. He'll be up and about again, tomorrow.'

She smiled, 'And coming tapping at this door first thing, I 'low, anxious to catch a glimpse o' this liddle maid. He'll have been missing her. And she's been asking for him. She do think the world of her Papa.'

'Aye, she do.'

I went through to the other room, but it was too early to go to bed yet; and besides, I was too shaken by what Leo had told me. That dream life would not stay buried, however hard I tried. I kept recalling what he'd said: 'If Francis had failed to provide, then obviously I would have made the upkeep of you and your child a charge upon the estate, just as I did with that girl at Pennings.' Those last words hit me with the force of a blow. I'd been so shaken I hadn't taken them in at the time – but I did now. I'd seen it in the estate records: there was a woman at Pennings with a child, who drew an allowance from the estate.

I'd noticed it when I was looking at the accounts while Mr Selby was ill. I'd meant to ask him about it, but then it had slipped my memory. Now I went out by the other door, straight downstairs and along the back corridor to the estate office.

The light was still on; Mr Selby looked up from his accounts. 'Lady Warminster, is anything wrong?'

'No – I just came to look something up.' I knew he was watching, but I had to know. Taking down the estate account books I began to search back. It began in the April of 1908, when a female child had been born to a Margaret Thomas. I carried the book over to Mr Selby and pointed at the entry. 'Thic maid, this Margaret Thomas, was her baby – was Lord Quinham the father of her child?'

Mr Selby's leathery face reddened. 'Yes, he was.'

'The baby, were it born a bastard?'

Mr Selby flinched before replying. 'Obviously. The girl was only seventeen.'

'Did Lord Warminster offer to marry her?'

Mr Selby stared at me as if I'd taken leave of my senses. 'Of course he didn't. In any case, the first Lady Warminster was still alive then. He wouldn't have been free to remarry.'

And then I realized I'd asked the wrong question. 'Why didn't Lord *Quinham* marry her?'

'Lady Warminster, as I said to your husband at the time, it was just a youthful peccadillo, these things happen. But obviously there was no thought of marriage – the girl was the daughter of the estate carpenter! It would have been totally out of the question.' As he said that I heard Frank's voice, from the past: 'Marry *you*! But you're a servant – how could I possibly marry you?' Mr Selby brought me back to the present. 'Lady Warminster, I'm so sorry, I'd completely forgotten. Please forgive me, I had no right to – ' His face was bright red with embarrassment.

I put my hand on his arm. ''Tis all right, Mr Selby, doan 'ee fret.' I made a big effort and asked, 'Is there a problem? You're working very late.'

He grasped at the straw I'd held out. 'It's the Home Farm accounts. I assumed you wouldn't have time for them this month, with your other duties. How is Lady Flora today?'

'She's doing very well – and she's sound asleep now, so I've got an hour or two to spare. Mebbe I could finish them off for you? You look fair worn out, Mr Selby. Have you had your dinner yet?' He hadn't, so I eventually managed to persuade him to go home for it, once he'd shown me where he'd got to in the accounts. Then I sat down at the desk myself.

For the next hour or so I made myself concentrate on the columns of figures; but when I'd ruled a neat line under the last total and cleaned my nib the other thoughts came crowding back. 'There was no question of marriage ' – just as there had been none with me. If Miss Annabel *had* died Frank still wouldn't

271

have been willing to marry me – not even to give my baby a name. I'd blamed Leo for not being Frank, rushing to my rescue at the last minute; but the truth was, Frank never would have come to my rescue, any more than he'd gone to the rescue of that girl at Pennings.

That bleak truth was more than I could bear; quickly I reminded myself of what he'd said that last time he'd been home on leave: 'If we were both free again then I would go down on my bended knee and ask you to marry me.' But I wasn't free, because I was Leo's wife – and I was Leo's wife because *he* was the man who'd come to my rescue that day. Although he was a lord, an earl, he'd still been willing to marry a servant. Whether his wife was the daughter of a French marquis or the granddaughter of a farm labourer, it made no difference to him. Even my bastardy didn't matter to him. No, Leo didn't care about my status or my birth: Leo was different. He'd willingly given me his name, simply because I'd asked for it – and because I'd spoken to him in the garden. I felt as though I were looking through the peephole of Flora's kaleidoscope, with the pattern changing as I watched. All at once the new pattern frightened me: I didn't want to think about it; besides, I was tired, and it was time for bed.

Next day Dr Matthews said Flora could get out of bed. She leapt up like a jack-in-the-box and he exclaimed, 'No leaving the room yet, young lady – we still need to keep an eye on you.' He smiled as she clambered up on to the window seat to see the world outside. 'You'll have your work cut out keeping her amused these next weeks. Now I'll go and release my other patient.' He grinned as he added, 'I don't know which of them has been the more trouble – eh, Lady Warminster?'

The doctor had barely left before Leo was pushing open the door. 'Papa!' Flora flung herself towards him on legs that still wobbled a little, but before she'd had time to stumble he'd crouched down to take her safely into the shelter of his steadying arm. At once she began chattering to him, telling him all her news.

Mrs Chandler winked at me then said, 'Now, my lord, no getting her over-excited. The doctor's only this minute said she can get up.'

I smiled as I added, 'I reckon there's someone else as didn't wait for doctor's permission before getting hisself up and dressed!' He glanced at me – then looked away, flushing. Yesterday he'd have made some retort, today he didn't. With a little sigh I left them together, and went down to see Mr Selby.

Over the next couple of weeks I hardly saw Leo, except when we were both together with Flora, and then she demanded all his attention. She wanted to go out and play, but obviously it was too soon; besides, she was still infectious. Dr Matthews said she would be until she'd finished peeling: poor Flora, she was shedding skin from her entire body – with great flakes coming off her hands and her feet. At first she was rather upset about it, but then Leo told her about lizards shedding their skins, and how they had lovely new fresh ones afterwards – and then we had to stop her pulling her scales off, she was so pleased about the whole idea!

In the meantime Leo had to go into Salisbury three times a week to have his arm massaged, though they hadn't taken his splint off yet. Dr Matthews said that was just as well; some army doctors got impatient, and didn't give the bones time to heal, but this way Leo should get the full use of his arm back again, and without its being crooked.

If the weather were fine Leo would go out into his rose garden or walk through the village or round the estate, so I hardly saw him. We did dine together every day, but he rarely spoke.

One evening he said to me, 'I'm not sulking, Amy, truly I'm not, it's just – ' He broke off with a small, helpless gesture.

I didn't know how to reply; I knew what was upsetting him, but I'd said all there was to say about it already. In the end I asked, 'How are the roses? I'm afraid there hasn't been the labour to keep them tidy this year.'

'They are a little unkempt – but as beautiful as ever.' He hesitated a moment, then asked, 'Why don't you come and see for yourself one day?'

'Aye, I maun do that. Only I am very busy; Mr Selby's not as young as he was and with Flora being ill I've not been able to give him a hand recently.'

'I quite understand.' He stood up. 'I'll give Nella her run now.'

'Leo, mebbe – '

'Yes?' He swung round so quickly he banged his splint. 'Damn and blast! I'm so sorry, Amy. Please forgive me. Yes, what was it you wished to say?'

Without looking at him I offered, 'Mrs Chandler said today as she'd sleep with Flora overnight if I wanted, then I could come back to my own bedroom, so if – if you did want to visit me there – '

'No, thank you, Amy. You've made enough sacrifices for my sake already.'

'But – '

'If I'm not prepared to offer you the child you want, then I won't take advantage of your generosity.'

'I don't mind.'

'But I do.' He was very decided. Maybe it was just as well he'd said no. I still had some figures to check through that evening. There wasn't even time to read the books that Leo gave me for my birthday; they were a pair of big green volumes with lots of paintings of roses and I knew I'd enjoy looking at them later, but now there was so much to do.

Soon after, the doctors took his splint off. It was quite a shock to see him without it. He'd managed wonderfully well with one hand all this time, even sitting on the floor to play games with Flora. She was getting very impatient at being confined to one room, now; she'd got bored with her toys and I had to be careful what I gave her because they'd all have to be burnt anyway: even the books, Dr Matthews said, to prevent infection spreading. Leo had brought her back new playthings from Salisbury. It did seem a waste, but better those should go than the old ones she and Rose were so attached to.

Rose! However busy I was I never stopped thinking of her; missing her was like an aching tooth. And she couldn't understand why she was only allowed to see me through the window of the cottage. She'd reach out her little hands calling to me, and I'd be in tears at not being able to touch her.

My heart leapt when finally Dr Matthews announced, 'Well, this little lady has definitely stopped peeling,' he tickled Flora's stomach and she laughed up at him, ' so I think we can assume that she'll no longer be infectious by the end of the the week.' He turned to me, 'It's time you disinfected your nurseries, Lady Warminster.' I rang for Clara at once.

It was a lot of work for the housemaids and Jesse. All the brass fittings had to be washed and well scoured with disinfectant, the furniture had to be pulled out from the walls and the curtains taken down and soaked in disinfectant. Next the windows were screwed tightly shut and paper strips pasted over the sashes, then more paper was pasted over the fireplace openings and round the door to the night nursery, before Jesse was sent in with a garden spray of water and orders to make sure every surface was nicely moist. Mrs Carter had sacrificed two old saucepans for the sulphur candles, and in each room these were balanced on top of up-ended flower pots set in large pails of water. Clara poured meths over the sulphur, set light to it – and left rapidly. As soon as she'd closed the door and gone on to the night nursery I pasted paper over the door cracks and sealed up the keyhole.

The fumigation took twenty-four hours, then another day was spent in a thorough spring clean with Jeyes Fluid before the estate carpenter arrived to repaint the walls, the woodwork and the ceiling. We kept fires lit and all the windows open for another couple of days, and then Dr Matthews told us that tomorrow, after Flora had had her bath, we could wash her hair with carbolic soap, dress her in clean clothes, and take her back to the nursery. The two sickrooms would have to be fumigated after that, which would take even longer as they were both papered, so that would all have to come off as well. By now Bertha was looking very long-faced, but I couldn't stop smiling all day: Rose, my beautiful Rose – she was coming home tomorrow!

At dinner Leo commented, 'You look very cheerful today, Amy.'

I smiled at him. 'Aye, I can hardly wait.' He smiled back – for the first time in a fortnight, it seemed like. 'And Leo, Dr Matthews says Flora can go outside tomorrow, so long as it's fine and she wears flannel next to the skin, so mebbe we could all come with you to look at the roses?'

His reply was formal. 'I would be honoured.' Then he stood up, 'I will take Nella for her walk now.' He was still so quiet and withdrawn. I wished now I'd been more appreciative of those evenings when he'd been confined to bed and had spent his hour with me acting like a spoilt child. At least I'd known how to behave then. And I hadn't minded because I'd known it had been partly a game. Partly, but not entirely; Mrs Chandler was right, he did need a lot of attention – only now he didn't seem to want it. But I couldn't stay low-spirited for long tonight – not with the thought of Rose coming back in the morning.

'Rose! Rose!' I ran across the cobbles and she pulled herself free from Ellen and ran to meet me. 'Rose, Rose! Oh how I've missed thee!' When at last I put her down she went straight to Flora. They'd often squabbled when they'd been together, but today they both seemed really pleased to see each other again. As Rose trotted along beside her sister, walking so sturdily now, I turned to Leo with a sigh. 'She's grown up so much these past weeks – she's not a baby any longer.'

The smile left his face, and it became set and still. 'I'm sorry, Amy.'

'Leo, I didn't mean – ' But he'd already walked on ahead.

We went down into the garden, and the roses danced in greeting, offering us their scent, their colour, and their beauty. They'd been neglected this last year, there'd been no dead-heading and precious little pruning, but they didn't seem to care. Those roses of his were as joyous as ever in all their untidy extravagance.

We came to the Blairii roses, and I stopped to gaze at their heart-breaking loveliness. 'They bist so beautiful – I'd forgotten, I should 'a come afore.'

He said quietly, 'You were too busy.'

'I be sorry.'

Quicky he replied, 'I didn't mean that as a criticism, Amy. You *have* been busy – very busy. Not just with nursing Flora: everyone on the estate sings your praises. I am grateful for all the burdens you have shouldered in my absence.'

But I shouldn't have forgotten the roses, his roses. I looked at him as he stood there, lop-sided, hump-backed: the Beast in his rose garden. And I asked, 'Will'st thee give I a rose?' Without a word he swung his ungainly body round and reached out one black-furred hand to snap off a single perfect pink bloom. Still in silence he handed it to me. Jokingly I dropped a little cursey, 'Thank 'ee, my Lord Beast.'

At once he exclaimed, 'I didn't mean to do it, Amy – I didn't mean to trap you.'

His voice was anguished, and hastily I reassured, 'I know that. Anyway, it dussent matter now.'

'But it does, it does!' He was shouting, and Flora and Rose turned round, their small faces alarmed.

I said, 'Leo, you're frightening the children.'

'I'm sorry.' I could see the effort he had to make to pull himself together, before turning and calling, 'Flora, Rose, see what Papa has found.'

I played with the children all morning, but even in my pleasure at Rose's return I couldn't get his face or his voice out of my mind.

By lunchtime the day was already overcast, but I left Ellen and Dora to settle my daughters for their afternoon naps and went down to find Leo. He was just crossing the hall.

'Leo, tis time to look at the roses again.'

Obediently he followed me round to the side door and out along the path – and then, of course, it began to rain.

'You'd better go in, Amy – you'll get wet.'

I shook my head. 'Likely tis only a shower. We'll go in the glasshouses first.'

I led the way into the nearest one – and then I wished I hadn't. There were no filled seed pans there now. No one had time to breed new roses while the war was on; but down at the end there were still a few bushes in pots – though not as many as there had been that evening I'd come in here with Joe Dempster. Joe, who'd kept begging me to marry him; and although I hadn't loved him I'd finally said yes. Then when I'd discovered I was already carrying Flora I'd been so relieved that I was betrothed to Joe – because it meant my baby would have a name. But first I'd told him the truth – and Joe hadn't wanted to marry me then. Instead he'd turned on me in anger and hit me, hard – and would have hit me again, if he hadn't been stopped by Leo, hidden from us by the rose bushes at the end.

Leo must have been remembering, too, because he suddenly said, 'Dempster was a good man with the roses.'

I turned to face him. 'Did you hear, that time – ?'

'Yes, I heard every word you spoke. I respected your honesty in telling him of your situation.'

When he said that, I felt ashamed and admitted, 'I nearly didn't tell him; I were tempted to deceive him. Since I'd found out about the baby I'd been frantic wi' worry – and I did so want a name for her, so she wouldn't be born like me. I know it were wrong, I shouldn't 'a been tempted, but,' I looked up into Leo's face as I confessed, 'I were so desperate for a husband.'

His face went rigid. Then he said, 'But not so desperate as to take me.'

I flinched from the bitter despair in his voice, then quickly gabbled, 'But I didn't know as I was being offered you. Thic doctor, he only said "Your precious 'my lord' has agreed to marry you", so naturally I thought he meant – I didn't *know* it was you, not until the service had started.'

'And then you cried out: "No!" But still I continued, and so bullied you into a marriage you never wanted – and don't want now.'

'*You* didn't bully me – it were just that I misunderstood the doctor. It weren't *your* fault.'

He was shaking, 'Yes, it *was* my fault! I should never have sent another man to ask you such a question – but I was a coward. I hadn't the courage to face rejection, not even from a desperate child. If only I'd come and asked you myself, then you would have understood whose hand you were being offered, and you would have said your "No" in time. As it is, you've paid for my cowardice ever since.' Swinging his ungainly body round he flung himself up the aisle and out of the door.

I stood looking after him – I tried to call out but I couldn't find my own voice: all I could hear in my mind was him, saying, 'If only I'd come and asked you myself, then you would have said your "No" in time.' But would I have said "No"? Suppose, just suppose, that he had come to me himself and said, 'I will give your baby a name – my name. But you will have to marry me to get it. Are you willing to pay that price?'

I didn't even have to ask myself what my answer would have been; I knew it. He'd been wrong, quite wrong, when he'd said: 'But not so desperate as to take me.' I had been that desperate.

Chapter Thirty-Nine

At once I began to move, running after him – but he was already halfway to the house, and he didn't look back. The rain had made the path slippery, I skidded and almost fell – but I didn't slow down, and I saw him go in through the side entrance. Shaking the raindrops from my hair I panted in behind, but by the time I reached the hall the library door had closed behind him. He had retreated to his lair.

In all the years we'd been married, only twice had I disturbed him there uninvited – but today I didn't hesitate. Pushing the door open I saw him crouched in his armchair, staring at the empty hearth. He must have heard me come in but he didn't even look up. Closing the door behind me I went and stood in front of him. 'You were wrong, Leo – I was that desperate.'

His head jerked up, 'What?'

'If you'd asked me, I would have said yes.'

He stared at me a moment, then turned away. 'I don't believe you.'

''Tis true.'

He shook his great head. 'You cried "No!" when you realized it was me, you cried out "No!"'

I caught my breath; I must be calm – to explain, to convince. 'Leo, I cried out "No!", not because it was you, but because it *weren't* him. I was expecting him. I'd even heard his footsteps – they were Mr Wallis's really, but I thought they were Frank's. I were imagining Frank standing there behind me, marrying me – so when *you* spoke instead, then o' course I cried "No!"'

'When *I* spoke.' His voice was harsh with bitterness. He didn't believe me, he didn't understand.

I tried again. 'Leo, if I'd known it were you, if you'd asked me yourself, I would 'a said yes. I were carrying a child out o' wedlock, an' I were desperate for a name for her, you know that.'

I saw from the small movement of his shoulders that he did know. He was wavering, I was beginning to convince him. Then his whole body tensed again as stubborn as ever, he repeated, 'No, I heard you, I heard you cry out: "No!"' But now it was the stubbornness of despair.

Patiently, gently I explained, 'That was the *first* time, when I was expecting him. But then they put my hand on yours and I felt the fur, the fur on *your* hand – so I knew it was you. When I were making my vows, I knew I were making them to you.'

He was silent. Then he said slowly, heavily, 'But knowing is not – consenting.'

And as I heard him say that it all became very simple. I said quietly, 'Then I consent now. Give me your hand.'

Dropping to my knees before his chair I took his hand, his black-furred hand, between both of mine and said, 'I, Amy, do take thee, Leonidas Arthur Hector, to be my lawful wedded husband. I will have thee and hold thee from this day forward, for better, for worse, for richer, for poorer, in sickness and in health. And I will love thee and cherish thee, honour and obey thee, until death us do part. Thereto I plight thee my troth.' Bending my head over his hand I placed my cheek against the thick silken hair on its back.

Through my cheek I could feel that his whole body was trembling, and it wasn't until he was still again that I raised my head. His crooked shoulder was bent awkwardly over so he could look down at me. I smiled up at him, but he didn't smile back, he simply continued to gaze down into my eyes. So lightly I said, 'Tis time thee kissed thy bride, Leo.'

Slowly, uncertainly, he bent down to kiss my cheek; but I turned my head, and it was my mouth which met his. His lips were soft and warm and gentle; I held mine close against them for a little while, then drawing away I said, 'There, my Leo, we do be properly married now.' Releasing his hand I rose to my feet, and he stood up too; he looked like a man who hadn't woken properly from a dream so I was brisk: 'Look, it's stopped raining, and there's a little patch of blue sky over beyond the cedar tree. I dare say the sun'll be out by tea-time. We could go and see thy roses now.'

Then at last he spoke, '*Your* roses.' Almost smiling he quoted: 'With all my worldly goods I thee endow.'

I said firmly, 'Our roses, Leo. Come along, then.'

All the rest of the day I felt very calm. I still loved Frank, nothing would ever alter that; but then, I'd loved Frank before Flora was born, too – yet that wouldn't have stopped me marrying Joe Dempster if he'd still been willing to have me. And no more would it have stopped me marrying Leo, either. If he'd come and offered I would have been astounded, bewildered, frightened, even – but I would still have married him, for the sake of my unborn child. And once married we would gradually have learnt to live together, just as we had done now.

No, the problem had not been the marriage, but the manner of our marrying. Leo was right, he should have asked me himself. Instead, the doctor's mistake had given me hope, revived my most precious dream – and my resentment at losing it had stopped me asking myself that one vital question, until today. Then I corrected my thoughts: no, it wasn't the resentment that had prevented me asking that question – it had been the dream itself. I'd wanted to go on believing that dream, believing that if Frank had been free he would have come to my rescue. It was only learning of that girl at Pennings that had finally made me face up to the truth about the past.

I'd been wrong in thinking that the past couldn't be altered. Obviously what had happened couldn't be – any more than the pieces of coloured glass in the sealed tube of Flora's kaleidoscope could be taken out and exchanged, but like the kaleidoscope the past could be shaken to make a new pattern. The same pieces of coloured glass, yet looking so different when you looked at them differently. I'd only wanted to see the one pattern: the pattern of Frank being willing to come to my rescue, had he been able. Like Clytie I'd wanted to believe that my sun god was perfect; even as I forgave him his faults so I'd pretended he was unflawed. But that pretence could only be maintained if I persisted in the other pretence – that the fault was my husband's, that he was the man who was flawed.

Then I began to smile; because of course Leo was flawed – we all were – but it shouldn't have stopped me loving him, because he was such a loveable man, and a man who needed love so much. And now I could give it to him, freely, willingly.

He was already up in the nursery when I went up, sitting on the sofa with a dark head pressed against one arm and a blonde head pressed against the other; he was reading our daughters their bedtime story. I stood still for a moment, looking at that blonde head, at Flora, who despite my sinful folly nevertheless had a name. His name. I felt a wave of pure, untarnished gratitude wash over me as I remembered the generosity of that gift he'd given me.

He was waiting for me in the hall before dinner as usual – but tonight he had chosen to wear full evening dress: high wing collar, stiff bow tie, starched white shirt front – all shining, gleaming white; while his tailcoat and tapered trousers were black as the night. He looked very splendid. I gazed up into his strong, craggy face and smiled. But he didn't smile back as he asked, 'Shall we go in now, Amy?' and even before he'd shaken out his napkin I knew there was something on his mind. My heart sank. Had his doubts come back? Had I not convinced him after all?

Then as Mr Tims left us alone with the soup Leo said, 'Amy, you cannot imagine the burden you have lifted from my shoulders today.' Then his face closed. 'But – ' I saw he was having difficulty finding the words to continue. At last he said haltingly – 'But – marriage is for the procreation of children.'

I tried to keep the excitement from my voice. 'Aye, Leo, so the prayer book do say.'

'I – I don't care a damn about the prayer book, but I do care about you.' And at once my excitement was quenched; he was afraid for me. Then I realized he was still struggling to say more. 'I care about your wishes, your desires, so if you – if tonight you want to – ' And this time my excitement took fire and became a leaping flame. He said quietly, 'I can see the answer in your face.'

'Please – '

'Then, I will try.'

Smiling up at him I leant forward so that his eyes dropped to my breasts – and were held there. I laughed with confidence and joy as I told him, 'Tis only right and proper, Leo, for today, tis our wedding day.' And all at once his face was ablaze with longing and desire.

We scarcely spoke again, then after the dessert he told Mr Tims, 'Her ladyship and I will take our coffee in here, tonight.' I nodded in agreement. He drank his coffee scalding hot then rose to his feet. 'Shall we walk for a little while, in the garden?' I dipped my head in answer. 'Then I'll call Nella.' I hadn't had time to drink my own coffee, but he hadn't noticed – and I didn't care.

We walked side by side along the damp paths; the sun was still up, a pale, watery sun, but there was warmth in it. I thought of next year, and how I would be holding a baby again, and before that there would be the calm months of carrying life in my womb. There'd been too many dying, too much death these past years; I wanted to bear new life. It was time.

As we came to the steps before the fountain and the Garland Rose, he began to walk down, but I paused at the top and stood gazing at the roses all around me, their blooms full and ripe with promise. He stopped and turned, waiting for me; and because of the steps his eyes were for once on a level with mine; and I saw how they were dark with longing – and uncertainty. I reassured him, 'Tis all right, my Leo, doan 'ee fret.'

Haltingly he said, 'Perhaps – there will be no child; women do not always conceive – when they wish.'

I smiled at him; then I took his hand and drew it to me and placed it flat against my stomach. 'Tis ready, my womb be ready for thy seed.' He snatched his hand back as though my belly were burning hot; his whole body was trembling. Firmly I told him, 'Tis time we went in to bed, my Leo. Nella – ' She looked up, surprised because her usual walk had been cut short; then resignedly she turned and padded after us. He didn't speak as we came back to the house and nor did I; all my thoughts and feelings were on what was to come.

We went straight upstairs. At my door I said, 'Now, don't be long, Leo. I'll be waiting for thee.' Turning the handle I went inside. I undressed quickly, but before I'd had time to get my nightdress on I heard his tap on the dressing room door. I pulled my dressing gown around me and tied the sash before calling, 'Come in.'

He came in still fully dressed in his evening clothes; when I moved towards him he backed away. 'No, Amy, I'm sorry – I can't. I can't give you what you want.' His whole body slumped, sagging in despair; all the earlier male desire, that longing, that excitement had gone – wiped out by fear. His grey eyes were hopeless, 'I looked in the mirror, and saw – myself.'

I said quietly, 'Dr Matthews said he was sure – '

'I know, and with my mind I believe what he said, but my flesh does not. I can't do it. I'm too damaged.'

Too damaged. But Rose, my pefect Rose, was upstairs asleep in the nursery to prove him wrong. So now I spoke to him gently, as to a frightened animal; as though he really were the great, sad bear he sometimes resembled. 'Doan 'ee fret, my Leo – I'll help thee.'

'But you can't – '

'Oh yes I can.' I was calm and confident.

He muttered helplessly, 'I can't even bring myself to take my clothes off.'

'Then I'll take them off for you. Sit thee down.' He looked round as if in a daze so I pulled up the firm, straight-backed chair I used for standing on to reach the top cupboard: he was such a big, heavy man. 'There, you sit on that.'

'But, Amy – '

'You just sit. You don't have to do anything else.'

He sat down, his hands hanging limply either side of the chair. I moved closer and began to undo his bow tie. Tossing it on the floor I ordered, 'Now bend thy head, so I can get at the back stud.' As he obediently bent forward I leant towards him, so that my breasts caressed his face. When the stud was out I gently but firmly tipped his head to the side again to release the remainder. His high white collar was soon on the floor with his tie and already I could see the first tufts of dark hair at his neck. My breathing quickened as I began to unfasten the buttons of his starched white waistcoat. Quickly I pulled it open and began to work at the tiny shirt buttons – but at the third I couldn't wait any longer; pushing the flaps back I slid my hand inside to fondle the warm hair of his chest. Stroking, caressing, I looked up into his eyes so close to mine and told him, 'I do so like thy fur, my Leo.' Very gently I kissed the tip of his nose as my fingers unfastened – four, five, six, seven – until all that dark silken hair was revealed and I could bury my face in it, kissing, caressing, with the rapid beating of his heart strong beneath my warm lips.

I'd been going to take his jacket off next, but his hand stopped me. So instead my fingers went to his braces, releasing them – and then moved on to his trouser buttons. He gave a murmur of protest, 'Amy – ' But I wasn't going to let him stop me now. 'Amy, it's no use, I can't make my – '

I put my finger to his lips. 'Shush, it baint thine tonight. Thy rod, tis mine – he do belong to me, and he'll do what I tell him, you just wait and see. But we maun get those trousers off first. Up you get.'

Obediently he stood up, and rapidly I pulled down his black dress trousers, with his braces flying after. Soon they were all tumbled on the floor with his underpants, and his black-haired legs stood strong as the trunks of two young oak trees. 'My shoes –'

'Never mind them,' I smiled, teasing, 'Nor thy socks – tis a cool night, best keep thy feet warm. Now, sit thee down again.' He sat, and I dropped on my knees in front of him. My voice was soft and reassuring, 'Now doan 'ee be afeard, I won't hurt 'ee.' But he was still frightened, so I knew I must be gentle. At first I knelt there, simply stroking the silken strands of hair that curled across his flat belly – but moving a little nearer to his rod with each slow caress. And already I fancied it was fuller, the curl of it becoming looser – as if it were aware of me before I'd even touched it. 'Don't be frightened, my Leo, I won't hurt him.' And as I spoke I slipped my fingers down into that warm soft nest of hair and then gently eased them up and began stroking his rod – and at once it responded to me, like a flower raising its head to the sun. The miracle had happened between my caressing fingers, and now life and the promise of life lay in the palm of my hand: soft as silk and strong as oak. And it began to beat for me.

Bending my head I kissed the full tip, and it jumped with pleasure and excitement in my hand. I kissed it again before untying my sash and climbing on to his lap. 'Do 'ee hold me steady, Leo. I maun help thee in.' So he held me, while I gently eased his full rod between my thighs and into the soft welcome of my cunny. For once my head was on a level with his, and I smiled into his grey eyes as I asked, 'There, don't that feel nice?' He looked at me as if he couldn't believe it, and I kissed the tip of his nose and eased myself further on to him until we were completely joined. I felt his rod inside me, warm and full of promise, and I drew it into me, holding it tight, tight as ever I could – and heard his gasp of pleasure. Slowly I released my grip, letting him go a little – and at once his hips began to move, pushing his rod deep into me again. I laughed, and taking hold of it squeezed it hard – and laughed again at the delight on his face.

We moved in rhythm now, rocking up and down in the chair together as though we were dancing. And then I felt him pushing harder and harder – so hard that for a moment I was frightened – then I let my fear go and surrendered to the strength of his seed. As he gave me that gift which I had so longed for I lifted my mouth to his, and we clung together until it seemed as if my whole body was on fire, burning with a heat that would never die down – and I cried out with the exquisite pain of that pleasure. When at last it was over I sagged down against his chest, limp and spent in the safety of his arms.

Afterwards we were both very shy. As I pulled away from him and stood up I quickly drew my dressing gown close around me. He turned his back as he stood up, and began hastily to retrieve his clothes from the floor. He was almost at the door before I ventured, 'Leo?'

He didn't look round as he replied, 'Yes?'

'Are you coming back for a cuddle?'

Still without looking at me he said, 'Yes – if I may.' And scuttled through to his dressing room.

While he was in there I pulled on my nightdress and tidied my hair before switching off the light and getting into bed. He came back in his pyjamas and climbed in next to me. We lay there, not touching for a little while, then I began to turn towards him and he moved to me – and we were in each other's arms again. We fell asleep still entwined together.

Chapter Forty

I woke very early. He'd already left me; I hadn't noticed his going but the pillow beside me was still hollowed where his head had rested. I lay in the warm nest of my bed drowsy and content.

I went up to the nursery first thing, just as I always did. I was sitting on the window seat with Rose on my lap and Flora beside me when the door opened. Flora called, 'Papa!' and ran to him at once. Rose strained forward in my arms, so I set her on the floor and we walked towards him, hand in hand. He crouched down to greet his daughters, then looked up at me, his face on fire. 'Good morning, Amy.'

My own blush answered his. 'Good morning, Leo.' We didn't seem to have anything more to say to each other, so we both turned our attention to the children.

Later I went down to the estate office and he went out to the glasshouses. I took the children out to see him before lunch, and then he left for Salisbury, to have his arm massaged. He was very quiet when he came back, but when I offered him tea in my sitting room he came at once. After the children had gone back upstairs he stayed while I sewed. I talked about the harvest, and the preparations we'd made; but since the weather had been so bad all the arrangements had had to be delayed. He listened, and made the occasional comment; but he was saying so little I fell silent myself, assuming he was waiting for an opportunity to leave. Instead he picked up one of the rose books he'd given me and began to leaf through it. Surreptitiously I watched him as he was reading: studying his grizzled dark hair that was always a little rumpled because of the curl in it; looking at his craggy face, so stern until it was transformed by his smile; his jutting jaw, his bushy eyebrows – I was aware of them all today. And suddenly I thought, already I may be carrying his son.

At dinner we talked only of the children and the roses; but whenever I looked up from my plate I saw that his eyes were on me. When he stood up to open the door for me after dinner I said, 'Leo?'

He swung quickly round, 'Yes?'

'Would you like to come to my room again tonight?'

'I – I – ' Then he gained control of his words, 'Yes, Amy, please – if I may.' He hesitated before asking, 'And may I come up for coffee now – with you?'

'Aye, o' course you can.'

It was raining again by the time we'd finished our coffee, but I put on my mackintosh and galoshes and we walked round the rose garden together, Nella by our side. When we got back we went straight upstairs.

He was wearing his dressing gown when he came into my room, and guessing why I said firmly, 'There's no need for you to bother with those fiddly little gloves now.'

He reddened, then said, 'I suppose it would be – shutting the stable door after the horse has bolted.'

I looked up at him from under my lashes. 'I reckon as thic horse has bolted in, not out.'

His face was scarlet by now, then he started laughing, too. But as I lifted the covers he said, 'I'm not sure – if I can – '

'Then just come for a cuddle. In you get.' Obediently he climbed in.

Of course, it was more than a cuddle, much more; and yet in a way it was still a cuddle: a deeper, closer, warmer cuddle. I didn't get the burning heat of the night before, but afterwards I felt so satisfied and content I exclaimed, 'That were nice – thank 'ee, Leo.' Pulling myself up until my face was level with his I kissed him, kissing the way I had done the night before, full on his lips with my mouth a little open, and he opened his, and our tongues touched and began to caress each other. I could have gone on like that for ever, except that I was getting out of breath. I drew away and settled myself down against his chest, before telling him, 'You know, I never realized afore that women could enjoy doing It. I thought it were only men who did.'

He replied very quietly, 'I have never felt such pleasure before, Amy, either.' I glowed with pride. Then, his voice tentative, he asked, 'But – did you really enjoy our making of love just now? Or are you – simply trying to please me?'

'I did enjoy it, truly I did.' Then because he seemed so anxious I added, 'In fact, I enjoyed it so much that I could do it all over again, this very minute.'

I felt him quiver with suppressed laughter; then he said, 'You know, Amy, I feel exactly the same way!'

It took me a moment to work it out, then I asked, 'Now?'

'In a few minutes, I think. But Amy, may I – touch you, first?'

I thought, but you *are* touching me – then I understood and told him, 'O' course you can,' and pulled my nightie up again. At first he only stroked my behind and then my belly – and by then I wanted him to stroke me lower down. I'd never have believed it of myself, actually *wanting* a man to touch me in my most secret places. But then, it was Leo, my husband – and he loved me. As I lay there I could feel his love in every gentle movement of his fingers, and reaching out I guided his hands down, and felt their warmth, warming my whole body. Now my own hand sought his rod, and as I heard his gasp of pleasure I drew it to me, into me – and so we loved again.

Afterwards, when I'd given him his kiss, I said, 'It were even nicer the second time. Thank 'ee Leo, thank 'ee so much.' And then I fell asleep in his arms.

He came to my room every night. Always he'd be a little uncertain as he stood by my bed: 'I'm not sure if – ' and I'd say, 'Just come for a cuddle, then.' But always it was more than a cuddle.

Afterwards he'd lie waiting for his kiss – and then he'd fall asleep. I'd lie warm and content beside him, remembering the excited anticipation on his face every evening as I invited him to my room; the exclamations of pleasure he gave as I held him inside me; and that final uncontrollable panting gasp of delight as he gave me his gift of love. And recalling all those moments made me feel so special, because I knew that for him there was no other woman: no other woman who could give him what I gave him, no other woman whom he wanted to give him these pleasures. There never had been, except *her*, and she hadn't loved him, or wanted him – so it was only me. 'The act of love should not take place except where there is affection and trust ... only within marriage.' And I was his wife, and loved him. Some nights that feeling of being special – precious – was so strong that I couldn't keep it to myself. I'd lean over and kiss him again and again, telling him with my kisses that I was here, beside him. And telling him, too, that if he wanted to perform his act of love, then I was there, and willing. Often he did want to, and so we would love again, fully and completely.

Once I fell so quickly asleep afterwards I was still sprawled across his body, his rod nestling damp against my cunny – and in the morning we both woke to find we'd begun to love again, almost without realizing it. I could tell he was as surprised as I was as I slid my hands around his strong buttocks and pulled him closer in.

When we'd finished I gave him his kiss and said, 'That were a nice way to say "Good morning", Leo – only you'd best slip back to your room now, because Bertha'll be up in a minute with my cup o' tea.' He went, still looking surprised – and at breakfast he kept sneaking little glances at me, as if he really couldn't believe what we'd just been doing.

We never had much to say to each other in the daytime; we talked to the children, but we only talked to each other about the roses, and not being able to start the harvest because of the weather. He still went to Salisbury three times a week and I was busy in the estate office, but we'd both find ourselves having breakfast together each morning, and he never missed lunch now.

One afternoon, a fortnight after I'd renewed my vows, I said, 'I've got to go up to the Home Farm to collect last month's receipts. He's been leading Mr Selby a dance for 'em, has Mr Arnott, using the weather as an excuse. If we don't get 'em off him afore the harvest starts it'll be weeks.' I stood up to go, and Leo stood up to come with me.

For once it wasn't raining. At the hazel copse we turned off the lane on to the cart track. It was very muddy, and I had to pick my way over the ruts. When he paused to wait for me to catch up I asked, 'Mebbe you could lend me your arm, Leo?'

'Certainly.' I slipped my arm through his, and drew him close to my side.

As he carefully shortened his longer strides to match mine I said, 'You aren't limping any more.'

'No, my leg is quite healed.' He added, 'And I have regained full use of my arm again.'

'Aye, you been lucky – ' I broke off, 'Look, there's Perseus – wanting his crust, I'll be bound.' The bull raised his huge head and then came padding over to the stile. 'I baint forgotten, Percy old boy – here it is, then.' I climbed up on to the stile and fed him, then I stroked his massive forehead, 'Thee bist a good boy, Percy.' I turned to Leo explaining, 'Percy, he's got every one o' the new heifers in calf. We're main pleased wi' him.' I scratched Percy in his favourite spot behind his ears, 'Baint you a hard-working old boy, then?'

Leo replied, his voice sounding slightly odd, 'I'm not sure – he would see it as work.'

'Tis what a bull's kept for. Now that Jersey bull, he's lazy. If he don't take to a heifer he'll only mount her the once. But Percy here, he'll keep at it. He do make a proper job of it – doan 'ee, my beauty?' I patted him again and he flicked his tail in reply. I turned to Leo and saw that he was looking at me with a very odd expression on his face. Seeing it, something came over me, I just couldn't help it. Reaching out to him I put my arms round his neck and drew him close so that my cheek rested against his – then I whispered in his ear, 'And thee dost make a proper job of it, too.'

I could feel his body shaking, and I thought for a moment I'd upset him – then I realized he was laughing. 'Amy! How could you!'

I nuzzled his ear, kissing it, and felt his arms tighten around me. Then a voice said, 'Afternoon, me lord, me lady.'

Leo jerked back so quickly I had to clutch at one of Percy's horns to stop myself overbalancing.

Mr Arnott said, 'I saw you was on your way, so I thought I'd come down and meet you. Your lady allus stops for a word wi' thic old bull. She's got him eating out of her hand, she has.'

Leo had recovered his composure. 'Yes, Arnott, she does have that effect. This weather's not improving, is it?'

Mr Arnott grunted. 'Getting worse, if anything. An' we were doing so well in June. Thought we'd really caught up on that bad winter, I did. I were going to ask your lady if those soldiers are still going to be free, if we has to put it off much longer.'

Mr Arnott and I discussed the harvest arrangements while Leo leant back against the top rail of the stile watching us, with Percy listening behind him. When we'd finished, Percy snorted and ambled back to his heifers. Mr Arnott looked after him approvingly. 'He's a good bull, that one, me lord.'

'Yes, so my wife has been telling me.'

'Keeps them cows in calf, he do – not like thic young Jersey.' He shook his head. 'Those young 'uns, they baint got no staying power.' Leo's face was a picture.

I said, 'That's just what I've been telling his lordship. Now Mr Arnott, have you got those receipts ready for me?'

He looked furtive. 'Aye, me lady, almost.'

I was firm. '*Almost* baint ready, Mr Arnott – you know that. Now, show me what you have got and I'll help you find the others. I want to take them back with me today.'

Mr Arnott looked at Leo, 'Proper slave driver she is, your lady.'

I retorted, 'If you'd rather do the accounts yourself, Mr Arnott . . .'

'No, no – '

I got all the receipts and invoices off him eventually; I'd learnt my way around his disorganization by now. 'If you'd just take the trouble to put them straight into thic liddle cubbyholes I labelled for you it'd be quicker in the end, Mr Arnott. Still, tis tidier than it used to be.'

He turned and winked at Leo. 'Easier to do as I'm told than be nagged every month, eh, me lord?'

Leo laughed, '*Much* easier, Arnott. I've discovered the same.'

On the way back I said to him indignantly, 'I don't nag you.'

'Not all the time.'

'Not any of the time!'

'What about when Matthews ordered me to bed?'

'That was different – you *needed* nagging then.' He laughed, and I added, ''Sides, I was right, because you're brave and well again now.'

His laughter stopped at once. Then he replied, 'Yes, quite well. And the medical board agree. I'm going back tomorrow.'

My arm through his dragged him to a halt. 'Back? Back to France?'

'No, no – light duties at first, in England.'

'Why didn't you tell me?'

'I was going to tell you this evening.'

I still couldn't believe it. 'But I thought you'd be at home at least until after the harvest – '

'No, I'm afraid not.'

'Couldn't you, couldn't you – ' I was going to say, 'just leave the army altogether.' After all, he was older, and he knew lots of people with influence, and that Lord Crawford had left and come back to be President of the Board of Agriculture. But even as those thoughts were rushing through my head I knew Leo would never leave the army, not while the war was still going on, so I simply said, 'Couldn't you ask for a bit longer?'

'I don't feel that I should ask for another special privilege. Remember that I should never have come home as soon as I did – others were not so fortunate.'

I walked on, fighting tears; it was the shock of him saying it so suddenly like that and just now, when – It was his hand that stopped us this time. Half lifting me off my feet he swung me round to face him.

'Amy, you must write as soon as you know – your condition.' His eyes watched my face, then he asked quietly, 'Are you already late?'

I shook my head. 'I'm not due till next Monday. But likely I won't be able to tell then. With Flora and Rose I weren't sure until I quickened.'

'Even if you are *not* sure, tell me if you have any grounds at all for suspicion.'

'But, if I am, wouldn't it be better if I didn't tell you till it was all over – to save you worrying?'

'No!' He was almost shouting. 'I am your husband, it is my *right* to worry. You must promise to be completely frank with me, Amy.'

I looked up at him – and remembered that he'd not been completely frank with me; and he was a big, strong man. 'How long do these "light duties" last?'

'I don't know.' He wouldn't meet my eye. 'Anyway, even if I am sent to France again – which wouldn't be surprising, given the present arrangements for the wounded – you can safely assume I'm at the base hospital.'

'Like you weren't last time.'

'Well – I ' He changed tack, 'It was probably better that you didn't know.'

'But I did know.'

He looked astounded. 'How on earth – surely Selby didn't betray my confidence?'

I said simply, 'Frank told me.'

'Good Lord – I could have sworn he wouldn't.'

'Well, he did.' I looked directly up at him. 'Leo, I'll promise to tell you on condition that you promise to tell *me* if you're sent to one of those field ambulances.'

'The personnel of a field ambulance do not face the same risks as front line soldiers.'

'Only there just happened to be a shell exploding – '

'Obviously there are times – but I really don't see the necessity of worrying you.'

'I'm your wife. Tis my right to worry about you.' He was silent, so I pushed home my advantage. 'I'll promise if you'll promise.' At last he dipped his head.

'What time do you leave tomorrow?'

'I'm catching the seven forty-five.'

'We'd best have breakfast early, then.'

'You don't have to get up – '

'Of course I do.'

We had tea together, and then we both went up to the nursery with the children. I only left him while we were dressing for dinner, and even then he came to the dressing room door and asked me to help him look for a collar stud he'd dropped. Dinner, coffee – then the last walk round the rose garden. At the top of the steps leading down to the fountain he asked me, 'What would you like for your Christmas present, Amy? Tell me, and I'll choose it on my way through Town, and arrange for it to be sent to you in December.'

'I want it now.'

He looked surprised, then he said, 'Certainly, if you'd like a cheque – '

I shook my head. 'I don't want money. I want a kiss.'

He was silent. I gave him a little push down the steps to bring his head on a level with mine, then put my arms around his neck and waited for his kiss. At first it was a warm, gentle kiss – like the one he'd given me when I'd renewed my vows. But then he kissed me again, and this one wasn't gentle: his mouth forced my lips apart, his tongue thrust into my mouth searching for mine – and all the time his hands strained my body against his. Then suddenly he broke away, setting me free. 'I'm sorry, Amy – I'm so sorry, I forgot myself.'

I reached out for his hand and took it in mine. 'Don't be silly, Leo. There's nothing to be sorry about. I'm your wife. We'd best go in now, tis time for bed.' He didn't reply tonight that he wasn't sure; it had been only too obvious during that kiss that he was sure, very sure.

He came to my room very quickly, and held me too tightly – almost desperate as he gave me his last gift of love. Afterwards we lay entwined together until we both fell asleep, still in each other's arms. Just before dawn he woke me, and in the pale early light we loved again. Then he left me.

He said goodbye to Flora and Rose, then I drove him down to the station. We waited together on the platform, but I couldn't think of anything to say, and he didn't speak, either. Then, just as the train was arriving he turned to me and said quietly, 'I love you, Amy.'

I looked back up at him and said, 'And I love you, Leo. Now, do 'ee take care.'

'And you, Amy – and don't forget to tell me.'

'Aye, I will. Now gi' I a kiss.' He bent his head and I kissed him full on the mouth. Then he walked away to the waiting train.

I stood waving goodbye until the last carriage had gone round the bend, then I went back home, to my children.

Chapter Forty-One

I did miss him, and so did the children; if only he hadn't had to go back so soon. Rose had only just got used to him, and Flora was upset: she kept asking when he was going to come home again, and when I told her not until next summer, she burst into tears. I shed a few myself as I was consoling her. It did seem an awful long time – and suppose they sent him to France?

But his first letter came very quickly – it had crossed with mine – he'd been posted to Netley again. I gave a sigh of relief. I read his letter again after I'd gone to bed, but it was as formal and restrained as his letters always were. I put out the light and turned over to sleep, but my bed seemed so big and empty now.

As soon as I awoke next morning I jumped up and went directly to the window: it was raining and windy again. My heart sank. Mr Selby said it was almost as bad as five years ago, and that had been one of the worst summers he'd ever known – but we hadn't been at war then. We could import all the wheat we needed in those days, but now we had to grow it ourselves. We *had* grown it; but we couldn't harvest it until the sun shone. With a sigh I went back to get dressed.

Down in the office we went over the arrangements again. The mattresses were ready filled with sweet-smelling hay, piled up in the corner of the reading room. Eight soldiers were to sleep there, while the others were to be billeted in the village. The older men and women had agreed to take them in, since they had the space. Maud Winterslow had refused at first, but then she'd changed her mind and demanded one for her spare room. As Clara said, Granny Withers had gone round telling everybody Maud was frightened of having a man in her house: 'And that soon did the trick.' We both laughed.

The soldiers were to take their meals in the schoolhouse, since school wouldn't be starting again until the harvest was over, so the desks had all been stacked up and trestle tables set ready. Mrs Carter was going to cook the meals on the big ranges at Eston, and then pack the huge saucepans in boxes of hay to keep them nicely warm. Mr Tyson and Jesse would take them down in the trap. At first I'd only asked Mrs Carter to feed the soldiers sleeping in the reading room, but then she'd produced menus for them all, insisting that it was just as easy to feed twenty as eight. And there was a further gain: it freed the older women to set the pots of the younger women on their ranges ready for when they came home from the fields. Because the soldiers couldn't provide enough labour, we needed women, too, especially now that the harvest had been delayed. We might have very little time when the fine weather eventually came – if it ever did come.

Jael had overhauled the self-binder and the two sail reapers so that we could cut three fields at once – but the reapers needed a lot more labour, because all the hiles would have to be tied by hand. We'd got more acres than ever under the plough this year, suppose we lost some of our crop? But we couldn't afford to, because so many of our merchant ships had been sunk by the U-boats, and their cargoes lost. Yet at lunchtime it was still raining, as though the weather was fighting on the side of the Germans, too.

I went along to the morning room and picked up the newspaper again. At breakfast I'd only had time to read the casualty lists, my heart in my mouth – but Frank's name hadn't been there. Now I saw that there was another great battle going on round Ypres. Suppose Frank was one of the men fighting there?

But in the afternoon Lady Burton called, and distracted me from the war.

'I'm so sorry I've missed Leonidas, dear – I couldn't come before, I've been away staying with Joan!'

I asked after Sir George, and she asked me about Flora – and then told me that the younger brother of the boy who'd gone down with scarlet fever had caught the infection too – and died of it.

I sat there, my hands trembling. 'Oh, Lady Burton, how dreadful!'

The minute she'd gone I went up to the nursery and hugged Flora and Rose. I could hardly bear to leave them to go back down to the estate office. As I wrote to Leo that evening, I remembered him watching with me in Flora's room as she tossed and turned in her delirium. I told him again how glad I was he'd been with me: 'I might have panicked, and let her down.'

'No, you would not have done,' he wrote in his reply – but I wasn't so sure. His letter was more relaxed today. He described how he still couldn't get over his relief that I would have married him if I'd known beforehand. 'You are still sure, Amy?' Yes, I was still sure, quite sure. I only wished I'd realized it long before, because it had been a great relief to me, too. Everything was much simpler, knowing that – especially now I hoped I was carrying his child again.

But that night I started bleeding. I knew, of course I knew, that it had happened before. I knew I was one of those women who did bleed for a couple of months even after I'd fallen; but I did so want a baby; not just for myself, but because it was *his* baby. I wrote and told him what had happened, as I'd promised, and he wrote back: 'I am aware that this occurrence does not necessarily have the same significance for you as for other women. Please send me another report next month.'

It was almost the end of August before Mr Arnott finally agreed that we could start harvesting the next day. 'I don't know whether we'll manage to get it all in, Lady Warminster, if the weather turns nasty again we just haven't enough hands.' After lunch I told Ellen what he'd said and she suggested, 'My Lady, my cousin Bet, she'd gladly help with the harvest, but her two are too young to be taken to the fields. I wondered if – '

So we decided to run a nursery in the reading room. Ellen and Dora were to be in charge, then Granny Withers and Maud Winterslow volunteered to help. There'd be twenty children in all, with Flora and Rose, and that freed fourteen more women for the harvest. Even Mr Selby shed a few of his wrinkles when he heard, until he found another difficulty.

'Arnott's still short of skilled men, though – '

'We'll manage, Mr Selby. We got to.'

He and I stood side by side in High Hams next morning. Mr Arnott spat on his hands, picked up his scythe and swung it in one flowing sweep; the first swathe of golden corn fell to the ground. The Eston harvest had begun. When that first track had been opened by hand the horses threw their great shoulders forward against their collars and began to pull the self-binder onto the stubble. Mr Arnott took off his cap to wipe his sweating forehead, then turning to the women he barked out his orders. Only when he was sure that everyone knew exactly what they had to do did he summon the waiting soldiers and lead them off to the next field. Their heavy boots tramped after him, in marching rhythm.

I was very busy the rest of the day. We supposed that we'd thought of everything before, but of course, we hadn't. There were problems to be ironed out, decisions to be made, ruffled feelings to be soothed; from Ellen's exasperated 'Really, my lady, those two squabble more than all the children put together,' as she glared at Martha and Maud, to Mr Arnott's, 'Some o' thic soldiers behave as though they're on holiday, they do. And look at thic gurt vule – took his shirt off! Don't he *know* as straw do scratch and sun do burn?'

'I'll go and have a word wi' him, Mr Arnott, and I dare say Clara'll have some soothing ointment.'

Then in the middle of the following afternoon, Dancer shed a shoe. The air around Mr Arnott turned blue. 'Sykes'll have to take him down the smithy. That Dancer, he's too lively for the boy – '

We'd got four horses pulling the self-binder, so Mr Sykes had been driving from Dancer's back, but his partner, Prancer, was a stallion – he needed firm handling, too. Then one of the soldiers volunteered, saying he'd ridden before, so Mr Arnott calmed down, but not for long. 'Ridden afore! Just you look at him, my lady!'

But I wasn't looking at the binder. I'd noticed Mary Tyson straightening up to look across the field, and when she nudged Jane Chandler I followed their eyes – and saw Frank.

He came striding across the stubble towards me, with the sun shining golden on his hair and his blue eyes smiling in his sun-tanned face. Mr Arnott's voice came from close beside me, but he could have been a hundred miles away for all I heard of what he said. I was listening only to that one voice as he said, 'Hello, Amy, and how are you?' His smile broadened.

I managed to stammer a reply as Mr Arnott touched his cap. 'Arternoon, me lord.'

'Good afternoon, Arnott. How goes the harvest? I see you've enlisted the help of a troop of Amazons.' He laughed, his teeth flashing white in his brown face.

Mr Arnott grunted. 'They're steady enough workers – but look at that one.' He nodded at the soldier astride Prancer, 'Said 'e could ride! Mebbe he can – on a milk float with a donkey. He baint no use on a binder with four proper horses, that's for sure. Be lucky if he sticks on till Sykes comes back.'

'Shall I take over, instead?'

Mr Arnott's face brightened. 'If you would, me lord, twould be a big help.'

'Here, Amy, hold that.' His cap came flying through the air, followed by the warm weight of his tunic. Then he was off, over the stubble, Mr Arnott having to lengthen his paces to keep up with him.

I watched as he sprang up into the saddle, I watched as he confidently took the reins into his hands, and I watched as that slim, straight back began to move forward.

The displaced soldier muttered, 'I've allus had stirrups before.'

'So's his lordship – but going without won't faze 'im – he can handle an 'orse, he can.'

And he could, he could. I stood watching, gripping the stiff khaki rim of his cap as if I'd never let it go. Then I walked over to the elm trees and sat down in their shade; Nella flopped down beside me.

I stayed there for over an hour, watching him riding slowly up and down that field. I told myself I had to stay, because he'd given me his cap and tunic to look after – but I knew that wasn't the true reason. I stayed because I couldn't bear to tear my eyes away from him. In his khaki he was all golden in the sunshine: if Apollo himself had come down to earth to help with the harvest, he would have looked just like Frank that afternoon. And so I stayed, watching.

The other women were watching, too. I saw it in the lift of a sun bonnet, the deliberately casual straightening up to glance at him – and then at me. But still I sat in the shade of the elm, nursing his tunic against my breast like a baby.

Mr Sykes arrived back with Dancer, the horses were changed round, and one sweating pair were taken off to rest. The man on the reaper picked up the stone jug of cider, and offered it to Frank. His bronze neck rippled as he swallowed, then he handed it back and wiped his mouth with the back of his hand. A word, a laugh, and then he'd left the men and was striding across to where I sat. Throwing himself down in the grass beside me, he stretched his long lean strength out in the shade. 'That's given me an appetite for the dinner you're going to invite me to, Amy – since I'm too late for tea.'

'Tis only rabbit stew and dumplings.'

'Good Lord – surely your new cook can do better than that?'

'She's busy cooking for the harvesters, tis the same as the soldiers are having.'

'Oh well, since I'm a harvester myself today, I suppose I must eat their humble fare.'

Rolling over on to his stomach he put a straw in his mouth, then narrowed his eyes to squint up at me. 'How are you, Amy? Beautiful as ever, I see. Summer suits you, it brings out the golden glints in your hair and makes your eyes look so warm and soft – Oh, she's blushing!' He broke off to laugh. 'I guessed it wouldn't take me long to bring a rosy flush to your face, my ripe, golden peach!'

He sat back on his haunches and sprang upright in a single fluid movement, then held out his hand. 'Up you get, Amy, I've asked Sykes to bring my horse back to the house later, so I'll escort you home – and then you must run me a bath or I won't even be fit to dine on rabbit stew and dumplings.'

I dropped his hand as soon as I was upright; I should never have taken it in the first place – and besides, the women were watching.

He walked beside me with long, easy strides until we reached the footpath. 'We'll cut through this way, those waggons have made a mess of the track.' Nella and I followed him obediently. As the path began to slope he said, 'Do you remember, Amy, those mornings when I used to meet you in the park?'

'Aye, I remember.'

'You always had a dog with you then, too. Let's pretend Nella is Earl.' She was padding along behind me: it could have been the sound of Earl's great paws. 'And let's pretend that you're a pert little lady's maid again and – how old *were* you that summer?'

'I was seventeen, going on eighteen.'

'You don't look any older now, so we don't have to pretend on that one. And I'm twenty-two and the world is at my feet, one long round of fun and excitement and pleasure. Let's pretend, Amy, let's pretend.' He smiled, and his smile was the boyish smile of that golden summer. And seeing it, I *was* seventeen again, and we were both young and free with no taint of sin or regret: free to walk together, free to laugh together – and free to love each other. He talked of dinners and dances and cricket matches and I gazed up at him adoringly, listening as I had listened then. So we walked on, until we came to the stile.

'Goodness, they've put a stile in Hyde Park – how very odd.' Putting his hand on the top rail, he sprang over in one lithe leap. Then he turned back to face me. 'Upsadaisy, Amy.' I climbed up on to the first step – and his hands reached out and caught hold of me round the waist. 'Over we come.' He swung me up and over the rail to set me down safely on to the other side. Still gripping my waist he looked down at me, his face very close, his eyes the same vivid blue – but they weren't the eyes of that laughing boy any more – and I was not that girl.

I broke free of his hands, calling 'Nella, Nella!' She bounded over to my side and crouching down I flung my arms around her neck. Without looking up at him I whispered, 'Tis too late, too late to pretend.'

He said softly, 'Yes, it is. And I should never have pretended then – that was my first mistake. How is Flora, Amy?'

So I told him how she'd been ill with scarlet fever, and how worried we'd been, and he listened quietly until we reached the house.

While he was in his bath Clara helped me brush his uniform. She didn't say anything, but the way she didn't say it made it quite clear how she felt.

I told her, 'Lord Quinham, he's been helping with the harvest. Dancer threw a shoe, and Prancer, he's not the easiest of horses to handle, so Lord Quinham, he . . . ' I knew I was talking too much.

When I finally paused she asked, 'Will he be staying the night, my lady?'

'Oh, he didn't say. I don't think – I don't know – ' Clara sniffed.

Up in the nursery Ellen didn't actually sniff, but she looked as if she wanted to. As I'd had to go down to the estate office first, Frank was already there, sitting on the window seat with Flora. We didn't leave until the dressing bell rang. Outside in the corridor I asked, 'Are you – where are you staying tonight?'

'At Ettie Burton's, but I told her not to expect me back for dinner. I'll see you later, Amy.'

I went down to tell Clara at once. 'Very good, my lady. Will that be all?'

I backed out of her room.

Frank was already waiting in the hall before dinner. He watched me all the way down the stairs. 'Mm, that dress is rather severe – but I admit you don't need the trimmings.' He extended one elegant black-clad arm. I placed my fingertips on it. 'Don't worry, Amy, I hardly ever bite women before dinner – shall we go in?'

When we were seated he said, 'Ellen told me the old man's only just gone back.'

'Tis twelve days since, now. He's been on sick leave. He were wounded in April.'

'Yes, I knew that – one hears things. Still, he's presumably fully recovered, since he's returned to duty. Hasn't he had enough yet? I'm sure he could have wangled his discharge.'

I shook my head. 'No, he won't leave, not till the war is over.'

'If it's *ever* over.' He added abruptly, 'Don't let's talk about that.'

'How long are you on leave?'

'The usual, about a fortnight – less travelling time, of course – they always sting you. I came over yesterday but I had certain – er – business – to attend to in Town.'

I said quickly, 'And today you came down to see Flora.'

'And you, Amy, and you.' I felt my cheeks becoming hot. 'And now I've seen you, I'd better say what I came to say, hadn't I?' His voice was light.

'What was that?'

'That I love you, Amy – totally, utterly.' And now his voice wasn't light at all.

'No! You mustn't – '

'I'm afraid I can't help it.' He smiled at my confusion. 'No, that's not true,

296

I'm not *afraid* at all – I don't *want* to help it. It's the most marvellous feeling in the world, being in love.' He leant forward, his eyes serious. 'Do you know, after Annabel cast me off I kept thinking of how I'd felt when I first fell in love with her – and I thought, I'll never feel that way about a woman again. But today, the minute I saw you standing in that field with your hair glinting golden in the sun and the tip of your delicious little nose just ever so slightly pink I thought: I love her, I love her! It was all I could do not to throw you over my shoulder and run off with you there and then. All at once, everything was right with the world. Crazy, isn't it? You're married to the wrong man, he owns my child, and there's the most godawful war on – yet when I leapt upon that horse I felt happy as a king!'

At last I found my voice. 'You mustn't, you mustn't. I be Leo's wife!'

The light in his eyes died down. 'I know. And he's been out there, and no doubt will be again before long, the way this latest little show's going. So don't fret yourself, Amy, I'll continue to play the game. I'll be totally British and stiff upper-lipped until the war ends, and then I'll be very French indeed and come and wrest you from him!' I opened my mouth, but he was still speaking, his voice darkening now. 'If I survive, of course, which doesn't seem very likely at present. I don't suppose I could keep going if it weren't for you, Amy, and the thought of you, afterwards. A man needs his dream, you know, when he's out there.' I held my tongue.

He reached for his wine glass and emptied it. Then he said, 'You were watching me in that field, weren't you? I saw you.' My face became warm. He went on, 'I also saw how the old biddies were keeping an eye on you, too. In fact, the air of Eston – outside the pure, sparkling atmosphere of your presence – is heavy with disapproval. I can't say it bothers me, but,' he shrugged, 'I don't want them tearing you apart the minute I'm gone, so I'll make it a very short visit this time. In any case, I'm going to Scotland for some shooting.'

''Tis a long way.'

'Yes, but I'm going by sleeper – and I won't be wasting the time sleeping, since I've engaged the services of a very fetching young actress as my companion for the trip. You see, Amy, I'm not concealing anything from you. Anyway you know what I'm like. That's part of your attraction, I suppose. You know all my faults, but you still love me, don't you, Amy?' I was fighting back the tears. He said softly, 'All right, don't get upset. You don't have to reply. Your eyes have already given me the answer, I've been reading it in them all afternoon.' He sat back. 'Now, if you don't want any more of that soup I'll ring for Tims, and we'll have a polite, civilized dinner together. You'll pour me coffee afterwards, and then I'll go back to Ettie – who explained that she would, of course, be waiting up for me. I'll be going up to town from there first thing in the morning – you may tell your servants that. Aren't I a good boy these days, Amy?'

I smiled at him, 'Aye, you are.'

He returned my smile. 'It's amazing what a war can do – and falling in love, instead of lust – that makes a hell of a difference, I've found. Now, tell me some more about my daughter. How is she getting on with her riding? By the way, Amy, I'd like a photograph of her.' He watched my face, 'Please, Amy, it would help so much.' I went to my desk and found a copy of the one of the three of us I'd had taken in Tilton for Leo. When I gave it to Frank he smiled, 'How did you guess I was going to ask for one of you as well? Thank you, my pet.' He took out his leather wallet, and after carefully slipping it inside, he buttoned it securely in his tunic pocket. I felt guilty giving him the photograph I'd had taken for Leo, but it was the only one of Flora I'd got. Frank glanced around. 'Not a very cheerful room, is it? Not even on a summer evening. Don't you find it rather oppressive?'

'I generally take my coffee upstairs, in my sitting room.'

'But I'm not allowed up there?' I could feel myself blushing. 'Don't you trust me, Amy?'

'I – no!'

He burst out laughing. 'That's a relief, otherwise I'd really think I'd lost my touch. Let it be the dull respectability of the drawing room, then.' He threw himself down in a chair. 'Black, no sugar, Amy, there's a pet.'

Over coffee he talked about France: not the war-torn France of today but the France of his childhood. I listened, fascinated, and he dropped unthinkingly into French. When I answered in the same language, he laughed, teasing me, 'My little peasant, straight from the country. One day, Amy, I'll teach you to speak French with a decent accent, then I'll take you to Paris and buy you hats – the most gorgeous hats in the world! Goodness, is that the time? I really must be going, or Ettie will be getting bothered. Do take me upstairs for one last peep at my daughter before I leave.' I took him upstairs and stood by his side as he gazed down at Flora's sleeping face. He breathed softly, 'She's beautiful, just like her mother.' I felt like Judas.

He went off to change back into his uniform, while I went down to wait with Mr Tims. At the door Frank took my hand and shook it solemnly. 'Good night, Lady Warminster – I have so enjoyed my dinner.' Then his voice dropped, '*Au revoir, ma chérie.*' His fingers stroked mine for a moment before letting go.

Out on the step he paused to call over his shoulder, 'I'll see you again before I go back.' Then running to where Mr Tyson waited with his horse he placed one foot in the stirrup, and swung the other over in a single graceful movement. Taking the reins in one hand he raised the other in farewell; then he was gone.

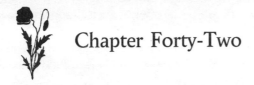

Chapter Forty-Two

How could I love two men? But I did. And how could I write and tell Leo that Frank had come to visit me – but I had to. It was a very difficult letter to write, though there was very little to say. After all, he did know I still loved Frank; there was no need to tell him. In the end I just wrote my usual letter, with news of the children, and then of the harvest. Then I added simply, 'Lord Quinham is on leave. He stayed at Belling for one night, and came over to Eston.' I explained how he'd helped with the self-binder for an hour or so, and that he'd stayed to dinner afterwards. 'He's going back to Town tomorrow morning, he said, and then on to Scotland. I'm sorry if you minded his coming.' There was nothing else I could say, so I just ended as I always did, 'Your obedient and affectionate wife, Amy.' I would send it off by the first post tomorrow.

He replied at once; I opened his letter with my heart in my mouth. After thanking me for my news of the children he continued:

> No doubt Arnott was grateful for Francis' timely assistance. I hope the weather in Scotland is as fine as it presently is in Wiltshire. Amy, I trust you. There was no need for your implied apology since I am confident that you did nothing to incur my displeasure. I know that in the past I have frequently behaved in an unreasonable fashion, but you never deserved my distrust then, and I am sure you do not now, and never will.

As I read those words I burst into tears of relief – and gratitude.

The weather stayed fine, the harvest was coming along well; and every morning when I awoke I would remember that Leo was still in England and Frank still on leave. The consolation of that first thought would stay with me all day as I made my round of visits.

I liked the schoolroom visit best of all, so I'd always spend some time there. Once Rose and Flora had brought me up to date with their news I'd sit and watch them playing with the other children, and maybe doze off for a few minutes. I was often sleepy nowadays and it was very peaceful in the schoolroom, with just the sound of the children playing.

One day as I was slowly waking up I overheard Maud Winterslow saying, 'Her ladyship's fair worn out these days, what with all the trouble of the harvest.'

Granny Withers retorted, ''Tisn't the *harvest* as has worn her out,' she became confidential. 'I 'low from the look of her as his lordship's left something to remember him by. Men!' She snorted.

'I reckon as how you're right, Martha.' Maud sniffed. 'They're all the same, men – they has their bit o' fun and then they're off, leaving the woman to pay the price.' Her voice rose. ''Ere, young Jem, you stop that nonsense – '

'Twere young Maggie as started it, Maud. You weren't looking – ' The rare moment of sisterly harmony was over. I pulled myself to my feet. I did so hope Martha was right.

After lunch I went up into the fields. Today they'd begun cutting Stowell End. I stood in the gateway watching the red sails of the reaper steadily turning, sending the pale golden oats falling to the stubble behind, to be collected up by the teams of women and soldiers. As the girl nearest to me bent over to tie her next sheaf, the ribbons of her sun bonnet fluttered in the breeze, and I saw that it was Hilda, Jael's pretty dark-haired daughter. Raising her head she caught sight of me and smiled. I smiled back; then her strong brown hands returned to their task.

Tugging the handful of stalks tight, she twisted the ends into a firm knot: the new sheaf lay beside its fellow. The soldier behind her swung them up as though they were made of thistle down. With one tucked under each arm he strode off over the stubble with all the easy, loose-limbed grace of the very young man. In one fluid movement he bent and stacked them in the hile then returned for more. Hilda looked up and I heard her soft voice teasing him, and his laughing reply. They were both so young and carefree I could hardly bear to look at them. In a few more weeks the harvest would be over. Where would he be then, that young soldier with his long loping walk and his vivid fresh laugh?

Turning away I went back down to the Home Farm. I found Mr Arnott in the stack yard. There were soldiers working there, too. A waggon was half unloaded, with two khaki-clad figures balanced on top of its golden corn, stacking the sheaves. I watched as smooth brown arms tensed to take the weight of the loaded pitchfork – and then there was a flash of gold as the sheaf swung up and over on to the stack. The arms relaxed for a moment before the strong muscles tightened again, and another golden sheaf soared into the air.

I said to Mr Arnott, 'They're a big help, aren't they – the soldiers?'

His eyes never left them as he replied, 'Aye – poor young devils.'

I read the papers that evening: there was still fighting round Ypres. The casualty lists were getting longer again.

The next day I stayed near the house because it was nine days since Frank had called, and I knew he'd be back again today or tomorrow. He came that afternoon. 'I'm catching the six ten, Amy, so I haven't got long. Let's go for a walk with Flora.' We went to fetch her from the schoolroom, and strolled with her up the leafy lane behind the church. His face was drawn and tired and he scarcely spoke, but when I fell silent he ordered, 'Don't stop talking, Amy – I want to remember your voice.' So I talked about the harvest.

After our walk we took Flora back to the nursery; she protested, but Frank was firm. 'No, Flora, I want to talk to your Mama now.'

Over tea I asked tentatively, 'What were it you wanted to talk to me about?'

He smiled at my question. 'That was just an excuse. I wanted you to myself for a while.'

I had to ask, 'Will they be sending you to that battle around Ypres?'

'God forbid, I hope not.' He grimaced. 'Do you know, before I went out for the first time I saw myself as going to lead men to victory, like a Medieval knight. I know better now. No one wins battles these days – they just die in the attempt.'

'Frank, if anything were to happen to you, do you think Miss Annabel would tell me?'

He looked surprised. 'She won't know. As far as the army's concerned I no longer have a wife. No, I've notified the authorities of the situation this leave, so they asked for my next of kin, and you know who *that* is – officially.'

'Leo! But he baint here any more.'

'But his wife is.' He watched my face before adding quietly, 'Don't upset yourself, Amy. I couldn't face the thought of your getting that telegram unprepared, so I spoke to Selby when I was last down here; it will go to him. So if – anything happens – you'll be the first to find out – after Selby, of course.' He continued conversationally, 'You'd better stop crying, Amy, or people will think I've been misbehaving again.'

'I can't help it.'

He reached out his hand to mine and squeezed my fingers gently. 'Thank you, my pet. You never know, it might be a convenient little Blighty one, like last time. Then you can run up to Town every day and feed me with grapes.'

As I poured him another cup of tea I asked, 'Did you have a nice holiday?' Then I remembered, and felt my cheeks go hot.

'*Not* the most tactful of questions, but since you ask – yes, enjoyable. The shooting was good fun too.' He laughed, then his face became serious. 'Amy, you don't need to be jealous of her. Men are different from women – remember that. To a man, a physical relationship is – just that, nothing more.' He began to talk about how many grouse he'd shot.

All too soon he glanced at his watch. 'I'd better go now, or I'll miss my train.' He stood up. 'I'll walk to the station. Put your hat on, Amy, and come with me as far as the lodge.' He didn't speak as we walked side by side together down the drive. Just beyond the lodge he stopped. 'We'd best say goodbye here, Amy – I don't want those old biddies in the village sharpening their tongues on you.'

He held out his hand. I took it, and we shook hands formally, but he didn't let go of mine. His blue eyes were very serious as he told me, 'I love you, Amy, don't forget that. Even if I took a thousand actresses to bed every day for a year, it would still be you I loved.' His smile flashed. 'Mind, I'd be in no state to demonstrate it, not after a year like that!' He gently flicked my cheek with his fingertip. 'Look after yourself, my pet.' With a parting wave of farewell he turned and walked off down the road to the village – and the station.

I gazed after him: slim and straight in his khaki uniform, a soldier marching off to war.

A fortnight later the soldiers of the harvest field were also ready to go: they had been recalled to their regiment. Their expressions were serious now; their time of grace was over. Mr Selby and I went down after they'd had their last breakfast at Eston, and stood at the door thanking each one personally as he left, shaking each strong warm hand in turn. Then the sergeant barked his orders, the men shouldered their packs and they formed themselves into lines, harvesters no longer. At the word of command, they wheeled round and marched off down the road, to the station.

In my sitting room that evening, I wept until my eyes were red and swollen; weeping for Frank, weeping for the soldiers of the harvest field, weeping for all the young men of England who had marched off to war.

Soon I was weeping again – for the young men of Eston. As the fighting continued in Flanders, so the telegrams began to arrive. Three times I went down to the village and sat in those neat bright kitchens weeping with mothers and wives. The fourth telegram was for Joe Dempster. I drove to see his mother one mellow autumn afternoon when the hedgerows were heavy with berries, and the leaves on the maples at the farm entrance already golden in the sun. His mother was quiet, reserved; she remembered and so did I. But I had to go: his father was one of the tenant farmers on the estate, and besides, I knew Leo would have wanted me to, because Joe had been a good man with the roses.

Two more Eston men were wounded, and we heard that Mr Parry, the agent at Pennings, had lost his right arm. We waited anxiously for news. Then the next letter came from Leo. It was from France. I had been expecting it, for the casualty lists were growing so long again – he would be needed out there – but still, it was a shock. There was no pretence this time. At the head of the letter he'd written in full: '2/1st Field Ambulance, 51st (Highland) Division.' He'd kept his promise and soon I would have to keep mine. I still wasn't quite sure, because I'd bled again, in September. But not very much, and I'd told him that. So I knew he would be waiting, as I was.

His letters became shorter, more formal still – I knew he didn't like their having to be censored. I would puzzle over the little he'd written, trying to imagine his life out there. I wished he'd write letters like Albie did to Ellen. Albie told her everything – no place names, of course, but otherwise he drew a picture with words, a picture so clear and vivid that you seemed to see it as you read his description. Albie wrote of love, too – despite the censor; I knew that because Ellen always carefully selected out certain pages before handing his letters to me to read. But Leo wrote only of the children, and the estate – and his roses.

I worried about him, and I worried about Frank: I loved two men – and both were in danger. One day Mr Selby might come to me, with a telegram in his hand – and the instant I saw him I would realise that it held the name of one of those two men I loved. There was no escaping the nightmare of that worry.

But then none of us was free from worry that autumn. I would sit of an evening with Ellen, talking of her younger brother and Albie. Clara would pop in, we would talk of her brothers, too – and of Jim. Jim was home now, but he wasn't the same Jim. Sullen and angry, he could not come to terms with the loss of his leg. He'd had a false one fitted at Roehampton, but he wouldn't wear it, saying that it hurt his stump, it was too heavy. Clara sighed, 'He wants to ride, does Jim, and run between the wickets again – he won't accept that he can't.' He grumbled at Clara and became angry at the least little thing, but if she didn't go down to see him for a day or two Jim's mother would catch me in the street: 'Jim's asking for Clara, my lady.'

I said, 'He sent her home in tears last time, Mrs Arnold.'

Her face crumpled. 'I knows, but he do care for her, even though he's behaving so bad.' She sighed. 'Clara's a good girl – nobody else'd put up with it.'

Clara did because she loved him. 'Just sometimes he says or does something like the old Jim – then I think as there's hope. I'd do anything, anything in the world, to make him feel better, my lady – because I love him.' So she put on her hat and coat and went down to visit him again.

I'd suggested he came back to his old job in the stables. I told him how Mr Tyson was getting old and forgetful, and although the boy was a good lad, he was only fourteen, so we needed Jim.

His face closed. 'No, thank 'ee, my lady. I'd be no use in the stables. I'm a cripple.'

Clara tried to persuade him, but he wouldn't listen. She came home crying. 'He said as he wished the shell had killed him. I don't know what to do, my lady, I really don't.' Nor did I.

I went to see Dr Matthews, to ask if Jim ought to go back to the army doctors, but he shook his head. 'Jim's body has healed, it's his mind that hasn't. Human beings weren't built to stand what these youngsters are having to face.' As I stood up to leave he asked, 'And how are you, Lady Warminster?'

'I – I be fine.' I felt myself blushing. 'Mebbe – I might want to see you next week.'

I waited all week, but this month I didn't bleed. I was going to send for Dr Matthews, but he arrived anyway, saying, 'I've had a letter from Warminster, he wants me to have a look at you.'

'I wasn't sure, I didn't want to worry him.'

'He's worrying already.' Dr Matthews questioned me, then I rang for Clara and he came along to my bedroom to examine me. 'Not that I think there's much doubt.'

He was smiling as he left. 'I'll write and tell him you're in good health. But shall I wait a day or two so you can give him the good news yourself?'

'Yes, thank 'ee, Dr Matthews, I'll write today.'

As soon as he'd gone I went rushing up to the nursery to tell Ellen; Clara was already there before me. In no time at all everyone knew. Mr Selby met me with a smile. 'I *am* so pleased to hear your news, Lady Warminster.' Mr Arnott pumped my hand vigorously. 'Make it a boy this time, eh, my lady? That'll bring a smile to his lordship's face.' As I began to climb the steps up to the farm office he rushed forward and seized my arm, 'Careful, now.'

When I went down to the village, women came down their front paths to have a word. Clara said, 'Everyone's so pleased – thinking of a birth. It seems like there's something to look forward to at last. Now, my lady, I'm moving this rug out. Thic fringe, it do ruck up at times, and we don't want you tripping over it.' She smiled again. 'An' Granny Withers reckons it'll be a boy this time, the way your face has filled out. Course, we all guessed near as soon as his lordship went back – but tis nice to be sure.'

And it was nice to be sure. I only hoped Leo wouldn't mind too much. I sighed; if only he'd not had to go away – I was sure he'd have come round to the idea if he'd been at home with me.

His reply came very quickly. It was in one of the special green-printed envelopes. I opened it nervously.

My Dearest Amy,

Thank you for your letter, which arrived today. Although your news was half-expected, the confirmation of those expectations was still a shock. Amy, I am the most illogical of men. Despite having so strongly expressed my opposition to the conception of another child at this juncture, I found that as I read your letter my dominant emotion was the most overweening pride. My anxieties were and are genuine, and as your time of trial approaches they will, I know, become acute, but today I luxuriate in the knowledge that I have fulfilled that most primitive of male desires, and begotten a child on the woman I love.

However, my present exhilaration is founded on more than simple pride. Amy, the child you are carrying is a symbol of our future. It is such a strange paradox that after so many years of despairing peace, now, in the midst of war, I have hope; the hope that you have given me. After the long years of blank endurance I now look forward again. I even dream, dream of our future. It is a very simple, domestic dream. It is summer, and we are walking in the garden together, our children gambolling like puppies around us. You are walking beside me, while your soft voice tells me all you have done that day.

That is all, Amy; I would ask for no more. But even that simplest of dreams is denied me, and so I must be content with memories: the memory of your smile as you hand me my coffee cup at breakfast; the memory of your intent expression as you sew; the memory of that quick flash of comprehension in your eyes as you learn a new skill; the memory of your face as you put Rose to your breast for the very first time.

So many memories you have given me: memories so vivid and so well-remembered that almost they satisfy me. Almost, but not quite. If only I had the Beast's magic mirror, and could see you now – but no, I deceive myself. Merely to see you would not satisfy me, either, because I want more than that. I want to hold you again, to feel your arms stealing round my neck, to feel your lips brushing my cheek in the gentlest of caresses, to feel your soft warm body opening itself to mine – I cannot go on. There is no guarantee that even this envelope will remain unopened, and I do not want other eyes to read of our making of love. That is too precious a secret – too secret even for words.

I love you, Amy, I love you. You came to me long after all hope had gone. Not just the hope of being loved, but even the hope of loving: and so I lived in the dark. I was a cripple, and you made me whole again, whole enough to love you.

But a man who has been damaged remains scarred; so when you offered me love I spurned it. I am so dreadfully sorry, Amy, so dreadfully sorry. I claimed to understand, but I hadn't understood. Or rather, I understood with my head, but not my heart – and so I spurned you. How I regret that now. This time, my head *will* rule my heart. I do understand; and so I ask you, beg you, to offer me that love again. I will not spurn it a second time.

Two hours later.

Even as I wrote this letter I did not know if I would ever send it. But I am sending it, and the fact that I am doing so is a measure of my faith in you. My defences are down, Amy; I have removed the last brick of that high wall I built around myself so long ago, and now I stand before you, naked and defenceless, trusting in your love.

I love you, Amy, I love you.

For the first time he had signed in full, the three names I knew he hated: 'Leonidas Arthur Hector, to whom Amy made her vows.'

Chapter Forty-Three

I read his letter over and over again; and every time I read the words he'd written the longing for his presence stabbed sharp as a knife. I wanted to reach out to him and take him in my arms; I wanted to kiss him, and then draw his head down to rest safely on my breast, where it belonged. But it was no use – he was in France, and all I had was my pen. Even as I picked it up I knew that it would not give him the comfort he needed:

Dear Leo,
    Thank you for your letter. Of course I offer you my love again. Even though you said you didn't want it, it was still there, waiting for you. I wish you could walk through the door now, then I'd be able to show you. It isn't easy to find the words to tell you, when you're so far away. I'm keeping brave and well, and tis the best of comfort to be carrying thy child. I've been dreaming a little too, dreaming of thy face when thee dost see thy son for the very first time.
Your loving and obedient wife, Amy.

It looked so short, but I'd said all I could.

When his reply came it was in a normal envelope. 'Thank you for your letter, I was most pleased to receive it.' That was all. The rest was as usual – formal, restrained. I sighed. It was strange that a man could write such different letters – but at least it was in ink. And there was one change: instead of his customary, 'Your affectionate husband' he'd signed, 'Your loving husband'. So maybe he had understood a little of what I'd wanted to say.

November arrived: I leant on the gate of High Hams watching the steam plough. I always stopped for a few minutes if I was passing; I was fascinated by the sight and the sound and the smell of those two huge engines at work. Judith Hawkins was driving the nearer engine. She stood on the platform, her knee bent under its sacking apron, her right foot in its heavy boot raised up to rest on the iron plating at the side. The shining steel rope hissed as it came winding on to the drum, drawing the huge plough behind it, and the exhaust chuntered sharp and fast with the effort it was making. I watched the smoke rise from the tall chimney and the tiny red sparks flying up with it – only to wink out against the pale blue of the winter sky. As the engine stopped working with a last dying huff the ploughman lifted his six bright ploughshares for the turn. Then I heard the bell-like tinkling of the gear wheels engaging as Judith began to move her heavy monster a few yards forward along the headland.

It was her father's turn now. And as his engine hauled the plough back on its return journey, Judith's strong body relaxed a little and she bent to throw more coal on the fire before reaching for her oil can. She raised it to me in a gesture of greeting, and I waved back.

Out in the field six more new furrows were steaily being carved out of the old stubble, and the rooks were flying cawing down to search them for treasures. I took one last deep breath of the mingled scents of freshly turned soil and drifting coal smoke and walked back over to the motor, and drove up to see Caleb, whose Dorset Horn ewes would be lambing soon.

A few days later I was dozing in the sitting room after lunch when Mr Tims knocked. A quick voice said, 'Don't bother to announce me, I'll go straight in.' I looked up, still mazed from sleep and Miss Annabel asked, 'How are you, Amy? under the weather?'

'No, I – Tis only that I be carrying again.'

She was silent for a moment, then she shrugged. 'Well, I suppose it's hardly surprising, since Leonidas was home all summer. I hope he gets a son this time, he certainly deserves one.' To my relief she changed the subject. She said she was on leave; she'd been visiting friends in Bath and was on her way back to Nether Court. 'So I thought I'd drop in for an hour or so. How is Flora now? Leonidas wrote and told me about her illness. You must have been dreadfully worried.'

'Aye, we were – but she's quite better now.'

'Good – children do bounce back, fortunately. I'll run up and see her in a minute.'

I took a deep breath and told her, 'He did come to see her, too – Lord Quinham.'

Her eyebrows rose. 'Did he? When Leonidas was still here? What a cheek he's got, after the damage he did last time!'

I explained hastily, 'No, twas after Leo had gone back.' Her eyebrows rose still higher so I gabbled, 'He didn't stay, Frank – he went to Scotland with a – ' I broke off and felt myself reddening before I finished, 'with a friend.'

'I hope he paid her well. Don't look so surprised, Amy. It's not difficult to guess when you've known Francis as well as I have – and had the misfortune to be married to him.' Then she gave a small, secret smile. 'Anyway, I can scarcely complain. I suppose what's sauce for the goose should be sauce for the gander, too.' She laughed, and lit a cigarette. 'Shall I tell you a story, Amy? Yes, why not? I've been longing to tell someone, and you're the very person to appreciate the irony of it.' She settled back in her chair.

'I wangled three days' leave in Paris in the spring. When I got there I went on a spending spree – bought a complete new outfit right down to the most delicious froufrou underthings. I was with a chum of mine the first day – a girl called Sylvia Benson – and she told me they made me look like a tart! But as I said to her, no one's going to see them, so who cares?' She laughed, 'I just felt like a change, you do when you've not been out of uniform for months. I saw Sylvia off to the south of France – her sister was convalescing there, she's a VAD – and then, since it was such a lovely evening I decided to go for a walk. I was just strolling along, the way one does when one's on holiday, when I suddenly had this sensation that someone was watching me. I turned to look and there was this young RFC officer, who'd obviously just arrived on leave. He was looking at me in a very interested way, and it was only then that I realized there were other women, just strolling oh so casually up and down too.' She laughed again. 'And he obviously thought I was one of them!'

'Oh, how embarrassing for you! Did you find a cab?'

'No, Amy, I didn't. I swung round so my petticoats rustled, lowered my eyelashes – and smiled at him. He came straight over – I was really quite flattered because some of the other girls were awfully pretty. And then, in the most appalling French he asked me if I was doing anything that evening. So I told him in my far better version of the language: "Not yet." He smiled, a most dashing smile, and offered me his arm.

I was open-mouthed with horror, but she continued calmly, 'He said: "Mademoiselle, I would be charmed if you would be my guest for dinner tonight, but you understand when a man has come straight from the Front . . ." Fluttering my eyelashes I squeezed his arm and assured him that yes, of course I understood – and had Monsieur le Lieutenant booked a hotel room yet? Whereupon Monsieur le Lieutenant indicated in his execrable French that he hadn't, but that he was about to do so immediately, and would be charmed if I would consent to share it with him before dinner.'

'Miss Annabel, whatever did you do?'

'I shared it with him before dinner.'

I just couldn't believe it. 'But – but – '

'I walked to the hotel on his arm and then stood there, bold as brass, while he collected the key. The hotelier was very polite, this being France, of course. As we went up the stairs I thought how lucky it was that I'd got my new underwear on, but it really wouldn't have mattered if I'd been in sackcloth bloomers that first time! He explained – with the utmost courtesy – that his desires were so pressing, he would be most grateful if I would excuse his urgency. It was incredible how he managed to convey such a delicate point with so little command of the language – but I assured him I *quite* understood, and I must say I do feel that all I've done to help the troops driving ambulances was probably less useful than the first five minutes I spent with that poor young fellow. Then we shared a cigarette – a rather brief cigarette, and – well, you can guess the rest, Amy. It was an extremely late dinner, but a very good one – he certainly knew how to do things in style – and then we returned to the hotel.'

'Miss Annabel – how *could* you?'

'Very easily, Amy, very easily.' She leant forward. 'Actually, my first thought when I saw him looking at me was: here's my revenge on Francis, because this young man – Con, he said, though I don't know whether it was his Christian name or his surname, and I never bothered to ask – he was the image of my dear about-to-be-divorced husband. Not in looks, though he was extremely good-looking, I wouldn't have indulged, otherwise – he had black hair and his eyes were a deeper blue, I suspect he had Celtic blood in him – but in every other respect he was the identical twin of Francis: the same devil-may-care manner, the same voice, the same accent – they may well have been at school together; they probably knew each other. That's why it was so irresistible. What a way to pay Francis back! I daren't tell him while the divorce is in process – but it'll be a temptation afterwards, if I should happen to run into him one day.' She laughed, but then her expression changed, became thoughtful. 'It's odd; originally I did it for revenge. I despised that officer because he was so obviously the epitome of Francis' type. Do you know, I even watched him write a postcard to his girlfriend. I peeped at the address while he wasn't looking – it's very convenient being a tart, one isn't handicapped by the usual scruples – and the poor girl was a VAD at Rouen, no doubt thinking of her handsome young officer all alone in Paris. No, the curious thing was, I actually enjoyed it. It was all so – simple. No messy emotions, just the coupling of two healthy young animals; I could never have been so unrestrained having an affair with a young man I knew. And to be fair to him, he – er – ' For the first time since she'd started telling the story she blushed. Then she said, 'Oh, why bother to be coy at this stage? After the initial onslaught he was obviously concerned that *I* should get some pleasure out of the events, even though I was only a tart. I must say I've never enjoyed physical intimacy in that way before. In fact I felt at the end as if I should be paying him! But I managed to restrain myself – it would rather have spoilt the act.' She thrust out her wrist where a gold bracelet glinted. 'Quite pretty, isn't it? I bought it with the money he gave me. I like wearing it, it's a charming memento of two happy days in Paris – not that I saw a great deal of Paris!' She laughed.

I closed my eyes for a moment before exclaiming, 'You didn't really take his money?'

'Naturally I did, Amy. After all, I earned it fairly. He was definitely satisfied. Indeed, he said if he were ever in Paris again he'd look me up. I was most flattered, an amateur like myself – and he was obviously a true connoisseur.' She threw back her head and laughed and laughed.

'You – you're shamming – '

'No I'm not, and you don't really think I am. Poor respectable Amy, I've shocked you to the core.' She stubbed out her cigarette. 'I really don't know how you ever brought yourself to allow the liberties you did to Francis.'

'I did love him.'

'Oh, it's far more sensible to do it for money, my pet – and a lot more fun.' She stretched languidly out in her chair. 'Aren't you going to ring for tea? And do send for darling Flora, I'm longing to see her – and Rose too, of course.'

She left straight after tea, but I just couldn't get over what she'd told me: Miss Annabel, doing something like that – and then saying she'd *enjoyed* it! And suppose she met that young officer again? If he was a gentleman she easily might – and then whatever would he say to her? I couldn't get it out of my mind for two whole days. Then it was pushed to one side by what Clara told me.

She came into my sitting room saying, 'Mrs Carter wondered about the fish – '

'Yes, I already told her, Clara.' Her face was working; I asked, 'Is anything wrong?' She just burst into tears. Jumping up I went to her. 'Is it Jim?'

'Aye – no – tis I – ' At first she was sobbing so hard she couldn't get the words out, then she said, 'I wasn't going to tell anyone, then I thought, my lady – she'll understand. I been so wicked.'

I got her sat down beside me and then she told me what had happened. 'Jim, you know what he's been like – so moody and down in the dumps all the time. Well, yesterday afternoon his Mam was out and we were on our own in the cottage, and all of a sudden he says: "You're allus fussing round me, Clara – would you do I a favour?" "Aye, Jim," I says, "Anything." And then he asked me to let him do – that.' Her voice dropped to a whisper, 'And I – I said yes. I couldn't say no to him. I love him too much. But – afterwards, I couldn't help it, I asked him: "Dost thee love I, Jim?" And he just looked at me as if he'd forgotten who I was. Then he shrugged and said, "I dunno, Clara. I just wanted a woman, and you was there, and willing, so I thought, why not?" ' She broke off, and began to sob again. 'I felt so, so – I felt as though I were no better than a loose woman.'

My arm tightened round her shoulder.

'Then he reached for his crutches and said, "At least I know I'm still a man – but it don't bring my leg back." And without thinking I looked down at his stump – and he suddenly starts shouting: "Don't look at it, don't look at it! Get out, get out!" So I just put my clothes on and came home.'

I asked, 'When are your monthlies due?'

'The beginning of next week. My lady, I'm worried sick about that, but I'm near as worried about Jim. It's as if nothing matters to him any more.'

'I'll write to his lordship – I mean, just to ask him about Jim.'

'Please – he'll know what to do.' Then she looked at me, her eyes all red and swollen. 'I feel so ashamed – my Mam'd never forgive me if she knew. And if – if I've fallen – ' She was shaking.

I said firmly, 'Clara, if anything's happened Jim'll marry you, I'm sure o' that.'

'But I don't want to trap him. Twere my fault – '

'Clara, it takes two to make a baby. It were him as asked you.'

'But a woman, she should say no.'

'What you did, you did out o' love. Now, we're going down to your room and I'm going to make you a nice cup o' tea – you'll feel better then.'

I wrote to Leo at once, and he replied by return of post.

It's time Tyson was pensioned off; he only kept going because of the war. Have a word with Selby who'll explain the procedure to you. In the meantime you go down and tell young Arnold I need him to start work at once. And insist that he wears that damn tin leg. If there is some genuine problem with it let me know, and I'll write directly to Crosby, asking him to arrange another visit to Roehampton.

Jim was sullen. 'How can I be a coachman? I can't ride any more.'

'Mr Tyson hasn't been on a horse thic side o' the old Queen's Jubilee.' I was firm. 'His lordship says as you maun start tomorrow.'

Mrs Arnold glanced at me, then her eyes went back to Jim; her hands nervously crumpled the skirt of her apron as she told him, 'You got to do what his lordship says, Jim. If he wants you to work in the stables you got to do it.'

Clara's monthlies came the next day, cramps and all. She was crying with relief when she told me, and I shed a tear or two myself. Jim had turned up for work that morning with a face as long as a tailor's yard, but by the end of the week he already seemed less grumpy as he led Flora out on Porridge. When I mentioned this to Clara she said, 'Tis the horses, Jim's always got on well with the horses.'

'An' I dare say as he's relieved there won't be no baby, too.'

Clara's cheeks reddened. 'I haven't told him. If he don't care to ask – '

'You'd best let him know, Clara. I be sure as underneath he's worrying.'

Clara came back later, her face calmer. 'Jim, he said as he was glad there weren't to be a youngster – not just yet.'

'Not just yet – oh, Clara!'

'Aye, he said as we'd best get married anyway, after what's passed between us. He's going to see Rector about banns today. He says as there's no point waiting.'

'Clara, I'm so pleased.'

She said quietly, 'It won't be easy, my lady, I know that. But I do love him.'

It was all arranged very quickly. The Tysons wanted to move down to the village to live with their eldest daughter, so Clara and Jim could have the cottage. Clara said to me, 'I'll be main sorry to give up the housekeeping, my lady.'

'Do you have to, Clara? The cottage is only over the yard.'

Her face lit up. 'I didn't think as you'd want a married housekeeper – but what about when the littl'uns start coming?'

I said firmly, 'We'll worry about that when it happens. Now, have you had any thoughts about what you're going to wear yet?'

Chapter Forty-Four

Clara married Jim at the end of November, as soon as the banns had been called. Maud Winterslow had made her a very smart costume dress in a fine russet wool with cream satin facings, and Clara asked me to go to Salisbury with her to choose a hat. We'd been to almost every hat shop in the city before I found the one I wanted and then I insisted on trimming it for her myself. I used four glossy pheasant's feathers and arranged them so that they curved over the small brim of the deep russet cloche and then curled up over her cheek. When Clara put it on, the port wine stain on her face had vanished, and she looked so pretty. There were tears in her eyes and she couldn't speak; she just took my hand, and squeezed it hard.

Even Jim seemed to cheer up a bit at the wedding, but his black mood was soon back again, and it was obvious poor Clara was having a difficult time with him. She said to me one day, 'I reckon as he only married me for the one thing.'

'It does matter to a man, Clara.'

'Aye, I do know. My Mam told me that. But if he'd just give me a civil word from time to time – sometimes he'll go the whole day without speaking to me – except for "Pass the salt" at the dinner table.'

I sighed. 'You maun be patient, Clara. He's not himself yet. Tis the war.'

'Aye, I do tell meself that. Of a night when he turns his back on me and starts snoring I deliberately makes myself remember how he was, that last year before the war started. He was nineteen, that summer – he asked me for a birthday kiss, just teasing, he were, but – ' her face softened. 'He were allus so cheerful, so ready with a laugh and a joke. I lie there, remembering, and then I says to myself: "Clara, the Jim you knew, he's still there, underneath, and he'll come back one day if you just give him time." It do help, thinking of him the way he was. And thinking o' you do help, too.'

'Of *me*?'

'Aye.' Her voice was quiet. 'I keep thinking of how it must've been for you, feeling the way you did about his young lordship, and then having to make a marriage with his father – and him a main difficult man to live with. As my Mam said to me when she was nursing Lady Flora, "It's not been easy for her, Clara, but you can see as she's learnt to love his lordship." ' Clara straightened her back. 'And I 'low tis easier for me, because I allus loved Jim – so I didn't have to fall out o' love with another man first.'

After she'd gone I sat very still; because it *was* time that I'd learnt to love Leo – but it wasn't true that I'd fallen out of love with Frank first.

I was thinking of what Clara had said about Jim when I went down to the village the next day. Mrs Chandler saw me, and invited me in for a cup of tea, and when we'd finished talking about Flora and Rose, and her Emmie's little Robert, I suddenly asked her, 'Mrs Chandler, what was his lordship like when he were a young gentleman?'

Mrs Chandler didn't seem surprised at my question. Her eyes narrowed as she thought back. 'He were tall and dark – such dark hair as he had – always a bit ruffled it was, as if the wind had got in it. When you looked at him, you could see he'd 'a been a handsome man, if it hadn't been for the twisting –' She sighed. 'You notice a humpback more in a young man, o' course. It seems so – wrong.'

'But what were he *like*?'

She gave a little smile. 'Impatient – yes, impatient. He'd got so angry with that stammer of his that he'd learnt to speak slowly to try and avoid it – but that was the only slow thing about him. He always wanted to do everything in a hurry – and he thought he knew all the answers, he did. He used to say to me, "If only people were *rational*, Grace, and considered before they acted," and I'd be having a quiet chuckle to myself, because he were one who *never* thought before he acted! Jump in, both feet first, that were his lordship when he were young. He was kind, always kind – and generous, but he didn't think. Sometimes he'd be kind in a foolish way, if you see what I mean, and then get upset because folk hadn't behaved as he'd expected.'

I said, 'He be still kind, very kind – and when I first came to Eston everybody said what a good landlord he was.'

'Aye. But he didn't trust folk any more by then – he'd lost his faith in others.' Her voice hardened. 'It were *her* as took that away from him, her first ladyship, whatever she did to him – it near destroyed him.'

Mrs Chandler fell silent for a little while, then she picked up the poker and drove it fiercely into the fire before looking up at me again. 'She were wrong for him, he shouldn't 'a married her – but like I said, he allus rushed in with both feet. And her manners were always so pretty, I thought at first she must've fallen in love wi' him. But then, after –' Her cheeks suddenly flamed red as the coals in the range, and she broke off.

I said softly, 'I do know, Mrs Chandler.'

'Aye – tis only right you should. I don't reckon as many would 'a guessed. Only I know him better than most. Beforehand, he were so excited about the little 'un being on its way, but then –' She shook her head. 'An' he were too big for his age, his young lordship. When you seen as many little 'uns as I has you gets to notice. One or two folk said as how his lordship must've anticipated, he were only young – but I knew he wouldn't 'a done that, 'cos he worshipped the ground that girl trod on!' She sighed. 'That were clear, from what he did, after her deceiving him like that. You'd think then she'd 'a bin grateful. Instead –' Mrs Chandler's voice rose with the same anger I felt. 'How could she, how could she 'a left him? I saw him, my lady, the day she went. He was on his way

313

to the station – but his face! I don't ever want to see that look on a man's face, not ever again.

'Next day, we heard she'd upped and left him, just like that, while he was away up in Lunnon. After she went it were as though the life had gone out of him. He weren't a young man any more. It was as though he'd built a wall round hisself, and were hiding inside it.' She added simply, 'He never trusted anybody ever again.'

Mrs Chandler sat back in her chair. 'He did get back to normal in the end – leastways, that's what folk called it, but tweren't normal to us as had known him afore. But then when he heard as she'd died – he was set right back again. He didn't get over that till Lady Quinham arrived. He perked up wonderful wi' her, only she left, too – ' Mrs Chandler broke off.

I admitted, 'That were my fault.'

She patted my hand. 'Clara said as they'd never be able to live in the same house together for long, not his old lordship with the young 'un, and she were right.' Her gaze was direct. 'When we heard as he'd married you, folk said – well, you can guess what folk said – but Clara, she spoke up for you, said as you were a good-hearted girl. So I were praying that for all you'd made the same slip as her first ladyship you weren't another light woman, and that things would come right at last. Only I thought as I was praying for a miracle, there.'

She reached out, and took my hand in hers. 'I'm not talking about love, that was only to be expected, a man of his age marrying a young woman wi' your looks. No, I'm talking about trust, that's different. It didn't seem he'd ever learn to trust a woman again – but he has. I can see it in his face when he looks at you – that wall he built, it's gone. He trusts you, my lady, altogether, all the time. I never thought it could happen, but it has.' She gently squeezed my hand, before standing up and saying, 'Now, thee maun get home and put thy feet up. I know you're a busy woman, but you're carrying his child, remember – so you got to look after yourself.'

All the way home I kept thinking about what Mrs Chandler had said, and although I was feeling a little weary I began my weekly letter as soon as I got back.

I sent it off early, and then two days later I wrote again: I'd quickened, and I wanted to tell him at once. I'd been driving back from the village under the Down when I felt that unmistakable fluttering. I drew over to the side of the road, then sat there waiting – and felt it again: the miracle of new life. I cried with happiness – and sadness, because he wasn't there to share it with me. So I wrote to him as soon as I got home.

He wrote back at once. 'I do hope you are looking after yourself. I worry about you: I know from Selby's letters how much you are doing. A woman with child should be nurtured and cossetted, not left to wrestle with government regulations and ploughing orders.'

But that was the least I could do, while our soldiers were out there fighting.

We'd captured Jerusalem from the Turks, but our allies the Russians had had another revolution – and now they'd made peace with the Germans, so they weren't our allies any longer. We had all been so hopeful in November when the church bells rang for victory at a place called Cambrai; but within a fortnight the Germans had advanced again – and the fighting round Ypres was as bad as ever.

It was such a bitter winter. Coal was in short supply now, so we saved all we had for the steam plough and only burnt wood in the house. I'd eat in the morning room wrapped in shawls, and then go up to the nursery after dinner to sit sewing there with Ellen, while Dora ran down to the kitchen. Everyone sat in the kitchen now, with the range – even Mr Tims.

It was cold for us, but how much colder must it be for Leo and Frank, without any fires at all? I packed up their Christmas presents in good time – I hoped Leo wouldn't mind my sending a parcel to Frank, but I had to, there was no one else. And I was his step-mother, after all. That thought didn't seem too strange now. Sometimes I felt as if I were so much older than him. When he'd been on leave last summer there had been times when he'd looked like a young boy – seeing him with Flora I could almost have believed they were truly brother and sister.

We had a very quiet Christmas. I went to church in the morning and prayed for the men of Eston, just as I did every Sunday; Leo's name was at the head of that long list. I worried about him all the time – and about Frank. At least I had my regular letters from Leo – when I held one in my hand I'd feel he was safe for a while – but from Frank, there was only the odd scrawled postcard addressed to Flora. And besides, I knew really that by the time letters and cards reached me, several days had elapsed, and anything could have happened. If Mr Selby ever asked to see me when I wasn't expecting him, my eyes would drop to his hand, to see if he was carrying a telegram. Would it happen, this week, next week? And if it did, how could I stand those few terrible seconds before I learnt which of them it was?

There hadn't been any more telegrams for Eston since we'd heard about Joe Dempster; then, at the end of December, I got a letter from Beat: Ned had been killed. I hadn't seen him since before Flora had been born, but he was my brother. I began to cry. When I'd pulled myself together I told Ellen, then I rearranged my business for the next day so I could go and see Beat.

A couple of days later Ellen had a letter from Albie. She didn't show it to me, but she said he'd decided to train for an officer. 'They've been suggesting it to him for months, only he didn't want to leave Ned. But now – '

'That is good news, Ellen, him doing so well.'

'Aye – but main thing is, he'll come home to do it.'

Ellen was usually so calm, but now her voice shook as she told me, 'Minute I get the letter saying as he's back in England, I'll be up on that table dancing a hornpipe!'

But the letter didn't come. Instead, one morning while I was up in the nursery, the door opened and Albie walked in. He didn't see me, he'd got eyes for nobody except Ellen. She looked up and saw him, then finished tying the bow of Rose's pinafore before rising to her feet and walking over to him. She put out her hand and he took it – that was all he did, take her hand – but at that moment I had to look away, as if they were loving in front of me.

Ellen's voice was quite calm as she said to him, 'I dare say you've not had breakfast yet – I'll send Dora down for a tray. Sit you down at the table.' She didn't dance a hornpipe, but then Ellen wouldn't; she wasn't that kind of girl. To give them a bit of time together I kept the children with me, but when Ellen came to fetch Rose and Flora for their morning walk, she said, 'Albie'd like to come with us, if you've no objection, my lady.'

'Of course he can, Ellen.'

Albie spent most of his time in the nursery. I told Ellen she could have the five days of his leave off, but Ellen said, 'There's no need, my lady – Albie and me, we both likes to spend time with the little 'uns.'

Albie said to me once, 'I don't think I could've kept going those days after Ned was killed, if it hadn't been for her. I'd just look at her photograph – and it was as if she were there with me, holding me close.' They'd spent so little time together, but with their letters they'd woven a web of love that was so strong and true you could feel the warmth of it filling the room as you came through the door.

Of an evening we'd sit lingering over our tea in the quiet nursery while Albie talked of the war. Ellen would shade the lamp, and in the shadows cast by the flickering fire Albie's face looked as it would look if he ever lived to be an old man. Yet his voice was still young: too young to have seen what he had seen, to have lived through what he had had to endure. Ellen said to me once, when we were alone together for a moment, 'He needs to talk of it, my lady, I know that – but tis main hard to listen.' She reached out and touched my hand. 'I don't think I could bear it, if you weren't here listening wi' I.'

Sometimes, I thought I could hardly bear it either, thinking of Leo out there now – and Frank, as well. Because I knew that what Albie was describing was what they'd endured too, and still were enduring. Hearing Albie talk of the mud, the slime, the men blown to bits beside him, the blackened dead shapes of what had been trees, and the evil grey pools of water ready to suck a wounded man under and drown him in filth – the war became so real and menacing that I almost expected to see its tentacles uncoil and creep out of the corner, to come slithering across the polished nursery linoleum towards me.

Albie's training was to be in Oxford. He said he'd run over to Eston whenever he could, 'If you don't mind, Amy.'

'You come whenever you can get away – there'll allus be a bed made up ready for you.'

Ellen told me that after the war Albie was hoping to become a school

316

teacher. 'So it will be a good few years afore we can afford to get married. We want to have everything ready for when the babies start coming.' She was so calm, so sure. I envied her that calm certainty.

Then my baby would start to make himself felt, and I wouldn't envy Ellen any longer. It was such a comfort, that winter, to be carrying Leo's baby inside me. By the end of January his movements were strong and lively. I was sure he was a boy, and each night, I'd lie there dreaming of the expression on Leo's face the first time he saw his son. It might even be not too long after the baby was born, because leave for ordinary soldiers was coming round a little more often these days. George Chandler had come home only ten months after his last leave, and Cyril Beeston had been home twice already since Easter. But then, he was an officer, like Frank. So perhaps one day before too long, Mr Tims would open the door of my sitting room and announce, 'Lord Quinham to see you, my lady.' And I would know he was safe.

But it didn't happen like that. Instead I was down in the estate office after lunch and I heard quick footsteps outside on the stone flags. The door burst open. 'Hello, Amy – Arnold said you were in here. Run up and put your hat on, I want to take you and Flora for a walk.'

I glanced at Mr Selby. 'Mebbe I could finish the figures later – '

'Of course, Lady Warminster.' His voice was formal, polite; he didn't meet my eye as he spoke.

'Come on, Amy – don't dawdle or we'll miss the best of the afternoon.' I stood up and walked to the door, very conscious of Frank's eyes on me. Outside in the corridor he said, 'You're looking decidedly – plump.'

'I be carrying.'

'I rather guessed that.' He shrugged, then smiled. 'Never mind, my pet, we all make mistakes.'

'It weren't a mistake.'

'I meant your marriage.' I opened my mouth to explain but he was striding on ahead of me, pausing only to call back over his shoulder, 'I'll see you up in the nursery.'

Flora was already dressed to go out by the time I arrived. She was perched on his knee and they were so alike that my heart jumped. He looked up and smiled his vivid smile. 'She gets more beautiful every time I see her – ' he glanced down at his daughter – 'don't you think so, Flora?'

He laughed at my blushes – and Ellen's disapproval hung heavy in the room.

We walked up the track that led to the Home Farm, with Nella padding along behind like a watchful chaperone. Frank was in such a lively mood that I ventured to ask, 'Has the war not been so bad, this winter, then?'

'It's been bloody awful, Amy – hence my cheerfulness at gaining a respite.' Suddenly he caught hold of Flora and spun her round and round. 'Eat, drink, and be merry, eh, Flora?' She squealed in excited delight.

Perseus and his cows had been moved down to a field closer to the park. He came up to the gate to see me, and I stopped to give him a pat. He whiffled into my palm, and then gave me a lick.

Lounging against the gate, Frank laughed. 'You do have a way with us males, Amy. Even bulls try to eat out of your hand.'

'Percy, he's main sweet-tempered.'

'But not a very elegant animal, is he? Still, he's obviously got it where it counts – you don't need a ring through his nose to see what his purpose in life is.' Reaching up, he patted Percy's massive neck. 'You're in clover, old man. Take my advice, and don't ask for a transfer to the Front.'

We had tea together, then he asked politely, 'Mind if I take my boots off and stretch out for a nap, Amy? I was travelling all night.'

He slept for nearly an hour while I sewed. From time to time I'd look up from my needle and study his face. It was far too thin, and there were dark shadows under his eyes.

Once he'd woken up, we talked for a while, then I asked, 'Are you staying to dinner?'

'Fraid not, Amy. Ettie Burton insists that I go back to dine at Belling. She gave me a pretty clear hint that dining here *à deux* would do some unspecified damage to your reputation. I pointed out that I'd dined here with you in the summer, but she assures me that dining in the daylight is quite different. To sit opposite you, eating under the glare of electric lamps would, she explained, give me "ideas". I didn't think it politic to tell her that those ideas were affected less by electricity than by the delectableness of your face and figure.' He glanced down at my non-existent waist before adding, 'So in point of fact, you're much safer now in February than you were last August. But don't be too cast down, Amy – *safer* I said – not safe – never that! But I think we can risk luncheon, don't you? *If* we're careful not to switch the light on!' Laughing, he stood up. 'See you tomorrow, my pet.'

Chapter Forty-Five

I tried to stay calm, working in the estate office all morning, but as I left to wash and tidy my hair before lunch I felt like a child released from school – and when I heard his footsteps in the hall, even the chilly drawing room seemed to become warm and alive.

Over lunch we sat chatting together easily, casually – like old friends. As he lit his cigarette at the end of the meal he said, 'It's so restful being with you, Amy. I don't have to put on a show or pretend.' He smiled. But when he'd stubbed out his second cigarette his face became serious. 'There's someone I want to see this afternoon. Will you come with me, Amy?'

'And Flora?'

He hesitated a fraction, then said, 'Yes, you're right. We'll go and fetch her.'

As we came out of the house I turned towards the village, but he didn't follow. 'No, Amy – this way.'

He led us round and along to the oak wood. We followed the main path, but beyond the turning to Leo's bathing lake he took the left-hand branch, and then he turned aside on to an even narrower winding route: and now I knew where he was taking us. Although it was a mild afternoon, I shivered as the dead leaves rustled emptily beneath my feet. We reached the hedge, and Frank walked along beside it, looking for the gap. When he found it he carefully pulled back the briars so Flora and I could slip through into the clearing beyond. Leo's Blairii roses were only leafless stems now, entwined over the crumbling stone walls of the ruined house. Flora gripped my hand tightly as we picked our way up the paved path and under the curved arch of the empty doorway. We followed his slim khaki-clad figure through the ruined hall and into the courtyard beyond.

She was still there, her head bowed protectively over the baby she was cradling in her arms: the child she'd never given Leo. And at that moment the child that I was soon to give him stirred in my womb, as if sensing my anger. But I didn't voice it to the man at my side, for he was her son, and he had loved her.

Frank stood looking at her for a long time, then Flora ran to him, seizing his hand, tugging at it. 'Uncle Frank, Uncle Frank – ' He looked down at her – then he stooped and swung her up in his arms, so that she could see the calm features of that sculptured face. '*Voici, ma petite. C'est ta grand-mère.*'

She looked puzzled, then reaching out she stroked the rounded marble arm. 'Baby – I want a baby.'

He smiled. 'Not yet, my Flora.' He set her gently down, and at once she was

319

off, eager to explore the delights of this new and exciting place. But Frank didn't move. He remained standing there, with his eyes fixed on the statue of his mother. When at last he spoke, his voice was soft and low. 'I wanted to see her again, before I went back. The likeness is extraordinary. He must have given the sculptor all the photographs he had.' He turned to me. 'I found it when I was still at school. I supposed he'd commissioned it in the first flush of their marriage, and then banished it here after she left him. But when I questioned old Thérèse, Maman's maid, she said no, he must have had it made after Maman left him. Thérèse asked me not to tell Maman about it, and I didn't – but I've never forgotten it.' Frank's voice dropped so low I could hardly hear. 'He couldn't keep her with him in the flesh, so he kept her in marble instead, here, where she couldn't run away from him. But why is she holding a child in her arms – it can't be me, surely?'

'Tis the child she promised him, but never gave.'

Frank was still for a second, then he said, 'Yes, Amy, you're right – I'm sure you're right.' He turned his head to where Flora squatted on the flagstones, investigating some treasure she'd found. 'So that's why he wanted Flora! What a fool I've been – I never understood. Annabel claimed it was because she was his granddaughter, but I knew *that* wasn't true. I understand now: not his grandchild, but hers – the grandchild of the woman he loved.' He looked round at the roses, so obviously planted in that courtyard, and trained up those ruined walls; and at the stone seat, carefully placed so a man could sit and gaze at the statue. 'It's like a shrine. How he must have loved her.' He broke off, 'I've always blamed the old man for the unhappiness he inflicted on Maman, by insisting that I be brought up as a Protestant, but – ' He gazed at the statue, 'I suppose it's only natural that he wanted to punish her for leaving him – when he loved her so much.'

I didn't reply. After a while he continued, 'I saw old Thérèse before Christmas. I had a couple of days of Paris leave so I went to visit her. I went to tell her what I would have told Maman, if she'd been still alive.' He turned and faced me directly, his blue eyes meeting mine. 'I went to tell her about you. That I loved you, and that one day I would persuade you to leave the old man, and come to me.'

'But – '

He ignored my interruption. 'I told her all my dreams and my hopes, and I told her, too, how gentle you were, how forgiving – and how good. So good that although you loved me you'd tried your best to be a good wife to the old man, and would never be unfaithful to him while he was away at the war.' He was smiling now. 'You know how it is, when you're in love – you want to talk about the object of your devotion. So I talked about you, mooning over your virtues like a lovesick boy.'

Then his smile faded. The self-mockery had gone from his voice as he continued, 'Later we fell to talking of Maman, and I said to Thérèse, "If only

Maman hadn't married the old man – he made her so unhappy." And she retorted, "But what of him, the man who was her husband? What of the unhappiness she caused him?" I couldn't believe I'd heard aright: Thérèse was always so loyal to Maman. She went on, "Do you think it's easy for a man to discover that the woman he loves has been deceiving him – and when he's forgiven her, and acknowledged her child as his own, to realize that she still loves her seducer? Think how you would feel in such circumstances, François."'

He paused and I saw pain in his eyes. 'Then she told me about something that had happened before I was born. I couldn't believe it at first – I didn't want to believe it – but it was true. Amy, have you ever looked at the past and realized that it's different from what you'd always assumed?'

'Aye. Tis like turning a kaleidoscope. The little bits o' glass are the same, but the pattern they make – tis quite different.'

He reached out and took my hand, pressing my fingers for a moment before letting them go. 'Yes, you understand – you always do.' His voice was low and sad. 'To discover that someone you'd idealized is fallible – no, worse than that, culpable, guilty of treachery – is very distressing.'

I felt so sorry for him – and so angry with her, she with her treacherous marble face, standing so calmly where Leo had put her. She'd betrayed him – and now she'd betrayed her son, too, even after her death.

Suddenly he exclaimed, 'I wish Thérèse had never told me!' Then, turning back to the statue, he added, 'If you've loved someone all your life, it's hard to stop. Even if, now, you despise them.'

He looked like a small boy who'd lost his mother and I tried to comfort him. 'But if they've always been kind to you, done what they thought were best for *you*, then, why should you stop loving them?'

He was silent for a little while, then he said, 'How wise you are, Amy – I do love you so much.' Then he shrugged. 'God knows, who am I to sit in judgement, after the way I've behaved?' Abruptly he turned away from the statue and called, 'Flora, come here. We're going home now.' She looked back over her shoulder in surprise, then jumped up and came trotting obediently over to take his outstretched hand.

As soon as we got in, he took Flora up to the nursery. She protested, but he was firm. 'That's what nurseries are for, Flora: to give grown-ups peace and quiet.' He grinned. 'You'll understand when you're grown up and have got that baby you wanted.'

Downstairs, he said quietly, 'But I wonder if I'll ever see Flora's children?'

Quickly I replied, 'I'm sure Leo wouldn't mind – '

'That wasn't what I meant, Amy, and you know it. Strange, that in the past one always thought one had endless years ahead – barring a freak accident, that is. Now I reckon it will take a freak accident for me to last until those years. Amy, if anything does – happen – will you promise me something?'

'Aye, if I can.'

321

'Will you tell Flora the truth – that I was her father?' When I didn't reply at once he said flatly, 'You'll have to, or she'll find out from someone else. Her parentage is no secret, is it? And I'd like her to think of me, sometimes. But it's not just for my sake, it's for hers, too. A child needs to know who its father was.'

I knew he was right. I dipped my head. 'Aye, I'll tell her.'

'Thank you.'

I couldn't help asking, 'Did she – tell you?'

'Yes. Her confessor said she must. He wouldn't give her absolution until she'd told me, so she did. After she died I went to him, my father, and told him I knew the truth. He said he was glad that I knew at last, but he asked me not to tell anyone of our true relationship. He said, "Let it be our secret, François," and I agreed. I realize now that it could never truly be a secret. Thérèse knew, and so did his own mother. Only at the time, I took him at his word and I never told anyone. But why should I keep his secret any longer, especially from you?' He paused briefly, then said, 'It was Mama's cousin, Uncle Jean-Paul – Great Aunt Clothilde's son.' His eyes seemed to look inward, as he went on, 'He'd always been there when I was growing up. I suppose you could say he'd been the hero of my boyhood – yes, you could say that. He taught me all the things a boy needs to know, played the father to me – but I'd assumed that was because his wife had only presented him with a succession of daughters – '

'His *wife*?'

'No, Amy, he didn't marry until after Maman and the old man had tied their ill-advised knot. Really, I should have guessed before that he was my natural father, because I knew that Maman loved him.'

My poor Leo. I felt a rush of pure hatred against that woman – but I couldn't express it, not to her son, as he told me, 'Maman had loved Jean-Paul as a child, and she never ceased loving him. Even at the end her face would light up when he came into the room.' He broke off. 'What's wrong, Amy? Why are you looking like that?'

'Did he love her in return, your father?'

'He said to me, on the day of her funeral, "She was the only woman I ever loved, François." '

'Then why didn't *he* marry her?'

Frank explained, 'Because there was no money. "Money is the root of all evil," so it says in the Bible – but lack of it causes even more evils, I've found. Uncle Jean-Paul had no money, and nor did Maman – that's why she was in London in the first place. She came of a very old family, but her dowry was pitifully small and dowries matter in France, even if a woman was as beautiful as Maman was. So my great-aunts brought her to England, where dowries are less important, hoping that she would catch the eye of some wealthy English gentleman. And she did – the old man's. Except that he wasn't old then, he was very young, and just down from Cambridge.'

'The great-aunts couldn't believe their luck when he offered his heart and hand – and all the land and money that went with them. Then came the discovery of my untimely conception, and they saw two fortunes slipping from their grasp: negotiations were just beginning for Uncle Jean-Paul's betrothal to the only daughter of a wealthy tin-pan manufacturer.' He sighed. 'I suppose if Maman had been a different sort of girl – or even if the nuns' instruction had covered more practical matters, such as the inevitability of the nine months' gap between conception and birth, instead of confining itself to the teaching of good manners and embroidery – ' He shrugged. 'But Maman was as she was, so she married the old man.

'I suppose I can't complain, I stand to inherit a great deal more from him than I ever would have from Uncle Jean-Paul. God, how the old man must have loved her, to acknowledge her child as his own, especially a son, an heir. Yet he did it. Though it's no wonder I always used to feel he wasn't all that keen on me. But he did his duty, in his ham-fisted way. He'd turn up at Eton from time to time, to take me out to lunch. He even turned up on the Fourth once. Maman had written to tell him she couldn't make it that year, then she arrived after all.' He closed his eyes for a moment. 'God, what an afternoon! It finished up with him bawling at her on the up platform of Windsor station. By then she was in tears and I could cheerfully have killed him. So I can't pretend I was sorry that the priest had insisted she tell me the truth about my parentage; though I could have done without having to promise to play the role of dutiful son to him. But,' his voice softened, 'poor Maman, she was so ill, I'd have promised her anything then – anything.'

His voice was husky. 'After she'd died Thérèse told me to send a telegram here, so he could come to the funeral. I said I would – but I didn't. She'd died in such distress – and it was all *his* fault. Maman was such a devout Catholic that in her eyes his decree over my religious upbringing had condemned me to eternal damnation. So I wouldn't have him at her funeral. I didn't send the telegram until it was too late, and the next day I came myself and told him how she died still desperately praying for my immortal soul. I told him exactly what he'd done to her; and when I saw the guilt on his face I was glad.' He looked up at me. 'Do you know, I rather wish I hadn't done that now – but it's too late for regrets.'

Leo, my poor Leo.

Frank continued, 'Don't cry, Amy. It's all a long time ago. Maman is dead and Uncle Jean-Paul is having a marvellous time in Paris, attracting the girls like wasps to a honey pot. He looks *so* extremely elegant in his smart uniform – and I've no doubt it will remain smart in the cushy desk job he's wangled for himself. Not for Uncle Jean-Paul the mud and the blood and the stink: those delights are reserved for me – and the old man. So the only decent thing I can do is keep my hands off his wife until this bloody show's over. I owe him that, at least.

'But the minute it *is* over I'll be here on the doorstep, ready to do battle for you – and I'll win, too. That's the only thing that keeps me going, Amy – the thought of you, afterwards.' His eyes closed, his face was haggard and drawn. I couldn't speak.

The children came down for tea, and he watched them with me, an indulgent smile on his face; but after half an hour or so I could see he wanted me to himself again, so I sent them back upstairs. He kicked off his boots and stretched out on the sofa opposite. 'Talk to me, Amy, in that soft, dove-cooing voice of yours.'

I kept my voice very low and soon he was asleep. When he awoke his face was the face of a young man again. He sprang up. 'Good Lord, is that the time? I really must be off, I'm meeting someone in Town.'

He dragged his boots on and came over to where I was sitting. 'Stay here in the warm, my pet. Tims'll let me out. Here, give me your hand.' When I held it out to him, he bent over it and his warm lips kissed the back of it. Then, without letting go, he turned my wrist over and put his mouth to my palm – and I felt the quick warm flick of his tongue before he finally released me, laughing.

I asked, 'Will you be coming down again, before you go back?'

'I think so, Amy, I think so – after all, you're my honey pot.' His blue eyes flashed their vivid smile, then with a parting wave he strode out of the drawing room.

There was still some time before I had to dress for dinner, so I sat there thinking of the woman who'd sat in this drawing room all those years ago. How could she have done what she had done to Leo? I could have understood the desperation of a woman deserted by her lover, but the French Countess *hadn't* been deserted. *Her* lover had been her cousin, who loved her back. But he'd been a poor man and she'd been too greedy and selfish to marry him, even though he was the father of her unborn child. So instead, she'd married Leo for his money and his title; then, having married him, she'd refused to pay the price. She'd left him, and gone back to her lover.

And Leo, abandoned, deserted by the woman he loved, had brooded on his deficiencies, on those unimportant physical peculiarities of his, until in time he'd come to believe that all women were repelled by him. But I wasn't repelled, and never had been. And when he came home again, I would hold him in my arms and show him I wasn't: I would show him how I loved him. Now I had to go up to my desk and write to him, and tell him that Frank had visited. Only this time I wouldn't be worried about his reply, because I knew he trusted me.

Chapter Forty-Six

Another telegram came the following week, to the village in the shadow of the Down: Caleb's grandson had been killed. I stood beside him as he told me of how Davy used to come up on the Down with him. 'He allus wanted to work wi' sheep, my lady – that were all he ever wanted. Then the war came, and he would go.'

'He went to do his duty, Mr Brewer.'

'Aye. And they killed him, they killed him.' He turned to look at me where I stood swelling with child, and said simply, 'I hopes as the liddl'un you're carrying, be a maid – and the mother o' maids.'

Frightened, I replied, 'The war'll be over afore long – so they do say.'

'There'll be another one, my lady, there's allus another one. Men, they baint like my sheep – they cassent live in peace.' He reached out and took my hand in farewell. 'Thank 'ee for going to see his mother, and my Becky. Twas a comfort to 'em to see your sweet face. But there baint no comfort for I. My Davy's gone, and all the tears in the world won't bring him back.'

That evening Mr Selby came to see me and I flinched as my eyes flew to his hand; but he carried no telegram. In any case, my last letter from Leo had been in ink so there was less need to worry. And Frank was safe, too – because he was still in England on leave.

I spent more and more time in the estate office: ploughing orders, price controls, pegging of rentals, powers of the Board of Agriculture – I felt as though I knew every word of the Corn Production Act by heart. I would struggle to interpret it and put it into practice while Mr Selby had to spend his days at the Executive Committee meetings. And then there was conscription to worry about, too. The country needed our wheat, but it needed our men as well. Still, it was a little easier for us on the Eston estate: because so many of our young men had gone already we had few more to lose; and the women were working in the fields, just as their grandmothers had once done, with young women from the Land Army alongside them now. The steam plough was busy every day, but it couldn't cope with all the extra fields that had been changed over to arable, and handling a plough was skilled work. Even the army had to admit that, so skilled soldier ploughmen were supposed to come back on special leave – but they hadn't turned up yet. And there were so many other jobs that needed doing at this time of year.

More German prisoners were being used on farms now. Some people were muttering about it, but when I asked Mr Arnott, he retorted that he was so far behind with the muck-spreading he'd take the Devil himself if he were willing to work: 'After all, he can use a pitchfork, can Old Nick.' So we applied for some German prisoners. It seemed an odd thing to do, but as Mr Selby said, 'The corn they grow tastes the same.' He looked very worn and tired these days, did Mr Selby, but he still worried about me. 'You must take care of yourself, Lady Warminster, at a time like this.'

I reassured him. 'I be brave and well, Mr Selby, and tis more'n two months yet.' But he insisted on bringing a footstool into the estate office, so to please him I sat at the desk with my feet up; and it did ease my tired legs.

In the middle of the afternoon he'd chase me out, 'You look exhausted, Lady Warminster. You really *must* go and rest.'

One day I was up in my sitting room lying dozing on the sofa, when I heard a voice saying, 'Don't wake her, Tims, I'll wait.' I opened my eyes and there was Frank, standing looking down at me. 'Hello, Amy.'

For a moment I thought I was still dreaming, then I began to haul myself upright into a sitting position. 'Are you going back already?'

'Not for another couple of days. I didn't mean to come down until tomorrow, but – ' his mouth twisted in an attempt at a smile – 'I couldn't keep away.' He dropped down on to the sofa beside me. 'I was up in Town and suddenly I – I just wanted to see you and Flora – to spend a few quiet hours with the pair of you. I hope you don't mind, Amy.'

'No, o' course not. I'll ring for her now.' I reached out my hand, but he stopped me by covering it with his own.

'No, not yet.' His fingers tightened round mine. 'Just you first, Amy – just you first.' And then I saw the tears in his eyes.

'Frank, what's wrong?' He shook his head as if dazed; and I reached out to touch his cheek. 'What's the matter? Tell me what's the matter.'

He looked at me and his face was the face of a man, but his eyes were the eyes of a desperate, pleading child. 'Maman's dead, Uncle Jean-Paul – ' He broke off to give a forlorn gesture with his hand. 'And Annabel, Annabel hates me, so there's only you. Amy, please – ' His blue eyes were vulnerable, imploring, so like Flora's when she was upset.

Gently I stroked his cheek, 'Tis all right. I'll look after thee – '

'Amy, tell me, please do *you* love me?'

So I told him, 'Aye, I do love thee.'

Still he looked at me, his eyes searching my face to see if I were telling the truth. I looked back, my gaze unflinching, because I knew that I was.

He gave a great sigh of relief, then he whispered, 'I'm so frightened, Amy, so frightened.' And all his young man's confidence had gone now as he cried, 'I don't want to die.'

I put my arms around him and drew his head down on to my heart. Pressing his face into my breasts he began to sob – great racking sobs that shook his whole body with their force. Stroking his soft golden hair I bent and kissed his damp cheek: murmuring, comforting, telling him of my love. And at last the shudders began to lessen and he lay quiet in my arms.

His long, lean body was sprawled across my lap, but still I held him – holding him for so long that I wondered if he'd fallen asleep, and did not dare ease my aching back for fear of disturbing him. Then he slowly started to pull himself upright.

His eyes were still red and swollen with tears but he made no attempt to hide them. 'I don't have to pretend to you, Amy, do I? I can tell you the truth. Out there, sometimes, I want to break down and howl like a frightened child, but I can't because of the other fellows, I can't let them down. And besides, I'm supposed to be an officer – I'm responsible for the men. They rely on me to set a good example, poor sods, so I can't break down. But with you, I don't have to pretend.' He put out his hand and gently touched my cheek. 'So thank you, Amy, thank you.'

Then he managed a smile. 'I can't let my daughter see me like this. I'd better run along and splash my face with cold water or whatever you girls do when the chaps have been unkind to you.'

When he came back he looked almost his old self. His hand rested lightly on my head for a moment as he passed the sofa. 'You are a pet, Amy, and I do love you. Now, where's Flora?'

She ran to him as soon as she came into the room. 'Uncle Frank, Uncle Frank!' She clambered all over him, bouncing on his knee, telling him tales of Tabby Cat and Porridge her pony; and then it was time for tea.

When Dora had taken a protesting Flora back upstairs again, he stretched out his long legs, saying, 'Sorry about that appalling exhibition I made of myself earlier, but the truth is, Amy, I'm not at all keen on going back.' He shrugged. 'Still, what must be, must be. Don't look so concerned, my pet, I'm over it now. May I dine with you this evening?'

'Of course.'

He put his hand up to cover his yawn. 'I've had rather a hectic time in Town. Mind if I snatch a few winks before dinner?'

'No, o' course not. Do you want to go and lie down in one o' the bedrooms?'

'No, Amy, I'd much rather sleep here with you.' His familiar grin flashed out. 'Since it's the only way I'm going to be allowed to, at the moment. Leave the lamp on – it won't disturb me. You can get on with your sewing or whatever you do at this time of day.'

I plumped up the cushions for him on the sofa while he eased off his boots, then I went and sat down in the armchair opposite with my sewing while he slept.

He wasn't asleep for long. It was barely half an hour later when, glancing up from my needle, I saw he was awake and watching me. He smiled lazily across at me. 'What more could a man ask for than to wake up and see a beautiful woman, sewing in the lamplight?' He pulled himself up and stretched his arms out wide before telling me, 'Do you know, whenever I woke in the nursery from my afternoon nap I'd see the same sight. Marie would be sitting beside the lamp, her hair shining like the colour of ripe wheat. She came from Alsace, so she wore her national costume – a dress of scarlet flannel, and over it a black velvet bodice, tight-laced. Whenever I was upset I'd run to her and she'd lift me on to her lap. Then she'd cuddle me better – just as you did to-day.' He bent down to pull his boots on. 'Let's pay a quick visit to your nursery, shall we?'

We ate dinner in the morning room, and he told me more about his childhood. 'Maman used to take me to Paris every autumn when I was small. She always rented the same apartment from some distant relatives who went to the country over those months. There was a balcony overlooking the street with flower boxes, and the minute we arrived Maman would have chicken wire set up along the iron balustrade, in case I fell over. Poor Maman, she was always worrying that some disaster would befall me! The apartment was on the sixth floor – there was a wide staircase with a red and green carpet, and a lift one worked by pulling on a rope. In winter, hot air came from slots in the wainscoting – I was fascinated. I thought it was done by magic. Then one day the concierge showed me the furnace in the basement – another illusion shattered! She meant to be kind, no doubt, but I'd much rather have continued to believe in the magic.'

I watched his face soften as he told me, 'There was a special lamp in the nursery with a red glass chimney that gave off heat. The warm glow of it was like a friend. When I was all ready for bed I'd sit beside Marie, waiting for Maman. She always came up to see me before going out to dine, or to the opera. She'd be wearing her evening dress, and her jewellery would be sparkling – and I'd think she was the most beautiful woman in the world.' He was silent a moment before saying softly, 'It all seems a long time ago, now.'

He left soon after dinner. 'You're tired, my pet – you need to rest. I telegraphed Ettie from Town and begged a bed there for the night. I'll borrow your dog cart, if I may. I'll return it to-morrow morning when I come.' I held out my hand, and he shook it formally. 'Thank you, Amy, thank you for this afternoon – and for just being – Amy.'

Next day I got up very early and worked in the estate office for an hour before breakfast. After I'd eaten I went back again, but not for long because Bertha came down to say Frank had arrived. He'd come early, as I'd known he would.

We went for a walk, just the three of us, closely followed by Nella. Coming back through the oakwood, Flora found a little clump of sweet white violets all in flower. Squatting down she carefully picked a tiny bunch and then held them up. 'For you, Uncle Frank.'

'Thank you, Flora my pet. My goodness, what a delicious smell.' She glowed with pleasure as he carefully arranged them in the buttonhole of his tunic.

We had lunch together, and then the children came down to my sitting room and he sat watching them play with their Noah's Ark. After Rose and Flora had gone back upstairs I rang for tea; I'd ordered it early, knowing he had to go back to London this evening – and after that, France.

It was France he talked of as we drank our tea and ate our hot buttered toast. Dropping into the language of his childhood he described how the nurses walked with their charges in the Bois de Boulogne – each one wearing the costume of her own province. He told me how Marie, when she was walking there, had always worn a great stiff black silk bow on her blonde head, with a black silk apron over her red flannel skirt – and the shining silver buckles on her shoes would flash as she walked. 'Marie used to tell me how she was especially proud to wear her costume, because it showed the Germans that they could never win the heart of Alsace, however hard they tried.' He paused. 'I wonder if her sons are fighting against me now – or whether they managed to escape and join the French army? Poor devils, if they're captured they're shot as deserters, you know – the men from the lost provinces that dare to fight for France.'

I shivered and at once he turned the conversation backwards again to his own past. The picture he painted was so vivid, I almost felt I was there, seeing it with him. He watched my face as he told me his tales, and if he saw that he'd used a word I didn't understand he'd tell me its meaning in English, before returning to his native tongue. 'You don't mind, do you, Amy? I like to talk to you in French,' he smiled, 'And besides, it means I can repay your "thou" with my "*tu*".'

'At tea time I would be dressed in my best and taken down to see Maman, who'd feed me with tiny oblongs of toast and jam. Whenever I dropped one down the front of my clean sailor suit she only laughed. And on Sundays the great aunts came and there would be cakes – chocolate eclairs bursting with cream, milles feuilles, cream puffs, delicious little tarts that melted in our mouth. I was allowed just two, and I'd spend hours choosing them, while Maman waited patiently to serve me.' He laughed. 'Ah, those were the days, two beautiful women always at my beck and call – what more could any male creature want?' He glanced at me sideways, smiling. 'I was spoilt, Amy, completely spoilt.'

Once tea was over he spoke in English again – and soon it was time for him to go. As I hauled myself out of my chair he said, 'Don't come downstairs, my pet. Let's say our goodbyes up here.'

I held out my hand but he shook his head. 'No, Amy, that won't do. Come here.' Gently he took me in his arms and I felt his lips on my cheek, then he drew back a little. But he was still holding me, waiting, hoping – but not asking. I knew he wouldn't ask, so it was I who raised my mouth to meet his. We kissed, a gentle parting kiss. Then with a final quick hug he released me and turned to go. But at the door he turned again, and stood there, briefly, just looking at me. As he reached for the handle he said, in a voice so low I could scarcely hear his words, 'Goodbye, Amy – my golden girl, my might-have-been.' Then he opened the door, and left.

Chapter Forty-Seven

I sat on in the stillness of my sitting room; it was growing dark, but I didn't put the light on. I recalled again the woman the sister had told me about, who'd loved two men – but she hadn't loved them in wartime: it had been easier for her.

At last it was my baby who roused me, kicking vigorously, telling me of his presence. My baby – Leo's baby. I stood up on legs that wouldn't stop shaking and made my way to the nursery. Rose came to meet me on her plump, sturdy legs, and I held her close, seeking comfort – then Flora was there too, demanding my attention, and so the evening passed.

Leo's letter arrived: still in ink, so I felt one of the tight bands of worry easing. Then a postcard came for Flora: 'Back in reserve, a pleasant enough village though damned chilly at this time of year.' Another band loosened a little. He must suddenly have remembered that it was supposed to have been written to a five-year-old, because he'd crossed out 'damned'; but only lightly, so I could still read it. Then he'd added: 'Tell your Mama that I was most grateful for her hospitality – with love, Uncle Frank.' But the 'Uncle' was written very light and small. I wanted to write back, but I knew I shouldn't. I had kissed him goodbye, and that must be enough.

Another telegram came to Eston village: Jim's cousin Len had been wounded. He'd been taken to Bristol and his mother went to see him there. She came back quite cheerful. 'He's over the worst, my lady. Tis only his arm – all bandaged up it is, and he says as it pains him, but he's so pleased to get back home he don't mind that.' Everyone went round saying, 'Baint it good news about Len Arnold?' And I thought how upset we'd all have been if it had happened a couple of years ago – but now, we were just so glad he was alive, and hadn't lost a limb.

The eight soldier ploughmen looked extremely cheerful, too, when they eventually turned up. 'Better'n France any day, eh, Stan?' But Mr Arnott wasn't so happy, because they'd missed the best part of the ploughing season, and he complained bitterly about their late arrival, as well as their inexperience. 'Call 'em ploughmen? One o' them's a barber and another's a counter jumper – used to sell pens and pencils, so he told me.'

'Well in that case, mebbe tis as well they didn't arrive earlier.'

He glowered at me, then gave a short bark of laughter. 'Aye, mebbe so.' He shook his head, 'I don't know where'd we be if we hadn't had our steam ploughing set – Butty Williams' daughter's worked like a dog, she has.'

I glanced down at Nella, sitting placidly beside me. 'Worked like a woman, you mean, Mr Arnott.'

He grunted. 'Be no holding you females, now you be a-going to get the vote.'

I shook my head. 'Not me, I'm a long way off being thirty yet.'

For a moment he seemed surprised. 'Aye, I suppose you are. I forgets as you're not much more'n a maid.' I must have looked insulted, because he added, 'Not as your *face* looks older, me lady, but you've got an old head on your shoulders.' He paused, and then added, 'I got to admit, when his lordship said as he were leaving you to take his place while he were away, I reckoned as he'd gone clean off his rocker – but you've not made a bad job of it, all things considered.'

I glowed with pride, but only for a second because he went on, 'Now, me lady, you got to move a couple o' them soldier chappies. You billeted 'em wi' Jack Hewitt's wife, and it just won't do.'

'But Mrs Hewitt said as she'd be glad o' the company.'

He looked me straight in the eye, 'Exactly, my lady. Hewitt's a good dairyman, even if he were a fool to marry that female of his. I don't want him coming back to find a cuckoo in his nest, and that's what'll be happening if you don't get thic fellows out sharpish.'

'But – '

'Elsie, she were seven months gone wi' young Jem afore they were married, and nobody were ever sure it were Jack's – not even Jack hisself. So you get 'em out o' there, me lady, afore there's more harm done.'

I went directly round and told Mrs Hewitt that the men would be moving down to the gardener's bothy at Eston. Her good-humoured face fell. ''Tis ever so dull of an evening wi' Jack away in the army – and them two, they be good fun.' Her voice became wheedling. 'Couldn't they bide a while longer? Some women, they're glad to see the back o' their man but – *you* knows what I mean, my lady.' She winked. 'After all, his young lordship visits more often than the old.' Watching my face, she said quickly, ''Tis only natural, my lady. A woman's got needs, same as a man – '

I broke across her words to snap, 'Send them down to the bothy at once. And if one of them so much as sets foot over this doorstep again you'll be out of this cottage, bag and baggage.'

Her face closed and her voice was sullen as she replied, 'If you say so.' She dropped an exaggerated bob of a curtsey before adding, 'My *lady*.'

My heart was thudding as I walked back to the motor: how dare she? How *dare* she? I collapsed on to the seat, shaking. Were the other women in Eston thinking the same thing and just not daring to say? After all, I'd been nine months gone when I'd been married and not with my husband's child, either. But it was Leo's child I carried now, and feeling his baby there, moving inside me, helped to calm the trembling of my legs, so that at last I was able to get out of the motor and go to find one of the men in the rickyard to swing the handle for me.

Clara grumbled a bit about having to cram two more beds in the bothy: 'Still, you were right to shift them two, my lady. Soon as I heard as Elsie Hewitt had offered to have 'em I knew there'd be trouble.' She leant forward and hissed, 'She were just the same at school – she'd go behind the dunnekins and let the boys look down her drawers for a farthing.' Clara's voice deepened in outrage. 'And by the time she were in Standard Five she didn't even ask 'em for the farthing!'

'I didn't realize she were that way inclined.'

'How could you, my lady? You're a foreigner to Eston.'

Clara's simple statement chilled me: no, I didn't belong even now. And were the women in the village always wondering if I'd let boys peep down my drawers for a farthing – or worse? What did they say behind the curtains when I walked past with Flora? If only it'd happened somewhere else – but there was no hiding it here: everybody knew.

Shortly after, twenty German prisoners arrived, along with their two British soldier guards. We put them in the pair of empty cottages behind the water tower, and one of the prisoners did the cooking. They drew their official rations from the main camp, but Mr Arnott and I didn't think they were enough for men doing heavy work all day, so he gave them several breeding pairs of rabbits and wire netting for an enclosure. I asked Mr Hicks to send all the surplus vegetables from the kitchen garden up there, too. We were lucky, since our prisoners were all Saxons or Poles who'd come from farms at home, so they were good workers. Though it used to upset Mr Arnott to see the two British guards just sitting under the hedge twiddling their thumbs.

Sometimes I wished I could just sit under a hedge doing nothing, too. I didn't sleep very well at night now. The baby seemed to wake up then, and when he finally settled down and I was able to drop off, there'd be the nightmares. Leo had written in pencil again, and I'd started dreaming of him. He'd be carrying his stretcher, plodding through the mud that was squelching and sucking and reaching up for him – and I'd know that the great German guns were about to fire; and he was there out in the open, weighed down so he couldn't run, and his heavy dragging steps would get slower over the greasy duckboards and the guns were about to fire – and I'd open my mouth to shout, to warn him – but no sound came. So I'd try to run forward to catch his arm, but I couldn't move, I could only watch in terror . . .

I'd wake up shaking and sweating with the sharp bite of cramp in my calves, and as I lay there in the darkness I'd hear Albie's low voice again: 'In August we went up to Dikebusch – it's just a few ruined buildings in the middle of a sea of mud . . . The Menin road has been so smashed by shells it's only a track now. I'd picked up an officer's revolver, so a transport corporal asked me to shoot his mule – it was being sucked into the mud. Poor brute, its eyes were rolling in terror. Some men couldn't get out either. If you slipped off those greasy duckboards . . . Château Wood they called it, I suppose it had been a wood once. Now it's just a few blackened stumps alongside a foul-smelling marshy lake. The shells were coming over and every so often they'd score a hit on one of those pathetic remnants of a tree. In Flanders even the trees are being tortured.'

I'd thought of Frank with his polished boots and his immaculate uniform in the middle of that desolation – and I'd thought of Leo. Every time Albie mentioned an ambulance car or stretcher bearers my ears strained. I listened, imagining Leo there as I heard of the tunnel under the Menin Road at Hooge where Albie had taken shelter alongside some RAMC stretcher bearers. I thought of him, too, in that concrete pillbox Albie described; it had been built by the Germans but was now used as an aid post by men from a field ambulance. Albie said it looked like a great toad squatting there, overlooking the pool of dark water that lurked at the bottom of the crater beside it. Dead water, dead as the bodies that littered the ground all around that vile crater.

I'd asked Albie if he'd seen Leo, but of course he hadn't, or he'd have told me the minute he'd arrived. 'But he couldn't have been far away, Amy, because I know the Fifty-First Division were there till the end of September. I was luckier: they pulled us out in the last week in August.' His voice became bitter. 'There weren't enough of us left by then to be any more use.'

Now I lay in the dark with Leo's child stirring in my womb, and thought of him, walking along that deadly track with the weight of the stretcher on his shoulder, hearing the moans of the wounded men, the squelching of mud clawing at his boots – and the scream of shells overhead. And although I was warm in my bed, I shivered, as he must be shivering out there.

But his next letter was in ink. He wrote that his unit was back at a large rest station, and they'd all been playing football.

> The men have been accustomed to playing the Association game, but the only ball they could obtain was one left behind by some officers, which was of the oval persuasion, so they insisted I must show them how to play rugby football instead. Consequently, I found myself kicking a ball again, and tackling. How I loathed it as a youngster; I swore I'd never go near another games field once I'd left school – and there I was, making a fool of myself! Still, the exercise was most invigorating, and I must say I preferred the more light-hearted approach to sport that prevails out here.

Putting my hand on my belly, I told my baby, 'Thy father, he's been playing football!' Tears came, but they were tears of relief.

I shed more of those tears the following week, because another postcard came for Flora, from Frank. 'Having a rest in some quite decent billets. Dampish, but there's good riding to be had round here.' So they were both safe, for a little while at least.

At the beginning of March, Albie managed to get over for a short visit. Ellen had taken the children out for their walk and I didn't know which way they'd gone. 'But they won't be long – you come upstairs for now.' I took him into my sitting room and he sat down in the chair opposite, looking grave and unfamiliar in his new uniform. I asked after the boys and Uncle Alf.

'Pa's back at a base camp – he had a touch of trouble with his rheumatics, thank goodness – but George'll be going out soon.'

'It doesn't seem possible, not George.'

'He was nineteen in December, Amy.'

I smiled, 'One of Aunt Agnes' Christmas babies.'

'Yes. It all seems a long time ago, doesn't it? We had some good times, didn't we, before Pa lost his job and Ma fell ill?' Suddenly he asked, 'Amy, when did *your* mother die?'

I opened my mouth, then closed it again. He said quietly, 'The same time as my mother. Isn't that right, Amy?'

'I didn't – I wouldn't ever have told you – Did Uncle Alf – '

'No. I worked it out for myself. But Ned always said you were her cousin's daughter. He didn't want to believe – that – of her.' He sounded so sad.

I said hastily, 'Tis only – that she did love too much – just the once. Her and my father, they were going to be married, but – '

I paused and Albie finished for me, 'But he died.' It wasn't a question so I didn't have to answer with a lie. Albie said quietly, 'Poor Ma,' and then we heard the sound of the children on the stairs.

As I lay in bed that evening I told my baby, 'Thy Dada, mebbe he'll be home soon.' My baby kicked vigorously in reply; I was sure he was going to be a boy. I was due the first week in May, Dr Matthews said – and the little worms of fear were already wriggling into my mind as I recalled the pain of it – I was such a coward. But perhaps Leo would be home on leave by then, and stay with me, helping me – like he had when Rose was born?

In my next letter I answered his usual anxious queries about my health and then wrote:

> It would be nice if you could come home just before the baby's born. They do say as leave is coming round sooner now. Mr Arnott reckons we'll get the ploughing done in time, though there's been problems getting enough coal. We've had to put off threshing some of the oats so Judith Hawkins and her father have enough for the ploughing engines . . .

When I'd finished all the news I signed off as usual, 'Your loving and obedient wife, Amy' – then the pen seemed to add of its own accord: 'I do hope I'll be seeing you soon.'

But a couple of days later Lady Burton told me that all leave was to be stopped. Her cheeks were pale and sunken under their two gallant patches of rouge as she explained, 'The Germans are going to mount a great offensive.'

My heart froze. 'You mustn't tell anyone, it's a secret – but everyone knows. Now they've beaten the Russians they're going to beat us.' Her hands were trembling.

I reached out and took them both in mine. 'They won't beat us, Lady Burton. We've got the Americans coming to help.'

She shook her head. 'They haven't arrived yet – they haven't had time. They have to be trained, you see, and the Atlantic's in the way. If only they could march on water – ' She broke off, and tried to smile. 'I'm being a silly old woman, aren't I? But, my dear, it's gone on for so long – and every time I see a telegraph boy I think, it's George – it's going to be George.'

It happened on the 21st of March. We didn't know at first, but the next day the paper said that a great battle had begun: the enemy had attacked along fifty miles of the Front. There was a map, too, and Mr Tims and I pored anxiously over it.

By Saturday, we knew that half a million of the enemy were trying to burst through the British lines, and on Sunday – Palm Sunday – the War Office sent a bulletin to the post office. It said that despite fierce attacks our troops were maintaining their positions, but on Monday morning *The Times* announced bleakly, 'The British retreat to the Somme Line. Paris bombarded.' Below, I saw the words, 'The 51st Division', and my heart stood still. 'Here, as elsewhere along the Front, the story is one of heroic fighting, whilst gradually falling back,' it read. 'Odds of nine to one.' Leo and Frank, both of them, were in the 51st Division.

Although it was the wrong time of the week I wrote to Leo; I didn't know if my letter would get to him, but I had to write. After the usual news, I finished, 'Do take care of thyself, and be sure to change thy socks if they should get wet.'

Then I wrote to Frank; it was only a short letter, but I had to write it.

> Dear Frank,
>   I'm thinking of you every day and praying for your safe return. Flora was talking of you only the other day. Do take care of yourself.
> Your affectionate Amy.

Tuesday: another map with a big bulging black area on it, marking the land we'd lost. By Wednesday, the bulge was bigger. Then on Thursday there was talk of the line holding firm – but on Friday, Good Friday, I looked at the map and saw that the bulge was a huge swollen belly covering yet more of France. But by Saturday, *The Times* said that the Allied line *was* holding, and in the second post there was a postcard from Frank. 'In the wrong ruddy place at the wrong ruddy time – as always, my pet. Don't worry, there's no point. Thanks for writing. *Je t'aime, Aimée.*'

No letter had come from Leo and I was almost sick with worry by Monday, when at last a muddied field postcard arrived. I read and re-read it, but there were only the few standard printed sentences to indicate that he was well, had received my last letter, and would write back at the first opportunity. Only the signature was in his own handwriting – and the date: it had been five days in the post. I sat staring at that neat 'Leo Warminster' so long that the letters blurred into one purple line. Then I went upstairs to give Rose her birthday presents.

On the Tuesday the paper said that the German advance was at a standstill – and in the afternoon post there was a letter from Leo.

> I must apologize for not writing at the usual time, and in pencil, but we have been rather busy and I have mislaid my ink. I do hope you are still well; do not work too hard, and please ensure that you rest with your feet up *every* afternoon . . . Do not be disturbed if there is another delay before you hear from me again; the postal services may well be disrupted by recent events.

As I read his words I felt relief warming me; then I noticed that under the signature he'd written two words in Greek. I fetched the lexicon from the library to look them up, but I'd already guessed their meaning: 'I love you.' I shivered with cold, because I knew why he'd written them.

Then on Wednesday the paper said the battle had died down. But the soldier ploughmen had been ordered to return to their regiments; they were going back to France. Albie was back there, too. So quickly had he been recalled, that his letter to Ellen telling her of his return had been written on the train to London. From Beat I learnt that George had gone as well; and on Friday there were reports of a new German attack, in Picardy. By Monday, the ominous black bulge had swollen again.

Tuesday brought a letter from Leo, in ink, and there was a scrawled note from Frank, too. 'The bad penny's still rolling, and on the move to a safer place, I hope and pray. Give my love to Flora, and write again, my pet.'

With a sigh of relief I picked up my pen and wrote a short, simple letter with news of the children, especially Flora. Then I wrote another letter to Leo, and posted them together.

The next day all my relief was wiped out. 'Battle front extended north and south . . . German advance to the Lys.' Thursday brought news of fighting around Armentières, and then I saw the headline 'Casualties in Medical Services evacuating wounded under fire.' I was shaking so much I could hardly set my cup down safely in its saucer.

Over the next week the fighting continued. I would sit in the office crouched awkwardly over the desk trying to concentrate on the yields of oats and barley – but all the time my heart and mind were in France.

Then, on Thursday, when I didn't think I could bear to wait any longer, the last post brought a field postcard from Leo. I held it in my hand, shaking. I knew why he'd had to send it – but at least he'd still been alive when he wrote that neat signature and date in indelible pencil. But the card had been four days in the coming. I wrote my reply that evening and took it down so it would go first thing tomorrow.

I didn't sleep well and I felt tired and heavy as I dragged myself down to the estate office next morning. Mr Selby's face creased in concern when he saw me. 'Lady Warminster, are you sure you shouldn't be resting?'

'I've been resting all night, Mr Selby.'

'But, in your present delicate state of health – '

'I'm not due for another couple of weeks or so. I'll just check those Pennings figures for you, and there's some letters to be seen to – '

My back was aching so much when I went up to see the children before lunch I could hardly bear the weight of Rose on my knee, but she was whining and grizzly, not like my usual cheerful Rose at all. 'Shush, shush – thy Mama's holding thee safe – '

Ellen smiled at me over my daughter's dark head, 'I 'low they do know when they're going to be pushed out o' the cradle.'

By the time Rose had settled, I was late for lunch, but it scarcely mattered, since it was rabbit stew again and I didn't really fancy it. I was just pushing the shoulder blade to one side and trying to hide the rest of the meat under it, when the door opened – and Mr Tims said, 'My lady, Mr Selby's here.'

Mr Selby was right behind him. As I stumbled to my feet my eyes dropped to his hand – the nightmare had come true. But perhaps a wound – then I saw the expression on his face as he told me, 'Lady Warminster, I'm afraid it's very bad news.' So I knew.

He came to the table and held the piece of paper out to me. I took it from him. 'Deeply regret . . . died of wounds . . . ' The letters danced and blurred before my eyes – until I dashed the tears away and read on. It was Frank.

Chapter Forty-Eight

I felt a moment of the most over-powering emotion – then it was swallowed up in grief. Grief for Frank – Frank so tall and straight and golden: Frank, striding across the harvest stubble; Frank springing so lightly up on to Prancer's broad back; Frank seizing the reins to ride, young and confident, between the sheaves of golden corn.

Frank – dead. That perfect, straight male body lay broken and tossed aside in the mud and slime that now was France.

Clara helped me weeping from the table. She was talking to me, and so was Mr Selby, but I couldn't hear them. I could only hear Frank's voice as I'd last heard it: 'Goodbye, Amy – my golden girl, my might-have-been.'

They took me up to my sitting room. As Clara knelt to light the fire Mr Selby hovered anxiously, his face drawn with distress. 'Should I telegraph Lord Warminster?'

I gazed up at him through my tears and it was Clara who replied, 'Aye, you'd best do that, Mr Selby. Tis only right he should know at once. And Lady Quinham.'

'I've only got her mother's address – '

'Best telegraph there, then.'

Mr Selby came and stood before me, and took my cold hand in his. 'Lady Warminster, I'm so sorry – if there's anything I can do?' I shook my head. I couldn't even find the words to thank him.

Clara sat with her arm around me, holding my unwieldy body close against hers as I sobbed. At last she said, 'You'd best try and calm yourself, my lady, for the sake of the child. I'll ring for Bertha to bring a cup of tea.'

As she made me drink the scalding sweet tea I whispered, 'I loved him, Clara – despite everything, I did never stop loving him.'

'I know, I know. You don't go cold on a man just because he behaves badly to you.'

She'd misunderstood. I didn't mean that, I meant – and that first moment came back and guilt swept through me. I thrust it away, walling it off; Clara was right, I must calm myself for the sake of my baby.

But it was as though something had snapped inside me. I was like a clockwork toy with a broken spring: I could only move at the bidding of others. Clara made me wash my face and took me up to the nursery. Flora ran towards me, as beautiful as he had been, and I wept anew as my daughters' frightened faces gazed up at me. Clara and Ellen led me to the couch so that Flora and Rose could cuddle close up to me; I couldn't even offer them a lap now, but their small arms gave me a little warmth.

The next few days were a blur of grief and grieving. Frank, running beside me in the park, Frank glorious and golden in the punt on the river, Frank striding into my room at Eston – Frank, the shining sun of my youth, lost.

A letter came from Leo. I held the envelope with fingers that shook; at least it was in ink, but when I opened it it was very short.

> Dear Amy,
>   I have received Selby's telegram. Such a tragic loss of a young life. However, we must remember that Francis died bravely, fighting to defend the country of his birth. I trust you and the children remain well, and that you are continuing to take adequate rest.
>   Your affectionate husband, Leo Warminster.

I went over to my desk at once, although the pen was so heavy I could hardly lift it, and my back felt as though it were breaking in two. I managed to write something; about the children, about the ploughing. Then at the end I wrote: 'Please take care – for the children and I do love thee.' The effort cost me as much as if I'd run all the way to the Home Farm and back again, without pausing for breath, but there were barely a dozen lines on the page. I couldn't think of any more, so I signed my usual farewell – and as I did so I realized that if another telegram came then it could only be Leo. Putting my heavy head down on the desk, I wept. *Oh Leo, Leo, why did you go?*

Dr Matthews came to examine me. As he left he patted my shoulder and said, 'Not so long now, Lady Warminster – only another two or three weeks or so.'

I looked up at him. 'But you said early in May. Likely the first week, you said.'

He squeezed my shoulder gently. 'That's only an estimate. It's impossible to be certain about these things, you know that. I'm inclined to think now that it could be rather later – I'll inform Warminster, so he won't get too anxious.'

Three weeks! Another three weeks of waiting – and I was so frightened already. Suppose something happened to me – and the other telegram came – the children – Flora had lost one father already – oh, Frank, Frank.

I went down to the estate office every morning, but the simplest tasks seemed to take me hours. Mr Selby wouldn't let me come back after lunch. Mr Parry would be back at Pennings soon, he told me, 'He's made an excellent recovery. In the meantime I can easily hold the fort.' So in the afternoon I would creep upstairs and lie on the sofa, tossing with grief and fear.

The next week there was only a field postcard from Leo – but it was at least signed in ink. I carried it round like a talisman, and when I showed it to Ellen she said quietly, 'He'll be busy, very busy – my lady.' She glanced at Dora then said, 'Jesse's just come back from the village. He says as Horace Drewett, Jael's husband's youngest brother, has been wounded, and so's Fred Smith. They dussent know how badly, yet.'

I knew I should go down to the village, but I couldn't, I couldn't. Two days later Eli Jenkins' younger son, Charlie, was reported wounded, too; but still I didn't go. I was a coward. Clara said, 'They'll understand, my lady, wi' you being so near your time.' But it wasn't that: I couldn't face their grief.

It was a couple of days later that Jim asked to see me in the estate office, his face grim. 'Clara's gone down to her Mam, her Emmie fetched her. I'd just come in with the trap so I turned it straight round – '

I broke in, 'Who is it?'

'Tis George, he's gone. And him with three young 'uns, too.'

I had to go and see Clara's mother, she'd been so good to me; and besides, Leo would have wanted it.

Jim took me down to Mrs Chandler's in the trap after lunch. They were all there: Clara and her sister Emmie, and Jane, George's wife. Poor Jane: remembering her laughing face in the harvest field I stumbled over the words of condolence, but they drew me inside and sat me down by the fire with a cup of tea.

The next day I went to see Mrs Jenkins and Mrs Drewett, and then Fred Smith's mother. My words were as clumsy as my body, but I had to go. I said to Mrs Smith, 'If he were really bad, likely they'd 'a sent for you – '

She shook her head. 'They're not sending for anybody now, my lady – tis too dangerous. They say as anyone can be moved, they're bringing 'em back – only,' her voice broke, 'there's no news of my Fred coming back.' I didn't know what to say in reply.

Another field postcard came from Leo. Again, he'd signed it in ink. I put it in my pocket with the first one, as if by carrying his signature around with me I could keep him safe. But I knew it was only a foolish fancy.

Albie wrote to say his battalion had been pulled back for a while, but Uncle Alf had been returned to the Front. Ellen's brother Dan had gone, too, although he was just eighteen; and Len Arnold was sent back to France, although he hadn't got full use of his arm yet. The army was so desperate that even men of fifty were being conscripted – though I knew they wouldn't have taken Leo, if he hadn't volunteered. But now he was out there and the Germans were still attacking, advancing – trying to capture the Channel Ports, Mr Tims said, and cut France off. If they did, our soldiers would be trapped in France – oh Leo, where are you?

I was overdue now: it was already the second week of May. Mrs Chandler had come to stay in Clara and Jim's spare room, and Dr Matthews dropped in every day. 'How are you, Lady Warminster? No swelling of the ankles? Good, good. I'll send a report to Lord Warminster, to ease his mind. It's difficult for a man, being away at a time like this.'

I cried, 'Why did he go? He didn't have to.'

Dr Matthews replied gently, 'He went to do his duty, Lady Warminster. We none of us can do more.' As Frank had done his, and paid the price. It was more than three weeks now since the telegram had come, and the pain and grief still numbed my brain and chained my legs with links of iron, so that in the morning I could hardly force my unwieldy body from my bed.

On the Thursday another postcard came from Leo. Not the printed form this time, just a plain postcard with a few words thanking me for my news written in his own hand – and in ink. I read it over and over again, before putting it in my pocket with the others; thank goodness it had been in ink again. But that evening as I sat at the dining table shifting from side to side on my chair to ease the niggling ache in my back, I thought, suppose he's guessed that I look for the ink? Last year while he was on sick leave, he'd talked of getting a fountain pen, but I'd said no – but perhaps now because I'm near my time, he's borrowed one to curb my fears. So my talismans were worthless. The tears spilled over, and I let them trickle unchecked down my cheeks. I was so tired – and so frightened.

I couldn't bear to be alone. I took my sewing up to the nursery to sit with Ellen and Dora. Mrs Chandler came up too, with Clara. They sat talking softly of George, of the time when he'd been growing up; talking of their past, which I hadn't shared. I sat in the midst of them, alone.

The ache in my back became stronger, until it was a band of pain around my swollen body, and I could scarcely drag myself along to the WC. As I crouched there, the flux came – and I knew it had begun. Pulling up my drawers, I began to sob, helplessly; I couldn't face it, I couldn't bear it – for I was a coward.

As I came back into the nursery, the first pain came sharp and biting and I cried out in panic. My cry woke Flora, who came running from the night nursery, her eyes wide with fear. 'Mama!'

She clung to my skirt, and behind her came Rose, with the same frightened face – and looking up I saw that fear mirrored in the other faces around: Clara's, Ellen's, Dora's – even Mrs Chandler had lost her usual calm. Flora's voice came again, louder, 'Mama!' A high-pitched wail of panic – and I heard Frank's voice, saying, 'Out there, sometimes, I want to break down and howl like a frightened child, but I can't, because of the other fellows – I can't let them down.' And no more could I. I was a coward, but I mustn't show it.

I crouched down, and put my arms around my daughters. ''Tis all right, Flora my pet – twas only a twinge o' the rheumatics, like Mr Tims do have.'

I watched her face clear, and then her frightened fingers relaxed their grip as Rose repeated, 'Matics?'

'That's right, my Rose. Now, you know Jim?' The blonde and the dark head both nodded. Of course they knew Jim. 'And the liddle cottage where he do live with Clara?' I glanced up at Clara, but I knew she'd say yes. 'Would you like to go and stay there, tonight, with Jim? Ellen and Dora'll be coming as well, o' course.'

Their eyes widened with excitement. Clara's voice broke in, 'I'd be main glad if thee wouldst, 'cos I've got to stay in the still room all night, finishing my jobs – and poor Jim'll be lonely if thee dussent go and bide along wi' him.'

341

Ellen's voice was coaxing, 'Why don't you come and help me pack?' They scampered after her into the night nursery.

I murmured to Clara, 'I don't want them to hear me.'

'No, tis the best thing. We should've thought of it afore. Jim'll make a fuss of 'em, mebbe roast a chestnut or two; we still got some left. I'll run down now and put clean sheets on the bed.'

I went down with the children and kissed them goodbye at the door of the cottage – they were too excited by then to notice my stifled gasp of pain. Mr Selby came hurrying over the cobbles: he must have been working late. 'Lady Warminster, how are you? Tims has just told me – ' His face creased with concern.

I said quietly, 'Doan 'ee fret, Mr Selby. Tisn't as though it 'ere the first time.'

He reached out to me and we shook hands firmly as he said, 'Good luck, Lady Warminster. I'll run home to say where I am then I'll be back. Tims and I will sit up together until you're safely delivered.'

My eyes prickled. 'Thank you, Mr Selby.'

Upstairs, Mrs Chandler had been busy in my bedroom: newspapers protected the carpet and mackintosh the bed. The blanket that had been specially baked in the kitchen range lay ready and waiting. I turned hastily away to look instead at the baby clothes, airing by the fire. It was burning brightly, with coal hoarded ready for this night by Clara. I shivered and at once Mrs Chandler fetched the screen. 'You get yourself washed and into your nightie, then put your nice warm dressing gown on.'

I did as I was told, but I didn't get into bed. 'I'll walk a while, Mrs Chandler.'

'Aye, you do that – it'll ease the pains.'

I was frightened, very frightened – but I knew I mustn't show it. I started to walk up and down, counting my paces. I walked slowly, weighed down by my baby, just as Leo might even at this moment be weighed down by a heavy stretcher: Leo, who'd gone to do his duty, just as I must do mine.

Dr Matthews arrived soon after my waters broke. He said it would be some time yet, but he'd stay. 'I've left word where I am – if I'm needed they can send up here.'

He looked tired. He wasn't a young man and he'd been up last night, too. I said, 'You'd best lie down next door for now, on Leo's bed. It'll likely be a long night.'

It was a long night – a long hard night. At one o'clock I was too tired to walk any longer, so I climbed up on the bed and knelt there, where Leo had held me in his arms. As my pains came closer I remembered his strength, and the comfort he'd given me when I'd laboured with Rose, but I had to labour alone now. Then I chided myself: I wasn't alone, Mrs Chandler and Clara were with me, and Dr Matthews was only next door. And it was easier for me – birth, not death; my poor Leo – but he was strong, so strong. Then the next pain caught me and doubled me up. Afterwards I murmured prayers of pleading: please, keep him safe.

At dawn I knew I had to scream – I panted disjointed words, explaining. Dr Matthews' voice was reassuring, 'Let it rip, Lady Warminster. The children are safely out of earshot.' So I opened my mouth and screamed, and let the pain dissolve into the pale morning light.

'Not long now – push, push!'

Panting, gasping, pushing, strong uncontrollable pushes, until I felt him begin to split me, wide. 'Stop pushing now – pant, pant – pant like a dog.' I panted like Nella and felt him force me open, thrusting through in the last slippery gush.

Dr Matthews exclaimed, 'It's a boy – you have a son, Lady Warminster, a perfect son.' And I heard his first, lusty cry and strength came flowing back into me. I reared up, reaching forward to seize him from the doctor and take his naked body into my arms. I hugged him to me, holding him safe. My son, my son – our son. Gazing down into his crumpled red face I searched for the likeness to his father, but he was completely bald, and I laughed. His hand reached up, his mouth opened, turning to my breast. Pulling back my nightie I murmured, 'Here, come to thy Mama, then,' and at once he took hold of me so that I was pierced with love and joy.

'A fine sturdy boy.'

'Aye, he's big, too, though that's not to be wondered at with him coming late. Her ladyship's lucky to have got by without a tear.'

He suckled greedily until the pain of the afterbirth came hard and fierce. I gasped.

'I'll take him now, my lady.'

'No, not yet – ' But they made me give him up for a little while.

'All over, now, Lady Warminster – we'll soon have you and the youngster cleaned up.'

Clean pads, freshly scorched, the binder firmly applied – and all the other remembered trappings of birth. Then Mrs Chandler helped me wash my sweaty body, slipped a clean starched nightdress over my head and combed and replaited my hair – until at last I lay back against the pillows, my son in my arms once more. I gazed down at his bright blue eyes, so wide and alert as they looked back at me. He was so beautiful, my son – and touching, stroking, caressing him, I told him of my love.

Clara tapped and came into the room, her face one broad smile. 'I've told everybody, and Mr Selby and Mr Tims have opened a bottle of port, if the doctor would like a glass. Stayed up all night, they did! And Ellen said as she'll bring the liddle maids up when her ladyship's ready.'

With a final kiss I gave him to Mrs Chandler, and she put him back in his cradle, so my arms were free for Flora and Rose. As soon as I'd hugged and kissed them, I said, 'Look what Dr Matthews has brought for you – a little brother!'

They both stared in wonder. Rose reached out one finger for a tentative prod, then Flora simply turned her back on him, and began to tell me about the popping chestnuts.

By the time Ellen had taken them off for their breakfast, Dr Matthews had come back for a final check. After he'd taken my temperature and pulse he said, 'Selby's telegraphing your husband. The message I gave him was: "Lady Warminster safely delivered of a perfectly formed son. Mother and child both doing well." ' He smiled. 'I don't want to leave him any scope for further worry – he's done enough already.'

'Thank you – and thank you for all you've done.'

His smile broadened. 'The pleasure is mine. There are few happier tasks than delivering a healthy child. Now it's high time you got some sleep.'

Mrs Chandler came round to the cradle and lifted out my sleepy son. 'You'll want him with you.' It wasn't a question; she understood. She handed him to me. 'Here's his little lordship, then.'

'His little lordship' – because my baby was Lord Quinham. The shock of that realization stabbed through my joy with the agony of loss. It was as though Frank had never been.

I turned my head so Mrs Chandler couldn't see my tears as she told me, 'I'll just be next door, my lady – you ring if you need anything.' Once she'd gone the tears fell, for Frank. My baby stirred and turned his face, seeking my breast. Automatically I gave it to him: the new Lord Quinham. It was right that he should be so called, for he was Leo's first-born son. But I had not forgotten Frank, and never would.

When Leo's next letter came it was in pencil. The tears came sliding down my cheeks yet again. I had so wanted him to be safe for a little while. I showed the pencilled address to Mrs Chandler; she patted my shoulder and said, 'But you got to remember, thic Americans've come. As Mr Tims says, they'll be a big help.' And then I felt ashamed, because she'd lost her own son so recently, and been so brave.

Leo's letter was very short; but I knew he couldn't help that, the way things were in France. He simply wrote that he was glad that I was safely delivered and that all had gone well, and told me to choose the baby's name myself. I felt rather crestfallen: I'd thought he'd want to do it. Then I scolded myself; he was too busy to think of things like that. So I named my baby after Granfer. He'd been Jack, but Jack was short for John, so John it would be – except that I called him Jackie.

Mr Selby was going to register the birth the next day so I asked Mrs Chandler to invite him in to see the baby. He came through the door very pink and embarrassed but I could see he was pleased to meet Jackie. When he'd admired him he asked, 'And a second name, Lady Warminster?'

I'd have like one of Leo's names, but I knew how he hated them so now I asked, 'I were wondering if you'd care to be godfather, Mr Selby?'

He blushed deeper. 'I should be honoured, Lady Warminster.'

'Then mebbe I could give him *your* name – I thought John Edward would go very nicely.' He did look pleased. 'And mebbe we could slip in a Leonard after that. Tis close enough to Leonidas, without being so close as to annoy Leo.' We both smiled.

He needed me all the time, did Jackie. If I put him down in his cradle for a little sleep, he'd cry for me the minute he woke up again. I'd have to be nursing him endlessly, although I was more tired than I'd been with Rose. Otherwise, I was really quite well and I knew I needed to get back to normal as soon as possible. By the end of the week I was up and dressed and in my sitting room: Mrs Chandler wasn't too happy about that, but Dr Matthews gave me permission. 'There's no point in your lying in bed if you're worrying all the time, Lady Warminster.' He did understand, did Dr Matthews.

So I wrote to Leo from my own desk, telling him what a wonderful baby Jackie was, and what we'd decided to call him, and how Flora had held him for a full five minutes while he'd been asleep. Rose had sat with her hand on his head, her big dark eyes round with the effort of staying still so long.

I couldn't go outside yet because I hadn't been churched, but at the end of the second week of my confinement I went down to the estate office carrying a sleeping Jackie in a laundry basket.

Mr Selby jumped up as I came in. He looked exhausted. When he saw me heading for my usual place he said, 'Lady Warminster, are you sure – ?'

'I'll just stay an hour or two, Mr Selby.' So we sat working together. Jackie woke up and began to whimper so I put him to my breast and drew my shawl around us both. Mr Selby glanced up, then looked hastily down again, his leathery face flushed. He'd soon get used to me feeding Jackie while I was at my desk.

I settled into my usual pattern of worry. The Germans had launched another attack, at the end of May. Within three days they reached the River Marne – the very place they'd been turned back at the start of the war. It was as if it was all to be fought again, and every order from the Board of Agriculture hammered home the same message. As Mr Selby said despairingly one day, 'They seem to be expecting another three years of war – but where will the men come from?'

Horace Drewett and Charlie Jenkins were on the mend, but although they'd brought Fred Smith back to England, he'd died in hospital in Bristol soon after his return. Just before their younger son had come back, Mr and Mrs Smith had received another telegram: their elder boy Arthur was missing. I asked Mr Beeston to church me early so I could go round to see Mrs Smith. My legs were shaking and I didn't know what to say but she was so brave.

'I didn't tell Fred about Arthur; he'd 'a been that upset. Instead I told him I'd just had a letter from him, and he was safe. It were a lie, but God gave me the strength to tell it.' Then she said softly, 'I'm glad you're safely delivered, my lady – and so glad as twere a boy. Mebbe it'll help his lordship wi' the hurt o' losing his eldest.' She looked at me directly. 'And I'm glad as the liddle 'un came when he did for your sake, too, my lady – because you must've felt the loss of his young lordship badly. When a woman's borne a man a child, whatever way it's happened, she feels she's given him part of herself. You'll be grieving hard.' I began to cry, and she finished up comforting me. She was brave, Mrs Smith – very brave.

The next time I went down to the village, I was on foot. I'd been to see Mr Beeston one evening to say that I'd like to delay Jackie's christening for a little while: 'They say as leave has started again – '

He finished for me, 'And you're hoping this young gentleman's father might be present at his baptism. Of couse we must wait – his lordship's son and heir –' Then he reddened. 'I mean – '

I said quietly, 'That's what he is now, Mr Beeston.' And when I came back through the village it was obvious everyone knew it. Even the older men came out of their cottages to look at Jackie. 'My, he's a sturdy youngster an' no mistake.' 'You done well there, me lady.' Jackie began to tug at my blouse and the men drifted politely away, back to their teas, but the women stayed clustering round me as I sat on the wooden seat opposite the green circle of grass at the head of the village street. 'My, he's a fine one, our liddle lordship.' 'Makes you feel as there's something to look forward to – I 'low his lordship were like a dog wi' two tails when he heard the news.' 'You been a good girl, me lady, giving him a fine son like that.'

Mr Arnott even brought the receipts down himself. 'I come to have a peek at the young 'un, see. My, but he's a big old boy for his age, and no mistake.' Jackie reached out and seized Mr Arnott's calloused finger. 'Strong, too – he won't let go o' the land when it's his.' He looked up at me, 'His lordship maun be main pleased wi' you, me lady, for giving him such a fine son.'

I knew Leo was, but you couldn't have told it from his letters. But then, he'd always written in that same formal, rather stilted style – I knew that he did so hate having to have them censored by his officer. I kept hoping he'd send me one of his other letters, the ones in the green printed envelopes – but those envelopes were difficult to get hold of, Albie had said. Likely they'd all been lost in the retreat.

Because it *was* a retreat, there was no doubt about that for all the papers' talk of a 'withdrawal from the outposts to the main battle zone.' We knew more of the truth now, from Albie, who was back in England, in hospital in London. Ellen had been up to visit him there. He hadn't been badly wounded, he told her: he'd only been sent back because there were too many wounded to cope with in France. He was very quiet, Ellen said, and he didn't talk much about what had happened, but he was going to get a medal, the Military Cross, for what he'd done. We were so proud of him.

And then we heard some even better news: Arthur Smith had been found. A message came from the Red Cross to say he was a prisoner of war in Germany. We were so relieved for his mother. I picked a big bunch of my golden roses and took them down to her. Normally I never picked the roses, because Leo didn't like them to be cut, but I knew he wouldn't mind this time. Besides, it was the rose he'd given to me.

I gathered a spray for myself, too, and put them in my sitting room. I'd look up from feeding Jackie and think about how he'd first given her to me, and the love in his eyes as he told me her name. Tears came as I recalled how I'd spurned him then, not wanting his love; but now I longed for it. I wanted to show him Jackie, and then to take him in my arms and show him how I loved him. I whispered, 'Thee must be a good patient boy when thy Dada comes home, for he'll want loving, too.' Surely Leo'd be back on leave soon?

But it was Mr Wallis who came first. He arrived during the second week of June looking very dapper in his khaki uniform: his three stripes had been joined by a crown, so he was a sergeant major now. He admired Jackie, and then I said, 'Clara'll be getting your room ready, Mr Wallis. You stay as long as you want.'

He saw me taking Nella out after dinner, and offered to carry Jackie for me. As we walked in the rose garden the flowers and their scents were so beautiful; I ached for Leo, who was not here to enjoy them. We sat down on the seat by the fountain. Looking round at the roses, Mr Wallis said, 'I can hardly believe it. When you're out there you get to think that's the only world there is.' He turned back to me. 'And how have you been getting on?'

I told him about so much of the meadowland having to go under the plough, and the problems with labour, and the prospects for the harvest. ''Tis such a worry, the weather at this time o' year.'

He smiled at me as he said, 'You've grown up, my lady.'

''Tis the war.'

He laughed grimly. 'Yes, it's had the same effect on me. I didn't think I'd got any further to grow – but I had.'

'Was it bad, when the Germans attacked?'

'Yes, Amy, very bad – I thought we were done for.' He added gently, 'I was sorry to hear about his young lordship.'

'Aye.' I let the tears flow, because I knew he understood.

He stayed for the whole of his leave. Clara said to me, 'He weren't as chatty as he used to be, Mr Wallis. Sometimes he'd be sitting in his chair in the Room as though he were miles away. But when I said that to Jim he told me, "We're none of us as chatty as we used to be, Clara. You wouldn't expect it, would you?"'

I took out Leo's last letter. It was short, but I'd been so relieved it was in pen I hardly noticed. Now I looked at it again and thought of what he must have been through these past months. No wonder he couldn't bring himself to write much – not that he'd ever written long letters. After all, he wasn't like Mr Wallis: he'd never been chatty in the first place.

But it wouldn't matter when he came home: then I'd hold him in my arms as he loved me, and cuddle him afterwards, too. The Sister had been right, there were more ways than words to tell a man that you loved him – though I'd tell him by words, too. Because he wouldn't be deaf this time.

His next letter came, written in ink this time; and the news of the war seemed a little less bleak. And as the roses bloomed, so hope did, too – though I hardly dared admit it, even to myself, just in case.

Chapter Forty-Nine

July came. The weather was so fine and warm, I took the children out into the rose garden after tea. We admired the tumbling pink frills of Dorothy Perkins, before walking on down to see Leo's favourite Blairii roses. Their last blooms hung lush and full-lipped above the drifts of their petals, covering the grass below. With a shout of glee Flora scooped up handfuls of pink and white, tossing them into the air; then she turned and began to run back up the sloping lawn, with Rose staggering after her. I followed more slowly, the weight of their brother in my arms.

Flora had gone in search of the bronze boy. When I caught up with her, she was perched on the flat marble rim of the fountain pool, gazing up at the plump dolphin. I stretched out a hand to steady her, but the water in the pool was only a couple of inches deep now: we'd had to turn off the fountain because of the war. I'd explained to Flora, but she still kept hoping that one day the silver stream of water would soar up again from the fish's mouth. With Rose pressing against my legs I looked across at the Garland: she'd flowered a little earlier this year, but her last clusters of fragrant white blossom still veiled the old apple tree. I looked around me: the roses were beautiful still, but they were already past their prime; if he didn't come soon – Rose tugged at my skirt, 'Horseys, horseys, Mama?'

We went to the stables, and then I took the girls back up to the nursery. I stayed there with them, and allowed myself a little time to sit in the window seat cuddling my baby. I was half dozing in the warmth of the sun, when all at once I heard Flora's shriek of excitement, and Rose echoing her. I looked up – and Leo was standing there in the doorway.

Heavy boots, soiled puttees, khaki tunic – even his grey hair was cropped so short that he looked like a stranger – but he was my Leo, and a warm tide of love flooded my body and swept up into my cheeks. With his son in my arms I stood up, and went across to him. He was bending over, his hand pulled down by Flora, but his eyes never left my face. As I came to him I reached up to kiss his mouth – but Leo, my shy Leo, turned his face, so it was the fast-growing stubble of his chin that grazed my lips.

'Welcome home, Leo.'

I put out my hand to his arm but he backed away. 'I must bathe and change at once. I'm lousy.'

With a smile I told him, 'I seen lice afore.'

He shook his head, his voice gruff. 'I'd rather you didn't see them again.' And of course, he was right, because of Jackie.

So I retreated a little and held out my baby, 'Leo, here he is – your son.'

He stared down at Jackie, who returned his stare suspiciously with his round blue eyes. 'He has – no hair.'

Laughing, I pushed Jackie's bonnet right back. 'He do have a liddle, but baint much, I 'low.'

'Rose was born with a full head of hair.'

I smiled up at him, remembering our joy at her birth. 'Aye, she were, but tis less usual, that. Jackie, he's only got a bit o' duck down, like Flora had.'

'Yes – like Flora.' She was swinging on his hand, trying to win his attention. 'How are you, my Flora?'

'Papa, come and see Porridge, and Tabby Cat – ' Rose was at her other side, reaching up to him. I didn't know how well she remembered her father, but she'd follow her big sister anywhere, would Rose.

He smiled down at his daughters and I gave way to them. 'I'll run your bath, Leo.'

'There is no need. Clara and Tims are making the necessary preparations.' He bent over the girls. 'Papa must wash first. It is very muddy in France.'

Flora's face fell, then she announced, 'I'll come down and sing to you. I can sing ever so loud, you can hear it through the door.'

Rose piped up, 'Me sing – me sing too.' He let them drag him out.

I left Jackie with Ellen, but by the time I got downstairs Flora and Rose were squatting either side of Nella in the corridor, shouting 'Three Blind Mice' through the bathroom door. I went on into his bedroom, but I could hear by the splashing that he was already in his bath. Mr Tims was just coming out through the connecting door, holding a bundle of clothes at arm's-length.

I went to take them from him, but he shook his head. 'His lordship said they were to go straight to the stables, because Jim'll know how to deal with them – and there's his boots, too.' He looked round for them, and quickly I went to pick them up. They smelt unclean, and as he took them from me Mr Tims shook his head mournfully, 'And to think how his lordship always had to have everything just so.'

For the next hour Flora and Rose followed him everywhere. They were so pleased to see him, and he was so interested in all their tales I hadn't the heart to send them upstairs, although it was long past their bedtime. I was out in the stables with them all when Dora came to say Jackie needed me. So I had to leave them.

Later, Leo came up and sat in the big wickerwork armchair as Ellen and Dora got the girls ready for bed. As soon as they were in their nightgowns Flora and Rose clambered on to his lap, demanding stories, and it was nearly dinner time before he could persuade them to let him go.

I said, 'I'm afraid tis only rabbit and lentil stew, so you needn't bother to dress for dinner if you don't want to.'

He looked quite put out. 'Certainly I will dress.'

So I went down to get changed, too. I would have slipped into his dressing room to see if he had everything he wanted, but he kept Mr Tims there all the time; I could hear their voices.

Clara waited at table herself, with Mr Tims. She looked so pleased, and she told me Mrs Carter had made a special trifle, and Leo's favourite anchovy tarts as a savoury. She must have started on them the minute he'd arrived.

I apologized for the rabbit stew again. 'We aren't supposed to eat butcher's meat more'n once a week. O' course, we can get liver and suchlike from the farm, only I like to share it out. The women are working so hard and the children are in the fields as well now school's out, so they need a meal every day.'

'I quite understand.'

He hardly said another word all through dinner. Over our carrot soup he looked up at me to say, 'I can scarcely believe I'm here.' Just like Mr Wallis. So I chatted about the children and the roses, while he just sat there, watching my face as he listened. It was not until Clara and Mr Tims had cleared the table and served the dessert that he suddenly spoke. 'I told myself out there that you could not possibly be as beautiful as I remembered – but you are. In fact you are even lovelier.' I blushed, but it wasn't so much what he'd said that gave me such pleasure – but the way he'd said it. He'd sounded so sad, from missing me all this time.

When he'd finished his apple I asked, 'Would you like to come up to my sitting room for coffee now?'

He reached for the bell. 'No, I think we'll take it in here, if you don't mind. Then perhaps we could go straight out – and look at the roses.'

I smiled at him, 'Aye, just like old times. Only mebbe I'd best run up and feed Jackie first – or we could take him with us, like we did with Rose.'

He replied quietly, 'No, I'd rather talk to you alone.'

I felt my cheeks become warm as I told him, 'Then I'd best feed him now. He does need a lot of nursing, my Jackie. Tis with him being such a big baby, I 'low. He weighed over nine pounds when he were born, but then, he was a couple of weeks late.'

'Was he?'

'O' course. You must remember.'

The door opened and Dora's head appeared round it. 'My lady, Master Quinham wants you.'

'I'm just coming, Dora.' I turned back to Leo. 'Don't you wait your coffee, Leo, I'll have mine upstairs while I'm feeding Jackie – unless you did want to come up to the nursery for yours, too?'

He shook his head. 'No. I fancy a cigar with mine.'

'Then I'll be down directly Jackie's settled.'

Upstairs, I began to worry a little. Jackie wasn't as placid as Rose had been. I'd have to put him in his cradle when Leo first came to my room, and Jackie wouldn't like that at all. Perhaps I should ask Ellen to keep him in the nursery for a while after bedtime; but when I looked at Ellen sewing serenely by the fire I couldn't bring myself to do it. Bending down I whispered into Jackie's perfect ear, 'You'll just have to be a good, patient boy.'

When he'd finished I gave him to Ellen. He grumbled but she rocked him soothingly and after a few minutes he settled; perhaps I could leave him upstairs for a while. When we came back from our walk I'd just run up and check, and if he was asleep, then I would ask Ellen.

As I came down the stairs I thought of walking in the rose garden with Leo, and could hardly stop myself from running. I was excited as a young girl. He was waiting for me in the hall. I wanted to reach up and kiss him, but Mr Tims was still there; Leo had obviously been asking him about Mr Wallis. Then as we came down into the garden, Leo was so eager to see his roses I had to almost run to keep up with him, but anyway, I'd decided to wait until he kissed me first – after all, I didn't want him to think me forward.

The roses near the entrance were so beautiful, but he didn't linger and I realized why: we were going down to see the Garland rose. As we came along the path to the steps I told him, 'Tis still in bloom, the Garland – though you've mebbe missed the best of it.'

'Yes, as I did before.'

I shook my head. 'No, you were here last summer, when it came into flower. But o' course, they weren't such a good show, then.'

We came down the first flight of steps, and I paused by the seat on the terrace there, but he went on down and crossed the lawn to the next seat, which overlooked the fountain. He stood beside it, waiting for me to sit down. The Garland was behind me now, but I could still catch the lingering trace of her honeyed-orange scent. Nella sank down on the grass beside me, but Leo stayed standing, looking down into the fountain pool, with its drift of leaves and muddied sediment. Apologetically I said, 'I'm sorry tisn't all clean and shining like it used to be, only there baint the labour to spare now.'

'No – of course not.'

He sat down, but leaving a little distance between us, so he could face me. He looked as if wanted to say something, but didn't know how to begin, so recalling the last time I'd sat here of an evening I prompted, 'Mr Wallis, he said it were bad when the Germans attacked.'

Leo replied quietly, 'Yes, it was very bad.' He paused for a moment, then began to tell me. 'We knew it was going to happen – but the reality is never what you've expected. You see, we hadn't experienced a retreat before; we'd been in pushes when the casualties were very high but a retreat – is different. Naturally the problem of evacuating the wounded in such circumstances is considerable, but that is less of a problem than the one of morale: suddenly we believed that we were going to lose. Beforehand we'd merely been doing the usual routine medical work that trench warfare requires, and I must admit that despite the imminence of the attack my thoughts were mostly with you. I was concerned about your coming trial.'

The thought of his concern warmed me, as he continued, 'Then the bombardment began. I'd expected to be posted to one of the advanced dressing stations: there were two, one at Doignies and the other at Beetroot Factory on the Baupame to Cambrai road. We'd been working on them for the past three months, strengthening them, digging a new accommodation for lying cases – the usual things. A total waste of time, as it turned out: since both ADSs were so heavily shelled in the first hours that they ceased to exist.'

My mouth dry by now, I asked, 'But – where were you?'

'I'd been transferred back to the relay bearer post at Beaumetz.'

'And were all the other men killed?'

'No, though they all became casualties, and the survivors were taken prisoner. But we didn't know that then. One of the MOs tried to get up to Beetroot Factory but had to turn back. Then a message got through, from Doignies, saying that they'd received several direct hits – gas shells had come over, too – and they had casualties needing evacuation. So we sent up three horse ambulance wagons. We got halfway there and suddenly saw a horde of men in field-grey uniforms advancing on us. I shouted to turn, but luckily the drivers had already begun wheeling the wagons round – fortunately none of the horses had been hit – and so we galloped hell-for-leather back to Beaumetz, and saved our wagons.

'After that we simply couldn't get through to those two ADSs. The telephone lines had long gone, several motor cyclists tried, but – ' He gave a small shrug. 'So we carried on dealing with local casualties. Nobody really knew what was going on. A rumour arrived that the grey uniforms had been spotted over the next hill, but we couldn't evacuate at that point, as we had no transport. So the MO said, "Any of you fellows know German? It could come in handy. What about you, Warminster, I thought you'd had some sort of education?" I told him, "Sorry, sir, I'm afraid I only know Greek." He said, "Fat lot of use that'll be. The Greeks are on our side!" And I replied, "In any case, it's ancient Greek," and we all laughed. What else could we do? Then the MO was shifted and I was left with a party of ten bearers at Beaumetz, with orders to act as an advanced dressing station as long as possible, and maintain touch with any of the regimental aid posts that were supposed to be still in front of us. But the next morning everything behind was moving back and we'd turned into a regimental aid post ourselves.'

I exclaimed, 'But, Albie told me, they be the ones right at the Front!'

'Yes, but since no one knew where the Front was by then it didn't make a lot of difference.' He stopped, and said almost brusquely, 'But I didn't intend to tell you all this. It was another story that I wanted – '

I broke in, 'But did you get back all right?'

'Obviously, or I wouldn't be here.'

'But how – '

'The division was eventually withdrawn from the line. Only six days after it had all begun, but – it seemed much longer.'

He fell silent, so I prompted, 'But you went back. Your next postcard was in pencil, too.'

He moved his shoulders again in one of his awkward, sideways shrugs. 'Another attack, another retreat, then we came out of the line again. It was a Thursday; I had some free time in the afternoon and I'd sat down to write you a letter. That was the treat I'd been promising myself if – ' he corrected – 'when, we got back, but I'd only just started when the MO sent a runner to find me. A staff car had turned up in camp, and the officer wanted to see me. It was Douglas Caister. We were in the same election in College – at Eton – I used to see him from time to time at the Club. He came over and put his hand on my shoulder, his face very serious as he said, "Warminster, I'm afraid I've some bad news for you."'

Leo's eyes lifted to mine, 'I thought at once it was you – though God knows how Caister could possibly have known that. Then he went on, "It's your boy, he was wounded in this last show, and he's pretty bad, I'm afraid." ' I shivered, although the night was warm. 'Turnbull, Francis' Colonel, had passed the information on to Divisional HQ – and told them I was out there too, with a field ambulance. Caister tracked down my whereabouts, and as he'd been coming in the same direction he made a diversion to try and find me. He gave me the position of the casualty clearing station where Francis was. It was only twenty kilometres away.'

I whispered, 'I didn't realize you were so close.'

'It isn't that surprising. After all, we were both in the same Division, Francis and I. Curious, since it's a Highland Division and neither of us are Highlanders. It was pure chance in my case: they needed reinforcements when I went out, but Francis – ' He paused before saying calmly, 'Perhaps it was the pull of the Auld Alliance. He was wholly French, after all. Caister said he was sorry he couldn't take me down himself, only he'd gone out of his way already, but he'd brought me a pass. He said, "You'll want to try and get to him, of course, Warminster." And I did.' The level tone of his voice altered a fraction as he said, 'I wanted to go to him. I'd promised – her that he would be as my son, but I hadn't been much of a father to him. I thought, this, at least, I could do. Caister suggested I borrow a horse, but we'd lost so many of ours already, there were none to spare. So one of the men found me a bicycle.'

'I didn't know you could ride a bicycle.'

'I can't. Or rather, I couldn't – I suppose I can now.' His voice dropped. 'You learn so many things in wartime. I kept coming off at first, but you get the hang of it in the end, it's only a question of keeping one's feet going round and round. The pavé is rather bumpy, but being further back at least it wasn't smashed up by shells. So I cycled.

354

'It was a strange journey. I recalled travelling through France before his birth. I didn't know then – Such high hopes I had for my unborn son – I was sure it would be a boy. He'd go into the army and make up for my failure. Then he was born, and I learnt that he wasn't my son at all, and my hopes were dashed. But as I pedalled that infernal machine, I thought, no, they weren't dashed. He *did* join the army, he's fought bravely, been out there three years, most of it in the front line. Caister had said, "You must be proud of him, Warminster," and I was, at last I was. I thought, if only I can get there in time I'll tell him so. I knew he was dying: Caister had made it quite clear, but I kept thinking, if only I can get to him, at least he won't die alone.

'That damned pavé. I had a puncture after about ten kilometres. I walked on some distance, pushing it – there was hardly any traffic. Then an ambulance car came up behind and offered me a lift. It turned out he was going to the CCS, so I threw the bicycle into the ditch and climbed up beside him. I was so relieved that I'd be in time after all. The CCS was in a former school. He dropped me off outside and I ran in. The sister was just coming out of the ward. I shouted, "Sister – Captain Quinham – he's my son, I'm his father – " Then I saw her face. He'd died half an hour before I arrived.'

I sat shaking, but Leo wasn't looking at me. He stared instead at the fountain, at the bronze boy, tarnished and green, at the dolphin's gaping mouth, empty now.

'His body had already been prepared for burial. She was apologetic, but she knew from my RAMC badge that I'd understand.' He turned to look at me again. 'There's no time for the dead, out there – the living must come first. The War Office had already been notified, the funeral was to be the following morning. They gave me something to eat and then found me a spare bunk in the men's quarters. I was very tired, but I didn't sleep: I couldn't stop thinking. I thought of you, and of Flora – and I thought of her, his mother. Over the years I've learnt not to think of her, but I couldn't help it that night. I kept remembering her face after he was born. She was so frightened of me, and I vowed I would never get angry like that with a woman again.'

He paused a fraction before going on in a low voice, 'I scarcely slept that night. I'd never expected to feel such grief, but he was still so young, and, in a curious way, since I'd seen him that time out there I'd thought of him as a comrade.'

Fighting back tears I told Leo, 'He did say the same about you.'

'Did he? I'm glad of that, because I felt guilt, too. I hadn't ever been a father to him in the true sense. I've understood that since Flora was born.

'The funeral was very early. They wheeled his coffin out under the Union Jack, and the Padre came to speak to me – then I saw that he was a Catholic priest. He told me, "Your son received extreme unction before he died." So Francis had entered his mother's Church at the end. She would have been glad of that.

'I stood at the graveside and watched his body being lowered into the mud of France. It was raining, raining heavily.' He lifted his head. 'Because of that rain I returned to the CCS – I hoped that they might have a piece of mackintosh sheeting, there's always some lying around. And then I recalled that I hadn't thanked the sister. She started to say, "He died peacefully," then her eyes dropped to my badge and she simply added, "more peacefully than many do." I thanked her again and turned to go, then just as I was leaving she called me back, "Sergeant, I have your son's last effects in my bunk. I was going to send them off today, but the way things are at present it would be safer if you took them with you now – unless, did he have a wife?" I said, "Not any longer, Sister." "I'll give them to you, then. It's only a small parcel." When she came back and put it into my hand she said, "They may be of comfort to you."

'I asked round and got a lift partway. Then I began to walk the rest, but the rain was still heavy and the mackintosh sheet kept sliding off my shoulder. Eventually, not too far from where the ambulance had dropped me, I found a YMCA hut. Just a small one, but it was shelter, so I decided to have a cup of tea, and perhaps hang around for another lift.

'I sat down with my mug, but it was too hot to drink, so I opened the parcel. His watch was there, the one I'd given him on his twenty-first birthday. I was surprised he'd kept it with him. Surprised – and touched. Then there were several photographs. One of them was of her, of Jeanette. She was – very beautiful. It was strange to sit there, in that place, looking at her face after so long. There was a wedding ring, too – I wondered if it was hers.'

'No,' I interrupted, 'it were Miss Annabel's, she gave it back to him.'

'Ah, I see. He'd also been carrying a missal, a new one – and tucked inside it were several letters he'd received. He'd kept them, the way one does. Then I found that he'd written several letters, too, and been carrying them around with him when he was hit. Men do that sometimes, in expectation of what may happen – what did happen.

'One letter was addressed to Annabel, a second to a captain in the French Army – and then I came to the third letter and saw written on it the name "Warminster" – and I supposed it was for me. I had an absurd hope that he had made his peace with me after his death – and then I saw that it was not my name, but yours. Not a letter to me, but to my wife.'

He reached into the pocket of his dinner jacket and held it out. 'Here it is, Amy.' He stood up. 'I will leave you to read it.' I sat with it in my hand while he walked over to the fountain, took out a cigar, lit it, and turned away so that his back was towards me.

I stared down at the envelope for a moment, then with trembling hands I lifted the flap and took out the letter.

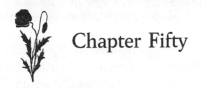

Chapter Fifty

BEF
March 17th, 1918

Ma chère Aimée

I told you last month that when this war was over, then I would come back and fight him for you, but if you're reading this letter you'll know I've finally lost that fight. I hope to God you never will read this and yet I can already see you holding it in your hand, with your pansy-soft eyes brimming with tears – because I think it's going to happen. I knew it even while you held me in your arms that last time. Other men have told me that they knew, and later events proved them right. I suspect that before long a shell is going to come over with my name on it. I'm sorry, Amy, because I know you'll be terribly upset – at least, I'm not sorry about your being upset, I want you to grieve for me – but I'm sorry for myself, because I wanted to live. I wanted the rest of my life. But above all, I wanted you.

Still, it's no use being morbid, Amy, even in an after-death letter. At least you'll have the baby to comfort you. I hope it's a son for your sake; and do you realize, he'll be Lord Quinham in my place? So it'll all come right in the end. And what could I offer you if I lived? Love – certainly, love – as much as you could ever want. You know that, you've known it for more than a year now, but I couldn't offer you respectable marriage: the Church and the law both forbid that. Annabel is divorcing me, and perhaps the old man would have divorced you, but a man may not marry his father's wife, and in law that's what you are. My dearest stepmama.

This past year I've been blaming him for marrying you, and so cutting us off from each other for ever, with only the prospect of an illicit union left to us – but that wasn't very fair, was it? The person I should blame is myself. If I had not seduced you, then he would not have married you. Finally I admit that it was my fault.

I told you once that I'd vowed never to feel guilt, but I realize now that guilt is the inevitable consequence of the human condition. No, I didn't think that one up for myself, Amy – it's not my style, is it? The priest said it after I'd made my confession. I've done it at last, I've joined Mama's Church. I should have had the guts to do it years ago. Anyway, it's done now, so perhaps I've made one woman happy, at least. Though God knows if she'll know. I suppose He does. I never thought about God before, but I do now; He's the only chap offering me any hope, and eternal life is a pretty good offer. Though they say there's no love-making in heaven: I'll miss that. But at present I think I'll take anything that's going, and be grateful.

This is a rambling letter, Amy. The priest told me to write it, to beg your forgiveness for the sins I committed against you, but I know I didn't have to do that, because you've forgiven me already. You always do, because you love me. I think those four short words you said to me last month gave me more comfort than all the words the priest spoke on the love of God. And the feel of your soft lips on mine – that was my absolution. I suppose what I've just written is blasphemy – but the priest assures me that the Church can cope with sinners like me.

I've got to write another letter now, to Annabel; a much harder letter, that one. You are carrying hope for the future, whereas I destroyed hers. But I must write it. Let me go and do it now, before I finish yours, then I've got something to look forward to afterwards. Writing to you is the icing on the cake, to be saved till the last!

Later.

It's written. It isn't good enough, but then I never was good enough for her, I see that now. I should have thrown my lot in with you in the first place: you've been a sinner, too, so we understand each other.

I want to thank you, Amy, because you've given me so much – especially this last year. I couldn't have kept going if it hadn't been for the thought of you, back there at Eston. You've been my treat, my reward for good conduct. Whenever I got my head down in one of those stinking dugouts, I'd make it all bearable by closing my eyes and thinking of you. I'd lie there, remembering your face as you played with the children, your voice as you spoke to Flora, your eyes as you looked at me. When things got really bad I'd pretend I was back in your sitting room asleep, and that when I woke up I'd see your face in the lamplight – just as I woke up and saw it on my last leave. Oh, Amy, I do love you, I love you so much.

Amy, I tried to write a letter to Flora, for you to give to her one day, but I couldn't do it. So would you tell her, please, when she's old enough to understand. Tell her that I was her true father, and that I loved her very much. I've written to Uncle Jean-Paul as well. I regret losing my temper with him last time I was in Paris. We're none of us perfect, and he is my father, after all.

Now I've written my letters I don't know what to do with them, but it occurs to me that I don't need to do anything, because they'll be sent back to Eston anyway, with the old man being listed as next-of-kin. So, Amy, would you send off the other two for me? I'm not even sure of her address now. Uncle Jean-Paul's is on the envelope – and would you send him a photograph of Flora, too? He always asks about her, and I think she's very like Maman was at the same age, so he'd like to see it. Perhaps one day you might even take her to France to meet him. It's asking a lot of you, Amy, I know, but then I always did ask a lot of you – and you always gave it, my generous Amy.

Aimée, je t'aime, toujours.
Your loving Frank.

I sat holding that letter, his last words to me, and I was overwhelmed with guilt. Oh, Frank, I did love you too.

Then the man in front of me began to turn round. He came and stood before me. 'Have you read it?'

'Aye.'

His voice was quite even as he replied, 'Yes, so have I.' And for the first time I realized that the flap of the envelope had been loose.

But Frank had written it to me, only to me. I exclaimed, 'You shouldn't have done that!'

'No, I should not. But like Eve I gave in to temptation, and like her, I have been punished. I sat there in that grimy canteen looking at the photograph of my faithless first wife – then I read her son's letter, and learnt that my second wife had been unfaithful, too.'

And only then did I realize the true nightmare. I looked down at the letter again: 'While you held me in your arms that last time', 'the feel of your soft lips on mine' – I looked up. He was watching me. I cried, 'No! No!'

He gestured to the letter in my hand, 'It is rather more convincing than Desdemona's handkerchief, I think.' He turned sideways with one of his awkward, lurching movements, and staring down into the murky fountain pool, recited deliberately:

'Roses have thorns, and silver fountains mud;
Clouds and eclipses stain both moon and sun – '

He turned back to face me directly as he completed,

'And loathsome canker lives in sweetest bud.'

Again I cried, 'No, no!'

He said, 'I knew that you loved him, but I did not imagine he would ever come to love you. I relied on his indifference – I was a fool. After all, I loved you, why shouldn't he do the same? And when he did, how could you help but respond?' He paused before adding, damningly, 'Especially now, when you had begun to desire the – sensual pleasures of the marriage bed.'

I tried to interrupt but he wouldn't allow me. 'No, Amy, it's not you who is to blame, but myself. Perhaps I made too many excuses for you.' Watching my face he asked again, 'Did you sin? Or did you merely love too well?'

359

I exclaimed, 'No – adultery, tis a sin!'

He looked down at me, his eyes dark in the shadow of the Garland rose as he answered, 'Yes, I think it is, because it is a betrayal, and all betrayal is a sin.'

'But I didn't – '

He interrupted me, quoting again. '*And the feel of your soft lips on mine.* Did you kiss him, Amy?'

'Aye, I did. I kissed him goodbye.'

'Just as you did me. But then, you are generous – generous with your kisses. Even as I came back today you tried to kiss me.' His tone dropped. 'As Judas did.' I began to shake. His voice was almost gentle as he said, 'Don't be frightened, Amy, I won't hurt you. I'm not angry with you. I told you, I vowed never to let myself feel anger again. The fault was not yours, but mine. I asked too much of you, and so you tried too hard to give it. You even tried to give me love.'

I cried out, 'I do love thee!' And for a moment he wavered, and everything hung in the balance.

Then he said, 'I asked *her* once, in this very place. I brought her down here, to this fountain, and I asked her, "Do you love me, Jeanette? Tell me that you love me." And she answered, "Yes." But she lied.

'At least you had the grace to maintain your pretence, and for that I am grateful. But you needn't pretend any longer. It will not be necessary. My folly is at an end.'

He took out his matches, and I watched him relight his cigar. He drew on it several times before telling me, 'I will, of course, acknowledge your son as my heir – just as I did hers.'

The nightmare deepened. 'But Jackie – he be *your* son.'

He paused to study the glowing tip of his cigar. 'Yes, I suppose that may even be true. You were always more generous than she was, Amy. That's why I loved you more. So much more that I didn't want to let it go. I sat there at that grubby table with his letter in my hand and thought, why shouldn't I continue to love her? After all, you knew what she was when you married her – *she* made no pretence. And he's dead now, while I am still alive – '

I heard the shadow of regret in his voice as he explained, 'I did try to be sensible, but it was quite pointless. Francis was wrong when he said he'd lost the fight. He's won it now, because he's destroyed my trust in you. And without trust, there can be no love.' Bending over, he stubbed the cigar out on the marble lip of the pool, then he tossed the butt into the fountain before turning back to me and asking, 'Shall we go in now? It's getting rather late.'

Stunned and shaking I followed him across the lawn and up the steps. I couldn't speak – what could I say? And he remained silent, too, until we reached the white gate that led out of the rose garden. Then he said to me, 'Naturally I will continue to offer you the protection of my name. I assume that you will not wish to leave Eston now that Francis is dead. In any case, there are

360

our daughters. I am sure you will agree that for their sakes we must maintain a façade of marital accord – in public. But in private we shall, of course, go our separate ways. Good night.'

He quickened his pace, but I followed him up to the side door of the house and through to the hall. 'But, Leo – '

'Goodnight.' He opened the door of his library and went in. Nella slipped through behind him, but as I moved forward he closed it shut against me.

I went up to my room and threw myself down on the bed. I couldn't even cry: I was beyond tears. I remembered Grammer, spurning me in the workhouse, but this was worse, much, much worse: because once he had loved me, and now there was nothing, not even anger.

I went to fetch Jackie; he'd be needing me. Taking him back downstairs I put him to my breast. I gazed down at his pale, downy hair, his round blue eyes – oh Jackie, even you have betrayed me – then I pulled myself up. Jackie was *Leo's* son; I *hadn't* committed adultery, I hadn't been unfaithful. But what was infidelity? I had listened to Frank when he told me of his love, I had held him, I had kissed him, I had told him I loved him.

In the morning I decided to go to Leo; to plead, to explain. He would be angry, but I'd endured his anger before; I could endure it again. He'd breakfasted early and Mr Tims said he was in the library. I tapped on the door and went straight in; he was sitting at his desk reading. He stood up and looked down at me; but there was no anger in his face, only indifference.

I whispered, 'Leo, that letter – '

He walked right past me and went to the door. He put his hand on the knob before speaking. 'We have said all that needs to be said. I do not wish to discuss the matter further. I will not intrude into your private rooms and I would ask the same consideration from you in return.' He opened the door and stood there waiting. I walked towards him and then stopped, to look up into his face. If he was still angry there was hope – but as I looked up into his eyes there was nothing there: only the reflection of myself, grown very tiny. He turned his head aside – and even that had gone.

And so it was. We dined together, and I tried to talk to him, but when he spoke it was only in front of the servants, and then always of the weather and the prospects for the harvest. Sometimes I took the children down to him, rather than letting Ellen do it; then Flora, my loyal Flora, would try to pull me with them, but he simply waited for me to go away. I went up to the nursery at the times when I knew he'd be there. He played with his daughters, but when I tried to join in he'd say, 'I think your son needs you.' And Jackie, sensing my distress, would be crying – and demanding me the more. Leo didn't look at Jackie: he didn't look at me.

Ellen knew something was wrong; I would see her small frown. Once she said, 'My lady, when a man has been away at the war tis a wife's duty to humour him.' I didn't answer, I couldn't answer. Looking down at Jackie in my arms, she said, 'Perhaps you should leave Master Quinham in the nursery with me while his lordship's at home.' But there was no point – and besides, I needed the comfort of him in my arms.

I began to wonder if Ellen was doing sums in her head. Frank had come over on leave so soon after Leo had left; Jackie had been born late. Were they all wondering, all the women in Eston?

Only Clara seemed to understand. She didn't know what was wrong, but she knew something was. 'My lady, men can be difficult when they've been at the war.' Without looking at me she said, 'Even if – even if there's been another woman, it doesn't mean – ' She broke off, uncertain how to go on.

I was so grateful that she wasn't blaming me, but I had to put her right. 'No, tisn't that. He wouldn't never do anything of that sort.'

She sighed, 'Well, they say as the war'll be over afore too long, now the Americans have come. Then, when he's home all the time I be sure as things'll be different.'

Mr Beeston came to ask about Jackie's christening. 'Now his lordship's home on leave, perhaps *you* could speak to him, Lady Warminster?'

So I spoke to Leo at dinner. The dessert was already on the table before I plucked up the courage to ask him whether Jackie should be christened during his leave. And then I only managed to do it because if I hadn't asked then, it would have been too late. He replied, 'If you wish it.'

'Mebbe the day afore you go back?'

'The Saturday? Yes, if you wish it.'

'I did tell you when I wrote, I've asked Mr Selby to be godfather, and I wondered if Albie could be the other. Jim, his brother, can stand proxy for him, Mr Beeston said. Then I thought of asking Miss Beeston to be godmother, she's been main kind.' I waited, but he only nodded in acknowledgement. Scarcely daring, I asked, 'And – will you come?'

He looked at me, his mismatched grey eyes expressionless. 'If you wish it.' Then he put down his fruit knife, dropped his napkin on the table and stood up. 'Is that all?'

'Aye,' I whispered.

I dressed Jackie in Rose's christening gown; there'd been no time to make another. I was so nervous, as I waited for Leo: suppose he wouldn't even go to the church with me? But he announced, 'We will follow the same procedure as before, except that I gather we should not use the motor.'

'No, tis because of the petrol restrictions.'

So went down in the carriage, with Ellen and Jackie. Beat came with Jim, but she'd said they could only stay for a couple of hours. I was relieved: I didn't want her sharp eyes to spot how Leo felt about me now.

By the time we arrived at the church, Lady Burton and Cynthia were already waiting. When Leo and I went over to greet them, Lady Burton drew me into her violet-scented embrace. 'How *proud* you must be, my dear.' Releasing me, she seized Leo's hand in both of hers. 'George told me, your dear mother would have been so pleased – and your father so proud.'

Leo began to lead Lady Burton away and Cynthia waited until they were out of earshot before drawling, 'I suspect that from what one used to hear of that old tyrant, nothing less than the VC would have satisfied him. But still, I do think it's rather fine of darling Lord Warminster. George says it'll be gazetted soon.'

'I'm afraid I don't understand,' I said.

Her eyebrows rose. 'Hasn't he told you yet? Oh dear, trust Mama to let the cat out of the bag.'

'Please – tell me.'

She bent low to whisper in my ear, 'Your gallant husband has won the MM. He did splendidly in that wretched retreat, George said. Come along, Amy dear – they're all waiting for us.'

We went back to the house and cut the cake Mrs Carter had made. When everyone had their glasses of champagne in their hands Leo proposed a toast, 'To my wife.' Then turning to where Ellen held Jackie in all his finery, 'And to my son.'

He behaved so well all afternoon, he even smiled at me whenever it was necessary, and I began to hope a little. I actually enjoyed dinner that night, since I'd invited Mr Selby and Dr Matthews and the Beestons, so Leo talked quite normally. They referred to the medal – Lady Burton had told everyone, of course. Leo was embarrassed by their congratulations. 'It was for the whole team. I was only named as the recipient because I was the NCO.'

Mr Selby said quietly, 'In charge.'

'Yes – ' Leo broke off, flushing.

Mr Selby smiled. 'Exactly.'

Nerving up my courage I told him, 'I'm very proud of you, Leo.'

'Thank you, Amy.' Then he asked a question about the estate, and he didn't seem to mind when Mr Selby and Mr Beeston included me in the conversation. He'd been so polite today, he'd even been using my name, so my hopes grew a little. Besides, I couldn't bear the thought of him going back to France, back into danger, without my kissing him, touching him, perhaps holding him in my arms; or at least giving him something, even if it were only physical release.

That evening, after I'd heard him finish in his dressing room I put Jackie in his cradle. I let down my hair and brushed it until it shone. Then I gathered all my courage and went through into Leo's bedroom. The light was on; he was reading in bed. He looked up and put down his book, but he didn't take off his spectacles. 'Yes, what is it?'

'I know you don't love me any more,' I said, 'only I thought, with you being a man, and seeing as I be your wife – ' He didn't move, his face didn't even change as he sat there. I stumbled on. 'I wouldn't speak, or even cuddle you, if you didn't want. You could just, just – ' I couldn't go on.

He spoke at last. 'No, thank you, Amy.'

I whispered, 'But – a man do have his needs.'

He was silent for a moment before replying, 'Living celibate for as long as I did, I learnt how to satisfy my own needs. I find that preferable, now, to playing the hypocrite.' I remembered him saying before, 'I decided that . . . the act of love should not take place except where there is affection and trust.' And now he felt neither of those things. Picking up his book again he said in a low voice, 'Go back to bed, Amy.'

Next morning he left. Mr Tims opened the door, then went outside, leaving us to say our goodbyes in private. Leo turned to me, 'Naturally I will ensure that a letter arrives regularly each week, as before.'

I looked up hopefully, 'You'll write?'

'I don't wish the servants to talk. I would be grateful if in return, you would send me regular news of the children.'

I said eagerly, 'Aye, o' course I will. I'll write regular – '

'Only with news of the children. To write – otherwise would merely cause pain to us both. Besides, what is the point?' He shouldered his pack and walked away, ungainly in his uniform. 'Goodbye, Amy.'

I ran after him. 'Leo – ' But he continued walking down the steps to where Mr Tims stood beside the dogcart, blinking in the sunlight.

'Leo – ' He turned round then, but only because the servants were there. I came up to him, but he didn't move. My voice faltered, and in the end all I said was, 'Do 'ee be sure and change thy socks if they do get wet.'

His reply was quiet. 'If you wish it.' He threw his pack up into the dog cart, and jumped up after it. Jim shook the reins and they rolled off.

I stood watching until the bend in the drive hid them from view. Then I stayed listening, straining my ears until the last clip-clopping of Bessie's hooves died away.

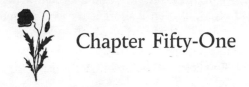# Chapter Fifty-One

I had loved two men, and lost them both.

I went back upstairs, back to my bedroom. I couldn't face anyone. I flung myself down on my bed, that very bed where he'd come to me and held me – and loved me. 'Affection – and trust.' For he *had* trusted me, once; but now he trusted me no longer. Then I forced myself to face the cold reality. Love, yes, but never trust. If he had trusted me, he would not have opened that letter. Although Frank must have hoarded my letters to him – the ones that Leo had found – there had been nothing in those letters to arouse his suspicions. They had expressed only affection and concern, and he already knew I felt those for Frank. Yet still he'd chosen to open that letter.

I stood up, stiff as an old woman, and went to my dressing table to take out the letter, Frank's last letter. I read it again. And as I read it, it was as though he were in the room with me, speaking to me. Oh, Frank, Frank – I loved you – forgive me, forgive me. The hot tears of grief and shame burnt my cheeks.

It was Jackie who brought me back to myself. I could not hide here grieving, I had children – a baby, needing my breast. Besides, soon it would be time for the harvest: I could not stay here weeping. I folded Frank's letter to put it away again, and saw beside it the other letter – Leo's letter of love that had taken me to France to find him. Now I took that out and read it once more, my heart heavy and hopeless, until I came to those words of his: 'When I am rational again, then I shall calmly burn these pages.' And as I read them I understood at last that he'd never intended to destroy it: that had been his farewell letter too, written before he went back into danger, written in the hope that if he were killed it would somehow find its way back to me. Oh Leo, Leo! I began to cry again, because I knew that he carried no letter next to his heart now.

I went along to the nursery to feed Jackie, then I took him down to the estate office. There was an hour before I had to leave for church and England was still at war, her people needing bread. Picking up my pen I began to calculate the harvest payments.

I wrote to Leo that evening. Only news of the children, as he'd commanded; I did not dare disobey. But I wrote very fully of what they'd done today, and I wrote of Jackie, Jackie who was his son, even if Leo would not believe it. I took my letter down to the hall table so it would catch the first post, then I went up to bed.

I was very busy these days: so much to prepare for the harvest, so many questions to answer, arrangements to be made for the soldiers we'd been promised – but however busy I was, Leo was always in my mind. Had he gone back to the Front? Was he still angry with me now? He'd said he would write – if only his letter would come. And after all, even a short letter would begin 'Dear Amy', and then I could start to hope a little.

It arrived sooner than I'd dared to expect, and it was written in ink. My heart thudding, I took it upstairs to open it. There was just one sheet.

18th July 1918

Your missive of the 14th instant has been received and the contents therein duly noted.

L.A.H. Warminster.

That was all. The small green shoots of hope withered and died. But I wrote back at once telling him all that the children had done and said. Then I signed it 'Your obedient and loving wife, Amy.' For though he no longer loved me, I loved him, and always would.

The next day I read over breakfast that British and French troops had launched an attack on the Germans. Among the British divisions attacking was the 51st. I trembled with fear.

The weather was fine, the harvest begun, but I never ceased waiting for that telegram. When, instead, his letter arrived, exactly a week after the previous one, I began to shudder with relief. There was only that same single sentence, written now in pencil. But at least he had been alive to write it, and the news from France was getting better every day. By the end of August our troops were advancing – and in Eston our harvest had been safely gathered in. We went to church to thank God for his bounty: we'd been lucky, because a couple of days later the weather turned very wet. One day hailstones fell as big as marbles, so any crops still in the fields were spoilt. In the garden the golden rose had come into bloom a second time, as she always did, but now her last petals turned brown and sodden in the cold, wet weather. As I stood looking at her ruined beauty I felt the tears of loss threatening; but I blinked them away and went in to write my weekly letter to Leo.

As I opened his reply I saw at once that it was more than just the one sentence; I felt a moment of excitement, but only a moment, because he'd simply added that he'd arranged for Flora to attend the small private day school at Tilton. She was to go in the mornings only for the first term, and Dora was to take her and bring her back. That was all.

I disobeyed him by taking Flora myself the first week, to ensure she was happily settled. I confessed to this in my weekly report, and wondered if he might be annoyed – but he didn't even bother to comment in his reply. Just the same cold sentence, 'Your missive of the . . . ' It was no use.

Albie went back to France in the middle of September, and soon after yet another telegram came to the village. John Davies, who everybody called 'Blinker', had died of pneumonia. Clara was crying as she told me. 'Poor old

Blinker, he sat on the bench behind me at school, and I used to hold my slate sideways, so he could copy my sums. He wasn't so quick on the uptake, wasn't Blinker, and he'd get the ruler most days, but he allus had a smile on his face. Blinker, he didn't never get out o' bed the wrong side of a morning.' I went to see Blinker's wife, and we wept together. Eighteen men had been lost now from Eston – when would it ever end?

But when I went up to the Home Farm late in October Mr Arnott told me the officer had just been round to check on the prisoners, 'And he said as we've really got thic Jerries on the run, me lady. It won't be much longer now.' He sounded so certain that I felt dizzy with relief; only the weight of my baby in my arms kept me steady. Mr Arnott reached out and tickled Jackie under the chin. 'Tis time your Dad came home and gave you a hand to sort out all them females you got nagging you in your nursery!' Jackie gazed up at him intently and Mr Arnott laughed. 'He's looking at me just like his lordship does – it don't half stand out, now his eyes 'a gone grey.'

I looked down at my son – and so they had. I hadn't even noticed: the colour had been changing so gradually.

Mr Arnott continued, 'My Mary's got the kettle on, if you'd like to step inside for a warm while I fetch them there plaguey bits o' paper.'

As I followed him inside I lifted Jackie to my cheek and whispered, 'Clever boy – clever, clever boy.'

It ended in November. Mrs Chandler came up to tell us, panting and with a stitch in her side. 'The message has come to the post office from Salisbury. Tis over, my lady, tis over. My John, my Horace – they'll be coming home – they're safe.' She began to sob. Mr Tims almost ran to tell Mrs Carter, and I went rushing to the estate office, 'Mr Selby, tis over. The war's over. Leo can come home!' I began to cry.

Mr Tims fetched a bottle of port up from the cellar and we all drank a toast to our brave soldiers. Jim drained his glass and then pulled himself upright. 'I'd best get back to the stables, my lady, thic news won't get the tack cleaned – or bring back my leg.'

Mrs Chandler didn't stay long either. She was very busy as several familes had gone down with the influenza so she had to get back to the village.

Mr Beeston arrived next: 'Should I ring the church bells, Lady Warminster? What do you think?'

'Aye, you ring 'em, Mr Beeston, for surely tis a great victory. But you'd best wait till after milking; Mr Arnott's very short-handed, what wi' the flu and all.' I put my hand on his arm. 'You maun be so relieved, knowing your Cyril'll be home again afore long.'

'I – I – ' He could barely get the words out. 'Lucinda and I can scarcely believe it.' There were tears in his eyes. 'Thank God – thanks be to God. But so many others will not be returning. We must never forget them, and their sacrifice.'

I said quietly, 'No, Mr Beeston, we won't.' That night, I lay and wept for Frank and all the other men who'd died. But in the morning I woke and said to Jackie, 'Thy Dada will be coming home soon.' And my heart was light from the lifting of that terrible burden.

The influenza was a specially bad type that winter and with some folk it turned to double pneumonia. Dr Matthews was grey-faced with exhaustion. Both his cook and his housemaid had fallen ill, so I asked Mrs Carter if she'd mind cooking extra portions to be taken down for the doctor. She offered to go down herself, every morning, so I suggested she stay there all day, since the doctor never knew when he'd be able to snatch a bite, and he needed to keep his strength up. Then Mabs and Lily Arnott both took to their beds, so I sent Sal upstairs to see to them and went into the kitchen myself, with Jesse to give me a hand with the washing up. That is, when Jesse wasn't needed in the stables, because Jim went down next, and Clara had her hands full nursing him. I worried about the children, but everyone in the nursery stayed healthy.

It seemed to be the young married women who were catching it most. Granny Withers and Maud Winterslow came up to the house, both very spry, and said, 'There's some folk not getting a bite to eat these days. You'd better get us organized, my lady, like in the harvest.' So we had teams of cooks and nurses and delivered food and medicine to families where the mother was in bed, and we did manage to get through our latest trial.

As Christmas came and folk began to get better, I said to Dr Matthews, 'It seems as if we've been lucky in Eston.'

'Yes, I think we have.'

I sighed. 'So many folk have been a-dying in other places. Tis terrible – after what they've already been through in the war.'

'I'm sure the war has something to do with this epidemic, too. Despite the Government's rationing programme many people have not eaten properly for more than two years now.'

'No one's gone short on this estate.'

He replied, 'Yes, and it's you we have to thank for that, Lady Warminster.'

Over in Tilton more than a dozen people died, but we were luckier in Eston and, by the end of December everybody who'd taken the flu was on the mend. But someone *from* Eston had died. Bob Wilson had been killed back in the Somme battle; now his eldest son, Toby, had caught the infection and died in hospital in Bristol. Mrs Wilson had been so relieved, thinking her Toby was safe, with the war having finished just before he was due to go out to France. But now she'd lost both her eldest son and her husband.

She was with Toby when he died, and she came straight up to the house the day she got back, and asked to see me. She wanted to bring his body back to be buried in Eston. 'You see, my lady, I'll never be able to visit my Bob's grave, but if – '

'Don't you worry, Mrs Wilson, we'll see to it for you. He'll be buried here in the churchyard, where thee canst take flowers to him, regular.'

Mr Beeston went to escort the coffin back from Bristol, and we waited at the station for the train. So many of us had lost our men and not seen them buried, that now it was as if young Toby belonged to us all. And he did. He'd been born and brought up in Eston, and worked on the Home Farm before he'd been called up. Everybody had liked Toby, he'd always been so cheerful and so willing.

Now his coffin was lifted off on to the waggon from the Home Farm, which Mr Arnott drove himself through the village. Mrs Wilson stood waiting at the door of her cottage, wearing her best black dress. 'I'll watch over him, this night.'

In the morning the soldiers came from the camp beyond Tilton, with the gun carriage. He'd died a soldier and he must be buried as one. At the church the sergeant barked out his orders and the firing party lined up outside, standing to attention while the six bearers carried the coffin into the church.

'Lord, thou hast been our refuge . . . The days of our age are three score years and ten . . .'

But Toby had been only just eighteen, and the war had already ended. Why, why . . . ?

We came out blinking into the daylight and made our way towards the empty grave.

'Man that is born of a woman hath but a short time to live . . . He cometh up, and is cut down, like a flower . . .'

Mrs Wilson bent her shapeless body forwards and the earth dropped from her hand. She was shaking and for a moment, seemed about to topple over the edge – then her brother tightened his grip on her arm and pulled her back.

'For as much as it hath pleased Almighty God of his great mercy to take unto himself the soul of our dear brother here departed . . .'

I shivered. It was cold, so cold, the day of Toby's funeral.

After Mr Beeston gave the closing words, it was very still at the graveside, with only the soft hiccupping of Toby's sister's sobs and the twitter of the birds. Then suddenly a hoarse shout rang out from the sergeant. Another shout and the firing party formed themselves into two lines, raised their rifles – and at the final command fired three volleys into the air. All the birds fell silent, and into that silence came the plaintive wail of the bugle, saying its farewell.

More shouted orders: then the firing party fixed their bayonets, shouldered their rifles and marched off, two by two. The pallbearers stepped forward and began to pick up the spent cartridges. I glanced at Clara, who looked back at me, equally surprised.

Mrs Wilson seemed dazed, but she still said proudly, 'He were a soldier.'

But as we walked back together I said to Clara, 'Why fire guns now, when he's back home? And couldn't they have left the cartridges, instead of going scrabbling for them like that?'

Writing to Leo that evening, I broke his rule. I wrote of the funeral, of Mrs

Wilson, and Toby's little sister crying, and the birds all frightened by the guns – and the men picking up the spent cartridges. 'Couldn't they have left them? It was a solemn occasion, and it did seem so undignified.'

He sent back his usual two lines, but underneath he'd added, 'I have sent my condolences to Mrs Wilson. As to your query, it is usual for us bearers to retrieve the spent cartridge cases, so that they can be refilled and used again.'

'Us bearers' – how many times had Leo carried out for burial the bodies of young men cut down and killed – cut down like flowers, even before they'd completed their first score of years. Cut down as Frank had been. I wept for him, and knew that in Eston that night other women were weeping too: weeping for their sons, their fathers, their husbands.

Please, God, bring my husband safely back to me. But then I rememberrd that he was not coming back to me. To his daughters, his home, his roses, yes; but not to me.

Yet in the morning I looked again at that extra sentence he'd written, written to me. Perhaps after all, there was some hope. So when I wrote again, I wrote a proper letter, more than just news of the children, and waited anxiously for his reply. It came. 'Your missive of the 3rd inst. has been received and the information *regarding the children* duly noted.' That was all, but the message was clear. Next week I wrote only of the children.

But still, underneath, I could not cease hoping. Now the war had ended, men were arriving home on leave, and soon it would be Leo's turn. Then, perhaps – I did not dare to give shape to my hope even in my thoughts but I knew it must have been there because of the despair I felt when Annabel crushed it.

She was demobilized at the end of January, and dropped in at Eston on her way to Bath. She referred to Leo, of course, saying that demobilization would be late for him, since he was in the RAMC, 'And there's still too much work for them to do.'

'But he'll be home on leave soon. They've all been coming.'

She looked at me oddly. 'Didn't he even bother to tell you? His home leave fell due a month ago, but he decided to turn it down.'

It was like a blow on the face. 'No – surely he couldn't have done that?'

'It is extremely unusual – but you don't look completely surprised.'

'I – I – Frank, he wrote me a letter, for after he'd died – and Leo read it.' Her face went very still. I whispered, 'He shouldn't have read it. It weren't addressed to him.'

'Maybe not, but he is your husband. Francis should never have written to you.'

'Twas only a letter asking me to forgive him – like the letter he wrote to you.'

'Was it? Just like mine?'

'I dussent know what was in yours.'

'No, and I'm not going to tell you.' Her face twisted in pain, then she sat up straight. 'Whatever his faults, he died bravely, and I'm proud of him.' She drew

370

off her glove and held out her left hand. Her wedding ring shone golden on her finger. 'You see, I'm wearing it again. He was my husband.' Quietly she added, 'As Leonidas is yours.'

I whispered, 'He did say as he wouldn't be a proper husband to me any more – he'd just pretend, for the sake of the children. But to say no to his leave – ' I broke off, to ask pleadingly, 'Didn't he – couldn't you – ?'

'I'm sorry, Amy, I don't think there's anything I can do.' Her voice was more gentle now. 'You know yourself, Leonidas is a man who take things – very hard. I only wish for his sake that – ' She broke off, to ask instead, 'Is Flora upstairs? I'm only making a flying visit, and I do want to see her.'

Annabel left after tea. I sat on in the dark. I felt cold, so cold. I admitted that until now I'd kept on hoping – not that he would ever forgive me, but that if I really tried I'd eventually be able to win him back. But now it was too late. I had no stomach to fight any longer. I wouldn't have the courage to approach him and I knew he would never approach me: he never had before, and he wouldn't now.

Sitting there in the dark, I accepted the truth at last: my marriage had finally ended.

Chapter Fifty-Two

But I still had my duty to do. As long as Leo remained away I must act in his place, and I did. Mr Selby went down with a bout of bronchitis soon after Annabel's visit so I was busier than ever – and I was grateful for the extra work. I didn't want time to think. Deliberately, I immersed myself in the present because I couldn't bear to think of the future.

But one day in February it was the past that came to Eston. I didn't realize at first. I'd taken the account books up to the sitting room to work on them there, because while Mr Selby was away I'd decided to save coal by not lighting the fire in the office. I was at my desk, with Jackie sound asleep in his cradle by the fire when Mr Tims appeared, his forehead creased with uncertainty. 'My lady, Madame Balsan wishes to speak to you. Are you at home?'

'Yes, o' course,' I replied automatically, before wondering, Madame Balsan?

She came in, an elderly woman dressed all in black; her face was strained, her eyes anxiously watching me. 'Good day, milady.' She paused, searching for words, her accent very strong. 'I travel from France, this last night.'

France? A message from Leo?

'Milady, I would demand you a question, if you please.' She paused again before asking, 'Do you have affection for your husband?'

I panicked – she was all in black – Leo! I exclaimed, 'Be he ill? You've seen him – where is he? He's not – ?'

Her eyes closed, she seemed to sway. '*Grâce à Dieu.*'

I caught hold of her thin arm. 'Madame, tell me, I must go to him, where is he?'

'I – I ' She was fighting for words. 'I not – ' Quickly I changed to French. '*Madame, où est-il? Vous l'avez vu récemment?*'

She replied in the same language, 'Milady, I have not seen your husband for many years. I do not come from him. To the best of my knowledge, he is well. It is you who I have come to see.'

I was shaking with relief. Finally I remembered my manners and asked her to be seated. She sat down on the very edge of the sofa, her eyes on my face as she asked, 'Milady, did he, François, ever speak to you of his mother's maid, who had been her nurse?'

Thérèse. She was old Thérèse. I said quietly, 'Yes, yes he did.'

She looked relieved. 'I am she, Milady – and I have brought you a message.'

Shock caught hold of me again. 'From Frank – François?'

She shook her head. 'No, from her – from Madame la Comtesse de Warminster.'

'But that's me!' Then I realized who she meant, and I exclaimed, 'But she's dead!'

'Yes, milady, she is dead these nine years now, and I mourn her every day. But before she died she sent you a message.'

I stared at her, recalling the beautiful Lady Warminster who had come to Borrell school. 'But how did she know where to find me?'

'Where else would you be, but here at Eston, milady – at the house of your husband?'

I was still bewildered. 'But – how could she know he would marry *me*?'

Thérèse looked puzzled. 'She knew,' then she corrected herself, 'She *hoped*, that he would one day marry again. And so he did, he married you. She did not know you, milady, how could she?'

But she did, for it was she who had sent me to him – Leo's first wife, who had deceived him, lied to him, and then left him. Without intending to she had sent me to Eston, by telling me I must be a lady's maid when I grew up and now she was sending me a message, a message from the dead.

I gathered my wits together to listen to Thérèse. 'Milady, I have been a long time coming, I know. But you see, when François told me of milord's marriage he told me everything: of the little girl of his begetting and of how your marriage came about without your willing it. And so it seemed there was no use in my coming. But then later, François came to see me when he was in Paris and told me you had borne your husband a child – and so I began to hope a little. But I could not come then, because of the war.'

She paused, her eyes dropping from mine. 'Only – when he came next, he was so happy because he said, he loved you now. And you – you still felt towards him as you had done before.' I felt my cheeks grow hot as she added, 'So my hope died. But then,' her eyes lifted again, 'then he told me that although you loved him you were a good woman, who talked of duty and would not break the commandments – and my hope came alive once more.' She leant forward, watching my face intently. 'François believed that once the war was ended he would win you from your husband, to become his paramour, but, I thought, surely a woman who is so strong as to deny the man she loves whilst he is in danger, will not weaken when peace returns? Milady, tell me, I am right, am I not? Even if François had lived, you would not have left your husband?'

'No, Madame, I would not.'

'Of course not – you truly care for him. I saw that in your face just now. But even without love, you would do your duty – just as my poor Jeanette did hers.'

I couldn't believe I'd heard aright. 'But she didn't! She left him, she left him!'

Thérèse shook her head. 'No milady, she did not leave him. He sent her away.'

'No! Frank told me: he said she left – '

'Yes, she left – because he sent her away. But she did not tell that to François, for she wished him to be a good son to the man who had given him his name.' She would not let me interrupt. 'Milady, I am telling you the truth: your husband sent my Jeanette away. I was here, in the bathroom, her maid, and he came into her room and told her: "Tomorrow I go to London, and when I return I will expect you to have gone." He shouted in anger, I could hear every word. She was frightened, and after he'd gone she said, "What shall I do, Thérèse?" I told her, "Do as he says, my little cabbage – I will pack." And so we left. But she did not leave him.'

I was floundering. She sounded so sure, but it couldn't be true. 'He loved her. Leo loved her!'

'Oh yes, he loved her. That is why he sent her away.'

I said, 'Madame, you talk in riddles – I do not understand.'

'No, nor did she – and I did not tell her. I would never have told her. But on her deathbed she discovered the truth and she wept, oh how she wept.' Thérèse put up her hand to cover her eyes. 'Then she told me I must make reparation, and so I have come.' Her hand dropped, her eyes held mine. 'But milady, *I* cannot repair the damage that was done, only you can do that, and I ask it in her name. *She* sent me, to ask you, to beg you.'

Anger simmered in me. 'Why should *she* care? She deceived him.'

'Milady, please, have charity. She was very young, and what she did, she did for love.'

My reply was blunt. 'She did not love Leo, her husband.'

The old woman's voice was low and sad as she told me, 'No, it was not he she loved.'

I pressed home my accusation. 'She shouldn't have married him.'

'No, she should not.' The old woman reached down to pick up her basket, her shoulders slumped. 'And I see now that I should not have come – it was too much to ask of you. I – I offer you my apologies.' There were tears in her eyes, and she was shaking as she rose to go.

Jumping up I went to her, and put my arm round her. 'Madame, you cannot leave now. You must be tired, you've come so far. Let me ring for tea – or coffee, if you would prefer. Come, sit yourself down again, here, where it is warmer.' She allowed me to lead her to a seat by the fire, and I rang for Mr Tims.

I didn't know what to say while we waited but luckily Jackie chose that moment to wake up. I lifted him on to my lap, kissing his sleepy face, greeting him, loving him. He smiled back at me, then his small hands reached up and tugged at my blouse.

When he was settled I looked up at my visitor. She was calmer now. I said, 'Madame, my daughters usually come to me at this time, but if you'd rather – '

'I should like to see his child, milady.'

As Mr Tims put down the tray the children came rushing in, their cheeks glowing from their walk, tumbling like young puppies onto the sofa beside me. 'Mama, I saw – ' 'Mama, Flora said – '

'Shush, your Mama has a visitor.' They turned to look at her – but her eyes were only for Flora. Thérèse was trembling. I said, 'Flora, go and say good afternoon to Madame Balsan.'

Flora slid off the sofa in a flurry of white petticoats and did as I'd bid her. Thérèse's voice was tremulous as she replied, '*Bonjour, ma petite.*'

Flora took her her cup of tea, but Thérèse didn't speak again. The children were clamouring for my attention. Old Thérèse seemed content to sit quietly sipping her tea, watching them, but after a while I rang for Ellen. 'But, Mama – '

'Shush, my pet, I have a visitor. I'll be up later.' I asked Ellen to take Jackie upstairs too, then turned back to Thérèse. 'I am afraid they are a little noisy, Madame.'

'Milady, I congratulate you, you have fine children.'

Politely I asked, 'Did you have a family, Madame Balsan?'

'No, there was only her, my Jeanette.' It was as if she had suddenly made up her mind, and she began to speak, the words coming so quickly that I had to concentrate hard to understand. 'I had been married, to a good man, and there was a child coming – our first. We were happy, milady, and then a little while before the child was due there was a storm. He went out to his cattle – to see they were safe. A tree fell on him, and although I was able to drag him in, he died. He was a big man, and perhaps because of that – I do not know, only the good Lord knows – but my baby was born and died. I had milk, but no baby. Then a neighbour came to tell me that Madame la Comtesse had given birth, so she needed a wet nurse for her new-born daughter. I went and put her to my breast, and from that moment she was my child. You understand, milady – you who feed your own children at your breast. Her mother ailed, soon she was dead – a childbed fever. My Jeanette never knew her. Her Papa lived longer, but when she was in her fifth year he, too, died, of the consumption. My poor Jeanette, she was delicate also, and when she pined – but I go too fast, we cannot see into the future. God is good.

'Soon after, she was sent away to the nuns. I wept, but it is the custom. Her aunts, Madame la Marquise and Madame la Comtesse, they let me stay at the château as a sewing maid. She came home for the holidays, and then I saw her. She would come running, her arms outstretched, her plaits flying, to me – her Thérèse. She was so gentle, so kind, so good – and so innocent.'

Her face changed as she exclaimed, 'Milady, he took advantage of her innocence! But I did not know; she told me everything, but she did not tell me that. If only I had been there . . . ' There were tears on her cheeks. 'She was seventeen, and she had come back from the convent for the last time; preparations were being made for her entry into society. She was sad to have left the nuns, but she was excited, too. She was only seventeen, milady, and she knew nothing, nothing.

'It was the only time I ever left her, but my own father had a seizure. I was the eldest daughter, so I was summoned home to nurse him. I was away more than two months, and when I came back she was – quiet, my Jeanette, but not unhappy. She had sinned, but she did not know it was a sin. She was so modest, so fastidious, that what her cousin had done distressed her – but she didn't know it was a sin. He told her that they were like a brother and sister, so what he asked of her was a little thing that would give him so much pleasure, so she had allowed him a liberty. Milady, those nuns, they were good women – but such fools!' Her voice was sharp and angry. 'They told her not to kiss; she would not let him kiss her, but he came to her room at night and held her close – she told me later that afterwards she thought it could not be right, so she begged him not to come again and he did not. I think, I hope, he was ashamed. It was a terrible thing to have done. He told her it must be her secret. She must tell no one, not even me, she must swear it. And because she loved him, she swore it.'

The old woman's hands were trembling. She gripped them tightly together. 'When I came back I noticed she did not bleed at the usual time, but I thought – I could not believe it, milady, she was so good. Besides, in France we are so strict with young girls, she had never been alone with a man except her confessor, and even then I waited at the back of the church. I slept in the dressing room, with the door open between us – but, of course, that night he knew I was not there.

'They told her, her aunts, that because her dowry was so small she must come to England to look for a husband, but she said to me, "I do not want an *English* husband, Thérèse," and she laughed. Then, for a moment, I did wonder – but she lived in fairy tales, my Jeanette. She would say, "I will marry a handsome prince one day, Thérèse," and laugh, so I thought she was dreaming. And so we came to England, and after a little while she met your husband.'

'In the park.'

'Yes. She was with a lady who knew him, and they were introduced. Jeanette was polite, she was always polite, my Jeanette – and that day, a postcard had come from Jean-Paul, her cousin, whom she loved, so she was happy, so happy.

'Your husband was heartstruck, and within a week he was calling every day. She was polite, always polite; the nuns had trained her well. Before long he called on her aunts and requested permission to seek her hand in marriage. As soon as he had left they sent for her and told her how lucky she was, to obtain a husband of birth, of title, and with estates, great wealth – and he did not want a dowry, because he loved her. She came running upstairs to me, panic-stricken. "What shall I do, Thérèse? They tell me I must say yes, but I can't, I can't!" So I told her, "Surely, if the young man is English, he is a Protestant." She gasped, she had not thought of that. She went back to her aunts and told them she could not marry a heretic. They were angry, very angry, but she was so devout that she stood firm, so at last they gave in – and in her relief she fainted. But it was not just relief, milady.

'I went down and unfastened her corsets, and then they saw, we all saw – the veins on her breast, the marks on her body. It was even there on her face, a shadow as from the wings of a great butterfly. I did not know then, but some women carry that mark. I'd seen it, and teased her that she'd been out in the garden without a parasol.' Her shoulders shook.

'It was terrible, milady, terrible. They were so angry with her. She could not withstand them. In the end she told them who it was who had come to her room. Her aunt, Madame la Marquise, was his mother. In her eyes he could do no wrong. Her other aunt had no son of her own, and she adored her nephew. So they told her, told my Jeanette, that it was *her* fault – all her fault. She had tempted him, led him astray; they spoke to her as if she was a woman of the streets. She had not known it was a sin before, but she knew now, and when she realized she was to have a child – her face – '

'But surely, she must have guessed, when she didn't bleed?'

Thérèse shook her head. 'No, milady, the nuns had taught her the most perfect manners, and how to sew the finest embroidery – but that was all they had taught her. She believed, my Jeanette, that the angels brought babies wrapped in their wings, and left them beside their mothers while they slept.' She sighed before continuing, 'You are a woman of the people, milady, as I was. On the farm, we learn. But young ladies, they must never know such things. She did not even see the changes in her own body. The nuns had taught her it was a sin to be naked, and she always bathed in a gown, as they had bid her. Even before me, who had fed her at my breast, she was never unclothed, never.

'If only she had been less modest we might have learnt how much time had passed since her cousin had visited her, but in her distress she became confused. They thought, I thought, that it was the last night I had been away, not the first. And she, she knew no more than the unborn babe she was carrying. She knew only that she had sinned, sinned grievously, so she asked to return to the convent as a penitent, to live in sackcloth and ashes, to scourge her flesh. But Madame la Marquise screeched like a fishwife: "You need a husband, not a cloister!" And at that moment I saw the flame of hope light in my Jeanette's eyes, until Madame la Comtesse added, "There is a husband coming for his answer tomorrow." I saw the flame die.

'I could not hold my tongue any longer. I said to Madame la Marquise, "Milady, should not he who begat the child be summoned?" She turned on me in a fury. "The sin is *hers*. She led him into temptation, she must pay the price." Then she told me she would turn me off if I dared to speak again, so I did not. But I listened, milady. They were too clever for her: they knew the way to my Jeanette's gentle heart. Madame la Marquise told her that if Jean-Paul were to marry her he would be condemned to a life of poverty. She had no dowry to speak of, the lands he had inherited were encumbered – if he married his cousin he would lose his birthright. How could she let him make such a sacrifice when the sin had been hers? They did not tell her then that the negotiations for his betrothal were already in progress; they spoke only of her duty to set him free.

'If you truly love Jean-Paul,' they said, 'you will sacrifice yourself for his sake, and marry this Englishman. Only in this way can you atone for your sin.' So she agreed to do just that.'

'That was wrong.'

'Yes, milady, very wrong. But I do not believe the sin was of my Jeanette's making.'

Still I didn't understand. 'But her cousin – *he* had not been brought up by nuns, surely he must have thought of what might have happened?'

'Do young men ever think, milady?' Her old eyes were shrewd. 'They take what they want, safe in the knowledge that it is not they who will have to pay the price. You know that, for you also paid the price.'

I whispered, 'But it was different for her. She was his cousin – and he loved her. He told Frank that she was the only woman he had ever loved – he told him that, after her death.'

Her voice hardened. 'It is easy to love the dead – they ask nothing of you – but the living demand a sacrifice, and that sacrifice Monsieur le Marquis was not prepared to make.'

I rushed to defend him. 'But if he didn't even know – '

She broke across my words. 'Milady, do you believe me to be so failing in love for my Jeanette that I did not think to tell him? Naturally I sent a message.'

'Perhaps it went astray.'

'That is what François tried to tell me. Always he had believed, as my Jeanette believed, that his father knew nothing until it was too late. And even when I told François about the message, that last time he came to Paris, he tried to defend him – his "Uncle" Jean-Paul.' There was contempt in her voice. 'But my words had sown the seeds of doubt, so he went to him, to the man who had begotten him, and challenged him. And Monsieur le Marquis was foolish, like a spoilt child he sought to defend himself by putting the blame on others. Milady, he had received not one message but *two* – the other was from his mother, telling him what had happened, and bidding him to stay away until Jeanette's marriage had taken place. And he did.

'When François learnt this he was angry, very angry. And so was I, when he came and told me what he had discovered. What she did, what my poor Jeanette did, was for love. What her cousin did! I can only be thankful that she never knew of his betrayal. It would have broken her heart.'

I remembered Frank talking to me at the statue. He'd been talking, not of his mother, as I'd believed then, but of his father. 'Someone you'd idolized' – as he'd idolized his Uncle Jean-Paul. My poor Frank. I asked quietly, 'Madame, since you had concealed the truth for so long, would it not have been kinder to conceal it still?'

She understood me, but she shook her head. 'Kinder to François, yes, but not to your husband.'

'But it could make no difference to my husband – '

She interrupted me. 'Milady, François planned to take you away from your husband, so I told him what I did because this time I wanted François to think of the harm he would do.' Her gaze did not waver as she went on, 'Your husband had lost one wife – I did not wish him to lose another, to the man he had treated as his son.'

'I would never have left Leo.'

'I could not be sure of that. I only knew that François, like his father, was very persuasive. But I also knew that in his heart he was a better man than his father could ever be. I hoped that, having understood the consequences of selfishness, he might, in time, have come to see the cruelty of what he planned to do.'

Grief and guilt made me exclaim, 'But he didn't have the time!'

'No. But he died bravely defending his country. He will rest in peace. But her, my Jeanette, she is not at rest. That is why I have come to see you today.'

She paused as if gathering her strength. 'Milady, you have blamed my Jeanette, I saw it in your eyes. It is natural. Your loyalty is to your husband. But surely you see now that she was more sinned against than she was a sinner.'

What Thérèse had told me had turned the kaleidoscope once more, sending the coloured glass spinning into a new pattern – but still I said, 'She should have told my husband the truth before she agreed to marry him.'

Thérèse was silent. Then she sighed. 'Yes, milady, she should. But you are strong and she was weak – as so many other women have been weak before her. She did not tell him. But she did tell him that she could not give him love; that all she could offer was respect. But he replied that he hoped to win her love in time, and for now he had love enough for both of them.' She said softly, 'He spoke the truth, milady. To forgive her as he did, to name her bastard son as his heir – that was very great love.'

'And yet you tell me that he sent her away.'

'Yes.' I could see her gathering her courage together. 'You must understand, milady, she was my nursling, my child. I would do anything for her.' Bending down, she fumbled in her basket, and drew out a slim leather-bound book, with a gold lock. 'She kept a diary, my Jeanette – it was her refuge. I did not know what she wrote in it – but, I could guess. She always kept it safe. You see, it has a lock; the little gold key she wore around her neck on a chain. Here it is, milady.' Reaching in beneath the high collar of her black silk dress, she drew out the key. Then bending forward, she pulled the fine gold chain over her head. Carefully, she coiled it up and rested it on the brown cover of the book. 'She always kept it locked – but I was her maid. One day, when she was in her bath and had left the key on her dressing table, I unlocked it.'

'You read it?'

'No. To this day I have not read one single word. She would not have wished it.'

'Then why ever did you unlock it?'

379

'Milady, I was here with her, at Eston. François was in the nursery, only a little older then than your son, who must now take his place. She went up to see him, as mothers do, and I – I took her diary downstairs and left it on your husband's desk. I did not know if he would read it, or simply give it back to her, unread. But a man who loves a woman wishes to know more about her, so I thought he would be tempted, and he was. Next morning, it had gone.

'It was gone for a day and a night, milady, the longest day and night of my life. She missed it, but I lied, telling her I had picked it up by mistake, and it was mislaid for the moment, but I would find it soon. She did not think too much of it, believing it to be locked. She trusted me, and besides, there were other things on her mind at that time.

'Early next morning one of the maids found it in the drawing room, and brought it up to me. I locked it before I called her. Then I gave it back to her, saying I had found it in my room. She did not write in it that morning, she simply put it in her dressing table drawer – and then *he* came, and sent her away. And now you must read it too, milady.' She held it out to me, but I didn't take it.

She stood up, and came closer. 'François told me you speak French. It was then I knew that I must come, that the Good Lord had made it possible. Take it, milady.'

Still I hesitated. Her face puckered in anxiety. 'You do read our language, milady – as well as speak it? I can speak a little English, but I cannot read it. Perhaps you – '

She looked so cast down that at once I reassured her. 'I am able to read the French language, madame.'

She gave a deep sigh of relief. 'Then truly, it is the will of God. Here, take it.'

'But – it is her private diary.'

'Milady, she wanted you to read it – to read what he had read. It was her dying wish. She said to me, "When he marries again, Thérèse, take it to his new wife, and ask her to read it, before you give me her message." Now take it, please, milady.' So I took it.

At once she picked up her basket. 'I will leave you, now. There is a woman in the village, the dressmaker. We used to talk of fashions when I was here long ago. I saw her on my way from the station, and she said if I wished for a room I could go to her. I will go to her now, and return to you in the morning.'

I managed to catch my scattered wits. 'You must go down in the trap. I'll send for it now.'

'Thank you, milady, you are kind, very kind. *Au revoir.*'

I stood uncertainly, and the kaleidoscope spun before my eyes until the coloured glass no longer made any pattern at all.

Chapter Fifty-Three

Putting the diary safely away in my desk, I hung the key round my neck, and went up to the children. But even as I bathed them and cuddled them and read their bedtime stories, part of my mind stayed with the tale Thérèse had told me.

Yet as I unlocked the diary later that evening, I still couldn't believe that she'd been telling me the truth. For so long I'd thought of the French Countess as a wicked deceiver – but the minute I started to read her diary I knew she'd never been wicked. Her exquisitely neat rounded handwriting was like that of a child. She was just a young girl of seventeen, going to England for the first time, excited yet nervous – and remembering her wonderful Jean-Paul, whom she adored. He had escorted them to Calais, and kissed her hand on the quay. She wrote that at that moment, her heart sang: he was so slim and straight and handsome. As the boat drew away from the shore she stood at the rail, watching him wave his hat in farewell – and his hair shone golden as the sun itself. Reading her words I felt as though I were standing there beside her.

Then came a word I did not know, so I went down to the library to find Leo's dictionary: the one he must have used to read this diary. The one where he learnt in those very first words that his wife loved another man. My poor Leo. But then I checked myself: by the time he'd read those words he already knew that – so why did he send her away?

Standing there in his library, I was sure I knew the answer: he'd sent her away for exactly the same reason that he'd tried to send me away. From reading this diary he'd learnt the story Thérèse had just told me, and so discovered that his beautiful gentle Jeanette had been forced into marriage against her will. That was why he had sent her away. My eyes filled with tears.

Picking up the dictionary I went to tell Mr Tims that I was going to bed early. I didn't want him staying up because the light was on in my sitting room: I would read the rest of the diary in bed.

But when I was in bed, her bed, I didn't want to read on. This was her personal diary, whose words she'd never intended to be read when she'd written them. I had no right to pry. Besides, I knew the story already, because it was the mirror of my own. So I didn't need to read it.

I was already closing the book when I recalled that the old woman was coming back tomorrow. I just couldn't tell her I'd refused the dying request of her foster child. And so, reluctantly, I began to read her Jeanette's story, the story I already knew.

Except that I didn't know it. I'd been wrong, quite wrong to think that. It was not the mirror of my story at all. No, it was a very different story, and worse, much worse than I could ever have imagined. So terrible was it that by the time my aching eyes had finished reading that exquisitely formed neat handwriting – which by the end was no longer either exquisite or neat – I was frozen with cold. And afterwards I lay huddled in that bed where he'd come to her as a young bridegroom, and I wept. Weeping for her, and weeping for him – and weeping for myself; because, at the last, I too had failed him.

I hadn't realized at first as I read her diary: in those early weeks it was only a simple catalogue of dances and dinners, plays and operas. She'd been taught English by Soeur Angelique, who came from England, and now Jeanette was happy because her aunts were pleased with her for speaking it so well. She liked to please people, Jeanette – that was clear from the way she wrote. It was clear, too, that she never questioned her aunts' decisions: the nuns had indeed taught her to obey. But she was glad to obey and so, those first few weeks she was happy. She didn't know what lay ahead, and nor did I – until that day in the park.

Even then I didn't realize at first; after all, I'd heard the story of their meeting before from Leo. The bumblebee had become entangled in the veil of her hat just as he'd told me, and after it had been set free she'd glanced up to see a young man, looking at her intently. Only it was not a young man she saw – but the devil. The devil called Asmodeus, who was prince of wantons, demon of lechery. Asmodeus, who had tempted Eve to sin. He had been painted with the other devils on the wall of the convent schoolroom: Jeanette had studied his picture in fear and loathing all the years of her childhood. And that devil, who had haunted her ever since, had had a humped back and a twisted neck, a distorted face and a lopsided body, which grew hair as thick as the pelt of an animal.

She knew Leo was really a young man, she knew it even as her chaperone introduced him as 'Lord Warminster'. She knew he was not truly the devil Asmodeus. Yet as he swept off his hat she saw that his hair rose up into untidy locks – just as it always did on devils, so that the curling menace of their horns might be concealed in their thick hair: black hair, Leo's hair!

He held out his hand to her, but she could not bring herself to take it. Instead she pretended that the bee had come back. Taking off her hat again, she'd shaken it – and one of the silk flowers had come loose, and fluttered to the ground. At once, Leo bent his twisted body and picked it up, then held it out to her. So she had to take it from him, that was only polite; but the next sentence seemed to be etched in acid on the page. '*Quand sa main a frôlé la mienne cela m'a donné la chair de poule.*' 'When his hand brushed mine I came out in goose flesh.' He had only brushed her hand, and she was wearing gloves, as he was. Yet even the lightest touch of his gloved hand had aroused her revulsion.

I'd had to read on to discover who Asmodeus was, but Jeanette had been so shaken by the encounter that she'd poured it all out to her diary the minute she'd reached home. It seemed that Sister Louise had given each of the children at the convent their own personal devil that they must especially fear. The devils: Beelzebub, Astaroth, Lucifer, and Asmodeus, had been allocated according to the personal failings of each girl, and the sin she was most likely to commit. Because Jeanette, even as a young girl, had been unusually pretty, her devil had been Asmodeus who tempted men to sins of lechery. Sister Louise had warned her that although Asmodeus had tempted Adam by appearing to Eve in the guise of a serpent, ever since he had used pretty young girls for this purpose, so she must always be on her guard against Asmodeus. And Jeanette, the obedient child, had forced herself to stand staring at the repulsive face and figure of Asmodeus so that she would be prepared. She had learnt his features so well that they had invaded her nightmares ever since.

Thérèse had done her best by telling her nursling that she was far too good ever to sin. Besides, would not the good St John the Baptist, Jeanette's name saint – name saint too of her cousin Jean-Paul – would not he protect her? And Jeanette had been comforted, because she knew that St John was the adversary of Asmodeus, so now she wrote: 'I know Lord Warminster is not really the devil; but if he is, good St John will protect me.'

That night when she awoke shaking with the nightmare again, she made herself think instead of Jean-Paul. Jean-Paul who was the very opposite of Asmodeus; Jean-Paul, so straight and slim and fair; Jean-Paul whom she loved, utterly and totally.

But Jean-Paul was in Paris, Lord Warminster in London; so it was Lord Warminster who kept appearing. She thought it chance, bad luck; but of course, I knew better – Leo was courting her. He didn't know that the merest glimpse of him filled her with loathing – because Thérèse was right, the nuns had taught her the most exquisite manners. All the nuns had taught them good manners, but Sister Louise had gone further: she'd made them each hold a finger to a candle and smile while the flame seared their flesh. 'For so the blessed saints went to their martyrdoms, *mes filles.*' Jeanette, who bore the name of the Maid of Orleans who'd been burnt at the stake by the wicked English, had held her hand in the candle flame longer than the other girls – and she had smiled as her flesh burnt. She still bore the scar, and she wrote of it with pride.

Then there was the day when Sister Louise had found the snake in the convent garden. She had commanded each of the girls to hold it, without flinching – and to smile as they did so. But they had not all smiled as Jeanette had smiled – and only Jeanette had lifted the snake to her lips and kissed it. Her flesh still crawled at the memory of that kiss. But she had done it, and Sister Louise had praised her for it. So she was sure now that Sister Lousie would have praised her when she allowed the young devil-man to take her hand and smile as she did so, though the bile rose in her throat at his very touch. It rose again the first time he peeled off his glove and she saw that dark mat of hair on the back of his hand – but still she had smiled; and anyway, as Thérèse pointed out to her when she cried out from her nightmare and woke that night, all men had hair on their hands.

Sometimes, Jeanette scolded herself for her foolish fancies. He was a man not a devil; his body might be twisted, but his skin would be smooth and fair under his clothes, just as she was sure Jean-Paul's must be. Like the marble statue she had seen in the gallery that day, the young man in the Grecian tunic, who had looked so like Jean-Paul . . . Eventually, she had gone back to sleep again, lulled by her memories of Jean-Paul, riding his horse into the stable yard at the château, and smiling down at her with his teasing smile. She had woken up happy, so happy that it had been almost easy to smile at Lord Warminster when they met him in the theatre that evening – but still, when he bent over her she wrote: '*Cela m'a fait frissoner.*' 'It made me shudder.' Jeanette, however, trained in the convent, had learnt to shudder inwardly while her face still smiled.

But he wasn't at the ball they went to the next evening and Jeanette wrote of it the following morning like an excited child. It had been so wonderful: the room, the lights, the flowers, the music: all so beautiful. Every dance, there had been partners begging for the honour of her hand; so many compliments, so much admiration – she could hardly wait for the day when she returned to France and could tell Jean-Paul that though other men had admired her, she thought only of him.

She had been writing at her desk in the window upstairs, and had seen a hansom stop, a young man get out – an unmistakable, crippled man. For a little while she had been frightened. But no summons came and soon after he'd left again, and in her relief she'd chided herself for her foolish fancies. It was the aunts he'd come to see, the aunts whose company he'd been seeking so assiduously these past days – not hers at all. Yes, Thérèse had been right: she was innocent; terrifyingly, frighteningly innocent.

But when she picked up her pen again that evening, innocence had fled for ever.

'I am with child. I have been so wicked. I have sinned, I tempted Jean-Paul and enticed him into evil. Sister Louise was right. I allowed the devil Asmodeus to tempt me, just as he tempted Eve in the Garden. And as Eve seduced Adam into sin, even so have I seduced Jean-Paul. But I will not let him suffer for my sin as Adam suffered for Eve's. I will endure the punishment myself, so that Jean-Paul may go free. Please, good St John, save Jean-Paul. I do not ask you to help me, I am too great a sinner. But save him, save his soul. Punish me instead – punish me, for I was the guilty one.'

Then later, the simple stark entry, 'St John has been good. He will allow me to pay the price of my sin, for my marriage to Lord Warminster will take place within the month. I understand now why he is in the shape of Asmodeus: he was always destined to be my punishment. For my punishment will be worthless, unless it is almost more than I can endure. But I will endure, for Jean-Paul's sake.'

And somehow, she did. Even that terrible moment when Leo first kissed her cheek. Only her cheek, because the aunts never left her alone with him. They did not always listen, but they watched, determined that their prize should not slip from their grasp.

The wedding plans were soon made: the marriage was to take place in France, to be followed by a honeymoon tour of two months, spent visiting Jeanette's relations. Although it was clear from the brief entries in her diary that Jeanette was going without protest to her martyrdom, it was also clear that the aunts guessed something, at least, of her physical repugnance for her intended bridegroom. They assured her that the young couple would be rarely alone on their honeymoon, and, of course, they would not share a bedroom, so she would not have to lie all night by his side.

She was resigned to her fate. Once, she wrote of her lingering hope that when they returned to France, Jean-Paul would be there waiting, coming to her rescue; but the aunts told her he would not be at the wedding, and she chided herself for being so selfish.

Of the deceit she was practising on Leo she seemed quite unaware. He was simply the agent of her punishment – the punishment that drew steadily nearer, until at last they were married.

I could hardly bear to read of that wedding night, and she could hardly bear to write of it. Disjointed words told of her revulsion and repugnance, but somehow she had managed to close her eyes and lie still, and let him do what he had come to do. But after he'd left her and returned to his own room she'd been violently sick before running to Thérèse, to weep in her arms. 'I am so dirty, so dirty – '

But then she had said, 'St John was so good, he helped me to endure.' Seeking to comfort her, Thérèse replied, 'And tomorrow night it will be easier, you will see.'

'Tomorrow night!' Jeanette, innocent, naïve Jeanette, had not realized that men had desires that rose afresh again each day. She had supposed that a husband simply lay with his wife once, to beget a child. Now Thérèse had to tell her the truth: that young husbands had needs, which must constantly be satisfied. She had become hysterical until Thérèse had promised that when three months were passed she would tell her husband his wife was with child, and then perhaps, because he loved her, he would leave her in peace. But in the meantime, she must endure. Jeanette wrote in a wobbly hand, 'I am not brave, I have no courage left, St John has deserted me.' She did not sleep till dawn, and then the nightmares came.

St John might have deserted her, but her husband had not. Leo was a young and passionate man – but he was also a kind man who loved his wife. When he saw her next morning he was concerned: she was so pale and ill. Stammering, he told her he had been too clumsy: he was a virgin, too, he admitted; he had not meant to hurt her, but he knew he had, so he would not come to her room the next night.

I wept, and gently stroked the page where she wrote of his kindness – Leo, my chivalrous Leo.

But to Jeanette one night's reprieve was nothing, with the torment of all the other nights to follow. She huddled in her bed, weeping with despair until St John gave her the answer – or so she believed. Over that night she turned her world upside down and convinced herself that endurance was not enough for her punishment. She must crave it, as Sister Louise had told the girls she craved the pain of the scourge. Jeanette would rather, much rather, it had been the whip for her, too; but her sin had been of the flesh, a sin of lechery and lust, so she must be punished by submitting to the lust of Asmodeus, the devil of lasciviousness and impurity. Except that he was not Asmodeus, but her husband who loved her. Only, over the next days and weeks Jeanette scarcely seemed to remember this. To her, he *was* Asmodeus, the devil sent from hell to punish her, and she embraced her punishment, because, as she wrote, 'Submission is not enough. I must draw the devil to me, urging him on to befoul my body over and over again.' And so she did.

I shivered as I read those words. She wrote like a girl driving herself to the edge of madness and beyond. 'Tonight I embraced the devil, and three times he befouled me. After he'd left I was weak, and I scrubbed myself all over, but it made no difference, all day his foul slime oozed from my body. It is a fitting punishment, for my soul is vile and unclean; so must my body be, too . . .

'When I was sick in the basin, Thérèse told me I must ask him to spare me, but I cannot do that; I deserve to be punished, over and over again . . .

'I close my eyes, but still I see Asmodeus under my lids, twisted and misshapen, the devil tormenting me – yet again and again I drew him to me. It is worse than the candle flame, it is worse than the snake, but still I must suffer. I have sinned, I have sinned . . .

'This afternoon we were alone and he wished to kiss me. How could I allow him to pollute the daylight? But I let him defile my lips. Afterwards I ran inside, and was sick. Thérèse has spoken to him now, and told him that the convent made me modest . . . He will not touch me again in the daytime. Asmodeus is a creature of darkness . . . He told me that the beauty of my body has enthralled him; I am a greater sinner than Eve, to provoke such never-ending lust in the devil. I am evil, so evil. I must be punished . . .'

When she wrote of the daytime, it was in the same clear rounded handwriting of those early entries, and it told a tale of dinners, and tea-parties, of bridal visits – but then the writing would become jagged and uneven as she wrote of the night. With the coming of darkness she lost her hold on reality. In the daytime, she knew that in truth 'Léonide' was her husband, but at night he became Asmodeus, and the natural scent of his sweat became the stench of corruption, the slippery gift of his seed became the foul slime that soiled her – and when she felt his loving lips caress hers, it was as though evil worms were crawling over her face. Over and over again, she wrote of this: to her, his kisses were the ultimate violation. Yet still she wrote, 'I smile, I smile.'

In September, they returned to Eston. Leo had had the drawing room redecorated for her, and her bedroom – this bedroom – made bright with flowered paper and new chintz curtains; but to her the greatest gift was the private bathroom he'd had installed for her alone. I knew that he'd arranged this so that she did not share his. Even though they had been married over two months now, it was clear that he always went to her wearing his pyjamas; she'd never seen him naked, for he was too shy. Jeanette had not been surprised at this for she herself always went to her bed clad in the most voluminous of nightdresses. No, the bathroom was welcome to her as a place where she could try to scrub herself clean from the pollution of his love-making. So her thanks were fervent – and he was pleased. He wanted so much to please her, to make her happy; instead, his very presence drove her ever nearer to the brink of madness.

After they had been back at Eston for a fortnight she wrote: 'I am like a puppet. The strings are pulled, I speak and perform as others expect me to, but underneath, the real Jeanette is dying, and I am glad. I am too weak; this punishment is more than I can bear.'

Then her reprieve came. 'Thérèse has told him I am with child and that he should not come to my bed. He has agreed.' I could read the relief in the very shape of her handwriting. For several weeks she gained a measure of peace. She helped Thérèse loosen her dresses; she had not shown her condition before but now at last she was becoming plump. She started to think of her child, even to sew for him. In the daytime she sat in the drawing room, and Leo came to her there, but he was often tied up in the business of the estate so he suggested she brought her sewing to the library while he worked, but she refused. Suppose a visitor came? Visitors were coming each afternoon to greet the new bride. She welcomed them: she liked to talk to people, of the weather, of France – besides, while visitors were there he would not try to touch her.

So she lived from day to day, calmer now that her nightly ordeal had ended, and only his evening kiss had to be suffered. Until one morning, while she was sitting alone with Thérèse, her baby kicked, hard – so hard that Jeanette jerked up in her seat. Thérèse noticed, questioned her, and paled, realizing suddenly that the baby would be born a scant five months after the wedding day.

Jeanette did not understand. Aunt Clothilde had told her it would be early, but that babies sometimes were early, so her husband would not be surprised. Thérèse exclaimed, 'Not *so* early!' Jeanette began to panic, so Thérèse calmed her. They would go back to France and her husband would stay here, on his estate. When the baby was born nobody would tell him. Then when Leo arrived, two or three months later, the aunts would pretend that the birth had only just taken place. Thérèse must have known by then she was clutching at straws, but Jeanette had believed her. Although she was carrying a child, she was still like a child herself.

So they travelled back to France. Leo escorted them, and then returned to

Eston. After this Jeanette wrote little in her diary. 'I grow heavy.' 'Jean-Paul has arrived with his new wife,' and a little spark as Jeanette added: 'She is very ugly.' Then she'd crossed the comment out. At the beginning of November Leo visited her; he told her he'd been seasick, but he didn't mind, because he was so glad to see her looking well and rested. The aunts told him Jeanette had been homesick and she wished her first child to be born in France. Naturally, he'd agreed that she might stay.

He came to see her again in November, and stayed for a week. The aunts tried to persuade him to go back to England – they must have been frantic by now. He left, then returned unexpectedly early. On December 1st Jeanette recorded his arrival, then wrote: 'I feel as if I have an iron band around my waist.' Her labour was about to begin – and Leo was there. The truth could be concealed no longer from him: her child was not his.

Chapter Fifty-Four

It was the end of April before Jeanette wrote in her diary again, and as soon as I began to read that next entry I saw that she'd finally grown up. 'Léonide is not a devil. He is a man, a good man, so very good. I owe him so much.'

At last she understood the full enormity of what she'd done. 'I was wrong, very wrong, to deceive him as I did. It was a second sin. But Father Vigot has explained to me that the proper way to atone for sin is repentance, not punishment. The Good Lord understands that we mortals are frail, and conceived in sin and born to sin, so in His wisdom he has ordered our atonement through penance. That is the way to put right the terrible wrong I have done to Léonide. My penance is to be a good wife to my husband. I must make him happy, and in doing so I will win him from his heretical ways and bring him to the true Church. Father has told me how a wife may make a husband happy: she must obey him in everything and submit herself to his desires with a pure mind.'

The priest had also said that even though her husband had been reared as a Protestant, he was a good man, a man worthy of respect. 'And when you have borne him children, respect will turn to lasting affection, I know it.'

In that moment, it seemed as though the priest were speaking to me. He was right, so right: it had happened exactly as he'd prophesied. Then the searing pain of my loss returned once more – because Leo no longer loved me.

I forced myself back to the story I was reading. She was writing the evening before Leo was due; she hadn't seen him since December, but tomorrow he would arrive early and take her and her son straight back to Eston. Now she wrote in a firm, clear hand of her determination to do her duty, and be a good wife to him. She even wrote of how 'Léonide' – she was always careful to call him that now – was an orphan, like her. But it had been worse for him for there had been no Thérèse to love and protect him. 'He must have been so lonely; how I pity him.' So much had she grown up that she was even able to write: 'Now I see the truth clearly. Léonide has such a need for love. I must give it to him, even though I cannot feel it myself. I have been such a foolish girl, so very foolish, to believe that he was a demon, not a man. So deranged was my mind, that I even supposed his body was twisted, his back humped – and that he had fur on his hands like an animal! How foolish I was, of course it was not so, how could it be?'

As I read those words my whole body grew cold.

'I still have the nightmares, but I know now that is all they are, nightmares sent by Satan to test me, and in the bright sun of the morning they wither and

389

fade. I have been remembering wrongly. How could any young man look as I remember? He is not really twisted sideways, it is merely a habit he has of holding his head a little cocked – as birds do when they listen to each other. Father Vigot is right: I was a hysterical girl all those first months. I see now that it was my hysteria which led me to believe that he had a humped back, when in truth he only stooped. His face – it was simply a trick of the light, which made one side look larger than the other. Of course his eyes are equal in size, or how could he see as well as he does? And his hands, they could not possibly be as I believed, for no mortal man grows fur. Tomorrow when he returns, I will cast aside my folly and smile; smile as a woman should smile at her husband.'

'I smiled.' The letters wobbled across the page. 'It was not a nightmare, but the truth. How *can* I do my duty? But I must, I must. He kissed me, and at the feel of his lips on mine my soul shrivelled. His kiss was worse even than I remembered; but I stayed still, and afterwards, I smiled. Blessed St John, help me, help me, I beg you.'

They were to leave that evening on the overnight ferry from Le Havre, so Jeanette would be safe for a little longer, in the cabin with Thérèse and her baby – and the new wet-nurse. The aunts had arranged that, and told the nurse that the baby had been born in February, the date Leo had registered him. Leo had already told Jeanette in December that he would do this, and that he would never reveal the true date of Frank's birth. So today he said they would put the past behind them, and make a fresh start. 'Perhaps by this time next year there will be a second child in our nursery, my dear Jeanette?' In wavering letters she'd written, 'As he spoke those words my heart turned to ice. Oh, what manner of monster will he beget on me?'

Her next entry was made at Eston, late the following evening. She had been sick on the boat. He had believed it to be the seasickness he also suffered from, but Jeanette knew it was not that. As their carriage drew into the driveway at Eston, nausea had overwhelmed her again; she had been sick the minute she stepped inside his house. He had been concerned, sending her straight up to bed and telling her he would see her the following morning – so she had won herself a brief reprieve.

She spent it pouring out her fear and horror to her diary. 'Father Vigot was right, he is a good man. It was not his fault he was born twisted. I must not blame but rather pity him – and I do, I do. From the first day I met him I have pitied him, so I never, ever, let him see how much I shrink from him. But now that is not enough: he wishes me to love him as his wife – and I can't, I can't. I know it is my duty, I must do it, but how can I, when my flesh crawls at the very sight of him?'

I managed to piece the story together at last. It was not exactly as Frank had told me, but then, how could he have known the full story? He only knew what Jeanette or Thérèse had told him; Thérèse more likely, since it was she who was to make the first move.

390

She told Leo that Jeanette was afraid that any child of their marriage would be born twisted, like its father, so Leo had offered to go and consult a doctor. The doctor had told Leo that his condition was likely to be passed on to any children – and then offered him the possibility of correcting his own deformities, by means of an operation. On his return from London he informed Jeanette he would release her from her promise, and remain her husband in name only. He gave her the key to his dressing room door, and told her to lock it against him. Then he told her that he would have the operation. She scarcely seemed to understand the risk he was undertaking; all she could feel was relief that he would never come to her room again.

He went to London for the operation, and when she went to see him afterwards he was able to look her straight in the eye. She wept with relief again.

She stayed at Eston with her baby while he was recovering, but she visited him regularly, sitting by his bed and reading to him. She even held her hand out to him in greeting each day. She wrote of that with pride – before adding 'Blessed St John is good, he gave me the strength to conceal my sickness.'

When he was due to come home she supervised the preparation of his bedroom herself, and ordered special dishes for his convalescence. Of an afternoon he would sit with her in the drawing room while she sat in the window seat and sewed. She kept telling herself that it was different now, because at last he was straight: but she never dared to look at his hands.

At tea-time the nurse would bring her François down for a little while. How beautiful her baby was, she wrote, and how grateful she was to Leo for saving her son from the terrible stigma of bastardy – so she must do her duty as his wife. Constantly, she wrote that it was easier now that he was normal.

The roses were in bloom; he asked her to walk in the garden with her. If she walked a little ahead, she wrote, she did not notice the way he lurched with his built-up boot, and if he put his hands in his pockets she could not see the black hair on them, so really there was scarcely any problem now. But the frequency with which she told herself that showed only too clearly that there still was, and as soon as the light began to fail she would always make some excuse and come in – because Asmodeus was the prince of darkness. Only in the daytime was he Léonide, her good, patient husband.

When I read that, I knew there would be trouble. Yes, Leo was a good man, and a kind man – I of all women knew that – but patient? He wasn't patient now, in his middle years; he could never have been patient in his youth. It must have been just the weakness lingering from his operation.

I was right. One evening, amidst the scents of the roses he began to talk of love. The shadows were lengthening, Jeanette had already tried to leave him, but he wouldn't let her go. She was frightened. To be near him was like being caught in a storm, she wrote; except that storms were cold whereas he was hot, so hot that when he came and stood close behind her she felt as though the flames of hell were scorching her body. He told her he would help her to improve her English accent by declining a verb as an example, which she must then repeat after him.

The verb he chose to decline was 'to love.' 'I love you, you love me. Now, you repeat that, my Jeanette.' She would not; she made some excuse and left him. But the next evening he pressed her harder. '*Do* you love me, Jeanette? Please say you do. Tell me, tell me that you love me!'

She exclaimed that she had a pain in her side, she must go in; she'd run away. Afterwards she wrote, 'Forgive me, St John, but it was not a lie – my whole body was in pain. But I must not lie to him of love, to lie thus would be a sin.'

Next day there was only the short stark sentence, 'I lied.'

Over the following weeks she set out to learn his daily pattern – so she could avoid him. At first she did this by ordering the carriage, calling on neighbours, like the Burtons; but he began to accompany her. He would ask Mr Tyson in the morning if she were going out, and then rearrange his day. So instead of using the carriage, she had learnt by the end of the summer to slip away and walk in the park or the woods. She preferred the woods because she felt safer there: he could not find her so easily. But sometimes he came looking for her, so she dressed in brown and covered her silvery blonde hair with a veil, walking softly and secretly as the shy creatures of the wood itself.

It was strange reading of that, because when I first came to Eston I had done the same. She had found the same places I had found, the sunny clearing where the golden rod grew beside the tumbling stream; the high hedge of briers hiding the ruined house – she took refuge there often, though there were no roses growing over the walls then, and no statue in the courtyard. But the stone seat was there, and often she sat on it in the sun and let her thoughts escape, drifting away from the prison that Eston had become.

But best of all, she liked the secret lake in the woods. It reminded her of the lake near the château, her home. Each year, Jean-Paul had taken her there for a picnic as her birthday treat. They had never gone alone, of course: Thérèse always came too, as chaperone. But Thérèse would sit nodding over her knitting needles in the sun while Jean-Paul taught Jeanette to play catch, or bat and ball. Every summer they had gone and always she would dream of that time, and of him. She still loved him, and she knew she always would. If ever it rained while she was out she would find her way to the lake, because there was a little wooden hut with a bench, so she could sit watching the rain dimple the surface of the pool, and imagine that suddenly Jean-Paul would come running up the grassy slope towards her, his face sparkling with raindrops, his mouth curving into his beloved smile.

An even smile. Not a lopsided smile like her husband's. It was that smile she'd noticed first. He'd looked up from his soup bowl and smiled at her. And as she made herself smile back she saw it, the unevenness. She told herself that it was her imagination, and the operation had made him straight, quite straight – but slowly, before her eyes, he was twisting again. Day by day his neck twisted a little more, and she watched in horror. Finally he admitted that the doctors had warned him that the operation might fail, that his torticollis might recur – and so it had.

Jeanette became frantic. Her nightmares returned, more strongly than ever. Thérèse tried to console her by saying that in truth he had never looked like a normal man. How could he, with his built-up boot and too-short arm? Why, even his face had never been as regular as other men's. But Jeanette had tried so hard to convince herself that she had almost succeeded in her delusion – but now all her hope was at an end. Her eyes began to play tricks on her: his smile of love became Asmodeus' leer of lechery, his man's hands became the curved claws of the devil – even the silky hair on the back of those hands seemed to be growing coarser and more rank. She started to imagine it creeping up from his knuckles, over his wrist up under the white cuff of his shirt until his whole arm was covered. She knew this was nonsense, and scolded herself for her foolishness – but her nightmares would not leave her. And his temper changed to become irritable and surly. He would shout at her in anger so she cringed away from him, then he would apologize, beg her forgiveness, and reach out to kiss her. Always she let him – but she knew her strength was failing.

Then, another reprieve. He wrote her a letter explaining that he would go away for a while, and when he came back he would spend less time with her. He asked for her forgiveness, and her understanding. He did not wish her to feel hurt or neglected, but he was a young man, with a young man's desires, so it was difficult for him to be near her and yet unable to express his love fully and completely. He assured her that he understood her fears about bearing his child, which he shared; so he hoped that she, too, would understand him if he spent less time alone with her. He finished by saying that he suspected that she found their unnatural life difficult also, so perhaps it would be easier for her as well.

Jeanette had written back at once assuring him that she would not feel hurt or neglected, and that yes, it would be easier for her, too. She was so thankful that she could admit the truth that I don't think she could imagine what he would read into her answer.

He went away but returned sooner than she expected. He told her he had missed her so much: even to be in the same house as her was a comfort to him; to share a table with her at meals was his greatest pleasure; but other than that – Hastily, she reassured him that she understood. Now she began spending longer than ever outside. It was a fine autumn, and she preferred to be out of doors; the house was a prison to her, she wrote yet again.

One morning in October she was woken up very early by a nightmare, the old nightmare of the devil Asmodeus. She sat shaking on the window seat watching the pale light of dawn bringing the safety of a new day, and decided to go out, now, away from the oppression of the house, and the man sleeping in the bedroom beyond hers. Even though he'd given her the key and she'd carefully checked each morning and evening that the door was locked against him, still the knowledge of his sleeping presence oppressed her. Quickly she dressed, left a note for Thérèse and went out into the pearly light of dawn. She set off for the lake in the woods, so she could dream of Jean-Paul. Her memories of him would ward off the demon for a little while.

When she reached the turning from the main path, she came to a barrier: it must have been left there by one of the men working yesterday. Pulling it aside, she slipped through and along the winding path. Noiselessly, she came to the edge of the clearing – a jay startled her, and she drew back behind the shelter of the hedge, beside the hut, wary as a woodmouse. But nothing stirred and she was just about to step forward when there was a rustling in the dead leaves, and a huge dark shape stepped out of the wooden hut. It paused in front of her, looking across the lake. Its back reared up in a great misshapen hump, its neck was twisted to one side, and the whole of its body was covered in thick black hair. The figure set off awkwardly, the humped shoulder dipping grotesquely up, down and up again as it began to move. Its head was still twisted towards the lake, but the front of its body was turned towards her now, and all of that, too, was matted in coarse black hair – save for the serpent of Asmodeus, rearing up between his legs; pink and evil, and ready to strike.

She could not move: she was frozen with terror. She could only watch as the creature climbed up on to the rock, stood poised a moment, its unequal arms uplifted in a dreadful parody of prayer before throwing itself down into the water. Then, and only then, did she turn and flee.

It was several days before she wrote of this, yet the terror of that moment was still with her, as it was still fresh in the ink today, all those years later. Asmodeus, with his twisted body and hairy pelt; Asmodeus, flaunting the serpent that had lured Eve to destruction; Asmodeus made flesh and brought to earth, to punish her for all eternity.

She'd been completely hysterical when she got back: Thérèse had put her to bed and called a doctor. It was before Dr Matthews had come to Eston; the doctor then was an old man who'd talked of a 'crisis of the nerves', and prescribed laudanum to sedate her. But in her drugged sleep the devil still tormented her relentlessly, for she had no defence against him now. She prayed over and over again to St John, but every time he appeared in her dreams his face began to twist and he became Asmodeus too.

Leo had regularly come to her room to enquire, and when he did so Thérèse always went outside and closed the door behind her, knowing that even the sound of his voice was a terror to Jeanette now. Then he sent for a specialist doctor from London, who came to examine and question her. She told him she had nightmares; she did not tell him what they were about, but at least he stopped the laudanum. Thérèse had suggested sending for the priest from

Tilton where Jeanette attended Mass every week, but Jeanette would not let her. 'I am a sinner. It is no use.' The doctor from London visited again. She admitted the nightmares were still coming, and he asked her if she were with child. 'No! No!' In her halting English, Thérèse explained the situation between Jeanette and her husband. The doctor listened, then prescribed another week of rest, but after that she must get up, eat downstairs, and walk a little each day. She was a young woman, he said, and she could not stay in bed for ever.

At the end of the week she prayed to St John to give her the strength to get up, and with Thérèse's help she did. The doctor came to see her again as she lay on her sofa in the bedroom, and told her that he now knew the remedy for her nerves and her nightmares. He had informed her husband of it, and when she was stronger her husband would pass the information on.

The next day she went downstairs and had lunch with Leo. Afterwards she was trembling and shaken, and he called Thérèse to take her back to her bedroom, but she had managed it: she had met him again. She wrote in her diary, 'The worst is over – and I smiled, I smiled.' Thérèse petted her, and told her how brave she was. Jeanette took comfort from her praise. 'Blessed St John gave me strength, and with his help I will hold the demon at bay.'

She dined with Leo for a week each evening, and each evening St John helped her to be strong, not to shrink from Leo's gaze, and even to smile at him. Because she knew that he was not really Asmodeus, but her husband. And every time that she looked down at the face of her beloved son she remembered how much she owed to Leo.

At the end of the week, as the dessert was served, Leo asked her if she were feeling stronger now. Yes, she told him, she was almost well. His face lit up with pleasure. Then he told her that the doctor had said that she must guard against such an attack again or she would damage her health permanently; but that if they followed the doctor's advice all would be well. Then she realised that his face had reddened, and he was stammering. 'Not yet, my Jeanette, but soon, then we will both be happier – '

Halting, stammering, but with excitement in his voice he repeated the doctor's advice. It was not healthy for a couple as young as they were to live without the release of the marriage bed. That was why Jeanette had fallen prey to nightmares and other morbid fancies. Without looking at her, Leo added that he knew from her behaviour during the first few months of their marriage that she desired marital conjunction, even as he had. So for her sake as well as his own he was delighted to be able to tell her that the doctor had informed him that there were – devices, which would allow him to act as her husband without the risk of begetting a child. As soon as she was fully recovered, he would be coming to her bed regularly again.

She looked at her husband as he spoke – and seemed to see the curled horns sprouting under his hair.

By now her handwriting was like the skittering trail of a frantic spider. I could hardly decipher it, but at the bottom I found written those final words: 'I smiled, I smiled.' There were no more entries.

Now I knew why Thérèse had left this diary for him to read. For *Leo* to read. He had read this! The full horror of it hit me. I'd been reading it from her point of view, trying to understand her feelings – but he'd read what she'd written of him. Now I understood why he'd sent her away – and that knowledge brought the bitter bile rising in my throat, so that I ran to the bathroom next door and retched in the basin where she'd been sick so many times before. Leo, Leo . . .

I wept until there were no more tears to weep. Yet still I sobbed on, sobbing myself into the hopeless sleep of exhaustion.

Chapter Fifty-Five

She came after breakfast, a small, hunched figure in black, with her basket in her hand. Standing by the door, she said, 'Milady, I see by your face you have done what I asked. So now you know why he sent her away.'

I cried out, 'You shouldn't have made him read it!'

Her face became stubborn. 'I did not *make* him read it, milady – he chose to read it.'

'But – '

She came closer, her voice dropping into a plea. 'Milady, you are angry, it is right that you should be angry – but she was my nursling, my child. She had borne so much, she could bear no more. I feared for her sanity, for her very life.'

'But surely, you could just have told him how she felt?'

She shook her head. 'He would not have believed me. He was a young man, in love: so confident, so sure that he could *make* her love him. What fools men are!' Her voice rose. 'Was I to stand by and let him destroy my child?'

'It wasn't his fault, it was the nuns'!'

'Yes, she went to them too young.' Her eyes looked inward, back to the past. 'Night after night, I sat up with her that first time when she came home from the convent. She was too frightened to close her eyes, and when at last I rocked her to sleep she would soon wake screaming of that devil – so even I could scarcely soothe her. I told her it was only a painted devil, but she believed the nuns, not me. She insisted that he was there, stalking her footsteps, lashing his serpent's tail, ready to destroy her as he had destroyed Eve in the garden, bringing all mankind to sin.

'Always, at night, that devil lay in the shadows, waiting for her. She never slept easy from that day on.' Thérèse lifted her head, to look directly at me. 'Your husband noticed that, milady. He spoke of it to me one day, not long after they were married. He said, "Your mistress does not sleep at night." I told him, "She has always been so; the slightest little thing will disturb her." So after that, he left her to sleep alone. I knew from his face when I told him how she was, that it would be a sadness for him to do that. He wanted to hold her in his arms as she slept, as men do when they love a woman. But because he loved her, he left her in peace. And at the end he loved her so much, that he sent her away.' Her voice quickened. 'Milady, if he were here today, I would fall down on my knees and thank him for that mercy. And Jeanette, in her heart, thanked him, too, as she thanked him every day for acknowledging her son.'

Bitterly I demanded, 'Then surely after what he'd done she could have kept faith with him, instead of betraying him with her lover?'

The old woman's eyes flashed with anger. 'Who told you that? Surely François never – '

'No, but he told me how she loved her cousin, so I thought – '

'Certainly, she loved her cousin, she loved him until her dying breath. But what you imply – never, never! Rather did she shrink from him who had led her into sin. Never would she stay in a room alone with him – she would not even let him kiss her hand. If you believe otherwise you still do not understand my Jeanette. She was good, so good – and she tried to do her duty to the end. Even when her husband rejected her, using harsh words, shouting at her to go away, to leave him – still she brought François to visit him. For weeks before we came she would be trembling with fear, but always she would come, year after year, until at last he ordered her to come no more. Then still she felt the guilt, for in the eyes of God he was her husband, even though he'd sent her away, even though he'd insisted that François be brought up a heretic. That last command hurt her, hurt her so deeply – but she obeyed. My Jeanette, always she obeyed.' Bitterness curdled her voice as she went on. 'She obeyed the nuns, she obeyed her cousin – and she paid for that obedience for the rest of her life.'

'My husband paid, too.'

'Certainly, milady. But Jeanette did not know how high was the price he paid, for I never told her what I had done – and I never would have. Only at the last, when she knew that she would soon have to leave this world behind her, she did as we all must do and made her preparations. So she looked through her possessions and found her diaries. She was going to burn them, and I was anxious to take them away – but first, she said, she must look again. And then she found it, in that diary you hold in your hand – a single black hair. Immediately, she remembered that day when her diary went missing, and how the next morning, he had come to her, his face grey as the winter sky, and sent her away. She had grown wiser over the years, my Jeanette, and she suspected the truth. She asked me, and then I told her what I'd done.'

Thérèse put her hand over her eyes, but I could see the single tear trickling down each withered cheek. 'I, I – ' She broke off, and it was a little while before she had command of her voice again. 'You see, milady, she had hoped – She was going to send François to ask the man who was his legal father to come and see her one last time, so she could beg his forgiveness for the terrible wrong she had done him. But she said, "I cannot ask him to forgive me now, Thérèse, for no man could forgive for that." Then she added in a whisper, "Poor Léonide, he had such a need for love and I, I – " She could not go on, milady, she was so distressed.'

Thérèse's voice was heavy with sadness now. 'But she forgave me. She was so good, so gentle, so kind – she forgave me. But then she made me promise a secret promise. She said, "Soon, I will set him free, that is all I can do for him now. He is not old yet, and surely he will marry again, and when he does you will know, because François will tell you. And then, Thérèse, I want you to go back to Eston, to his new wife. She will be an English lady, of that I am sure, but English ladies, they learn French. So I wish you to take this diary of mine, and ask her, in my name, to read it."'

Thérèse looked at me directly. 'You were not born a lady, yet you still speak French. St John has been good to my Jeanette at last, and so you have read it.'

'Yes, I have read it.'

'Good. My Jeanette said to me, "Thérèse, when Léonide's new wife has read this diary of mine, please, give her this message from me."' The old woman paused a moment to gather her strength, and when she spoke again it was as if I were listening to that same sad sweet voice I'd heard so long ago in Borrell. '"Madame, you who are now Léonide's wife, please, I beg of you, give him the love I cannot give."'

There was silence. Then Thérèse, her face calm and untroubled now, continued, 'Milady, I did not come at first because you had borne François a child, and then I could not come because of the war. But the war is over, and I see by the tears you shed for him last night that you love now the man who is your husband. So you will be able to do what my poor Jeanette could not do – and now, at last, she may rest in peace. Thank you, milady, thank you.'

She stood with her head held high, as if a great weight had been lifted from her shoulders – while my heart cried out: 'But I can't, because I have lost his love.' Only my lips did not move.

She spoke again. 'Thank you, too, milady, for letting me see her – my Jeanette's granddaughter. I will pray for her every day, that she may be happy. I will pray for you, too, milady, with your sweet face, for I know you are as good as my Jeanette.' Still I did not speak. 'Au revoir, milady.'

Picking up her basket she turned to leave. I could only whisper, 'Au revoir, madame,' and then I was alone, alone with my thoughts.

I understood so much now. If only I'd understood before. And I should have done; the clues had all been there, but I'd been so wrapped up in my own troubles I'd not bothered to read them. I'd realized, of course I had, how much he hated his deformities, but I'd not worked out why. I'd known she'd never loved him, but I'd never guessed at the depths of her revulsion. I should have done; after all, he'd told me himself once: 'I won't touch you – I'm too damaged to touch any woman.' Even Frank had hinted at the truth. When he'd told me that Leo was not his true father, he'd mentioned at the same time that Leo's conjugal demands had been almost more than his mother could stand when they were first married. But I'd taken no notice, because he'd been talking of Jeanette as a woman already carrying a child when she married, and terrified that her husband would guess. And I'd known, too, that she loved another man, so her distaste for her husband's advances had seemed quite natural. Even then I'd assumed she'd concealed that distaste, to avoid his guessing her secret. And so she had done, hiding her true feelings, deceiving him constantly – until he read her diary.

My Leo, however must you have felt when you learnt the truth? Oh, Leo, whyever did you read her diary anyway? And why did you read Frank's letter? Why couldn't you have trusted me? But I knew the answer already – I held it in my hand. How could he ever trust another woman after reading of Jeanette's deception? At that moment I hated her, hated her as I'd never hated in my life before. I raised her diary, and flung it away from me, throwing it with so much force that it crashed against the fireplace. As it slithered down into the hearth I cried, 'You destroyed him, you destroyed him!'

But slowly my hatred drained away. She hadn't meant to destroy him, she'd tried so hard to do her duty; but he needed more than duty from her – as he still did from me. Leo needed love, boundless love, and I hadn't given him that until too late. I hadn't even realized the full depths of his need until now – when he'd already lost his faith in me. So I was as guilty as she was.

I went straight up to the nursery. Flora was sitting on the window seat, her blonde hair shining in the pale winter sun. Flora, Jeanette's granddaughter, the child of her beloved son, whom I had loved for so long – and the bitter taste of betrayal rose in my throat. I forced it down and shut my mind against it. But I couldn't shut Jeanette away, and I didn't even try to. Over those next few days I felt so close to her, remembering how she'd lived in this house where I now lived, walked in the garden where I now walked, and borne the name that now was mine.

I just couldn't leave her diary alone: it drew me as a candle flame draws a moth, which returns to singe its wings over and over again. She had written of her own feelings but now as I read it again I saw Leo's, too, through her words. Leo, eager, passionate, laying everything he possessed at her feet – a young man in love. I would never see him like that, and I grieved for the past we had never shared.

Sometimes I daydreamed. Suppose I'd met Leo earlier, before I'd met Frank? Suppose, just suppose, that rather than going as lady's maid to Miss Annabel I'd come instead to Eston, to be housemaid here. I might have met him in the garden, just as I had, and seen him as the kindly Beast. But then there would have been no handsome prince in my life before him, so like Beauty I would have lived in his house, walked in his garden – and come to love him. Clara would have let me help her clean his library in the morning, and if he'd woken early, and come down for a book, perhaps, then I'd have seen him. Or maybe we'd have spoken in the courtyard about Nella: I'd have made friends with her, of course. Gradually he'd have got used to me, learnt to trust me and then, perhaps, like the Beast with Beauty, one day he'd have asked me to marry him.

I pulled myself up sharply. Don't be foolish, Amy: you were simply a servant, he'd never have married you! Then I almost laughed, because, of course, he'd married me anyway, when I'd been even lower than a servant, a disgraced servant – but he'd still come to my rescue. And there lay the answer. He would only ever have married me if I had been in need of that kind of help – and to be in such need I had to have loved another man first. And not any man, but only Frank, his first wife's son. It could only have happened that way, because otherwise he'd never have had the confidence to propose to any woman, not even a servant. After all, when it came to it, he hadn't had the courage to propose to me, he'd sent the doctor to do it for him.

'So confident,' Thérèse had said, speaking of Leo, but she was wrong. He'd never had the confidence of a normal man – not even when he was young. Thérèse hadn't realized that, but I could read it there: the uncertainty lurking beneath the surface. The uncertainty of a child who had lost his mother, and been rejected by his father; the uncertainty of a man who knew that he would never look like other men.

After all, he'd never knowingly let Jeanette see him unclothed; from the very beginning he'd come to her bed in pyjamas, just as he always had to mine. He knew I didn't see him as Jeanette saw him, he knew that to me he was Beauty's kindly Beast, whose silken hair I'd loved to stroke – but still he'd never intentionally let me see his naked body. If perhaps as a young man he'd married a woman who truly loved him then he might have been coaxed, gentled into the confidence of other young men. But instead he married Jeanette, and read her diary; and after that he'd been too damaged.

No, I was wrong. Not too damaged, because still he had learnt to love me – and loved me even more. But I had failed him as well – and now it was too late.

I turned to the children for comfort. Flora was so happy to be going to school, and Rose couldn't wait to join her. Jackie was still my baby, though he was drinking from a cup now in the daytime because I had had to leave him when I went round the estate or over to Pennings to see Mr Parry. Decisions had to be made about the Home Farm there, and Leo had written to Mr Selby to say he was too out of touch these days to judge the state of the market, and we must decide. So Mr Parry and I discussed the different options, trying to weigh the likely benefits arising from the good price for cereals, that the government was still guaranteeing, against the possible gains from a return to more pasture. Back home, I sat down and worked out all the varying implications; it was a relief to have something else to worry about.

There were problems to tackle at Eston, too. Although the war was over, the government regulations were still in place and labour shortages continued, since demobilization was taking longer than expected. But the men were slowly coming back.

When I called at Belling at the end of February, Sir George had arrived home on leave. Lady Burton kissed me in a cloud of excited violet scent.

'We're going to instal central heating, the winters have been so cold. George is leaving the army for good, then he'll be at home all the time – my dear, I'm so happy.' She rang the bell. 'Tell Sir George that Lady Warminster is here.'

When he arrived his tall gangly young son was with him. Sir George took my hand. 'Lady Warminster, how delightful to see you.' His brown eyes looked searchingly into mine as he continued, 'I saw Leonidas a couple of months ago, in France.'

My heart jumped. 'Was he well?' He didn't reply for a moment and I exclaimed, 'He baint ill? You must tell me if – '

'He appeared to be quite recovered from that wretched flu. It was only a mild attack.'

'I – I didn't know he'd ever had it.' I was on the verge of tears.

He said quietly, 'I expect he didn't want to worry you.' I couldn't answer. Sir George's voice was kind as he went on, 'The RAMC have been very busy, but I'm sure it won't be too long now before he's demobilized. And mother's planning to hold a big dinner party once I've finally left the army – so we'll expect you both.'

'Thank you.'

Lady Burton demanded my attention – she'd dropped a stitch in her knitting. When I'd picked it up for her she started talking to Geoffrey about Eton. I remembered that Sir George had been there at the same time as Leo so I turned to him and said, 'Leo was at Eton with you, wasn't he?'

'That's right, we were both tugs, so we saw a fair amount of each other, even though I was in the election below.'

'*Tugs*?' I asked, bewildered, thinking of Albie pointing them out to me on the river.

'King's Scholars – so we lived in College, instead of one of the houses.' He smiled at my bemused face. 'They speak a different language at Eton. You'll discover it all when your youngster's old enough to go.'

He looked so relaxed today, that I ventured another question. 'What was Leo *like* at Eton?'

He looked back at me for a moment before pulling himself up out of his armchair. 'Come along to my study, Amy, and I'll show you something.'

What he showed me was a photograph. I stood there, holding it as carefully as though it were made of the most fragile porcelain. Leo was at one end of the back row: I could see him clearly. He looked so young. His hair was black and he'd turned his body so that he could look straight at the camera; defiantly, as if daring it to frighten him.

Gazing down at that young vulnerable face, I said softly, 'I didn't think he'd ever have let a photograph be taken.'

'No. I suspect he wasn't all that keen on this one, but it would have looked odd if he'd backed out, and he's never been a coward. So he went through with it. Would you like to keep that picture?'

'Oh please! Thank you, thank you so much. But won't it leave a patch on your wall?'

He laughed. 'Only in that dark corner – that's why it's not faded at all. In any case, Mother's planning to redecorate when she gets her precious radiators in.

No, you keep it.' I hugged it close to my chest. Sir George propped himself up against the desk, clearly not in any hurry to get back to the drawing room. So I asked again, 'But what was Leo *like* then?'

He thought for a moment. 'Young, eager, clever, passionate. He wanted to put the world to rights and he was always in a hurry. Too much of a hurry: he'd never stop and think, just jump in with both feet.' Then he added, 'He was still the same when he came down from Cambridge. He saw a girl in the park, fell in love, and married her. He didn't stop to think.'

I didn't know how to reply. I looked down again at the photograph of Leo, with his white tie, black tails – and lopsided face. 'Didn't he hide from people in those days?'

'Not at Eton, no. He was happy there. He wasn't keen on team sports – anything involving a ball put him at a disadvantage, obviously. But he had a natural bent for scholarship, and then there was the swimming – he's an excellent swimmer, of course.' His voice became reminiscent. 'I remember once, looking at him on the bank, at Boveney Weir, and thinking what an ungainly figure he cut, all tilted to one side, with his hump; and then he dived into the river and at once he became all grace and swiftness like an otter, swimming as though the water were his native element.'

'You don't have a photograph of him swimming, do you?'

Sir George burst out laughing. 'I'm afraid not, Lady Warminster. You see, at that time, even in the Thames we bathed in the buff. If a boat came along when we were on the bank we simply jumped back into the water – that was our only concession to modesty. Geoff tells me a bathing dress is obligatory these days – another sacrifice in the name of progress, I suppose.'

I gazed down at the picture in my hands of the boy standing awkwardly on his built-up boot, his head for ever twisted – and imagined him with his silky black hair clinging to his body like sleek wet fur, swimming in the water, easy as an otter. I said softly, 'So that's why he had the lake made deeper at Eston – but he doesn't swim now.' I felt the tears prickling under my eyelids, threatening to fall.

Then Sir George began to speak again. 'Some time after his first wife left, there was a curious story going the rounds. Mother picked it up from her maid. A local youngster who'd had a drop or two too much, went after a rabbit in the woods over at Eston. He heard splashing in the lake, went to have a look – and arrived back in the village here scared out of his wits, babbling some tale of a strange creature in the water. He said it was a huge black beast, covered in fur.' He paused for a moment. 'So I think Leonidas did still sometimes swim – but only at night, when no one could see him.'

Sir George's eyes never left my face, but when he spoke to me again, I thought at first he'd changed the subject; then I realized he hadn't. 'Do you know, Amy,' he went on, 'Your predecessor, the first Lady Warminster, was a beautiful woman, with the most exquisite manners, but I noticed once that she would never allow her husband's shadow to fall on her. She avoided it so subtly, it was only chance that I noticed it, but once I had noticed I saw it was her invariable practice. She couldn't bear to let even his shadow touch her.'

I couldn't control my trembling. 'You're cold, Amy; come back to the drawing room. Mother will be wondering where you've got to.' He held out his hand, and I took it. It was warm and strong, and he gave my fingers a little squeeze before telling me, 'You've got to make allowances for the war, Amy – just be patient. I'm sure things will sort themselves out when he comes back. He does need you, you know, even if he won't admit it.' He smiled before releasing my hand. 'And after all, you don't mind stepping in his shadow, do you?'

I couldn't answer, because I knew that he would never even let me as close to him as that, not now.

Mr Wallis came back at the beginning of March, to become our new butler. Mr Tims was getting old and the responsibility had become too much for him. But he said he didn't want to retire altogether, as he'd have nothing to do all day, so he was staying on as under-butler to Mr Wallis. But I insisted he must only work half of each day – these last years had taken their toll. Mr Wallis and I decided not to go back to footmen. I'd written to Leo to ask him what he preferred but he'd replied curtly, 'The running of the household is Lady Warminster's decision, provided that either Tims or Wallis is available to fulfil *all* my valeting requirements.' My heart sank; he wouldn't even allow me to brush his clothes for him now.

Lily Arnott asked if she could train to be a parlourmaid and wait at table, so Clara's young cousin Joan was to start as housemaid. It was just as well we'd got everything sorted out, because the next minute I went down with tonsillitis.

For several days I felt dreadful. My throat was so painful and I had a temperature. Dr Matthews ordered me to bed and banned the children from my room, for fear of infection – so Jackie had to be fully weaned. I felt so low Clara kept popping in and out all day, trying to cheer me up. Even when my throat improved and I could talk again I was still very miserable: I kept thinking of Leo not wanting me any more. I'd managed to write my usual letter before taking to my bed, and I sent a message to Mr Selby that he wasn't to mention I was ill when he wrote his weekly letter. 'In case his lordship worries,' I croaked to Clara – but really it was in case he *didn't* worry; I couldn't bear the thought of that.

One afternoon towards the end of the week, Granny Withers arrived. She said she'd heard I was down in the dumps so she'd come to perk me up. With a creaking of corsets she settled herself down and took out her knitting. ''Tis a muffler for my Edie's youngest boy.' She peered at me from shrewd dark eyes. 'My, you do look low, my lady. Had to wean your little 'un, I hear – I dare say as you're missing the comfort of him.'

As I lay there watching her gnarled fingers busy with the clacking bone needles it was as if I were a little girl again, back in Borrell with my Grammer. Not Grammer as she was, but Grammer as she might have been, as other girls' grammers were. In her neat black dress with her white hair tucked up under her mob cap she was calm and unchangeable: she looked so wise and safe and good. I should have had more sense: I knew Granny Withers better than that by now.

The tears of weakness oozed from my eyes as I admitted, 'Aye, I do be missing Jackie.'

She shook her head. 'You'll see, it'll be for the best in the long run. Once his lordship's home you won't have time for nursing.' She finished her row and flicked the knitting round. 'First weeks he's back you'll hardly have your drawers back up afore he'll be tugging 'em down again. They're all at it, them as is home already – taking their last four years' ration all in one go, they are.' She sniffed, then leant forward to advise, 'Fact is, if I was you, my lady, I'd leave me drawers off altogether for a few months. Save you a lot of trouble, that will.'

'But Mrs Withers, I can't – '

She wagged her finger at me. 'I know. As I allus says meself, a wife shouldn't spoil her husband, or he gets to take her for granted. But you've been going wi'out, too, so this once, you just enjoy yourself.' She put down her knitting. 'You can allus pull him back into line when there's another youngster on the way and you don't feel the need of it so strong yourself. You don't mind if I smoke a pipeful, do you my lady?' She rummaged in her pocket.

'No, o' course not, Mrs Withers. Only, only – ' And with me feeling so weak and her sounding so wise and all-knowing, I told her. 'He says as he won't come to my bed any more.' I had to repeat myself – she couldn't take it in at first. 'And he says, too,' my voice was breaking as I told her the final terrible truth, 'he says as he doesn't love me any more.'

She stared at me blankly, 'What's that got to do with it? You've kept your looks, and he's a man.' Her jaw dropped. ''Ere, in that wounding, he didn't lose his balls, did he?'

'What?'

'Well, see, there's thic fellow over Tilton way – piece o' shrapnel took 'em both off, clean as a whistle. Still got his rod, but it baint no use any more, floppy as a piece o' wet washing, it be.' Then she shook her head. 'No, he can't 'a done – 'cos he got that little 'un on you *after* he were wounded.' She snorted. 'I know that fork-tongued hussy Elsie Hewitt tried to say as you'd been with his young lordship again, but folk knows as that were nonsense. Arnott near turned her out of her cottage, he were so angry. Said as he'd seen you with his old lordship hanging round his neck a billing and cooing like a liddle turtle dove.' Granny Withers shook her head again. 'Nar, plenty o' girls make a slip or two afore they're married – but once they gets a ring on their finger then they settles down respectable.' She snorted, ''Cept for Elsie Hewitt – and now she's trying to drag you down wi' her.'

'I baint never committed adultery.'

'No, that's what Maud and I thought. A little fornication, now, tis only natural – specially when a girl's as pretty as what you are. I know, I were a looker, too, in me salad days. But I can tell you was brought up proper, and adultery, tis a commandment. You wouldn't 'a broken one o' they commandments.'

'He thinks I did.'

'Well, he would, wouldn't he? Men are like that – fools, every last one on 'em.' She snorted indignantly. 'Fancy 'im telling you you got to go wi'out! All right for him, he went years wi'out a woman, he's used to it! But you, at your age, you wants your bit o' fun. Besides, it baint good for your health to go wi'out. And he's your husband, so tis his duty to provide.' She glanced round my bedroom. 'You know, my lady, I allus thinks as gentry makes a rod for their own backs, wi' these gurt big houses, tis too easy for a man to keep out of his wife's way. You wouldn't have a problem if you shared a bed wi' 'im, as the Good Lord intended.' She shrugged. 'And then 'im, he's allus been one to cut off his nose to spite his face, just like his father before him. So I knows what he'll do, he'll go on depriving hisself, just to make you suffer.'

She was right, it was hopeless. I began to sob. Her voice was brisk: 'Now, now, me lady, let's have none o' that. Tears won't help – where's your backbone?'

'But you said there's nothing I can do about it.'

'I never said nothing o' the sort. O' course there's something you can do about it; there always is. First thing, stop fretting yourself. After all, you never know, he might come walking in here first night he's home, and give you such a welcome as by morning you'll wish he were back out there again, so's you can get a bit o' peace.'

I shook my head miserably. 'He won't.'

'No, I don't reckon as he will, either – knowing him. No, likely as not he'll still be sulking when he comes home, so you'll have to make the first move.'

'But I did afore – I went to his room when he was on leave, and – he sent me away.'

'You'll have to be a bit smarter than that, my lady. 'Ere, you stop fretting about it now. I'll go straight round and have a word wi' Maud and we'll put our thinking caps on. Just you wait 'n see – we'll sort things out for you, we will. Now, Clara'll be here in a tick wi' the tea-tray, so you dry your eyes and let's have a proper smile.'

I did manage a smile because she'd given me hope, at last.

The next day I was so much better that Dr Matthews said I could get up, and by the following week I was out and about again.

On a beautiful spring day at the beginning of April there was one single extra sentence on my weekly letter from Leo. 'Be so good as to inform Selby that I

406

shall be returning to Eston in a fortnight's time.' He was coming home, Leo was coming home. Despite everything, my heart leapt with excitement.

That afternoon, I went to the ruined house. As I stood in the courtyard gazing up at the marble statue of the French countess, I seemed to hear her speaking to me as she had so long ago in Borrell. But this time her sweet sad voice was pleading, 'Please, give him the love I cannot give, for Léonide has such a need for love.'

I looked up at that lovely marble face and told her, 'I will try again, I promise.' And for a moment her lips seemed to curve into a parting smile.

Chapter Fifty-Six

I would win his love again, I would.

But I didn't know how I was going to do it, because he didn't want my love. I saw it in his face as he came through the door. He didn't even look at me. Mr Wallis stepped forward. 'Welcome home, my lord.'

'Good to see you, Wallis. And you, Tims.' He shook them both by the hand.

Mr Wallis tried to help me. 'Her ladyship's been waiting this past half-hour, my lord.'

And only then did he turn and say, 'Good afternoon – Amy.' But his eyes were looking over my shoulder.

There was a sudden eruption of shrieks, 'Papa! Papa!' Flora launched herself down the final steps; Leo ran forward and caught her just in time.

'Flora – my Flora!'

Ellen, pink-faced, still hung on to Rose's hand. 'I couldn't stop her, my lady.'

''Tis all right, Ellen, her Papa did catch her afore she fell.'

Everyone seemed to be in the hall at once: Clara, Bertha, Lily, Joan, Mr Selby, Dora with Jackie in her arms. I even saw Mrs Carter peeping through from the back, dabbing her eyes with her apron, and Jesse shouting in her ear, 'He's back, his lordship's back,' while Sal and Mabs jumped about, trying to see over his shoulder. Leo spoke to everyone, and shook them by the hand – but he didn't touch mine.

And that is how it was: as though there was an invisible brick wall between us. He was polite, always polite, especially in front of the servants and the children; though I think Flora knew. She was only just six, but very quick for her age. Sometimes she'd say, 'Mama likes Porridge, too, Papa,' and turn to hold out her hand to me.

But he'd shake his head, 'Your Mama is busy,' and that was that. At least he took Jackie with him. The first time he picked him up my heart was in my mouth: I thought, if Jackie bawls – but he didn't. He'd got used to men: Mr Wallis and Jim were both very good with him, so now he looked up at Leo with his round grey eyes and smiled. And his father smiled back; I was almost faint with relief. But Leo didn't smile at me.

I tried to behave the same as always in front of the servants, but I know I didn't fool Mr Wallis. Ellen would probably have realized, too, except that all her attention was on Albie. He was planning to go to a training college and learn to be a teacher using a special grant for ex-officers. He told me Leo had suggested he apply to him for any funds that were needed. 'Very decent of him, Amy, but I hope it won't be necessary. I'd prefer to make my own way. It'll mean a long engagement for us, but Ellen understands.' He was staying with her family in the village; Mrs Watson had been very anxious that he should, then they'd all be able to get to know one another. So although Ellen was as careful of the children as ever, the rest of the time she only had eyes for Albie.

Clara knew, of course. I spent time in the still room with her, now Leo was back visiting the estate or in the office with Mr Selby. It was his place, after all. Most of the men had returned now, and we still had the German prisoners of war, so there was plenty of labour. Things were getting back to normal. I met Judith Hawkins in the village one day wearing a print pinafore and her own boots again: they seemed almost dainty. We stopped for a word and she told me, 'Seems like I'm in the family way again, me lady, now Jem's back.'

'That is good news, Mrs Hawkins.'

She just looked at me. 'My youngest's already left school. I thought at my age – ' Leaning closer she put her mouth to my ear. 'Truth is, I miss thic there big engines, I do, even though it were a dirty job now and then. Now they men's back, they won't let us women near anything bigger than a mangle.'

She lifted her basket on to her hip. 'Lost your job, too, I hears. Shame – you was good at it, too, same as I was.' She sighed. 'Tweren't all bad news, thic war.' I walked on to the draper's to get some needles. I supposed it would be nice to have time for sewing again. My sigh echoed Judith's.

I was coming up the street again when Maud Winterslow peered round her curtain and beckoned. By the time I'd lifted the latch and gone in she was at the foot of the stairs. 'Now, you go on up to me workroom, and sit yourself down, while I fetch Martha.' Obviously they were on speaking terms for the time being.

I went up to the front bedroom, which Maud always insisted she used as a workroom because the light was better. It was, but as Martha never tired of pointing out, the view was better too. You could see the whole village street from Maud's upstairs window, right up to the circle of green at the end where folk would meet to pass the time of day. There wasn't much going on in Eston that got past Maud.

I glanced down at her sewing. I couldn't work out exactly what it was, but it looked like some sort of camisole, made of satin. But it wasn't long enough, and it was boned. I picked it up to take a closer look.

Maud and Martha came clattering back up the stairs. When she saw what I was holding, Maud said, 'That's for you. We'll have to try it on, they got to fit just so, them things have. I've got a good eye, but there's nothing like doing a proper fitting.' She went over and drew the lace curtains across.

'But whatever – '

'Tis a bust bodice, I've told you afore.' She rounded on her sister. 'Martha, if you maun smoke in my workroom, at least have the manners not to drop your ash on my clean rug.'

Granny Withers winked at me before settling her clay pipe more firmly between her two blackened stumps of teeth and her behind more comfortably into Maud's best armchair.

Maud turned her back on her. 'Now, let's get down to business. First, we'll have to check your legs.'

'My *what*?'

'Your legs, my lady, your legs. If you was wearing your skirts a fashionable length like them painted hussies over by Salisbury, we wouldn't have to ask. Proper let yerself go, you have, far as yer clothes are concerned. Never mind, me and Martha'll get you smartened up again. Now, lift up your skirts.'

Bemused, I did as she told me. 'No, higher – above your knees.'

Martha sat up straight to inspect. 'Mm, very nice – couldn't have shown a better pair meself when I were your age.' She smirked. 'I told Maud we wouldn't have no trouble there, 'cos your ankles are so slim. Slim ankles, shapely calves – that's the rule. Make a note, Maud: "Hemline high." Now, slip your blouse off.'

'Mrs Withers, I don't know – '

She fixed me with her sharp old eyes. 'He's still playing hard to get, baint he – his lordship?'

'Well, I – '

'No use pretending to us: we asked Clara. When I said as you'd already told me you got problems, then she let out as she reckoned they weren't over yet.' She leant forward, pipe clenched between her teeth. 'Now, is he warming your bed, or isn't he?'

'I, I – ' then I confessed sadly, 'No.'

She shook her head. 'Then you have got problems.' She turned to Maud. 'I mean to say, he's been away near on for a year. You'd expect, even if he weren't speaking to her he'd 'a been up her a few times by now.' I closed my eyes. Granny's voice was kindly. 'Don't you worry, me lady – Maud and me'll sort it out. We'll soon have 'im up to scratch again, eh, Maud? Now, you get your blouse off, my lady.'

Meekly I did as I was told.

Martha snorted. 'Cotton! Cotton's gone right out o' fashion for underwear – and so's threaded ribbon – and what's that you got underneath? Not a corset! What do you want corsets for – your stomach baint dropped? And them drawers! No wonder he's not trying his luck. Couldn't find his way in, I 'low.' She cackled.

'Now, Martha, you're getting coarse.' Maud stood up and walked all round me, clucking her satisfaction. 'She's got a nice little figure, she has, just like one of them Gibson girls – round at the top and round at the bottom. We got something to work on there, Martha.'

'You're right, Maud, we have.' And they did.

The bust bodice they produced lifted my breasts a good three inches and made them seem even fuller. Maud tweaked a dart here and there, then declared herself satisfied. 'That'll do nicely for the dinner party.'

410

I asked, 'Dinner party?'

'That's what we're doing all this for, thic dinner party over at Belling. Clara told us. End of the month, baint it? I dare say as the weather'll be getting warmer by then, but if it baint, you'll just have to put up with it.'

I didn't follow at all, but I said, 'It'll be warm at Belling, there's radiators being put in.'

Maud paused to smile at her sister. 'Ah, looks like it's meant, eh, Martha?' She turned her attention back to me, 'Now, don't go putting your hems up afore – we don't want to spoil the surprise for him.' She went over to consult the calendar. 'Next Monday all right? It'll take the whole day.'

'What will?'

'Going up to Town, o' course. We need help with this little job.'

So we went up to London on Monday, all three of us. I asked Leo if he would mind if I went to visit a dressmaker, just for the day. He replied, 'It is of no consequence to me *where* you go, or for how long.'

I cried myself to sleep that night, and decided I wouldn't go, there was no point. I'd wear my old blue velvet to the dinner party, it still fitted, more or less. Only I didn't dare tell Granny Withers and Mrs Winterslow, so I was there on the platform to meet them on the Monday. They looked very smart, both wearing black silk dresses and neat matching toques. Maud had made Granny leave her pipe at home, and she was still grumbling about it.

We went to a dressmaker in New Bond Street. 'She dresses a lot of titled ladies, does Molly, and them Gaiety girls come here, too – them 'as've been clever enough to persuade some gentleman to pay their bills for 'em.' Maud swept through the door and announced to the saleswoman, 'Madame d'Hiver is expecting us.'

The two old ladies seemed very confident in London. I'd heard in Eston that they had acquaintances there, but I'd always assumed some folk in the East End, not a friend who owned an exclusive court dressmakers in New Bond Street. And she obviously was the owner: I'd been in enough dressmakers with Miss Annabel in the past to know that. In fact, I'd been in this very one.

Madame d'Hiver recognized me at the same time, but was too discreet to let more than a flicker of an eyelid show it. 'Good morning, Lady Warminster – I trust we shall be able to meet your requirements.' She turned to my companions, 'And how are you, Aunt Maud, Aunt Martha?' I stared in surprise as they offered their wrinkled cheeks and the stately Madame d'Hiver bent to kiss them. She must have been over fifty, but she was still a very good-looking woman with smiling dark eyes and hair that was only just beginning to turn grey. She reminded me of someone – I couldn't think who it was – then I realized it was Maud. So she really was their niece: that explained her name.

Madame d'Hiver beckoned to her assistant to come forward. 'This is the dress, Lady Warminster. Aund Maud sent your measurements, but obviously we need to try it on.' I gasped in disbelief. It wasn't a dress – just a scarf of rose-pink charmeuse.

'But – '

Maud snapped open her capacious handbag and whipped out the bust bodice. 'There you are, my lady. You got the step-ins, Molly?'

Madame held out a wisp of transparent silk crepe – georgette it was, of a paler pink than the dress. 'I've put a suspender belt and a pair of stockings ready – that's all you'll need.'

As I walked through the dressing room door in a daze Martha called, '*Everything* off, mind,' then, 'Now, Molly, find me one o' your cigarettes. Old misery guts here made me leave my baccy behind.'

'You can't come to Town with a clay pipe, Martha Withers.' I could hear them, still bickering, as I stripped off. I put on the bust bodice, and the filmy georgette chemise – at least I supposed that's what you called it, though it was like no chemise I'd ever seen before. Then I realized they'd forgotten something, and putting my head round the door, said, 'There's no drawers.'

Maud called, 'Do up the ribbons, them's camiknickers,' and went back to her argument. I looked down: on the hem of the camiknickers there was a narrow flap of silk crepe and two pairs of slender satin ribbons – that was all. I tied them together and then looked in the mirror – you could see everything through those camiknickers: not just the hair between my legs, but even the golden-brown colour of it, too.

I seized the stockings, which were of sheer silk. I would have looked more decent with bare legs, what with the sheen of them when they were on – but they did feel lovely. The suspender belt was just a narrow strip of satin ribbon: I undid the flap and fastened it on. I was feeling quite reckless by now.

I couldn't believe the dress. It was in two shades of pink satin, one blending into the other, but there was less material in it than one of my usual chemises. There were no straps at all, just fine gold chains barely wide enough to cover the ribbons holding up my bust bodice. The design was very simple, but the soft satin was embroidered with a sinuous line of gold flowing down to the golden fringe round the hem. Taking a deep breath I pulled it over my head; with a sensuous whisper of silk it slid smoothly down to embrace my hips. I looked up, into the mirror – and for an instant it was as though I saw myself through Leo's eyes: bare shoulders above, long silken legs below. And in between, although the dress fell straight, the cut was so clever that instead of concealing the full swell of my breasts and the curve of my hips it subtly emphasized them. I turned slowly round – and knew that I simply had to wear it to that dinner party at Belling.

I picked up the band of matching pink ribbon, and tied it in place round my head. Then with one last glance in the mirror I tilted my chin and walked out of the dressing room.

At once the bickering stopped; in the total silence that followed, I twirled round so that the golden fringe flew out over my knees – then I smiled. Martha said loud and clear, 'That's it, Maud, we're in business.' I felt as if I'd passed Standard Five all over again.

Madame d'Hiver sailed forward. 'A little adjustment here,' tightening the satin fractionally over my hips, 'and I think we'll lengthen the straps. Just a glimpse more – '

Martha nodded approvingly, 'You're right, Molly, whatever the fashion papers say, a man likes to know as there's plenty o' tittie ready and waiting for him. Stands to reason.'

Maud broke in, 'I think that hem could go a twitch shorter. What do you think, Martha?'

'You're right, Maud, she's got the legs for it.'

'And the slit in the skirt, she can take it higher. What do you say?'

Martha's eyes narrowed through the smoke from her cigarette. Then she nodded decisively. 'Aye, Maud, she can.'

We bought the shoes at Harrods. They were made of gold brocade with narrow tapering toes and elegant curved Louis heels – the highest I'd ever seen. The fastenings were shining gold ribbons crossing over at the ankle and tied with bows either side. They made me buy two pairs: 'You'll have to practise walking in them – so you'll need a spare pair.'

When I tried to protest at the expense, Martha swept my objections away. 'He can afford it. 'Sides, he's the one who'll get the fun out of 'em. All you're likely to get is a ricked ankle.'

She hustled me on to hosiery. 'Six dozen pairs o' silk stockings, miss; flesh tint, finest gauge, Lord Warminster's account.'

'But Mrs Withers, they cost so much – '

She snorted. 'Let 'em pay for his pleasures. You got to have spares, my lady – once he gets his great paws on them, they'll be laddered in no time.'

I couldn't look the shop assistant in the face.

Martha dismissed me as we came out of the drapery department. 'Maud and me have got a few little odds and ends to fetch. You go and pop in on your Auntie and we'll see you back at the station ticket barrier, Plymouth diner, three forty-five.' Meekly I went down for a cab.

Beat said, 'You got some colour in your cheeks, today, Amy, and no mistake.' She grinned, 'Comes from having his lordship home again, I'll be bound. I got to admit that when Alf came walking through that door safe and sound, me heart give a little jump – even at my age.' She nudged me. 'Nice to be able to warm yer feet in bed again, ain't it, Amy?' I just smiled back, because I didn't know yet. But I would, I would.

Maud and Martha were at the station. They looked very cheerful, and they'd accumulated a fine collection of parcels; the porter holding them seemed quite cowed. 'Molly'll send the dress down tomorrow, we'll have a rehearsal Thursday, that'll give us a coupl'a days to sort out any last-minute hitches.'

'Rehearsal? But I'm not going on the stage.'

They cackled. 'We don't want no slip-ups on the big night, do we?'

When Mr Wallis opened the door, he said, 'You look more cheerful, my lady. I can see your day out's done you some good.'

I reached up to whisper in his ear, 'Maud Winterslow wouldn't let Granny Withers take her clay pipe so she smoked *cigarettes* instead!' He burst out laughing, and I joined in.

I laughed again when Martha suggested at the rehearsal that *I* should learn to smoke. She waggled her pipe at me. 'Gives a woman a bit o' sophistication it does.'

I had a sudden vision of myself at Belling in my beautiful rose-pink dress, producing a clay pipe from the tiny matching satin bag and tapping the dottle out on the elegant gold heel of my evening shoe, before rounding off the performance by stuffing it full of shag. I said, 'Well, if I could mebbe borrow your pipe, Mrs Withers – '

She was outraged. 'Not a *pipe*! One o' them long holder things.'

Maud winked at me. 'She's having you on, Martha, but all the same, one o' them holders would look elegant.'

I was firm. 'No, I'm sure his lordship wouldn't like it.'

'Pity. Still, seeing as you're not used to smoking, I suppose it might take your mind off your flirting.'

'*Flirting*?'

'O' course, you got to make him jealous. Now, me and Maud'll give you a few tips. You don't need many; you're a natural, you are.'

I exclaimed indignantly, 'I don't flirt.'

Maud winked at Martha. 'Hark at 'er! And did you see her ladyship with old Zeke Taylor yesterday?' They both burst out cackling.

'I was wishing him happy birthday – his eighty-eighth!'

'I knows – an' I reckon 'is best birthday present was you putting your hand on his arm and fluttering your eyelashes while you looked at him with them big goldy-coloured eyes o' yourn, your voice soft and cooing like a turtle dove as you wished 'im all the best. He said to me after you'd gone, "Martha," he said, "if I'd been sixty years younger I wouldn't 'a let his young lordship get near 'er. Come to that, if I'd only been twenty years younger, I'd 'a given 'im a run for his money.' She paused, 'Well, I dare say as that's how he'd 'a put it in polite company. No, you're a natural, me lady – though Grace Chandler, she won't have it as you're a flirt. She says it's what the picture papers call charm, because you behaves the same wi' women. But what me and Maud are a mite worried about is that you don't do it to other men, when his lordship's around. Then tis only 'im as gets the full treatment, and that won't do at all. On Saturday evening you got to work at the others and take no notice of 'im.'

'But tis *him* I – '

'I knows that, but you don't want to let *him* know. He's taking you for granted, that's what's happened. I tell you, if you were a Gaiety girl he'd be there waiting at the stage door every night, supper at Romano's, piling on the presents, hanging on your every move – and thinking he was lucky if he as much as got his hand up your skirt once in a while. As it is, 'cos he can have whatever he wants whenever he wants, he don't want it. Men!' She spat accurately into the hottest part of the fire.

'Martha!'

'Just 'cos you can't spit, Maud, nor never could.'

I stood up. 'I'd best go now, the children'll be expecting me – '

Martha raised a bony finger and waggled it at me. 'Now just you remember, no letting 'em jump the starting gun afore the big race. You play hard to get till you're on the way home on Saturday night. *Then* you can start snuggling up to him in that liddle motor o' his'n. Get your leg wedged in close to thic pedals so everytime he has to put his foot down on it, he gets a nice good feel of it. If you've done the job proper he'll be foaming jealous by then and main glad as tis him as is the one who's got the right to take you home. Then, once you're back in to his library, offer to fetch his cigars – and drop the box all over the floor.'

'Why ever should I do that?'

Martha turned and looked at Maud. 'Reckon as she must've found them three young 'uns of 'ers under a gooseberry bush, eh, Maud? She's that wet behind the ears 'erself.' She turned back to me, with exaggerated patience. ''Tis so's you can *bend over* in front of 'im – legs straight, backside tipped up in the air – that way you'll show 'im what you're wearing underneath.'

'*Not* wearing underneath, more like, eh, Martha?' They both cackled again.

'I really must go, Miss Winterslow – ' I almost ran to the door.

'We'll be up on Saturday to dress you,' Maud called after me.

On Saturday Clara came up to the nursery to tell me they'd both arrived. 'They said as they'd go straight up to your bedroom, my lady.'

I ran down to find them sitting either side of the fire, toasting their toes. Two such sweet old ladies: I felt a rush of affection for them, they'd been so kind. 'You stay in the warm, I'll just go and have my bath.'

Martha's head jerked up. 'When did you have the last one?'

'Yesterday.'

'That'll do, we don't want you washing all your scents off.'

'Oh, I haven't got any perfume. You didn't say – '

'You're not putting any of that fancy muck on, it's your natural juices we're after.' Her voice was firm. 'My lady, when a bitch is on heat and looking for a mate *she* don't go round dowsing herself with Eau de Colony, do she? She's got more sense, she knows what pulls the dogs to her.' I closed my eyes. 'Now, we been turning it over atween us. Thic there actresses, they takes a razor to their armpits, and Maud was wondering about yours, so just slip out of your blouse and lift your arms up.' Helplessly I did as I was told. Martha peered at me, then shook her head. 'No, Martha, she's got a nice little bit o' golden fluff there – we'll leave it be. After all, we don't want to make his lordship feel out of it, do we?' She leant forward. 'Ere, is it true what they says, as he grows hair all over hisself?'

I said, 'Not *all* over, Mrs Withers.'

'Well, he wouldn't have any on his – '

I interrupted loudly, 'Not on the soles of his feet, no.'

They both rocked with laughter. 'You're quick, you are, tonight.' 'Sharp as a knife!' 'Now, get behind the screen, out of the draught, and put your glad rags on.'

'Isn't it a bit early?'

'Warm enough in here. We told Clara to make the fire up.'

So I got dressed. First the flimsy silk crepe, then the soft pink satin; by the time it slid with its seductive whisper down over my hips my excitement was rising – and my confidence was rising with it. Once I'd strapped on the golden shoes I felt like Cinderella going to the ball.

I came out to display myself to the old ladies: Maud tweaked and adjusted, to make sure the inner straps were all secured under the fine gold chains, then stood back with a nod of approval. 'You'll do. Now, you see to your hair, though I still thinks, if only you'd had it shingled – '

'His lordship likes my hair long.'

'You're too soft with him, me girl, that's your trouble.'

As I piled my hair up the hairpins slid in just as they should; nothing could go wrong tonight, I was sure of it now. Carefully I fixed the satin band and the silk rose – a rose for Leo.

'I'll wear the diamond necklace he gave me.'

'You will not. We don't want no distractions – nasty, glittery things, diamonds. You got a skin like a ripe peach, and we want it to show.'

I looked in the mirror and giggled; there was rather a lot of it showing. I slipped my engagement ring on; they wouldn't stop me from wearing *that*. Behind me, Maud opened her large handbag. 'Now, *I'm* going to paint you. I've had more practice than Martha.'

'Paint?'

'Rouge, eye black, touch o' powder – nothing fancy.'

'But I can't wear *paint*!'

'Just a touch, we don't want to over-gild the lily. Sit round this way, under the light. Martha'll get on with your manicure.' I didn't seem to have any choice.

When they finally released me, I rushed over to the mirror. Maud had been very skilful, you could hardly tell – and yet it made such a difference. Eyelashes were darker, cheeks pinker, my mouth fuller and redder. I looked exactly like Leo's painting of Aphrodite, and I smiled her full, confident smile before saying, 'Oh, Miss Winterslow, you *are* clever!'

She smirked. 'I learnt to paint in the days when nobody didn't ever admit to it, so it had to be done with a fine brush.'

I looked down at my fingernails: now they were a pretty polished pink, and the five diamonds of Leo's ring sparkled beside them.

'Thank you, thank you so much.'

Clara tapped at the door, 'Five minutes, my lady.'

Martha called, 'Come and have a look, Clara.'

Clara came in, then stopped suddenly. 'Oh, my lady – you do look so beautiful!'

I felt the warm glow of confidence. 'Is his lordship downstairs yet?'

I was almost out of the door before Granny Withers' claw clamped on my shoulder. 'Back! The unveiling's going to be at Belling, not here. Molly sent this.' Maud was already fetching a long black velvet cloak out of the other wardrobe. 'She's stitched in a nice little inner pocket for your shoes – you can put your ordinary ones on for now, and we'll tuck in a spare pair o' stockings, in case yours get laddered in the motor on the way. Clara, you go and tell his lordship she'll be down on the dot, and not before.'

The cloak covered me from head to foot. They fastened it and then checked that all my finery was fully concealed. Madame d'Hiver had even thought to stiffen the edge of the hood so that it jutted forward like the brim of a sunbonnet – hiding my face in its shadow. I drew my gloves carefully on, then solemnly shook the two gnarled old hands.

'Good luck, my lady, we'll be thinking of you.' 'Remember, now; don't let him catch a look at you till you're arrived. And we'll be nipping down the backstairs for that bite to eat Clara's kindly offered us. Come on, Maud.'

I was almost running as I sped along the corridor and down the stairs to the hall.

Chapter Fifty-Seven

They needn't have worried about Leo seeing me, because he was already outside. The engine of the motor was running and he was waiting impatiently by the open passenger door. As soon as I was in he slammed it shut, stalked round to the driver's side, climbed in – and we were off. He hadn't even said good evening. Yesterday I'd have hardly dared say it myself. To-day, cocooned in my chrysalis of black velvet, with my satin wings folded close around my body, I said confidently, 'Good evening, Leo.'

'Good evening.' He sounded grumpy; my heart sank. By the time we turned into the drive at Belling it was down in the toes of my sensible shoes. Besides, I'd never been to a dinner party before. Up until tonight I'd been concentrating so hard on what would happen when he brought me home afterwards that I hadn't had time to get nervous about the before. Now I was nervous; I shifted uneasily, and he asked, 'Are you – cold?'

'No, but I'm a mite frightened. I've never been to a dinner party afore.' I corrected quickly, 'Before.'

He was slow to reply but at least there was a reply. 'No doubt you will know a number of the other guests. And it is a *public* occasion.' The slight emphasis told me he was going to behave like my husband while we were at Belling, at least. I relaxed a little.

As the motor swept round the final curve of the drive and drew to a stop outside the imposing pillared entrance I saw that every window of the great house was blazing with light. A footman came quickly down the steps to swing open the door of the motor; behind him, Belling rose up so huge and impressive that for a moment I was overcome by panic. I glanced round. 'Leo – '

Without looking at me he said, 'I will wait for you in the hall.' Relief sent me almost running up the flight of stone steps. Inside, a housemaid was waiting ready to direct me up the stairs to the bedroom that was being used as a ladies' cloakroom. I opened the door nervously but it was empty except for Lady Burton's maid, Barnes. With a smile she came forward to help me off with my cloak. She stepped back with it, and I was warmed by the sincerity in her voice as she said, 'My lady, if I may presume to say so – you look beautiful.'

Thanking her, I bent to check my stockings; they were still unladdered. Dropping down on to a chair I carefully slid my golden shoes on to my feet, crossed the ribbons and securely tied the bows: Cinderella had come to the ball.

As I stood up I felt so light – light as a butterfly unfolding its damp wings and stretching them to the sun for the first time. I didn't seem to care that I'd no drawers on and a skirt so short my silken knees showed through the golden fringe. I pirouetted round in front of the mirror, all rose pink and glowing gold. A quick tuck and smoothing of my hair, a final adjustment of that silken rose, and I was almost dancing to the door.

My hand scarcely brushed the bannister as my golden toes skipped down the stairs. Skimming down the final flight my eyes were fixed on the huge black back of Leo, standing in the hall. I waited until I'd reached the last few steps, before calling softly, 'Leo.'

He began turning, saw me – and stopped abruptly. I jumped off the last step and almost ran to where he stood. He stared down at me, as I looked up at him. I smiled – but he just kept staring down at me. Then he demanded, 'Have you been painting your face?' He sounded angry.

I felt my smile falter as uncertainly I asked, 'Don't you – like it?'

'I, I – ' His hand went to his stiff white collar, tugging at it as if he was almost suffocating.

Forlornly, I offered, 'I could wash it off if you wanted.'

'No – it's – I was merely taken by surprise.' His eyes dropped down to fasten on my dress. He looked astounded.

'Do you like my new frock?'

'It's – very fashionable.'

I told him proudly, 'That's 'cos it came from London.'

'Ah – I see.' He tugged at his collar again. Then he said, 'I – er – suppose we'd better go in.'

He'd spoken more words to me this evening than the entire fortnight since he'd come back. I was so grateful to Maud and Martha. Then I heard Sir George's voice behind us. 'Leonidas, has Lady Warminster – ' I moved forward to greet him, and as soon as he saw me he exclaimed, 'Amy, my dear, how lovely to see you – and how stunning you're looking tonight. I simply must claim a host's privilege.' Putting his arm right round my waist he kissed me on the cheek; his moustaches tickled my ear. He stood back. 'You do look beautiful, ravishingly beautiful – doesn't she, old man?'

He turned to Leo. My heart was in my mouth and my eyes on his face as I waited for Leo's reply. Then he said, 'Yes, she does,' and my whole body glowed with delight.

Sir George was so kind. He put his arm round my shoulders and shepherded me into the drawing room. 'Here are Leonidas and Amy, mother.'

Eyes swivelled to where we stood, voices stopped – there must have been close on thirty people in the room – then Lady Burton surged forward. 'Amy my dear, how smart you look.' The voices began again, but in that moment I'd seen them: two skirts as short as mine. I heaved an inward sigh of relief as I was kissed in a cloud of violet scent, then the perfume changed to heliotrope as Cynthia pecked my cheek. Sir George seemed to have forgotten he'd kissed me already and his moustache tickled my other ear, then I saw Mr Selby behind him, looking rather shy and lonely so I went up and put my arms round his neck and kissed his weather-beaten cheek. He instantly went bright red.

Another voice said, 'Good evening, Amy.' It belonged to a young man with flashing blue eyes and black hair, whom I'd never seen in my life before. His smile broadened, 'Now we've been introduced, perhaps I could join the queue?'

His blue eyes sparkled with mischief and I was stepping nervously back when to my relief a voice behind me bellowed, 'No!'

All the other voices fell silent again at Leo's shout, then Sir George said smoothly, 'Amy you've met Fellowes, I think – and he and Leonidas are old friends, of course,' I heard the voices around us resume their conversation again as I turned with relief to shake the hand of a gentleman I knew from the War Agricultural Committee. We all talked of farming until dinner was announced.

Sir George bent over me, 'I'm taking you, Amy, and Leonidas takes Mama.' I put my hand on his arm, while behind us the other guests formed their pairs, and we led the procession out of the drawing room. I felt so excited, I whispered to Sir George, 'Tis the very first dinner party I ever did go to.'

He patted my hand comfortingly. 'Don't worry, Amy. I'll look after you.'

I gasped as we entered the dining room. My eyes could hardly take in its splendours: the gleaming whiteness of the damask, the glitter of silver, the sparkle of glass – and everywhere the scent and colour of flowers. 'Oh – tis beautiful!'

Sir George put his hand over mine again. 'I'll tell mother you liked it: she'll be so pleased. Here we are, you're in the place of honour tonight.'

'Thank you – and thank you for being so kind.'

'There's no need to thank me, Amy – your pleasure is my reward.' He smiled, and I smiled back. Sir George was so nice.

As I sat down I realized there was some confusion over who was to sit on my other side. A tall fair man picked up the place card with a frown. 'But I'm sure Ettie told me – '

The dark-haired young man from the drawing room shook his head. 'My place old man, isn't that so?' He turned to the footman behind him and winked.

The footman replied gravely, 'I believe so, Mr Finlay.'

Mr Finlay made shooing motions to the fair man. 'Off you go, Bertie. Our hostess must have changed her mind.'

'But look, Conan old fellow – '

Mr Finlay stayed firm. 'There's a space down there.' It was obvious he wasn't going to budge.

I suggested, 'I daresay as Lady Burton had second thoughts about her seating plan.'

Mr Finlay turned his flashing smile on me. 'I was sure you'd agree.'

The asparagus soup arrived, and after we'd both tasted it he commented, 'Better than the usual standard of cooking at these country house dinners, don't you think?'

I admitted, 'I don't know, I've never been to a dinner party afore.'

'You *haven't?*' He looked astonished, then said, 'That would explain why I've never seen you before.'

I suddenly recalled Martha's instructions and lowering my lashes, I murmured, 'Mebbe you have, and don't remember.'

He swung right round to look at me. 'My dear Lady Warminster, I can assure you that if I had seen you for one thousandth of a second on the other side of Trafalgar Square on Boat Race night,' his voice dropped, 'I should have remembered you.' His vivid smile flashed out again.

By the time the soup plates were being removed I knew Martha and Maud would have been proud of me; but then, I'd been so lucky, for Mr Finlay was a very easy man to flirt with.

Over the trout he asked, 'Am I correct in assuming that the rather large gentleman sitting on our hostess' right is your husband?'

'Yes. He's just come back from the war. He went, though he didn't have to, o' course, with being over age, but he joined the RAMC. He was wounded carrying stretchers in France, then they made him a sergeant – *and* he got a medal.' I finished proudly.

'Splendid show. Er – he's *very* large, isn't he?'

'Yes.'

'And he does have a rather piercing stare, doesn't he?' I glanced at Leo as Mr Finlay continued, 'Or glare, perhaps, would be more accurate. In fact, he seems to be using it on me in what one might almost say was a hostile fashion.'

Leaning closer to Mr Finlay I whispered, 'Does he look – jealous?'

'Mm, I think you might well describe him as looking jealous, Lady Warminster.'

I smiled. 'Good.'

'Ah, you're obviously a lady who enjoys playing with fire – we should get on famously. Would you like him to be even *more* jealous?'

'Yes, please.'

'Well, I think we could arrange that.' Mr Finlay moved even closer, so that his shoulder was almost touching mine. His mischievous grin flashed out. 'But if he becomes violent, can I rely on you to throw yourself between us? I'm the most awful coward, you know.' He laughed; after a moment I joined in.

A voice interrupted from my left. 'Finlay, old man, I think it's *my* turn now to enjoy Lady Warminster's smiles.'

'Now, now, Sir George, no pulling rank, we're not in uniform any longer.'

Sir George leant forward. 'True – but I *could* tell your hostess that you'd bribed one of her footmen.'

Mr Finlay started laughing again. 'Touché! Oh, very well, you may have her until the lamb.'

As we started on our roast duckling and salad Sir George asked, 'Amy, do I gather that you want to make Leonidas jealous?'

'Yes. Mrs Withers and Miss Winterslow said I should.'

'Well, I do agree with Finlay that you're playing with fire – but a gentleman must always oblige a lady.' He moved closer, and gazed fully into my face. 'Do you know, you have little golden flecks in your eyes.'

I smiled back. 'And *you've* got little red veins in yours.'

He threw back his head and laughed out loud. 'Oh, no, Amy, that *won't* do. You didn't say that to young Finlay, I'll be bound.'

'He hasn't got them. But,' I put my hand on Sir George's sleeve, 'he hasn't got a moustache, either – and I do so like the way it tickles my ear when you kiss me.'

Sir George smiled broadly. It turned out that he was just as easy to flirt with as Mr Finlay – and while I was flirting with him I could sneak little glances at Leo at the other end of the table. He didn't seem to be saying much to Lady Burton – or the lady on his other side, although she was very young and pretty, and obviously more than ready to talk to him. Instead, he just sat there scowling. I broke off flirting with Sir George to say anxiously, 'Leo does look a mite angry.'

'My dear Amy, jealousy and anger go hand in hand. You can't have one without the other.' The champagne bottle came over my right shoulder, but Sir George murmured to the butler, 'Lady Warminster would prefer water from now on.' He explained to me with a smile, 'I suspect you're going to need a clear head tonight.' I was rather sorry, since I liked the way the bubbles tickled my nose.

As soon as the saddle of lamb was carried in, Mr Finlay interrupted us, 'My turn now, I think.' The lady on the other side of him didn't look at all pleased; he was very good-looking, as well as being so easy to talk to. While he was being served with cauliflower I took the chance of sneaking another glance at Leo. He glowered back.

I was sneaking a lot of glances at Leo by the end of the meal: he did look so big and distinguished in his evening dress – and I saw so little of him these days. Luckily it was Sir George's turn over the dessert, and I knew he understood.

Then Lady Burton caught my eye, and gave a tiny nod. As I began to stand up Sir George muttered, 'Amy, take my advice: don't overdo it. He hasn't taken his eyes off you this past half-hour.' My heart gave a little skip of delight; he'd been looking at me, at me!

I ran up to the cloakroom to check that my paint hadn't smudged. As I came back into the drawing room I heard Lady Burton saying, 'No, *not* a Gaiety girl – ' She broke off to beckon me over. 'Amy dear, I don't think you've met Madeleine Keneally, have you? She and Cynthia are *such* friends. Madeleine has a little one in the nursery, just the same age as your Jackie.'

I sat down beside Mrs Keneally. It was a relief not to have to flirt, and she was so kind. We talked about our children and then she leant closer. 'My dear, if I may ask, how have you kept your figure so, er, upright – after nursing?' I told her about Maud's bust bodice, and she said she'd go and order half a dozen the next day. Maud would be pleased.

Then the door opened for the gentlemen to arrive. I looked up eagerly, but Leo didn't come in until last, with Sir George, and by then Mr Finlay and the fair young man – who'd been introduced as Mr Baxter – were sitting either side of me on the sofa, with Geoffrey Burton hunched up on a footstool at my feet. Geoffrey was trying to grow a moustache like his father's, but it hadn't got very far yet.

The footman came in with fresh coffee but Leo still stayed at the other end of the room, talking to Sir George and Mr Selby. There were several people in between – I had to crane my neck to see him – but whenever I did, I saw he was looking in my direction. I sat back, satisfied. But I couldn't help wondering when it would be some other lady's turn for Mr Finlay and Mr Baxter. I could see flirting was a pleasant enough way of passing an evening but I was beginning to run out of ideas; I'd really much rather talk about farming or the estate.

Then suddenly Sir George appeared in front of me. 'Excuse my interrupting, Geoff old chap, but if I might just have a word with Lady Warminster.' He bent down to me. 'Amy, I think Leonidas' cup needs refilling.'

I jumped up in the middle of Mr Finlay's sentence. 'I must go – ' and almost ran across the room to Leo. His empty cup was on the table beside him. Picking it up I took it over to the tray, but the footman wasn't there, so I poured the coffee myself, added a dash of cream and one spoonful of sugar, just as he liked it, then carried the cup carefully back and held it out to him.

His bushy eyebrows drew together in a frown. 'What's that?'

'Sir George said your cup was empty.'

He stood there, just looking down at me. Then a slim dark figure appeared on my right. 'Any more coffee going?' It was Mr Finlay.

Another figure took up his position to my left, and Mr Baxter exclaimed, 'Now, now, this won't do at a dinner party. Can't have husbands monopolizing their wives – especially not a wife who looks like yours, Warminster old fellow.'

Suddenly the cup was knocked out of my hand and coffee went flying. There was a bellow of rage – I'd never seen Leo like that. Then I couldn't see him at all because I was hurtling through the air. As my stomach hit his shoulder the breath was knocked out of me. I clutched wildly at his hump but his arm was clamped tightly round my thighs so I wouldn't slip off. The room had gone completely silent. I was moving – moving very fast and jerkily past all those upside down faces – except it was I who was upside down: Mr Selby's look of horror, Lady Burton's jaw dropping, Geoff Burton's eyes goggling as he slid sideways off the footstool – then, behind me, I heard the silence broken as a voice called, 'Well held, sir!' It was Mr Finlay.

Then we were out through the door and heading across the hall. A footman carrying a tray gasped, 'My lord – '

'Get upstairs at once and fetch Lady Warminster's cloak.' The next minute I landed with a bump on the butler's chair. 'Stay there!' I froze. Leo came back in his overcoat just as the footman came leaping down the stairs with the black velvet cloak. Leo snatched it from him and throwing it round my shoulders, commanded, 'Outside!' I scuttled out under the portico, but my ankle turned on my slender gold heel and I began to fall. Seizing my arms he half lifted me down the steps to where the motor was already being brought round. As Sir George's chauffeur climbed out one side, I was tossed into the other. Leo flung himself into the driving seat and we were moving off while the footman was still closing the door.

Leo drove back like a madman. We came hurtling up to the Eston turn-off, there was a groan of brakes at the corner, then the next minute we were lurching round into the drive. I sneaked a look at his face in the light from the lodge windows: his jaw was clenched with fury. Thank goodness Mrs Whittles had left the gate open, otherwise he'd have driven straight through it. Another groaning of brakes, the scatter of gravel and we juddered to a halt. 'Get out!' He was shouting at the top of his voice.

I stumbled out, teetering on my golden heels. Seizing hold of me round the waist he swung me off my feet and up the steps. There was a loud peal of the bell: Mr Wallis hadn't expected us back so early. He opened the door. 'My lord, is something the matter – '

Leo just shouldered past him, pushing me in front, then he almost carried me up the stairs to the landing. My cloak dropped off, and he kicked it savagely to one side. I went over on my ankle a second time and he swept me off my feet and clamped me to his chest. I could hear his heart drumming under my cheek as he carried me along the corridor to my bedroom. Inside, he kicked the door shut behind him, strode over to the bed and dropped me down on to it.

I looked up at him – so big, so strong, so full of fury. Not an act of love, but of lust. Terrified, I began to cower away. Then I remembered: *Give him the love I cannot give*. Yes, I loved him, however he felt, I loved him. So it wouldn't be lust – but love. Lifting my arms, I held them out to him.

His huge hands began to tear at his braces, unfastening them. The buttons of his trousers flew open and along with his underpants they fell to his knees. The golden fringe of my dress flicked my thighs as he tossed it back, the two little bows were torn off – then he was on me. The weight of him drove the breath from my body, yet still I opened myself to him. And so we came together.

But even as he used my body my heart and my mind said: I love him.

Soon he realized his weight was too much – Leo, who never hurt me – and then he raised himself up on his elbows. It was all very quick. His grunt of pleasure sounded more like a cry of despair, and then he lay sprawling sideways across my body as he spent himself within me.

We lay joined for a long time: time to feel the silken hair of his belly damp on mine; time to feel the slippery satin of my dress, split open to the waist where he'd torn it in those first frenzied moments; time to listen to his rapid breathing ease and slow; and time to hear his voice, low now and sad, murmur, 'Such civil war is in my love and hate.'

He left me without another word. After I heard the dressing room door close behind him, I struggled up and stumbled over to the mirror. I stood there, tugging at my torn satin skirt, trying to rub the dirty black streaks from my face where the tears had run and smeared with the rouge. I looked cheap and tawdry. Even my golden sandals had lost their shine, but the flimsy ribbon straps were still tied tightly round my ankles. He'd never even bothered to take my shoes off. Realizing how I must have looked to him, the hot tears of shame spilled over to run burning down my cheeks.

Carefully I took off my diamond engagement ring and put it safely away. He'd loved me once. Then I went to the bathroom he'd had built for the French Countess and washed myself all over, just as she had done. But I wasn't sick with disgust as she had been, because I loved him, and always would.

I lay awake for a long time, wondering if just possibly he might come back for a cuddle; but he didn't. 'Love and *hate*.' Then I thought that there might be a child conceived tonight, conceived in anger – but no, in love, because I loved him. And just before I finally fell asleep I thought: 'Love and hate, *love* and hate.' So there was still a chance.

Chapter Fifty-Eight

But by morning my confidence had waned, and then when I got up Mr Wallis told me Leo had already left the house. 'He's gone up to Town for the day, my lady, but I gather he will be dining at home tonight, as usual.' After last night I could hardly look Mr Wallis in the face, but he was smoothly professional, the perfect servant. 'Shall I tell his lordship you were asking for him, when he returns?'

'No, no – don't bother, thank you.'

Martha Withers and Maud Winterslow appeared soon after breakfast, their faces alert and inquisitive. 'How did you get on, my lady?'

'Did he warm your bed for you?'

'Aye – but that were all.'

'All! What more do you want?'

'I – I'd have liked a cuddle.'

Martha looked at Maud. 'Some folk are never satisfied.' She turned back to me. 'There's women in Eston been married fifty years and never had a cuddle – leastways, not from their husbands!' She dug Maud in the ribs and they both cackled.

Maud asked, 'Thic dress did the trick then? Get noticed over at Belling, did it?'

I replied, 'Aye, it did – only it were a little tight in places. Mebbe it would 'a been more suited to a Gaiety girl.'

Martha nodded. 'Well, o' course, that were the idea. No good looking like a lady if you want to catch a man, is it? You got to look a bit fast. And you did.' She was smirking. 'Fast as a hare with the hounds at her heels. I says to Maud, yesterday evening, I says, "That'll get his lordship jumping – or he's not his father's son."'

Maud broke in quickly, 'Have you got it hung up safe, thic dress? If you let me have it I'll freshen it up for you.'

I felt my face going hot, as I admitted, 'I'm afraid it – got a mite torn.'

Martha exclaimed, '*It* got torn! I don't reckon as it tore itself, eh, Maud? Somebody tore it, they did.'

'Ripped it right off her back, more like.'

'It weren't her *back* he were interested in, Maud.'

I said hastily, 'Not ripped *right* off – '

Martha snorted, 'Never even gave you time to get your clothes off. Well, I can't say as I'm surprised, my lady, the way you looked last night. Left boot polish on the bed linen he did, I shouldn't wonder. Still, he always was a hothead, just like his – '

'Shush, Martha. Now, my lady, tis time we both got off home again to put our Sunday best on, ready for church.' Maud leant forward and waggled her knobbly finger at me. 'You look a mite washed out today, so this afternoon you'd better have nice lie-down.'

'*On* your own!' They both cackled their way to the door.

I went up to the nursery and cuddled Jackie. Oh why had I let them persuade me to dress like that, to behave like that? Before, he'd simply been indifferent – now he despised me.

I didn't lie down after lunch, of course. Instead I went reluctantly over to my desk. I knew I had to write and thank Lady Burton for the dinner party – but what could I possibly say? I sat staring at the blank piece of paper while the ink dried on my pen. Eventually I managed to put how much I'd enjoyed the evening – but it was like writing a lie. I simply couldn't get that last horrifying upside-down journey out of my mind. There'd been all those people there: so many ladies I hadn't known – and even worse, several gentlemen I had; gentlemen I'd met from the county War Agricultural Committee, who'd treated me as a responsible person. Then there was Mr Selby, who'd looked so shocked, and Lady Burton herself – whatever must she be thinking today?

I got the letter finished somehow, and had just sealed the envelope when there was a tap at my sitting room door; it was Mr Wallis. 'Lady Burton has called, my lady. Are you at home?'

'I, I – ' What could I say? I'd never been able to tell the conventional untruth. 'You'd better show her up, Mr Wallis.'

As he withdrew he said softly, 'Wallis, my lady – *not* Mr Wallis.' I hardly heard him, I was so hot with shame. Whatever would she say?

'My dear, *how* we women did envy you! *What* a sensation Leonidas was last night – quite, quite splendid! That dark, brooding presence, then suddenly, sweeping you up and off just like that! So, so romantic – young Lochinvar throwing you over his saddle – or am I thinking of the wrong story? Well, rather older Lochinvar, then. But he quite put those young puppies in the shade, they simply don't have the – the – ' Her search for an appropriate word failing, she took my hands and squeezed them. 'Have you made it up yet, dear? George did whisper in my ear this morning that things had been a little – difficult – between you and Leonidas, so George was just a twitch worried when you both left so – er – precipitately. But I said, "You don't know women, my dear. Amy will be completely *bouleversée*. There wasn't a woman in that room who wouldn't have changed places with her last night."' She suddenly stopped. 'Well, dear, have you? Made it up, I mean?'

Guileless blue eyes were fixed on mine. I could feel my cheeks burning, but I just didn't know how to answer. She spoke for me. 'Of course you have, I know you have. You looked quite irresistible in that little pink dress – the men couldn't keep their eyes off you. George was *so* taken. Maureen Seeton was quite jealous at dinner – although she and Geroge have been devoted to each other for years.'

427

My mind slipped sideways, even more in a whirl. 'But – Mrs Seeton, she – her husband – '

Lady Burton looked surprised. 'Surely you'd realized, dear? Maureen is such a good – er, friend, of my George's. Cecil has his own hobbies.' She leant closer. 'Chorus girls, you know. She and Cecil understand each other perfectly. Fancy your not knowing, dear – Leonidas really should have dropped you a hint, it's so easy to be a little tactless, otherwise. But then darling Leonidas was never noted for his tact. As Maureen said last night, "Fancy a man sweeping his *wife* off in such an enthusiastic way!" We all laughed, but I know she was envious really, dear, because I heard her saying to George later: "*You've* never thrown me over your shoulder like that," and Geroge said, "If your legs were as shapely as little Lady Warminster's I might just consider it." And Maureen was *not* pleased. *So* tactless of George – and rather unwise, I thought. You see, dear, when a woman's not actually married to a man she can close her bedroom door on him – of course, some wives do that, too, but I know *you* wouldn't, dear. Besides, the mood Leonidas was in last night, he'd simply have kicked the door down – so romantic.'

She stood up to go. 'Now, don't forget to send me an invitation to the christening.'

'But, Lady Burton – '

'Another little boy would be nice, don't you think, dear? As I said to Madeleine after you'd left last night, fortunately Amy is *such* a good little mother. Now, I simply must go, dear. I'm on my way to the Deanery, but I simply *couldn't* pass without dropping in to see how you were today.'

I tried to collect my scattered wits. 'I was just writing you a letter of thanks.'

She raised her hands. 'Oh, my dear, you don't need to thank *me* – we should be thanking *you*. It quite made the evening, *so* thrilling. No one could talk of anything else after you'd gone – no need to fall back on boring old bridge yesterday! Goodbye, dear. Love to Leonidas.' She was soon gone, leaving only a lingering trace of violet scent.

I sagged down on the sofa. He had wanted me – wanted me so much he'd picked me up and carried me off, even in front of all those people. Despite my turmoil, new hope fluttered in my heart.

But at dinner that evening he never spoke. I tried to talk to him but he wouldn't answer. When at last the servants had left, I watched hopelessly as his black-furred hands angrily wrenched the peel off an orange. Then his head lifted and his brows drew together in one glowering frown as he asked, 'Why? Why did you do it?'

I whispered, 'Do what?'

He was almost shouting by now. 'Why did you behave like a tart?'

Stumbling, I tried to explain. 'Because – because Mrs Withers and Miss Winterslow told me if I flirted you'd be jealous – and then afterwards, you'd act like a husband to me again.'

'Why did you want *that*? Why? Why?'

'Because I – I – '

Furiously he interrupted me. 'What a stupid question to ask *you* of all women. It's always the same answer with you: you want another child.'

I was astonished, I'd forgotten all about that. 'No, I don't – at least, not so soon.'

'Then why? Why?'

Looking straight into his blazing eyes I told him, 'Because I do love thee.'

All at once there was silence. Then, his voice lower now, he said, 'Yet you were unfaithful to me.'

'No, no! I did never commit adultery – you maun believe I.'

'Tell me, Amy, why must I believe you?'

My voice was firm now as I told him, 'Because I never did tell you a lie.'

Quietly he replied, 'No, not even when I wanted you to. You wouldn't tell me that you loved me, when you didn't.'

I dipped my head in agreement. 'No, I wouldn't. But I do love thee now.'

'Then why did you do what you did last year?'

I felt as though I were poised on a knife edge. 'He were upset so I did hold him, and I did kiss him – but it were only the one kiss, the one afternoon. That were all.'

He pressed me further. 'And now you're sorry – you *are* sorry?' His eyes were intent on me, demanding the answer he wanted. But I couldn't give it. It would have been so easy to give it – but I had to tell him the truth.

'No, I'm not sorry.' His whole body stiffened in reply. 'I'm sorry you read his letter, and I'm sorry you've been upset – very sorry. But I baint sorry I did what I did. It weren't a sin. I did it with love, and he needed love. He were frightened, frightened of going back there; and he knew he were likely going to die. So he needed the arms of a woman who loved him.'

There was silence. I was completely hopeless now; but it was true.

His voice was so low I could barely hear his reply. 'Amy, who never lies. Even when the truth hurts more than I could ever have believed possible.' He got up, and walked out.

I sat there, looking at the orange he'd peeled but never eaten. All I could feel was despair.

He left very early the next day. He hadn't told Mr Wallis where he was going, or when he would be back – if he ever would be back. I kept trying to convince myself that he couldn't have gone for ever, that he must come back, because of the children. And he'd taken Nella with him; surely – ? But underneath I wasn't convinced. I delayed dinner as long as I dared, but he didn't come, so Mr Wallis suggested that I eat by myself in the morning room. I could hardly swallow the food Mrs Carter had sent up. At the end of the meal Mr Wallis offered, 'I'll wait up for him, my lady. You go to bed.'

'No, I'll wait up.'

He hesitated before saying, 'But – he might not come back tonight.'

I said, 'I'll still wait up, just in case.'

'Then I'll light the fire for you.'

I was glad of it. Although it was nearly May the night was chilly and I was so cold.

It was after midnight and I'd almost given up hope when I heard his footsteps outside. I half stood up, uncertain what to do. Then he tapped at the door. My voice quavered as I called, 'Come in.'

'Wallis told me you were still up.' He walked over to the fire and held his hands out to its warmth. Nella flopped down exhausted on the hearthrug and I saw that Leo's boots were coated with chalky mud. He must have been walking all day on the Downs.

I ventured, 'Would you like a drink?'

'Wallis is bringing a tray up.'

He dropped down in the armchair – his armchair, which I'd drawn forward ready – and sat gazing into the flames. Mr Wallis arrived very quickly, set the tray down with a wink of encouragement to me, then left us alone. I poured Leo's coffee, added cream and sugar, and carried it over to the small table beside his chair. Without looking at me he commented, 'You're up very late.'

'I – I were waiting for you. Only – ' I hesitated a moment before admitting – 'I were afeared you might never come back.'

Slowly, very slowly, he turned to face me. 'You are my wife, and the mother of my children. Furthermore, I accept that yesterday evening you were telling the truth, and that you have never committed adultery.' A flame of hope flared up; but then he added, heavily, 'In the technical sense, that is.' The flame began to flicker uncertainly. 'But emotionally, it was still adultery – adultery of the heart. Do you understand that, Amy?'

Those words snuffed out the flame. 'Aye, I do understand.'

His eyes never left my face, but I couldn't bear to look at him; now it was I who stared into the flames flickering in the grate. As they blurred and fused into one, he began to speak again. 'I, too, have a little confession to make. My leave fell due after Christmas.'

I looked up at him. 'Aye, I know. Annabel told me. She said – she said as you preferred to stay in France, on duty.'

He picked up his cup and drank before replying, 'In France, yes. On duty, no. I spent my leave in Paris.' Watching my face intently, he continued, 'I went to the bank, found myself a tailor, had a suit adapted – and became an English gentleman again. Quite a delightful sensation to be wearing clean linen, decent clothes, and to have money in my pocket. Paris is a city dedicated to pleasure, you know, Amy. So I decided it was high time I partook of those pleasures. Time to enjoy the simple pleasures of the flesh: good food, good wine – and a woman.' I froze. 'Not, of course, a "good" woman – that would be a contradiction in terms, wouldn't it, Amy?'

His eyes never left my face, but I couldn't reply, so he continued, 'Fortunately, George Burton was attached to Paris HQ at the time, or I'd have scarcely known how to go about it. Quite absurd, a man of my age visiting a house of accommodation for the first time – but George was totally *au fait* with the procedure. He kindly made all the appropriate arrangements, even supplying me with the necessary protectives, so you see you're in no danger of infection from our – er – marital interlude of the other evening. Another cup of coffee, Amy, if you'd be so kind.'

I went to fetch him his cup, refilled it, and returned it to him. 'Thank you.' He drank again, then set it down. He was crouched in his chair like a huge cat that plays with a mouse – releasing it for a brief moment of freedom, before pouncing again. He was almost smiling as he asked, 'Surely you're not surprised?'

I looked at that great paw waiting to slam down on me again and replied quietly, 'But you told me once that to perform an act of love you believed there should be trust and affection.'

'Yes, I did say that. Rather naïve of me, don't you think? I know better now.' The paw came slamming down. 'As you no doubt recall, I had no problem performing with *you* on Saturday night.' I flinched. He continued, 'I'm sure you'll be relieved to know that I've decided to resume marital relations. After all, as I told myself today, it would be extremely foolish of me to deny myself the relief which access to your body can afford. And I do have access to your body, don't I?' He waited, and for a moment I saw a flicker of uncertainty in his eyes.

At once I replied, 'Aye, you do.'

The cat was confident again now; this mouse would not escape. He pressed me harder: 'Any time I choose?'

'Aye, any time you choose.'

He put down his coffee cup. 'Then I choose now.'

I stood up. 'I'll go and get to bed, then.'

'No, Amy, I said now.'

'*Here*? In my sitting room?'

'Yes, here, in your sitting room. After all, you held *him* in your arms here, didn't you?' He watched the tell-tale flush on my face. 'You held him because – he loved you. Now you can hold me because I – *lust* after you. That's why I no longer need respect or trust or – affection – because it will not be an act of love, but an act of lust. Come here, Amy.'

I stood up and walked across to where he sat. Standing by him, I looked down at the lines on his face, the bushy eyebrows, the dark pouches under his eyes – but his eyes were masked and I couldn't read what was in them. When he ordered, 'Sit on my lap,' I could only obey.

The arm that came round me was like an iron band. He said, 'I'm rather sweaty, but I dare say you can put up with that?'

'Aye.'

'Amy, who never says no. Unbutton your blouse, please.' I did as he bid me. 'Now – your – er – undergarment.' Again I obeyed. He slid his hand inside and cupped my breast, then said, 'Yours is very soft – compared with that girl in Paris. Presumably she hadn't borne children.' I didn't flinch. Black fur brushed my bare breast as he slowly withdrew his hand and dropped it to my knee. 'Would you be so kind as to separate your lower limbs?' I opened my knees and his hand slid under my skirts, and now I felt the black fur touching the bare skin above my stocking as his fingers fumbled with the leg of my drawers, trying to find a way in.

I whispered, 'Shall I – take them off?'

'It would be more convenient, since you are obviously attired in a traditional garment today, rather than the lingerie of the Paris demi-monde.'

Standing up, I turned my back on him, while under the shelter of my skirt I began to unfasten the buttons. He continued speaking, 'As you *are* my wife I would prefer it if you usually wore more conservative apparel – but those would prove something of an obstacle tonight.'

My drawers dropped to my ankles. I stepped out of them and picked them up – then stood holding them in my hand, uncertain where to put them. He reached out and took them from me, staring at the long white cotton legs and narrow lace trim. Then he spread them out on his knee, as if to inspect them further. 'I didn't realize women's drawers had flaps in them.' He sounded surprised.

'Miss Winterslow says as they're very old-fashioned – only if you like 'em best, o' course I'll always wear 'em.'

Suddenly he crumpled my drawers up and flung them away. 'Come here.'

I went back and sat down on his lap again. He didn't move, so I asked, 'Shall I open my legs again?'

'Please.'

Slowly his hand crept back up between my thighs and touched my cunny. He started to fondle it. Very quietly he said, 'You don't shrink from me either, do you, Amy? It's ironic, because I would never have dared to visit a woman of that type if it had not been for you. You gave me the confidence, and so I was able to approach her.'

His hand was still moving, searching. I offered, 'Shall I open my legs wider, so you can – ?'

'Please, Amy.'

I shifted, and at once his finger came inside me. 'You don't mind my – er – fondling you in this rather intimate fashion, do you?'

'No, o' course not.'

'I do find it – rather arousing.'

His finger moved as if searching; there was a sudden firm pressure – and I gasped.

'So women are all alike. That was a little piece of advice George gave me, about predisposing a woman beforehand. Poor Amy, I was appallingly ignorant when I first came to your bed, wasn't I? I really must apologize now.' Slowly his finger withdrew, and he said, 'I find I need rather more than arousal now, Amy. Perhaps you would be so kind as to unbutton me?' I reached for his waistcoat but he caught at my hand. 'No – don't bother with that. Just the – er – relevant area.' I unbuttoned his trousers, then his underpants – and his rod burst out. I jumped. For a moment we both sat staring at it, until he said, 'Perhaps you would – sit astride me now?'

'Aye, o' course.'

I knelt with my knees either side of him on the chair. His hand moved uncertainly, and I realized it was an awkward manoeuvre for him so I offered, 'Shall I put it in?'

'Thank you, Amy, if you would. I'll just rearrange my garments first.'

He unfastened his braces so that he could ease his trousers down a little, and I saw the black silken hairs on his belly – that the woman in Paris had seen – and for a moment I couldn't do it, I simply couldn't. But he was waiting, and I loved him. Whatever he'd done didn't make any difference, I loved him – so I took his rod in one hand and felt it beat in my palm as I slipped it very tenderly inside my body. 'Is that comfortable for you?'

'Very, thank you, Amy.'

Pressing my knees close against his hips, I put my arms around him. At once he began to move in a strong, steady rhythm. It wasn't at all comfortable for me: it had been easier in the straight-backed bedroom chair the night Jackie had been conceived; he'd still loved me then. I thrust the thought away from me. Although my eyes were on a level with his, I couldn't bear to look into them so I dropped my lids and concentrated on moving in tune with his hips.

It seemed to take him a long time to reach his peak, but when his breathing told me he was nearly there I tightened my whole cunny to give him that extra squeeze I knew he liked – and at once I felt him beginning to spend. That girl in Paris, *she* wouldn't have known to do that – except that, being so experienced, she would. So even that little triumph was denied me.

His spending finished, but he didn't seem to want to leave me, and there was no need since he wasn't using the little glove. So I knelt on, holding him, with my face resting against the bristly stubble of his cheek until finally he slipped out. At that moment I felt shame, for he had used me in lust – but then I thought, no – *I* love him, however much he despises me. I love him, and always will.

His low voice was very close to my ear as he said, 'Thank you, Amy. I'll be able to sleep now.' Then the pressure of his hand on my bare behind told me it was time to slide off his lap.

Retrieving my drawers I pulled them on with my back to him. When I turned round he was standing up, with his braces refastened and trousers buttoned. Nella's head lifted, and as he bent to stroke her he said, 'Good night, Amy.'

I walked to the door, but before leaving I looked back and saw him, slumped now in the chair, his face grey and haggard with exhaustion. *Give him the love I cannot give.* My hand dropped from the door knob and I went back to him. Bending down I kissed him gently, full on the mouth. 'I do love thee, Leo.'

His voice was hardly more than a whisper as he told me, 'You'd better go to bed now, Amy. You must be tired.' So I left him. In bed I thought of her, that girl in Paris. How many times had he gone back to her, fondling her small firm breasts, spending himself in her welcoming cunny? Then I thought, but it doesn't matter, because I love him.

Chapter Fifty-Nine

I tried to sleep, but I couldn't. I just lay staring into the darkness, until I heard the tiniest of sounds – the dressing room door had been opened, very gently. I saw the shape of him standing there, and whispered, 'I'm still awake.'

Hesitantly, he ventured a single step in to my room. 'I thought – you might be sleeping by now.'

'No, I'm awake.'

Pulling myself up, I reached for the bedside lamp and switched it on. He was still fully dressed. His voice uncertain, he asked, 'Then – would you mind if I came in – and talked to you for a little while?'

'No, o' course not. Come and sit down.'

'Thank you.' He drew up a chair next to my bed, then his hand gestured to the lamp. 'Would you mind – switching this thing off? I would find it easier to talk in the dark.' At once I turned it out. There was a silence for a little while, then he said, 'There's something more I wish to tell you, about that visit I made in Paris.'

'No, no, I dussent want – '

'I must tell you, Amy.' His voice was decided; so I had to listen. It took him a long time to get started; he was having difficulty finding the words. 'After – the summer, I was very angry with you. Then, when I met George, although he didn't suggest that I – ' He stopped and began again. 'I was aware that despite his own commitment, George had not refrained from indulging his desires whilst he was abroad. So I thought, why shouldn't I do the same? She has betrayed me, so why shouldn't I betray her? What's sauce for the goose is sauce for the gander.'

He drew a deep, unhappy breath. 'I didn't know whether, when it came to the point, I would be able to – perform – but she was a pretty girl, and totally professional. Her manner, her clothes, her underwear were all – most arousing, and I was aroused, extremely aroused.' My heart sank like a stone. 'She made me feel like a – normal man. And as the moment of consummation came closer I wanted her, I wanted her badly – ' He broke off.

I could only whisper, 'Tis all right, I understand.'

'No, you don't, you're not a man. You could not feel the lust, pure and simple, which I felt at that moment.'

'I know as a lot o' men do go to women like that.'

His voice was low now. 'Yes. But I had never done so before. And at the finish, I could not.' My ears were straining in the darkness as he continued, 'Not – *couldn't*. I was obviously able. In fact,' he said bluntly, 'I was about to

435

enter her. But I – my mind, my emotions, wouldn't let me. I just got up off the bed, rearranged my clothing, and left.'

I was shaking, and he could see it in the dim light from the window. He sounded surprised as he asked, 'Did the possibility of my infidelity mean so much to you?'

'Aye.'

'But if you had ever united with Francis, he would never have been physically faithful to you.'

I knew what he said was the truth. 'Aye, and it would've hurt, hurt bad – but it would only have been physical relief for him, whereas wi' you – '

He sounded almost amused as he said, 'I can assure you, Amy, that it would have been physical release for me, too – and one that I badly needed at that moment. I was calling myself all sorts of a fool as I tramped the streets of Paris afterwards. Several times I turned round and started to go back. After all, I'd paid her well. But I imagined she'd probably be engaged with her next client by then, and that thought disgusted me sufficiently to make me turn away once more. I told myself that was why I hadn't gone through with it – purely from disgust. Just because you had done what you did, why should I drag myself down to the same level? But underneath, I suppose I knew even then what the true reason was, only I wouldn't admit it to myself, and I haven't been admitting it ever since.'

I could feel their warmth now: little sparks of hope were being kindled. Then he said, 'Amy, it's no use.' And with those words he doused the sparks, instantly, so that I shivered with cold – but he was still speaking. 'I can't fight it any longer, I realized that this evening. I've had to face up to the truth at last: whatever you are, whatever you've done – I love you.'

My body was so still I could scarcely breathe as his low voice asked, 'Did you sin – or did you love too well? Do you remember when I first said that to you, Amy?'

'Aye, I remember.'

'I suppose I recognized even then that only a girl who loved too much could have any over to spare for me.'

'But, Leo – '

'It's all right, Amy, I understand. And it doesn't make any difference, I still love you. I've been trying to fight against it for so long now – but it's no use, I can't stop loving you. I finally realized that this evening. You came back, and kissed me; and at that moment it was all so simple, so blessedly simple. I loved you, I couldn't help loving you. There is no remedy for love.'

I reached out to him, and he took my hand, clasping it firmly in his. But his voice was sad now as he told me, 'Yes, I love you – but I was wrong, it isn't simple, Amy, not simple at all. *Such civil war is in my love and hate.*'

I protested, 'But if you love me, you can't hate me!'

His grip on my hand didn't falter as he told me, 'I'm sorry, Amy, but I can.

436

I don't want to, I want to forgive and forget – but I'm not very good at doing either. I went to that woman in Paris because I wanted to punish you, and when I realized that I still felt love for you, as well as the other emotion, then I couldn't bear to admit it to myself. Instead I pushed the knowledge away like a shameful secret. I allowed George Burton to assume that I'd done what I planned, and I was angry with myself for not having gone ahead. I called myself a fool because love is weakness, and I didn't want to be weak – not after what happened before. I loved once before, Amy, when I was young – and it almost destroyed me. I can't begin to tell you what I went through those years after Jeanette went. I thought, I believed, that I could never love again – and then I did and – '

He broke off, but I didn't risk speaking. After a few moments he continued, 'So I came back determined that I would *not* love you any more, that there would be nothing between us, nothing. Only you were too seductive.' His voice dropped. 'No, I could have resisted that – but you were too loving. Tonight – and on Saturday. Your face in the hall at Belling – I was going to shout at you, order you to wash off that foul paint, but then you smiled at me, like a child proffering a present. You were so like a happy, expectant child that I just couldn't do it. But over dinner,' his voice deepened in anger, 'That young scoundrel! And you, gazing up at him, your hand on his arm! And the others, every man in that room – ' His breathing quickened. 'Watching you then, I realized the full enormity of my folly. I am deformed, but you are beautiful – and you're almost three decades younger than I am. I'd never seen you in company like that before, and all at once I understood the sheer absurdity of my loving you. And then, your behaviour: is that how you always behave with other men, if I'm not there to watch you?' His hand tightened on mine, crushing my fingers.

'No, no! It were *because* you were there, watching. Mrs Withers told me, and Maud – they said I should flirt to make you jealous.'

'Well, you certainly succeeded in your objective. I behaved like a stag in the rutting season.'

'I wanted you to notice me.'

'And did you also want me to take you against your will?'

I flinched from the words, but the warmth of his hand still gripping mine gave me the confidence to contradict them. 'But you didn't, you know you didn't. I were willing, and I held my arms out to you.'

'Yes, so you did.' There was wonder in his voice. 'You knew what I intended to do, and yet you held out your arms to me. Do you know, I couldn't have gone through with it otherwise. You looked so frightened when I dropped you on the bed, that I was going to leave you – and then – ' His voice faltered briefly before gaining strength again. 'And then you held your arms out to me, but I used you like a whore.' His tone was bitter with self-contempt.

437

I exclaimed, 'No, it weren't like that! It can't be like that because – ' my voice dropped – 'because you do love me.'

His reply was quiet. 'But I don't trust you.'

'I told you, I did never commit adultery. I told you the truth.'

'I know, I know, and with my head I believe you – but in my heart I am betrayed. Yes, I love you, but I wish I didn't.' I couldn't answer. 'Sometimes,' he went on, 'I even wish I was back in France. Out there I didn't need to think, there was no point in thinking, no point feeling, because there was no future. You couldn't survive if you hoped for a future. The only way to cope was to live from day to day, hour to hour, minute to minute – and not to think. Now the war is over and I'm back here with you I can't stop thinking – and feeling. I know I'm a fool to feel as I do, but I can't help it. Every time I look at you I'm torn in two by love – and hate.'

Gently he loosed his fingers, and put my hand away from him. 'Amy, you said that you wished me to act as a husband to you – but I don't think that I can. I can't act in lust but – I can't act in love, either.' I couldn't speak. He said gently, 'I'm sorry, Amy, but I am as I am.'

At last I whispered, 'I do love thee.'

'I know, Amy, I know.' He sounded very tired. 'You've tried so hard. You renewed your vows, you even came to France, to save the dying Beast.' He moved, restlessly. 'You were wrong, you've always been wrong about that. I'm not the kindly Beast who simply falls in love with Beauty, who longs for her to love him back – and when she does, breaks free from the spell cast upon him.'

I admitted, ''Twas my fault, because there was another handsome prince, and he was going back to the war – '

He shook his head as he stood up. 'Don't blame yourself, Amy. The damage was done long before you were ever born. I realize that now. Another woman put a spell on me. No, not a spell – let's tell the truth for once. A curse. Real life is not a fairy tale, Amy: no mortal woman could lift such a curse, not even you. There is no happy ending.' And with that he left me.

I'd failed. Jeanette had put a curse on him. She hadn't meant to, and when, at the end, she'd realized the true nature of that curse she had sent Thérèse to ask me to lift it – but I'd failed.

In the morning I realized I'd failed a second time. There was blood on my nightdress: my monthlies had started. Even his seed had rejected me.

He came to the nursery early, while I was still there. We both stayed with the children a little while, then he set Jackie down and stood up. I'd been about to leave myself, but now I hesitated, unsure if he minded me following him down to breakfast, or whether he'd prefer me to keep out of his way. Then he asked, 'Are you coming downstairs, Amy? It's nearly breakfast time.' At once I jumped up.

Outside the door he asked, 'Are you not well this morning? You look very pale.'

I looked up at him, so I could watch his face as I told him, 'This morning, my monthlies started – wi' cramps'n all, so I be sure I'm not, I'm not – ' The expression on his face was one of relief. I whispered, 'Doan 'ee want another baby?'

He said simply, 'No.' Watching my face he added, 'You told me on Sunday that you didn't, either.'

'No. Only I thought, I thought, if I, if we – ' I stumbled to a halt.

He said softly, 'Children must exist for their own sakes; they cannot be expected to put the world to rights for those who beget them.' I knew he was right, but still I had hoped.

He didn't speak at breakfast, and when I followed him out of the morning room he went straight across the hall and into the library, closing the door firmly behind him. I went up to my sitting room and tried to concentrate on my sewing – but I couldn't get that closed library door out of my mind.

Give him the love I cannot give. I imagined her lying in her bed, her face pale and drawn as she sent her last despairing message. To me. But I'd failed, and now there was only that library door, closed against me.

Closed, as it always was, because the library was *his* room, which I never entered, save with his permission, or at his invitation. Then I jerked upright, because it had been just the same with Jeanette. He'd invited her to sit with him there when she'd first come to Eston. But she'd made excuses never to go in, and he'd stopped asking. He *knew* she never went in there – yet he'd found her diary lying on his desk, where Thérèse had left it. Thérèse probably didn't know that Jeanette never normally entered the library; or perhaps she knew, but didn't care. She had to leave the diary somewhere where he'd be sure to read it – to think he'd been *meant* to read it.

My heart was hammering: I'd been so stupid all this time. I'd kept thinking of her diary as being like Frank's letter, which he'd wilfully opened – but he'd done that because he didn't trust me. Her diary was different. Even the fact that it had a lock, which had been left invitingly open, would have made him believe that it had been left there intentionally for him to read. And left not by Thérèse, but by Jeanette, his wife.

The pieces of coloured glass in the kaleidoscope were tumbling into a terrible new pattern. For him to have read of her revulsion was bad enough, but to have believed that she'd wanted him to read it! Oh, Leo, my Leo. I sat huddled in my chair, shuddering with the pain he must have felt. But it was more than pain she had inflicted upon him, it was the curse he had spoken of last night. A curse too heavy for me to lift, so heavy that only one person could lift it: the person who'd first placed it on him. Even if he'd allowed me to give him the love she'd asked me to give, it wouldn't have been enough. He needed to know that *she* hadn't left the diary for him to read. But above all, he needed her message. And Thérèse had gone back to France, so only I could tell him.

I went downstairs and knocked on that closed library door. He didn't look at all pleased to see me. 'Leo, may I have a word with you? Tis important.' Grudgingly, he waved me to a chair. I took a deep breath and began. 'In February, before you came back from the army, I had a visitor from France – Madame Balsan, Thérèse.'

His body went quite still, and I saw by his face that he knew already. What a fool I'd been: of course, someone would have mentioned it; she'd lived here once, lots of people must have recognized her. I waited a moment to see if he'd admit it. Then slowly he said, 'Tims told me she'd been here.' He looked directly at me. 'I assumed she'd brought some final keepsake – from Francis.'

I'd been even more of a fool. Obviously that's what he would have thought, and these past weeks he'd been brooding over those suspicions. I shook my head. 'No, what she brought me weren't from him, but from his mother – the French Countess.'

He was so still now, I could hardly tell he was breathing. I didn't know how to go on, but then he offered me the opening I needed. 'Am I – to be allowed to know – the nature of this – object?'

'It were her diary.'

'Her diary!' He shied like a frightened horse.

My reply was swift. 'Leo, it were Thérèse who left it on your desk for you to read. The French Countess, she never knew, she never knew you'd read it until she lay dying.'

'What?' He was astounded as he exclaimed, 'But I thought–I was sure that –'

'No!' The words came tumbling out. 'She were going to try and do her duty, but Thérèse knew she were in such a state, and that you *didn't* know, because she'd been pretending to you. So Thérèse thought, if you realized how Jeanette felt, you wouldn't ask her to act as your wife again.' I paused to draw breath, 'Leo, I know it were cruel, terrible cruel of Thérèse to do what she did, but Jeanette, she were like a daughter to her. If it had been my Flora, or my Rose, I might likely have done the same. And Thérèse, she'd never read that diary – she didn't know what were in it, she didn't realize how – ' I stopped suddenly as I saw the stricken expression on his face.

'Leo, *she* told Thérèse to ask your next wife to read it.'

'Did you read it?'

'Aye. Jeanette wanted me to.'

He put his head in his hands. I heard the bitterness in his voice as he said, 'So that my next wife would learn to hate me, too.'

'Leo, she *didn't* hate you.'

He raised his haggard eyes to me. 'You read it. Don't you lie to me, too.'

I looked directly into his eyes. 'It was your body she hated – not you.'

'Can I separate myself from my body? I would if I could, but I can't.' His voice was still bitter as he said, 'So now you know that I forced myself over and over again on a woman whose flesh crawled at the lightest touch of my hand.'

'But you didn't know – how could you know? The nuns, they taught her to pretend.'

'Those holy deceivers!'

Anger was mingled with bitterness now and as I heard it I understood and exclaimed, 'So *that's* why you wouldn't let Frank be brought up in her Church!'

'Was it? Or was it because I wanted to punish her – as Francis claimed? By now I hardly know myself; perhaps he was right.' So great was the despair in his voice I reached out my hand to him, but his eyes held mine as he told me, 'After reading that diary, I felt for her what I now feel for you – love, and hate.' My hand drew back. 'History has repeated itself, Amy. We none of us can escape the past, can we?'

Quietly, I replied, 'No. But we can see it differently.'

He shook his head. 'That's not possible. You did what you did, you felt what you felt – '

'I don't mean *my* past, I mean yours, and hers. Surely it does make a difference to you, knowing that it weren't *her* as left that diary for you to read?'

His voice dragged. 'How – can it? When she didn't even allow me to attend her funeral.'

'That were nothing to do with her – that were Frank. In fact, afore she found out about you reading that diary she were going to send for you.'

'To *send* for me?'

He sounded as if he hardly dared believe what he'd heard. 'Aye, when she knew she were dying she wanted to see you, to ask your forgiveness.'

He asked uncertainly, 'For her – infidelity?'

I shook my head. 'No, she never committed adultery, any more 'n I did.'

I could see him grappling with the new pattern that was forming. 'Then why did she desire my forgiveness?'

'For deceiving you when you were to be married.'

'But – I had forgiven her for that.'

'She'd still have felt it.' I knew I was right, but I also knew that there'd been more. 'And she wanted to ask your forgiveness for not being able to love you as a wife should love a husband.' His eyes never left my face. I added quietly, 'I dare say, too, as she wanted to thank you, for giving her son your name, only – then she found out that you'd read her diary, and so she told Thérèse as no man could forgive that, so she didn't send for you.'

'If only – if only she had.'

Quickly I told him, 'But she tried to do the next best thing, she sent a message to *me* instead – to your second wife.'

Very slowly he asked, 'And may I know the nature of this message?'

'Aye. I'll tell you exactly what she said to me.' And I spoke her words, just as Thérèse had spoken them to me. 'She said, "Madame, you who are now Léonide's wife, please, I beg of you, give him the love I cannot give."'

His eyes closed, and he began to shake, shaking with relief.

Then, when at last he was calm again he looked up at me and said in a voice full of sadness, 'But you can't give me that love, either.'

'Leo, I can give it to you – but you won't take it.'

Standing up, I turned away, to leave him alone with his memories.

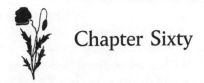 Chapter Sixty

I didn't see him again until the afternoon. I was up in the nursery with the children, and he came to see them. Flora and Rose went running to him, as they always did, and Flora reached him first – and as he looked down at his first wife's grandchild I saw the expression on his face. He'd made his peace with Jeanette at last. With her: but not with me. Looking up from his daughters, his voice was formal as he asked, 'Would it be acceptable if the girls accompanied me to the Home Farm this afternoon? That is, if you have no other plans for them. I need to see Arnott.' He left without another word. He loved me, but he couldn't forgive me. A tear dropped on Jackie's downy head. It was hopeless.

And yet, there was an understanding between us now. Over dinner, he spoke to me; only of the weather and the children, but we were speaking. When the servants had left us alone with dessert and he began to peel his usual orange, I saw that he was watching me. He said quietly, 'I will try, Amy. I will try to be sensible, and come to terms with the past.' He sounded so unhappy that I couldn't find the words to answer as I fought back my tears.

When he'd finished his orange he stood up, went to the door and opened it for me. 'I will drink my coffee down here. Don't wait up, since I shall be taking Nella for a long walk afterwards. Good night.'

With a murmured reply I walked past him, out into the corridor – and heard the door close firmly behind me. Doubt, suspicion, resentment: they'd all been there, in his face; but I knew that underneath there was love, too.

Over the next weeks I felt as though I were walking on eggshells. I needed to show him my love, yet I had to be so careful not to intrude. I waited for him to make the first moves, which was so difficult because in the past I'd always made them. Yet slowly, he did make them: an invitation to the office, to discuss some matter of estate business with him and Mr Selby; a suggestion that I bring Jackie up to the Home Farm, too, when he was taking the girls up there; a request to take his coffee in my sitting room; even, a walk in the rose garden together.

One evening, as I walked beside him in the garden, shy as a young girl, I told him those dreams of mine – of a different past, a shared past. He listened in silence, then shook his head. 'No, Amy.' Tipping his face back a little further to watch the rushing clouds as they chased the crescent moon across the sky, he admitted softly, 'Do you suppose that I haven't dreamt, too? But the past cannot be changed; especially not our past. Because I was as I was, I could never have offered myself to any woman.'

'Unless she were desperate.'

'Yes. It could only have happened the way it did. Accepting that should make it easier for me to face the consequences. I am trying, Amy, I am trying.' Ahead of us a nightingale began to sing; together we turned and walked towards that beautiful soaring song – and came to the golden rose, my rose. Already the first buds had opened, and I bent to breathe in her lemony scent. Standing behind me he said, 'I gave you a golden rose, but it is the red rose which is the symbol of love and passion.' Gently he began to quote: ' "If you want a red rose, you must build it out of music by moonlight, and stain it with your own heart's blood." ' He turned to face me before adding, 'The light of the moon, the song of the nightingale – they're not enough. I must learn to give you that final gift, too.' His hand brushed mine for a moment, but before I could respond it had dropped down to pat Nella's golden head. 'Come along, Nella, it's time we went in.'

We went back to the house, and upstairs to our separate bedrooms. Granny Withers was right: it would have been so much easier if we'd shared a room, and a bed. But Leo was as he was. Nothing had ever been easy for him since the day he'd read her diary – or before, right back to the day he'd been born. He'd been branded then, just as I had been. So I understood. But as I lay in my lonely bed I ached to take him in my arms; only I knew he was right: he had to come to terms with the past himself.

That night my monthlies started. Although I knew there had been no hope of a child this month, still it seemed a sign of the distance between us. There was not even any reason to tell him. In the darkness I allowed myself the luxury of tears.

By the morning I felt sick and ill, and I was already bleeding heavily. Although I knew I should have grown out of my fear of blood by now, I still hadn't. Always it brought back the memory of Dimpsey, her eyes desperate and begging me to save her before the pig-sticker's knife came slicing down.

Leo had already been to see the children before me, and when I went down to breakfast Mr Wallis said he'd just left. 'I believe he's going over to Pennings today, my lady.' Walking over to the hotplate, I lifted up the lid of the first dish – and saw rashers of bacon. I was gagging as I dropped the cover down again. Although I managed to force down some toast, I still felt very queasy by the end of the meal.

I was down with Clara in her room when Leo rapped at the door. Putting his head round it he said without looking at me, 'Amy, Selby was coming over to Pennings with me, but now he says he's rather tied up – and that in any case you'd be more useful than him, since you've been dealing with Parry recently. So he suggested that I ask you.'

At once I said, 'Of course I'll come – if you want me to.'

He didn't say he did, he merely barked, 'Go and tell the children then, I'll bring the motor round at once.' The door closed with a bang.

Clara turned to me. 'Weren't that thoughtful of Mr Selby? I know he's been worrying about you, my lady.' Her face became concerned. 'Only, you don't look so well – '

'Clara, I must go.' But as I went upstairs to pack several clean towels and a piece of mackintosh in my basket I wished it had been yesterday, or tomorrow.

I said my goodbyes to the children as quickly as I could, but even so, Leo was looking impatient. He frowned at my basket. 'We're not going for a picnic. Parry will be lunching with us.'

'No, tisn't food – ' Seizing the basket from me, he tossed it into the back and stalked round to the driver's side.

At the lodge he turned right instead of left. 'Leo, we'll miss the train.'

'I've decided to drive over there for a change.'

'Oh. Do you know the way?'

'There are signposts, aren't there?' Sounding very grumpy, he muttered, 'I can't imagine what Selby had to do today that was so important.' I huddled down further into my seat. If there'd been room, I'd have crawled right under it.

In his temper, he took the wrong turning at Warminster. 'Why weren't you looking, Amy?'

'I be sorry – only I dare say we could go down that lane and thread across – '

At once he put the motor into reverse, turned and drove all the way back to the town. It was probably just as well, because by the time we saw a sign saying 'WESTBURY 2 MILES', I knew I was going to have to ask him to stop.

'Leo – please, there's a station at Westbury. Could you let me stop and get out?'

There was a furious silence for the next couple of miles, then he exploded: '*When* you arrive back at Eston tell Selby to get over here on the next train!'

I couldn't think what he meant at first, then realizing I exclaimed, 'I don't want to catch the *train* – I just need to use the lady's room.' He looked so disconcerted I'd have laughed if I hadn't been so anxious. The station was some distance outside the town and by the time he drew up in the forecourt I was convinced there must be a red patch on my skirt. I threw myself round to grapple for my basket, managing to thrust myself at the door just as he opened it from the outside. I tripped and would have fallen if he hadn't caught hold of my elbows – but the basket tumbled to the ground, and the towels spilled out on the gravel.

He stood staring at them. Then his face went brick-red. He looked at my scarlet cheeks, crouched down suddenly, and seizing the towels, rammed them back under the mackintosh and thrust the basket into my hand. I began to hurry towards the station building; he overtook me, almost running, and by the time I got to the ticket office he'd already bought a platform ticket. He pressed it into my hand and I felt the hard edge of the penny that was with it.

I emerged to find him waiting outside on the platform. 'You should have told me, Amy. I wouldn't have dragged you all this way.'

445

'Tis all right. 'Sides, I wanted to come with you.'

He glanced at me sharply, before saying, 'You don't look at all well, you know. I should have noticed before. There's a train back to Eston in half an hour. Perhaps I should put you on it.'

'No, no – please.' I was almost crying, but I couldn't help it.

He said gently, 'Poor Amy, you're trying much harder than I am, aren't you? Very well then, we'll carry on – and I'll endeavour not to shout at you.'

'I dussent mind – so long as tis not too loud.'

He smiled, then reached down to take my basket – and as he did so our hands touched. Only for a moment, but I knew that moment had been intentional, and I felt a stirring of relief.

He didn't lose his way again until we were almost there. He muttered under his breath, then we came to another signpost at a crossroads. He glared at it, then pointed at one of the boards. 'We'll take that one – then you can direct me the rest of the way.' I followed the line of his broad finger. The sign read simply 'BORRELL'. He swung the wheel of the motor to the left and we began to bump along the narrow lane.

We came to the little tin chapel first, right on the edge of the fields. I cringed back as if from Grammer's voice, harsh and angry, 'You, you be a sinner.' Desperately, I tried to stem the flood of memories.

The road straightened, and Leo increased his speed a little. We passed the small brick chapel, the road to the hall, the big stone church, and the graveyard behind it where Grammer and Granfer lay buried. The road curved round and there was the school. It was mid-morning break and the children out in the yard came running to the low wall, staring at the strange motor. Post Office, shop, Mr Wilcox the cobbler's, the horses waiting outside the forge – we drove slowly past them all; so slowly, I even heard the hiss of steam as the wheelwright fitted a new iron tyre. Next came the pond, and Dummy Drew's old cottage, still looking ragged and unkempt – 'Which way now, Amy?'

'Left – do 'ee go left at the beerhouse.' It was difficult to get the words out, for the memories crowding in. Oh Granfer, Granfer – how I did love thee –

Leo turned into Hill Lane, dropping down into low gear as he saw the road running down to the bend. I could see the top of the ash tree, even taller now – then we came round the corner and there was our cottage. Granfer's roses had gone for ever but up in the thatch was the little window in the loft, where I'd lain all that winter after Dimpsey was killed. Dimpsey, Dimpsey – and the floodgates wouldn't hold any longer. I tried to picture Granfer, and his roses – but all I could see was Dimpsey lying on the bench beneath the apple trees, her golden flank heaving with terror. Dimpsey, her eyes fixed on mine, begging me to save her. And the bitter taste of betrayal rose in my throat.

'Ah – there's the sign for Pennings.' He turned the motor right, on to the high road. 'Not much further now.' He pressed his foot down, and we sped away leaving Borrell behind us: but not my memories, clinging to me close as burrs.

Leo said, 'I'm sorry we hadn't time to stop at Borrell, so you could have had a look round. Another day, perhaps – '

'No! No! I don't want to go back there, not ever.'

He glanced at me searchingly, but I turned my head away. He didn't speak again until we were drawing into the stableyard at Pennings, then he said quietly, 'You look as white as a sheet, Amy; you really shouldn't have come today. Ah, there's Parry.'

Mr Parry came striding over from the estate office, his left hand outstretched. 'Good morning, Lady Warminster, how nice to see you. And you, Lord Warminster, so glad you're safely back.' He shook Leo's hand vigorously.

'Morning, Parry. How are things with you?'

'Mustn't complain, Lord Warminster, mustn't complain. Now, I'm sure you'd like a drink after your journey, Mrs Taylor's prepared the morning room – or would you prefer refreshments in the office?'

'The office will be quite satisfactory, thank you, Parry. But first, Lady Warminster wishes to run along and tidy her hair.' He reached into the motor for my basket. I took it from him gratefully and hurried off through the house to the cloakroom. As I was changing my towel in the WC I began to shake: the blood, Dimpsey's blood, spurting out – I could barely force my trembling fingers to obey me.

Back in the office Leo and Mr Parry were standing talking by the window. Leo turned at once. 'I ordered tea for you, Amy – I suspected you'd prefer that.' I managed to smile at him, and he drew up a chair. 'Sit down, now.'

It was easier once the talk turned back to business. Leo studied the plans. 'I see you've already started to put a considerable acreage back under grass.'

Mr Parry said, 'Lady Warminster's very keen on that.'

Leo turned to me, eyebrows raised. I explained, 'The war's over now, and there's all these new ships being built. I reckon as soon there'll be a lot o' grain coming in, from Canada, and Australia.'

Leo replied, 'But the government's still guaranteeing good prices for corn.'

I drew a deep breath. 'I don't reckon as they'll keep on doing it. They didn't afore the war, whichever party it were making the decisions. And the war cost 'em a mint o' money, so it don't make sense, keeping the price of English grain up, when there's cheaper waiting to be bought elsewhere.'

I watched Leo's face anxiously. He nodded. 'You're taking a pessimistic view, Amy, but I'm inclined to agree with your reasoning.' I gave a sigh of relief. He continued, 'Now, what exactly do you propose for next year?'

I glanced at Mr Parry, who nodded encouragingly. 'Well, we thought as we'd best . . .'

So we talked on, of pasture and plough, herds and crop yields, until it was time for lunch. I wished Mr Parry hadn't ordered ham. I wished even more that he wouldn't keep discussing pigs while I tried to eat it; but of course, that was what we were there for. So I forced myself to take part. I saw Leo watching me

447

over the meal. After I'd come back from the cloakroom again he hung behind Mr Parry and murmured, 'Amy, if you want to stay and rest in the house this afternoon – '

'No, of course I'll come out wi' you. The fresh air'll do me good.'

We visited a couple of the tenant farms, then finished up at the Home Farm. I'd almost enjoyed the afternoon: Leo had discussed the problems and plans with me as if I were his equal. His questions were searching and I had to think hard about my answers. He suggested several alterations in our plans, but when I admitted, 'Aye, you're right, I hadn't thought of that,' he said, 'Don't look so cast down, Amy. Remember, your experience has all been gained in abnormal times – but generally your assessments are shrewd.'

Mr Parry exclaimed heartily, 'I knew you'd be happy with Lady Warminster's plans, she has a clear grasp of essentials. As I always say to Selby, she should have been born a man!' He slapped his knee and laughed. 'But I couldn't expect *you* to agree with that, eh, Lord Warminster?' He didn't seem to notice that Leo wasn't laughing. 'Now, I told Hayter we'd just drop in at the lodge, some roof problem he wanted you to look at. The man's a bit of a fusspot, but he's always been a good worker, so if you wouldn't mind – '

'Not at all.'

We drew up at the lodge. While Leo and Mr Parry inspected the roof, I had a word with Mrs Hayter. Her two grandchildren from the Home Farm were staying with her while their mother was confined. They came up to me shyly; when I bent down to greet them, little Jenny whispered, 'Us wants to show you something, me lady.' Her brother Tom nodded his brown head excitedly. One small hand gripped each of mine. 'Will 'ee come wi' us?'

I smiled back down at them. 'Aye, o' course.'

They dragged me round the back of the house and down the brick path between the bean rows. It was only then I realized where they were taking me. I hung back; but small hands tugged mine, anxious to show me their treasure. 'Do 'ee look, me lady – ' I let them lead me on; I would look once, just to please them. We reached the sty. 'Baint she beautiful! The small girl's face was proud and excited, just as mine must once have been. 'Look at her, me lady.'

I nerved myself to take one hurried look – and couldn't tear my eyes away. I stood, frozen, as beside me the happy voices chattered on. 'Granfer said as we could name her, so we called her Goldie. Do 'ee come here and say good day to her ladyship.' Pointed ears pricked up. 'See, she do know everything we says.' She came, tip-tapping across the pen on her small dainty feet, to stand gazing up at me from her friendly, inquisitive eyes. Bright, happy eyes, fringed with golden lashes – my Dimpsey's eyes.

'Do 'ee give 'er a scratch me lady.'

'Behind 'er ears, she do like that.'

Children's voices, but the present had faded. I was the child again, now. Dimpsey, my beautiful Dimpsey, how I love you – I heard heavy footsteps behind, and my voice, thin as thread, cried, 'Granfer, help I – ' But I knew he wouldn't, he couldn't . . . A different voice spoke: 'Amy, it's time we – ' I swayed, hands caught me, arms held me. Children's voices, anxious, frightened; Leo's voice, calming them. But I was back under the apples trees: Dimpsey lay in front of me, her dainty little feet bound, her eyes fixed on mine – begging, pleading. The sharp knife slicing down, Dimpsey's red blood spurting up – her eyes, her eyes hopeless now, and full of despair at my treachery. Then the knife came down a second time and my legs gave way and I began to fall . . .

Leo carried me back to the motor. I crouched in the seat, my fingers locked on the edge of his jacket. There was anger and regret in his voice as he exclaimed, 'As soon as they told me where the children had taken you, I came – but I was too late, too late.'

I was gagging again as we reached the house. Leo carried me straight in to the cloakroom and set me down on a chair by the basin. The sickness subsided a little, and I huddled there, still shaking. He squatted down on his haunches beside me, and took my cold hand in his. Then he said, 'So Dimpsey was a Tamworth pig.'

'However did you know?'

'Obviously I deduced she was a pig – but I assumed a black and white one because of her name.'

I whispered, 'I did call her that 'cos Granfer brought her home in the dimpsey, just afore it went dark. She were only a baby, she were the dilling. Her Mam couldn't feed her, so I fed her, wi' milk from a bottle. I fed her like a baby – ' I couldn't go on.

But he did. 'So, being a loving child and a lonely child, you made a pet of her. How old were you then, Amy?'

'Eight, going on nine. So I were doing the chores by then. I used to feed her, and fetch the milk for her as well. I'd bring sow thistles and dandelions too, and liddle snails. She liked snails, did my Dimpsey. I used to climb in her pen and put my arms around her neck and whisper in her ear, telling her secrets. She understood every word. She were a lovely pig, my Dimpsey. Only then – '

He finished for me. 'Autumn came.'

'I did try. I caught leaves for wishes, I jumped and jumped – and every time I caught one, I wished as November wouldn't come. But it did, it did!

'Thic evening, she were lying there on the bench, her liddle feet bound up, and she were frightened – but then she thought as I were going to save her. She were looking at I, begging I. Only I couldn't, I couldn't – and the pigsticker, his knife came down and she screamed, just like a baby. She screamed – only she weren't dead. Her blood spurted – but she weren't dead, and she looked at me – her eyes – I hadn't saved her, and she knew it, she knew it. And then they killed her.'

His warm hand gripped mine; his voice was kind but sad as he told me, 'You should have stayed indoors and covered your ears.'

I replied miserably, 'Grammer'd made I go out, to carry the can. I had to hold the can, to catch her blood for the puddings – she made I keep stirring – '

His fingers tightened on mine and I saw the anger in his face, but I knew it wasn't me he was angry with.

I whispered, 'I did boil her blood, I made the puddings – but I wouldn't eat her, I wouldn't eat my Dimpsey. She lay on the slab in the larder, while Grammer were curing her, and I mopped up the brine as ran off from her body, but – ' My eyes were wide as I told him, 'But I didn't eat her, I *didn't* eat my Dimpsey.' My voice quickened, desperate to explain. 'When I were ill in the loft Granfer sent Emmie Rawlings to tell I as he'd switched the flitches one night, when Grammer were sound asleep – so Grammer never knew. Rawlingses, they had a black and white pig thic year, and twere him as I ate.' I exclaimed again, 'I never did eat my Dimpsey.'

His eyes held mine, and though his voice was pitched low it was very firm as he said, 'Amy, you've never lied to me before. Don't lie to me now.'

'No – no – ' My voice wavered into a frightened silence.

But his was unyielding. 'Tamworth hams are very distinctive. And besides, a woman of your grandmother's age and experience would have been able to tell the flitches she'd cured from those of her neighbour. And you were an intelligent child, so you must have known that, even then.'

I didn't answer. I tried to shake my head. How could I tell him the truth – the truth I'd never admitted, not even to myself? But his voice was a command now. 'Amy, tell me the truth.'

In agony I cried out at last, 'Aye, I did eat her, I did eat my Dimpsey!' And now the knife was slicing into me, the pain of it more than I could bear as it lanced into the abscess, tearing it apart – and releasing the poison. My stomach began to heave.

He moved very quickly. I was on the floor, kneeling, over the bowl, even as the sickness erupted. Above me his voice was calm. 'Don't fight it, Amy – let it come up.' His hands were firm on my shoulder, holding me, supporting me through the violence of my sickness. I saw tiny pieces of ham floating in my vomit, and gagged again. 'That's enough, Amy, quiet – quiet now.' His hands holding me, calming me, until at last the retching ceased. Reaching up, he gave the chain a sharp tug: the water came rushing, tumbling down, sweeping the last fragments of ham away – and taking the poison with them.

I crouched, drained and empty, until he lifted me up and carried me through to the chair by the washbasin. He bathed my face with cold water, then held the glass to my lips. 'Just rinse and spit, Amy.' Hollow and weak, I sagged back against him. 'Shall I take you along to the morning room now?'

But the nausea rose again as I tried to stand up. 'I – I – no, the closet, please, the closet – ' He helped me back there and I was sick again, but it was only bitter bile now. I stood up, swaying, my hand against the wall. 'I still feel queasy – I'm not sure if – ' I looked at the WC bowl, scared of leaving it.

'We'll stay here a little while longer, then.' He sat down on the floor, bending his knees and bracing his feet against the opposite wall before drawing me down on to his lap.

I whispered, 'You'll get cold, sitting on the tiles.'

I heard the hint of a smile in his voice as he told me, 'I've sat in far colder places, these past few years.'

'But – '

'Don't fuss, Amy.' He bent his head and kissed my damp forehead. And in that moment, I knew. Because it was a husband's kiss: a quick, casual confident kiss of reassurance – and of love. Not hate: just love.

As I lay in his arms trembling with relief everything seemed very strong and clear. The rough texture of his tweed jacket under my cheek, the steady beating of his heart, the gurgling of the cistern refilling – even the lingering smell of vomit told me I was alive, and safe.

At last I whispered, 'I ate her, I ate my Dimpsey.'

Leo said quietly, 'It didn't make any difference to her by then, she was dead.'

'But I didn't save her, when she were still alive.'

'Amy, there was nothing you could do. You had no choice, you were only a child.'

And it was there, where it had been since last year, another shameful secret, hidden deep with Dimpsey. The other betrayal – but now there was nothing to muffle it. So I told him the truth. 'But I wasn't a child when the telegram came.'

I felt his whole body stiffen. Then he said, very softly, 'It's all right, Amy. I understand. Do you feel able to get up yet?'

'Aye, if I can hold your arm.' He set me on my feet, and held his arm out to me.

Mr Parry was waiting in the morning room, his face creased with concern. Leo told him, 'Lady Warminster will rest for a little while, until we've sorted out the last few items.' He turned to me. 'Don't worry, Amy – I won't be long.'

He came back quite quickly. 'Parry asks, do you wish to stay over here tonight? He can offer a bed.'

'No! I want to go home.'

'Then would you prefer to travel by train? It would be a lot faster.'

I shook my head. 'No, thank 'ee. I'll come in the motor with thee.'

'Very well. We'll take a pail with us, just in case. You'd better go and change your – er – dressings now, and we'll stop at Warminster again on the way back if necessary. I'll go and bring the motor round to the front.'

We didn't go back through Borrell. We turned the other way outside the lodge and he drove on a little way in silence. Then, with his eyes fixed on the road, he said, 'Amy, yesterday you told me of your dreams, of what might have been. I replied that I, too, had dreamt. But my dreams were slightly different from yours. Do you remember telling me once of how, after your grandmother had spurned you, you came to Pennings? And wept in the garden there?'

451

'Aye, I remember.'

'Since then I've occasionally indulged in a day dream: dreaming that I'd come to Pennings myself that day, and found you there, weeping, a desperate child. So desperate that perhaps you would not have noticed – my deformities. Or even believed I truly was your fairy-tale Beast.' He almost smiled as he said that. 'Then I would have rescued you, and taken you to Eston. I'd have arranged for Grace Chandler to offer you a bed with her youngsters, but always I would have been there, too, taking care of you, protecting you. And then perhaps one day, when you'd grown up – ' He broke off with a decisive shake of his head. 'No, it couldn't have happened like that.'

I exclaimed, 'But it could've done, if you'd found me that day.'

'No, it could not. Because when you grew older, sooner or later you'd have met Francis – '

'And fallen in love with him.'

'Yes. And by then you'd have been old enough to know how I felt, and so you would have been torn in two by love and loyalty. As you have been for so long now.'

I couldn't bear to hear the sadness in his voice. He said gently, 'It's all right, Amy. Don't cry. As I told you, I do understand. At last, I understand.' His warm hand covered mine for a moment. 'You look tired.' He drew into the side of the road. 'You're very tired, so I'm going to put you into the back seat now, and I want you to try and sleep. It's all been too much for you today, hasn't it?'

He was talking to me as if I were Flora, and like Flora, I obeyed.

Much later, his voice woke me. 'We're home, Amy.' I blinked myself awake as he came round to help me out of my side. By the time I'd walked slowly up the steps the door was open, Mr Wallis smiling, 'Good afternoon, my lady.' Then I heard the shrieks of excitement, 'Mama!' 'Mama!' 'Mama!' They tumbled down the stairs – Dora following with Jackie in her arms. I was hugging and kissing them as though I'd been away for a fortnight. Then it was Leo's turn for their welcome.

As soon as the excitement was over he announced, 'Bed, now, Amy. You can have supper in your room.' I didn't argue; I still felt weak and shaken. When he held his arm out to me I clutched at it, gratefully.

At my bedroom door he said formally, 'I must apologize for having hurt you, by forcing you to make that admission.'

'You were right to do it, Leo. Twere time I did face up to the truth.'

'Yes,' he replied quietly, 'we all have to confront the past eventually. Good night, Amy.' He turned and left abruptly, and my heart sank. It was only just gone six o'clock, but he'd said goodnight already, so obviously he didn't intend to come and say it later. I'd begun to hope again this afternoon, because he'd been so kind, caring for me. But then, he'd been caring for folk all these past four years, it must be simply a routine for him by now. I'd been wrong that moment in the WC: it had just been my wishful thinking.

452

Chapter Sixty-One

I slept the clock round and more; I didn't wake until my morning tea arrived. Clara brought it. 'His lordship's asking how you were, so I said I'd bring your tray up myself.' She smiled. 'Your colour's back, my lady.'

'I do feel better for the long sleep.'

She nodded. 'Aye, he said you never so much as stirred when he peeped in last night.' Suddenly I felt a lot more cheerful; Clara's grin was sympathetic. 'They do start coming round in the end.'

But he'd already left the nursery when I went up, and although he came in for breakfast he hardly spoke to me once he'd said he was pleased I was feeling so much better. His own face was drawn: he didn't look as if he'd slept well, if at all.

It was only after he'd drained his last cup of coffee that I learnt what was on his mind. He asked abruptly, 'Amy, have you still got her diary? I wish to re-read it.' When I hesitated, he continued, 'I know what you're going to say, but as I told you yesterday, we must all face up to our past eventually. It's time I did so, too. But I'm older than you, so my past begins earlier – with Jeanette.'

I tried to prevent him. 'But, you've read it already.'

His eyes were watching my face. 'So it is as bad as I remember. But don't worry, Amy, it can't be worse. So please, may I borrow it?'

I tried again. 'Mebbe you've forgotten your French. After all, that time you took me to France, you made a mistake about the train – '

He broke across my excuses. 'I've never had any problem with the written language.' He gave a half-smile, 'And my command of the spoken has also improved these last years, since I found myself appointed unofficial interpreter for the unit.' The smile faded. 'Amy, it's no use your trying to protect me: there are even worse ghosts for me to confront than those in my first wife's diary, but let me at least try and come to terms with them first.' I went to fetch it.

I didn't see him again all day. When he finally came to my sitting room after tea his face was grey and haggard. He handed me the diary. 'Thank you.' He watched as I took the key from my blouse and locked it. Then he asked, 'Would you come for a walk with me, before dinner?'

'Aye, o' course. I'll just tell the children.'

I expected he'd want to walk in the rose garden, but instead he headed straight across the park to the wood; and then I realized where he intended to go.

The evening sun was slanting golden across the brier hedge and into the clearing. Several of his Blairii roses had already opened their pink blooms in a sheltered corner of the south-facing wall, but he walked past them, across the uneven flagged floor of the ruined hall and out into the courtyard, where she stood.

I didn't dare speak. I watched his eyes seek her beautiful face, and I turned away from the pain I saw in them. Her expression was so calm, so serene: as if even now, she were hiding her fear and revulsion from him. Yet they'd been there, always.

Quietly he said, 'It was hopeless, wasn't it?'

I came to stand beside him. 'Aye. You were right to send her away.'

'Yes.' His voice twisted in sorrow. 'There was nothing else I could do, having once committed the terrible crime of marrying her.'

'It were the aunts who made her marry you. That weren't your fault.'

He shook his head. 'No, Amy – my fault, too. I realized that, reading her diary again today.'

'But – '

He interrupted me. 'She was weak, defenceless; but she did have one weapon, and that was her religion. The first time I read what she'd written, I saw only the damaging consequences of those beliefs of hers – but they gave her strength, too. And they would have given her the strength to refuse me.'

I exclaimed, 'She did, afore she knew about the baby, then – ' I stopped, but it was too late now, so I had to tell him the truth. 'The aunts gave in, but she fainted, and that's when they found out she was carrying.'

My voice died away at the hurt in his face, but he said only, 'I wondered if that had been the case.'

'But *they* forced her then, so it still weren't your fault.'

'Oh yes it was, Amy. You see, in cases of mixed marriage it is a strict condition that the children of the union should be brought up in the Roman Catholic faith; the priest asks the Protestant partner for a promise to that effect before the marriage. No such promise was asked of me. I realized why, later: her aunts were women of great influence. But at the time I felt only relief, because I never had the slightest intention of allowing my children to be reared in the Roman faith – I'd always felt it to be corrupted with superstition. But Jeanette never knew my feelings. She assumed that a promise had been made, and I allowed her to persist in that assumption, because I feared she would refuse to marry me if she understood my true intention. So I deceived her, Amy, even as she deceived me. And in so doing, I deprived her of the only weapon she had the strength to fight with.' His voice was low and anguished now. 'I fell in love with her, I married her – and I destroyed her.'

Quickly I shook my head. 'No – it didn't make any difference. She needed a husband, just like I did – ' I faltered to a stop, because now I saw the truth, just as he had.

'No, not like you, Amy. Francis was already married by the time *you* knew you needed a husband. Besides – '

454

I said quietly, 'I were only a servant.'

'Yes – to him. But the father of Jeanette's child was free to marry her, and was her social equal. His mother would have had to give in eventually, if Jeanette had refused to marry me. Then, she could have married the man she loved.'

But still I tried to console Leo. 'Only, her cousin didn't want to marry her – not even when he knew about the baby. Thérèse sent him a message but he stayed away, like his mother told him to.'

'Good God! How could any man have behaved so despicably?' Then he shook his head. 'No, Amy, he'd still have had to marry Jeanette, to prevent the scandal. She was his cousin, remember.'

I retorted, 'But fancy being married to a man as had let her down like that. And he'd have been unfaithful, too. She'd have been so unhappy.'

Leo looked straight at me as he asked, 'Do you think she was happy with me?' There was no answer to that. His gaze shifted back to the statue, to her. 'And then I made her suffering still more acute by refusing to allow Francis to be reared in her faith.'

'It were understandable, when you found out about the way she'd been frightened by devils. And anyway,' I said quickly, 'he joined her Church at the end.'

'Yes, he did. But too late to give her the peace of mind I'd denied her.'

I looked at her calm face. 'But if what she believed were true, she'll know about it, and be happy at last.'

Leo replied quietly, 'And if she was wrong?'

I could only offer him the bleak truth. 'Then, she's dead now, so it don't make any difference.'

There was such sadness in his reply. 'So now I can never put right the wrong I did.'

The tears blurred my vision so I could hardly see the child in her arms: the child. For she held a child – just as I had. Her son's child. Safe now, at Eston. I said quietly, 'Leo, you've put it right already. You put it right when, instead of turning me out of your house, you sent me to Kew and you put it right when you married me to give my baby a name.' I turned to look at him directly. 'It wasn't just because I spoke to you in the garden that you married me, was it? It was because of her, too – for her sake. Because I were in the same state she'd been in, only worse. I had nobody – except you.' Watching his face, I knew I'd hit on the truth.

Then he shook his head. 'But it isn't possible to redeem the past, is it?' His eyes went back to the statue. 'It was too late for Jeanette.'

'But it weren't too late for me. And she hoped it weren't too late for you; that's why she sent me her diary – and the message.'

'Ah yes, her final plea. Which you cannot fulfil, because I will not let you. Let's go back, Amy.' He turned and left her in peace. Fighting back my tears, I followed him out of that quiet courtyard, back through the ruined house and into the wood.

As we left the shelter of the last trees, he paused a moment to look at me. 'You're still very pale, you know, you're not over yesterday's upset yet.' He reached out, our hands met, clasped – and then his fingers loosed their grip. 'Facing up to the past isn't easy, is it? So thank you, Amy, for helping me lay the ghosts of my first marriage. But you can't help me with the ghost of my second; I have to do that myself, and I can't do it yet.' I couldn't reply as I walked on beside him.

Outside the library door he said, 'I suspect she would wish you to destroy that diary now.'

'Aye. I should've done it before.'

'No. I'm glad I was able to read it again. I had buried the memory of it but – underneath, it was still there. I feel better now that it's out in the open.'

I knew exactly how he felt. 'It were the same for me, yesterday. Tisn't good to hide these things, and pretend. The poison, it do stay there, festering. It needs to be opened, like an abscess. Tis only then the healing can begin.'

His whole body stiffened. When he finally spoke his voice was so low I could hardly hear. 'I've been selfish again, I simply haven't been thinking of you.' He looked at me, his expression almost desperate. 'Just give me a little more time, Amy.' Before I could reply the library door had shut behind him.

He didn't speak over dinner, hardly seeming to hear my occasional tentative remark. Afterwards he went straight out with Nella. 'Don't wait up for me, Amy. I'll be late.'

But it wasn't much after eleven when his footsteps passed my door, though I was already in bed. My sitting room had seemed very lonely; but once I was in bed, I couldn't sleep, so I was sitting up reading. I heard him come into his dressing room. Then the door opened, 'May I come in, Amy?'

'Aye, o' course.' I put my book down. 'I decided that if your light was still on, I would come and talk to you tonight.'

'Do 'ee sit down.'

'Thank you.' But before he did so he carefully positioned the chair so he could see my face. He hesitated, and I could see him draw a deep breath before he began. 'Amy, for both of us there is more poison yet, isn't there? You didn't just feel guilty over betraying your pig, did you? There's been another betrayal since, hasn't there?'

'I – I – ' I was frightened. I didn't want to admit that he was right.

But he wouldn't be stopped. 'You almost told me yesterday, at Pennings. You said, "But I wasn't a child when the telegram came." You were referring to the other betrayal, weren't you? When the telegram came – telling of Frank's death.'

I still wavered. My heart was beating so fast that I could hardly breathe, but his voice was inflexible. 'Amy, you must tell me. Tell me what happened when the telegram came.'

I whispered, 'The news were so bad, and you were both o' you out there. I kept reading the paper, imagining the guns. I were so worried – ' I couldn't go on.

But he was strong, too strong for me. 'Amy, tell me. Tell me the truth.'

My voice was a wail of despair. 'I didn't want him to die!'

'No – because you loved him.'

'Aye, I did love him.' I felt the tears on my cheeks. 'Only, when Mr Selby came with the telegram I thought it were going to be you.' I swallowed, and my voice came faster. 'Before, I'd think of it happening, imagine Mr Selby holding the telegram, and the look on his face – and me not knowing which of you it was. It were my nightmare. So when it happened, and Mr Selby said, "I'm afraid it's very bad news," I should have been prepared, been thinking that it might be either of you. But when the time came, all I could think, was that it were going to be you.' Leo's face was carved from granite, as I cried desperately, 'I were so sure it were *your* name I were going to read that when I saw his – I felt – ' I stopped. I couldn't bear to admit that terrible shameful truth. I began to sob.

'Tell me, Amy, what did you feel?'

I looked up into his mismatched grey eyes and told him, 'All I could feel – was relief.'

'Relief!' He was shouting.

Hastily I excused myself. 'It were only for a moment. Then I grieved, I grieved so much. But you see, before I read it – ' my voice broke at the memory – 'I'd been so sure it were you. And then afterwards, I were so ashamed, because he loved me.' I was shaking, yet even in those first moments I felt relief again, because I'd faced up to the truth at last.

I was almost calm when Leo eventually spoke; but his voice sounded odd and strained. 'Amy, all this time, I've been thinking it was the other way round.'

I was bewildered. 'The other way round?'

'In France, after I read that letter he'd written, and learnt how he'd come to love you, and planned to take you away – '

'But, Leo, I wouldn't never have left you.'

'Amy, you wouldn't have had to leave me, if the name on that telegram had been mine.'

The kaleidoscope started to turn, spinning faster and faster as he said, 'I imagined your thoughts in those moments before you read it, knowing already that one of us had been killed. And I imagined you, in those moments, praying that the name you read would be mine.'

I stretched out my hand to him. 'Oh, Leo, I'd never've wanted that, never. Even if – '

'Even if?'

'Even if I'd wanted to go away with him. But I didn't, I wanted you. I wanted you to come back to me. That were why I felt the way I did – but it were only for a moment.'

457

I began to weep. I felt his arms come round me, lifting me on to his lap, and I clung to him, sobbing and sobbing. When I looked up, I saw the tears on his cheeks, too. I gazed up at him, at Leo who'd believed all this time that I'd wanted him dead – and yet had still loved me. And I had been blind, too: I'd known at the end that I hadn't loved Frank enough, but I'd thrust the thought from me in guilt and shame, instead of understanding why. The kaleidoscope fell into its final pattern.

I drew my head back and said, 'I did love him, Leo.'

'Yes, I know.'

'Only it were a different kind of love. I was only a girl when I met him, and he were so young, too. But now, I be a woman grown, and tis thee I love.' I drew his head down to mine, and kissed him gently on the lips. Then we simply held each other close.

Chapter Sixty-Two

At last he murmured, 'You'll get cold, Amy, I'd better put you back in bed.'

My arms tightened around his neck. 'I dussent want thee to go.'

'And I don't want to leave you, either,' he said softly.

'Then, mebbe if you slipped your suit off, so as not to crease it, you could lie beside me under the bedclothes.' I sensed his hesitation, so I added quickly, 'O' course, if you'd rather not, while I've got my monthlies – '

His quick kiss reassured me. 'I'll go and get ready for bed. I won't be long.'

He came back in his pyjamas and climbed in beside me. At once I took him in my arms. He was shivering. 'Thee bist cold.'

He murmured, 'No, Amy, it's relief. This last year – ' He broke off, then admitted, 'In my worst moments I believed you hated me, would still have hated me even if it had been my name on that telegram. Hated me, because even my death would not have set you free to marry Francis. I could never forget, that by forcing you into marriage I had cut you off from him forever.'

I gave him a little shake. 'Leo, you're being silly. You *didn't* force me into marriage, you know that. And even then it weren't a true marriage – not till I made it one. That were my decision, not yourn. Now, tis time thee didst forget thy foolish fancies – and tis time, too, we went to sleep.' Drawing his head down on my breast, I gently stroked his soft hair until the slowing of his breathing told me that he slept.

He left me at dawn. After he'd gone I lay awake and wept, weeping for Frank; but behind my tears was relief, because Leo's fears were over, and finally he believed that I truly loved him.

Those next days were our time of healing. We both had to accept the sorrows of the past.

'I let him down, Amy. I'd promised I'd be as a father to him – but I wasn't.'

'I let him down, too.'

'Not until the end, and then he never knew.' He reached out his hand, and we sat with our fingers entwined until the children came in search of us. Those days we were always together: in his library; in my sitting room; the estate office; and in the rose garden. We'd grown so far apart this last year, now we had to find each other again. It was a quiet time: we spoke only the odd disjointed sentence of regret, and explanation, and love. But we took comfort from each other's presence – and all day we were never apart.

At night we would go to our separate rooms, and get ready for bed. Then he would tap on the connecting door and come in, wearing his dressing gown over his pyjamas – to show me I had a choice. He'd tell me, 'I've just come to say good night, Amy.' And I'd reply, 'Why don't you come under the cover for a little while, just for a cuddle?'

'Thank you.' His dressing gown would drop to the floor, but never his pyjamas. The most he'd allow was for me to unfasten the buttons of his jacket, so I could rest my cheek on the silken hair of his chest. My shy Leo. Jeanette, who'd avoided his shadow in life, still cast her own shadow over him in death.

On the Saturday, as I held him in my arms, I said, 'Likely my monthlies'll be finished by tomorrow evening.' I felt his body tense and his breathing quicken. Then, remembering what Granny Withers had said, I suggested, deliberately casual, 'Seeing as you've got your dressing room for shaving and suchlike, why don't you use my room for sleeping? It'd save on the laundry.'

At first he didn't reply. Then he said, as if making a joke, 'Despite the appalling rises in taxation over these last years, I don't think we need to economize to that extent, Amy.' His breathing slowed as if he'd fallen asleep, but I was sure he hadn't; he just wanted me to think he had, so I wouldn't suggest sharing a room again. Her shadow. But it wasn't just her shadow: he'd arranged these rooms with their carefully separate bathrooms long before he'd read her diary. Yet at Eton he'd swum naked in the river – but, of course, they were all boys at Eton. He didn't mind men seeing him, it was women he avoided, even his wife. I sighed: why couldn't he realize that I wasn't Jeanette, who'd been frightened by devils? Still, I could understand how he felt after having read her diary, especially the way she'd gone hysterical after she'd seen him with no clothes on by the lake. Poor Jeanette – and in that moment I knew the answer. She'd asked me to give him the love she couldn't give, and so I would.

He'd left me by the time I woke the next morning, but the sun was already slanting through the gap in the curtains. It was going to be fine. I would ask him today.

After lunch we were walking in the garden when he exclaimed, 'It's so warm this afternoon, we can almost see the roses unfolding their petals.'

At once I seized my chance. 'Leo, seeing as tis so hot, why don't you go for a swim in the lake, and cool yourself down? I'll come with you, to hold the towels.'

He stopped so suddenly I bumped into him. His voice was abrupt. 'No, I have no bathing dress.' He began to walk on, very fast. I ran after him. 'But you don't need one. You never wore a bathing dress to swim in at Eton. Sir George told me.'

'Damn George! Don't be stupid, Amy. I can't swim in front of you in the buff.'

'Why not? I am your wife.'

'It's out of the question,' he snapped.

He was in a thoroughly bad mood by now, but I wasn't going to give up. I said loudly, 'Leo, I do find it strange that a man like you as were so brave in France, winning a medal n'all, should be too frightened to go for a swim in front of his own wife.'

That threw him off course. It was a little while before he replied and his voice wasn't angry any more. 'Amy, you told me once you were an arrant coward about toothache; I'm an arrant coward about this.'

I said softly, 'Leo, I do love thee. Dussent thee trust I?'

I could see the struggle in his face. Reaching out to him, I took his hand in both of mine, clasping it firmly. He began to stammer, 'I – I' At last he got the words out. 'After tea – not till after tea.'

He'd have been better agreeing to go at once. I could see him getting more and more worked up all afternoon. When the children had gone back upstairs after tea, he turned to me, his face anguished. 'Amy, are you *sure*?'

'Aye, I'm sure.'

'But suppose – you see me – and loathe me?'

'Leo, I've seen you once already, don't you remember?' As his face went brick red I added briskly, 'I'll run along and fetch the towels, and a rug for me to sit on.'

Behind me he shouted, 'And my dressing gown. I must have my dressing gown – '

He never spoke a word as we walked across the park together, with Nella padding beside us. We entered the wood and still he said nothing, until we came to where the path turned off to the lake. There he stopped, and said quietly, 'I'm frightened, Amy.'

I stretched up, pulled his head down, and kissed him. 'I do love thee, Leo.' As soon as I'd released him he went over to the old hurdle, tugged it out of the undergrowth, and set it to bar the path behind us. Then he strode on to the lake.

When we arrived he took the dressing gown from the bundle and went straight into the small hut. I walked along a little further and spread out the rug on the grassy slope. Then I sat down on it, facing across the lake.

When he came out of the hut his dressing gown was wrapped tightly round him. Without looking at me, he walked off in the other direction, making his way round the side of the lake to where the boulders were piled up above the deep water. He gave Nella the word, and she went streaking off, but my eyes were on Leo as he climbed up the giant's stair of rocks to the one at the top, which jutted out over the water. On strong bare feet he walked forward along its level surface to the very brink. He stood there a moment, facing me; then all at once he shrugged the dressing gown from his shoulders, raised his arms, and dived in.

Sir George had been right: he was as easy as an otter in the water. I felt for a moment the most overwhelming anger at the French Countess for destroying all that grace and power; then I forgot everything in the pure joy of watching him. He swum out to the centre of the lake, reared up, plunged down – and disappeared. For a moment I was frightened, until his sleek dark head broke the surface; lifting it high, he shook the shining drops from his face, before plunging once more. There in the centre of the lake he was leaping, turning, playing; all for the sheer joy of feeling the water on his body. And the confidence of him! I knew now that he'd swum since she'd left, must have been swimming while he'd been married to me; but secretly, alone save for Nella, who plunged and frolicked with him now. Swiftly he turned his lithe, powerful body and began to swim to the opposite bank. The trees hung low over the water there, and reaching up one strong dark arm he snapped off a stick and threw it skimming across the surface of the lake. Nella surged in pursuit, and Leo went chasing after her. The golden dog was so at ease in the water – but not as graceful as the man racing beside her.

No, not a man, but the Beast – the Beast in his natural element at last. And as he leapt up and threw the stick again and dived smoothly after it, my eyes filled with tears, for the Beast was beautiful, so beautiful in the water.

The stick was thrown once more, then cast aside. The time of play was over. He began to swim straight as an arrow, back and forth across the lake. A quick curving turn and then he was heading back again with the strong flowing movement of an otter. Six times he swum the length of the lake, then he turned for the seventh time – and began to swim towards me.

I stood up and walked down the slope to meet him, towel ready in my hand. When he saw me waiting there, his steady progress faltered for a second, before continuing in its straight line towards me. He reached the shallower water, his feet found the bottom, and he stood up. As he emerged from the water I saw the shining strands of black hair clinging to his body like wet silk. There was no concealment now: when he started to wade towards me all his male strength was revealed to my gaze.

With one vigorous step he was out of the water and striding across the pebbly shore and up on to the grass where I stood waiting. I held out the towel but he didn't take it. Instead, he dropped to his knees and bowed his whole lop-sided body. He was ungainly again, now that he'd left the water. He could only bend sideways, not forwards; but still he dropped his head lower, to bare his humped back before me.

Gently but firmly I towelled him dry, drying him as so often I'd dried his babies after their baths. Then I told him briskly, 'Come up to the rug now, my Leo, so I can dry the rest of you.' So then it was I who knelt, kneeling in worship at his feet as I dried his strong legs – and that which lay between. Next I dried his buttocks, then his chest, and last of all, his face, so I could kiss him as I rubbed the water from his damp hair. His voice was quiet as he said, 'Not a handsome prince, Amy.'

I whispered, 'Tis the Beast I love, my Leo. And the Beast in the water, he were so strong and graceful. I never seen anything so beautiful in all of my life.'

I saw joy transform his face, then he took me into his arms, and my whole body was yielding to his. There beside the lake we loved; a loving so close that it was as if our two bodies became one.

Afterwards, as we lay still entwined, he murmured, ' "I am not thine, I am a part of thee." ' His voice was alive with wonder as he told me, 'When I first read those words I did not believe they could be true for any man; yet they have come true for me. Oh Amy, Amy, I want to shout your name to the skies – I love you, I love you!'

We walked back through the wood hand in hand. As we left the shelter of the trees I expected him to slip his fingers from mine – but he didn't. We were still holding hands as we arrived back at the house. Mr Wallis met us in the hall: I saw his flicker of surprise swiftly suppressed as he said, 'My lord, Sir George has telephoned. He wishes you to call him back.'

Slowly, Leo disengaged his fingers from mine. 'I suppose I'd better go and see what he wants.' He lobbed the bundle of damp towels to Mr Wallis, 'Sort those out for me, Wallis,' then turned to me. 'Stay here, Amy, I won't be a minute.'

But it was more than five minutes before he came back, looking rueful. 'Amy, I've said I'll go over and see George. Maureen Seeton's given him the push and he's feeling very low. He's on his own in the house, so he asked me to dine with him tonight.'

'Oh.' I felt so deflated, and Leo's expression reflected my feelings.

'I know, Amy, but I had to agree. He was very good to me after – ' Then he paused, and said firmly, 'After Jeanette's departure.'

'When will you be back?'

'I don't know. George seemed pretty cut up about the whole affair. You'd better not wait up for me. You run up to the nursery while I throw my dinner jacket on. The children will be wondering what's happened to us. I'll see you up there.'

We had five minutes together with the children, then I kissed him goodbye outside the nursery door. 'You have an early night, Amy: you look tired, and I suspect it will be well after midnight before I get back.' I felt sorry for Sir George, but I did wish he'd asked someone else to keep him company. Then I scolded myself, I had no right to be so downcast. After all, I'd see Leo in the morning.

I went to bed at the usual time and fell asleep straightaway. Much later I was woken by Leo's voice. 'I'm back, Amy.' I opened my eyes to see his white shirtfront, then all at once my bedclothes were thrown back and I'd been scooped up into his arms. Before I knew what was happening, he'd carried me through the dressing room and dumped me on to his bed. He pulled the covers up over me. 'Go back to sleep, Amy, I won't be a minute.' As I watched he began to undress. Jacket, tie, waistcoat, braces, shirt, vest – all flew off in different directions. His trousers and underpants dropped to the floor, he stepped out of them, tugged off his socks with the suspenders still attached, and tossed them over his shoulder. Then he strode towards the bed, naked.

463

As his hand reached for the light switch, I asked, 'What time is it?'

'Five past three – time you were asleep.' The light snapped off.

As the mattress bounced under his weight I said, 'I've woken up now,' and reached out to him.

His arms drew me close, enfolding me, tightening into a satisfyingly warm hug as he told me, 'I've been longing for this moment all evening.'

Belatedly I remembered to ask, 'How was Sir George?'

'I hope he was more philosophical about the whole business by the time he'd downed a few brandies. I never liked that woman, in any case. I told him he was well rid of her and it was high time he settled down and got married again. So he asked me to introduce him to your sister. Give me a kiss, Amy.'

I exclaimed, 'But, Leo!' then his mouth covered mine and I gave myself up to the pleasure of his kiss. He tasted of cigars and brandy, and when he finally drew his head back I asked, 'Are you drunk, too?'

'Not with wine: just with love. Give me another kiss. Mm, that was delicious. Have you really woken up?'

'Aye, I only went to sleep till you came home.'

'You are wonderful, Amy – wonderful, wonderful. Let me show you just how wonderful you are.' His hands tugged at my nightdress, pulled – and went on pulling until it was right over my head.

From beneath the muffling folds I told him, 'You should have untied the ribbons first!' He was laughing so much I had to find them myself. When I'd got them undone he gave a last heave at my nightdress, and then I was as naked as he was. I launched myself triumphantly into his arms.

'Oh, Leo, don't that feel nice?' Kissing, caressing, revelling in the feel of his warm skin on mine – I could have gone on for ever, but turning over on his back he lifted me astride him and slipped his rod in where it belonged.

His hips moved under mine, and I felt the warm pleasure of him there and murmured of my delight until that delight grew so great I had to cry out with the sheer joy of it.

Afterwards I lay on his bare chest in a trance of happiness, listening to his voice telling me of his love and joy. At last he turned on his side, drew me close against his heart, and pulled the covers up over us both. Only then did I remember: 'But, Leo,' I said, 'I don't *have* a sister.'

It was too late, he was already asleep. So I closed my eyes, and surrendered to sleep as well.

The light falling on my eyelids as the curtains were drawn back woke me – I lifted my head just as Mr Wallis turned to face the bed. Both our jaws dropped, then I dived down to burrow under Leo's arm. Mr Wallis had regained his composure as his level voice asked, 'Shall I tell Bertha to bring her ladyship's tea-tray in here, my lord?'

'Thank you, Wallis. In future she'd better bring mine, too, since her ladyship will be sleeping in here from now on.'

'Certainly, my lord.' I heard Mr Wallis' footsteps head towards the door.

'Oh, and Wallis – don't come back. I'll shave myself this morning.'

'Certainly, my lord.'

As I heard the door opening, Leo called, 'And tell Mrs Carter to delay breakfast; we'll be late down.'

'Certainly, my lord.' The door closed with a gentle click.

I emerged from Leo's armpit, my face hot. It became even hotter when I saw my discarded nightdress lying where Leo had tossed it last night, next to his own tumbled heap of clothes. I exclaimed in horror, 'Whatever did Mr Wallis think?'

'I simply can't imagine, Amy.' Leo stretched lazily, and drew me back down against his side.

'Am I really to move into your bedroom?'

He corrected, '*Our* bedroom. Yes. While I was driving back from Belling last night I decided you were quite right: it *is* time we economized on the laundry.' He pointed, 'You can put your dressing table over on the far wall, so I can lie in bed and watch you prinking and preening.'

'I don't – '

His lips silenced me. When I drew back he said, 'Give me another kiss, Amy. And another one – *Da mi basia mille.*'

'Is that Greek?'

'No, Latin. It means, "Give me a thousand kisses" – that should just about last me until lunch time. Mm – '

When he paused for breath I asked, 'Why did you tell Mr Wallis to put back breakfast?'

'So I can say good morning to you properly. Up you come, now.' In a moment his rod was safe inside me.

'There, it do slide in easier with practice.'

'You're quite right, Amy: practice is the thing – lots and lots of it.' Then the teasing note left his voice. 'Oh, Amy, Amy –'

Afterwards I lay breathless in his arms as he caressed my hair and kissed my cheeks. When finally he released me, I said, 'I'll light your Etna, then I'll have to go next door to dress.'

But I'd only just got my petticoat on when he called me back into his dressing room. 'I can't find my cuff links.'

'They're here, just where they always are.'

'You put them in for me.'

'On one condition – '

'What condition, Amy?'

'That you give me a kiss for each link.' We didn't stop kissing until the water in the Etna was about to erupt. I watched while he worked up the soap, lathered his face and picked up the razor labelled 'Monday'. As he wielded it he said, 'Do you know, Amy, it makes me feel very married, having my wife standing in her petticoats, watching me shave.'

'You are married, *very* married.'

He laughed again. 'I suppose so, with three children.' He glanced at me with a smile, 'And no doubt a fourth soon on the way.' I blushed.

When he'd finished his shave he patted his cheeks dry with the towel, then held his arms out to me. 'Come here, Amy. My fifty-sixth kiss is overdue.'

When he finally let me go I said, 'I reckon it's nearer seventy, now.'

'Nonsense, that was only one – pauses for breath don't count.' His hands on my shoulders swung me round. 'It's time you got dressed.' With a pat on my behind he sent me off to my bedroom.

He lay sprawled on my bed while I put the rest of my clothes on. 'You attire yourself in far too much underwear, Amy. Next time you visit that dressmaker I'll come with you, and choose something new – perhaps one of those abbreviated diaphanous garments that you wore to the dinner party.'

'It weren't decent.'

'Quite.' He chuckled, and I didn't know how to reply.

I buttoned the placket of my skirt and sat down at my dressing table to do my hair. In the mirror I saw him watching me; when the last hairpin was in place he came towards me, and his large hands rested lightly on my shoulders as he bent to kiss the nape of my neck. Then his cheek came to rest against mine, as he crouched beside me. We gazed at our two faces, reflected in the dressing table mirror. He said softly, 'Beauty – and the Beast.' His voice was sad. 'Forever the Beast – I'm sorry, Amy.'

Quickly I turned, and my mouth found his. We clung together for a long time. Then he murmured, 'Amy – thou art my sun, my moon, my stars, my world. How I do love thee.' His lips gently caressed mine once more before he straightened up and said, 'The children will be wondering what's happened to us. We'd better get up to the nursery.'

My voice was brisk. 'Aye, we'd better. You'll have to have your other nine hundred and forty-one kisses in the garden, after breakfast.'

He began to laugh. 'But Amy, I'm not sure I can wait that long!'

Chapter Sixty-Three

And so it began, our time of love and roses. When we walked together of an evening, every rose in his garden seemed to share our joy: their colours were brighter, their scents sweeter, and their petals had opened more fully to the warmth of the sun. I was like a rose, too: basking in the glowing heat of his love. There were no secrets between us now, no suspicion, no doubt, no fear – just love. Love in the touch of his hand, love in his voice – and love in our hearts.

We spent each day together: in the nursery, in the garden, in the estate office, up at the Home Farm – and down at the lake. He taught me to swim that year, and I learnt the joy of silken water on my bare skin. He began to teach me Greek, too, in the library of an evening. Once I said to him, 'What should I teach thee, Leo, in return? Mebbe to do accounts?'

'I'm not sure I'd be as quick with those as you are with your Greek. In any case, why should I bother, when I have you to do them for me?'

'Thee bist as idle as a cuckoo!'

He smiled, a lazy, contented smile. Then his expression changed, and became serious. 'Amy, you've already taught me the most important thing of all.'

'What's that?'

'You've taught me to love again.'

Later I whispered, 'I'll never get the endings of these verbs learnt if thee dost keep kissing me all through the lessons.'

'*You* started it that time. Anyway, we'll have to close our books. Nella's becoming impatient.' Lifting me off his lap he set me on my feet and stood up himself. 'Let's take her for her walk in the garden.' He held out his hand to me, and together we went out into the scents of the evening. It was our time of love and roses.

Harvest came. Once more I sat under the shade of the big elm tree in High Hams, watching Rose and Jackie tumbling with the other children, while Flora swung on Leo's hand as he talked to Mr Arnott. Then all at once she was away, leaping across the stubble, to her brother and sister. I smiled to see her bounding energy: I was so sleepy these days. My eyelids drooped.

'Well, I reckon as we did a good job there, eh, Martha?'

My eyes blinked open. Granny Withers and Maud Winterslow stood in front of me in their best boots and sunbonnets, looking very pleased with themselves. 'We just stepped up to see how his lordship's harvest were going, and by the look o' you this afternoon, me lady, there'll be another crop fer him in the spring.' She dug her sister in the ribs. 'Been busy sowing his oats all summer, he has!'

'*Who* has, Mrs Withers?' Leo loomed behind her.

She wasn't a whit abashed. 'You have, me lord, and by the look o' thy lady there they baint fallen on stony ground, neither.' She cackled and Maud joined her, before ordering, 'Come along, Martha, we want a word wi' your Annie while we're here.'

Leo dropped to the grass beside me. 'Perhaps you'd better check with Matthews before that pair of harpies pass it all round the village.'

I nodded. 'We'd best be sure, I suppose.'

His fingers curled round mine, and his smile was full of tenderness. 'You're sure already, Amy. I can see it in your face.'

'Are you pleased?'

'Very. I think it's the right time now, don't you?'

I rested my hand on the curve of my belly, 'Twouldn't make no difference if it weren't – thic baby's coming anyway.' He laughed, then bending over he kissed me on the lips in full view of the busy harvest field. There was a confidence about him this summer that I'd never seen before.

He lay back on the grass again and said, 'It's time we had a dinner party, Amy. Talk to Clara about it tomorrow. We'll hold it at the end of September, while Annabel's here.'

A dinner party – at Eston! I felt so excited. Then I exclaimed, 'But, Leo, what shall I wear? All my evening dresses are out of date, 'cept for the pink one, and I'm not sure if – '

He chuckled, 'No, you'd better not wear that! It wouldn't do for the host to throw the hostess over his shoulder and make off with her in the middle of his own dinner party!'

'Oh, Leo, you wouldn't do that.'

He turned over so he could look at me fully, then he whispered, 'I might, Amy, I just might.'

Blushing, I said hastily, 'Well, in any case it was rather a snug fit, even then, so I dare say as I won't even be able to get into it, by the end o' next month.'

'No.' He sounded very pleased with himself. 'And since it is I who must take responsibility for the new and most delightful ripening of your figure – ' he waited for my blush to deepen, and when it did he smiled again, a proud, possessive smile – 'then, my sweet Amy, the least I can do is buy you a new dress. As soon as the harvest is finished we'll have a day in Town together.'

We went up to London on the early train, so we could spend the morning in the British Museum. Leo wanted to show me the Elgin Marbles from the Parthenon; then after lunch there was to be the dressmaker's, followed by a visit to Kew. At the Museum I thought the Greek sculptures were beautiful, but I was even more fascinated by the homely bits and pieces in the Egyptian rooms: it was like a miracle to see the toys that children had actually played with all that time ago!

We had lunch in the Ladies' Room at his Club and as we drank our coffee at the end of the meal I exclaimed, 'Oh, Leo, I *am* enjoying today!'

His smile was indulgent. 'And you've still got your visit to the dressmaker's ahead of you.'

'Oh, but I thought you were coming, too.'

'Indeed I am, after what you chose when left to yourself. In fact I'm beginning to wonder if we should be going somewhere else.'

I shook my head. 'We can't do that. Granny Withers and Miss Winteslow'd never forgive me if I didn't get my new dress from their niece.'

'Their *niece*?' He sounded very surprised.

I explained, 'Well, Madame d'Hiver called 'em both "Aunty", and seeing as *l'hiver* means "the winter" I reckoned as she must be their brother's daughter.'

'But the two Winterslow brothers – ' He broke off looking quite agitated, then asked, 'Amy, how *old* is this woman?' I hesitated, knowing he was a mite sensitive about his age, but he said it himself: 'About my age – perhaps slightly older?'

'Aye, that'd be about right. She has started to go grey, but mostly her hair's still black.'

He suddenly jumped up. 'We'd better be on our way, she'll be waiting for us.'

'I only said sometime after lunch, when I wrote.'

But he was already halfway to the door. I hadn't even finished my coffee. Still, I didn't mind, I was flattered that he was so interested in choosing my new dress.

Except that when we arrived there, he was much more interested in Madame d'Hiver than my dress. And although she was as businesslike as usual, I could see she was quite taken with Leo, too. By the end of the fitting I was distinctly put out by the way she and Leo kept sneaking glances at each other. Then, to cap it all, as we were leaving he asked her if she'd ever visited Wiltshire. She replied that she'd only been to Pennings, just the one time – out of curiosity, she said.

Leo pressed her. 'Have you never visited your – er – aunts in Eston?'

'No, Lord Warminster, they prefer to run up and see me in Town.'

Leo's voice was hearty. 'You really should come down to Eston one of these days – and when you do, you must call on us. We'd be delighted to see you, wouldn't we, Amy?'

Madame d'Hiver blushed, actually blushed – at her age! It was all I could do to mutter, 'Yes.'

He never said a word in the cab all the way to Kew, and we were halfway to the Palm House before he bothered to ask, 'Are you pleased with your new dress, Amy? I think the colour suits you.'

I replied tartly, 'I didn't think as you'd even *noticed* the colour, what with you being so busy making eyes at Madame d'Hiver all the time!'

He came to such a sudden halt he almost wrenched my arm. 'What on earth do you mean?'

'Well, it were obvious as you'd taken more'n a passing fancy to her.' I knew I sounded huffy, but I couldn't help it.

'You're not *jealous* of me, are you, Amy?' He sounded as if he couldn't believe it.

'Why shouldn't I be? You're *my* husband, not hers.'

'You *are* jealous!' He sounded so pleased I could have hit him. Then he started laughing. 'But, Amy, she's the last woman in the world you need to feel jealous of – since I rather suspect she's my sister!' I just stared at him, as he continued, 'When I read my father's personal accounts after his death, I discovered that he'd settled a substantial sum of money on a certain young woman, so I deduced that there'd been some degree of intimacy – ' He broke off to add regretfully, 'But I never realized there'd been a child as well. I do wish I'd known.'

D'Hiver – *Winter*slow – 'Maud!' I exclaimed.

He shook his head, 'God forbid! No, not Maud – Martha. Didn't you know she was a housemaid at Pennings for a short while, some five years before my mother's death?'

I was completely stunned. No wonder Madame d'Hiver's face had seemed so familiar the first time I'd met her!

Then I realized Leo was swinging me round and heading off in a completely different direction. 'But I thought we were going to the Palm House.'

'No, Amy. First we are going to the rhododendron dell, which, since rhododendrons are out of season at the moment, will I trust offer an area of privacy and seclusion where a middle-aged man may kiss his wife – his beautiful young wife who is actually *jealous* of him!'

'But – '

'Don't worry, Amy. I assure you that by the time I've finished you will be in *no* doubt as to the warmth and constancy of my feelings for you.'

We never did get to the Palm House.

But when I was curled up in Leo's arms that night, I remembered what he'd told me, and started to do sums in my head. Five years before Leo's mother had died Leo's father had been sixty-four at least – and Martha, now, she'd been seventy-four last birthday, so she must have been only eighteen! Poor Martha! To be seduced like that by her employer; she wouldn't have dared to say no. Why, he might even have forced her! And to have fallen for a baby, too. I knew she'd not been married until she was twenty-three, so it must have been dreadful for her before that – the disgrace! And then, worst of all, having to leave her little girl behind in London – no wonder she was a bit sharp-tongued sometimes.

Leo must have been thinking about it overnight, too, because while he was shaving he asked me if I'd go down and have a word with her. 'I may be building castles in the air, Amy, so I'd be grateful if you'd try to glean some more information. Perhaps if you just dropped a discreet hint – '

I dropped in on Granny Withers that very afternoon.

As soon as I'd checked that the door was properly latched I said, 'Mrs Withers, we went to see Molly yesterday, and afterwards his lordship told me all about you and his father.'

'Huh! Just like a man. Wagging tongues, they got. I never knew a man yet as could keep a secret.' But she didn't seem all that bothered. 'Mind, I'm surprised he needed to tell you. I'd have thought as you'd already 'a noticed the likeness and worked it out for yourself. Like a cup o' tea, me lady?' I sank down into the chair. Her ginger tom leapt up with a wail of protest. 'Mind Tibbles now – '

As soon as the kettle was on the range she sat down in her rocking chair opposite. She sighed, 'Aye, it were a long time ago, now.'

I exclaimed, 'Oh, Mrs Withers, it must have been dreadful for you, Leo's father seducing you like that!'

Granny Withers bridled. '*He* didn't seduce *me*! Twas the other way round.' I gaped at her as she began to fill her pipe. When it was drawing to her satisfaction, she went on, 'First time I saw him riding into the stableyard at Pennings I thought, that's the man fer you, Martha, I thought. Lovely figure he had, back straight as a ramrod, and his thighs – ! They don't make 'em like that nowadays! Soon as he was off that horse I was running out into the yard, accidental, like. Then I pretends to start, as if I've only just caught sight of him, and I makes me curtsey. He stops and asks me me name, and gives me a civil word – and I can see by the way he was looking at me as he were liking what he saw as much as I were. So I gives him another smile, and another curtsey – taking good care to let him see as me ankles were up to the standard of the rest of me. Then he goes striding off, and I stood there watching him, with me legs all of a tremble! I thought, Martha, tis up to you now.'

She leant closer. 'You see, my lady, I knew from the other girls as he weren't one for catching the maids behind the door and giving 'em a kiss and a fondle – too much of a gentleman he were, to get up to them tricks – so I knew as it weren't going to be easy. But then, I've allus been one fer a challenge, I have. So I starts keeping me eyes and ears open and afore long I sees me way to it.'

She puffed on her pipe. 'He were an early riser, wi' being in the army so long, I dare say, and sometimes he'd be down in his study while it were being cleaned of a morning. So I ups and swaps wi' Sarah Carter as was third housemaid – she had her own fish to fry, did Sarah. So there I am the next morning cleaning the grate in his lordship's study when he walks in. He notices, and says, "What are you doing in here, young Martha?" I says, bold as brass, "I asked Sarah to swap wi' me, me lord." "Did you now," he says. "And why would that be?" "'Cos I 'as a fancy fer the company a girl might find in here of a morning."

'Well, his eyebrows come together and he says, 'You're a forward hussy, you are, young woman, and no mistake!" So I says, "Forward, maybe, me lord, but I'm not a hussy." Then I looks at him meaningful and says, "Leastways, not yet!" So he says, looking at me from under them bushy eyebrows of his, "So

471

there's some young man as might persuade you to deviate from the paths of virtue, eh, Martha?" "He's not a *young* man, me lord – and he won't need to do much persuading!" He starts laughing, then he says, "I like a girl who knows what she wants."

'Next thing, he walks over to the calendar and says, "Martha, you're only young, so I'm giving you fair warning." He jabs his finger at the date and says, "It's the second today. You got three weeks to change your duties back again. But if you're still here on the morning of the twenty-third, then I can tell you now, you'll be losing something, as once it's gone, it's gone for good. Do you understand?"

'I looks up at him, and says, "Aye, me lord, I understands." So he puts a cross on the calendar, nice and clear so I can see it, then he sits down at the desk and starts working, humming to himself, he was.'

I was open-mouthed. 'Mrs Withers, however did you dare?'

'He liked a girl as could stand up fer herself, he did.' She gave me a wink. ''Course, thic next three weeks I didn't make it easy fer 'im.'

'No, o' course not, wi' you still being just a young maid.'

'Aye. Every morning, I'd be in there flouncing and flaunting meself in front of him as I cleaned me grate and dusted thic there high shelves – never been so clean afore or since, I'll be bound – I give him such a tease them mornings! I could see he were soon regretting putting that cross where he had! But he kept to his word, he were a real gentleman, he were.

'Anyway, come the twenty-third, I were down there at the crack o' dawn – but he were there afore me!' She sighed reminiscently. 'Ah, he were a fine set-up man, he were.' She smiled, 'You never forget the first time, do you, me lady?'

I let out my breath. 'Just fancy, you seeing him on his horse and falling in love wi' him, just like that!'

Granny Withers looked furtive. 'I wouldn't exactly call it "love", me lady. You know how the Good Book talks about the lusts of the flesh? Well, I reckon as my flesh lusted after his – and his after mine. We understood one another, we did.' I could feel my jaw dropping even further. 'Thic water's boiling.' She creaked to her feet and busied herself with the teapot.

When she was sitting down again, I prompted, 'And Molly?'

'Oh, ar, I reckons as I fell for Molly that morning. Well, at first you don't know no better, do you? And men, *they're* not bothered.' She sniffed.

'But didn't her ladyship find out?'

She looked shocked. 'O' course not, he'd never have done nothing to hurt her. Thought the world of her, he did. So did I. Such a sweet lady she was – too sweet for his lordship, I used to think. He needed a woman as'd shout back at him. Men, they're all bullies if they get the chance.'

'Leo isn't.'

'You don't give him the chance, do you, now? And quite right, too. Now where was I? Oh ar, in Lunnon.'

'*London?*'

'Nice little house he found for me there. He'd allus spent two or three days a week up there anyway, so no one was any the wiser. Maud come, too, to make it all respectable, like. She took care o' Molly when she arrived. I weren't ready to have my wings clipped, but Maud, she's allus been the steady one. His lordship paid for her to learn her dressmaking, so she could have a career.

'Aye, five years it were, and we had some good times, we did, him and me. Then your lordship was born and his lady died – and he was broken. Turned into an old man overnight. So he made me an 'andsome settlement, and I came back to marry Dan Withers. Allus had a soft spot fer Dan, I had. Maud, now, she stayed in town till Molly were grown up. She liked the bright lights, did Maud. But me, I'd had me fling, so I were ready to settle down. Now, this tea'll be brewed, my lady, so I'll pour you a cup.'

I kept looking at her as she drank her tea, thinking of what she'd just told me. I couldn't wait to get home and tell Leo the whole story. I knew he'd be shocked to hear about her seducing his father, and so was I, of course – but I couldn't help feeling a sneaking admiration for Granny Withers, all the same. She was a wicked one, she was!

I was nervous before the dinner party, but everything went off very well. I could see Sir George was rather taken with Annabel. Leo seemed quite intent on matchmaking, but I told him I didn't think it would be any use, after what she'd said to me the day she'd arrived. She'd been telling me how she'd been climbing mountains in Switzerland all summer, then her face had changed and become shadowed. 'I've been trying to get clean again, Amy – but I can't.'

'Clean?'

'After Paris. I don't know what came over me that time. "Sauce for the goose", indeed!' Her mouth twisted with self-disgust. 'All I did was lower myself to Francis' level – and let him down.'

'But – he did do the same.'

'I know, but he didn't know any better, I realize that now.' She looked up at me, 'I went to see his "Uncle" Jean-Paul, you know. I thought – oh, I don't know what I thought. But after I'd met him I felt I understood Francis at last. How could he have been other than he was, with that man playing the father to him? He did, you know – Francis told me that. I remember him saying, "Uncle Jean-Paul was the one I always went to when I got into a scrape. *He* never preached or blamed. He'd just say, 'There's only one rule that matters, François: never get found out!' Then he'd laugh, and get me out of whatever mess I'd got myself into that time."'

She leant forward, her eyes dark with anger. 'Do you know, Amy, Francis told me once that on his sixteenth birthday Jean-Paul took him to his own favourite brothel! "To learn to be a man." How absolutely disgusting! It's only now that I realize what effect that kind of attitude must have had on Francis.

His behaviour was only to be expected, whereas I should have known better than to prostitute myself the way I did.' She shuddered before adding, 'Still, given the casualty figures in the RFC I don't suppose I'll ever have to meet that man again.' Her eyes closed for a moment.

I didn't know what to say to comfort her, but immediately she changed the subject. 'I can see you've made it up with Leo.'

'Aye, he does understand now – about Frank.'

'Actually, Amy, I intended to try and intercede for you if he was still being awkward. I was going to point out to Leonidas that you had had the generosity to do what I should have done.' She looked at me directly, 'Now, I can only thank you for giving Francis the comfort you did.' Her voice dropped. 'I went to see his grave, you know. I thought it was the least I could do. I stood there beside that simple wooden cross and I felt – so proud.' Her eyes glistened with unshed tears. I knew they'd remain unshed: she was so brave, Annabel.

Before she left she said, 'You know, it's time you told Flora the truth, while she can still remember Frank. She's his child, and he died bravely. He has a right to be remembered by her.'

I glanced at Leo. He said quietly, 'Yes, Annabel, you're right. We owe it to him.'

We told Flora together. Her blue eyes widened with surprise, soon followed by uncertainty. She turned to Leo, 'Papa?' Her voice was an anxious question. He held out his arms to her and she ran to him. As he drew her close I said softly, 'Papa was Uncle Frank's father, so he's your Granfer as well as your Papa.' Safe against his chest she nodded, satisfied. The other secret, the secret of Frank's birth, she would never be told.

Frank was very much in our thoughts that autumn because Eston, like every other village and town, was planning its war memorial. Ours was to be on the green at the head of the village street, where we could see it every day.

There was sadness, but there was hope, too. Other women were carrying babies, just as I was, and in November Clara told me her hopes had turned to certainty. Her face was radiant as I hugged her. 'Oh, Clara, I be so pleased for thee!'

She laughed, 'It's took so long we was wondering if we were doing it right!' Then she became serious. 'Mebbe tis as well I didn't fall earlier. I 'low as Jim needed all my loving at first. Now he's as thrilled as I am.'

Christmas came. We took all the children to church with us in the morning. Leo came with me to church sometimes of a Sunday now, and when he'd been two weeks running in January, Mr Beeston murmured to me after the service of the value of a good woman's influence. Leo was eavesdropping unashamedly and I could see he was trying not to laugh. Then Mr Beeston turned to Leo and asked him if he'd be prepared to read the lesson next week. Leo's smile vanished, he snapped, 'No,' and marched off up the lane without even waiting for me. Poor Mr Beeston looked as if he was going to burst into tears.

I put my hand on his arm. 'Don't you upset yourself, Mr Beeston. He didn't mean to be unkind. Tis because of his stammer. It's almost gone now when he's just talking to folk in a room, but he couldn't do something like read a lesson, in public.'

The war memorial would be finished at the end of February. At the beginning of the month Leo and I went down to the meeting in the schoolroom to discuss the arrangements for the dedication and unveiling. Mr Arnott said, 'His lordship here has kindly drawn up a list o' likely gentlemen, as us might ask to perform the ceremony.' He read out the names of a number of the men who'd helped our forces to victory. When he'd finished he asked, 'Now, would someone like to make a proposal?'

Mr Hale stood up, cleared his throat loudly and announced, 'Us wants to propose his lordship.' There was a chorus of 'Seconded' from the other members of the committee and Mr Arnott said, 'Any other proposals?' There was total silence. 'Right, carried unanimously. His lordship will unveil our memorial.'

Leo looked at me, his face agonized.

I said, 'Mr Arnott, tis usual to have generals and suchlike.'

Ellen's father turned to Leo. 'My lord, we dussent want a general, we wants you. Tis only fitting, seeing as you went, just like they did. You were out there with our sons – and then you lost your own boy, too. So we wants you to do it.'

Heads nodded in agreement all round the table. There was a long silence and then at last, Leo dipped his own head in assent.

I said to him on the way home, 'Leo, there doesn't have to be a speech. You could just pull the cord, and let Mr Beeston get on with the prayers. You don't have to make a speech.'

He answered, 'Yes, Amy, I do. If they had the courage to die for their country, the least I can do is have the courage to honour them as they deserve.'

He spent hours agonizing over that speech, but I knew that composing the words wasn't the problem; it was the speaking of them that he dreaded.

The ceremony was to be in the morning. Annabel had arrived the day before, and now she sat at the breakfast table with us, calm and composed. Flora was downstairs with us, too, today. She held her back proudly straight, because she knew that one of the names on that long list was that of her father.

Leo left the table and went into the library to study his speech one last time. At ten o' clock I went in to find him. 'Tis time, Leo.' Reaching out for his hand I squeezed it comfortingly, and smiled. His fingers responded to mine but there was no answering smile on his face.

We walked out together on to the front steps. The governess cart drew up with Jim holding the reins and Mrs Carter sitting beside him. Ellen climbed up to join them, and as soon as she was seated Leo swung Jackie up on to her lap; Mr Wallis helped Mr Tims in next, then Jim cracked his whip and they rattled away. Mr Wallis shut up the house, as all the other servants were already gathered outside with us, wearing their best clothes. The gardeners came from their bothy, their boots and medals shining, and we all began to walk down the drive, and on to the village, to where the bronze memorial stood muffled in its shroud.

The whole village was waiting there, everyone wearing their best Sunday clothes: the younger men with their service medals pinned to their jackets, just as Leo's were pinned to his. They parted to let him through, and he climbed up on to the dais erected in front of the memorial. Mr Beeston followed him, with Mr Arnott and Mr Selby, the churchwardens, by his side. Then Annabel was helped up to the chair set ready for her. I should have been on the dais too, but I'd refused. I wanted to be where Leo could see me, and besides, there were the children; so now I went and stood to one side, with Flora.

Leo's face was like that of a statue, old and stong as time. But I knew that within his breast his heart beat fast with fear. As I watched, the other men stepped back, leaving Leo alone at the front of the platform. I saw his eyes searching for mine, seeking my support. As they rested on my upturned face I smiled to him, and for a second he held my gaze. Then, tilting his head so that he could look out at all the assembled people of Eston, he opened his lopsided mouth and began to speak.

The tears came to my eyes. For the hesitation was there, as always it must be: but there, too, in his voice, was courage. And now that courage gave him the strength to speak out loud and clear, in honour of our dead.

'Today we remember those we have lost, as we remember them every day. We do not need a monument cast in bronze to remind us, because we will never forget them. But they, they deserve a memorial, so that their children, their grandchildren, and all the generations that come after them may look on their names – and remember. The stranger, too, and the traveller who passes through our village – he must see this memorial and learn how these men, our men of Eston, answered their country's call. Leaving their homes, their families, their farms, their fields, they went to do their duty – and paid with their lives.'

Stepping forward, he pulled hard at the cord and the black curtain fell away to reveal a soldier of bronze. He was standing straight and proud in the sunlight, wearing his pack on his back and holding his rifle ready by his side. He gazed out over the village and the woods and the fields he'd fought to defend, and now would never see again.

On the plinth were inscribed in bronze panels the names of the dead. In a strong carrying voice, Leo began to read out that roll of honour:

'George Leonard Chandler; Edward Davies; John Davies; Herbert Dawson; Joseph Albert Dempster; Francis Peter Jean Fitzwarren-Donne, Viscount Quinham; George Hale . . .'

When he'd finally come to the end of that long, sad list Leo waited a moment before reading the inscription beneath it: 'They gave their lives that we might live in peace.'

Then, moving forward, he raised his hand, and pointing to the soldier cast in bronze, he said, 'This statue is the symbol of he that you lost. Look at him and remember. Remember your son, as I remember mine. Remember your husband. Remember your brother. Remember your grandson.' His voice dropped, and he looked down to where the children stood in front of us, Flora beside them, 'And remember your father.' Then his head lifted again as he commanded us all, 'Remember – and be proud.' His voice rang out, strong and powerful.

'There is no fitter end than this.
No need is now to yearn nor sigh.
We know the glory that is his,
A glory that can never die.'

There was silence, broken only by the soft sound of women weeping. Then Leo stepped back, and the Rector moved forward to take his place. 'Let us pray . . .'

That afternoon we walked in the garden, just the two of us, together. Annabel had taken Flora out in her new motor, and Rose and Jackie were up in the nursery with Ellen; our next child lay safely under my heart.

Leo's voice was sad. 'I should have been more understanding of Francis. I regret so much the anger and the bitterness, that last time he came here – '

I said, 'Leo, you did see him again, out in France. So you didn't part in anger.'

'But I wish – oh how I wish – that I'd been in time before he died.'

'You tried. You tried.'

He was searching for words. 'Amy, I am glad now, that you sent him away – with love. Thank you.'

March arrived, and I waited for my baby. I'd told the children that their new brother or sister was growing safe inside me, until he was big enough to come out. Flora and Rose were full of excitement, but Jackie looked extremely dubious about the whole business, and kept trying to climb on to what was left of my lap.

Leo reassured me, 'Don't worry, Amy, I'll make an extra fuss of him while you and the girls indulge in infant worship.'

I shifted, trying to ease my aching back. 'I'll be glad when tis all over.'

'Yes, so will I.'

'You'll stay with me?'

'Naturally, if you want me to.'

I reached out for the comfort of his hand. 'Yes, I want you to.'

Our second son was born on the morning of 15th March. Leo was by my side as he gave his first cry, and it was Leo who put him into my arms for the first time: my beautiful, sturdy son – how I loved him.

By the evening I was rested and longing to see my other children. Jackie flung himself into my arms while the two girls hung over the cradle. 'Look at his little fingernails, Rose!'

'*Nice* baby!' They were both entranced.

I eased Jackie over to the edge of the bed. 'Here's a new brother for you, Jackie.'

He frowned, then announced, 'Don't want! Don't want!' Turning, he buried his head in my breast.

Stroking his soft hair I looked up at Leo, who smiled reassuringly. 'Give him time, Amy.'

Rose and Flora climbed up on to my bed and tucked themselves in beside Jackie. Flora looked at me expectantly. 'Papa said we could have our story down here, 'cos you can't get out of bed yet.'

Leo retrieved the book from the floor, where Flora had dropped it in her excitement over her new brother. 'Here it is, Amy.' He drew up a chair and sat down beside the bed. 'Flora, it's your turn to choose tonight. Which is it to be?'

Flora said firmly, ' "Beauty and the Beast".'

So I began to read the familiar tale: ' "There was once a very rich merchant, who had six children, three sons and three daughters . . . "'

I read of Beauty's trembling arrival at the enchanted castle, of the Beast, and his kindness to Beauty – and her growing affection for him. Then, I read of how she nearly forgot the Beast – until she came rushing back to find him lying senseless by the stream, and bring him back to life.

I continued, ' "She looked down at the Beast, who loved her. And he was so strong, and yet so kind and gentle, too, that she fell in love with him." ' There was a sigh from my daughters. Looking up from the book, I finished, 'So then Beauty married the Beast, and they lived happily ever after.'

Flora's voice rose in protest. 'But, Mama, that's not right – there was a clap of thunder, and lightning, and the magic fireworks. You've got the ending wrong.'

I looked across at Leo and we exchanged smiles as I shook my head. 'No, Flora, that was only a fairy story – my story is true.'

Eston, Wiltshire
March 15th 1920

PERTH AND KINROSS DISTRICT LIBRARIES